TWICE UPON A TIME

Twice Upon A Time

BY

I. Hicks-Mudd

PUBLISHED BY

Orr-Fenwick Productions
East Hanney,
Oxon. OX12 0HN

*First published 2005
by Orr-Fenwick Productions,
East Hanney.*

Printed and bound by Parchment (Printers) Oxford.

ISBN 0-9550341-0-8

© 2005 I. Hicks-Mudd

*For my sister Kate and my friend Greta
in gratitude for their encouragement,
also my cousin Sarah
for her help with the research,
and especially to
Thea,
whose splendid reaction
to the final draft of the story
encouraged me to go ahead with publication*

ACKNOWLEDGMENTS

The author would like to thank BBC Written Archives at Caversham for providing details of wireless programmes and news bulletins referred to in the text; also the Imperial War Museum whose staff have been very helpful in the checking of dates and other facts and for permission to reproduce some of the war-time posters. Thanks are also due to the directors of Beales Department Store in Bournemouth for information and help, in spite of the fact that their company records for the period were destroyed by enemy action in May 1943. Of great help also was the Library and Archive of the *Bournemouth Echo*, who supplied detail of cinema and theatre programmes, as well as enemy action in the Bournemouth area during the autumn of 1940.

AUTHOR'S NOTE

ALTHOUGH A GREAT MANY of the locations described in this story actually exist, Seabourne Preparatory School, and all of the pupils and staff therein, together with other characters in the story, are purely imaginary, and any resemblance to any person, living or dead, is purely coincidental.

However, several of the incidents described—for example, a certain exploit of Maggot's—*did* actually happen (many years earlier), but names have been changed as I have no desire to offend or embarrass any friends or or members of my family—living or dead!

A number of events that actually occurred during the autumn of 1940 have been worked into the story, to give young readers a taste of some of the things children had to endure on the '*home front*' during the Second World War.

References to the French Resistance and the *Special Operations Executive* (SOE) have been 'tailored' to suit the plot, but have been based on the exploits of SOE agents in France in during a slightly later period of the war. The doings of SOE have been included in the story to show how very ordinary people, women as well as men, did very extra-ordinary and exceedingly brave deeds that helped to bring to the Allies their eventual victory in 1945.

For the sake of historical accuracy I ought to point out that SOE was only formed in June 1940, and did not actually send any agents to France until well into 1941. The first woman agent to be sent to France was Yvonne Rudellat (code-name *Jacqueline*) who landed from a felucca in July 1942; she died in the terrible Belsen concentration camp in April 1945—one of the thirteen brave SOE women who were either executed by the Gestapo or died and never saw their homes and families again.

As far as I know, there were no agents of SOE or the resistance with the code-names *Loir* or *Lièvre*; neither was there a resistance circuit known as *Chapelier Fou*, nor was there an escape line led by an agent known as *La Maîtresse*. The *Messages Personnels* on the BBC did not begin until July 1941 at the suggestion of one of the first SOE agents, Georges Bégué; However they were to become such a vital link in SOE's work that I have included them as an extra dimension to the story (albeit slightly out of time).

I should also point out that the rationing of sweets and chocolates did not come into force until July 1442, but it was to become so much a part of the wartime child's life that I brought it forward to 1940 (when there was a definite shortage of all types of confectionery).

Finally, I am happy to reassure readers that, during 1940 (or any other period), neither was the Matron of Boscombe Hospital called Drusilla Prudence Dawes, nor was the Vicar of All Saints called the Revd Algernon Pugh; both characters, like all the others in the story, being mere figments of my imagination.

I.H-M.

CONTENTS

Chapter 1	Friday the Thirteenth	7
Chapter 2	Peregrine Dormitory	16
Chapter 3	War's Bitter Taste	21
Chapter 4	First Morning—Later	26
Chapter 5	Harry Gordon	34
Chapter 6	Harry Moves In	43
Chapter 7	Things That Go Bang in the Night	52
Chapter 8	"Best Friends"	57
Chapter 9	Saturday	63
Chapter 10	Harvest Festival Howler!	74
Chapter 11	Our Windy Walk with Bendy Wendy	81
Chapter 12	Grave News	86
Chapter 13	At the Hospital	92
Chapter 14	The Message on the Wireless	98
Chapter 15	Another Night in the Shelter	103
Chapter 16	Tuesday	109
Chapter 17	Choir Practice	118
Chapter 18	Troubles	124
Chapter 19	Consequences	129
Chapter 20	Wet Start to the Weekend	138
Chapter 21	Super Sunday—Misery Monday	145
Chapter 22	Confession	151
Chapter 23	Despatches from the Front	157
Chapter 24	Half-term Begins	164
Chapter 25	Patients' Progress	171
Chapter 26	The Beak Arranges a Treat	176
Chapter 27	The Outing	182
Chapter 28	Harry's Sunday Shock	188
Chapter 29	By Train to Brockenhurst	194
Chapter 30	"Operation Lollipop"	202
Chapter 31	Half-Term Ends—	207
Chapter 32	—And the Rest of the Term Begins	213
Chapter 33	November—into December	218
Chapter 34	Bomb-site!	223
Chapter 35	Safe Once More	230
Chapter 36	Friday the Thirteenth—Again	236
Chapter 37	Saturday the Fourteenth	243

CHAPTER ONE

Friday the Thirteenth

'BUT *THOSE* AREN'T *MINE!*' I protested, as the lady held out a pair of navy-blue knickers for me to put on. 'I wasn't wearing *those* when I got here last night. You *can't* make me wear THOSE—I'm a *BOY!*'

The lady looked surprised. 'Yes, dear. Of *course* you are. And *I*, am the Lord Mayor of London. Come along now, child,' she said impatiently in her Scottish voice and shaking the knickers at me. 'I've no time to argue just now. Put your drawers on at once, before I get cross!' So, reluctantly, I stepped into them and she pulled them up high under my nightgown, almost lifting me off my feet in the process. Then she whisked the nightie off over my head, and there I was, gobsmacked, and naked save for that pair of thick, baggy, navy-blue knickers, which had a small pocket on the front of the right leg. I could feel the tight elastic round the legs cutting into the flesh half-way up my thighs. As she pulled a vest over my head I wondered what the pocket was for. 'Now then,' she said. 'I'm sure you're able to finish dressing on your own. Do you know how to tie your tie?'

'Yes,' I replied quietly, pushing my arms through the arm-holes of the vest and tucking it in. It was queer, unlike any vest I had ever seen before, having two tapes sewn inside, one over each shoulder and hanging just below the hem, front and back, with a sort of button sewn on each end. I wondered what had become of my T-shirt and Y-fronts.

'Yes, *Matron!*' she said sternly, fixing me with her beady eyes. 'You wee girls seem to have no manners nowadays!' She rolled the "R" of *'girls'* making it sound like *'Gir-ruls,'* and VERY disapproving.

'Yes, Matron,' I replied meekly, but added belligerently; 'but can't you understand? I'm a *BOY!*'

'So you said, Alexandra! Come along now, stop all your nonsense *this instant*, and finish dressing like a good wee girl.' She swept out of the room, leaving me wondering what kind of nightmare was happening me—*Alexander Francis Muir.*

*

Let me introduce myself properly and explain how I, a boy, came to wake up wearing a girl's nightdress. My name really is Alexander Francis Muir and I *am* male! Yes, truly! I am usually called Alex, and ever since both my parents were killed in a 'plane crash when I was seven, have lived with my grandmother in Southbourne, and attended St. Alloysius' School for Boys.

To begin at the beginning. It was September 1974; I was ten and a half years old and it was the beginning of the last week of the long summer holiday. I can remember the exact date, it was Sunday the eighth, and Gran and I had just got back home from All Saints Church where I sang in the choir. I had spent much of that holiday sailing in the boat of my first cousins, Nick Colquhoun (pronounced *Cahoon*) and her sister Jackie, in Christchurch Harbour. Their dad, my Uncle Dougal, Mum's elder brother, was a captain in the Merchant Navy so was away at sea most of the time, "driving his oil-tanker!" as Nick used to say when she was younger. She is three weeks older than I and Jackie is two years younger. They are very tomboyish, and behaved and looked more boyish than girlish. Nick had been christened Nicole, after her French great grandma, and Jackie, Jacqueline, however, both flatly refused to answer to those names. At a time when most children went around with longish hair, many people could not be certain what a child was unless it was wearing a skirt or dress! As Nick and Jackie usually wore jeans or shorts, people regularly mistook them for boys. Once when we were playing together a lady, discovering they were girls, and seeing me similarly dressed in jeans and a t-shirt, asked, horror of horrors, if I was a girl too; I tried to think of a polite answer, but it was not easy, and Nick spared my blushes replying, very firmly, that I was *very definitely* a boy, before I could say anything. If the weather was bad and we could not go sailing, we usually played together, either at my house or theirs, or we settled down and read in one of our bedrooms.

I was also a keen cricket fan, Hampshire having won the County Championship the previous year, and I often went to watch them when they were playing in Bournemouth. I went to their match against Somerset at the end of August, and we should have won—probably clinching the championship for a second year—but the rain came and the match was drawn. A pity as the last match of the season, against Yorkshire, never even started—rain again.

Sometimes, if Nick and Jackie were away or being 'good little girls' visiting elderly relations, as a last resort, I played with the kids next door, Tim, who was nine and at my school, his bossy eleven-year-old sister, Susan, and her—equally bossy—best friend, Christine, who had just reached eleven and lived round the corner.

As soon as we had finished lunch that Sunday, Gran told me she had to go into hospital for an operation, and realising that I would be anxious about her assured me that it was quite a routine operation she was going to have.

'Don't worry, Alex, my precious,' she said. 'I'll be fine, and Great Auntie Margaret is going to come and look after you. She'll be arriving on Thursday, so I can show her the ropes. She will look after you splendidly, you know how fond she is of children.'

I shuddered. 'Must it be G.A.M? Couldn't Auntie Connie come instead?'

You'll have guessed that Great Aunt Margaret was very far from being my favourite auntie. She was Granpa's eldest sister, very strict and I was sure she had disapproved of boys ever since she had been the headmistress of a girls' school in Ipswich. Great Auntie Connie was completely different, a kind, jolly lady who was tremendous fun to be with.

'I'm sorry, my precious,' said Gran, (she insisted on calling me her "precious," even in front of my school-mates, which was *so* embarrassing) 'Auntie Connie's away just now, so I'm afraid it *has* to be Auntie Margaret. Doctor Matthews said he could arrange for you to go to Colvin for a short while, but I thought you'd prefer to stay at home so I persuaded Auntie Margaret to come.'

Colvin had been a school until about ten years ago. When it closed, the buildings and grounds were bought by a charity for use as a children's home.

'When are you having your operation, Gran?'

'Monday the sixteenth, my precious pie,' she replied. I cringed, thankful that neither Tim nor any of my school-friends were around. 'But I have to go into hospital on Friday afternoon so they can do some tests first. When Auntie Margaret arrives on Thursday I can show her where everything is, and tell her about your likes and dislikes. It'll give her a chance to settle in, as she's had nothing to do with children since she retired from the school.'

'How long'll you be in hospital?' I asked, wondering how long I was to be left to the tender mercies of G.A.M.

'About two weeks, then I'll have to go to a convalescent home for a while, my precious.' She put a hand on my arm and gave it a squeeze. 'You mustn't worry, precious, Auntie Margaret knows all about children. Don't forget she was the head of a school in Ipswich for many, many years.

'But *Gra–an!* It was a *girls'* school!' I said, disdainfully.

'But that doesn't mean that she doesn't know how to look after a boy just as well. Anyway, you don't hate girls, precious; look how often you go and play with Susan and Christine.'

'True,' I replied glumly. 'But they always want to play such soppy games.'

'Nick and Jackie are girls, my precious,' she reminded me.

'Ye-es, but they don't count; they seem like *boys*, even if they *do* have to wear dresses sometimes; and Nick's hair's the same length as mine.'

'But yours is quite long for a boy,' said Gran. 'It's so pretty, I often think it's a pity you aren't a little girl.' (I knew she was going to be *really-really* embarrassing now!) 'You'd have been *such* a pretty little girl.'

I felt myself blushing; 'Oh, *Gra–ann! I wish* you wouldn't keep SAYING that!'

'You know it's just my little joke, precious,' she said with a twinkle in her eye. 'If your hair was just a little longer, you'd be the spitting image of your poor Auntie Alexandra when she was your age. She was such a brave little girl.'

Auntie Alexandra had been her daughter, Alexandra Frances Muir, my Dad's twin sister, who had died of pneumonia during the second world war when she was at school. I had been christened Alexander Francis after her.

The last week of the summer holidays passed quickly. Being a choirboy, I had to sing at a wedding on Saturday afternoon and earned an extra fifty pence pocket money. Most of Sunday was taken up with church services. Monday was spent sailing with Nick and Jackie; we sailed down to Mudeford, and had a picnic near the Black House, said to have once been the haunt of smugglers. This would be the last chance I would have for a sail this hols, as Nick and Jackie would be going back to their boarding school, Spettisbury Manor, on Wednesday. On Tuesday, Gran took me into Bournemouth to buy some new clothes for school, and Nick and Jackie came to tea. Auntie Kate, their mum, came too and while we kids had a glorious picnic up in the tree-house in the garden, the grown-ups stayed indoors talking about dead gruesome operations. We were glad to escape that, believe me!

On Wednesday I went to the station to see Nick and Jackie off to school. It was strange seeing them all prim and proper in their navy-blue school uniforms. After the train had gone, Auntie Kate drove me back home and stayed for lunch. Gran had been making the arrangements for G.A.M's arrival, dusting and polishing the spare room, and making sure there was plenty of food in the 'fridge, so she was glad not to have me 'under her feet' as she put it. Auntie Kate offered to drive us to the station to meet G.A.M. next day, and Gran said that would be really kind of her.

The telegram arrived at lunch time—not long before we were due to leave for the station. G.A.M. had fallen downstairs, broken her hip, and was in hospital so she couldn't come. Yippee! Auntie Kate said she would have had me to stay with her, but she had already promised to go and look after an elderly aunt who was dying of cancer.

Great Aunt Margaret's accident had come as a bolt from the blue on the very day that she was supposed to come to look after me. It meant that alternative arrangements had to be made in a hurry. I had hoped to be able to stay with Auntie Kate but as she was going to be away, that was out of the question. In the end, our doctor, Dr. Matthews, arranged for me to stay at Colvin, where he was on the Board of Trustees, and there was a guest room available for short-stay visitors. The doctor was going to take me to Colvin himself, but he had been called out to an accident, and as it was getting late, Auntie Kate stepped into the breech and drove me there in her Renault 16TX. Everything had been done in a rush, and it had been nearly midnight when we finally arrived. After Auntie Kate had left, having dropped me off, the Colvin matron discovered that Gran had forgotten to pack my pyjamas. All the spare ones Matron had were too small, and all she could find that was my size was a girl's pink nightie! So, much to my horror, she had insisted I wear that. I agreed *only* after making her promise that I would have to wear it for just that one night, and she would never, *ever*, tell anybody. She made me a cup of cocoa, and when I had finished it, put the light out, and left me to go to sleep cuddling my old one-eyed teddy bear, Edward Bear Esquire.

*

Next morning I was wakened by the loud clanging of a bell. When I opened my eyes it was still pitch dark. Where was I? I felt strange, not my usual self. I turned over. The bed felt foreign and hard, and had sheets and blankets—my own bed had a duvet. And why was I wearing a nightdress? I hugged Edward Bear Esquire tightly. As I lay there, half-awake, things began to come back to me. I was having to stay at Colvin, a local children's home, for a short time because Gran had to go into hospital for an operation and Great Aunt Margaret who had been coming to look after me had fallen over and broken her hip so she was in hospital too. But I still could not understand why it was so dark. Did the bell ring before dawn? There was no sign of light coming through the pale blue curtains I remembered Matron closing the night before.

The door opened and light from the passage spilled in. A lady came in. 'It's half past seven, and time you got dressed.' She crossed to the window, drew the curtains and let up a black blind to let in a watery morning sun. Even so, the light was bright enough to make me blink; but my eyes were soon accustomed and I could see she was wearing nurses' uniform and her reddy-brown hair done up in a bun. The night before, Matron had been wearing ordinary clothes. This was a different lady so I thought she must be Matron's assistant. I glanced around the room. It was not quite as I remembered it from the night before; the paint was dingier, and I was sure that the black blind had not been there.

'Time to get up,' said the lady in nurse's uniform. She had a Scottish accent. 'There's *watter* to wash with in the jug on the wash-stand.' She pointed to a china jug standing in a matching bowl. 'Get dressed as soon as you've washed. You've got twenty-five minutes before the breakfast bell rings. Don't forget to scrub your neck!' I looked round for my clothes. They were laid neatly on the chair by my bed, but there was something strange about them; they certainly did not look like the ones I had been wearing yesterday. Where were my jeans? and what was that cardboard box with the long loop of string attached to it?

'What's happened are my clothes?' I asked.

'They're on the chair where you put them when you undressed last night,' replied the lady in nurse's uniform. 'You're looking at them. Up you get now! I know it was very late when you arrived, and you'll be feeling tired, but we must press on. I shall be back in five minutes to see how you're doing.' With those words she poured some water from the jug into the bowl and left the room.

I looked around me. It was undoubtedly the same room, yet it was different somehow. I pushed down the sheet and blankets, got out of bed and went over to the wash stand. I was sure there had been a proper wash-basin with hot and cold taps there last night. The water was icy cold. I washed and dried my face, hands and neck. I looked for a tube of toothpaste, but could not see one; just a round flat tin about six centimetres across labelled "Gibb's Dentifrice". Inside was a block of a pink stuff. I brushed my teeth with plain water, then I went to the chair to get my clothes.

But they were NOT mine! They were *girl's* clothes!

I opened the cardboard box. Inside was an odd looking black rubber thing with a cylindrical bit, a clear window and straps. I could just remember Dad showing me a picture of one once. I was fairly sure it was a gas mask.

I didn't know what to do so I sat on the bed, still wearing the pink nightie, to think things out. I was still tired and was feeling peculiar. I could not put my finger on it, but I was certain that something very queer had happened during the night. I picked up Edward Bear Esquire; he looked younger and had *two eyes!* When the nurse-lady returned I was sitting on the bed, cuddling him.

'Come along now, dear!' she said. 'You've no time to cuddle Teddy! Buck up! Are you unable to dress yourself, then? I'd have thought that a big girl of ten would able to dress herself. If you cannot, I suppose I'll have to help you!' She collected the pile of clothes and put them on the bed beside me. 'As it's your first day I'll help you; but just this *once,* mind!' It was at this point that she held out those awful navy-blue knickers for me to put on! They were a bit like the ones Nick and Jackie wore, only much baggier! 'Come along now, Alexandra; be a good girl.'

After she left I had to think. Did she really call me "*Alexandra?*" Did she really say "Good *GIRL?*" What had happened? Why did I feel so peculiar? I could feel my hair was longer, reaching easily to my shoulders! Last night it had covered my ears and, only just, reached the nape of my neck. What had happened? A sudden, terrifying, thought struck me. *Had I actually changed sex?*

Could it be true? *Was* I now a girl? I had to find out. As soon as the door closed behind Matron, a quick look was enough to confirm my worst fears—there was absolutely nothing "boyish" in those knickers! The unthinkable HAD happened! Last night I had fallen asleep as a boy, and woken up this morning as a girl!

It was the most horrible nightmare. Panic grabbed me; I felt wobbly at the knees and had to sit on the bed again. My heart thumped and I felt sick. Why had this *happened* to me? What would I do when I wanted to wee? I wished Nick was there, she'd laugh like a drain, but at least she'd be able to tell me some of the things I needed to know.

I thought Matron would be back soon to see how I was getting on, so decided to carry on dressing. I picked up the white shirt; it was waist length, with buttons all the way down and elastic at the waist. There was name-tape sewn in it telling me it belonged to Alexandra Frances Muir—*my dead auntie!* Did that mean I had actually become Dad's twin sister, who had died as a schoolgirl?

I slipped the shirt on. It buttoned up on the wrong side; it felt a bit queer doing it up that way. I released my hair which had become trapped inside the collar, and began to tie my tie; it was navy-blue with narrow green and gold diagonal stripes. Just as I straitened it and turned down my collar Matron returned.

'Buck up, lassie! Have you not put on your tunic yet?' she said, picking up the navy-blue gymslip. 'My! You *are* a slowcoach, Alexandra. Anyone would think you'd never dressed yourself before!'

I nearly told her I hadn't! Not in *girls'* clothes anyway!

'Arms up!' she ordered. I raised them and she dropped the gymslip over my head. It was of the old-fashioned type, with a square yoke and box pleats, like one I had seen Mum wearing in photos of her at school. 'I'll leave you to tie your girdle, put on your socks and shoes and see to your hair. Be quick about it now; the bell for breakfast will be ringing at any moment. I realise you arrived very late last night, that you're a new girl, and it's your first day, but I *hope* I shall not have to help you get dressed after today. Don't forget to take a clean handkerchief and to carry your gas-mask at all times.'

'Yes, Matron—I mean, no, Matron!' I felt myself blushing.

She stalked out, leaving me to tie the "girdle" round my waist and put on the white ankle-socks and black lace-up shoes. The bell rang while I was brushing my hair. A fair girl with two long plaits, and wearing the same old-fashioned pattern of navy-blue tunic as mine, came in. She gave me a friendly smile. I reckoned she was a bit older than me. She had her gas mask box slung over one shoulder.

'You must be Alexandra!' she said, and without waiting for me to reply added; 'Welcome to Seabourne Prep. I'm Jennifer Pendleton, your dormitory monitress. Scottie—er—Matron, Miss Scott asked me to take you down to the eatery; that's what we girls call the refectory—the dining room. You'll be moving into my dorm., *Peregrine,* after brekker. Scottie says you arrived so awf'ly late that she didn't want to wake us, so she put you in here—the sick-bay. Hurry up, or we'll be late!. Don't forget your gas-mask.' She looked me over. 'You look fine, except you haven't tied your girdle the right way; you do it the same way as you knot your tie. Let me do it for you.' She undid it and quickly re-tied it, so the knot and the two long ends were on my left-hand side. 'Were you a boarder at your last school?'

'No, I was a day-bo—*girl*.' I only just stopped myself from making a ghastly blunder in time! I followed her out, feeling more than a little embarrassed. It felt very strange wearing a skirt, less restricting than shorts or jeans, and as a gust of wind whistled along the corridor, much draughtier! We joined the queue of other girls, all wearing the same uniform, carrying gas-masks and scurrying towards the top of the stairs. One or two of them stared at me inquisitively, making me feel even more self-conscious. Evidently I was now a boarder at the Seabourne Preparatory School for Girls, where Auntie Kate had once been a teacher, and which had been closed down in the summer of 1964, about four months after I had been born. I pinched myself to check I was not dreaming. I felt it! At the bottom of the stairs we turned right along another passage towards an open door.

'In here,' Jennifer told me. 'No talking until after Grace.' Inside, there were about thirty girls, all standing at their tables, and each one with a gas mask box slung round her neck. Jennifer signalled me follow her. When she reached her place at the top of one of the tables, she pointed to an empty place next to her. I looked at the other girls around the table; they all seemed to be about my age.

A young grown-up, whom I supposed to be one of the teachers, entered and stood at the head of the top table. She cleared her throat and all the girls looked down and closed their eyes. *'For what we are about to receive may the Lord make us truly thankful,'* she said. Her voice sounded more like a schoolgirl's than a grown-up's.

'Amen,' chorused the assembled company. There was much scraping of chairs and benches as everybody sat down. Only four of the ten or so tables were

occupied, each with between six and nine girls; there were six of us at our table with one empty place.

'This is Alexandra—Alexandra Muir,' Jennifer announced to the others at the table. 'She arrived frightfully late last night. She was a day-bug at her last school, so it's her first time as a boarder. Now, Alexandra, meet the other members of Peregrine dormy. By the way, Alexandra's a bit of a mouthful, may we shorten it to Sandra, or Sandy or something? My friends call me Jen-Pen or Jenny.'

'I'm usually called Alex at home, Jen-Pen—unless I'm in trouble!' I replied truthfully. Jenny grinned. 'I'd hate to be called Sandra, it sounds too soppy and girlie-girlie for words!'

'Alex it is then,' said Jenny, smiling. 'On your left is Roberta MacGregor; she comes from Scotland, and we usually call her *Rob Roy* after her famous ancestor.' Rob Roy gave me a friendly grin as Jenny went on: 'At the far end of the table is Nancy Blackwell, who's vice-monitress of Peregrine and the red badge on her tunic means she's captain of the Third Form at present. Opposite you are our twins, Dilys and Emily Willis.'

'We know them as Dilly-Willy and Milly-Willy,' said Rob Roy.

The twins giggled, and I looked at them to see if I could tell them apart. 'How will I know which of you is which?' I asked, when I had decided I could not.

'Lots of people can't,' giggled one. 'So if you call me Milly-Willy, I'll just say I'm Dilly-Willy!'

'And if you call me Dilly-Willy, I'll say I'm Milly-Willy!' giggled the other. 'I've got a small mole on my right cheek. Mole and Milly both begin with M. It'll help you to remember.'

'I'll try,' I replied, 'but I might get mixed up and call you Moley-Willy!' A number of giggles from around the table made me feel much more cheerful.

While Jenny had been introducing me to my new school-mates, a small, rotund lady in a flowery pinafore, and pushing a large trolley, had been serving porridge to the girls at the next table before coming to us. She put a plate in front of Jenny, sprinkled a teaspoonful of sugar and splashed a small amount of milk on it. Then she did the same for the Willis twins.

'No sugar for me please, Gladys,' said Rob Roy.

'I ain't forgotten, Rober'a,' said Gladys, in a strong cockney accent. 'But 'ow yer can eat it wiv salt beats me.' She put a plate in front of Rob Roy and turned her attention to me. 'Now, 'oo've we got 'ere? A *noo* girl? Wot's yer nyme, ducks?'

'Alexande—,' I began to reply automatically and then remembered I was now a girl and managed to change it in mid-word to; 'Alexande-*RA* Muir.'

'D'yer like sugar'n milk on yer porridge, Alexandra?'

'Yes, please,' I replied. She slopped porridge on a plate, added the sugar and milk, and put it in front of me. 'Thank you very much,' I said, and took a spoonful. It was awfully hot and I had to suck lots of air in to cool it down.

'I'd blow on it if I were you, Alex,' said Rob Roy.

'Yes, *do* be careful,' said Jenny, 'I burnt my mouth with it once and got a blister that was absolutely gigantically painful.'

'They're a bit mingy with the sugar and milk, aren't they?' I remarked.

'*Don't you know there's a war on?*' said Jenny. 'I'm jolly glad we didn't have an air-raid last night. I'd have gone barmy if we'd had a third night on the trot in the air-raid shelter.'

'Spug-bug says she's *sure* the Jerries bomb Bournemouth by mistake, thinking it's Southampton,' said Dilly-Willy.

'They must be im*mens*ely stupid!' said Milly-Willy. 'Don't *you* think so, Alex?'

I only half heard, because I was digesting what I had just learned. Spug-Bug? *The Jerries?* That's what Dad used to call the Germans. The war? *Which* war? Not the first world war, because everyone called the Germans *Huns* then; so it must be the *second* world war, 1939–1945? *I then knew I must have travelled back in time!* But to which year?

'Sorry,' I said, 'I was trying to work something out. What did you ask?'

'Aren't the Jerries absolutely im*mens*ely stupid?'

'Oh! Errr—Yes,' I replied. 'Who's—er—Spug-Bug?'

'Our form-mistress,' replied Roberta. 'But, of course, we don't call her that to her *face*, we wouldn't *dare*. Actually her name's Miss Spurgeon, she's really top-hole. You'll meet her when she takes register before prayers.'

'I wish she was still *my* form-mistress,' sighed Jenny. 'We've got Pretty Polly—Miss Parrot—worst luck! She's horrible, *and* she keeps a gym-shoe in her desk drawer to whack us with.'

'I'll never be able to remember all you've told me—' I said, feeling bewildered. 'I'm a bit confused, having got here so late last night. What's today's date?'

'Well, it's Friday the thirteenth—' said Dilly-Willy.

'—of September—' continued Milly-Willy.

'—nineteen-forty.' Her twin added the information I wanted most of all.

Nineteen-*forty!* A quick bit of mental arithmetic told me that I had travelled back in time thirty-four years! My face must have shown some alarm, because Jen-Pen exclaimed; 'Golly, what on *earth's* the matter, Alex? You look as if you've just seen a ghost!'

I didn't think she was very far wrong!

CHAPTER TWO

Peregrine Dormitory

THE REMAINDER of breakfast passed quickly. A slice of toast, spread with the tiniest cube of margarine and a thin film of marmalade was accompanied by two cups of weak tea. I learned that butter, margarine, marmalade, milk and tea were strictly rationed. The butter ration was four ounces per person per week. I was draining my last drop of tea when somebody called 'Stand,' and there was much scraping of chairs and benches as we all stood up. *For what we have received may the Lord make us truly thankful,'* said the young teacher. I found out later that she was Miss Bendall, the gym and games mistress.

'A-men,' we replied and then we filed out, table by table, and went back upstairs to make beds and tidy dormitories. Jenny took me to our dormitory. *'Peregrine,'* said the door-plaque. Inside were seven cubicles, each one with curtains drawn around it.

'Although there are seven cubies,' Jen-Pen explained, 'there are only six of us in here this term.' She drew back one of the curtains. 'This is yours. Scottie will probably have unpacked for you, she usually does for new girls.' Inside the cubicle was a bed with a pale blue counterpane and a chest of drawers with a small mirror and a photograph on top. I recognised the photo as the one of Dad as a boy that I had last seen yesterday on Gran's mantelpiece. A blazer, a spare tunic and two dresses, a warm one of navy-blue velvet, the other blue gingham check, like those Nick and Jackie wore in the summer term, all on coat hangers—hung on a rail. Jenny opened the middle drawer.

'Yes!' she said. 'Scottie has put everything away for you; in here, your blouses and undies. Socks, stockings and hankies are in the top drawer. Keep your drawers tidy, whatever you do. Scottie gets fearfully ratty if she finds them in a mess.' She pushed the drawer closed, and picked up the photo.

'Who's the boy in the kilt?' she asked.

I was ready for *that* question. 'Oh, he's Rory, my twin.'

On the bed was Edward Bear Esquire. Now I understood why he looked so much younger. He was, in fact, thirty-four years younger. Jenny picked him up. 'He's lovely!' she said. 'Does he have a special name, or is he just Teddy?'

'He's Edward Bear Esquire,' I replied. 'He used to belong to an auntie when she was a little girl.' I added, forgetting that I, myself, was now that Auntie.

'Hello, Edward Bear Esquire,' giggled Dilly-Willy. 'You *do* sound posh!'

'D'you like being at Seabourne Preparatory School—' giggled Milly-Willy.

'—with all us *glamourous* girls?' tittered the first twin.

'Of course he does!' said Jen-Pen, giving him a kiss on his nose. 'I'll tell you what, Alex, if you watch me making my bed, you'll know what to do when you have to make yours tomorrow.'

'I'll help you if you like,' I offered. 'I always make my own bed at home.'

'Jolly dee!' said Jenny. 'With two of us, it'll take no time at all. Scottie insists we do hospital corners and we have to turn our mattresses every Saturday.'

'Matron—Scottie seems very strict,' I said.

'Och! Her bark's worse than her bite,' said Rob Roy. 'She's a wee darling really, just like a soft-centred sweetie. But don't forget to dust your cubie, Alex; forgetting that is the other thing that makes her ratty.'

'Yes,' said Jenny, as we pulled up the blankets on her bed. 'I'll show you where the dusters and wax polish are kept. Watch how we make hospital corners.' She went to the foot of the bed and took hold of the corner of the blankets. She laid it across the bed diagonally and tucked in the bit that was still hanging down. Then she let the first bit hang down again and tucked it all in. 'There, that looks neater.' She watched while I did the other side. It was really quite easy.

'Is Alexandra Muir in here?' came Matron's voice.

'Here, Matron,' I called. 'Jenny's just showing me how to make hospital corners.'

'Will you come to your own cubicle, now please?' asked Matron. 'I'd like to show you where everything goes, and how I expect it to be kept. Woe betide you, my girl, if I ever find it untidy. I cannot *abide* slovenly wee girls.'

'Yes, Matron—I mean—*NO*, Matron.'

'One thing more, Alexandra,' said Matron, after she had shown me where she had put everything away. 'You shouldn't have left your hair loose. We don't allow girls with long hair to have it draped round their shoulders. You ought to have plaited it; if Miss Plenderleith sees you with it straggling like that, you will get a misconduct mark.'

'I don't think I can plait it on my own, Matron. I've never had plaits before.'

'Never mind, I'll do it for you, as it's your first day,' she said, smiling. 'Come here, my lamb, and bring your brush and comb.' She looked kindlier when she smiled. I found my brush and comb in the top drawer and gave them to her. She brushed my hair very vigorously and plaited it into two neat pigtails, each with a dark blue ribbon at the end. I wondered what Susan and Christine would say if they could see me; even worse if my cousins Nick and Jackie could! Mind you, Nick would probably think it was a tremendous giggle, and laugh like a drain. But they would never see me like this, because they would not be born for a quarter of a century or more. 'There now, lassie!' said Matron, as she finished tying the ribbon on the left plait. 'That looks much smarter, doesn't it?' She gave my arm a friendly squeeze. 'Jennifer Pendleton?'

'Coming, Matron,' replied Jenny, poking her head through the curtains of my cubicle.

'Jennifer Pendleton,' said Matron. 'I realise it's your first term as a dormitory monitress, and that the term is less than a week old, but that's no excuse for not telling Alexandra that she should have plaited her hair.'

Jenny flushed, saying; 'Sorry, Matron, I meant to, but forgot.'

'And what does "sorry" mean, Jennifer?'

'It means "I won't do it again," Matron.'

'Just make sure you don't. As Alexandra's not had pigtails before, I'd like you to teach her how to plait them.'

'Yes, Matron, gladly.'

'Good girl. Now off you pop and show young Alex the ropes. Show her what you were shown when you were a new girl.'

'Yes, Matron,' replied Jenny. 'Come along, Alex, I'll show you round before the day-bugs arrive. What sports did you play at your last school? Hockey? Lacrosse? Netball? Tennis? Cricket? We had a wizard under-twelve lax team last year, won every match.'

'Cricket in the summer,' I replied. 'I really-really enjoy playing cricket.'

'What about the winter?' asked Jenny.

'Football,' I replied without thinking.

'*Foot*ball?' exclaimed Jenny. 'But football's a *boys*' game. I didn't know girls *could* play football.'

'Why not? I did!' I said. 'Anyhow, the rest of the team were boys. We all looked much the same and Alex is a also boy's name—'

'Coo! What a wizard wheeze,' said Jenny, as we reached the bottom of the stairs. 'That's The Beak's study,' she told me, pointing to a door to our left, on the opposite side of the hall.

'*The Beak?*' I queried.

'The Headmistress, Miss Plenderleith. She'll want to see you today. She's a jolly decent sort; you'll like her.'

'Why d'you call her The Beak?' I asked. 'Does she have a beaky nose or something?'

'Heavens no!' laughed Jenny. 'I don't know why she's called it. She's been known as that for as long as I've been here.'

'Have you been here a long time?'

'Ever since I was seven,' she replied. 'I'll be twelve on Guy Fawkes Day. I've had a wizzo time here and will be jolly sad when I've got to leave and go to another school.'

'Have you been a boarder all the time?' I asked.

'No, I was a day-bug for the first three years. We used to live very close by—in Watcombe Road. Daddy's in the Navy, and when he was given command of a cruiser, we had to move to Pompey.' She must have seen me frown. 'Portsmouth, y'know. Anyhow Mummy and Daddy decided that as I was so happy here, I could stay on as a boarder if I wanted to.'

'Golly, aren't you jolly worried your dad might get killed?'

'Yes, but I've got used to it now,' she said. 'So's Mummy. There're thousands and thousands of women and children who dread the knock at the door, in case it's a telegram bringing bad news. Is your daddy in the war?'

'No, he died in an aeroplane crash when I was seven,' I said

'Oh, I'm sorry. I bet you miss him, don't you?' replied Jenny, giving my arm a squeeze.

'It's all right, it seems quite a long time ago now.'

'What about your mummy, is she doing something for the war effort?'

'Yes, she's doing something rather hush-hush in the War Office, and might have to go away at a moment's notice, which is why I've come here as a boarder.' I had worked out that if I was now Dad's twin sister, Gran would be my Mum, and I knew she'd been a Special Operations Executive wireless operator, working with the French resistance during the war, so therefore my Mummy was doing something rather hush-hush.

We were now walking along a covered way with a scrap of garden on the left. Jenny pointed at a door on our right. 'That's the day-bug's changing-room where they hang their hats and raincoats and change before gym, sport or "music and movement".' A girl with fiery red hair, cut in a bob, rather like Nick's, was coming along the covered way towards us. 'Hey! Maggot!' called Jenny. 'Come and meet Alex. She arrived during the night and spent it in the sick-bay. She's in the third with you.'

The redhead stopped. She was a cheerful girl, a bit taller than me, her long legs emphasised by the shortness of her tunic, which fell short of her knees by about ten centimetres.

'Hiya!' she said cheerfully. 'I'm Margot Burton, but my chums all call me Maggot.' She held out her hand.

I shook it. 'Hello, Maggot, I'm Alex Muir.

'Sounds as if you should be a boy!' said Maggot. 'Lucky you! I wish *I* had a boy's name. I wish I was a boy like my twin brother.'

'Alex played football at her last school,' said Jenny. 'Her name's Alexandra, actually.'

'I used to play football with my brothers,' said Maggot. 'But when I got too good for them they wouldn't let me play any more. Typical boys! I say, Jen-Pen, have you seen Weevil around? I must find her before lessons. *Toodloo,* Alex, see you later.' She waved and dashed off.

'Who's Weevil?' I asked, intrigued.

'Her best friend,' said Jenny. 'Actually, her name's Evelyn. We used to call her Eevie-weevie, which became Weevie for short, and then Maggot thought of Weevil. Maggot and Weevil seem to go so well together, don't you think?'

I laughed. We returned to the main hall where we found Rob Roy, who had just come downstairs. 'Hello, you two,' she said. 'Have you been shown everything now, Alex?'

'I'm just going to show her the gym,' said Jenny, 'Then you can take her to the third form room. I checked the class lists on the board and her name is just below yours.'

They showed me the gym, a large room with wall bars along one side and two ropes hanging from the ceiling. There was a piano and gym apparatus, and at the far end, a platform with a table and eight chairs ranged along the wall behind it.

'This is where we have prayers every morning,' said Jenny. 'The chairs are for the mistresses. We have to sit on the floor, worst luck. Do you like gym, Alex?'

'Yes,' I replied. 'We called it PE. Our teacher was really nice. He'd been an army physical training instructor, and was married to the French teacher.' I suddenly realised she might have thought this a bit odd, so added; 'I should think he'll have been called back into the army again by now.'

'Coo! Fancy having a *man* to take you for gym,' said Rob Roy. 'How embarrassing. Didn't you mind?'

'No, not a bit. Never thought about it, I s'pose.' I could hardly tell her I was a boy at my last school.

'Miss Bendall takes *us* for gym,' said Rob Roy. 'Her christian name's Wendy so we call her Bendy Wendy, She said Grace at breakfast. We've got gym first period after break. I must go and get my blazer from the dormy, then I'll take you to our form-room. Golly! look at the time! A quarter to nine already! The day-bugs'll be here in two ticks.'

'What time's assembly—I er—mean—prayers?' I asked.

'Nine o'clock on the dot,' replied Rob Roy. 'We'd better hurry or we'll be late. I've still to polish my shoes.'

We scampered upstairs to Peregrine, and Rob Roy dived into her cubicle, while I went to mine. I took the blazer from its hanger and put it on; there was a fountain pen in the top pocket. I found a clean hanky and shoved it in one of my blazer pockets. I could hear Rob Roy brushing her shoes still, so I waited outside her cubicle.

'Come away in,' she called. 'I'll only be half a tick.' I went in and sat on the end of her bed. She finished cleaning her shoes then crouched down and put them on. Then she took a clean hanky from her top drawer, hitched up her skirt and stuffed it into the little pocket on the front of her navy knickers.

'So *that's* what it's for,' I thought, stood up and transferred my own hanky from my blazer pocket. Then I smoothed out Rob Roy's counterpane where I had been sitting, and we were ready.

'All set, Alex?' she asked. 'Let's go and meet some of the day-bugs!'

CHAPTER THREE

War's Bitter Taste

IN THE SHORT TIME we had been upstairs, the school had become a hive of activity. Day-girls were arriving in droves, and as soon as they had taken off their wet raincoats and hats and hung them in their changing room, they made a bee-line for their form-rooms. There was a hubbub of eager voices; discussing what they had heard on Children's Hour, complaining about the war and last night's prep, swopping juicy bits of gossip or speculating on what the day ahead held in store. Many were saying how glad they were that there had been no air-raid last night, as disturbed nights made everyone sleepy and cantankerous next day.

A second after we entered the form-room, everybody stopped talking and watched as Rob Roy handed me over to Nancy Blackwell, the form captain, whom I had met at brekker and in the dormitory. She took me to the desk that had been allocated to me. The girls had heard there was to be a new girl in the form, and they crowded round to be introduced.

'This is Alexandra Muir,' said Nancy, '—but she prefers to be called Alex. She's a boarder.' She turned to me. 'You've met Maggot, now meet Evelyn Cochrane—Weevil—her best friend. They're always up to mischief and Spug-Bug calls them *The Grubbies* when they're particularly naughty. Last term Maggot filled her bike-basket with horse-manure and chucked dollops of it at a croc of Saint Aloysius' boys as she cycled past and made several of them cry. The beastly master in charge of their croc sneaked on her to The Beak.'

'Golly,' I said, looking at Maggot with even greater respect. 'What a super thing to do!' She grinned impishly, and I wondered what she would have said had she known that I was a St Aloysius' boy from thirty-four years in the future.

'I thought it was rather fun,' said Maggot. 'Looking back on it, it was worth the six of the best The Beak gave me.'

'She gave you the cane?' I said.

'*Rather!*' Maggot replied. 'Six on the bare botty! Couldn't sit down for ages.'

Nancy turned to a plumpish, jolly girl. 'This is Barbara Goodbody. Actually she's in the fourth, and is just visiting us. We call her Goody-two-shoes, or Goody for short.' She looked vaguely familiar, but I couldn't think how. 'And this is Sue Spender; her nickname's "Garters".'

I frowned; 'Sue Spender—Garters?' At last the penny dropped. 'Oh! I see, *Suspender!*' and giggled girlishly—surprising myself as I had never giggled girlishly before. 'Hello, Sue, I'm sorry I laughed, but I couldn't help it!'

'That's all right, Alex, I am just glad nobody calls me Suspenders!' Two other girls sniggered, so I guessed that they might be new, too.

Then Nancy introduced a pretty, fair-haired girl with pigtails and a clear complexion. 'This is Sarah Nickerson; she's the vice-monitress of Eagle Dormy. She hates being called Sarah and as there's another Sarah in the form we usually call her Sally or Nicky—one girl, who's left now, used to call her Nickers—'

'Without a "K",' Sarah added hurriedly, with a friendly grin. 'But most people call me Nicky. Hi, Alex. Welcome. I wondered who you were when you came to brekker with Jenny. Is it actually true that you actually played *football* with boys at your last school?'

'Yes—and it was brilliant fun.'

'Coo!' exclaimed Nicky. 'Frightfully brave of you; I'd've been absolutely *petrified!* Shall I introduce her to the other Eagles, Nancy?'

'Yes, please, Nicky. They're your crew, after all,' Nancy replied.

'Come on, Alex, meet Miss Patricia O'Halloran,' said Nicky, turning to a round-faced girl with a snub nose, freckles and carroty hair. 'A wild Irish colleen, if ever there was one. You'll not be surprised to learn that we call her Paddy.'

'Hello there, Alex,' said Paddy in a rich Irish brogue, pumping my arm up and down violently at the same time. 'Didjer really play footy at your last school? Honest injun?'

'Yes, really-truly-honest-injun.' I was glad the bell rang at that moment, because I was afraid my arm might break off if Paddy kept pumping it any longer. We stopped talking and went quickly to our places. I looked round at my new classmates and realised that I did not know any of the day-girls yet.

The door opened and a mistress bustled in. She was slim and pretty, with auburn hair and a kind face and laughing eyes.

'Good *Mor*-ning, Miss Spurgeon,' chanted the class.

'Good Morning, girls. You may sit down,' she replied, so we did. 'Now, before I check the register and we go into prayers, I would like to introduce a new girl who has joined us today, Alexandra Muir. Would you please stand up, Alexandra, so all the form can see you? I'm sure you've been introduced to some of the girls already, and within a week or so you'll know everyone by name.'

I stood up and everybody looked at me. I felt very self-conscious and knew I was blushing as their eyes bored into me. I wondered how long I could keep up the pretence before someone found out that I was not who they thought I was.

After what seemed like an eternity Miss Spurgeon said, 'Thank you Alexandra, you may sit down now. I believe you prefer to be called Alex. Is that so?'

'Yes, Miss Spurgeon,' I replied rather quietly, still blushing.

'Speak up, dear, don't be shy. I can't hear you if you mumble.'

'Yes, Miss Spurgeon,' I said, louder, and blushed even more.

'That's more like it,' she said. 'Did they not teach you to speak up at your last school?'

'Oh *yes*, Miss Spurgeon,' I answered boldly.

'Good girl. That's *much* better. I shall call the register now.' She took a book from her desk drawer and began to call our names. 'Sarah Ackroyd—?'
'Present, Miss Spurgeon.' She put a tick against Sarah's name.
'Margot Burton?'
'Present, Miss Spurgeon,' answered Maggot.
'Evelyn Cochrane?'
'Here,' replied Weevil.
'I beg your pardon, Evelyn.'
' 'M sorry, Miss Spurgeon! *Present,* Miss Spurgeon.'
'Hannah Dürnberg?'
'Present, Miss Spurgeon.'
'Margaret Frost?'
'Present, Miss Spurgeon.'
'Stephanie Graham?'
'Present, Miss Spurgeon.'
She soon got to me and called, 'Alexandra Muir?'
'Present, Miss Spurgeon,' I replied boldly, and she flashed a smile in my direction as she ticked my name in the register. I thought Spug-Bug was rather nice.
As soon as she had finished, she closed the register with a snap and looked up again. 'Just one absentee; does anyone know why Judy White's not here today?'
There were mutterings of; 'No, Miss Spurgeon,' just as the bell rang again.
'Quiet now please, girls!' said our teacher. 'Form captain and door keeper, please.' Nancy sprang to her feet, and went to the door followed by Jane Wright, a serious-looking girl with spectacles. Jane opened the door and stood to attention beside it. 'Now girls, have you all got your hymn books? Alex, you will have to share with Roberta until you've been issued with one of your own. Come along, girls, fall in behind Nancy.' There was the noise of tip-up seats springing up; '*Quiet*-ly please girls! Margot Burton! You re-*vol*-ting child! What *have* you got on the back of your tunic?'
'I don't know, Miss Spurgeon.'
'No! Don't look *now,* girls.' Miss Spurgeon looked pained. 'Get back into line at once! After prayers, Margot, go straight to Matron and ask her for a clean tunic.'
'Yes, Miss Spurgeon.'
'Margot, you are quite the *grubbiest* little girl that it has been my misfortune to encounter.'
'Yes, Miss Spurgeon,' replied Maggot, going bright red.
'Right you are, Nancy, quick march. Left-right-left-right.' We marched into the gym for morning prayers. A number of much younger girls and small boys were already there, standing in rows in front of the dais. 'They're the juniors—the remove and second-formers. Boys can stay till they're nine.' Rob Roy hissed in my ear, earning a scowl from Spug-Bug as we took our places behind the second form. The fourth and fifth forms followed and stood behind us. The mistresses were all

seated on the dais, waiting for Miss Plenderleith. A small, tired-looking old man with a bald head, fringed by wisps of greyish-white hair, sat at an old upright piano, a hymn book open on the music-stand. Moments later, the Headmistress, The Beak, swept in, her black gown billowing behind her, a sheaf of papers, a prayer book and a hymnal, all held in her right hand. There was the noise of scraping chair legs as the mistresses stood up.

'Good MOR-ning, Miss Plenderleith,' the pupils chanted together.

'Good morning, everybody.' She was looking serious, and gave a little cough behind her hand. 'Children,' she began, 'I have just received a very sad piece of news; Judith White's father was shot down over the Channel yesterday.' There were several gasps of horror. 'He was still in his burning Spitfire when it plunged into the sea.'

So that was why Judy White had not come to school.

'We shall stand in silence for one minute,' said The Beak; 'To honour Flight Lieutenant White, and all those brave men and women who have given their lives for our country in this dreadful war.'

During that minute's silence, I suddenly remembered that today was Friday the thirteenth.

When the minute was over, Miss Plenderleith announced; 'Hymn number 257, *I Heard the voice of Jesus say.*' There was much turning of pages as we found the right place. Finally The Beak looked up and there was instant silence. 'Thank you, Mr. Grubb.' The little grey man played the first line of the tune, paused and started again, this time with everyone joining in with the words. Afterwards we remained standing. Then we said the Lord's Prayer, and after a couple of other prayers read by Miss Plenderleith, she said; 'You may sit.' The mistresses sat on their chairs and we all sat cross-legged on the floor. A round-faced mistress with pebble glasses and a lisp, wearing a maroon suit, read a short passage from Saint Paul's second Epistle to the Corinthians and sat down again.

'Any of you who listened in to the news on the wireless this morning,' said Miss Plenderleith, 'will have heard that during a four-hour air-raid over London, a German aeroplane dropped five bombs on Buckingham Palace.' There were more gasps. 'One hit the chapel, and two others damaged the inner quadrangle. More bombs fell in the grounds. But you will be pleased to hear that Their Majesties, the King and Queen, were uninjured and, after examining the damage, they went on a tour of London to inspect the bomb damage suffered by others. The King said that he and the Queen now had personal experience of what others had suffered from the German barbarity.' After several more notices, she asked us to stand and said; '*The Grace of Our Lord Jesus Christ and the Love of God and the fellowship of the Holy Ghost, be with us all evermore. Amen.*'

We marched back to our form-room in silence, appalled by the news. Several girls were crying and even though I had not yet met Judy, I felt a lump in my throat and stinging behind my eyes. It was my first bitter taste of what it meant to be living in a country at war. Back in our form-room, we sat silently at our desks staring the blackboard, on which Miss Spurgeon had written "Friday 13th September 1940" in flowing copperplate handwriting. Our first lesson was supposed to be dictation, according to the timetable on the notice board.

'Girls,' said Miss Spurgeon, 'I know we all feel deeply about Judy's loss. All but our new girls will remember Judy's daddy at Sports Day at the end of last term. He was a lovely man and a wonderful father to Judy, and he will be sorely missed by everyone. There are others among us who have lost a father or a mother, and I know of at least one pupil in the school who has lost both, so those girls will know how Judy will be feeling. The Headmistress says that, all going well, Judy will be back with us on Tuesday. So-o,' she took a deep breath, paused and sighed; 'On Monday, I shall make a collection so we can buy some flowers for Judy and her Mummy. Therefore, instead of spending all your pocket money on your sweets ration tomorrow, if you could spare a penny, or even a ha'penny, it would mean we could buy a really pretty bouquet for Judy to take home on Tuesday. I'm sure I can rely on you all.

'Now, girls, dry your eyes, and put your hankies away because I want to cheer us up a little. Instead of dull, boring old dictation, I'm going to read a story from *Winnie the Pooh*.'

'Jolly dee,' said Nancy. 'Please, Miss Spurgeon, can we have the one about the hefferlump trap?'

'Hands up those who would like that?' asked Spug-Bug. Nearly every hand went up, including mine. 'Right, hefferlumps it shall be. Oh—before I begin—Alex, Miss Plenderleith wants to you see later. Don't worry, it's only so that she can welcome you personally to Seabourne Preparatory.'

'Yes, Miss Spurgeon.' I made sure I spoke out this time.

'Good girl. Now, are we all sitting comfortably? Here goes then.' She began reading; '*One day, when Christopher Robin and Winnie-the-Pooh*—' We sat and listened, many of us with our elbows on our desks, our chins resting on cupped hands, and lost ourselves in the story, which Miss Spurgeon read so beautifully.

You could have heard a pin drop.

CHAPTER FOUR

First Morning—Later

THE SECOND LESSON WAS MATHS. The hefferlump story had put us in a happier mood and most of us were able to put Judy's tragedy to the back of our minds. However, as soon as Miss Parrot came into the room it was plain to all that she was in one of her moods. I recognised her as the mistress in the maroon suit who had read the lesson at Prayers. She was small, frumpish and round-faced, with faded orange hair, parted in the middle, and buck teeth. Her pebble glasses made her look pop-eyed. Polly was far from pretty!

I remembered what Jenny had said, and wondered if she carried a gym-shoe around, or if she kept one in each form room. It was algebra on Friday; evidently it was a new subject to the form. We were about half way through the lesson, and poor Dorothy Clark could not make head or tail of it. Dotty Dot, as she was known, was 12 years old, large, lumbering and lazy, and rather dense at the best of times. Pretty Polly was getting more and more ratty, her eyebrows raised, eyes looking even larger and "poppier" behind her pebble glasses and her buck-teeth seeming to thrust even further forward, as she stared at poor Dotty.

'Are you an imbethile, Dowothy?' lisped Miss Parrot, going red in the face. 'If two x, pluth thwee y equalth thirteen, when x ith two,' she bawled, 'Surely it'th not beyond your pea-thized bwain to be able to work out the value of y!' The unfortunate Dotty burst into tears. 'Well!' said Miss Parrot, 'If *you* cannot work it out, p'waps thome other girl can give me the anthwer.'

I had done algebra before and found it easy. My hand shot up instantly, with several others.

'You, girl!' Miss Parrot pointed at me. 'You're new, aren't you? What'th your name?'

'Alexandra Muir, Miss Parrot.'

'Tell me the anthwer, Alecthandwa Mew-er?'

'It's three, Miss Parrot.'

'Cowwect. But you don't need to "Mith Pawwot" me all the time. "Mith" ith quite thufficient.'

'Yes, Miss Parrot—I mean yes, Miss!' My reply brought a snort from the back row. Pretty Polly stared past me, trying to spot the culprit. An outbreak of sniggering came from the area of the Willis twins, Lucy Parker, and Cecilie Poole, titterers all. A number of the girls in the front row turned round to see what was causing such merriment.

'Face the fwont!' thundered Pretty Polly, starting to lose her wool. 'Face the fwont! ALL of you, thith inthtant!' I stole a quick glance round when she was not looking at me. Weevil was sitting at her desk, wide-eyed, with eyebrows raised and a set of false buck-teeth sticking out beneath her top lip.

'Evelyn *Cochwane!*' thundered the irate teacher. 'Come here at *onthe!*' Weevil strolled to the front, grinning toothily. 'You howwid little Madam! What are you?'

'A howwith lickle nadan, Niss,' said Weevil, unable to speak properly with the fake teeth in her mouth.

'Give me those thith inthtant.' The mistress held out her hand and Weevil spat out the teeth and handed them over. 'I am confithcating thith until the end of term.' She put them in her handbag and Weevil began to go back to her place. *'Thtand thtill!* I've not finithed with you yet, young woman!' She opened the mistresses' desk and took out a huge gym-shoe which looked bigger than my old PE teacher's size 14s. 'Bend over the dethk!'

Weevil obeyed. Miss Parrot pulled up Weevil's tunic. From my desk in the second row I could clearly see the shape of several books inside Weevil's knickers. Miss Parrot was so ratty that her glasses must have got steamed up, and it seemed that she had not noticed Weevil's "padding"! It was hard not to giggle as six strokes of the gym-shoe were given, and Weevil went back to her desk. As soon as she had turned her back on Pretty Polly, she stuck out her tongue and grinned.

The rest of the lesson passed reasonably quietly. As soon as the bell went for break and Miss Parrot had gone, everyone dissolved into helpless laughter, while Weevil bent over the desk again and Maggot, with great ceremony, removed five exercise books, one by one, each one getting a cheer from the rest of the form. How Miss Parrot didn't see them I'll never know!

*

During break we all had a bottle of milk before going into the playground for some exercise. The milk came in small bottles holding one-third of a pint. We drank it by pushing a hole in the cardboard disc that sealed the bottle, and putting in a straw.

When we had finished, we had to put the empty bottles in the crate and the used straws in the wastepaper basket. Then, as it had stopped raining, we had to go out in the fresh air. As it was the first time I had been out-of-doors in 1940, I wanted to look at what the road outside the school looked like.

I was getting on well with Rob Roy who was quite like me in many ways. She was ten and enjoyed the same sort of things as me, like sailing and swimming. She had never played football, but was demon on the lacrosse field. I liked Nancy too; she had had her tenth birthday in the last week of the summer term. She was quiet, studious and responsible, but even so had a great sense of humour. It was she who had thought of calling Sue Spender Garters, and Cecilie Poole Cesspool. As we strolled towards the bushes that grew between the lawn and the boundary fence, we were joined by another Scots girl.

'This is my best friend, Jemima Stewart,' said Rob Roy. 'She's Puddleduck or Puddles to her friends. She's in the fourth and has a wee brother, Hamish, who's nine.'

'He came to our sports day last term wearing his kilt,' said Nancy, 'and Maggot and Weevil spent the whole day trying to peer up it. Talk about em*barrass*ing!'

'In the end,' said Rob Roy, 'Moo-Cow, that's Mrs. Cowley, our form mistress last term, got so fed up with the exhibition they were making of themselves, she gave them a hundred lines each.'

'My Dad was born in Scotland.' I said, thinking of my real Dad, and not thinking that as his twin sister in my present life, I must have been born there as well. We reached the fence, and could just see over it into Southbourne Road where it joins Belle View Road. It looked almost the same as in 1974, but the lamp-posts were different and two sets of parallel overhead wires, running along the line of the road were strung between them. A horse-drawn baker's delivery van plodded wearily past and a yellow number 22 trolleybus glided silently into Belle View Road bound for Tuckton, emitting a faint whine—Of course—the wires were for the trolleybuses. I could just remember them, before they were withdrawn in 1969, when I was five, and wondered why these clean, almost silent, buses should be replaced by noisy, smelly diesels. Another, a number 21 from Christchurch, bound for Bournemouth Square via Fisherman's Walk and Boscombe, stopped opposite the school gates.

We gazed at the outside world for a few more minutes, then strolled back towards the school house. A long line of girls were playing tag, and some were skipping to chants of *"I-am-a-little-orphan-girl"* or *"Rasp-ber-ry, Straw-ber-ry, Goose-ber-ry Jam"*. A few had tucked up their tunics to do handstands against a high wall; another group were having a 'sevenses' competition—bouncing a ball against a wall and catching it again, doing something in between like spinning round or clapping hands and then bouncing it again, this time under one raised leg. Some others were playing catch with a tennis ball. Many were just strolling around in small groups, like us, chatting.

Soon, Kate Jackson, the head girl, came out of the front door ringing the bell for the end of break. We formed up into lines and filed back in, form by form.

'We've got gym with Bendy Wendy,' Nancy whispered to me when we were inside. 'Come on, I'll show you where our changing room is. The day-bugs one is down the covered way, but ours is next to the gym.' In the changing room, Rob Roy, Maggot, Weevil, Nicky, Paddy and the Willis twins, to my horror, had taken off their tunics and shirts and were busy lacing up their gym-shoes.

Sudden panic gripped me! It had never occurred to me that I would have to do gym wearing only my vest and knickers! I had often changed into sports kit in front of classmates as a boy; but now I was a girl and had to undress in front of girls for the first time. Help! I felt very self-conscious and vulnerable, afraid I might give myself away. After taking off my tunic I glanced round furtively, expecting everyone to be staring. *But nobody was taking any notice.* Only *then* did I realise that, to them, I was just another ordinary schoolgirl like themselves. I would only stand out if I behaved oddly. With some relief I took off my shirt and put on my gym-shoes. Even so, I still felt shy and self-conscious as I joined the line and we trooped into the gym.

We were greeted by Miss Bendall, tall and slim and wearing a short, faded, bottle-green gym-tunic that made her look like a gawky, overgrown schoolgirl. 'Jolly good show, boarders,' she enthused. 'Beaten the day-bugs to it again, eh?'

'Hello, Miss Bendall,' said Nancy, 'This is Alex, Alexandra Muir, who got here late last night. She used to play football for her last school—with *boys!*'

'I say, jolly *decent* show, Alex! Like Harry eh?' She clapped me hard on the back, making me stagger slightly. 'We should try to get a footer side going here, don't you think. Ah! here come the day-bugs. Fall in, chaps, and stand still, then I can see if you're all here.' She counted heads. 'Where's young Harry today?'

'Please, Miss Bendall, she's just coming, Miss Bendall,' said Peggy Frost.

I could not place Harry. 'Who's Harry?' I asked Cecilie Poole in a whisper.

'Henrietta Gordon, the girl with the short hair, cut like a boy's,' hissed Cesspool. 'She's Scotch and the most terrible tomboy; and she *always* dresses up as a *boy* at home, and she went to a *boys'* school till they found out she was acksherly a girl!'

'Golly! How long's she been here?' I asked, liking the sound of Harry.

'Since the beginning of last term,' said Priscilla Smith. 'Her last school *really* thought she was a *boy* all that time.'

'Yeth,' lisped Lucy Parker whom, I soon discovered, loved gossip. 'And, d'you *know*, she'd *never* worn a fwock before she came here? She wath *ever*-tho wough and has had to *learn* how to behave like a pwoper little girl!'

'Stop chin-wagging, Lucy Parker! Jack, go and light a firework under Harry, will you?' Bendy Wendy told Peggy Frost. 'It can't take her all this time to change. Tell her from me that if she doesn't hurry up, I'll give her a lateness mark.'

Stephanie Graham put up her hand; '*Please,* Miss Bendall? Pul-*ease,* Miss?'

'What is it, Steve?' asked the gym mistress, slightly irritated.

'*Please*, Miss Bendall, 'tsbout *Harry*, Miss Bendall. She asked me to tell you that the laccy in her—in her…in her…er—*unmentionables*,' a blushing Stephanie coyly whispered the word, 'broke while she was changing, so she's gone to Matron to get it mended.'

'Thank you, Steve,' said Miss Bendall as Angela Fitzpatrick exploded into giggles and her chummery of day-girls sniggered and nudged each other gleefully. 'I don't think it's *at all* funny, Angela. Quiet now! Settle down, *please*, chaps. *Cecilie Poole*, control yourself THIS INSTANT, or take a misconduct mark! It's not the sort of thing that *nice* little girls should find the least bit funny!'

' 'Msorry, Miss Bendall,' said a sullen Cecilie Poole, her cheeks turning scarlet.

'I should *think* so too! Now! Form up in four lines facing me.' We obeyed. 'A little bit further apart; stretch those arms out so you can't quite touch the chap next to you. Arms down now. Aa-tenn-*shun!* Come on, chaps, chins up, shoulders back, chest *out*, tummies *in!* Arch those backs! That's good, Rob Roy, and you,

Alex. Well done, Jack; and Steve. Oh *dear!* What *are* we going to do with you, Dotty? I said tummy *in*, not stuck out like that; it makes you look expectant!' There were sniggers. 'Quiet, Weevil! You may share the joke with Maggot later. Right now, chaps! Running on the spot! Are you rea*dee?* Bee*egin!* Hup-two-three-four—hup-two-three-four—hup-two-three-four—hup-two-three, and—*stop!*'

A leggy, athletic-looking girl, her dark hair cut short like a boy, came in. 'Sorry I'm late, Miss Bendall. I had a bit of a problem.'

'Ah! There you are, Harry,' said Miss Bendall. 'Did Matron fix you up okay? Jolly dee! Lucky it happened before we started, eh?' Poor Harry blushed to her hairline and Lucy Parker and company sniggered and nudged each other yet again. Miss Bendall stared hard at them, making them stop instantly and turn scarlet.

'Oh, yes, thank you, Miss Bendall,' replied Harry, lowering her eyes coyly and showing her long eyelashes. I felt sympathetic towards her and thought she looked the sort of girl I would like to have as my friend. After all we'd both been at boys' schools before coming to Seabourne Preparatory!

'Fall-in in front of Alex, there's a good chap, Harry.'

As she came to the front of my line, I gave her a friendly smile. She relaxed, giving me a really chummy grin in return, and I felt sure we would be friends.

'Stride jumps, with arms raising sideways,' announced Miss Bendall. 'Rea-*dee?* Bee-*gin! Stride*-t'gether—*stride*-t'gether—*stride*-t'gether—*stride*-t'gether—keep—up—Dott—ee,—*stride*-t'gether—*stride*-t'gether—stride—and—*stop!*'

After that we did some other exercises and then we climbed the ropes. Harry and I raced each other to the top; she won—just! But I could vault higher over the horse than she could.

Miss Bendall dismissed us five minutes before the bell, so we had time to change back into tunics and tidy ourselves for the last lesson before lunch. Also, I had to meet The Beak, the Headmistress, Miss Vera Plenderleith.

∗

My appointment with The Beak was at twelve o'clock, a quarter-of-an-hour after the next lesson began. It was history, which was taught by Mrs. Griffiths, the fourth-form mistress. When she entered we were sitting quietly at our desks, as she put up with no malarkey whatsoever. She was a gaunt, stern-looking lady, with greying hair, cut in a severe bob, wearing a tweed suit, thick stockings and brown lace-up shoes. Her children, Gillian and Victor were both pupils at the school. Gillian was thirteen, and in the upper fifth, and Victor, who was eight, was in the Remove. I discovered later that she was a widow; her late husband, serving in the Royal Navy aboard the cruiser HMS Exeter, had lost his life during the Battle of the River Plate in December 1939.

As soon as she entered the room, the hubbub ceased. She strode to the front of the class and put her books on the desk.

'Good Morning, gels,' she said.

'Good Morning, Mrs. Griffiths,' we chanted in reply.

'Now, gels, before we start, is Alexandra Muir here?'

I put up my hand and stood up. 'Present, Mrs. Griffiths.'

'Good. I'm glad you've arrived at last. Welcome!' She smiled and her face changed instantly to that of a kind and caring lady. 'I hear your journey here was rather fraught and hair-raising. It must have been somewhat unnerving being on a train as it was bombed. Still, you've survived and it's something you'll be able to tell your own children about one day. Now, don't forget that you've to see the Headmistress at twelve o'clock, so keep an eye on the time.'

'Yes, Mrs. Griffiths, I will,' I replied.

'Good gel!' She glanced round the class as she opened one of her books. 'Now, gels, in our last lesson we learned about the time of Queen Elizabeth, and we will be returning to her later on.' *(Elizabeth? Which Elizabeth? I was about to ask when I remembered it was 1940 so there had only been one. Elizabeth II was still only a princess. I must be* very *careful!)* 'But first, who can remember the *mnemonic*, that little rhyme, we learned to help us remember the kings and queens of England?'

Several hands shot up, accompanied by squeals of '*Please*, Miss, *me*, Miss.' Mrs. Griffiths—whom the girls referred to as Grif-Bug, looked around the class, deciding which of her pupils to pick. It was almost as if she had a box of chocolates, and was deciding which one she fancied most. 'Sarah Nickerson.'

'Thank you, Mrs. Griffiths,' said Nicky standing up. She clasped her hands tightly behind her back and rattled off at speed; '*Willy-Willy-Harry-Steve, Harry-Dick-John-Harry-three—*' She ran out of steam, frowned, and made little turns left and right, clasping her hands even tighter, showing her embarrassment.

'Stuck?' asked the history mistress, raising an inquisitive eyebrow.

'Yes, Mrs. Griffiths—'m sorry!' replied Nicky.

'Never mind, dear, a good try. You may sit down. Can anybody go any further? No, Dilys Willis, don't cheat by looking it up in your book! I was wondering if any of you dunderheads could still remember it all.' She looked round the class, but had no takers until Harry put her hand up. 'Can *you* finish it, Henrietta?'

'I'll try, Mrs. Griffiths,' said Harry. '*One, two, three Neds, Richard two, Henries four, five, six, then who? Edward four, five, Dick the Bad, Harries twain and Ned the lad*—Oh *blow!* I'm sorry, Mrs. Griffiths, but I can't remember the rhyme after that, but I know it's Mary, Elizabeth and James the sixth—I mean—the *first!* You see, they didn't teach us much about the English kings at my Scottish school!'

'Very good, Henrietta, that was a valiant effort,' Mrs. Griffiths said. 'I want you all to learn it again as part of your preparation tonight. Alexandra, you may copy it from someone's book during preparation this evening and learn as much of it as you can.'

'Yes, Mrs. Griffiths,' I replied.

'You'd better skip along to the Headmistress's study now,' she told me. 'We mustn't keep her waiting, must we, dear?'

'Yes, Mrs. Griffiths—I mean *no*, Mrs. Griffiths.'

'Put your books away in your desk, that's a good gel.'

'Yes, Mrs. Griffiths.' I put the books away and as I closed the lid, it slipped from my hand and shut with a bang.

'Please try to close your desk *quiet*ly, Alexandra!' Mrs. Griffiths said sharply.

'Yes, Mrs. Griffiths, 'msorry, Mrs. Griffiths,' I said, feeling myself blushing red hot, and fled as quickly as I could.

*

'Come away in,' came the answer to my knock. I opened the door and, timidly, entered The Beak's study. I felt nervous, just as I did when I had to see the headmaster at Saint Aloysius'. Miss Plenderleith, sitting at her desk, peered at me over the top of her pince-nez. As soon as she saw me, she stood and held out her right hand to me. I grasped it and shook it as firmly as I could.

'Hello, Alexandra, welcome to Seabourne Preparatory!' She spoke with very slight Scottish accent. She smiled. 'My! That's a good firm handshake for a lassie; I can see we're going to get on famously. I can't a*bide* people with handshakes that are like a bit of wet fish! Let's sit down, shall we?' She nodded towards two easy chairs. She was elegant and distinguished-looking, of medium height, with greying hair. She had a kind face, and the sort of expression that gives you confidence. I was sure that she was somebody I could trust, who would do anything to help anyone in difficulty.

As soon as she had sat down, I perched, rather nervously, on the edge of the other chair, my knees tightly together, and my hands clasped, on my lap.

'Well, Alexandra,' she continued, 'Or would you prefer me to call you Alex? I believe that's what you're called at home, isn't it?'

'I like Alex best, Miss Plenderleith.'

'Very well, Alex it shall be. Now, my dear, you can't be very comfy perched right on the edge of the chair like that, why not sit on it properly and relax. I'm not going to bite you.' She smiled as I shuffled into a more comfortable position, and smiled back at her. 'That's more comfy, isn't it?' I nodded.

'Well, my dear, I'm jolly glad to meet you at long last, and all in one piece, too! From what Matron tells me your journey must have been quite an ordeal, what with Waterloo being closed due to the bombing and having to catch your train at Wimbledon. I won't ask you about it, and if I were you I wouldn't say anything about it to the other girls. I don't mind if you tell your best friend, if you have one, but ask her not to spread it around. How is your dear mother? I had gone to bed when you arrived last night and was so sorry to miss her. It's such a long time since I saw her.'

'Oh, she's fine, Miss Plenderleith. She couldn't come down with me, but when she saw me on to the train she sent you her love. We were in London together during an air-raid, after the train journey from home, so I don't think I want to tell anybody about it just now.' I could hardly have told her that it was not me on the train. It was news to me that Gran was an old friend of Miss Plenderleith.

'I think that's very sensible, my dear. I believe this is the first time you've been at boarding school.' I nodded. 'You'll probably find it a wee bit strange at first, having no parents to take your problems to or ask for advice. That's where we come in; Matron, your form mistress, Miss Spurgeon, and, of course, myself. If there's anything you're not sure of, or want to know, please don't be afraid to come and ask. We're not monsters, we're here to be your friends and to look after you in much the same way as your parents.' She smiled. 'You'll find we're a happy little community—rather like an overgrown family.

'Now, I'm sure there are lots of things you want to ask, but if you're like the other girls, you've probably forgotten most of them just now. Don't worry, my door is always open if you want help. Is there anything you'd like to ask now?'

I thought for a moment or two. 'What do we do after lessons, and what time do we go to bed?'

'I'll answer the easy one first. Third form bedtime is half past eight. You must be in bed by then, but you may read until lights-out at a quarter to nine. Now for the hard one! When afternoon school finishes at four, most of the day-girls go home; those who stay behind to do preparation join you boarders for tea and a cake at a quarter past four. After tea, you have preparation until ten past five, when the day-girls go home. You may then listen to Children's Hour on the wireless in your common room, read, chat or play board-games like Monopoly until high tea at half past six. After high tea, the fifth formers do second preparation while you and your chums are free to play until bedtime.'

'I see; thank you, Miss Plenderleith.' I was not sure whether all this had sunk in, but at least I knew what to expect.

'I'm sure you'll not remember it all. Jenny, your dormitory monitress, will help you if you need any advice. Now is there anything else I can tell you?'

I thought for a few seconds; 'Are we allowed to go shopping on Saturday?'

'Yes, after luncheon; as long as you ask permission from Matron or me. At least two of you must go together, and you *must* wear school uniform. Of course, being in uniform, you must behave properly, and act in a manner that is a credit to the school. You get your pocket money from Matron just before lunch on Saturday. On Sunday we go to All Saints Church for Matins, unless you are going out for the day with parents or friends.' She glanced at the small wrist-watch she was wearing. 'Gracious me, how time flies, it will soon be lunch time. Skip back to your form room and tell Mrs. Griffiths that I'm sorry to have kept you away from her history lesson so long. I hope you've enjoyed our little chat, and that it has been helpful to you. I always find it helps me to get to know my new girls.'

Obviously this was the cue for me to leave, so I stood up.

'Thank you, Miss Plenderleith, I feel a lot happier now.' Nancy had told me that we were expected to curtsy when we left the head's study. She had shown me how to do it during a short lull in gym. 'Good-bye, Miss Plenderleith, and thank you very much.' I said, performing a very unsteady and clumsy curtsy, before leaving her study and closing the door quietly behind me.

CHAPTER FIVE

Harry Gordon

By the time I returned to our form-room, it was nearly half past twelve and Mrs. Griffiths had just finished setting our prep. I passed on Miss Plenderleith's message, returned to my desk, and had hardly sat down when the bell rang for the end of morning lessons. Immediately there was a clapping of books as they were snapped shut and several girls had opened their desks preparatory to putting away their books.

'And who told you you could go, Margot Burton?' Mrs. Griffiths fixed Maggot with a steely eye. 'Or you! Evelyn Cochrane! The lesson is not over until I say so.'

'Sorry, Mrs. Griffiths,' said Maggot. 'I thought——'

'Well you thought wrong. Take out your history book again and open it at the page on which we were working, and when you have found it bring it to me. The rest of you may put your books away, quietly mind, and go out to play.' There was a low babble of voices as desks were opened and books put away. 'Alexandra Muir?'

I closed the lid of my desk, quietly this time. 'Yes, Mrs. Griffiths?' What did she want? Had I done something wrong?

'Come and see me now. I won't keep you a minute.' I went and stood by her desk, hands behind my back. 'As it's your first day, and you missed most of the lesson, instead of doing the prep I set the others, will you copy out the mnemonic, about the kings and queens of England since 1066 and learn it by heart in time for the next history lesson?'

'Yes, Mrs. Griffiths. Thank you, Mrs. Griffiths.'

'You're welcome, my dear, how polite you are. You may go out to play now.'

'Thank you, Mrs. Griffiths,' I replied, trying another curtsy before heading for the playground.

'Margot Burton, have you found that page yet?'

'No, Mrs. Griffiths, I'm still trying to find it; it seems to have disappeared!' replied Maggot. It was ten minutes before a sorry-looking, tear-stained Maggot arrived in the playground.

*

Most of the day-girls went home at lunch time; those that did not, stayed to have school dinner with us. Of the third-formers staying for dinner, I knew only three to speak to, Harry Gordon, Angela Fitzpatrick and Priscilla Smith, "pretty and birdbrained," was Nancy's description of her. "Prissy," as she was known, tittered at the least thing and was shocked by the more down to earth girls like Rob Roy, Harry and Nicky. The dinner bell rang at ten to one. I had been kicking a ball around with Harry, Nicky and Rob Roy. It seemed I was not the only one who enjoyed playing football, as Nicky and Rob had played it with their brothers, and of course Harry had played for one of the teams at her boys' school. We went inside quickly, washed our hands and then queued up outside the eatery. There was an appetising smell coming from the kitchen.

'Och, it smells like fish 'n chips,' said Harry. 'Not too bad at all.' You could hear she was Scots when she said things like "och," or "too" which sounded more like "tue." I really liked Harry; I guessed she was the same age as me, and we liked the same sort of things. What I liked about her most of all was her bluntness; she called a spade a spade, and I was to find out that she always stood by her friends.

It was not long before the door was opened and we filed in to take our places. As boarders, we sat in the same places as we had at breakfast, but we could invite a day-girl to join us if there was a spare place at our table. As there was a spare cubicle in our dormitory, there was a spare seat at our table, so we asked Harry to eat with us. We stood silently, waiting for Grace, which was said by one of the pupils at lunch-time. It was Rob Roy's turn, so she made her way to the top table.

Miss Plenderleith, who always presided at lunch, called for silence. Then we heard Rob's clear voice reciting the Selkirk Grace;

> '*Some hae meat and canna eat,*
> *Some canna eat that want it.*
> *But we hae meat an' we can eat,*
> *Sae let the Lord be thankit. Amen.*'

We sat down, and as soon as Rob Roy had joined us, Harry, sitting between Rob and me, began talking about Scotland.

'Well done, Rob,' she said. 'That reminds me of St Mungo's Academy, my last school. We always said that Grace at dinner-time.'

'Did you really go to a boys' school?' I asked. Gladys put a plate with a small bit of fish and some chips on it, in front of me. 'Thanks, Gladys.'

' 'Fcourse I did!' Harry replied. 'It was absolutely spiffing!'

'But how did it happen?' I asked. 'What did your Dad say about it?'

'Daddy died before I was two,' said Harry. 'Thank you, Glad.'

'You're welcome, ducky.' said Gladys. ' 'Scuse me, Rober'a, so I c'n put yer plate dahrn.'

'Mummy'd have liked me to've been a boy,' Harry explained; 'So she put me in a kilt like lots of wee boys in Scotland; I liked my hair short, it's easier to keep tidy, and Henrietta's an awfu' mouthful, so it got shortened to Harry, and people just presumed I was a wee boy. When I went to kindergarten, Mummy forgot, *accidentally on purpose*—I think—to tell them I was a girl. I say, Rob, can you pass the salt please? Thanks, and I always preferred playing with trains and boy's toys rather than dolls. Sorry, Alex, did you want the salt too? and when I had to go to a bigger school I ended up at a boy's school. 'Twas all a bit of an accident really; it just seemed to happen!'

'What about school uniform, did you wear shorts?' asked Rob Roy.

'Heavens no! I wore a kilt, lots of us did. I only had to wear shorts for gym, football 'n things like that, like everyone else.'

'So what are all those rumours about wearing boys' things at home?' I asked.

'My *kilt* of course, *dumb* cluck! Ye dinna want tae believe a' the things ye hear, Alex, ma wee hen,' she added putting on a strong accent, and grinning at me.

'And the short hair?' I asked.

'Got used to it, I s'pose,' she replied, 'It's quicker in the morning than your pig-tails—forbye, it's much easier to wash.'

'So, when did you leave Scotland?' I asked.

'Last April. Mummy's work meant we had to come south. She's doing something terribly hush-hush at the Civil Service.'

'Is she? So's mine—my Mummy—I mean.' I said. 'So you didn't have to leave your last school because they discovered you were a girl?'

'Good gracious me, no!' She laughed. 'They knew I was a girl when I started there. They liked me, and I knew many of the boys who'd be in my class, so they saw no reason not to take me. I'm as good any boy of my age in a fight. It'd have been different if I'd been a frilly, giggly sort of girl, like Prissy or Cesspool.'

'I ought to've been born in Scotland,' I said, thinking of my male life. 'But Mummy and Dad had to move to England before I arrived.'

'Muir's a good Scots name right enough,' she said, and added with as grin; 'but being born in England saved your train fare south! What d'you think we'll get for afters?'

'Stodge and custard probably,' replied Rob Roy. 'It is usually stodge on Friday.'

'I wish this war was over,' said Harry. 'How long do you think it'll last?'

'It'll—' I was about to say it would go on until May 1945, but just stopped myself in time. I had to be careful not to give myself away.

'Some say it'll be over by Christmas,' said Rob Roy. 'But they said that last year; and in the Great War, too. Here comes our pudding now—Och no-*oh!* It's *Frog-spawn! Ugh! Groo!* I *hate* tapioca! You've gone very quiet all of a sudden, Alex.'

'Sorry, Rob, I was just thinking, that's all.'

'Careful, Alex!' laughed Harry. 'Don't work your brain-box too hard!'

'You three are thick as thieves,' said Jenny. 'Will you pass your empty plates down to this end please, then Glad can clear them away to the scullery. It hasn't taken long for you and Harry to make friends, Alex—'

'Sorry, Jen-Pen,' I said, 'I've been ignoring you.'

'Don't worry,' she laughed, 'I'm glad you're making friends so quickly. How's your Mum, Harry?'

'She was fine when I left home to come to school this Morning.'

'Give her my love, will you.' said Jenny, 'And tell her I can still remember the super lunch we had when you had me out for the day last term.'

'She'd like to do it again,' replied Harry, 'but the ration's awfu' wee. Ah! here's the pudding. Thank you, Glad.' She took a spoonful and made a face. 'Tapioca's *ugsome!* Frog-spawn's a good name for it! I say, it's Saturday tomorrow; is there a lax match, Rob?'

'No, just a practice game.'

'That's good, I need lots of practice,' said Harry. 'D'you play lacrosse, Alex? Oh no, you played footer at your last school like I did. You must ask Miss Bendall to let you play lax.' I suddenly realised I didn't think I had a *crosse*—a lacrosse stick.

'I lost my crosse when the train was bombed.' I said, glad Nick had tried to teach me how to catch with hers. 'My cousin Nick taught me a bit about lacrosse during the holidays.'

'What an up-side-down family you seem to have, Alex,' said Jenny. 'Girls who play football and boys who play lax!'

'Oh, Nick's a girl, but she won't answer to her full name. She's a bit like Harry in some ways and she taught me how to catch and cradle during the hols.'

'That's a start,' said Harry cheerfully, 'and there's bound to be a lax stick you can borrow. Miss Bendall has hundreds of them.'

We stood while Kate Jackson said; '*For what we have received, may the Lord make us truly thankful.*' We all added '*Amen,*' and then went out into the playground again until the bell rang for afternoon lessons.

I was feeling a bit tired and very perplexed, which was not like me. But I reckoned that going to bed so late and waking up quite early was a good excuse for being tired. And discovering that I had changed sex and travelled back thirty-four years, was enough to confuse anybody! I could not for the life of me think how it had happened, and I hoped I'd be able to travel back to my own time and be a boy again. Knowing that Aunt Alexandra had died during the war, made it vital that I return to 1974 as soon as possible. But how? And what had happened to the real Alexandra? Had she gone to the future and become a boy? All these thoughts were churning round my brain as I strolled around the playground with Rob Roy and Harry, who had been chatting away to each other.

'You're very quiet, Alex,' said Harry, putting an arm round my shoulders. 'Is something wrong?'

'Not really,' I lied. 'I'm a bit tired, that's all. It must be the journey and going to bed so late.' I was warming to Harry; beneath her hearty tomboyish exterior was a heart of gold. 'It was jolly kind of you to ask. I say! Wouldn't it be great if we three could sit together in class.'

'I'd like that,' said Harry. 'Who sits next to you now?'

'That small, thin, solemn girl, Ruth—Ruth—Ruth—thingie!'

'Loader,' said Harry. 'Toady Loader. She's a horrid wee goody-goody swot.'

'I am sure she'd love to swop with you,' said Rob Roy, 'I know she wants to sit in front 'coz she loves to suck up to the mistresses.'

'Let's ask her,' said Harry, 'And if she says yes, we can ask Spug-Bug.'

'Let's ask Toady-Loady now,' I said, 'And if she agrees, you can swop places before geog.'

'Toady goes home for lunch, and never gets back before five to,' Harry said. 'If we ask Spug-Bug, she could tell Toady to change places with me.'

'There's Spug-Bug over there,' I said, seeing her coming out of the front door. 'Let's ask her now.'

'Okay,' said Rob Roy. 'Last one there's a sissy!'

We rushed full tilt, almost knocking over a girl trying to do handstands at the edge of the lawn. 'Miss Spurgeon! Miss Spurgeon———!'

'Hello, you three. I see you've made some friends already, Alex. What are you all so eager about?'

'Please, Miss Spurgeon,' said Harry, 'Please could I swop desks with Toa—er, *Ruth* Loader, so I can sit next to Alex?'

'As long as you promise not to chin-wag in class,' said Spug-Bug with a smile. 'I know Ruth wants to sit in front; she asked me only yesterday, and I said I'd try to find somebody to change places with her. I'll tell her I told you to swop. If we go and do it now, you'll be sitting together for Miss Tripp's geography lesson.'

'Gosh thanks, Miss Spurgeon. You're a brick.' said Harry, trying to crush our form-mistress in a bear-hug. 'You're *really* spiffing and top-hole!'

'So are you, Harry,' laughed Miss Spurgeon, giving her a hug in return.

*

The desk swop was quickly done. Spug-Bug supervised us, so by the time the bell rang for the start of afternoon lessons, Harry was installed next to me, and Toady Ruth was thrilled to bits to have her desk where the mistresses could see how clever she was!

'Who takes us for geography?' I asked my new friend.

'Sweaty Lettie! Miss Tripp—Miss Leticia Tripp,' she replied, 'The Remove's form mistress. She's very roly-poly, and in hot weather her lessons are unbearable. She perspires terribly, and when she bends over you to see how you're doing, the pong can be unbelievably overpowering!'

'Aye,' Rob Roy said, 'Once last term it was so bad that Maggot and Weevil, who had to sit at the front so the mistresses could keep an eye on them, drenched themselves with cheap scent. It was so strong you could smell it from the back row!'

'Crikey! What did Miss Tripp say?' I asked.

'We don't think she ever smelled it,' answered Rob Roy. 'We reckon she can't smell, and that's why she's so whiffy herself!'

'Golly, I hope she doesn't come too near,' I said.

'Don't worry,' said Harry, 'It is only on hot days that she has odouriferous oxters!'

'Oxters?' I queried.

'Armpits,' said Harry. 'We call them *oxters* in Scotland. Is what old Grif-Bug said, about you being on a train that was bombed, really true? That must have been a bit scary.'

'Yes,' I replied, and sensing danger added; 'Actually, I'd much rather not talk about it.'

She gave my arm a reassuring squeeze. 'Don't blame you. I wouldn't either.'

I had hardly finished speaking, when *Sweaty Lettie* waddled into the room. Harry wasn't kidding about roly-poly! With each step she took, a different part of her wobbled, and her pink face reminded me of strawberry blancmange!

'Good afternoon, girls.' She had a squeaky voice, that did not match her size. I caught Harry's eye, and she grinned.

'Good after*noon*, Miss Tripp,' we chanted. Did I *really* hear Harry and Rob Roy say *Miss Drip?*

It was a rather boring geography lesson. We had to draw a map of Italy. I got on fine making the outline in pencil—all the pencils were plain, unpainted wood and stamped "WAR DRAWING"—but when I had to ink it in, I had a problem; I had never used a "dip" mapping pen* before, and kept getting blots of ink on my map. Harry and Rob were doing fine. I suppose they were used to dip-pens. We coloured our maps with wax crayons. I guessed that felt-tips had not been invented in 1940.

I tapped Harry on the shoulder and whispered; 'I wish I had a b—,' and stopped myself from saying "*biro*" just in time, and felt a bead of sweat on my forehead. I took out my hanky and wiped it away. 'Phew!' I thought. 'That was a near thing.'

Harry was looking at me, but couldn't say anything because Miss Tripp was watching us. Seeing the blot on my map, she passed me a piece of blotting paper. I nodded my thanks, glad my slip of the tongue had gone un-noticed; she must have thought I was asking for blotch! My map of Italy showed several "archipelagos" that did not exist! After the lesson, Harry said I should send it to Hitler so he could try to capture all my non-existent "Inkipelagos!"

After geography we had needlework, which was taught by Miss Gillespie. She was a sweet, bird-like little lady wearing woollies that she had obviously knitted herself, all in creams, greys and mauves to match her cream and mauve complexion and grey hair. She got flustered by the slightest thing, and would potter round muttering; 'Oh dearie, dearie me! Oh, dearie, dearie me!' So it was inevitable that she was known among the school's pupils as Silly Gilly.

Not surprisingly, I had never done needlework before. I discovered later that the real Alexandra was supposed to be rather good at it. During that first lesson, I couldn't even thread a needle, let alone do anything with it! I whispered to Rob Roy and Harry that I couldn't see the eye in the needle, because I was so late the night before, so Rob threaded it for me. Miss Gillespie gave us each a small square of white cotton for us to hem all round the edge to make a hanky. Harry was very nimble fingered, and in spite of her tomboyish attitude was obviously good at it. When she saw the hash I was making, she insisted we swopped over. Hers was all

---

* A fine-nibbed pen which had to be dipped in the inkwell built in to all school desks at that time

but finished, and she was so quick that she soon had done mine. I felt rather guilty because it seemed like cheating.

Towards the end of the lesson, one of the senior girls came in. 'Excuse me, Miss Gillespie,' she said.

'Why, it's Brenda Gunn,' said Silly Gilly. 'How nice it is to see you, Brenda, dear. I used to teach your mummy when she was a little girl, you know. She was such a sweet little thing. And what may I do for you, dear?'

'Please, Miss Gillespie, Miss Plenderleith says could you spare Henrietta Gordon for a few minutes? She wants to see her.' Harry looked at me, her brow furrowed. It was the first time I had seen her frown.

'Of course, dear. Run along, Henrietta, dear, there's a good girl. We mustn't keep Miss Plenderleith waiting, must we, dear?'

'No, Miss Gillespie,' replied Harry, still looking worried. She glanced quickly in my direction, and I showed her I had my fingers crossed. She grinned, and followed Brenda out. I glanced at Rob.

'I hope she hasn't done something awful or that it's bad news,' she whispered. Not knowing, I shrugged my shoulders.

*

The next lesson was Nature Study, with Mrs. Cowley, Moo-Cow or Moo, as she was known affectionately. Apart from prep, it was the last lesson of the day. We were well into the lesson by the time Harry returned, very excited and smiling, so we guessed that The Beak had not sent for her to tick her off.

'I am sorry I'm late, Mrs. Cowley,' said Harry, 'I had to see Miss Plenderleith. She says she's sorry she kept me so long.'

'That's all right, my dear. We are drawing the parts of a flower. Take one from the jam-jar and sit down as quickly as you can, that's a good girl.'

'Yes, Mrs. Cowley.' Harry took a flower from the jar and made her way back to her desk. She sat down, grinned at me, then wrote something in her rough book and smuggled it to me under the desk. I glanced at it. She had written, '*I am not a day-bug any more!*' in her neat handwriting. I passed it to Rob, and we both looked at Harry.

I could hardly wait for the end of the lesson to find out what it was all about. It was an interesting lesson, and Mrs. Cowley was a good teacher. The other members of the form, who had mostly just come up from the second, were clearly very fond of her. Even Maggot and Weevil behaved themselves and worked hard.

By the time the bell rang for the end of lessons, all the bits of the flowers we had dissected had been swept up and put in the waste paper basket. The day-girls, except those who stayed behind for prep, were in a rush to get home for tea. As soon as we had put our books away, Harry dragged us out into the playground.

'I'm a boarder!' she said excitedly, and did a cartwheel on the grass. 'Isn't that absolutely spiffing? I wanted you both to be the first to know. And I'm going to be in the Peregrine dormitory with you.'

'That's wonderful,' said Rob Roy, 'But why so sudden? I hope nothing's happened to your Mummy?'

'Och no! She's got to go away on a special sort of job,' Harry replied. 'She knew it was likely to happen at almost a moment's notice. It's just happened a bit sooner than we expected, that's all. She's bringing my things round after prep. I'm so excited.' She sprang into a hand-stand and began walking across the lawn on her hands, the skirt of her tunic cascading over her head so she was unable to see where she was going and bumped into Nancy.

'What on *earth's* come over you, Harry? The Bombardier's eyes are popping out of his head on stalks! You really ought to've tucked up your gymmer before doing that!' scolded Nancy.

'Who's the Bombardier?' I asked.

'The gardener and general factotum, Mr Perkins—*Perky*,' replied Rob Roy. 'He's Gladys's husband. He was a bombardier in the last war.'

I glanced round at the Bombardier, a tall, elderly, red-faced man with a bushy white moustache and snow-white hair. He had the upright bearing of a proud old soldier. Harry stood up again.

'Hiya, Nancy!' she said, grinning. 'Was I giving the Bombardier an eyeful? Never mind! He must've seen our navy knickers millions of times! Have you heard the news? I'm not a day-bug *any* more, I'm going to be a *boarder* from now on! Isn't that absolutely *spiffing?*'

'*And* she's going to be with us in Peregrine,' I added. 'That makes us seven.'

'Welcome aboard, Harry,' said Nancy, clearly delighted.

'Your servant, Miss Blackwell,' said Harry, making a sweeping gesture with her right arm and bowing low. 'Gosh, I'm starving! It must be nearly teatime. Let's go and wash our hands, and I'll move my coat, shoe-bag and sports things to *our* changing room. Last one there's a sissy!'

*

Tea was very informal. It consisted of a cup of tea and a cake or bun. Gladys served it through a hatch from the kitchen into the passage outside the eatery. After helping Harry move her things from the day-bugs' changing room to ours, a queue had already formed. There was a buzz of conversation as clusters of girls chatted about this and that. The news of Harry's sudden promotion to the ranks of the boarders had spread like wildfire, and was greeted with enthusiasm by all who liked her. Only girls like 'Lulu' Parker, Prissy Smith and Cesspool, who disapproved of Harry's cheerful, honest, "hail-fellow-well-met" attitude, showed no interest. Maybe it was because Harry seemed to be at least half boy, whereas each one of that gang was more than one hundred and ten per cent girl, and soppy, catty and spiteful with it.

For our tea that day we had an iced sticky bun. As sugar was on the ration, I learnt it was a great treat to have anything with icing on the top. Nancy and Harry nibbled their bun from the bottom, saving the top with the icing until last. The tea was weak and came out of the urn with milk already in it. It had a funny taste, making me pull a face.

'What's the matter, Alex?' asked Harry.

'The tea tastes a bit funny,' I replied.

Harry tasted hers. 'Aye, it's pretty *ug*some,' she said. 'They've used condensed milk from a tin, or dried maybe.'

That came as a shock to me—used to unlimited quantities of such things as milk, eggs, sugar, butter and cheese—to discover that they were all severely rationed. The daily milk ration was half-a-pint per person, with an extra third of a pint for children at school. Our sweets ration was four ounces per week.[†] Sweets were so valuable that they were used as money! Janet Peak, a tubby second-former, had a pretty butterfly brooch that Prissy Smith fancied. Janet loved sweets, so Prissy paid for the brooch with four bull's-eyes.

We passed our empty cups through the hatch. The clock in the hall said twenty past four, so as there were ten minutes before prep, we went out in the fresh air again. I had finished my bun, but Harry and Nancy were still nibbling theirs, trying to make it last as long as possible.

'Gosh, Alex! You ate your bun jolly fast,' Harry scolded me; 'We don't often get a treat like this. I can't remember when we last had iced buns, can you Nancy?'

'Not this term anyhow,' replied Nancy, taking a tiny bite. 'You really ought to try to make it last longer, Alex.'

' 'Msorry,' I said, feeling suitably ticked off. 'I'll make it last next time.' I was learning fast that in wartime one could not take things like iced sticky buns for granted—such treats were to be savoured for as long as possible.

Harry made her bun last until about two minutes before the bell went for prep. After she had eaten the last tiny morsel, she licked her fingers so as not to waste any stray icing that might have stuck to them then pulled out her hanky to wipe them dry.

'Well!' she said with a contented smile, 'That was ab-so-*lute*-ly spiffing!'

We did prep in our form room, supervised by a senior, usually a prefect from the upper or lower fifth. That day it was Brenda Gunn's turn. She was captain of lacrosse as well as a being a prefect, and her nickname—naturally—was Bren-gun.

''T'snot *just* because of her name,' Nancy explained to me, later; 'but also because she's such a wizard shooter of goals!'

Harry lent me her history note book so I could copy out *Willy, Willy, Harry, Steve*. I had to be able to recite it, word perfect, at next Tuesday's history lesson, if I was still in 1940 next Tuesday. A sudden thought struck me; it could almost be about our form—*Dilly, Milly, Harry, Steve!*—but I must not, on any account, recite that to Grif-bug. And then I had another thought; I could be thankful I had not gone back any further in time as I did not think I could ever have coped with life in 1066—as either a girl or a boy!

[†] Less than 125 grammes

CHAPTER SIX

Harry Moves In

As soon as the bell rang for the end of prep I gave Harry back her history note book. When we had put our books away, the two of us headed for the hall. 'Mummy'll be here in a few minutes with my things,' Harry said, looking at the clock. 'Let's go and meet her at the gate.'

'Okay,' I replied. We were not allowed to use the front door, so we made for the covered way went out by the back entrance, past the day-bugs' cloakroom and loos. I was still wondering why this had happened to me, and whether I would wake up tomorrow back in 1974, as if nothing had happened or if I would still be in 1940. It might seem odd, for although I was keen to return to 1974 and my boyhood, I had begun to enjoy being a 1940 schoolgirl; it was a new experience. I was living life as it had been for Mum and Dad when they were ten. I had also made at least two good friends, Harry and Rob Roy. Deep down, I hoped I might stay a bit longer; after all I was encountering, first hand, what my friends in 1974 could only learn about in our history lessons.

'Penny f'your thoughts, Alex.' Harry's voice brought me back to consciousness.

'Not worth that much,' I replied. 'I was just thinking——'

'Secret thoughts?' she asked.

'Sort of,' I replied with a shrug, wondering what Harry would be like in 1974. She would be forty-four, old enough to be my mum. 'It's funny, we met only this morning, and yet I feel I've known you for ages and ages.'

'Me too!' she replied. 'I'm glad we're in the same dorm.' She linked her arm through mine and we strolled towards the front gate. We were not allowed to go outside the grounds without permission, so we stayed just inside and watched the comings and goings outside. The last of the day-bugs who had stayed for prep were going home, some on foot, some catching a trolleybus, others riding their bikes.

'G'night, Harry, g'night, Alex,' It was Peggy Frost wheeling her bike past us.

'Are you coming to lax practice t'morrow, Jack?' I asked.

'*Rather*. G'night, both.' She got on her bike and rode away.

'How's your Mummy coming?' I asked Harry after Peggy had ridden away.

'Taxi. My trunk'd be much too difficult to get on the bus.'

'There aren't many cars about, are there?'

'Not now the basic petrol ration's been stopped,' she replied. 'You can only get it if you're someone important—like a doctor. Most cars have been laid up until the war's over.' A large black car was slowing down, its "trafficator", a little arm like a finger, rose up between the front and back doors, pointing left, and glowing orange. 'That looks like Mr Knox's car now. Aye, that's him; *Maman* usually uses his taxi.'

The car, a Sunbeam with a long, straight bonnet and tall radiator, slowed almost to a stop as it turned into the drive. Harry waved and the car stopped. The driver, an elderly man wearing a chauffeur's cap and small round spectacles, wound down the window. 'Hello, young Harry. Want a ride on the running board?'

'Yes please, Mr Knox. And please may my friend Alex have one too?'

'Certainly.' said Mr Knox. 'Hop on, both of you. Hold on tightly, now.'

We stood on the steps, Harry on one side, and me on the other, while Mr Knox drove slowly to the front door of the school. When the car had stopped we jumped off and Harry opened the back door for her mother. Mr Knox got out and went round to the back of the car where Harry's trunk was strapped on the luggage rack.

'Hello, Harry, *ma chérie.*' Mrs. Gordon was elegant and pretty, like a grown-up Harry, with the same determined set of the jaw. It was obvious where Harry got her good looks.

'*Maman!*' exclaimed Harry flinging herself at her mother and giving her an enormous hug and showering her with kisses. 'This is my new friend; she's called Alex and she's a new girl and we're in the same dormitory.'

'Hello, Alex,' said Mrs. Gordon, holding out her hand for me to shake. 'My, that's a good firm handshake for a girl. Has Harry been showing you the ropes?'

'Yes, Mrs. Gordon,' I replied.

'And now she's going to show *me* the ropes, aren't you, Alex?' said Harry, linking arms with me and giving my hand a squeeze.

'I've only spent one night here so it's very new to me too.'

'You can look after each other, can't you?' said Mrs. Gordon. 'Now, how do we get your trunk in, *chérie?* Ah—here's Matron, she'll tell us what to do with it.'

'Good evening, Mrs. Gordon,' said Matron. 'Perkins will carry it up in a wee minute; he's coming just now. Alexandra, please would you take Henrietta and Mrs. Gordon up to Peregrine. I'll join you up there in a jiffy.'

'Can you wait for a few minutes, Mr Knox?' asked Mrs. Gordon. 'I should only be about ten minutes at most.'

He touched his cap: 'Very good, Madam, I'll wait.'

I led them upstairs. 'Alex's daddy died in an aeroplane crash,' Harry told her mother. 'She doesn't know exactly what her mummy does, do you, Alex?'

'Only that she works at some government office in London. They need her because she lived in France when she was a girl, and speaks fluent French.'

'*Maman aussi, n'est-ce pas, Maman?*' said Harry. 'Lived in France I mean; and you work in some hush-hush government office too.'

'Yes. What's your Mummy's name, Alex,' asked Mrs. Gordon.

'Mrs. Muir,' I replied, 'Or do you mean her christian names?'

'They begin with M and F, don't they?' asked Mrs. Gordon.

'*Oui, Marie-Françoise,*' I replied, amazed. 'How did you know? My granny's French. I had to come here because Mummy's got to go away somewhere, like you.' (*I was glad Gran had told me a bit about what she did in the war. Now I was* in 1940, such knowledge might be useful. She had parachuted into France to work as a radio operator with the French resistance, receiving dispatches from and sending messages back to England.) I wondered where she was at this moment; England or France?

'Sssh!' said Mrs. Gordon putting a finger to her lips. 'Marie-Françoise and I are old, old friends; we were at the same school, like you and Harry.' We arrived at Peregrine dormitory and I held open the door for Mrs. Gordon. 'Thank you, Alex. This is very nice. Which is your cubicle, *chérie?*'

'This is Harry's cubie,' I said, opening the curtain. 'Next to mine.'

'That *is* nice, I'm glad you're together. I know you're going to be great friends—like Marie-Françoise and I. You've got a twin brother, haven't you, Alex?'

'Yes, Rory. He's at boarding school up in Scotland.'

I could hear footsteps approaching. Mrs. Gordon turned round as Matron came in. 'Perkins is bringing your trunk up just now,' she said. 'I'll unpack for you tomorrow morning, Henrietta, but I shall take out your night-clothes and dressing gown for now, and clean linings for the morning. You'll also need your sponge bag and a towel forbye. Don't worry, Mrs. Gordon, she'll be just fine. She and Alexandra are firm friends already.'

'Before I forget, Miss Scott, here's Harry's identity card, her ration book and her pocket money,' said Mrs. Gordon, handing a buff envelope to Matron.

'Thank you, Mrs. Gordon,' said Scottie. 'That saves me asking for them.' She took the envelope and left us alone. It suddenly struck me that I must have a ration book and an identity card too and wondered what they looked like.

'I'd better be going now, *chérie*,' said Mrs. Gordon. 'I still have to pack my own things. I shall leave you up here with Alex, *chérie*; don't come and wave good-bye. I hate waving good-bye. *Embrasses ta maman.*'

She bent down. Harry flung her arms round her neck and kissed her, several times.

'*Prends garde, Maman, je t'aime très, très beaucoup,*' she said with a perfect French accent. '*Au revoir, Maman. C'est meilleur que* "good-bye," *n'est-ce pas?*'

'*Oui, ma chérie, vraiment. Je t'aime très, très beaucoup aussi.* Now promise me you will look after each other, and when I see Marie-Françoise,' she said turning to me, 'I shall give her your love, Alex, *ma chérie*, and tell her that our two brave little girls are together, and are going to be *grandes amies. Au revoir, tous les deux.*' She gave me a hug and kiss, and Harry a final kiss and hug, '*Au revoir, chérie, à bientôt.*' Then she turned and headed towards the stairs without looking back.

'*Au revoir, Maman, prends garde. Je t'aime.*' A solitary tear rolled down her cheek. I offered her my hanky but she had already pulled out her own from under her tunic. 'Well, it's just us now,' she said, and she threw her arms round me and burst into tears. And that made me cry too.

We were still consoling one another when Scottie returned, followed by the Bombardier with Harry's trunk. When she saw we had been crying, Scottie came straight to us and put an arm round each of us.

'Come on, you two,' she said in a gentle voice. 'Let's dry those eyes, shall we?

You won't want to look all tear-stained when you go down to high tea.' She hugged us both at once. 'I know I said I'd unpack your trunk tomorrow, Harry, but why don't you both help old Scottie do it now? You unpack, and I'll put away and it'll be done in two wee shakes of a haggis's tail! Go and wash away those tears, and we'll do it before high tea.' We both felt better as we headed for the bathroom. So Scottie wasn't the battleaxe that she appeared to be. Underneath she was kind and gentle, like a mother, just as Jen-Pen and Rob Roy had said.

'It's queer, isn't it?' Harry said.

I glanced at her, puzzled. 'What's queer?'

'That our mummies know each other, and are going to work together.'

'And were at school together,' I added. 'Yes! I s'pose it *is* a bit queer.'

'I hope they're going to be all right; the blitz in London is really frightful. It'd be just too awful if anything happened to either of them. I hate this war! Och, bother, I forgot my towel.'

'Use mine,' I said, handing it to her.

'Thanks,' she said, and was her cheerful, bouncy self again. 'I'm sorry I blubbed like that; sissy and weak of me. You won't tell the others, will you?'

'It'll be our secret,' I replied, 'And Scottie's. Wasn't she nice? I shan't be so scared of her now, will you? Let's go and help her.'

*

It did not take long to put Harry's things away. We took her clothes out of her trunk and passed them to Scottie who put them away where she liked them to go. Mrs. Gordon had packed Harry's kilt for her to wear when we didn't have to be in uniform. Scottie hung it up with Harry's spare tunic and two frocks.

'I'm everso proud of my kilt,' she said. 'It's a real *boy's* one, and the Gardon tortan of course.' She giggled; 'I mean *Gordon tartan!*' Then I dissolved into giggles as well. Even Scottie chuckled, and I knew then that my first impression of her, when I awoke that morning, had been completely wrong.

'My twin brother's got one,' I said. 'Half a sec! I've got a photo of him in my cubie.' I pushed through the curtains separating our cubicles, and got the picture of Dad as a kilted boy.

'Golly!' said Harry, 'you're awf'ly alike. Without pigtails you could be him.'

'There now, all done!' said Scottie, putting away Harry's spare towel. She closed the trunk and put it outside for the Bombardier to collect. 'Why not go and run around outside for ten minutes before high tea. You'll not be allowed out afterwards as it'll be getting dark. By the way, did you know that you're both down to have baths tonight? Eight o'clock sharp, and *woe betide* you if you're late!'

'Yes, Scot—' Suddenly, I felt myself blushing. 'I'm sorry—I mean—Yes, Matron.'

She smiled. 'You may call me Scottie, if you like. It's only day-girls who have to call me Matron.' She pretended to box our ears. 'Away you go, the pair o' ye; afore I change my mind!' We scampered downstairs and out into the playground.

Outside, they were playing French cricket, so we joined in. Harry was very good, and it took ages to get her out. She always managed to stop the ball from hitting her legs. In the end I managed to bowl her with a googly, and it was my turn to bat. I was getting on quite well when the bell called us in for high tea. It was a sausage and a bit of fried bread, followed by a slice of greyish bread, I think it was supposed to be white, spread with a scraping of margarine and red jam of indistinct flavour, then a rock cake that was true to its name, and finally, a mug of warm, flavourless tea to wash it all down. I vowed that if I ever returned to my own time, I would never, ever, complain about school food again.

We spent the hour between high tea and our bath-time in the junior common room, which was for boarders in the third form and below. Inside we found Sally Nickerson from Eagle dorm., lying on her tummy, propped up on her elbows, reading a book. It was my first time in there, Harry's too. It was a friendly room with a coal-burning stove in the fireplace, a large table with chairs round it, and four arm chairs and a sofa. There were several framed photos on the walls and a colourful recruiting poster for the Women's Land Army; Gran had told me about how "Land Girls" had kept the farms going in the war. To the left of the fire-place was a large bookcase containing a huge selection of books. This was the "Junior Common Room library." An exercise book, dangling at the end of a string, hung alongside. I was just able to make out the words "*Library Register*" written on a label stuck to the front. A notice pinned to the wall nearby said; '*Books removed from the Junior Common Room must first be entered in the Library Register.*' Another said; '*Please replace books on the correct shelves when you have finished with them.*'

Hearing the door close, Sally looked up. 'Hi*ya!*'

'Wotcha, Nickerson!' said Harry, cheerfully.

'Wotcha, Gordon!' answered Nicky, sticking her tongue out at Harry.

'Hi*ya*, Sally,' I said. 'What's that you're reading?'

'*The Bumper Book for Girls.*' she replied. 'Full of tales of derring-do—schoolgirl heroines catching spies and saving England from the clutches of evil foreigners, or riding off on horseback to fetch help for an injured friend.' She turned the page.

'Sounds highly improbable,' Harry remarked.

''Tis,' answered Nicky, 'but it's quite exciting all the same. There's a picture here of two girls riding bareback in gymmers. Imagine! It must be *fright*f'ly tickly!'

'*Gymmers?*' I queried.

'Oh, you *know*, Alex,' said Nicky, '—gym tunics.'

'Oh, yes! 'fcourse,' I said. 'Silly of me!'

Harry was looking along the bookshelves. 'Hey, Alex! There are some first rate books here; loads of *Just Williams*, and *Chalet School*, Elsie Oxenhams and Angela Brazils, and Arthur Ransomes—my favourites! I say, his latest one, *Secret Water's* here. I haven't read that yet. I've got all his other ones at home. I like them because the children in them seem more real than in most stories, and do the things I'd like to do.' She took out *Secret Water* and started browsing through it.

'Hey, Nicky!' said Harry. 'Can you lend me a pencil f'ra mo.? I'd like to take this one out.'

'There should be one hanging on a string,' replied Nicky.

''T's okay! Found it!' Harry said. 'I was being a clot!'

'I enjoy *Swallows and Amazons* books too,' I said. 'And *Just William.*' I had never heard of Elsie Oxenham, but I knew Nick liked *Chalet School* books. I glanced along the shelves and selected *The Chalet School in Exile* by Elinor Brent-Dyer which looked very new. I knew Nick had a copy which had belonged to her mum; she said it was really exciting and had told me that I ought to read it. As a boy I thought that boys who read girls' books were girlish and sissy so I refused. 'But now that I *am* a girl,' I thought to myself, 'it doesn't matter if people think I'm girlish!' So I took it down and went to sit on the sofa by Harry and began to read.

After twenty minutes Rob Roy came in. 'Hello!' she said. 'Where IS everybody?'

'Don't know,' replied Harry. 'We've not been here very long.'

'Anybody like to play a game of something?' asked Rob Roy.

'What've we got,' I asked.

'Monopoly, Ludo, Happy Families, Snakes and Ladders, Snap—'

'Not enough time for Monopoly,' said Harry. 'Alex and I've got baths at eight o'clock. How about Snakes and Ladders?'

'That'd be fun,' I said, 'What d'you reckon, Rob?'

'Fine,' replied Rob Roy. 'How about you, Nicky? D'you want to play too?'

'Okay,' she replied. 'Just let me finish this paragraph.'

*

At five to eight Scottie put her head round the door. 'Alexandra Muir, and Henrietta Gordon,' she said in mock severity; 'I hope you've not forgotten your eight o'clock baths.'

'Golly!' exclaimed Harry. 'We're not late, are we, Scottie?'

'Not yet, you're not, but you *will* be if you don't go upstairs *toute de suite.*'

'Just coming, Scottie,' I said. I had been winning, but my last throw landed me on a snake's head, taking me back almost to the start. I put my tiddly-wink in the box.

Harry had thrown six and arrived at the bottom of a ladder which took her into the lead. 'What a swizz, I could've won!' she said joining me by the door. 'Lead on, MacDuff.'

While we undressed, Scottie went to run our baths. 'Don't forget we're not allowed to have more the water than four and a half inches deep,' she told us.

'Blinking *war!*' exclaimed Harry as we walked to the bathroom in dressing-gowns and slippers, our gas masks hanging round our necks. In the bathroom there were three baths, each one in its own curtained cubicle, and six wash-basins.

'Alex,' said Scottie, 'Tie your plaits on top of your head so you don't get your hair wet, there's a good girl. I haven't time to dry it for you tonight. You don't need to, Harry, with your boy's haircut.' Barbara Goodbody, the plump fourth-former who was monitress of Merlin dormitory, arrived to use the third bath. 'Come along, Goody-two-shoes, you're almost late.'

'Sorry, Scottie,' replied Goody. 'Susan Morgan was feeling homesick, and crying her eyes out, so I gave her a bit of a cuddle.' Susan was one of the three boarders in the Remove, who were all in Merlin.

'Good girl,' said Scottie. 'The poor wee mite's finding it a bit hard. I'll go and give her a cuddle myself. She's only just seven, and it's the first time she's been away from her mummy. To make it worse, her father was shot down over enemy territory and taken prisoner just two days before term started.'

'Poor wee lassie,' came Harry's voice. 'It must be awfu' hard for her. She's so young.'

'Aren't you in that bath yet, Harry Gordon?' called Scottie. 'Or do I have to come and put you in it, Miss, like I have to with the babies?'

There were sounds of splashing from Harry, as she sat down in the bath. 'I'm in now, Scottie,' she said.

'About time too,' came the reply. 'I hope you're all able to dry yourselves properly. Don't forget to dry between your toes, and brush your teeth. I must go to wee Susie now. I'll be back to tell you to get out. And remember to clean the bath when you've finished. The girls coming after you won't want to find a dirty tide mark—or a sopping-wet floor.' She left, closing the door behind her.

'Harry?'

'Yes, Alex.'

'I wonder what happens if there's an air-raid while we're in the bath? It could be jolly awkward.'

'I don't know,' she replied. 'Perhaps we rush naked and sopping wet to the shelter! Do *you* know, Goody?'

''Tnot happened yet,' answered Goody. 'Thank goodness!'

'Famous last words!' said Harry.

*

When we returned to Peregrine the other girls, except for Jen-Pen who, being fifth-former, had a later bed-time, were getting ready for bed. Rob Roy had passed us on her way to the bathroom. The Willis twins were chasing each other around in their vests and navy-blue knickers, giggling, and uttering gleeful squeals of girlish glee. Nancy, as vice-monitress of the dormitory, was doing her best to control them. '*Stop* it, you two,' she was asking. 'Stop it at *once*! If Scottie comes and catches you fooling around, she'll probably give us all misconduct marks. *Please,* twins. Be decent—*please?*' she pleaded. 'Scottie's *sure* to hear the row you're making.'

At this point, Harry caught hold of Milly and clamped a hand over the girl's mouth. Then, lifting the astonished twin off her feet, carried her into her own cubicle and dumped her on the bed. Dilly stopped in her tracks and watched open-mouthed. Harry made a move towards the second, now-silent, twin, but the mere threat was quite enough, for Dilys was scuttling towards her cubicle when Scottie came in.

'*Dilys Willis!*' thundered Scottie, fixing her with an angry stare. 'Was it *you* making that *appaling* row just now? And what do you think you are doing prancing around in your liberty bodice and drawers, squealing like an imbecilic piglet. Do you want to catch your death of cold? And *you*, Henrietta Gordon, I'm *surprised* at you. I thought *you* had more sense! Take a misconduct mark each, and go to your cubicles this instant.'

'Msorry, Matron,' said Harry meekly, going very red.

'Yes, Scottie,' said Dilly.

'Don't you *"Yes, Scottie"* me, Miss! I am *most* displeased with you.'

'I'm sorry, Matron,' said Dilly turning bright red and looking down at the floor as if she wanted it to swallow her up.

'And what does *sorry* mean, Dilys Willis?'

'It means *I won't do it again*, Matron.'

Then Milly came out of her cubicle. 'Please, Matron,' she said meekly, 'you mustn't give Henrietta a "miss.", Matron. Pul-ease, Matron, I'm ever so sorry. I was being noisy too, until Henrietta made me stop. She was only trying to make Dilly stop when you came in. Pul-ease, Matron, you *mustn't* punish Henrietta. 'T's not fair and you can't give Dilly a "miss." without giving me one too.'

'Well, Emily,' said Scottie, 'That makes quite a difference. Thank you for owning up. I must say, Harry, I was surprised to find you involved; you're not the giggly type. I'm sorry I misjudged you, and hope you'll forgive me. Thank you for taking matters in hand.' She smiled, putting a reassuring hand on Harry's shoulder and giving it a squeeze. 'I can see that you're going to be a good influence.'

Rob Roy returned from the bathroom, to find Harry blushing for the second time that day.

'Thanks for owning up, Milly,' said Harry, putting a hand on that girl's shoulder and smiling. 'Scottie, I've been a clot, and left my libr'y book in the JCR. Please may I go and fetch it?'

'All right, but be quick, there's a good girl. Now, you silly Willises, off you go to the bathroom *now* please, or you'll each get a lateness mark as well. Alex and Rob Roy, you'd better get into bed, or you'll catch cold. I'll be back to put your light out shortly.'

I went into my cubicle and picked up my clothes, which lay where I had dropped them on the bed as I undressed. I folded them up neatly and put them on my chair, wondering if I would be needing them again tomorrow. I hung my towel on the rail at the foot of the bed, then took off my dressing gown and put on the pink night-dress I had been lent the previous night, in 1974! Would I return to boyhood that night, or would I still be a girl when I woke up in the morning? Why had all this happened to me? I was confused, terribly scared, and not very happy. I sat on my bed, picked up Edward Bear Esquire and hugged him. He made me feel a bit better.

I don't know how long I sat like that, but it could not have been more than a minute or two, when I felt a hand on my shoulder. I looked up. It was Harry.

'What's the matter, Alex? Is there anything I can do? Are you feeling homesick?'

'A bit, but I'm tired mostly; it was awf'ly late when I got here last night. I'll be better after a good night's sleep, and jolly glad when Friday the thirteenth's over.'

'Me too. I'm a bit homesick too,' she admitted. 'D'you know, this is the first time, ever, in my life that *Maman* hasn't been around to kiss me good-night?' She sat on the bed beside me, and suddenly, looked forlorn. 'I *do* hope mummy'll be all right in London with all those horrible air-raids.'

I put an arm round her shoulders. 'Don't worry, she'll be just fine, mark my words. We'll both see our mums again soon.'

She turned and grinned shyly. 'I say, I like your teddy. Hello, Teddy.' She tickled him under his chin. I passed him to her and she kissed his nose.

'He belonged to an auntie when she was a little girl,' I said, still forgetting that I was now that auntie. 'He's called Edward Bear Esquire.'

'Is he? How *frightfully* aristocratic-sounding!' She giggled just as Rob Roy's head appeared round the curtain.

'I shouldn't let Scottie catch you in Alex's cubie if I were you, Harry. We ought to be in bed by now.'

'Okay, Rob! Thanks,' replied Harry. She stood up, kissed Edward Bear Esquire once more, gave him back to me, grinned, and went back to her own cubicle. I climbed into my cold bed and snuggled down under the bedclothes with Edward Bear Esquire. I wished I had borrowed that book from the JCR library, like Harry.

I heard footsteps come into the dormitory. 'Are you twin idiots behaving yourselves now?' It was Jenny. 'Scottie told me she'd given you each a "miss." tonight. You've let Peregrine down; you *know* we were trying to get through the whole term without any of us getting any misses.'

'We're really sorry, Jen-Pen,' said one twin.

'Really, *everso* sorry, Jen-Pen,' said the other. 'Honestly—.'

'All right. Just *don't do it again*. I want Peregrine to win the prize for the best behaved dorm. this term.'

'Yes, Jen-Pen,' said the twins in unison.

'Welcome to Peregrine, Harry,' said Jenny. 'Settled in O.K?'

'Fine thanks, Jen-Pen,' replied Harry.

'Good. You'll find it a bit strange at first, so let me know if there's anything I c'n do,'

'Thanks, Jen. I will.'

Next she put her head through my curtains. 'Everything all right, Alex? Settling in O.K? If there's anything I can do, don't be afraid to ask.'

'Fine. I just wish I'd borrowed a book from the JCR library. I won't forget tomorrow.'

'Jolly dee!' Jenny went and spoke to Rob Roy and Nancy before she went to her own cubicle and got ready for bed.

Before long, Scottie came to put the light out and wish us good-night. My first day as a schoolgirl in 1940 was over.

CHAPTER SEVEN

Things That Go Bang in the Night!

I WAS DREAMING. A FIRE-ENGINE was dashing to a fire, clanging its bell. Somewhere in the mayhem I could hear a voice calling; 'Wake up! Wake up, girls! The siren's just gone! It's an air-raid warning!' I opened my eyes to find the light on and Scottie giving orders, like a general commanding his troops; 'Come along, girls! Quickly now! Quickly! Put on your warm woollies, drawers—*and* linings, please—dressing gowns, socks and *outdoor* shoes. Make sure you wrap up well! Take the rug from your bed and DON'T FORGET YOUR GAS MASKS. Form up by the door, and walk to the shelter in an orderly manner. Chivvy your girls along, Jenny, and remember, *walk* to the shelter. No running please!'

I was out of bed when Jenny came to check I was awake. 'Hurry up, Alex! Put on your warmest things, extra layers if you like, then bring your rug and gas mask and line up by the dormy door.'

'Okay, Jen-Pen,' I replied, wide awake now; I felt uneasy as I pulled up an extra pair of knickers under my nightie and put on socks and shoes. I was fumbling with a shoe-lace when Jenny looked in again. 'What's the time?'

'Don't know,' she replied, 'but Scottie'll tell us. Here, let me tie that lace for you; you're all fingers and thumbs! You'll find it easier if you try to stay calm. The first air-raid's always the worst.' She squatted down and tied the lace I had been struggling with. 'Is that all right?' She smiled reassuringly, and went to chivvy somebody else, meeting Harry as she left my cubie. 'Well done, Harry, jolly dee! Got your gas mask? You remembered to put undies on?'

'Rather!' replied Harry. 'At least two of everything!. Come on, Alex, I'll help you fold your rug, then you can me help fold mine.'

'Thanks.' We folded our rugs and formed a queue. I took Edward Bear Esquire with me. Jenny called the roll and ticked off our names as we answered.

'Good,' she said. 'All present and correct. All got your gas masks? No talking until we're in the shelter. Follow me.' She led us downstairs, out of the front door and across the playground to the underground air-raid shelter hidden among the bushes on the far side. We could hear the drone of aeroplanes overhead and the noise of the anti-aircraft guns firing. Searchlight beams criss-crossed the dark sky in their quest to pin-point the approaching enemy.

Miss Plenderleith stood at the top of the stairs that led down to the shelter. She was wearing a tin helmet with her hair hanging in a thick plait down in front of her left shoulder. Her dark red dressing gown was supplemented by a long mauve woollen scarf wrapped several times round her neck and she had her gas mask box slung from one shoulder. As we filed past her, she ticked our names on her list.

'Well done, Peregrine. First again! All got your gas masks?' she asked. 'Good! Go inside and sit down. Wrap up warm won't you.'

'Yes, Miss Plenderleith.'

The shelter consisted of two underground chambers, joined by an archway. The walls were made of concrete and lined with brick that had been white-washed. Light came from two dim electric bulbs and hurricane lanterns stood by for use when the electricity failed. Long benches lined the walls and in one corner a trolley was stacked with enamel mugs. We sat on one of the wooden benches, Harry on one side of me, with Rob Roy on the other, and were joined by Jemima Stewart, Puddleduck, and her crew from Eagle dormitory.

'Hiya, Puddles,' said Jenny. 'What a palaver, eh?'

'It's a flipping nuisance,' said Jemima, stifling a yawn. 'Three o'clock in the morning. I ask you! What a terrible time to drag us out of bed. I wish somebody'd shot Adolf Hitler at birth. How long d'you think it'll be before the all-clear?'

'It could be hours,' said Rob Roy, 'like it was on Wednesday; or just a few minutes. I hope Gladys makes cocoa again tonight.'

'That was spiffing, wasn't it?' said Nicky. 'I wonder if—' Her words were drowned by a crunching explosion that felt too close for comfort. The lights flickered.

'*Crivens!*' exclaimed Harry. 'That was close. What did you say, Nicky?'

'I was just going to say, "I wonder if any bombs will drop near us tonight!" Nicky replied. 'Ah! Here comes Mag-Bags with the babes.'

A girl of about twelve led several much younger girls, shepherded from behind by Goody-Two-Shoes and Bendy Wendy. All the little ones looked anxious and very frightened. Several of them were crying, and all were clasping dolls or teddy bears tightly to their chests. I felt very sorry for them.

'It must be very frightening for them,' I said, none too easy myself, but unwilling to admit it.

'They're mostly second-formers.' replied Rob Roy, 'And three from the remove. Some of them are only just seven.'

'Why's she called Mag-Bags?' I asked.

'Her name's Margaret Bagnall,' explained Puddles. 'We used to call her Maggie when she first came, which is what she's called at home. Then Jen-Pen called her Mag-Bags one day, and she's been that ever since. Ah, here are the Goshawks.'

Goshawk was the senior dormitory. Six seniors led by Brenda Gunn came in and straight away mingled with the juniors, ready to comfort them. The head-girl, Kate Jackson, brought up the rear, and finally came Scottie and Gladys with a huge urn.

'Hoorah for Gladys!' shouted Milly-Willy. 'Is that cocoa?'

'Nah,' said Gladys, keeping a dead pan face. 'Scotch whisky!'

'But I don't think I like whisky,' said Dilly-Willy, looking disappointed.

'Dumb cluck!' exclaimed Harry. 'Can't you tell you're having your leg pulled?'

'That 'ad you on good'n' proper, di'n'it, ducky?' laughed Gladys. With Scottie's help she lifted the urn on the trolley, then found themselves somewhere to sit. Miss Plenderleith closed the door, took off her tin hat and went to sit with "her babies," as she called them.

'Now, girls,' said Miss Plenderleith. 'Shall we practise our gas mask drill?' She pointed to a large green and white poster pinned to the back of the shelter door. "Gas Attack", it said. Then she opened her box, took out her gas mask and demonstrated how we should put them on. We followed suit, and our dormitory monitresses checked that we had done it right. Mine began misting up and soon everything looked fuzzy through the oval window.

'Didn't you spit on your gas-mask window, Alex?' Jenny asked.

I had never put a gas mask on before. 'Sorry, Jen, I forgot,' I fibbed.

'You'd better do it now,' she said. I took it off and spat on the inside of the window. 'Now spread it round with your fingers.' I did so, and put it on again. It was much better now. Maggot and Weevil were pretending to be monkeys, scratching their armpits and searching for imaginary fleas. The little ones thought this was hilariously funny and muffled giggles could be heard coming from inside their gas masks. Even some of the older girls laughed when Weevil caught an imaginary flea on Maggot, and mimed putting salt and pepper on it before eating it! I must say that in our gas masks we all looked a bit like monkeys so Maggot's and

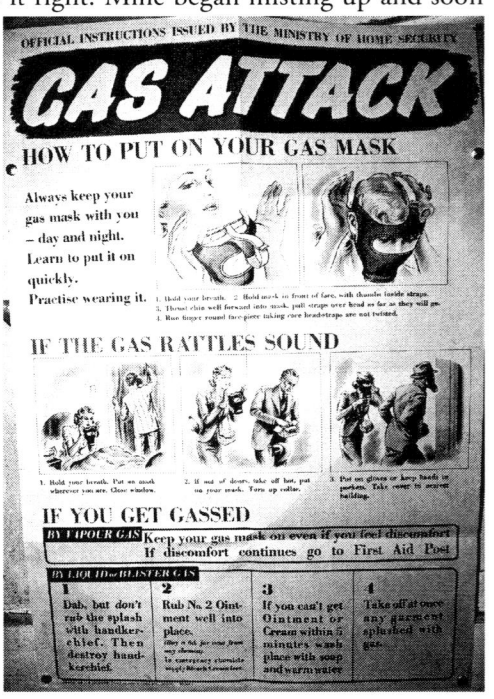

The poster pinned to the back of the shelter door

Weevil's mime was rather fitting. The two youngest, Susan Morgan and Greta Ransom, both only just seven, and small for their age, had red Mickey Mouse gas masks. When we had all been inspected, Miss Plenderleith took hers off and told us to put ours back in their boxes.

'Well now!' she said, 'Shall we pass the time until the "all-clear" by having a sing-song? How about *One man went to mow* to start with?'

'Ye-esss!' came the answering chorus. After twelve men had well and truly mowed the meadow, we went on to sing *Run Rabbit, Run*—a current popular "hit", *This Old Man he Played One*, (He played knick-knack with Bren Gunn!) and *Ten Green Bottles Hanging on the Wall*. Then Harry, Puddles and Rob Roy, sang a Scots one I had not heard before; *Three Craws Sat upon a Wa'* (Three crows sat upon a wall). We all laughed when they sang a fourth verse, which began '*The fourth craw wasna' there at all!*' which Scottie and The Beak joined in.

'Well *done*, gair-rls,' said The Beak, putting on a special posh Scots accent and rolling her "rs" like Scottie often did. 'I've not hear-rd thet one since I was a wee gair-rl in Kelvinside. How about wetting our whistles now, Scottie?'

'Good idea,' said Scottie. 'Gladys has found some bickies she didn't know she had. No, girls! Sit down! Dormitory monitresses come and hand the cocoa round to everybody. 'Mag-Bags, you may pass the bickies round, that's a good girl. Two each *only*, please, girls, and no seconds. Remember there's a war on!'

'Golly!' said Harry, when she had got her cocoa. 'I've read about midnight feasts in school stories, but I reckon this is much more fun.' She had barely finished speaking, when an enormous explosion shook the ground. Everyone flinched, the lights flickered and went out, and the tin mugs on the trolley rattled. Several girls screamed.

'Gor' blimey! Tha' woz a bit close!' said Gladys. 'Not 'arf i' wozn't. I got some matches 'ere.' She struck one and it flared up. Reaching up, she lit one of the hurricane lanterns. 'I 'ope it wozn't the school.'

'So do I,' said Miss Plenderleith. 'I ought to go and look.'

'Don't go out just yet, Vera,' said Scottie, who was comforting two of the little ones. 'There might be another one. Gladys, pass me your matches and I'll light the other lanterns.'

It was very cosy by lantern-light. It seemed to make it more exciting somehow. About five minutes later, the door opened, and Gladys's husband, came in. He was wearing a black tin hat with a big white 'W' painted on the front. We gave him a cheer and he blushed!

'Beggin' yer pardon, Miss Plenderleith,' he said, after regaining his composure, 'That big'un was down Tuckton Road a bit. I thought you'd like to know the school's OK.'

'Thank goodness for that, Bombardier,' said Miss Plenderleith. 'Has the "all-clear" sounded yet?'

'Not yet, Miss Plenderleith. I c'n still hear one of them beggars buzzin' around up there. I 'ope 'e gets shot down inter the sea.'

'Would you like a mug of cocoa, Bombardier?' asked Scottie.

'Very kind o' you, Miss Scott,' said Mr Perkins, 'But I'd best be gettin' on now.'

'Come on, Bombardier,' said Miss Plenderleith, 'It'll warm you up nicely, especially if I ask Matron to put a drop of something warming in it. Did you bring your medicinal flask with you, Morag?'

'Oh! You mean my special cough medicine?' said Scottie with a twinkle in her eye. 'Come now, Bombardier, Matron's orders!'

'Well,' said the Bombardier, 'If you twist me arm, "I don't mind if I do," like that Colonel Chinstrap on *ITMA* says. But I still gotta go and 'elp the poor so-

'n'-sos what got bombed.' He took a mug from Scottie and drank it down quickly. 'You was bang on, Miss P. Jus' what the doctor h'ordered. Ta h'everso! Keep yer chins up, girls. G'night all.' Then he left, shutting the door behind him.

'Right,' said Miss Plenderleith. 'Let's have another song. How about *She'll be coming round the mountain when she comes?*'

After that we sang *Ilkley Moor bar t'at*, and then, just as we finished singing *I'll sing you one-oh, Green grow the rushes-oh*, the lights came on again and we heard the "all-clear" siren moaning its message that it was safe to go back to our beds.

'Right you are, girls,' said Miss Plenderleith, 'Lets go back to bed, shall we? As it's Saturday you can have an extra hour in bed. Will it mess up your arrangements in the kitchen, Gladys?'

'Nah, Miss P, I c'n do breakfuss' for nine o'clock easy. I'll be glad to 'ave the extra hour meself. These air raids will be the deff o' me so they will!'

The hall clock said a quarter to five as we trooped upstairs again. Once back in our dormitory, we helped each other put the rugs back on our beds and in about three minutes flat we were all tucked up ready for the lights-out for the second time that night.

'Alex?'

'Yes, Harry.'

'That was good fun wasn't it?' she said. 'D'you think it's always like that?'

'Quite often, it is,' said Jenny.

I could hear footsteps coming along the passage. They stopped at our door. 'Are you Peregrines all back safely?' It was The Beak.

'Yes, thank you, Miss Plenderleith,' we called. She looked in each of our cubicles to check we were all right, tucked us in, then went back to the door.

'Good-night, Miss Plenderleith,' we called.

'Good-night,' replied the Head. 'Sleep tight.'

'And see the bugs don't bite,' said Harry. There were giggles from the direction of the twins.

'That's enough of that, young Harry,' chuckled Miss Plenderleith. 'You're not at your *boys*' school now. Don't you know that bed-bugs are not allowed to come to boarding schools for young ladies?'

'No,' I remarked. 'Only Maggots and Weevils!' Everybody, including Miss Plenderleith, exploded into fits of giggles.

'All right, all right,' laughed Miss Plenderleith, and when she had stopped laughing, added, 'You've had your joke. Please try to get some sleep now. Remember, you've got lacrosse practice at half past ten. Good-night, everybody.'

'Good-night, Miss Plenderleith,' we replied together.

'Good-night, girls,' she repeated as she switched off the light.

CHAPTER EIGHT

"Best Friends"

'KER-LANG, KER-lang, KER-lang, KER-lang.' The jangling of the bell woke me. I took a moment or two to gather my thoughts, opened my eyes, and rolled on to my back. I heard the door open. 'Wake up now, Peregrines,' came Scottie's voice, so I knew at once that I was still in 1940. 'It's after half-past eight. Show a leg there.'

'Righty-oh, Scottie!' came Harry's clear voice from the next-door cubicle. I heard Scottie leave. I was still half asleep and had just closed my eyes again and yawned, when something landed on me. 'Come on, Alex, show a leg! It's Saturday, and we haven't got any lessons!' I opened my eyes just as Harry was about to pull the bedclothes off me. I clung to them, but to no avail, and flopped back on to the pillow. Having pulled them off, she jumped on me again and knelt astride my tummy, sitting back on my legs and pinning my shoulders down with her hands. 'Now Alex, are you going to get up now, or do I have to tickle you?'

'How can I get up with you sitting on top of me, you great lump?' I replied. Her fingers began moving as if she was going to tickle me. I had always been horribly ticklish, and the mere threat was enough to make me squirm. 'All right! *All right!* You win! I'll get up. Are you as bouncy as this *every* morning? You're worse than Tigger in the Pooh stories!'

'Not at home,' she said, 'I haven't got any brothers or sisters to bounce on. Come on, let's go and wash. It's Saturday and we've got lax this morning.' She got off me, sat me up, picked up my dressing gown and tossed it to me.

'Put it on and come to the bathroom or we'll be late,' she said, just as Rob Roy put her head round the curtain.

'Good morning, you two,' she said. 'Did you sleep well?'

'Good Morning, Rob,' said Harry. 'We're fine, aren't we, Alex? Did you sleep okay, Rob?'

'Fine thanks. But I could've done without the air-raid,' replied Rob Roy. 'Are you all right, Alex?'

'Yes, as soon as this animal stopped bouncing on me,' I said, aiming a playful punch at Harry. I picked up my sponge-bag and towel, and we linked arms and went to the bathroom.

'What do we wear on Saturdays?' Harry asked, when we were back in the dormitory again. 'Gymmers or home clothes?'

'Gymmers,' replied Jenny. 'We're allowed to change into our own things before high tea, if we want to, but most of us don't bother. We may wear home clothes after church on Sunday, as long as we're not going out later.'

We dressed quickly, but when I tried to plait my hair, I got into an awful muddle. I began all right, and then something went wrong so I began all over again. I was cursing and muttering under my breath when Harry popped her head round my curtain.

'Don't tell me I should have it cut short like yours,' I told her. 'I never had pigtails before I came here, so I never learned how to plait the stupid things!'

'D'you want some help?' she asked. 'I'll plait them for you if you like. After all, that's what best friends are for.'

'But I thought you'd never had pigtails,' I replied.

'Neither have I, but that doesn't mean I don't know how to plait 'em. Pass me your brush, I'll have to start again.'

'I was going to ask Jen-Pen to let me watch her doing hers,' I said. 'Ouch! don't tug so hard, you're worse than Scottie.'

'Sorry, I didn't mean to hurt you. D'you have a ribbon, or d'you use laccy bands?'

'Here's a ribbon,' I replied, passing one to her.

'Can you untie it please? If I let go, your pigtail'll come undone.'

I pulled at the knot and gave her the ribbon. She did not take long to do the other one, and we went downstairs together. At the foot of the stairs, she put a hand on my arm and held me back.

'Alex?' she said, 'I know I hadn't asked, but I hope you didn't mind me calling you my best friend just now. I meant to ask you last night, but there were too many people around. So will you? *Please?*'

'You want *me* to be your best friend? But what about Rob? I thought *she'd* be your best friend. After all you're both Scots and you only met me yesterday.'

'I know, but I've never had a best friend here. When I was a day-bug, I couldn't ask a boarder to be my best friend. Anyhow Rob's been here since she was seven, and she and Puddles have always been best friends. You're the first girl here that I've liked enough to ask to be my best friend. I loathed it when I first came here. You see, I looked a bit like a boy wearing a frock, and girls like Prissy, Cesspool and Toady kept whispering horrid things behind my back, and making up beastly, spiteful stories about me; like telling people that I wasn't a girl at all, and should go back to my boys' school. They made me terribly unhappy and I often went straight home and to my room to cry. I never told *Maman* about it, or let her see I'd been crying.' She slipped her hand into mine. 'I've never told that to *anyone* before. Pul-*ease* be my best friend, Ally—'

'Only if you'll be mine,' I said, grinning and giving her hand a squeeze. She grinned and squeezed back. 'I wanted to ask *you*, but I was scared to in case you had a best friend already. I felt so sorry for you in gym when Cesspool and her spiteful gang were sniggering about you. I say, shouldn't we prick our fingers and let our blood mingle or something?'

'Clot!' she laughed, 'It's blood brothers that do that. Hey! Let's be blood sisters?

What a spiffing idea! Shall we?'

'Yes, do let's,' I replied. 'I say, shouldn't we be going to brekker. By the way, when's your birthday?'

'Twenty-fifth of March, when's yours?' said Harry.

'Same day. What a coincidence? I'm ten and a half.'

'Me too! Gosh, Ally, that's spiffing! You see—we've *got* to be best friends!' She linked an arm through mine and we walked happily to the eatery. Jenny, Nancy and Rob Roy already in the queue, waiting for the breakfast bell to ring.

'I see you managed your plaits, Alex,' said Jenny.

' 'Fraid not,' I admitted. 'Harry did 'em for me. Please would you show me how you do yours?'

'Yes, 'fcourse. It's frightfully easy once you get the knack.'

'Thanks, Jen-Pen. Who gives us our pocket money?' I asked.

'Scottie,' replied Jenny. 'Just before we go into lunch.'

'What do we do about sweets coupons?' asked Harry. 'We can't buy our sweets ration without our Ration Books.'

'Scottie's got an arrangement with Mr. Pitcher at Fisherman's Walk,' said Jenny. 'She sends him a list of girls who want sweets. If you want sweets, she snips the coupon out of your Ration Book, and pins it to a piece of paper with your name on. Mr. Pitcher takes the coupon and lets us buy what we're entitled to.'

As I had not come across rationing in my own time, I had no idea that it was so complicated. 'Crikey!' I said, 'What a huha! I always asked Mummy or Gran to get mine for me.'

'Well it's either that or go without,' said Jenny. 'A word of advice; if you want your ration to last as long as possible, buy something small and light. You get a lot more jelly babies in a quarter of a pound than you do toffees, or bon-bons.'

'What about chocs?'

'They count too,' said Harry. 'Choc drops are the best to go for. If you suck them, you can make them can last for simply ages.'

'What about Smar—' The brekker bell interrupted me. I was about to say "S*marties*," but suddenly thought they might not have been invented. I felt myself blushing as we filed quietly into the eatery. We had to stay silent until Grace had been said. It was lucky the bell rang when it did, for I might have had to explain my way out of an awkward spot. We stood in our places, waiting for Brenda Gunn to say Grace.

'*Benedictus benedicat*,' said Bren-Gun in her Captain-of-Games-voice. No sooner had we sat down, than the room filled with chattering voices. Harry sat between Jenny and me, with Rob Roy was on the other side of the table, on Jenny's right, facing us. Soon, Gladys came round with the porridge.

'You 'ave yours with milk an' sugar, don't you, Alex?'

'Yes please, Gladys,' I replied.

'What about you, 'Arry?'

'I have mine with salt—please, Gladys' replied Harry.

'Lumme! You ain't Scotch an' all are yer, ducks?"

'Aye, hen. Borrrr-rn and brrrr-red.' replied Harry rolling her Rs in a strong Scots accent.

'An' oo's you callin' 'en?' asked Gladys, putting a plate of porridge in front of her. 'Cheeky young madam!'

'Well you called me ducks,' protested Harry. 'In Scotland we call people we like, hen.'

' 'En indeed!' said Gladys. 'Yore askin' for a clip round the lug'ole, my girl. Garn wiv yer. I dunno, 'en eh? Rober'a, will you be 'avin' salt on yours as per usual, ducks?'

'Aye, hen, that would be chust fine,' said Rob Roy, taking a leaf out of Harry's book.

'Blimey, don't you start an' all. We'll 'ave Bonnie Prince blooming Charlie 'ere next!' She gave Rob Roy her porridge.

'*Tappa let, a Gladys*,' said Rob Roy.

'What the 'eck's that in aid of?' asked Gladys.

'I only said "Thank you, O Gladys," in Gaelic,' said Rob Roy.

'Garlick eh! I'll give you *O Gladys!* Whatever next? D'you want porridge, Emily?'

'I'm Dilys; and yes please, O Gladys, Hen!' giggled Dilly, 'I'd love some porridge—with milk and sugar, please.'

'Don't you *'EN* me my girl!' said Gladys, splodging a dollop of porridge on Dilly's plate, 'Or you'll get *'EN* on your B.T.M., and then you won't be able to sit down for a fortnight!'

After serving Milly and Nancy, Gladys moved on to the Eagles' table. 'Poor old Glad,' said Jenny. 'We really oughtn't to rag her like that. Look! Maggot and Weevil are having a go at her now.'

The rest of brekker passed uneventfully, and when we had put our plates, cups and cutlery on the trolley, Harry, Rob Roy and I made our way back upstairs. Harry was bubbling over.

'Rob! Ally's agreed to be my best friend,' she said, putting her arm round me, and squeezing me tightly. 'I'm so happy; and you'll never guess; we were born on the very same day.'

'I'm jolly pleased for both of you,' replied Rob Roy. 'As soon as I saw you two together yesterday, I knew you were going to be best friends.'

Back in the dormitory Scottie was distributing clean sheets and pillow-cases. 'Clean beds today,' she said, 'And you must turn your mattresses. Now, you two.' She put an arm round Harry and myself; 'As you're both new, you won't know that we put on clean night-clothes when we change the bed-linen. Before you put any dirty things in the laundry basket, check that they're all marked with your name. Let me have any that aren't, and I'll sew a name-tape in for you.'

'I'll do it for her, Scottie,' said Harry. 'We're best friends now, and best friends always help each other.'

'You'll have to be careful, young Harry,' laughed Scottie. 'That sort of thing doesn't fit in with being a tomboy, you know.'

'I meant it, *really*,' said Harry. 'I'd like to do it for my best friend.'

'All right, Harry,' said Scottie. 'You're a strange wee lass. But I'll tell you something, you're one of the nicest wee girls that I've known at this school. But don't let that go to your head now! I'm glad you're best friends, you suit each other.'

Harry blushed, and lowered her eyes.

'Really, Harry, just because I say something nice about you, is no reason to go all girlie and coy. Come along now, *tempus fugit!* I suggest you help each other turn your mattresses. You'd better get on before I say anything else to make you go coy and demure. Why not you let your hair grow a bit, Harry? Without that boyish short-back-and-sides you'd be very pretty. Look how pretty Alex is with her longer hair and she's just as tomboyish as you. Do you know, when I wakened her yesterday morning, she insisted she was a boy?' Now it was my turn to blush. 'Heaven help me! now I've made the other one go all coy and girlie. I can't win!' She was laughing as she left the dorm.

'She really *is* jolly decent, isn't she?' said Harry. 'I was scared stiff of her when I was a day-bug. When the laccy in my pants broke yesterday, I was petrified when I had to go and ask her to mend it. I stood outside her door for ages, holding them up with one hand, with the other hand clenched, ready to knock.'

'I wish I'd seen you,' I laughed. 'You must've looked so funny!'

'I s'pose I must,' she replied, grinning impishly. 'I think Scottie's a jolly good sport.'

'She is, isn't she?' I said, stretching full length on my bed with my hands behind my head. 'She's right, you know. You'd be really pretty with longer hair.'

She sat on the edge of my bed, picked up Edward Bear Esquire and cuddled him. 'I wish I'd brought my teddy with me. I left him at home because I thought the other girls would laugh at me. D'you *really* think I ought to grow my hair?'

'Yes.'

'Okey-doke, I'll do it, and that'll be one in the eye for Prissy, Cesspool and Co. Come on, let's get our chores done—we've got lax at half past ten. I say, did you really tell Scottie you were a boy?'

'Yes,' I replied quietly.

'But why? You're a girl. I've *seen* you are. Did you *really* think you were a boy?'

'Yes—No—Oh, I don't *know*! Maybe I *dreamt* that I was a boy in another life.' I let my eyes close. How could I tell her the truth? If it *was* the truth? It was so utterly weird and unbelievable. I could only think that I had returned to a previous incarnation, because if I had not come back from the future, why did I have such vivid memories of 1974? When I looked in the mirror, my own, familiar, boy's face looked back at me, and yet, I was now undeniably a girl! In my

1974 male life I had a small birthmark in the shape of an "M" on the side of my right thigh. As I dressed on this, my second morning in 1940, that same birthmark was there and yet my body was now undoubtedly that of a girl. How had this happened to me? Why? I could think of no reason. What I knew for certain was that the person whom I become, my father's twin sister, died when she was still a schoolgirl. Must I live out the rest of this, her life, before I could return to being a boy in 1974?

Whatever the truth, I was certain that telling Harry would wreck our friendship. Should I have let our relationship happen? What would happen to her when I returned to my own time?—*if* I was to return to my own time! I felt very lonely, yet sensed a tremendous bond with this stout-hearted girl, whom I had met for the first time only the day before, and yet whom I felt I had known for considerably longer than just one day.

'Come on, Ally! Wakey-*wakey!*' said Harry anxiously. 'Pul-*ease,* Al-*leee*, don't go all peculiar on me. I'm Harry, your best friend. Remember?' She shook me gently. I opened my eyes and saw the anxiety of her voice reflected in her dark eyes. Once before, I had seen a similar distress in the dark eyes of my cousin Nick.

'I'm okay,' I replied. 'I was thinking, that's all. Sorry!' I pulled her down on top of me and we wrestled happily, until we fell off the bed, and ended up rolling on the floor in a giggling tangle of arms and legs. We picked ourselves up, dusted each other down, and then got on with the job of turning my mattress and re-making my bed with clean sheets and pillow-slip.

After helping Harry with hers, I went back to my cubicle and picked up the pink nightie that Mrs. Brownlow, the matron at Colvin, had lent me. I presumed there would not be a name-tape in it, indeed I hoped there wouldn't be somebody else's name-tape in it. There was not. But there *was* one that said *Alexandra Frances Muir!*

CHAPTER NINE

Saturday

BY GIVING EACH OTHER a hand, the after-breakfast chores were soon done. Scottie brought me a name-tape, but it wasn't needed. Still, I was puzzled as to how the night-dress lent to me in 1974 had got my aunt's, *now my own*, name-tape sewn in it. It was just another of those queer inexplicable things that had been happening to me over the past twenty-four hours or so.

Since breakfast, the sky had clouded over, and it looked as if it might rain. Five of us from Peregrine had decided to go to lacrosse practice; Jen-Pen, Nancy, Rob Roy, Harry and me. We were not surprised when the twins decided to give it a miss; they were not of the sporty type, being more akin to Prissy and company as far as taking exercise was concerned. We met in the boarders' changing room at twenty five past ten. Nicky, Puddles, Mag-Bags and Paddy from Eagle dormy had beaten us to it. We were ready and changed by the time Miss Bendall arrived on the scene.

'Jolly good show, chaps!' she remarked. 'Has anyone seen Bren Gunn?'

'I'm here, Miss Bendall,' came a stentorian voice from behind a row of lockers. 'I'll be with you in half a mo.'

'Jolly dee, Bren,' said Bendy-Wendy. 'That's eleven so far. Are any more boarders coming, apart from you chaps?'

'Peg-Leg said she'd be coming, Miss Bendall,' said Jenny. 'She asked me to tell you that she'd be a few minutes late.'

'Maggot and Weevil said they'd be coming when I asked them,' said Mag-Bags.

'They're so scatterbrained, you can never rely on them,' said Bren Gunn. 'Jacko said she'd try to join us for the last hour. She's got a job to do for The Beak first.'

'I know,' said Miss Bendall, 'The Beak told me a few minutes ago. Kate's going to be such a good head girl. She takes her duties very seriously. I say! Why don't you chaps go out and start warming up, while I light a squib under those day-bugs.'

'Please, Miss Bendall?' I put my hand up.

'Yes, Alex.'

'Please, Miss Bendall, I haven't got a lacrosse-stick—a crosse, I mean; mine got lost when the train I was on got bombed on the way here.'

'Don't worry, Alex, I've got one you can borrow.' She went to a large cupboard and opened it. An assortment of crosses, cricket bats, tennis rackets and hockey sticks cascaded to the floor. 'Oh *fiddle!*' she exclaimed. 'I *am* a silly sausage! It *always* does that! Come along, chaps, lend a hand to pile them all back.' She picked out a suitable crosse for me and then we put the rest back in the cupboard and went outside to do some warming-up exercises under the direction of Bren Gunn.

Miss Bendall soon arrived with the day-girls. She divided us into two groups, experts who went with Bren, and novices who stayed behind. As I had never played before, I joined in with the novices, and was surprised when Harry joined me.

'I thought you'd've been an expert,' I remarked.

'Not I! I've never played the game before this term.' And reading my mind she added, 'I played cricket last term.'

Bendy Wendy showed us how to catch and throw the ball with our crosses; also how to cradle the ball in the net so it didn't fall out while we ran.

'It seems odd not having a boundary, or a touch line,' Harry remarked as we ran together, practising cradling.

'Maybe it's because the game began with the red indians,' I suggested.

After about half an hour, Bendy Wendy suggested having a game, boarders versus day-bugs. Sadly, after we had been playing for about twenty minutes it started to rain. We boarders were leading two-nil, so were declared the winners. Harry scored one of our goals and Puddles the other.

Back in the changing room, Harry's grin spread from ear to ear. It was her first game and she had scored.

'Well done, you,' I told her. 'You were brilliant!'

'I wouldn't have scored if you hadn't sent me that super pass,' she said. 'It was really *our* goal, not just mine. Don't we make a *smashing* team?' She took hold of my hands and danced me round and round in circles, until we became dizzy, and had to support each other, before collapsing in a giggling pile on the floor, just as Miss Bendall came in.

'Jolly good show,' she said, and then, seeing us, added, 'Oh! Golly-gosh! What are you chaps doing? Are you feeling all right?'

'They were doing a victory dance,' explained Rob Roy. 'I think they got giddy and collapsed in the giggling heap you see.'

We stood up. The changing room still seemed to be going round and round, so we sat on the bench next to our lockers, until our giddiness subsided, before getting dressed again.

'Well, chaps!' Bendy Wendy said to us. 'Do I take it that you enjoyed yourselves? Are you sure you've never played before?'

'No, never, Miss Bendall,' replied Harry, buttoning her blouse. 'They don't play lax at boy's schools. We really enjoyed ourselves, didn't we, Ally?'

'That's right! You both played footer, didn't you?'

'Yes, Miss Bendall,' I replied, looking up at her from a crouching position as I tied a shoelace. 'Do we play matches against other schools?'

'We play against Southbourne High occasionally,' she replied, 'but they're more of a *netters* school. I'm trying to arrange some lax fixtures with other schools.'

'Do we play netball?' Harry asked, as she pulled her tunic over her head. 'After all there're goal posts in the playground.'

'Not officially,' replied Miss Bendall, 'But sometimes we play instead of doing gym when the weather's decent. Why? Would you like to try? What d'you all think?'

'*I* would,' said Jen. 'My elder sister plays for her school.'

'Me too,' said Rob Roy. 'Would you, Puddles?'.

'I played at Laurel Bank, my school in Glasgow,' she replied, 'So you can count me in; what about you, Nicky?'

'Ra-*ther!* How about it, Bendy?' replied Nicky.

'Oh gosh, Nicky,' said the gym mistress, blushing, 'I wish you wouldn't call me that while day girls are around.'

'I'm sorry,' said Nicky, 'but Harry's a boarder now—and so's Alex. I certainly wouldn't call you that in front of *day*-bugs.'

'Oh, righty-ho then,' said Bendy Wendy. 'Who's coming for a hot drink? I asked Gladders if she could manage some cocoa to ward off the jolly old cold.'

*

Scottie dished out pocket money at half past twelve. As we waited patiently for her to arrive, we gazed out of the window at the steadily falling rain.

'I don't fancy walking to Fishermans Walk in all that rain,' said Harry. 'D'you s'pose we could take a bus.'

'It'd cost money,' I replied. 'How much is it on the bus, Jen-Pen?'

'When it's raining Scottie gives us a special bus-ticket,' said Jen-Pen. 'A scholars' penny return—like the ones given to the day-bugs who live too far from school to walk or 'cycle.'

'I used 'em last term, till I got my bike,' said Harry, 'But when it was wet I took the bus, because once I got so soaked biking that I squelched every time I sat down!'

Emily Barker, one of the second formers, exploded into a fit of the giggles.

''T's not funny, Puppy,' said Harry. 'You just try riding a bike into heavy rain in a dress. The rain reaches some jolly uncomfy places, I c'n tell you!' she added frankly. Emily giggled again and sniggers came from the Willis twins.

'Why did you call her Puppy?' I queried. 'I thought her name was Emily.'

'Because her name's *Barker*, you dumb cluck!' said Harry. 'You like being called "Puppy", don't you, Emily?'

'Woof-woof,' came the reply amidst much giggling.

I aimed a playful punch at Harry, just as Scottie came to give out pocket money.

'Fisticuffs, Alexandra?' she said with mock severity. 'Are you trying to knock out your best friend? My spies tell me that the two of you have been brawling on the changing room floor like a pair of drunken sailors. Maybe you *are* both boys, after all!' She winked at us, so we stood in mock innocence, with shoulders back and hands clasped tightly behind our backs. 'What shall we do with them, girls?'

'Send 'em to Saint Aloysius' with the other boys,' suggested Jenny, good-humouredly, 'and stop their pocket money.'

Harry dropped on to her knees and pulled me down by her. 'Oh no, Matron! Not *Saint Ally's Wash House!*' she pleaded, '*any*thing but *that!* Maggot'd pelt us with *you-know-what!* Have mercy, have mercy upon us miserable offenders.'

'*Saint Ali's Wash-House,* indeed!' chuckled Scottie, and we all collapsed laughing. 'I shall always think of it as that now! How can I ignore such an impassioned plea? Maybe we'll let you off this time. Come on, you loonies, you're as bad as Maggot and Weevil! No, not as bad, you are *much* worse! *And* you're holding up the pocket money queue.'

It didn't take her long. She had a book that showed how much we each had for the term, and how much each of us was allowed each week. I had fifteen shillings to last the term, and I could have up to ninepence a week, leaving some for emergencies. Fifteen shillings in old money is 75p. in decimal, and ninepence, just under 4p. Harry was getting sixpence, so I decided it was enough for me too. In 1940, I discovered that sixpence could buy as much as I could with 25p. in 1974.

We each decided to give a penny towards Judy White's flowers, so Scottie gave us each a shiny sixpence and a large old penny, and a penny return bus ticket and my sweets coupon. She had pinned them to a piece of paper on which she had written my name. We gave the flowers' penny back to Scottie to keep safe. As we went into lunch, Harry and I were discussing upon what we should spend our shiny new sixpences.

*

We were allowed to go to the shops after two o'clock. Before leaving we had to pass Scottie's inspection; clean hands, faces and knees, tidy hair and uniform, with polished shoes, wearing raincoats, school hats and gas-mask cases. Weevil was sent to change her tunic because she had a tear in the one she had on.

As we walked up the drive, it was raining harder than ever, and the easterly wind made it even worse. We turned up the lapels of our raincoats and buttoned them close under our chins.

'I'm jolly glad we aren't walking to Fisherman's Walk,' Harry said, as we crossed the road to the bus stop. We were soon joined by Maggot and Weevil, Jen-Pen and Mag-Bags, Puddles and Rob Roy and several second-form boarders under the watchful eye of Kate Jackson—Jacko, the head girl. It was not long before a yellow trolleybus glided silently round the corner and stopped beside us. It was a number 22A from Crossroads to Bournemouth Square.

As soon as it stopped, a door at the front opened and a lady got off. We had to get on by the platform at the back. A red-faced conductress—a *clippie*—stood at the bottom of the spiral staircase that wound its way to the top deck. Hanging round her neck were the tools of her trade—a square, shiny metal, "Bell" ticket punch on the left-hand side of her tummy, and a many-pocketed leather money pouch on the right. In her left hand she held a wooden rack with stacks of different-coloured tickets held in place by spring wire clips.

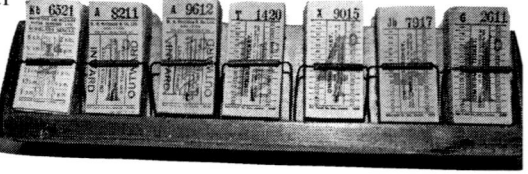

A bus conductor's ticket rack

We rushed upstairs. The only passengers on top were two women sitting near the back, talking loudly about *"ow terrible it all was."* One, with her hair in curlers had a cigarette dangling on her lower lip that wiggled up and down in time with her words.

'—and 'ow that Lord Wilton—*y'know*, Else—the Minist'ruh' *Food*,' she paused to take a drag of her cigarette; ''ow on *earth* 'e expects one and tuppensaypenny-worth o' meat to last a 'ole week, I dunno, I reely dunno. Disgustin' *I* calls it.'

We scampered past, to sit right at the front and soon the sounds of our own voices drowned the women's grumblings. Harry and I shared the long seat over the driver with Rob Roy and Puddles. It was meant for three grown-ups so there was plenty room for four girls. No sooner had we sat down, than we heard the clippie sing out; 'Hold very tight, please,' and ring the bell twice to tell the driver to start. When she came upstairs we gave her our tickets. She put them in the narrow slit at the top of her ticket punching machine and pushed down a lever at the bottom. There was a "ting" and she handed the ticket back, with a neat round hole punched on one side. When she had punched all our tickets, she went back to the lower deck by the front stairs.

We had passed the Emmanuel Church and the top of Carberry Avenue, and as the trolleybus slowed for the next stop, the clippie sang out; 'Irving Road.' A lady Air-Raid Warden got on, our clippie called, 'hold very tight, please,' the bell went "ding-ding", and we were off again. As we branched left up Southbourne Grove we heard; 'Grand Avenue next stop.'

'D'you know?' said Harry, 'That in Scotland, boys wearing kilts aren't allowed to go upstairs on the trams or buses? 'T's true, isn't it, Puddles?'

'Aye, sure enough.'

'It's jolly unfair,' said Harry, 'Girls're allowed on top.'

Maggot said; 'I s'pose that as you went to a boys' school, you weren't allowed to travel upstairs either?' Harry nodded.

'But you're a girl,' said Weevil.

'Aye,' Harry replied, 'but I had short hair, wore a school cap, and looked like a boy in the kilt, so I was treated like one.'

'Why don't they let boys in kilts go upstairs, Harry?' asked Freda Carter, a mischievous second-former with all the makings of another Maggot. 'Is it so people can't look—?'

'*Huisht*, Freddie!' Puddles cut in, scowling fiercely.

'You mean it's *true?*' squealed a delighted Freddie at the top of her voice. 'They *acksherly* don't w——'

'*Freda Carter!*' Kate Jackson interrupted hastily. '*Shush!* You *mustn't* ask things like that in public; it's very, *very*, VERY rude! Another word on the subject and I shall give you a misconduct mark. D'you understand?'

'Yes, Kate,' mumbled the usually bubbling Freddie, adding loudly; 'but all the same, they must find it *frightfully* chill——'

A Bournemouth trolleybus circa 1940

'*Freddie!*' said Jacko sharply. 'What did I say just now?'

'Not to say another word or you'd give me a "miss", Kate,' said a contrite Freddie, turning bright pink. 'Please don't give me a "miss". I'm *ever* so sorry, Kate.'

Jacko smiled, and squeezed Freddie's hand to show she was not cross with her any more.

'Come on, Ally, our stop next,' said Harry, standing up and heading for the front staircase. I followed her down, and stood by the glass partition between us and the driver's cab.

'Fishermans Walk,' called the conductress. The bus slowed down and when it had stopped, the driver pulled on the hand-brake, making a "*Krrrrrrrrrrr*" noise. Then he pulled a handle on his side of the partition to open the front door. We jumped off right outside W.H. Smith's. First stop, the sweet shop. We crossed the road and walked about twenty-five yards back down Southbourne Grove.

'Here we are,' said Harry, unbuttoning her raincoat. The sign over the shop announced;

"A. W. PITCHER"

and beneath, in smaller letters,

"*CONFECTIONER AND TOBACCONIST.*"

Inside, a man in army battledress was buying a packet of Woodbines. 'Thanks, Arthur,' said the soldier, taking his cigarettes and the change. Before leaving the shop he removed the cigarettes from the packet and put them into his cigarette case. 'It's good to be back. Pity I could only wangle forty-eight hours leave. Still,

I was lucky to get away at Dunkirk. A lot o' my mates got took pris'ner.' He gave the empty Woodbine packet to Mr Pitcher. 'Comes to somefink when we 'ave to save old fag packets so they c'n be sent back to be refilled, eh, Arthur? Dunno wot's gonna 'appen next. 'Tseems the *brass* is expecting 'itler to invade any day now. I only 'ope the 'ome Guard's on its toes!' He turned round and nearly trod on us. 'Sorry, girlies, I didn' see yer there! Come for yer sweetie ration? Don't let old Arthur 'ere diddle yer. Cheery-bye, Arthur, see yer next time.'

'Righty-ho, Fred,' laughed Mr Pitcher. 'So long as Hitler's not here, eh?' He turned to us. 'Well, young ladies, and what can I do you for today? Oh, hello, Master Harry, I didn't recognise you in school uniform. I don't think I've ever seen you looking like a *real* girl before, I'll have to start calling you Miss Henrietta—ha-ha! Where's your mum today? You usually come in with her.'

Harry had gone very pink. 'Oh—er—she's had to go away to London for a bit, so I'm a boarder at school now, Mr Pitcher. This is my best friend, Alex.'

'I'm very pleased to meet you, Miss Alex,' said Mr Pitcher, 'And what would you like? There's not nothing like the selection I had before the war. I just got a new jar of jelly babies in, and one of chocolate drops; I couldn't get any Smarties this week, but I've got some Liquorice Allsorts, if you like those.'

So you *could* get Smarties in 1940! 'Please may I have two ounces of chocolate drops,' I said, 'And, er—er—two ounces of jelly babies, please, Mr Pitcher.'

He put a two ounce weight on the back of the scales, unscrewed the lid of the large jar and poured chocolate drops into the pan of his scales. The needle moved quickly towards the middle of the scale's window. He stopped pouring. Then he took one more chocolate drop out of the jar and added it to the pan.

'And an extra one for luck,' he said, giving me a smile and a wink. 'We mustn't give you pretty little girls short weight, must we?'

He tipped them into a paper bag and, holding the top corners, swung it over twice to twist them to keep it closed. 'Now the jelly babies!' After weighing them he passed me the bags. 'Let me see now; that will be tuppence-ha'penny for the Cadbury's chocolate drops and a penny-three-farthings for the jelly babies; that's fourpence-farthing altogether, please, Miss Alex.'

I opened my purse, took out my sixpence, and gave it to him with the piece of paper with the coupon pinned to it.

'Thank you, my pretty little one, and—a penny-three farthings change,' he said, smiling. 'How's that?'

I felt myself blushing burning hot as he gave me a penny, a ha'penny and a farthing change. I scowled to try to hide my embarrassment and thanked him before putting the change in my purse and my sweets ration in my mac pocket. I waited while Harry bought hers.

'Gosh, Ally!' said Harry, when we were outside, 'You blushed like billy-o in there, and why did you scowl so?'

'Well he called me Miss Alex and his *pretty little one!* Nobody's *EVER* called me that in my en*TIRE* life before. It's enough to make ANYBODY blush!'

'But, Ally,' she replied, 'You shouldn't have scowled so fiercely; we're supposed to be pleased when people say nice things like that to us. Anyhow, I agree with him; you *are* pretty.'

'Don't *you* start,' I said, with a grin, 'or I'll bash you up! Anyway, you blushed like billy-o too, when he said it was the first time he had seen you looking like a real girl.' I made to punch her arm.

'Naah—naah—na—na—naaah,' she chanted, dancing out of the way. 'You can't catch me for a wee bawbee!' Then she took my hand and led me back to W. H. Smith's, where the lady behind the newspaper counter let us browse through some of the comics. After that we crossed the road and waited for a trolleybus to take us back to school.

*

The very second we got off the bus at the stop outside Emmanuel Church, the heavens opened. It was stair rods, cats and dogs, and coming down in buckets all at the same time. The easterly wind had freshened to a full gale and was driving the rain straight into our faces. The stop was about a hundred yards west of the school gate, and from there to the school building was another hundred.

'Come on, Ally,' said Harry. 'Let's run for it.'

We put our heads down and ran into the gale. I never saw the puddle until I trod in it. It was the first time I had run in the rain wearing a skirt, and was not expecting water to splash where it did. Suddenly everything below my waist felt very soggy, cold and uncomfortable.

'Oh, flipping *HECK!*' I screeched at the top of my voice. Harry stopped dead in her tracks and turned round, looking alarmed. When she saw me walking with my legs wide apart, clutching my skirts, she hooted with laughter.

'What's the matter? she asked as I waddled towards her. 'You're walking as if you'd wet yourself. Couldn't you wait till we got back to school?'

'I *have* wet myself! But *not* the way *YOU* think,' I replied. 'I wasn't looking where I was going and trod in that rather deep puddle back there and it splashed where I didn't expect it!'

'Clumsy clot!' she said, grinning. 'Come on, the sooner we get back into school, the sooner we can both get dry.'

*

Scottie was gazing out of her window and saw us as soon as we rounded the corner of the drive where it opened out into the playground. No sooner were we in the changing room taking off our wet raincoats, hats and gumboots, than she was fussing round us like a mother hen.

'It's not fit out there for man nor beast,' she said. 'You poor wee drookit mites! Like two drowned rats, so you are. Why on earth didn't you shelter until the rain eased a wee bit?'

'It started coming down in buckets just as we got off the 'bus,' said Harry. 'We were rushing back as quickly as we could when Ally wet herself!'

'Could you not have waited?' asked Scottie; then she saw Harry grinning. 'Och, you two! *Honestly!*'

' 'M afraid I *did* wet myself, Scottie,' I admitted, 'But not *that* way! You see, we were running back and I wasn't looking where I was going and clottishly trod in a rather deep puddle and it splashed up my skirt!'

Scottie burst out laughing; 'Och! You funny wee lass, you'll be the death o' me! Go straight upstairs and change straight away. You may put on your home clothes now if you like. Then bring me all your wet things and I'll see they're dried properly. Off you go, *toute de suite!* I don't want you catching cold. Be sure you dry yourselves *properly* before you put on dry things—put on clean linings too, the ones you've got on are bound to be damp and dampness down there is the best way to catch a chill. By the time you've changed it will be time for tea.'

'I thought she'd give us an awful row,' I said, as we reached our dormitory.

'So did I,' admitted Harry. 'I think she's spiffing! A jolly good sport, don't you?'

'I think she is too,' I replied, letting my wet clothes fall in a heap on the floor. 'I think she's one of the kindest ladies I've ever met.'

'So do I,' agreed Harry, 'she's absolutely ripping. I can't think why I used to be so scared of her.'

'Probably 'cos you were a day-bug and didn't really know her,' I suggested.

'And they say that you never hear good of yourself when you eavesdrop,' said Scottie, appearing with two large bath towels. As she came into my cubicle I had just stepped out of my soggy linings and was standing, shivering, wondering what to do next. She wrapped one of the towels round me and took the other to Harry.

Scottie returned to my cubicle. 'Come here, my wee Alex,' she said. 'Let me dry you before you catch your death of cold, you silly wee goose!'

She rubbed me dry and then found me something to wear; my aunt's midnight-blue velvet dress with long sleeves, smocking on the front and a white Peter Pan collar and cuffs. Harry put on her Gordon kilt and a dark green jumper.

'I'll see you downstairs in ten minutes for tea,' Scottie said, picking up my wet things and leaving my cubie. Alexandra's dress buttoned at the back, and I found it rather hard to do up. As I was taking so long, Harry came looking for me.

'Let me help,' she said, when she saw me struggling. 'Turn round!' Her nimble fingers did me up quickly and then she shook out the pleats of my skirt so that it was hanging evenly. I was learning there is more to being a girl than just putting a dress on, so I made a mental note to remember to do that myself next time.

'Thanks,' I said, when she had finished. 'You're ever so kind to me.' She put her arms round my neck from behind and gave me a strangling hug.

Downstairs in the eatery, a hot cup of tea was just what the doctor ordered. Saturday and Sunday tea was better than weekday teas because there were no day-girls around; so instead of just a cake or a bun, we got a hot-buttered crumpet, a jam sandwich, a slice of slab-cake and real milk in our tea.

As we ate, we gazed out of the window, watching the rain, still pelting down. The warmth of the room made the windows steam up and we had to wipe them from time to time to see out. Over tea Harry told me about her life in Scotland. She had brought some snaps that had been taken while she was at St. Mungo's Academy. In her class photo, she had to point out which "boy" was her, as about a third of them were wearing kilts. She even wore a sporran.

After tea we went to the JCR, where Children's Hour was coming from the wireless in the corner. The room was really cosy since the Bombardier had lighted the stove. We sat on the hearth rug, hugging our knees and gazing into the glowing embers. When we were warm enough, Harry bagged us two places on the sofa. She settled down to read *Secret Water*, and I went to see if *The Chalet School in Exile* was still where I had put it back the evening before. It was, so I signed it out to myself in the Library Register, and joined my best friend on the sofa to read until the high-tea bell rang. I was soon absorbed once again in the story of an English girls' school in Austria faced with the threat of the nazi take-over of that country in 1938 and the problems which resulted. It was really exciting, with a party of the Chalet School girls being spied on while going back to school on the train and having lots of narrow escapes as they flee the Nazi menace; I realised Nick had been right and that I would have enjoyed reading it in my boy's life.

Saturday high-tea was bacon and tomato on fried bread. The bacon was rather salty and mostly fat and I think the tomato had come out of a tin. Afterwards, we returned to the JCR and read our books on the sofa again. We were joined by Rob Roy and Puddles who, as a fourth-former, was entitled to use the senior common room, but preferred to spend her spare time with her best friend.

'Shove up, you three,' said Puddles, 'make room for wee me.' Even though she was a fourth-former, she was not yet eleven, so felt more at home with us third-formers; anyhow, being in the third, Rob Roy was not allowed in the senior common room.

Nearly everybody was wearing home clothes; it turned out that Harry and I were not the only ones to have got soaked. Only the Willis twins were still in uniform; they hated going out in the rain, preferring to stay indoors which, that day, had been the wise choice. Nicky was there too, curled up and almost hidden in the big winged armchair while she read her book. Maggot, Weevil, and Paddy were on the hearth-rug playing Monopoly and Florence Cox, a cheeky second-former, was playing Ludo with Freddie, her best friend, and two others. Looking up and seeing Harry, Florence stood up and came over to us. 'Hawwy?'

Harry stopped reading and looked up. 'Yes, Flossie.'

'Can I see the snaps you showed Alex and Wob Woy at teatime?'

'What did you forget to say?' asked Harry.

Flossie thought for a moment, then said; '*Please* will you show me them?'

'*That's* better,' said Harry, picking up her album. She turned the pages, while Flossie scrutinised them carefully.

'Oooh, look at that castle!' squealed Flossie with delight.

'That's Edinburgh Castle,' Harry said, turning the page. 'And these ones were taken inside. See that huge gun? They fire it every day at one o'clock sharp.'

'Why?' asked Flossie.

'To tell the good folk of Edinburgh that it's one o'clock.'

'Can't they just look at a clock?' asked Flossie.

'Well, they could, nowadays,' replied Harry, 'But in the olden days, before every house had a clock, it was a jolly good way to tell everyone it was lunch-time.'

'Yes, I s'pose so. Is it everso vewy loud?'

'Yes, ever-so very, *very* loud,' said Harry.

'Who's that girl standing by it?' asked Flossie.

''T's not a girl, but a boy called Calum who was my best friend at St Mungo's.'

'Why'th he wearwing a thkirt?' Flossie began lisp when she got interested.

'It's a kilt——' Somebody was fiddling with the wireless and suddenly there was a sneering voice saying; '*Chairmany calling, Chairmany calling.*'

'It's that *awful* Lord Haw-Haw,' said Nicky. 'Turn the beastly traitor off. We don't want to listen to *his* poisonous rubbish.'

The voice was saying; '*English women and girls, frightened of injury from splinters from our German bombs, are asking milliners for hats made from tin plate covered with silk or velvet—*'

'*Fiddlesticks!*' exploded Harry. 'What utter *ROT!* Turn that lunatic *off!*' Her words were unnecessary, as Maggot had got up and her hand was already on the switch.

'Surely nobody believes what he says, do they?' I said.

'Some people are stupid enough to believe everything they hear on the wireless,' said Maggot. 'They think that if it's on the wireless it's the Gospel truth.'

'Is he really a lord?' asked Freddie.

'No,' replied Nicky. 'He's a British nazi who ran away to Germany before the war. His real name's Joyce.'

'But Joythe ith a girl'th name,' said Flossie.

'Not when it's a surname,' said Nicky. 'His christian name's William, *if* he's a Christian, which I doubt!'

'Oh,' said Flossie. 'I *thee*,' she added doubtfully.

'My big brother's called Evelyn,' said Freddie, 'after Grandad.

'Poor chap,' said Maggot. 'I bet he gets teased at school.'

'He did, till he mashed the form bully at boxing,' replied Freddie proudly.

By eight-thirty, I was eager for my bed so Harry and I went straight upstairs as soon as we heard the bell. I remembered my book this time and after a wash, and brushing my teeth, I snuggled down in bed, listening to the wind howling in the trees and the rain crashing against the window panes as I read about the doings of Joey Bettany and her friends in Austria. Soon I felt very cosy, warm and safe in the cocoon of my bed. When we said our prayers that night, I doubt there was a single one of us who did not pray for a peaceful night—without another air-raid.

CHAPTER TEN

Harvest Festival Howler!

ON SUNDAY, the getting-up bell was rung at eight o'clock, half an hour later than on weekdays. I was barely out of bed, when Scottie appeared with our tunics, dry, pressed and looking smart for church.

'Here you are, Miss Gordon! And don't say I'm not kind to you.'

'Thank you, Scottie,' I heard Harry say. 'Golly! That was jolly quick. I never thought you'd have our gymmers ready so quickly.'

'Good Morning, Scottie,' I said when she came into my cubie. 'I'm sorry I was so clottish getting wet like that yesterday; thank you for being so nice. I thought you were going to be cross.'

'Don't be a chump,' she replied, 'I knew perfectly well it was an accident. You're not the kind of girl to do a thing like that on purpose. I should imagine that you'll watch where you're treading next time.' When she had gone, Harry came to check that I was out of bed.

'Oh! You're up,' she said, disappointment clouding her face. 'I came to bounce on you again, like I did yesterday!'

'No need to be Tigger today; I had a good night's sleep. Is it still raining?'

''T'snot,' she said. 'I can see out of the window from here. Come on, Ally. It's time to go to the bathroom.' I picked up my towel, then we linked arms and went together.

*

Sunday brekker was special. It was when we had our weekly egg. The Ministry of Food rationed every man, woman and child in the country to just one egg a week—if you were lucky. We had our porridge first, and then one girl from each table went to fetch the boiled eggs from the kitchen. The eggs were cooked table by table so that we would all get runny yolks. That Sunday, 15th September 1940, it was Rob Roy's turn to be our waitress.

As soon as we had finished our porridge, we stacked the plates for her to take back to the kitchen, and as soon as Gladys saw her coming she would put the eggs on to boil. The toast was already cut into fingers, and spread with *real* butter as it was Sunday.

Even after only two days in 1940, experiencing the privations of war-time food rationing, I vowed that when I got back to my own time—*if* I got back to my own time—when things were plentiful—I would never grumble about food again.

Rob Roy brought the eggs in a napkin-lined basket. Each girl took one and put it in her egg cup. I watched the others. This was one of the highlights of their week. They had not had an egg since the previous Sunday, whereas Gran had given me two for my breakfast on Thursday. How I wished I could go forward to 1974 and back just to bring enough eggs for every girl in the school to have one whenever she wanted.

'This is our best brekker of the week,' said Rob Roy, dipping her finger of toast into the yolk. 'I think we ought to keep hens, like Akkers's mummy does, then we could have eggs more often.'

'That's right,' said Jen-Pen. 'Mrs. Ackroyd's allowed to buy chicken meal so long as she supplies a number of her neighbours with their weekly egg ration. All the scraps, and peelings are boiled up and mixed with meal to feed the hens. Lucky Sarah gets an egg quite often. The Bombardier keeps a few hens too.'

'Why not suggest we get some hens at the next boarders' council, Jen-Pen,' said Nancy from the other end of the table. 'The government's doing everything it can to encourage people to produce their own eggs.'

'That's a super-dooper idea, Nancy,' replied Jenny. 'I'll mention it to Jacko when I see her after brekker and she can ask The Beak. Every girl could adopt a hen. Then we'd have lots of eggs and be able to sell some to pay for the meal. Gladys must have loads of potato peelings and instead of sending them to the pig man we could feed them to our hens. D'you remember the rhyme?'

'Dearly beloved brethren, isn't it a sin?' said Harry.
'To peel the potatoes and throw away the skin,' added Rob Roy.
'The skin feeds the pigs,' said Milly-Willy.
'And the pigs feeds us,' said her twin.
'Dearly beloved brethren, isn't it thus?' Harry, finished off the recitation.

We resumed the slow eating of our eggs making it last as long as possible, and savouring each delectable mouthful. When we finally finished, we turned the empty shells upside down in our egg-cups to make them look as if we had never eaten them.

'It's a game we play with Gladys every Sunday.' Rob Roy explained. 'Look, she's coming to clear away now.'

'Oh, you *naughty* girls,' said Gladys, 'You 'aven't eaten your luverly eggs again, and them on the ration too!' She went to Jenny, picked up a spoon and gave the egg a resounding bash, making a huge dent in the top. 'There you go, 'aving your poor old Glad on again!' and she burst into hoots of laughter which made her wobble like a jelly.

'I wonder what it's like having big bosoms like Gladys?' asked Dilly-Willy, once Gladys was out of earshot. 'They really must get in the way most awf'ly.' Milly-Willy giggled.

'As you'll probably grow up to be a big fat lady with big fat bosoms yourself, you'll be able tell us all about it, *won't* you, Dilys Willis?' said Harry, a look of disgust clouding her usually cheerful face. 'I think that's a mean, horrible thing to say!' As soon as Harry had turned away, both twins stuck out their tongues and thumbed their noses at her.

After our morning chores, we all went to our common rooms to write letters to our parents. Harry and I sat at the table, next to the wireless set. We had never had to write letters home before and we both found it quite hard to get going. I got as far as *'Darling Mummy,'* and stuck! Harry managed about the same, so we compared notes and then decided that all we had to do was to write about what had happened during the last couple of days. In the end I managed to write nearly two full pages about our night in the air-raid shelter, becoming best friends with Harry, lessons and lacrosse practice. And then there was our trolleybus trip to the shops at Fisherman's Walk to buy our sweets ration, and how we got caught in a cloudburst just as we got off the bus; I knew she would giggle like mad at my silliness in not seeing the deep puddle and getting myself so wet that I had to change all my clothes! I ended by sending lots of love and saying how much I missed her and hoping everything was going well. It came quite easily in the end and both of us managed a really newsy letter. When we had finished we compared our efforts and had a good think—just in case there was anything else we should have told our mums about which we could add as a P.S.

…had a good think—just in case there was anything else…

The rain that had fallen overnight had left many puddles behind, but when the sun broke through the clouds, the playground sparkled with countless tiny stars and the puddles began to steam gently as they dried. The remaining clouds were scurrying away, leaving bigger and bigger patches of blue sky, and when the time came to assemble outside for the walk to church, there was scarcely a cloud to be seen so Scottie told us that as it had turned out such a grand morning, we could go to church wearing just our blazers, without raincoats, if we liked. 'I had a wee word with the Bombardier just now,' she explained, 'and he told me he was sure the weather was set fair and it was going to be sunny for the next three days.'

'That's a jolly good reason for wearing our macs,' Dilys said, gloomily.

'You c'n never believe *anything* predicted about the weather,' added her twin.

'And even when we had weather forecasts on the wireless they were *always* wrong,' proclaimed Dilys. (*Until this moment I had not known that weather forecasts had not been broadcast since the war started.*)[†]

'What twin Doubting Thomases you are,' said Harry. 'I'm not wearing mine.'

'Nor'm I,' I said as The Beak came out of the front door.

'Good morning, girls.'

'Good morning, Miss Plenderleith,' we replied in chorus.

[†] It would have been extremely stupid to broadcast information of military significance to the enemy.

'Now, girls,' said The Beak, 'Form a crocodile; Merlin in front, then Peregrine, Eagle, and Goshawk at the back. You may talk quietly among yourselves on the way to and from church. But I don't want to see any malarkey or giggling. Is that understood?'

'Yes, Miss Plenderleith.'

'Kate, please will you count heads to check that everybody's here.'

'Yes, Miss Plenderleith,' replied the head girl. She went along the crocodile. counting. On reaching the end of the line, she frowned. 'Twenty eight; there's somebody missing.'

'Will the girl who's not here please put up her hand,' said The Beak. After a few seconds silence the penny dropped and we burst out laughing. 'All right, girls, simmer down now! Dormitory monitresses, check if anyone is missing from your brood.' She paused while the head of each dormitory checked numbers. Puddles put up her hand. 'Yes, Jemima.'

'It's Amanda Hardy, Miss Plenderleith,' said Puddles.

'Oh! Has anyone seen Amanda Hardy?' asked Miss Plenderleith.

'She was in her cubie making her bed, the last time I saw her,' said Paddy, in her Irish brogue. 'But I've not set oyes on her since.'

'Kate,' said The Beak to the head girl, 'Have a quick scout round and see if you can find the wretched child, but don't be long or we won't have enough time to walk to church.'

Jacko dashed into the school just as Miss Bendall was coming out.

'You haven't seen Amanda Hardy, have you, Miss Bendall?'

'No, Jacko, 'fraid not. I've just come straight from my room.'

Two minutes later Jacko returned with a sullen looking girl.

'You are late, Amanda Hardy!' Miss Plenderleith said sternly. 'And *where* do you think you have been?'

'Pleathe, Mith Plenderleith, I wath being ecthcuthed.'

'You should have thought about being *excused*, as you put it, five minutes earlier,' said The Beak. 'How is it that all the others—even the tinies in the Remove—manage to *be excused* in good time for us to leave punctually, and yet you, Amanda Hardy, thirteen years old and in the fourth form, can not?'

'I don't know, Mith Plenderleith,' lisped the hapless Amanda, her face going purple with embarrassment, and starting to cry.

'Then, I suggest you find out. You will take a lateness mark, walk with the remove to and from church. Furthermore, you will go to bed at the same time as them, for the rest of the week. You should know better at your age; so let this be a lesson to you.'

'Yeth, Mith Plenderleith, I'm evertho thowwy, Mith Plenderleith.' Amanda curtsied and, dabbing her eyes with a hanky, took her place next to Freddie, who made her hold hands. The other juniors, were nudging each other and sniggering. In such a mood our crocodile set off on the half-mile walk to All Saints Church.

After some fairly brisk walking, we arrived with about three minutes in hand. As we entered the church, Harry and I both took off our hats, earning a frown from Scottie.

'We ladies are supposed to keep our heads covered in church,' she hissed. 'Neither of you are being boys just now!' She shook her head as if pitying us. So we put our hats on again and filed into the pews that were reserved for us at the front of the congregation. I knew the church well, and was delighted to see it decorated with masses fruit and vegetables for Harvest Festival, one of my favourite services, which we had had on my last Sunday in 1974. It was like having the same treat two weeks running.

The organ struck up the processional hymn, *Come, ye thankful people come, Raise the song of harvest home*, and the choir, wearing royal-blue cassocks like the ones we wore in 1974, processed from the vestry, down the south aisle to the west door, then up the nave to the choirstalls. I felt very strange sitting in a pew, dressed as a schoolgirl. Because of wartime shortages we had to share hymn- and prayer-books. I shared with Harry, but I knew the order of service well, having sung it every Sunday since I was seven, so I hardly had to look at the prayer book at all. The sung versicles and responses were second nature to me, and being accustomed to singing out, my voice was louder than any of the other girls.

As the vicar made his way to the pulpit for the sermon, I noticed that he had a bad limp and recognised him; The Reverend Algenon Pugh, or Peg-leg Pugh as we called him behind his back, who in 1974 was the cherubic old vicar who was about to retire. He had lost a leg in a motorbike accident before the war, so was not fit for military service. How could this scrawny man, whose adam's apple waggled up and down on top of his dog-collar, turn into the roly-poly, pink-faced and absent-minded old man I knew in 1974?

Mercifully, his sermon was short, as it had been in 1974. His 1940-sermon was almost word for word the same as he had preached in 1974, the only difference being references to the war and rationing which were unsuited to 1974.

At the end of the service, after the blessing I sang the Amen with the choir, much to Harry's horror. Then came the recessional hymn, *We plough the fields and scatter,* during which the choir and clergy returned to the vestry; I was enjoying myself so much that I forgot I was not a choir-boy, and in the last verse, *We thank thee then, O Father*, I launched into the soaring descant we had sung at our 1974 Harvest Festival the Sunday before. This was, to say the least, a bit of a clanger, considering I was now in 1940, and the descant would not be composed until 1973! I got a few strange looks from the direction of the choir as they filed past in procession, scowls from my schoolmates, and Harry kept digging me in the ribs and looking very embarrassed.

When we filed out of the church, Mr Pugh was outside the west door shaking hands with everybody. When he saw me, he beamed and asked my name.

'Alexandra Muir, Sir.'

'Well, Alexandra, you have a beautiful voice, better than many of the boys in our choir.'

'Thank you, Sir,' I replied. 'I love Harvest Festival; it's one of the best services for singing. That and the service of Nine Lessons and Carols at Christmas.' Then I suddenly thought the service of lessons and carols might not exist in 1940.

'Quite, quite,' he said wringing his hands and stooping over me as he answered. 'It's such a pity you're not Alexander, ha-ha, because if you were a *boy*, I would have you in the choir immediately. Where did you learn that splendid descant?'

I had to do some rapid thinking. 'Oh, er—I learned it with my twin brother; he's a choirboy and I helped him to learn it. They sang it at their Harvest Festival last Sunday.'

'Quite! Quite!' He was wringing his hands again, and spotted The Beak approaching. 'Aah! Miss Plenderleith, I was just telling Alexandra that it's such a pity that she isn't a boy. With her beautiful voice she would be perfect in the choir. She has an amazingly well developed treble, so clear, as good as any boy's I've heard, even in some of the cathedral choirs. Indeed her voice has a strength and edge to it that I have only heard in boys voices up to now.'

'Is there any reason why she should *not* sing in your choir?'

He wrung his hands again and made embarrassed little bows; 'I am err—afraid that err—having a err—*girl* in the choir would be err—frowned upon by the err—the err—diocesan powers-that-be——'

'Diocesan powers-that-be? *Fiddlesticks*, Mr Pugh. Fiddlesticks, I say!' said The Beak, irritably. 'Don't you realise there's a war on, and women are doing men's jobs in the armaments factories, working as railway porters, bus-drivers and all manner of things hitherto regarded as purely men's work! Come along, Alex, we ought to be going now, we've taken enough of Mr Pugh's time already.' The Reverend Mr. Pugh visibly cowed at this verbal onslaught from The Beak.

'Good-bye, Alexandra,' said the vicar, regaining his composure and clasping my hands between his own and bowing. 'Thank you for singing so beautifully. I'll look forward to seeing you when I come to take you for scripture on Tuesday.'

'Goodbye, Sir,' I said, and managed a wonky sort of curtsy.

'Well, Alex, I must say you do sing rather well,' said The Beak as we joined the rest of the girls. 'Your voice must've had some training to sound so clear and true.'

'Thank you, Miss Plenderleith. I used to go to choir practice with my brother and also used to sing in the choir unofficially, except when the bishop or other big-wig was there.'

The Beak chuckled. 'Well done, little girl! Some of these men are too big for their boots. Was I too hard on poor Mr Pugh, d'you think? Would you like to sing in the choir?'

'Rather!' I said. 'It seems jolly unfair that I am not allowed to, just because I'm a *girl*.'

'Well said, young lady,' said Miss P. 'In that case, I think I might try just a little more arm-twisting; perhaps I should be a bit gentler next time! What a pity your hair's not short like Harry's, you could easily be taken for a boy then.'

I looked up at her and grinned, and she smiled and winked.

We formed a crocodile again and began the trek back to school. Harry slipped her hand into mine as we set off. 'What did Pughie want?' she asked. 'And where did you learn to sing like that? You knocked the choirboys into a cocked hat.'

'He said it was a pity I wasn't a boy, because if I was, I could join the choir. The Beak said 'Fiddlesticks! and didn't he realise there was a war on, and women were doing men's jobs in the factories, and trains and buses,' which made Peg-leg Pugh wring his hands even more.'

'What a *super* name for him,' giggled Harry. 'But where did you learn to sing like that?'

'With a church choir,' I replied truthfully. 'With Rory,' I lied. 'My hair wasn't always this long.' We looked at each other and grinned. She squeezed my hand.

'You mean *you* used to let people think *you* were a boy too?'

I nodded. 'Of course! Rory and I are awf'ly alike, and when I had shorter hair people could hardly tell us apart. So I often used to go to choir practice in his place so he could go fishing.'

'I *knew* we were alike! I can *see* you as a boy,' Harry said grinning. 'Would you like to be in the choir? It seems jolly unfair that you can't, just because you're a girl.'

'I'd love to,' I replied, 'Especially at Harvest Festival and Christmas. Oh, and Easter too, 'fcourse.'

'What did the other choirboys think when you turned up instead of Rory?'

'I don't think they realised,' I lied. 'At least most of them didn't. The ones that knew me kept quiet so Rory didn't get into trouble.'

'What a lark!' she said, giving my hand another squeeze. 'Tell me, what was that high bit you sang in the last verse of *We plough the fields and scatter?*'

'The descant? It's a high harmonising part the trebles sing, while everyone else sings the normal tune in unison. It comes from the times when the monasteries had singing boys as well as monks and used to chant everything in plainsong.'

'Golly, you know a t'rific lot about it,' said Harry. It was my turn to squeeze her hand this time. We walked in silence for a while, I was thinking about the past hour, and how I hated having to pretend to Harry. I wished I could tell her what had really happened. We crossed the top of Carberry Avenue, marched past the Emmanuel Congregational Church, where the congregation was just leaving, and turned in at the school gates.

As we took off our coats, hats and blazers, and hung them in the changing room, the smell of the Sunday dinner wafting in the air, made us all feel hungry.

CHAPTER ELEVEN

Our Windy Walk with Bendy Wendy

WE HAD ROAST BEEF for Sunday lunch, or so we were told! A small, greyish sliver with an edging of pale yellowish fat adorned our plates. It was cut so thin, that if you held it up to the light you would probably have been able to see through it! Beside it lay a dollop of watery, over-boiled cabbage, two roast potatoes, and a flabby slab of something that was pretending to be Yorkshire Pudding! It was all swimming in a brown, watery, tasteless liquid that was an insult to the noble name of gravy.

Actually the roast potatoes were scrummy. The meal had begun with a watery liquid of indistinct flavour which, we were told, was vegetable soup. The pudding was orange jelly with 'mock cream'. The jelly was jolly good, but the mock cream was aptly described by Harry as being '*Ugsome*, and thoroughly deserving to be mocked!'

After lunch some of us went for a walk with Bendy Wendy. Jenny told me that our gym mistress had only left school in July 1939, and was not yet nineteen. As a schoolgirl she had excelled at all games, and when she left it seemed the ideal career for her. Seabourne Prep was her first job and she behaved almost as if she was still a schoolgirl, wanting to be "one of the girls". She liked to treat us as younger sisters, and out of school hours, asked us boarders to call her Bendy, her nickname ever since she first went to school as a little girl.

It was a bright sunny day blowing an easterly gale. Apart from Harry and I, there was Jen-Pen, Mag-Bags, Puddles, Rob Roy, Nicky, and Paddy O'Halloran. We walked up Stourwood Road and crossed over the Overcliff Drive to the grass-covered cliff top. Up there we were met by the full force of the wind and were glad the elastic under our chins stopped our hats blowing off. The wind was behind us, and it was our skirts that were the problem, and poor Bendy was suffering most. She was wearing a pretty frock with a full skirt that came just below her knees. She had to use one hand to hold on her hat, and the other one to hold down her dress.

'If you had a bit of laccy under your chin like us,' Mag-Bags told her, 'You wouldn't have to hold on to your hat all the time.'

About a hundred yards ahead was a bandstand, where some soldiers were doing the things that soldiers do. Bendy was in front, chatting with Jen-Pen and Mag-Bags. Suddenly there was a tremendous gust, stronger than before. As the skirts of our tunics billowed, we made a grab for them with both hands, holding them down with difficulty. Poor Bendy was still holding her hat on with her right hand and was unprepared for such a gust. Before she could do anything, her skirt blew inside out. It wouldn't have mattered if it had been only us behind her, but at that instant we were passed by two big boys on bicycles. As poor Bendy struggled to control her skirt, one of the boys gave piercing a wolf-whistle, and the other whooped for joy.

'Lovely view, sweetheart!' crowed one, riding off.

'Pink's my favourite colour!' cackled the other, following his mate.

Poor Bendy went purple with embarrassment. 'What horrid, vulgar boys! They must have been errand-boys! Decently brought up chaps would've averted their eyes, and said nothing.' Ahead was a small pagoda-like shelter and she suggested we sit down for a while, while she got over the shock.

It was pleasant sitting there; we were out of the wind. Bendy soon regained her composure and became her normal cheerful, overgrown-schoolgirl-self again. She was even able to make a joke about it. We stayed there for about ten minutes, then set off again towards the bandstand about a hundred yards ahead.

'I say, chaps,' said Bendy. 'It's the Home Guard. Let's go and see what they're up to, shall we?' As we marched over to them, I suddenly remembered *Dad's Army,* the hilarious television programmes back in my own time and wondered if the real *Dad's Army* was as hopeless and bumbling as Captain Mainwaring and Co at Walmington-on-Sea? When we approached them, two were standing guard on the bandstand itself, while the others were down below and seemed to be practising taking their rifles apart and putting them together again, under the beady eye of an elderly sergeant who had two long rows of medal ribbons on his battledress blouse. Seeing our approach, they stopped what they were doing and watched us. Several of them seemed to know Miss Bendall.

'Hello, Wendy, nice to see you,' said the sergeant. 'Turned out nice again; but it's still a bit windy, Wendy.' He winked at her, and she lowered her eyelids coyly. 'Cor! It didn't half blow in the night. The lads in B Comp'ny almost had to anchor themselves down, to stop 'em bein' blown over the bloomin' cliff.'

'Gosh, Mr. Evans! I *say!*' She looked down at the ground shyly, uncertain what to say. She seemed to be feeling awkward, shifting her weight from one foot to the other and flapping her hands as though she was unsure of what to do with them.

'An' we nearly 'ad a nasty h'accident,' said Mr Evans. 'Poor ol' George Turner was standing sentry up top,' he pointed to the sentries on the bandstand, 'When Jim Spear come in to clean 'is rifle. Well, the clot had left one up the spout, so when 'e pulled the trigger before starting to clean it, it went off. 'T'were pointing upwards and the bullet went through the floor up top, missing poor ol' George by no more'n a coupl'a inches!'

'Gosh! Oh golly-gosh! How absolutely *frightful*,' said Bendy. 'Poor Mr. Turner!'

We thought it was hilariously funny and hooted with laughter. ('Just like *Dad's Army* on TV—they don't like it up 'em,' I thought to myself and wished I could have told Harry about it.)

'No chaps, pul-*ease!*' said Bendy, frowning. 'It's *not* funny! A few inches either way, and poor Mr. Turner might have been killed, or had some of his bits and pieces shot off!' Then she added, hastily, 'You know; hands, arms, legs or, that sort of thing!'

We all looked at each other wide-eyed, eyebrows raised, and our lips tightly closed, bottling up laughter until we could hold it no longer, and exploded into raspberries of hysterical mirth.

'Really, chaps!' said Miss Bendall, nonplussed; 'I really can't see what you find so funny. Come along now, if we don't press on, we'll be late back for Sunday tea.'

We said good-bye to the Home Guard, and continued on our way. Further along, a cliff-lift, which in peace-time ran between the Overcliff Drive and the promenade below, lay dirty and chained up. The paint of the car at the top station was cracked and peeling, and several of the windows were broken. It looked rather shabby, forlorn and sad.

Suddenly, the sound of anti-aircraft fire came from behind us, startling me. Seconds later, an aeroplane flew past towing a round target behind it.

'Look, chaps!' exclaimed Bendy. 'The ack-ack boys are practising. They aim at the target and try to shoot it down.'

'Do they ever shoot down the 'plane by mistake?' asked Nicky.

'Good gracious, Nicky!' Bendy was appaled. 'Our chaps would *never* shoot down one of our *own* 'planes. It's only the Jerries that do that sort of thing.'

Further along the cliff, looking down at waves crashing on the beach, I noticed long criss-crossed spikes poking up out of the sand. 'Miss Bendall?' I asked.

'Yes, Alex. And do call me Bendy when we're out of school like this. Please, I think it's so much friendlier, don't you?'

'Please, Bendy, what are those spikes sticking in the sand?'

'They're anti-tank defences, to stop the Jerries driving their tanks up the beach, should they invade. You can't see from here, but there's barbed wire all tangled up among the spikes to prevent enemy soldiers getting through. Also, as there are probably mines on the other side, it stops silly little girls and boys from going and getting themselves blown to smithereens.'

*

As soon as we were back at school, we rushed upstairs to change before tea. Harry said we should wear each others' clothes, as a sign of our friendship. So when we went down to tea I was wearing her kilt and jumper, and she had on my midnight-blue velvet dress. In the common room after tea, we sat in front of the fire hugging our knees, listening to Children's Hour on the wireless.

High tea was Welsh rarebit which I really enjoyed because I love cheese. Afterwards I tried reading in the common room, but could not concentrate on my book, so I went upstairs to the dormitory quite early that evening. I had to think things out.

As soon as I was in my cubicle, I folded back the counterpane and took off Harry's kilt and laid it carefully on the chair by my bed. Then I picked up Edward Bear Esquire, lay on my bed and gazed up at the ceiling, cuddling him. He was a friend to whom I could tell my secret troubles.

I had now spent three days in 1940, and was very worried that I had overdone it in church. Also, I had to keep inventing stories to cover awkward situations I got myself into, and was not sure if I could remember which story I had told to whom. It was getting too complicated, and I wished I could be myself again in 1974. But then I wouldn't see my best friend any more. I had never had a proper best friend at school before; I was really quite a solitary boy, and when I had a problem would share it with Edward Bear Esquire. Now I had Harry; she was the sister I had never had. But how could I tell her my troubles? She would think I was loony! The thought of losing her made me unhappy. Actually I was finding my new life very interesting; I had discovered that a girl's life was very different from that of a boy, particularly in 1940. Things I had taken for granted as a boy, such as singing in the church choir, were closed to a girl, even if her voice was as good as any boy's. People treated me so differently as a girl; I was sure Mr Pitcher would never have put an extra chocolate drop in the bag if I had been a boy, and he certainly wouldn't have winked and called me his "*pretty little one*".

I was still gazing at the ceiling when Harry came looking for me. 'So *that's* where you're hiding,' she said. 'I was worried about you. You'll catch cold lying around half-undressed like that; you ought to've put your dressing gown on.'

'I came up here to think things out,' I replied. 'Edward Bear Esquire always knows what to do. He's been my friend as long as I can remember.'

'You keep retreating into your shell.' She sat by me and took hold of my hand. 'You're like a broody old hen. Are you feeling homesick? You can tell me; or is it very secret and private? I wouldn't tell anyone, best friends don't give away secrets.'

'I think it's too secret and private,' I replied, 'even for a best friend. P'raps another time'

She looked at me, smiling. ' 'T's all right,' she said. 'But you know I'm here if you want help. D'you know, you looked jolly nice in my kilt, you must borrow it again.'

'I liked wearing it and you looked really, really pretty in my best frock,' I answered, glad to change the subject. 'Yes, do let's swop clothes again.' We grinned, then laughed, and any tension that might have come between us, quickly evaporated.

It was not long before the bed-time bell. Before going to her cubie, Harry asked me to undo the buttons at the back of her (or rather my) dress. She shrugged it off her shoulders, stepped out of it and laid it on my bed. As I passed her kilt to her, I noticed the name-tape sewn in the back of it; 'Harry C. Gordon' it said.

'What does the "C" stand for?' I asked.

'What "C"?' she asked.

'On your name tape,' I replied. 'What's your middle name?'

'Oh, *that* "C"—Catriona.' She pronounced it '*Ca-tree-uh-nuh*', with the accent on '*tree*'. 'It's Gaelic for Katharine.'

'It's a nice name,' I told her. 'What my Granny would call a "pretty name". It suits you. I'm glad you've got *one* name that you can't turn into a boy's name. You know, when you're grown up "Auntie Harry" would sound ever-so queer, wouldn't it, Catriona?'

'It would, wouldn't it?' she laughed, happily. 'You may call me Catriona when I've grown my hair. What's your "F" stand for?'

'Frances. I only need to change the "E" to an "I" to make it into a boy's name.'

'I could call you Fanny, but I won't. It doesn't suit you.'

'If you called me Fanny, I'd bash you up.'

'That's funny, Fanny.' She stuck out the tip of her tongue 'I bet you would too! Aunt Fanny sounds pretty awful, like a potty relation in a soppy story like the ones Prissy and her chums read.'

'Uncle Fanny would be even worse if I was a boy called Francis!' I giggled.

'Uncle Frank'd be okay,' she said, smiling, and then suddenly frowned. 'Lessons again tomorrow. And we've got maths with Polly first lesson, worst luck! *Groo!* How *ugsome!* she pulled a face. 'What a horrid way to start the week! Come on, let's go to the bathroom now; then we'll have some extra time to read before lights-out.'

'All right, Bossy Boots! I'm coming,' I replied putting on my dressing gown.

'You don't mind, do you?' she asked. 'I've always wanted a brother or sister to boss around!'

'Not at all,' I replied, linking arms with her. 'I've never had a sister to boss me around. I boss Rory like anything. I quite like being bossed by you.'

*

Shortly after lights-out the siren wailed again and we all had to trail out to the shelter again.

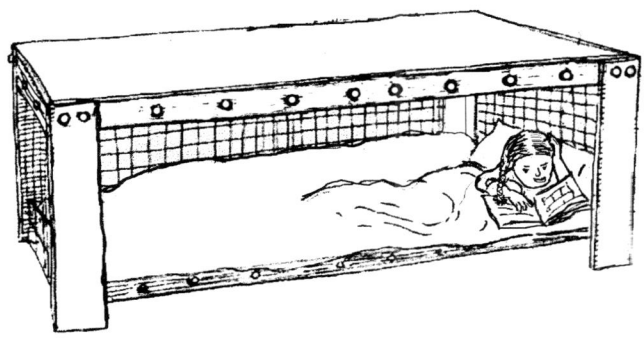

The "Morrison" air-raid shelter for use in the house.
It was made of heavy sheet steel with strong wire mesh sides
and the top could be used as a table

CHAPTER TWELVE

Grave News

THE AIR-RAID had been a long one, so at breakfast most of us were still half asleep. We had to go to the shelter just after nine o'clock and it was not until almost six o'clock that the all-clear sounded. After cocoa and biscuits in the shelter, we tried to sleep, but it was a fitful sleep sitting on the benches, and several of us rolled off on to the floor more than once.

When the rising bell rang at half-past-seven nobody felt like getting up. A weary-looking Scottie woke each of us to make sure we did not go back to sleep, reminded us it was Monday, and that we had to put on clean clothes.

I felt fresher after a wash. Everyone was strangely quiet during breakfast, and even Gladys was subdued as she served the porridge. Poor Bendy Wendy looked terrible; Greta Ransom had had a nightmare just before the siren sounded, and was so upset that Bendy cuddled her throughout the raid.

At prayers, The Beak looked sombre. 'You will all be distressed to hear that Caroline Baxter, whose first term with us this is, and her mother were injured when their house received a direct hit on Friday night. They are both in Boscombe Hospital, who told me that Caroline had received shrapnel wounds and is "comfortable", but her mother was very badly hurt. I'm sure you will all think about them in your prayers. Yesterday, German raids on London were the heaviest of the war so far. The enemy sent over 200 bombers, escorted by about 400 fighters; but our Spitfires and Hurricanes shot down more than sixty of them.' She paused while we cheered. 'Remember Mr. Churchill's words less than a month ago; *"Never in the field of human conflict, was so much owed by so many to so few."*' There was more cheering. 'Now, let us pray.' We said a special prayer for Caroline and her mother to have a speedy recovery, and then the rest of prayers followed.

After prayers, Harry was quiet. 'Poor wee Caroline,' she said and wiped a tear from her cheek. 'She's such a sweet little girl. Auntie Jane, her mummy, is a friend of *Maman* and we often went to see them. Caroline's ever so shy till she knows you and Auntie Jane asked me to keep an eye on her. I hope the shrapnel hasn't hurt her face.'

I put an arm round Harry's shoulders. 'D'you think Scottie, or The Beak would give us permission to visit her in hospital?'

'We can ask,' replied Harry, 'but I don't know if I'd be brave enough to look at her if she's terribly badly hurt.'

'Same here. But if *you* were injured and in hospital, I'd come and see *you*, how ever much it might upset me, because it could make you feel better.'

'You're absolutely right!' She set her jaw resolutely. 'I'll ask Scottie during break.'

'We'll go and ask her together,' I said. 'You'll need me there to look after you.'

'Thanks, Ally. You're the best best-friend anyone could have. What I don't understand is how she got injured, because she sleeps in a Morrison shelter.'

'Is that the one people dig in their back gardens?' I asked.

'No! The sort you have indoors; the metal table things with thick wire-mesh sides, like a cage. Her mattress and bed-clothes, were inside and she slept in it every night. During a raid Auntie Jane got in with her and put up the sides.'

'I suppose if they got a direct hit, the shelter-cage-thingy could have got damaged.'

'Poor wee soul,' said Harry. 'I do hope we can visit her.'

'I'm sure we'll be allowed to,' I replied, giving her hand a squeeze.

*

It was a subdued third form that assembled after prayers that morning. When Miss Parrot came in, we were sitting quietly, with our arithmetic books open at the page about vulgar fractions, the subject of the lesson on the previous Thursday. I had been issued a tatty, dog-eared, arithmetic book which had once belonged to: "Beatrice Davies, 68 Watcombe Road, Southbourne, Bournemouth, Hampshire, England, Northern Hemisphere, The World, The Solar System, The Universe." On the cover of a new arithmetic exercise book I wrote: "Alexandra Muir, Form 3, Arithmetic," in my best handwriting, and opened it at the first page.

After we had chanted 'Good morning, Miss Parrot,' we were told to recite the 7- and 8-times tables. I was glad that my 1974 school believed in the old-fashioned way of teaching maths, making us learn our tables by heart. I wondered what Miss Parrot would think of the pocket calculator which had appeared in 1973!

As I was a new girl, Miss Parrot wanted to find out how much I knew, so she asked me to recite the twelve times table. After I had finished she went on with the rest of the lesson which was about HCF's and LCM's, Highest Common Factors and Lowest Common Multiples, which I had learnt before.

'Well, Alecthandwa,' she lisped. 'I underthtood fwom weports fwom your pwevious thchool, that you were backward for your age in mathematicth. However, in algebwa last Fwiday and awithmetic today, you've shown that you have a good knowledge of both thethe thubjects for a girl of your age. If you were looked on ath being backward, those who were good must have been geniuthes—or ith it genii?'

Then she turned to face the blackboard, Harry put her hand on my leg and squeezed. I glanced at her and she grinned. When the bell rang at the end of the lesson, the form stayed quiet.

'Well girlth!' Miss Parrot said. 'I must thay it'th been a pleasure to teach you thith morning. It just showth that if you twy, you can do it. Even Maggot and Weevil—' she paused, looking straight at them, '—oh yeth, girlth, I know your nicknameth, even Maggot and Weevil have been well-behaved. I hope Weevil hath not been too uncomfy thitting on the bookth with which she hath padded her undergarmenth!' She grinned a vampire-like grin, and we all burst out laughing; all except Weevil who had gone bright red. 'Maybe you won't need to wear armour in future!'

'Golly!' said Nancy, when Polly had gone. 'She must be human after all. She's certainly got the measure of you, Weevil. You won't get away with the book trick again.'

It was English with Spug-Bug next. She began teaching us about parsing sentences. It was new to all of us, and after she had explained it, she gave each of us a sentence to divide into subject and predicate. After Nancy, Garters and Prissy parsed simple sentences for her, she wrote, "*Fido buried his new bone in the garden*," on the blackboard and looked at me.

'Now, Alex! It's your turn,' she said. 'First of all; what is the subject?'

' "Fido", Miss Spurgeon,' I answered.

'Well done,' she said. 'So the predicate is?'

'"Buried his new bone in the garden"?' I replied uncertainly.

'Good girl, Alex' she said. 'The predicate is what is stated about the subject. In other words?' She looked round the class; Harry's hand shot up. 'Yes, Harry?'

'The verb and the object, Miss Spurgeon,' replied Harry.

'Correct,' said Miss Spurgeon. 'Do you all understand that, girls? If you think of the verb as the doing word and the object as the part of the sentence that has something done to it, you won't go far wrong.'

We remained attentive throughout the lesson. Miss Spurgeon was a good teacher who always managed to make her lessons interesting. Just before the bell rang for break, she set some of the parsing exercises in our English Grammar book for prep.

'Before I go,' said Spug-Bug, 'Would any day-girls who wish to give money towards the flowers for Judy and Mrs. White please come and see me now.' Angela Fitzpatrick's right hand shot up. 'Yes, Angela?'

'Please, may I be excused, Miss Spurgeon? It's *frightfully* urgent!'

'If you're quick. I don't want to wait around long as I've a lot to do during break.'

'Please, Miss Spurgeon,' said Sarah Ackroyd, waving her hand in the air. 'May I be excused as well?'

'If you *must,* Sarah,' sighed our form-mistress. 'I hope the rest of you can wait until after you've seen me.'

*

As soon as we'd drunk our milk, Harry and I went in search of Scottie. We found her in the sewing room, checking that what the laundry had returned was the same as she had sent last week.

'Hello, you two,' she said. 'What can I do for you?'

'Please, Scottie,' said Harry. 'It's about Caroline; Mrs. Baxter's a friend of Mummy's, and she asked me to keep an eye on Caroline; she's a bit timid and shy till she gets to know you. She's very sweet and I'm ever so fond of her.' She wiped a tear from her cheek.

Scottie put an arm round her. 'Of course you are, my lamb,' she said sympathetically. 'What would you like to do?'

'We wondered if we'd be allowed to visit her in hospital?' I said, when Harry could not answer.

'If that's what you'd like to do, I'll see what I can arrange. If they say she can have visitors, I'll take you both this afternoon. I'd planned to go and see the poor wee mite myself, and if you know her and her mother, it would be a kind act. I'll clear it with The Beak, if the hospital says it's all right.'

'Thank you, Scottie,' said Harry, doing her best to smile

'I must warn both of you,' said Scottie, 'That she might not be very pretty to look at. Her injuries sound quite nasty—'

'We don't mind,' said Harry, 'Do we, Ally?'

'No,' I said. 'I'd like to go, even though I don't really know her.'

'You're kind lassies,' said Scottie. 'I know you're both going to be a credit to us. Now go and wash those tears away, Harry, and have a run around outside.'

After Harry had got rid of any evidence of her tears, we went out into the playground. We did not feel much like anything energetic, so we just strolled around talking. We were near the air-raid shelter, when we heard somebody crying.

We searched around and eventually found Hilary King, a little boy in Caroline's form, hidden in the bushes, and crying his eyes out. According to Harry, Hilary was Caroline's best friend. His mother was a widow and had to go out to work; so in the holidays he played with Caroline while Mrs. King was working. Harry used her own hanky to dry his eyes and we did our best to comfort him. When he was sobbing a little less, we took him up to Scottie's room.

'You *are* being good samaritans today,' she told us. 'Did you know his father had been killed at Dunkirk, poor wee chap. He's such a timid little boy, and he worships Caroline, you know. Some of the children here, girls as well as boys, can be terribly cruel if they think a boy is a bit of a sissy, or feeble or different. His name doesn't help, especially when the other Hilarys at the school are both girls.'

'He was all alone, crying and crying,' I said. 'He'd hidden in the bushes in the bushes by the shelter and we heard his sobs. We had to look *ever* so hard to find him.'

'I'll look after him now,' Scottie said, 'And try to contact his Mummy. He can help me until she comes for him.' The bell rang as she spoke; 'There's the bell! You'd better go or you'll get lateness marks. If you would be kind and pop into the remove and tell Miss Tripp that Hilary is here with me, it will save me the trouble.'

' 'Fcourse,' said Harry, smiling again, 'we'll come and see you at lunch time.'

'Not if I see you coming first,' laughed Scottie, aiming a pretend clip round Harry's right ear. 'Go on, away with the pair o' you, or you'll be late.'

We told Miss Tripp about Hilary being with Scottie, and then joined the rest of our form for the next lesson, which was Art, and after that, French.

In art we were asked to draw something we had seen over the weekend. Harry drew the aeroplane towing the ack-ack target. I drew a trolleybus; Rob Roy said I should have drawn Bendy Wendy and the errand boys, but I said I thought it would be unkind, and anyway, I couldn't draw people.

The French mistress was a lady called Mrs. Foster. In spite of her very stolid British name, I had been told that she was a very French lady. An old friend of The Beak, they met as teachers in the same school in France. Just after founding Seabourne Prep, Miss Plenderleith was joined on a camping holiday in the Lake District by Mademoiselle Yvette Bonchoses (as she then was). Mr Foster was camping at the same place. He and Yvette fell in love, married two weeks later, and the new Mrs. Foster took the post French mistress at Seabourne Preparatory School.

I had not met Mrs. Foster yet, as she did not teach on Fridays, and she had not been at prayers that, Monday, morning. Nobody took any notice as, Harry said, she often cut prayers if she did not have an early morning lesson; so we were surprised when The Beak arrived to take us for French. 'I'm afraid you will have to put up with me for a while, in Madame Foster's absence.' Harry put her hand up. '*Oui, Henriette, qu'est ce que c'est?*'

'*S'il vous plaît, Mademoiselle Plenderleith,*' said Harry. '*Qu'est ce qui est arrivé à Madame Foster?*'

'For those who did not catch what Harry said,' The Beak said, 'I shall repeat it for you. She asked: "*Qu'est ce qui est arrivé à Madame Foster?*" Who can translate that for me?' She looked round the class, and as I put up my hand I caught her eye. 'No, Alex, not you; I know you can do it. Let someone else have a go.' She looked round the class; several hands were up. Ruth Loader was waving hers urgently, almost punching the air above her head, desperate to answer. The Beak nodded at her; 'Yes, Ruth.'

'Please, Miss Plenderleith,' said Toady, looking very smug. 'Henrietta asked when Mrs. Foster will be arriving back.' Harry and I glanced at each other and grinned.

'No, Ruth! Harry didn't ask me that. You should've listened more carefully.' Toady looked downcast, and there were gleeful nudges and winks all round. Miss Plenderleith looked around again. 'Maggot. You can tell me, can't you?'

'Yes, Miss Plenderleith. Harry asked; "What has happened to Madame Foster?"'

'Thank you, Maggot. Remember, Ruth, that the verb *arriver* also means *to happen* or *to occur*. Madame has gone to assist an elderly relative in need of succour, and I expect her to be away for the rest of the term.'

When the lesson was over, Miss Plenderleith asked Harry and me to accompany her back to her study. We waited while she put her books down and sat at her desk. 'Now, my dears,' she said after gathering her thoughts, 'I'm sorry for keeping you waiting and away from your play-time, but Scottie tells me that you would like to visit Caroline and Mrs. Baxter in hospital.'

'Yes pul-*ease*, Miss Plenderleith,' replied Harry. 'Mrs. Baxter's *Maman's* friend and she asked me to keep an eye on Caroline, so I thought I ought to go and see them, as *Maman* is away. Alex says she'd like to come too. In fact it was really her idea.'

'—Scottie tells me that you would like to visit Caroline and Mrs. Baxter in hospital—'

'The hospital has agreed that you may visit Caroline,' said Miss Plenderleith, 'and think it will help her recovery. But you will *not* be allowed to see Mrs. Baxter, because she is under special observation in an isolation ward. Scottie's going to take you this afternoon.'

'Thank you very much indeed, Miss Plenderleith,' said Harry.

'Now, don't tell anybody why you are missing afternoon lessons,' Miss Plenderleith told us. 'If anyone asks, I shall say that you have been taken to the dentist for a dental examination. You may tell your close friends where you've been when you return. Make sure you are clean and smart, and remember that when you are seen in public, you are representing the good name of the school.'

'We will, Miss Plenderleith,' I said. 'Won't we, Harry?'

'*Rather!*' agreed Harry.

'I know you'll be a credit to us,' said Miss Plenderleith.

CHAPTER THIRTEEN

At the Hospital

AT A QUARTER TO TWO we were waiting at the bus-stop with Scottie. The wind that had blown so fiercely the day before, had dropped, and gone were any clouds. The sun was shining and Scottie said we could go without raincoats. We had to wait barely five minutes before a number twenty-one came whispering round the corner.

'May we go on top please?' Harry asked Scottie.

'Ooh, yes! May we?' I asked eagerly, then added; 'Pul-*ease?*' and gazed up at her.

'All right!' she laughed. 'How can I say no when you make eyes at me like that? Go on, the pair of you.'

We raced up the stairs and rushed to the front seat. Scottie followed more sedately and sat beside us. On the single seat to our left, sat a schoolboy of about our age. He was wearing a grey flannel suit, with shorts coming almost to his knees, and on his head was a dark green school cap with a yellow badge on it. I recognised it at once, Saint Aloysius, my 1974 school. He scowled fiercely at us and made a face, so I reckoned he didn't like girls.

I nudged Harry and put my mouth near her ear. 'I don't think he likes us,' I whispered. 'P'raps he's one of Maggot's victims!' She tried not to giggle, but it escaped as a spluttering sort of raspberry. Scottie raised her eyebrows and we both had a fit of giggles. The Saint Aloysius' boy gave us an even more disapproving scowl. Seeing him alone on the bus set me thinking. In 1940, children, even girls, went around on their own, walking, riding bikes, even on the buses, without grown-ups. In 1974, such a thing was almost unheard of. 'It's not safe,' our grown-ups told us, '*Because there are horrid strangers who would enjoy doing nasty things to you!*'

'Ally, you've gone all peculiar on me again!'

'Sorry, I was thinking.'

'I can see,' she said. 'There's an enormous bubble coming out of the top of your head saying "Thinks!" Just like they draw in *The Beano.*'

'Honestly. You two,' said Scottie, raising her eyebrows.

'Fares please, *I thang-you—*' bellowed a voice behind us.

'One and two halves to Ashley Road, please,' said Scottie.

The clippie pulled one buff-coloured, and two off-white tickets from her rack and punched each one in turn. 'Sevenpunsay'p'ny please, Ma'am,' she said, handing the tickets to Scottie. 'I thang-you.' She took the shilling that Scottie offered, put it into her money pouch, and counted the change into Scottie's hand. 'A hayp'ny makes eight and a penny is nine, and thripp'nce makes a shilling, I thang-you, Ma'am.'

'May I see the tickets please, Scottie?' I asked.

'You funny wee girl, Alex,' she said. 'You're just like a wee boy in so many ways. Here you are. Keep them if you want to, but have them ready just in case the inspector comes round.'

'Gosh thanks, Scottie, you're a smasher,' I replied. There was a threepenny-ha'penny one and two tuppenny ones. I put them safely in my purse and put it back in my blazer pocket.

'I'll give you a smasher, my lass,' she laughed.

'D'you know, Scottie,' said Harry, 'she's *ever* so like Calum, my best friend at St Mungo's. He collected bus tickets. Maybe that's why I like her so much. Yet when I was upset she was really sweet to me. And she's everso ticklish. When I tickle her she giggles and wriggles even more than Cesspool. Don't you, Ally?'

'Really, Harry!' laughed Scottie. 'What a terrible name for the poor girl.'

'Well her parents shouldn't have christened her Cecilie,' said Harry. 'With Poole as a surname, it's asking for trouble! It's the same for her wee brother Gordon, in the remove; somebody called him "Lily Pond" in the playground the other day.'

'Sorry, Harry, I don't get it,' I said. 'Gordon Poole doesn't sound anything like lily pond.'

'Say Gordon Poole quickly,' said Harry, 'though why they have to insult the fine old Scots name of Gordon, beats me.'

'Gordon Poole, Gordon-Poole,' I said. 'Oh I see-ee, *Garden* Pool! I think that's jolly clever.' I laughed, and so did Scottie.

'I shall always think of him as Lily Pond from now on,' Scottie said. 'Poor wee boy, he doesn't stand a chance against the likes of you two! Gracious! We've passed Fishermans Walk already. Look on the left, there's Mr North's shop, where we buy our provisions. We'll soon be at Pokesdown.'

'Darracott Road, next stop,' the clippie called from downstairs. The St Aloysius boy stood up, stuck his tongue out at us, and went down the front stairs. We were on our way again as soon as he had got off. The next stop was at the end of Seabourne Road where it joined Christchurch Road. On a building across the road, big white letters on a bright vivid green background proclaimed,

"SOUTHERN RAILWAY" and
"POKESDOWN STATION",

except "POKESDOWN" had been half-painted over. To our left, a large low building had a sign saying "BRITISH RESTAURANT". We waited while another trolleybus crossed in front of us before we turned left and followed it towards Boscombe. We passed the Savoy Cinema which was showing two pictures; one was called *The Chinese Bungalow*; the other, *Death Chase*, starred somebody called Ronald Reagan.

'Ashley Road next stop,' sang the clippie.

'Come along, my scallywags,' said Scottie. 'This is our stop, mind you don't tumble down the stairs.'

Boscombe Hospital was on the left as we walked up Ashley Road. As we went in through the entrance we were greeted by that unmistakable hospital aroma; a cocktail of disinfectant with a dash of ether, carbolic soap, floor polish and boiled cabbage. Behind a desk, sat a large lady wearing spectacles and a dark green dress. Scottie told us to wait while she went to ask the way to Caroline's ward. The large lady peered at us over the top of her specs as if we were something disgusting the cat had dragged into her nice clean hospital. I felt myself withering under her stare and squeezed Harry's hand. She squeezed mine back.

We were both relieved when Scottie had been told the way and we could get away from those piercing eyes.

'Cripes!' said Harry. 'That lady really gave me the creeps!'

'I wonder if she puts her broomstick in the bike shed when she gets here in the morning?' I said.

Scottie smiled. 'Aye, she looks a bit of an ogre. She even made me feel about two inches big.' We came to some stairs. 'Up here.'

'How many flights up do we have to go?' I asked.

'Just the one,' said Scottie. 'The children's ward's along the corridor on the right. You know there will be other children who are air-raid casualties, and some of the poor lambs may look a wee bit gruesome. Try not to stare.'

'We will,' I said, feeling butterflies in my tummy. I glanced at Harry and she squeezed my hand, she must have them in her tummy, too. We reached the first landing and waited for Scottie to lead the way. Ahead of us was a long corridor with double doors on either side. After passing two sets of doors we stopped by the third. Scottie pushed one side open and waited for us to go in. It was a large room, with beds down each side. Some had screens erected round them. It was like a giant version of our dormitory. A nurse in a dark blue uniform frock with a stiffly starched white apron and head-dress sat at a central desk. Hearing the door, she turned and saw us standing, rather timidly, just inside the door.

She smiled, and seeing Scottie, beamed, and rushed over and hugged her. '*Scottie!*' she exclaimed. 'What a *lovely* surprise.'

'Emily Tranter!' replied Scottie, beaming. 'You're the last person I expected to see! I thought you'd retired from nursing, and yet here you are as ward sister.'

'I *had* retired, but the war means that nurses are in short supply. I'm surprised you're not off nursing at the front. What brings you here, and who are these pretty girls?'

'Och I've got my hands full with the likes of these,' she said, nodding at Harry and me. 'About thirty of them.' Sister Tranter showed some alarm. 'No-no!' laughed Scottie. 'They're not mine! I'm matron at a girl's school in Southbourne. These are two of my best girls; Harry with the boy's crop and Alex with the pigtails.'

'They sound as if they ought to be *boys* with names like that,' laughed Sister. She winked at us and smiled. 'So, what brings you ladies to my ward?'

'You've got one of my wee day-girls here, Caroline Baxter,' said Scottie. 'Harry's a friend of the family.'

'Oh, yes, Caroline,' said Sister. 'She's doing nicely. She sustained a shallow scalp wound—where the shrapnel must have nicked her as it flew past—and a nasty wound in her right leg, where a piece lodged and fractured her fib. Had it been any bigger, she could have lost her leg.'

I felt a shiver ran down my spine, making me shudder.

'Mr. MacDonald, the consultant, operated on the leg as soon as she was brought in. He's given her the piece of shrapnel—"scrapnel" as she calls it— and she's got it in a jar by her bed, bless her. She's so proud of it, the funny little mite. Come along, Harry and Alex, I'll take you to her.'

She led us down the ward. Caroline was in one of the beds at the very end by the window. There were children in all the beds, all wearing white hospital nightgowns. One little boy had both legs in plaster, and a girl had her neck in a sort of support thing and an arm in plaster. Another had his or her head swathed in bandages, with just a nose and mouth showing. Some of the beds had screens drawn round them. I supposed that the doctors and nurses didn't want visitors to see the children in them, because they were so badly injured.

'Here she is,' said Sister. 'Caroline, I've brought some friends to see you.'

She was sitting up in bed with her head swathed in turban-like bandages, doing a jigsaw puzzle on a trolley that bridged her bed. She looked up, and seeing Harry, broke into a beaming smile. 'Harry!' she exclaimed. 'How lovely to see you.'

'Hiya, Caroline,' said Harry, bending down to give her a kiss. 'This is Alex. She's a new girl in my form and we're best friends; she appeared on Friday. And, I'm a boarder now; we both are. I say, you look just like an Indian potentate with a turban, doesn't she, Ally?'

'Rather' I said. 'How are you feeling, Caroline?'

'All right, but my leg hurts quite a lot,' she replied. 'Oh, hello, Matron, have you come to see me too?'

'Yes, my lamb,' said Scottie. 'How are you feeling now?'

'A little better, Matron, but my leg hurts quite a lot,' she said.

'You poor wee lamb,' said Scottie, giving her hand a squeeze. 'And before you say anything else, no more calling me "Matron". You may call me *Scottie* like my two scallywags here—'

'Was it very frightening?' Harry asked, 'waiting to be rescued I mean. I'd've been scared out of my wits.'

'I don't 'member anything about it,' replied the little girl. 'They said I was knocked un—un—'

'Unconscious?' I suggested.

'Yes, unconscious. I can just remember waking up in the amb'lance. Mummy was on the other bed.' All of a sudden she looked haunted; 'Poor Mummy, she had blood all over her. I hope she's not going to go to Jesus.'

'I'm sure she'll get better soon,' said Harry, squeezing her hand. 'I say—can I see your leg in its bandages?'

'Yes, if Matr—*Scottie* can pull the bedclothes back. Acksherly it's in plaster. Look, Harry! This is my piece of *scrapnel*. Isn't it super? Mr Mac—er—the doctor who took it out, said I could keep it for ever and ever and ever.' She took a jar off her bedside cabinet and passed it to Harry.

'Coo-oo!' Harry exclaimed. 'What a whopper! That's absolutely spiffing, isn't it, Ally?'

I nodded, and Scottie smiled and pulled back the bedclothes so we could see Caroline's plaster. It stretched all the way from her foot, right up the top of her thigh. Her toes were sticking out of the end.

'Look, I can wiggle my toes.'

'So you can,' I agreed. 'Scottie, have you got a pencil?'

'I *think* so.' She searched her handbag, and took out a diary that had a little pencil stuck down it's spine. 'I suppose you both want to sign her plaster.'

'Yes, please,' I replied. 'It is all right, isn't it?'

'Of course,' laughed Scottie.

'Will you do it too, please, Scottie?' asked Caroline.

'If you'd like me to, my lamb,' she replied. 'Now then, what shall I say? I know.' She began to write, right down near Caroline's toes. When she had finished, she stood back to admire her handiwork. 'Aye!' she said. 'That'll do just fine.'

'What have you written, Scottie?' asked Caroline. 'It's too far away for me to see. You read it for me, please, Harry.'

Harry read. '*Lang may your lum reek. With love from Scottie.*'

'What does "lum-reek" mean?' asked the patient. 'Do I have a lum-reek?'

'You'd better tell her, Harry,' Scottie said.

'It's an old Scots saying,' explained Harry. 'In English it would be, "Long may your chimney smoke." It's like saying *good luck*.'

'You stay with Caroline and write your messages,' Scottie said. 'I'll just pop and have a quick word with sister.'

'It's ever-so nice of you to come and see me,' said Caroline, when Scottie had gone. 'How did you know I was here?'

'Miss Plenderleith told us at prayers this morning,' I said. 'We said a special prayer for you. As soon as we heard, Harry wanted to come to see you, so we asked Scottie. Miss Plenderleith sends her love, and Hilary sends his too. We found him hiding in the bushes, crying his eyes out. He was terribly upset.'

'Poor Hilary,' said Caroline. 'He's my best friend, you know. He's very shy and so gentle; not like the other boys in our form, so I look after him at school. He often comes to play when his mummy's working; sometimes we dress up and do plays, or play mummies and daddies with my dolls. What are you writing on my plaster, Ally?'

'Get well soon, lots of love from Alex,' I replied.

Then Harry wrote '*I would have cut it off! Lots of love, Harry.*'

'Really, Harry—' laughed Caroline, when she read it 'I think you're teasing me! You wouldn't cut it off, would you?'

'Well-ll,' said Harry, ' 'mnot sure—P'raps if it hurt really, really, really, *really* badly. Then if I cut it off it wouldn't hurt any more.'

'Oh, Harry, you are funny,' giggled Caroline. 'If it was cut off, I would have to hop everywhere.'

'No you wouldn't,' I said. 'You could have a wooden leg like Peg-leg Pughie or Long John Silver.'

'You could be Short Caroline Baxter,' said Harry. 'And have a parrot sitting on your shoulder, but that'd be rather difficult 'cause they're on the ration at present!'

We were all laughing when Sister Tranter returned.

'So, parrots are on the ration, are they?' she chuckled. 'I don't think I've got any parrot coupons in *my* ration book. I'll have to write to the Minister of Food and complain! I came to ask if you would like a cup of tea? I know Caroline would.'

Harry looked at me. 'Shall we?' she asked.

I nodded. 'That would be super. Thank you, Sister—'

'Milk and sugar?—'

'Yes, please,' we replied.

About five minutes later, she returned with a tray. There were three cups of tea on it, some bread and jam and three pieces of Battenburg cake.

'Here you are,' she said. 'You can have a tea party.'

'But what about the rations?' I asked.

The Squander-Bug

'I'm sure there are lots of people here in hospital who can't eat their cake,' said Sister. 'And it'd be such a pity for it to go to waste. We don't want the *Squander-Bug* to get it, do we, girls? Go on, you tuck in and enjoy yourselves; and be blowed to the ration, I say. You are helping my patient to get better.'

*

We were not allowed to visit Mrs. Baxter. Scottie had been to see her while we were having our tea party with Caroline. We asked about her on the bus home, and all Scottie would say was; 'Poor soul—I'm glad it wasn't me. I could *murder* that Hitler—'

Harry gripped my hand tightly. 'Sh—she—she's going to die, isn't she, Scottie?' she asked, anxiously.

There was no reply, but I saw Scottie squeeze Harry's other hand.

CHAPTER FOURTEEN

The Message on the Wireless

THEY WERE JUST FINISHING TEA when we arrived back at school. We went straight to the cloakroom to hang up our hats and blazers, then directly to our form room as it would shortly be time for prep. We were soon joined by Rob Roy and Nicky.

'How was the dentist? You were an awful long time,' Nicky said with a grin. 'Or was it one of Scottie's *wee expeditions?*'

I looked at Harry. She grinned and said; 'Aye, it was one of Scottie's "*wee expeditions*" right enough.'

'I thought so,' said Rob Roy. 'The dentist is the usual excuse The Beak uses. The day-bugs think you really did go to the dentist, but we guessed you went somewhere else.'

'I bet you went to see Caroline what's'ername in hospital,' said Nicky. 'How was she?'

'Jolly cheerful, considering,' replied Harry. 'She said her leg hurts a lot. A piece of shrapnel flew into it and broke one of the bones. She was lucky not to lose it.'

'Poor little girl,' said Nicky screwing up her face. 'How I *hate* war! It's so un*fair*.'

'The surgeon gave her the bit of shrapnel he took from her leg,' I said. 'She's got it in a jam-jar and is really proud of it. She's also got a small injury on her head and that was bandaged up like a turban.'

'How about her mummy?' asked Rob Roy.

'They wouldn't let us see her,' said Harry, gravely. 'Scottie saw her though. All she would say was she was glad it wasn't her. I th–think she's going to d–die—'

'Poor wee Caroline,' said Rob Roy. 'What'll happen to her? I've heard their house was almost completely flattened, so I s'pose she'll go to an orphanage or something—unless she's got a granny or someone she could stay with.'

'She's got a granny and grandpa in Brockenhurst,' Harry said. 'They went to see her yesterday. Her dad's in the Merchant Navy.'

'If her Gran lives in Brockenhurst, she won't be able to stay at school here,' said Nicky; 'unless she comes as a boarder.'

'I say, you two,' said Harry, 'You won't say anything to anyone else, will you? The Beak said we could tell you, but she doesn't want it spread around just yet. You know what the silly Willises are like—and Maggot and Weevil.'

*

After prep Harry and I went outside for a stroll. We didn't feel much like talking, because we'd both been shaken by what we'd seen at the hospital. I had never seen the horrors of war in the flesh. In my own time, I had seen reports on the television news about the war in Vietnam, and the recent troubles in Northern Ireland, but it seemed unreal, distant, like a film. When you leave the cinema, or turn off the TV set, you are back in your own world again and the troubles are far away. The thing about a real war is that it's still there when you come out of the cinema.

'I hope Auntie Jane—Mrs. Baxter—doesn't die,' Harry said. 'She's so nice, helpful and kind, and she doesn't talk down to you like most grown-ups, but treats you as an equal; like Mummy, *she's* never talked down to me.'

'I hope Mrs. Baxter doesn't die too,' I said. 'Can you remember your dad?'

'No,' she replied sadly. 'I was two when he died. I've got a photo of him in my cubie. If your dad died three years ago, you must still remember him.'

'Yes, but it seems long ago now. I can remember the good times; days by the sea, building huge sand castles with tunnels and canals which we floated wooden toy boats in. Going for walks in the country, things like that.' (*Daddy and Gran had told me about the wonderful times they had before the war with Alexandra, and had shown me pictures of them in the family photograph album, so I could see them in my mind's eye.*)

'Those poor boys and girls in hospital,' said Harry. 'Did you see the one whose head was bandaged, with only a nose and mouth showing? For an awful moment I thought it might be Caroline.'

'Yes, and it could so easily have been you, or me,' Just then Jacko came out ringing the bell. 'There's the bell for high tea. Let's go and wash; last one in the wash-room's a sissy!'

We scampered towards the back entrance and into the washroom where we found Maggot and Weevil squeezing bars of soap at each other. One narrowly missed Harry who was not amused. Neither was Jacko who was right behind us.

'Margot! Evelyn! Stop that at *once*, or I'll give each of you a miss.",' said the Head Girl. 'Why is it that you two *always* have to behave as if you were about four years old? Go and get a mop and rinse the floor where you've dropped the soap, and made it slippery. And if it makes you late for high tea, you'll just have to face the consequences.'

'Yes, Kate, 'm sorry, Kate,' said Maggot, blushing bright red.

'Well, Evelyn, don't you have something to say?' asked Jacko.

Weevil hated saying sorry. 'Sorry, Kate,' she mumbled.

'Well, then, what're you waiting for?' said Jacko, 'you know where the mop's kept, so get it and mop up before you're late for high tea. Did you know that Miss Plenderleith's the duty mistress tonight.'

'Oh, lawks!' said Maggot, barging past and nearly knocking me for six. We washed quickly and went to wait outside the eatery.

'I wonder what treat Glad's cooked for us tonight?' asked Rob Roy, just ahead of us in the queue. 'I bet it's something like macaroni cheese.'

'Ugh!' exclaimed Dilly-Willy.

'Boiled intestines in sick!' said Milly-Willy.

'You *nauseous* child!' said Jen-Pen. 'If that's all there is, we've still got to eat it. Now

I'll be thinking of what you said, and it'll seem even worse than it usually is!'

Harry grinned; 'Boiled intestine in sick is better than some of the sights we saw this afternoon,' she whispered in my ear.

'Shouldn't whisper, Hawwy Gordon,' said Flossie. 'My mummy says it's wude.'
'Oh, does she?' said Harry. 'Who was whispering to me last night in the JCR?'
'That was diff'went,' said Flossie blushing. 'No 'twasn't, was it? Sowwy, Hawwy.'
'All right, Flossie,' laughed Harry, ruffling her hair. 'I'll forgive you.'
'Stop it!' exclaimed Flossie. 'I've just bwushed it. I hope you haven't messed it up.'
'It looks just fine, Flossie,' I said. I had barely finished speaking when the bell rang again and we filed into high tea.

It *was* macaroni cheese, but I couldn't taste any cheese.

*

After high tea we went to the common room, bagged the sofa, and read for a while. Some of the "babies" were playing snakes and ladders, and Rob Roy and Nicky were lying on their tummies on the hearth-rug, gazing into the fire. The wireless was on and I was listening to it with half an ear, as most of my attention was on the adventures of Joey Bettany and her friends escaping from the Nazis.

I'm not sure what made me look up from my book. Maybe a piece of dud coal made a spitting noise and everyone stopped talking. From the wireless came the sound of a drum beating three short beats and one long one, Morse Code for "V"; 'Dum-dum-dum-*Dummm*—dum-dum-dum-*Dummm*—dum-dum-dum-*Dummm*—' Then the announcer said; 'Here are tonight's personal messages for our friends overseas. Rupert Bear will leave a present for Bill Badger in wild woods. *Tout va bien avec Lisette.* The Brown Fox has returned safely to his lair. *Loir et Lièvre feront un rendezvous avec le Chapelier Fou ce soir.* Tante Claudine sends love to her nephews and nieces. The Tom Cat can see in the dark. La Maîtresse will give French lessons to her pupils tomorrow. That concludes the personal messages for tonight.' Then came the drum-beats once again; 'Dum-dum-dum-*Dummm*—dum-dum-dum-*Dummm*—dum-dum-dum-*Dummm*—'

'Our *Maîtresse* won't be giving us any French lessons tomorrow!' said Nicky. 'She's looking after an aged relation.'

The mention of *Loir* had made me prick up my ears; *Loir* was the name Gran had been given as her "code name" in the resistance. She had taken me to France after Mum and Dad had been killed, and we paid a visit to some of her wartime resistance comrades. They told me about many of their exploits, which made me feel very proud of my Gran.

'That sounds a bit rummy to me,' said Harry. 'I wonder what it's all in aid of?'
'Don't you *know?*' I whispered. 'They're special coded messages to the French Resistance.' No sooner had I said the words, than I knew I shouldn't have said anything. She did not seem to think it was anything out of the ordinary, but I was sure she might wonder how I had come to know about matters of great strategic secrecy about which no ten-year-old schoolgirl ought have knowledge. *Loir*—the

French for *dormouse*—had been Gran's nickname when she was a little girl in France. Could *Lièvre* possibly be Mrs. Gordon?

'Harry, does your mummy have a nickname?'

'Don't know. Why?' She looked puzzled, her lower lip jutting forward slightly.

'You mustn't say a word about this to ANYBODY,' I hissed, "cos it's awfully secret and if it got out it could get us both into the most *terrible* trouble.'

'Let's go where we can't be overheard,' she whispered. 'C'mon, we'll go to our form-room; we can pretend to be looking something up for tomorrow's lessons.'

'Okay,' I replied. We got up from the sofa and as Harry hauled me along the corridor she turned to me and whispered. 'What's so awfully secret? You're being frightf'ly *cloak-and-dagger*, Ally, and what on *earth* has Mummy's nickname got to do with it?'

'I s'pose I shouldn't *really* tell you,' I replied, "cos actually it's t'rifically hush-hush and all to do with our mums' work.' She frowned as I continued; 'You know that the Germans have occupied part of France?'

'*Oui, Grand-mère Henriette est encore là-bas.*' she said. '*Maman et moi, nous avons fait une visite à Grand-mère en Oradour il y a un an*; just over a month before war was declared. She lives in Vichy France—the part that the *boche* haven't occupied. *Yet!* I reckon they will, though. I s'pose that foul traitor Petain is a wee bit better than the *Boche*—but only just! The way he gave in and made peace with Hitler makes me feel ashamed of the bit of French blood I've got.'

'You're being frightf'ly *cloak-and-dagger*, Ally…'

'Golly, I bet you're jolly glad you got out before war was declared.' I said. 'Well anyhow, I don't know if you know this, but in the occupied part there are groups of French people, men and women who are doing their best to disrupt and resist the Jerries.'

I had her full attention; 'What sort of things?'

'Sabotage. Like blowing up railway lines, bridges, electricity pylons, ammunition dumps, petrol and fuel depôts, derailing troop trains, cutting telephone wires; all those sorts of things. It's called the Resistance. Others are helping our pilots who get shot down over enemy territory to escape back to England to fight again.'

'But what's it got to do with *Maman?*—*Oh, Christopher Columbus!* Her jaw dropped, her eyes were suddenly very large and very round and anxiety clouded her face. 'D'you mean to say *they* might be going to France to work with this resistance? Can you tell me what it's got to do with those queer messages?'

'They're sort of coded messages for the resistance. Did you hear the one that said, *"Loir et Lièvre feront un rendezvous avec le Chapelier Fou ce soir?"*' She nodded. '*Loir,* the French word for *dormouse,* is Mummy's code name. It was her nickname when she was a little girl in France.'

'I can't remember Mummy saying if she had a nickname,' Harry replied. 'All her French friends call her *Annie-Colette.*' Then her face lit up. 'Hey, just a minute! Uncle Bill calls her "Hare" sometimes. *Lièvre* is French for *hare*. But who's *le Chapelier Fou,* the Mad Hatter, with whom they're going to make a rendezvous?'

'I don't know; must be somebody who's already there.'

'But, Ally, how do *you* know about all this *secret* stuff?'

This was the question I'd been expecting and worrying about. I had to make something up on the spot. How I hated fibbing to her. After a moment I said, 'I shouldn't know about it, really, but one of Mummy's friends, who lives in the unoccupied part of France, came to see us a little while ago. He was telling her about it and I'm afraid I overheard. Mummy taught me enough French for me to understand quite a lot of what they were saying. When he'd gone I asked her about it, and she told me I must never repeat what I'd heard.'

'So what's the meaning of the message?—' she asked, very anxious now.

'I think it means that *nos mamans* are going to parachute into France tonight, to meet *le Chapelier Fou.*'

'Oh, *Heavens!' she* exclaimed, grabbing of my hand. 'Please, God, they'll be safe. What'd happen if the *boche* caught them?'

'I don't know,' I replied. 'I don't like to think about it. It wouldn't be very nice for *them,* and we could both end up as orphans.'

'They're really are top-hole, aren't they?' said Harry. 'I feel t'rrific'ly proud of them, don't you? I wish *we* could go and join the resistance. The *boche* would never suspect children. We must try to listen to the messages every night, and pray for *nos mamans et la résistance aussi.* And we must keep it very, *very* secret. *Attention à ça que tu dis ici; les murs ont des oreilles—*'

'Yes, *"walls have ears,"* like it says on those posters with Hitler's face all over the wallpaper; *"Careless talk costs lives".* Shall we go back to the common room now? Betcha someone's baggy-ed our places on the sofa.'

CHAPTER FIFTEEN

Another Night in the Shelter

AT BEDTIME that night I felt an even closer bond with Harry. We didn't need to talk much, but seeing Caroline and the other injured children in hospital had affected us both. How easily it could be us lying there—or any of our school friends. And now there was the possibility that both our mothers might be parachuting into enemy-occupied France in a few hours' time, to do dangerous but vital work, right under the very noses of the Nazis.

I wished I had not told Harry about our mothers' war work; she would be so anxious, not knowing if she would ever see her *Maman* again. It was different for me, because I knew that Gran had survived, in spite of being captured by the Gestapo in August 1943. Luckily a friend helped her escape, and after many weeks on the run, moving only at night and lying low by day, they reached the Spanish border and eventually got back to England safely, bringing three RAF airmen who had been shot down over France with them. I did not know if the friend who had helped Gran to escape had been *Lièvre*, or even if she survived the war. How terrible if *Lièvre* had been one of those who were captured, tortured by the Gestapo, and put in front of the firing squad.

We asked if we might go to bed early, because we did not feel much like being jolly in the common room. When we asked, Scottie did not ask us why. Usually, if you asked to go to bed early, she stuck a thermometer in your mouth to see if you were poorly, and dosed you with unspeakably awful medicine. but she had seen the same upsetting sights that we had at the hospital. And she knew that both our mothers were involved in "*something hush-hush in the civil service,*" so she may have put two and two together.

Up in the dormitory, I fetched Edward Bear Esquire, and we sat together in Harry's cubicle. She showed me more of her photos (or snaps, as she called them), taken in happier, more carefree times. There were several of her at St Mungo's, looking very much the schoolboy, complete with blazer and school cap. Anyone looking at her photos would never guess that the boy in them was really a girl! Some of them showed her playing cricket and football. Her mother was a keen photographer, and there were some fine action shots. One of them showed her hanging by her knees about ten feet up a tree; I could only just see it was her, because her face was almost completely hidden by her kilt! Gazing up at her admiringly were about a dozen small boys, mostly wearing kilts, and four little girls in frilly party frocks.

'That was at my seventh birthday party,' she said sheepishly. '*Maman* was hopping mad, and I got well and truly spanked for that prank. I suppose 'twas a bit silly really, I could easily have fallen on my head. But at least she took a snap of it.'

'Who could have fallen on her head?' asked Scottie, putting her head through the curtains. 'Pity you didn't, Harry Gordon, it might have knocked a bit of sense into you.'

'Oh, Scottie,' I said, rushing to my friend's defence. 'You can't say Harry's silly.'

'No, of course not,' said Scottie. 'Can't you tell when I'm pulling your leg yet? I came to find out how you were. I was very proud of you both this afternoon; I told The Beak so. She told me she's rather pleased with you too; but don't let that go to your heads!'

'Lots of people visit friends in hospital,' I said.

'We were just saying we wished we could do more,' said Harry. 'It could so easily have been us, or any of our friends, lying there in hospital, injured and mangled.'

'You both seem to have quite old heads on those ten-year-old shoulders of yours,' said Scottie. 'Maybe it has something to do with your both having lost fathers. Or did *you* nearly drop on your head too, Alex? You've got a twin brother, haven't you?'

'Yes—Rory. He's fifteen minutes younger than me.'

'It's a pity you couldn't be at the same school,' said Harry.

'Well, we couldn't really have him here as a boarder,' said Scottie. 'I don't some-how think he could do a Harry Gordon in reverse; after all, Harry, you were a day pupil at your boys' school.'

Harry frowned, and then grinned. 'Oh I see, you mean for him to pretend to be a *girl*; no boy would do that. It'd be far easier for Ally to pretend to be a *boy*. I think she's more than half-boy anyhow—' She put a hand on my shoulder. 'But if she hadn't come here, I'd never have had such a spiffing best friend.'

I'm afraid I have to admit that I blushed. 'Well I think the same about you,' I said, squeezing her hand. 'Did you want us for anything special Scottie?'

'Well, I don't know if you count coming to my room for a cup of cocoa and a bicky, as special,' she replied. 'How about it?'

'Och, Scottie,' said Harry, 'You bonny wee angel, jus' try tae keep us awa'.'

'Yes, please,' I said. 'I am sorry to say the macaroni un-cheese was not the nicest thing Gladys has given us. I s'pose it must be jolly hard for her to cope, with rationing and all.'

'I hear the Willis twins have a special name for it,' Scottie said. 'I didn't hear what it was exactly, but I'm told it was something utterly revolting.'

'*Boiled intestines in sick!*' said Harry pulling a face. 'Jen-Pen said it would put her off macaroni cheese for life.'

'I can't say I blame her.' laughed Scottie. 'I must say I've never liked macaroni cheese much. Well! Are you coming for cocoa or not? It's half an hour until the rest will be coming up to bed—and it's Maggot's and Weevil's bath night.'

'Heaven help us!' said Harry. 'The bathroom'll be flooded.'

'And we'll have to pick our way between the horse doings,' I added.

Scottie laughed and aimed a pretend clip round my ears—which I ducked.

Scottie had a nice room; it was quite big, with three dark red, comfy-looking armchairs ranged round the fireplace. The deep window bay, with dark red velvet curtains drawn round it, had a round table at it's centre. In one corner the bed was covered by a dark red counterpane. On the mantelpiece, there was a clock in the centre with a pair of silver candlesticks at either end and a number of framed photographs in between. A small table to the right of the fireplace, had a table lamp and several more framed photographs on it. We went to look at them and saw they were mostly of girls wearing Seabourne Prep uniform.

'That's my *Rogues' Gallery*,' Scottie explained. 'They're the girls who've done something special while they were pupils here. They're what The Beak calls my "Best Girls". You'll see that most of them are more senior than you. I asked you here, not just for a mug of cocoa, but to ask you if you would allow me include you both in my Gallery.'

Harry tried to say something, but when she opened her mouth, nothing came out. 'That's the first time I've seen Harry Gordon lost for words!' laughed Scottie, before I could say anything, either.

'I don't think we've done anything *special*,' I managed to say at last. 'We only did what we thought would help someone get well again.'

'But we haven't really done *anything*; not special,' said Harry. 'We only visited a wee girl in hospital.'

'That's a lot more than some of my girls did,' Scottie said. 'And I've a feeling you two are going to do a great deal more. Please will you let me take your photographs tomorrow? I have three shots left on the spool I took in Scotland during the summer holidays.'

I looked at Harry, and took her hand. 'We would be very honoured Scottie,' I said, 'Wouldn't we, Harry?'

'Yes, we would,' confirmed my friend. 'Please may we have a picture us together?'

'Of course you may, my scallywags,' said Scottie, coming to stand behind us and putting her hands on our shoulders. 'Now how about that cocoa, I think I hear Gladys coming.' There was a knock on the door. 'Come away in, Gladys.'

Gladys entered carrying a tray with three mugs of cocoa and a plate of biscuits on it. ''ello, Alex, 'ello, 'arry,' she said. 'Wotcha bin doin' to get this honour?—'

'They've been very kind, and very brave girls,' said Scottie. 'And a great help to someone who's suffering greatly just now.'

'I knoo they was nice kiddies, first time I saw 'em, Morag. A reel credit to us they'll be, mark my words. I'll be orf now. I 'ope we 'ave a quiet night tonight, wivout any air-raids.'

'Amen to that, and thanks,' said Scottie. 'Good night.'

'Good night, Glad,' I said, 'And thanks.'

'Yes, thanks, Glad,' said Harry. 'Good night,'

'G'night, all.' She left, closing the door quietly behind her.

'Come on now, you two,' said Scottie, 'Don't just stand there looking gormless. Sit you down and tuck in. I must just pop out and see that a couple of my wee bairns are in their baths. I'll be back in two shakes of a wee haggis's tail—'

*

There was an air-raid that night. Scottie roused us just before midnight. I had quickly got into the routine, and so had Harry. As we traipsed downstairs and out across the playground, I was wondering just how long we would have to stay in shelter that night.

'I wonder whose home will be destroyed tonight,' Harry said. 'I hope it's nobody we know. In fact I hope no one's home gets bombed.'

'Poor Caroline,' I said. 'What will *she* be thinking? It must have been so frightening for her. If it had happened to me, I'd have been petrified. I think she deserves to be in Scottie's Gallery a lot more that we do—'

'I agree,' said Harry, 'Shall we tell Scottie?'

'Yes, we must,' I replied and lowered my voice; 'Harry? I've just thought; our mums could be parachuting into France at this very moment?' She tried to say something, but her voice was drowned by the sound of aircraft overhead and ack-ack fire. We looked up, but could see nothing but searchlight beams criss-crossing the dark sky in the hope of pin-pointing one of the marauding Jerry bombers. Suddenly, one of the beams picked up one of the aeroplanes.

'Look, Harry,' I shouted so she would hear, 'they've got one of them. The other searchlight's on it as well now. Oh, shoot the so'n'so down!' I screeched even louder. 'Go on—What're you waiting for?' We had just reached the top of the shelter stairs, where Miss Plenderleith stood resplendent in her dressing-gown, mauve scarf and tin hat, checking our names as we arrived.

'Did that blood-curdling screech belong to you, *Master* Muir?' she asked, peering at me over her pince-nez. 'Or maybe it was *Master* Gordon, your partner in crime!'

'Oh no, mith, it wath him,' said Harry lisping and pointing at me. 'You know I'm only a thweet ickle girlie.'

'Says who? You're as bad as each other!' laughed Miss Plenderleith. Then looking at us more seriously, added; '*En passant, c'étais très bien fait, cette après-midi. Bravo, tous les deux*—'

'*Vous trouvez, Mademoiselle?*' said Harry, '*Mais nous n'avons fait rien du tout.*'

'*Allez vous en, mes enfants, tous les deux—*'

'*Oui, Mademoiselle*,' said Harry trying to bob a curtsy, but tripping over her nightdress and might have fallen down the shelter steps if I hadn't grabbed her. Miss Plenderleith hooted with laughter, and Harry grinned sheepishly.

Down in the shelter, Goody-two-shoes and Mag-Bags were already there with their "babes." 'Hiya, Mags, hiya, Goody,' said Harry, cheerfully, 'Can we help *avec vos petites?*'

'Greta's rather unhappy,' said Goody, who had a sorry-looking Edith Hill on her knee. 'Would you like to look after her, Alex? Harry, p'raps you'd go and see to Susie. Scottie says you visited Caroline Baxter in hospital this afternoon. How was she?'

'Jolly plucky and cheerful—in the circs,' said Harry, 'but some of the other children were *much* worse, and it could so easily be *us*.'

'I know, that's the awful thing about this war,' said Goody. 'I *hate* it.'

'Me too,' I said, making for Greta, cowering in a corner, wrapped in her rug. 'Hello, Greta, if you make room for me next to you, we can have a cuddle.' She looked up and smiled, then stood so I could put my rug on the bench. Then we both sat down, I put an arm round her, and we wrapped the rug around us.

'I feel better now you're here, Alex,' she said. I noticed Susie's tears being dried by Harry and grinned at her. She grinned back.

'Why d'you have a *boy's* name, Hawwy?' I heard Susie ask.

'I don't really; Harry's short for Henrietta.'

'Oh! But shouldn't Henwy short for Henwietta?' said Susie.

Harry smiled. 'I s'pose it should be, but I like *Harry* better.'

When everyone had arrived, Jacko and Bren-Gun took charge of Puppy and Fanny, and Jen-Pen was comforting Flossie. Margaret Legge, or Peg-Leg as we called her, one of the prefects in the upper fifth, was trying to persuade a stubborn Freda that she should cuddle up to her.

'But, Freddie,' Peg-Leg was saying, 'I want *you* to cuddle *me*, 'cause I'm everso scared. Look, here comes Scottie, she'll tell you what a cowardy-custard I am, won't you, Scottie?'

'Indeed,' she confirmed. 'You look after Peg-Leg for me will you, Freddie?'

Freddie looked at Scottie, not sure if she was serious or not. Scottie gave Freddie a knowing wink. 'Righty-oh, Scottie,' said the bold, tomboyish Freddie. 'She'll be alright with me.'

'I knew I could count on you, Freddie,' said Scottie. She was trying not to laugh when she came to check we were all right. We watched with amusement as Freddie tried sitting Peg-Leg on her lap, and then deciding that if she was to give Peg-Leg a cuddle, it would be easier if she, Freddie, sat on Peg's lap after all. 'I bet you were as stubborn as Freddie, weren't you Harry?' laughed Scottie. 'I'm glad to see you're making yourselves useful.'

'Ith Gladyth here yet?' demanded Amanda Hardy. 'D'you know if she'th bwinging uth any cocoa? I'm ever-tho thirthty.'

Unfortunately for Amanda, The Beak, who had just come in and was taking off her tin hat, heard her question. 'Do you always think of yourself first, Amanda? What a selfish little girl you are. We would all be more pleased with you if you were to think of other people first for a change.'

'Yeth, Mith Plenderleith,' said the unhappy Amanda, looking as if she was going to cry. 'I'll twy. I pwomith I will, weally, Mith Plenderleith.'

'See that you do. Here comes Gladys now. Make room for Gladys now, girls, we don't want her to trip and spill the cocoa do we?' The Beak made her way to the corner where Goody was comforting Edith. 'Hello, Goody,' she said. 'Is there anything I can do? What about little Muriel? Why is she sitting all alone?'

'She wouldn't let anyone cuddle her,' said Goody. 'She's even more stubborn than Freddie. She's having one of her sulks.'

'Leave her to me,' said Miss Plenderleith. She slowly worked her way to the corner, offering words of comfort to each girl as she passed, until she reached where Muriel, who was seven, was sitting, sucking her thumb and scowling. 'Hello, Muriel, is that a nice, tasty thumb? I'm sure you'd rather have one of Gladys's bickies, wouldn't you? Would you like me to tell you a story?'

Muriel looked apprehensive, and shrank into her corner. Miss Plenderleith sat beside her, and began her story. Slowly Muriel relaxed, and in next to no time she was sitting happily on Miss Plenderleith's knee and listening in rapt attention. I watched, and looking back, I feel very honoured to have had the chance to know such a wonderful lady.

Rob Roy, Nicky and Puddles helped pass the cocoa round, and Maggot and Weevil went round with the biscuits. Amanda Hardy and the Willis twins stayed huddled in a corner, looking sorry for themselves. I glanced at Harry. She smiled. Young Susie was cuddled up close to her and fast asleep.

The all-clear sounded—eventually—at half past two.

CHAPTER SIXTEEN

Tuesday

IT WAS TO BE POETRY with Miss Spurgeon in the first lesson after prayers on Tuesday. I was worried, because poetry was something I had avoided if possible, having any normal boy's opinion that it was sissy and girlish, and usually about fairies at the bottom of the garden! It put me in a bit of a quandary, so I asked Harry what she thought about it as we dressed that morning.

'Poetry?' she said. 'Funny you should ask that, I was going to ask you the very same thing.'

'Hard cheese! I asked first.'

'Well, when I started at St Mungo's, I thought it was terribly soppy and girlie-girlie, like all the boys did; until the day the English master introduced us to the most *amazing* poet ever, William McGonagal.'

'Never heard of him,' I said. 'Why is he so brilliant?'

'Because he wrote the most terrible poetry in the world!'

'I thought you'd go for Robert Burns, or somebody Scots.'

'Och, McGonagal was a Scot, born in Dundee, and lived there all his life. I'm going to ask Spug-Bug if I can recite one of his poems today. What are you going to recite?'

'Crikey, will I have to recite something?' I replied. 'How *awful!* I don't think I know any poems by heart.'

'You must know *one*,' said Harry. 'What about Casabianca? You must know that! "*The boy stood on the burning deck—*"'

'*With a pound of sausages round his neck,*' I continued. 'D'you mean that one?'

'No! You *muckle sumph!* she giggled. '"*Whence all but he had fled;
The flame that lit the battle's wreck
Shone round him o'er the dead.*"

'Where on earth did you learn that extraordinary version?'

I was just about to say 'at my last school,' then thought better of it. 'Oh! Rory taught it to me,' I lied. 'He was told it by one of his chums at school.'

'How does it go after that?' she asked.

'I dunno, I've forgotten.' (Actually, I didn't know if there was any more of it.) 'Do I have to recite from memory?'

'Well, if you don't know anything by heart, she'll probably let you read something you like, a poem about something you enjoy. What d'you like doing in the hols?'

'Sailing,' I replied.

'I've a book of poems in my desk,' said Harry. 'I'm sure there'll be something nautical in it. In fact I *know* there is; one of my favourites, it's by a chap called Allan Cunningham who died about a hundred years ago. Oh *bother!*

'What's the matter?' I asked.

'I've just pushed my heel through one of my socks. *Botheration!*'

'Put another pair on.'

'My other pair's got holes in both socks, and my third pair's at the laundry. I'll have to wear stockings. What an absolute bind!'

'D'you want to borrow a pair of my socks?' I asked. 'I've got two extra pairs.'

'What an angel you are, Ally,' she said, coming into my cubie in her tunic and one holey sock.

'They're in the top drawer. Help yourself.'

'Ta everso, I'm sure,' she said, imitating Gladys' cockney accent. 'D'you want me to plait your hair while I'm here? You can put your gymmer on afterwards.'

'Yes, please.'

'One good turn deserves another,' she replied.

*

Harry found her poetry book for me after brekker, on our way do our chores. When I had made my bed, dusted, and made my cubie tidy, I sat down and leafed through the small volume. It was titled *Palgrave's Golden Treasury*, and was quite old. Harry had put a bookmark in the page with the poem she thought I would enjoy. As I read it through I realised I had heard Gran—or "Mummy" as I was now beginning to think of her—reciting it; it had been a favourite of Alexandra's (the real one), and Mummy had chosen it as the basis for her "poem-code"‡ which she used when transmitting her wireless signals back to England from France. It seemed a remarkable coincidence that Harry had suggested it to me, and I felt it would was a good omen for our mums on their dangerous missions. When Harry came into my cubicle just as I finished reading it for the second time.

'What d'you think?' she asked.

'I really like it,' I replied. 'Let's walk round the lax pitch before prayers, then I can read it aloud a couple of times. We've got half an hour to spare, and it's a gorgeous morning.'

---

‡ S.O.E. wireless operators (or *pianists,* as they were often called) each used a personal poem-code devised for them by the code room at H.Q. This was based on a poem, chosen by the agent, that they knew, or which was easy to memorise. From this poem the agent chose five random words from which to work out a *"transposition key"*. This key was then used to encode the signal. The *transposition key* words were given as an *indicator group* at the beginning of the signal, and each subsequent signal sent by the agent would use five different words for the *transposition key*. The teleprinter operator receiving the message in London would have a copy of the agent's poem and from that could decode the signal as soon as she (all the teleprinter operators were members of the F.A.N.Y.) had identified the words of the *transposition key*. The use of very well-known poems, such as *Casabianca*, was discouraged as they would be equally well known to the enemy code-breakers. Poems were often written specially written for agents so that the enemy would have no chance of knowing the words. (This is too brief an explanation, but if you are interested in S.O.E. codes read *Between Silk and Cyanide* by Leo Marks, published by Harper Collins, which tells the full story.)

As we left the dormitory, we bumped into Scottie. 'So *there* you are!' she said, 'I've been looking for you so I can take your pictures.' She waved an old-fashioned box-camera at us.

'Scottie,' I said, 'We've been thinking about what you asked us last night.'

'Yes,' said Harry. 'We thought Caroline should be included in your Gallery instead of us. She's been ever so much braver than we have.'

'I thought you'd say that,' Scottie said. 'I said so to The Beak this morning. Don't worry, she'll have her picture there when she gets better. I'll take one of all three of you together. Are you coming out so I can take it before the day-girls arrive, or do you want the likes of Dotty Dot staring gormlessly at you?'

'Gracious no!' exclaimed Harry. 'That would be the absolute terminus! Buck up, Ally! Scottie's going to take our picture.' We went round to the front of the school which was in the sun.

'Now!' said Scottie. 'I want a nice one of you together. Now, put your arms on each other's shoulders.' We stood about half a metre apart and I put my left hand on Harry's right shoulder and she put her right hand on my left one.

'Like this?' we asked, both grinning from ear to ear.

'No, you loonies!' she laughed. 'Stand close to each other and put your arms round each others shoulders properly.' We did as she asked. 'That's much better, now stand still, and look at me. No, don't put on those imbecile Dotty-Dot-like grins, just smile naturally. That's better. Hold still now!' The camera clicked. 'That'll be lovely. Now, if you just let me take one of each of you on your own, then you can do whatever it was you were about to, and I can drop the *fil-um* into Boots when I go shopping later.'

'Please may we have copies, Scottie?' I asked. 'We'll pay you for them, won't we, Harry?'

'You can save your pennies!' said Scottie. 'They will be my treat.'

'Thank you, Scottie,' we said in unison.

'You deserve it,' Scottie replied. 'You're good, kind wee gir-rls. Now off you go and get ready for school, or you'll be late.'

*

When we got to our form-room, several of the day-bugs had arrived already. I remembered their faces from yesterday and Friday, but found it hard to put names to all of them. However, there was one face that was new to me—a girl with fair hair, cut in a page-boy bob with a dark green ribbon, who was wearing a black arm-band on the left sleeve of her white blouse. Harry spotted her straight away.

'There's Judy,' she said. 'Come and meet her; you'll like her. She's the nicest of all the day-bugs.' We made out way between the desks to where Judy was talking to Nancy and Maggot. She saw us before we reached her, and smiled at Harry.

'Judy,' said Harry, giving her a bear-hug. 'I was so sorry to hear about your Dad. Are you sure you feel well enough to be at school?'

'Hiya, Harry,' she said. 'Thanks! I'd rather be here at school; it'll help me think about something else, although I'm getting used to it now. I always knew it could happen, so I was sort of ready for it. How's your mummy? Please give her my love when you get home this evening.'

'I haven't seen *Maman* since Friday,' said Harry. 'She has had to go away on some hush-hush job, so I'm a boarder now. And this is Alex Muir, my best friend; she arrived on Friday and she's a boarder too. Ally, this is Judy White.'

I held out a hand to Judy. 'Hello, Judy, I was really sorry to hear about your Dad.' We shook hands.

'Thank you, Ally. Welcome to Seabourne Prep,' she said. 'I wondered who you were, as soon as I saw you coming in with Harry. So you got here on Friday?'

'About midnight on Thursday night,' said Nancy. 'She was ever so late, and had to sleep in the sick-bay that night. The first thing we knew about her was when she appeared at brekker on Friday.'

'She was in a train that got bombed!' Harry said. 'Weren't you, Ally?'

'Yes, but I don't like to talk about it.'

'I don't blame you, Ally. Poor *you!*' said Judy. 'And fancy you being a boarder now, Harry. I've only been away two days, and everything seems to have changed.'

I liked Judy instantly, and especially the way she called me Ally. She was really friendly, and very pretty, with a ready smile, even in her grief for the dead father whom she had worshipped. More day-girls had arrived and were crowding round her to offer their sympathy. She was beginning to look strained when Spug-Bug arrived. We hastily took our places.

'Good morning, girls.'

'Good morning, Miss Spurgeon.'

'First of all, welcome back, Judy. We were all so very sorry to hear about your daddy,' said our form-mistress. 'Are you sure you can cope with school?'

'Thank you, Miss Spurgeon,' said Judy. 'I'd rather be here. It helps keep my mind off things. At home, all I can do is sit around moping, thinking about what has happened.' She smiled to show she was all right.

'Brave girl,' I thought, as Spug-Bug checked the register.

At prayers we sang another of my favourite hymns, *Immortal, Invisible, God only wise*. I did not sing out as much as I had in church, as I felt rather self-conscious about my singing now, and did not want to draw attention to myself.

As we returned to our form room, I turned to Harry, as always at my side. 'Well at least there's no more news about Caroline or her mummy, so I suppose no news is good news.'

'Hope so,' she replied.

We were all ready for Spug-Bug's poetry lesson when she came in.

'Well now, girls. Poetry.' she paused. 'Instead of the usual thing where I set you a poem to learn by heart, we'll do something different for a change. Instead of repetition, we are going to read some poetry. Now I know that most of you know a poem that you can recite, but today I want you to read a poem that you do not know by heart. I got the idea from Harry who's keen on the works of William McGonagal, a strange poet who was born in 1825 in Scotland—hence Harry's interest. His poems are not well known south of the border, although he is held in high esteem in his native city of Dundee. He thought of himself as a genius, but his poetry may sound a bit odd to our ears. Harry has chosen to read the poem he wrote about the Tay Bridge disaster that happened on the 31st of December 1879. It tells us how this beautiful new bridge collapsed during a storm, just as a train, on its way to Dundee from Edinburgh was crossing it. Are you ready, Harry?'

'Yes, Miss Spurgeon.' She stood up, opened her book, cleared her throat and began; '*The Tay Bridge Disaster* by William McGonagal.' She spoke in a much stronger Scottish accent than usual, rolling her R's with great relish.

'Beautiful Railway Bridge of the Silv'ry Tay!
Alas! I am very sorry to say
That ninety lives have been taken away
On the last Sabbath day of 1879,
Which will be remember'd for a very long time.'

There was a giggle from Weevil. 'Stop giggling, Evelyn,' said Spug-Bug, 'it was written in all seriousness. And you, Emily and Dilys, can wipe those idiot grins off your silly faces. Carry on, Harry.'

''Twas about seven o'clock at night,
And the wind it blew with all its might,
And the rain came pouring down,
And the dark clouds seemed to frown,
And the Demon of the air seem'd to say—
"I'll blow down the Bridge of Tay."
When the train left Edinburgh
The passengers' hearts were light and felt no sorrow,
But Boreas blew a terrific gale
Which made their hearts for to quail,
And many of the passengers with fear did say—
"I hope God will send us safe across the Bridge of Tay."'

Harry read on, the story unfolding dramatically, with Boreas braying angrily as the train sped on with all its might towards the Tay Bridge.

'So the train mov'd slowly along the Bridge of Tay,
Until it was about midway,
Then the central girders with a crash gave way,
And down went the train and passengers into the Tay!
The Storm Fiend did loudly bray
Because ninety lives had been taken away,
On the last Sabbath day of 1879,
Which will be remember'd for a very long time.'

'Right, stop there a minute, will you, Harry,' said Spug-Bug. 'Now girls, what do you notice about this poem?' She looked round the class. 'Yes, Roberta.'

'It doesn't scan properly, Miss Spurgeon,' she replied.

'Right,' said the mistress. 'Now so far there have been two mentions of *Boreas*. Who knows who Boreas was? Yes, Jane Wright.'

'Please-Miss-Spurgeon-Boreas-was-the-Greek-God-of-the-north-wind-Miss-Spurgeon,' she said all in one breath. She was the youngest in the class and a very serious and brainy little girl with spectacles, whose father taught Latin and Greek at St. Aloysius'.

'Quite correct, Jane. Harry, you may read the rest now.' Harry read through to the end, declaiming the most dramatic bits with gestures of her right hand, her left being used to hold the book. At the end, everybody clapped. Several other girls read their poems, and eventually it came to my turn.

I stood up. 'My poem doesn't have a name, but it's by Allan Cunningham. Er-Hmm.

> 'A wet sheet and a flowing sea,
>   A wind that follows fast
> And fills the white and rustling sail
>   And bends the gallant mast;
> And bends the gallant mast, my boys
>   While like the eagle free
> Away the good ship flies, and leaves
>   Old England on the lee.'

After two more verses I sat down.

'Thank you, Alex,' said Miss Spurgeon, 'You read that very nicely.'

There was enough time for two more readings before the bell at the end of the period. We had scripture with the Rev'd Mr. Pugh next, and then Geometry with Polly Parrot after break.

At the end of morning school, Nancy presented the flowers to Judy so she could take them home to Mrs. White. It was a pretty bouquet, and Judy was very pleased.

For lunch we had sausages and mash with dried peas that hadn't been soaked enough. Maggot and Weevil whooped for joy and asked us all for our peas to use as pea-shooter ammunition. I shall not reveal where they put their "ammo." for safe keeping! The treacle pudding and custard we had for afters was really scrummy. Unusually, there was even a bit left over, so we could have second helpings.

In the afternoon we had history first period, at which I successfully recited *Willy, Willy, Harry, Steve,* to Grif-Bug without a single slip. She was pleased that I had taken the trouble to learn it properly, particularly when one or two of the others could still not get through it without mistake. Then we had singing. I had not met Mr. Grubb, the music master, having only seen him in the distance at Prayers, and did not know that he was organist and choir master at All Saints, or that he had heard my descant on Sunday and wondered who had sung it. The Beak had told him about me so, as soon as we arrived in the music room, I was asked to sing some scales. I hung back, because I was not sure how I was going to explain how I, a ten-year-old schoolgirl, had the voice of a trained choirboy.

He took my reserve for shyness, which made Harry giggle. Mr Grubb was very kind, so I went and stood by the piano as I had done so many times before at choir practise.

'Now, Alexandra: I believe it's *Alex*, that you prefer to be called?'

'If you please, sir,' I replied.

'Well, you *are* a nice polite girl. It's usually only in boys' schools that I get called "Sir". Now, Alex, shall we begin with C major?' He struck the C above middle-C on the piano. 'Would you sing "*na*" down one octave to middle-C?' I sang this with no trouble. 'Now, how about C minor?' I sang C minor. He took me through all the scales and tested my range. He was pleased I was able to sing a top-C (two octaves above middle-C) without squawking.

'I can't go much higher, Sir,' I said.

'You'd find it easier if you were more relaxed,' he said. 'Can you read music?'

I nodded; 'Yes, Sir.'

He handed me a sheet of paper with some lines of music on it. 'Would you please sing the third line to "*na*" unaccompanied. I'll give you the first note.'

I could hear the first note inside my head, so I began to sing before he had given it to me. When I had finished, he struck the note I should have ended on. I had sung it spot on the correct pitch. Mr Grubb peered over his spectacles at me.

'Very good. You appear to have perfect pitch,' he said.

'Not really, Sir,' I replied, 'but I can remember pitch quite well. The last scale I sang was B major, and this began a major third down, on G.' I saw Harry grin.

'Very good,' said Mr. Grubb. 'Now I'd like you to try something else.' He handed me a flimsy booklet; it was a vocal score giving voice parts and organ accompaniment. The cover said *Hear My Prayer, by F. Mendelssohn Bartholdy*. It was an old friend, the very solo I had sung at the wedding at All Saints on the last Saturday of the summer holidays, just over a week ago, in 1974.

'I know this,' I said. 'I helped my brother learn the solo part for when he had to sing it at a wedding.'

'Would you like to sing some of the solo part for me now?'

'Yes, please, Sir,' I replied eagerly. 'But won't it sound odd without the choir?' I felt tense and excited, like I did when I was going to sing solo in church. I glanced through the score, reminding myself of the tune, and didn't notice Scottie and Miss Plenderleith sneaking in quietly and sitting at the back.

'Begin at bar number 156—I've pencilled in some of the bar numbers—and sing to bar 183 where the choir comes in. I'll accompany you on the piano.' He looked at the rest of the form; 'This is quite a well-known piece, girls, so some of you may recognise it. Your parents may even have the gramophone record of Master Lough of the Temple choir singing it.' I found the place and saw the familiar words. He struck B on the piano. 'Now face the rest of the class, Alex. Take a few deep breaths first, then I'll give you a bar for nothing and you come in. Ready?'

'Yes, Sir,' I replied, and took a deep breath as he counted out one bar, then I began to sing; '*O for the wings, for the wings of a dove! Far a-way, far a-way would I rove!—*'

It's a great piece to sing, and I really enjoyed myself, as always. Singing was easy for me and I enjoyed showing off! I didn't sing it as well as I had previously, when I was a boy. I made a nasty noise at the first top G and forgot to snatch a breath at one point, so I ran out of puff on a long B two bars from end. In the last bar, Mr Grubb sang the first few notes of the bass part, and when we had finished, the girls all clapped like mad.

'Very good, very good,' said Mr Grubb, taking my hands in his. 'Well done, Alex, well *done*,' He held up a hand to stop the clapping, just as Harry called '*Encore!*' much to my embarrassment.

'I'm sorry, I was careless and made a couple of silly mistakes, Sir. I squawked the top G in the third bar, and forgot to snatch a breath here,' I pointed to the score on the piano, 'so I didn't have enough breath to sustain this long B.'

'Never mind, you sang it very well,' he said. 'I can't get over your voice; it's got the timbre, the edge, the clarity and strength that, up to now I have only ever heard in a trained choirboy; never before in a little girl. If I hadn't known, I'd have sworn a boy was singing. You have a great gift, young Alex.'

'Thank you, Sir.' I felt embarrassed and looked at the floor.

It was then that The Beak and Scottie stood up and made their way to the front of the class. The Beak gave me a huge smile, and Scottie was dabbing one eye with a hanky.

'Well done, Alex,' said Miss Plenderleith. 'You've made Matron cry, and sent tingles running down my spine. Well, Mr Grubb does she sing well enough for your choir?'

'Oh yes, indeed,' said Mr. Grubb. 'I'm sure I'll be able to persuade Mr. Pugh; we have been down in numbers ever since the Holman boys were killed in an air-raid during the summer. Would you like to sing in the choir, Alex?'

'If you think I'm good enough, and would like me to, Sir.' As a girl, I was really rather pleased to be striking a blow for the my new sex. As a boy I disapproved strongly of girls singing in church choirs, and would have been horrified if one joined our choir in 1974; but after all, this was war-time and lots of females were doing jobs that had previously been only done by males. 'I'll have to be a probationer first, won't I, Sir?'

'I don't think so,' he replied. 'You've proved to me that you have the voice and the necessary musical skills to be a full chorister straight away.'

'Thank you, Sir. Would you like me to come to choir practise this week? I'd have to ask permission from Miss Plenderleith.'

'I think Alex can take that as granted, can't she, Matron?' said The Beak.

'It was so beautiful,' said Scottie, dabbing one eye. 'Of *course* she must go to choir practise.'

'And now, Mr. Grubb,' said Miss Plenderleith, 'We've taken up enough of your time and must let you get on with the rest of your lesson.'

After they had gone we sang some English folk songs, *The Miller of Dee* and *The Hunt Is Up*. I earned a jab in the ribs from Harry when I sang; '*And Harry our king, Is gone hunting to bring his beer today*', instead of '*deer to bay!*'

Our next period was gym, and while we changed the others asked how come I sang like a boy. I found it all very embarrassing, and was glad when Bendy Wendy came and asked us if we would like to have a go at playing netball for a change.

*

After prep that evening, Harry and I went to the common room to read our books. We bagged our usual corner of the sofa, and as it had been a fine, warm day, there was no fire, to save coal for when it would be essential.

After a while we turned and looked at each other, and both said 'I wonder..' at the same time. We laughed, and Harry said, 'I wonder what our mummies are doing now?'

'Just what I was going to say,' I said. 'By the way, after I sang this afternoon, you had the very same expression on your face that Mummy has when she hears Rory and I singing.'

'Well, I felt just as if I *was* your proud mummy, my clever wee Ally. I thought your singing was absolutely topping!'

'I'd have sung better if I hadn't been showing off—I've never squawked a top G before; a top C maybe, but never a top G—'

'You certainly seemed to impress wee Grubby, when you sang the unaccompanied bit without him giving you the first note. And now you're going to sing in the choir, you clever wee girlie, you—'

'Oh, shut up!' I felt myself blushing again, so I jabbed her playfully on the arm and changed the subject; 'What shall we do after high tea? I hope there's no air-raid tonight. I wouldn't mind going up to bed early.'

'Neither would I—' she said, as the bell rang for high tea.

*

We had a quiet night without having to visit the shelter, so we woke up bright and fresh after a full night's sleep. At prayers that morning The Beak told us of the tragic sinking of the liner *S.S. City of Benares*. She had been torpedoed by a Jerry U-boat, killing seventy-seven British children being evacuated to Canada where they would be be able to see out the rest of the war safe from the blitz. Shortly after this tragedy the government decided that no more child evacuees should cross the Atlantic to Canada or America on account of the constantly growing U-boat menace.

CHAPTER TWENTY

Choir Practice

On Thursday I had high tea early, so that I could go to choir practice at the church. I took a trolleybus, on my own, to Fisherman's Walk. As I walked down Beresford Road to the church, I was feeling rather nervous, as this would be the first time that I had, as a girl, been alone in the company of boys. From my other existence as a boy, I knew that choirboys held strong opinions about their choirs being infiltrated by girls!

It was still less than a week since I had woken up in 1940, and discovered that I had changed sex. Without Harry to "hold my hand," I was wondering how I would cope if the boys started ragging me. I was only too aware of what my school friends and I had inflicted on some poor unfortunate girls in 1974. Now the boot was going to be on the other foot, (with a vengeance!) and I felt rather uneasy and decidedly vulnerable. Yet thinking of Harry gave me courage; after all, she had thrived in the company of boys as the only girl, albeit a very tomboyish one, and she herself had said that I was more than half boy. If only I could have told her how near the truth she was. If *she* could do it, I told myself, as I reached the church door, so could *I*. After all, I had one great advantage over Harry, I had *been* a boy, and *she* hadn't. I was there to be a chorister, and so were the boys, so what did it matter that I was wearing a gym-tunic and they were in short trousers?

I opened the church door, took a deep breath and gathered myself together. How many times had I walked through that doorway? It was familiar territory; only the circumstances and the people were different. Once inside, I headed for the vestry. I walked down the stairs, took another deep breath and went in. Inside I found about twenty boys and Mr Grubb, who turned to me and beamed.

'Come in, come in,' he said. 'I'm so glad you could come. Now take off your hat and coat and I will introduce you to everyone.'

As I unbuttoned my raincoat, I realised that from habit I had buttoned it on the boy's side. Mr Grubb took it and my hat and hung them on the very same peg that I hung my school cap and blazer on in 1974. The boys were all staring, and I felt very self-conscious. Mr Grubb put a hand on my shoulder.

'Come and meet the other trebles,' he said. 'There are one or two who have not arrived yet, but you'll meet them later. Now, boys, last Sunday you might have heard a splendid descant to the last verse of *"We plough the fields"*. I told you it was sung by someone called Alex, and Alex was going to come and join us. Well boys, I would like you to meet our new chorister, Alex—Alex Muir.'

'But, Sir!' protested a plump boy of eleven or twelve with red hair and freckles. 'He's a GIRL!' He spat out the word *"girl"* as if it described the most loathsome and despicable thing he had ever known.

'How very clever of you to notice, Kenneth,' said Mr Grubb, with a heavy dose of sarcasm that made the boy visibly wither in front of his friends. 'I would not have thought that a boy of your low intellect would have noticed any difference. I trust you will remember what I said to you the other day about fighting!' Kenneth went beetroot-red, and the boy that was my inner-self felt a bit sorry for him.

'As I was saying before I was rudely interrupted,' said Mr Grubb, 'This is Alex; she has recently come as a pupil at Seabourne Preparatory School, where she is a boarder. I have it on the best authority that she played football for her last school in a team in which the rest of the players were boys, mostly a couple of years older than herself. I'm not sure how many of *you* have been picked for your school football team. Rumour also has it that her right hook is as good as any boy of her age, so I wouldn't suggest you try anything out on her—Kenneth Duncan!' He looked over the top of his half-glasses at the blushing boy. 'You might come off worse. I'm sure you'll all make her most welcome, and that she will add strength to our singing. I suggest you think of her as just another treble, like yourselves.'

I listened to this speech, and immediately felt happier. This wise little old man had somehow realised what my feelings would be, and had nipped any trouble in the bud by telling his boys that I was just as good as they were and probably better in some ways.

He took me round and introduced me. I recognised one of them, Alan Fraser, who was in the Remove at Seabourne. He was very musical, and popular with everyone. It was fun to meet Alan as a boy, as I knew him as a grown-up; his son was head boy on my side (the decani) of the 1974 choir. He smiled and shook my hand with great enthusiasm.

'I'm glad you came, Alex,' he said. 'Mr Grubb told me that you were joining us when I had my piano lesson yesterday.'

Another "Seabourne-ite," one that I was not so pleased to see, was Julian Quinn, the only boy among twenty girls in the second form. He was a mummy's boy with curly blonde hair, blue eyes, and was small and delicate for his 10½ years. The girls in his form did not like him, and despised him for being a sneak. He was also such a sissy that they usually called him Julie-Ann.

'There now, *Julie-Ann*,' said another boy, John Wilson, who I later discovered had left Seabourne Prep at the end of the summer term. 'Isn't it nice for you that you're not the only girl in the choir now.'

'Thyut up,' cried Julian. 'I'll tell my mummy on you.'

'*Tell tale tit, your tongue shall be split! and all the little dickie-birds will get a little bit*,' three young probationers chanted rhythmically.

'Boys! *Boys!* Calm down, *please*,' said Mr Grubb. 'Let's warm up our voices before the men get here, shall we? Alex, please take your place in the Decani, between Alan Fraser and Ian Roberts.' He went to the piano, and put his hymn-book on the music desk. It was the very same piano that was there in 1974, but it looked a lot newer now.

'Right then, boys, may we have some hush, *please*. Paul Jones, remove that sweet from your mouth. You can't sing possibly properly sucking a gob-stopper—Spit it into the wastepaper basket—Oh all *right*—put it in your hanky if you *mus*t. I pity your poor mother!' Mr Grubb might give the impression of being a doddery old codger, but he was as sharp as a needle, and ruled his choirboys with a rod of iron.

Two late-comers arrived, hot and flustered. I recognised them instantly—they were both in the remove at school, Oliver Davies and Andrew Clegg. 'Sorry I'm late, Sir,' panted Andrew. 'I got a puncture, and had to push my bike.'

'Sorry I'm late, Sir,' said Oliver. 'I was with Andy so I walked with him.'

'All right,' said Mr Grubb, 'I forgive you this time. Quickly now, take your coats off and join in. We were about to do some deep-breathing exercises and sing some scales and arpeggios. Is everyone else ready?' When we had finished the deep-breathing he looked round. 'C major.' He struck the C an octave above middle C on the piano and we *na-na'd* down the scale; then came D and E, each time getting higher and higher. He was very thorough, pulling up anyone who sang off-key and making them sing on their own. I sang a horrid squawky top C, and he made me sing it several times on my own until I rose above it and hit it spot on. When satisfied that we had warmed our voices up, he opened his hymn-book.

'We'll run quickly through evensong first,' he said. 'We will be singing Walmisley's *Mag and Nunc*. Sorry, Alex, I am referring to the *Magnificat and Nunc Dimittis*; we'll run through it when the men are here.'

'That's all right, Sir,' I said. 'I know *Walmisley in D Minor*. The trebles split into two parts in a couple of places, don't they, Sir?'

Several of the boys gave me quizzical looks, and Alan, beside me, grinned and whispered; 'One-nil to you, Alex!'

'Splendid. Yes, we split down the middle—Cantoris and Decani. Decani take the top line,' said Mr Grubb. 'Now turn to hymn number 477; *The day thou gavest, Lord is ended*. The tune is *Saint Clement*, I'm sure you all know it.' He played through the tune while we found the place in our hymn-books.

'Ready? I'll give you a full bar for nothing; come in on the third beat of the next. I want to hear a good attack; you begin with the altos on D.' He struck the note on the piano and raised his right hand to conduct. 'One—two—three—one—two—' We came in as he said 'Three.'

We sang through all the hymns and psalms for evensong and matins, and Merbecke's 1550 setting of the Holy Communion service (which followed matins once a month). When the lay clerks (the men who sang alto, tenor and bass,) arrived, we ran through them again as a full choir, before tackling Walmisley's *Mag and Nunc*.

Once the boys realised I could hold my own, and sight-read music as well as any of them, most accepted me. When we had finished, I was shown round by Derrick Ackroyd, the head chorister and leader of the Decani. He had been at

Seabourne Prep until he was nine, and his younger sister Sarah was in my form. We got on well, and both he and the leader of the Cantoris, Christopher Hickingbottom, complimented me on my singing. After Mr Grubb had found a spare cassock and surplice to fit me, I was free to go.

As I left, Kenneth Duncan was waiting outside. I had decided I did not care for Master Duncan, and I didn't think he liked me. His elder sister Pamela was in the upper fifth at our school. She was a big strong girl, good at sports, who bullied her plump little brother unmercifully.

'I *hate* girls who spoil our fun,' he said, 'so I'm gonna bash you up.'

As he lumbered forward, I side-stepped and, accidentally on purpose, left a foot in his way. He sprawled on the ground face down. 'I'm *so* sorry, did I trip you?'

John Wilson, John Spender, Oliver Davies and Alan Fraser, who were watching, grinned. I caught sight of Julian Quinn dodging out of sight behind one of the gravestones. Alan offered to help me.

'No thanks, Alan, leave him to me,' I said, as Kenneth struggled to his feet and rushed me again. This time I punched him as hard as I could in the tummy, and as he doubled up I brought my knee up under his chin. He fell as if pole-axed. When he got up his nose was bleeding and he began to cry. The boys who had expected to see a girl "put in her place", cheered and slapped me on the back. None of them, particularly Kenneth, gave me any trouble after that.

John Wilson, holding out his hand said, 'Shake! I'm sorry I compared you to Queen Julie-Ann earlier. I was wrong. Not many of us boys'd've taken on Kenneth like that. Well done, ye! You're as tough and good as any boy in the choir, except one and *she* doesn't count.' I assumed he was referring to the unfortunate Julian.

'That's okay, John. I'm used to fighting with boys,' I told him absolutely truthfully. Some days later, Kenneth's sister Pamela told me that her little brother had been ragged unmercifully by the boys in his form at Larkfield School because, not only was he hen-pecked by his sister, but a girl younger than he was had given him a bloody nose and made him cry.

When I got back to school, Harry was waiting.

'I'm glad you're back, Ally,' she said. 'I was worried about you and wondered if you'd be all right on your own with all those boys.'

'Why shouldn't I be?' I answered. 'You held your own at a boys school. I really enjoyed myself, especially afterwards. I gave Kenneth Duncan a nose-bleed and made him cry.'

She looked at me. 'You mean Pamela's odious wee brother? I've only seen him once or twice. He looks revolting.'

'That's the one. And yes, he *is* revolting.'

'Well *done*, Ally!. What a swizz I wasn't there to see it.' She gave me a clap on the back. 'Tell me what happened.'

'After we'd finished, he was waiting for me outside and said he wanted to bash me up, and rushed at me. As he got near I side-stepped and tripped him. The next time he rushed at me, I punched him as hard as I could in the tummy, and he doubled up, so I brought my knee up under his chin. He collapsed in a heap, and then slunk away blubbing, with blood pouring from his nose. The other boys seemed to enjoy it—they all cheered—John Wilson told me I was as tough as any of the boys. I came back on the bus with Alan Fraser and three of the others. Two, Bob Smith, and John Spender, Garters's brother, are both in the same form as Kenneth at Larkfield; betcha he gets ragged like anything. The other was that unfortunate Quinn boy in the second form, cowering behind a gravestone and had watched me bashing-up Kenneth. On the bus he was gazing at me like a love-sick puppy.'

'Oh, Queen Julie-Ann!' scorned Harry. 'Poor old *you*. She's more *girlie* than any *girl* in the school, even the likes of Prissy and co. He was cracked on *me* last term, worst luck! But tell me about the singing; how did it go? Did you manage okay? Did you get on with the boys all right?'

'Help! One question at a time,' I replied. 'It went jolly well, and I managed as well as any of them, and I got on well with most of the boys. I liked Derrick Ackroyd, Sarah's big brother who leads the Decani, and Chris Hickingbottom, leader of the Cantoris. Although we practised the hymns for evensong, *I'm* only going to sing at matins for a week or two. Let's go and find Scottie, I promised I'd tell her how I got on.'

She was in her room. We knocked and waited. 'Come away in,' she called. She was sitting in her chair, and darning a large hole in a sock. She looked up as we entered, and smiled. 'So, Alex the wanderer has returned. How did it go, my lass?'

'Fine, thank you, Scottie,' I replied. 'It was smashing. And I got on really well with the boys. Most of them didn't seem to mind that I was a girl, and treated me just as if I'd been a boy, like them; they were really nice. I am in the Decani, on the right hand side as you face the alter. Derrick Ackroyd, Sarah's big brother, leads us. I really like him. He's fourteen, and worried his voice is going to break soon. It'll be a shame, 'cos his voice is *really* good, clear and strong, easily the best in the choir. The Cantoris leader, Chris Hickingbottom, is nice too, but he's not nearly as good a singer as Derrick.'

'*ALLY!*' exclaimed Harry. 'You never told me you'd fallen in love with Derrick Ackroyd!'

'I haven't *fallen in love* with him, you dumb cluck!' I protested, feeling myself blushing. 'All I said was he's jolly nice chap.'

'Look, Scottie! She's blushing and she's gone all coy!' said Harry.

'Oh shut up, Harry!' I said, feeling even more embarrassed. She put her arms round me and gave me one of her bear hugs.

'I'm sorry, Ally, I was only teasing.'

'I know.' I aimed a playful punch at her.

'Derrick's certainly scored a hit with you, young lady,' said Scottie. 'I'm glad you got on well with the boys. I was a wee bit concerned in case any of them made trouble for you. That malevolent wee brother of Pamela Duncan can be a right wee pest when he's a mind to it. I meant to warn you about him.'

'Och, Ally dealt with *him* good and proper,' said Harry proudly. 'He tried to bash her up in the churchyard afterwards, and he ended up going home in tears with a nose-bleed. He'll be the laughing stock of Larkfield tomorrow. Serve him right too.'

'He didn't hurt you, did he, my pet?' Scottie asked anxiously.

'Never gave him the chance,' I replied, and told her what had happened.

'Good for *you*,' chuckled Scottie, with a twinkle in her eye. 'I'm glad you can take care of yourself, but I don't think we'll tell The Beak—she might not approve of one of her girls engaging in fisticuffs.'

'What! Me?' I put on my most innocent expression, gazing at the ceiling, with arched back, arms stiffly behind me and my hands clasped tightly together.

'Don't you try that "*butter wouldn't melt in my mouth*" act on me, my lass. It doesn't work,' laughed Scottie. 'You're both bundles of mischief. Come here, the pair o' ye.' She put her arms round both of us and gave us a hug. 'Having the likes of you, makes all my hard work worth while. And talking of hard work, Henrietta Catriona Gordon, I've got a wee bone to pick with you, young woman! What, do you call this?'

She held up a sock. I recognised it as the one that Harry had put her heel through on Tuesday morning.

'It's a sock isn't it, Scottie?' said Harry assuming the same innocent posture as I had a moment or so earlier.

'It *was* a sock, *Miss Gordon*, and what's more, one of *yours*, so don't come the innocent with me, my lass. I really ought to make you darn it yourself. You might be more careful with your things then,' Scottie said, trying to look stern, but the severe expression suddenly broke into a smile. 'Go on, the pair o' ye. I can't bring myself to be cross with you. Your old Scottie's just a softy who loves you both. I'll come and say good night later.' She patted each of us on the behind and we left her room just as the first bedtime bell rang.

'Harry,' I said.

'Yes, Ally.'

'I was only saying that Derrick's a decent chap. *You're* my best friend.'

'I know, and *you're* mine. D'you realise, that tomorrow it'll be a whole week that we've known each other.'

'Yes, I got here at just before midnight a week ago, so your first night in Peregrine was mine too. I slept in the sick bay my first night.'

'And all this time,' laughed Harry, 'I thought you were an old-stager. We're both as new as each other. Last one in the bathroom's a sissy.'

*

We had no air-raid that night—for the second night running.

CHAPTER EIGHTEEN

Troubles

FRIDAY THE TWENTIETH dawned dull, and I did not feel like getting up one bit. I had now been in 1940 exactly a week, and was beginning to worry that I might never get back to my own time. My problem was that I had no idea how I had got into this peculiar situation. I had woken in the small hours, and had lain awake brooding on it for some time. As I lay there, things that Gran had told me about the war began to come back to me. Something had happened to my Auntie Alexandra and a school friend; it was all so hazy that I couldn't remember any details. Suppose my voyage back to 1940 was pre-ordained, and I had come back to 1940 for a special reason? If so, I would not be able to return to my own time until I had completed whatever task it was I had to perform. These thoughts were whirling round and round in my head until, finally, I drifted back to sleep again.

So when I was wakened by the first bell, I was still feeling rather tired. But I wasn't allowed to lie in, because Harry was even more her bouncy, Tiggerish self than usual, even though I would have liked to doze until Scottie rang the second bell. 'Come on, Ally!' demanded Tigger, pulling my bedclothes off me. 'If you lie there any longer, you'll be late for brekker. And if you want me to do your pigtails, you'd better hurry up. Mind you, it's about time you did them yourself. If a pudding like Dotty Dot can do it, you should be able to do it standing on your head.'

'Okay,' I replied, 'I'll do them myself today. I've got to learn to do it sometime. Suppose you were ill? I'd have to do them then.'

'All right, I'll stay and watch you.'

'No!' I replied firmly. 'You'd put me off.'

So that Friday morning she left me to it. After struggling with them for what seemed a lifetime, regretting my bold stand, I managed to do them after a fashion. I was leaving the dormitory, on my way down to brekker, when I bumped into Scottie.

'What on earth have you done with your hair, my lamb?' she asked. 'You can't go into brekker like that, The Beak would throw forty fits! You normally do them so neatly.'

'Not me, Scottie,' I said, looking up at her. 'Harry usually does them for me, but I wanted to try by myself today, without her looking on.'

'Come here,' she said, 'I can't let you go down like that. Old Scottie'll do them for you in two wee shakes of a haggis's tail. Would you and Harry like to visit Caroline in Hospital again this afternoon? Ask her and let me know after brekker so I can fix it with The Beak.' Her nimble fingers quickly plaited my hair, and she had one side done before I could answer.

'Yes, I'd love to, and I'm sure Harry would,' I said. 'I'd like to talk to some of the other children. Some of them looked so unhappy, I'd like to try to cheer them up. We're too young to fight the boche, as Harry calls them, but it's something we can do to help towards winning the war.'

'That's thoughtful of you,' she replied. 'You're a good-natured, kind lassie. Speak to Harry and see what she thinks. There you are, Miss Muir, how do you look now?' I looked at myself in the mirror.

'Tidy, Ma'am, thank you, Ma'am,' I said, trying to curtsy and overbalancing.

Scottie caught me before I fell over. 'Go on, you loony,' she laughed. 'Off to brekker before you're late.'

I got to the eatery with a minute to spare. Harry was already there, waiting for me. She scrutinised the finished job.

'Very *good*, Ally. Well done!' she declared as we sat down after Grace. 'You won't need me to do them any more. You've made a really excellent job of them.'

'No, I *haven't!*' I replied. 'You're right, I'm useless! Worse than Dotty Dot! Scottie took one look at my efforts, and said The Beak would throw forty fits if she saw me! So she did them for me in "two wee shakes of a Haggis's tail." Please will you do them for me again tomorrow?'

''Fcourse I will.'

'Harry?' I said, after I'd swallowed a mouthful of porridge. 'Scottie asked if we'd like to visit Caroline again this afternoon. I said I was sure we would, but I'd ask you, anyway. D'you know, ever since Monday, I've been thinking about the other children there. I thought we could visit some of them at the same time. As girls, there's not much we can do to help win the war, but this is something we can do.'

'That's a super idea!' she replied. 'P'raps some of the others would like to join in. We could all do one visit a week, and not visit only children, there are probably lots of older people who would like to talk to us. Jen-Pen, what would you say to visiting some of the children who are in hospital because of the bombing?'

'I'd love to,' said Jenny; 'As long as it doesn't get in the way of exam work. We could ask Scottie to organise a rota. And I know someone who's sure to want to join us, and that's Goody-Two-Shoes.'

'Yes!' said Harry. 'She would be great. Look how she mothers her wee ones in the shelter. We'll ask her after brekker.'

'Go and ask her now if you like,' said Jenny. 'For a good cause like that, the prefects wouldn't mind.'

'I'll go when I've finished my porridge,' said Harry.

*

Goody-Two-Shoes thought it was an excellent idea too, so she came with us to see Scottie after brekker.

'Would you like to come along with Alex and Harry this afternoon?' asked

Scottie. 'Of course you will have to clear it with Mrs. Griffiths. I'll ask her for you if you like.'

'Would you, Scottie?' replied Goody. 'That'd be super. I can think of several girls who might like the chance to help. Mag-Bags and Jemima, for a start.'

'And Rob Roy, and Nicky,' said Harry. 'And when Ally told Jen-Pen, she was awfully keen, as long as it doesn't interrupt her swotting for Common Entrance. As Ally said, it's something we can do to help our country's war effort.'

'That's what I thought when Ally suggested it,' said Scottie. 'I'm sure The Beak'll agree that it's something you can do. Mind you, we'll have to restrict the number of visitors at any one time, because hoards of schoolgirls running riot in a hospital would cause chaos in next to no time! I would think six or so at a time would be ample. I'll ring the Matron; she's an old friend and colleague who was the sister of my first ward after I had qualified as a staff nurse. Her name's Miss Dawes, Miss Drusilla P. Dawes, so you can imagine what we young staff nurses and the patients called her, can't you Harry?'

Harry frowned. I could almost hear the cogs in her brain whirring round and round. Slowly a wicked grin spread across her face. 'Dru P. Dawes,' she giggled.

'Droopy Drawers?' chuckled Goody. 'Oh Scottie! I'll never be able to keep a straight face if I meet her.'

'Aye,' said Scottie, grinning, ''Tis unfortunate what some parents unthinkingly inflict upon their children.'

'Poor lady,' I said. 'I bet she got a hard time at school.'

'And you three'll be getting a hard time at school if you don't go and do your morning chores,' said Scottie. 'The bell for prayers will be going and your beds won't be made.'

*

At prayers, we sang *New every morning* and after we had said *Our Father* together, Miss Plenderleith said a special prayer for Caroline and her mother.

Back in our form room, Dotty Dot had a note to say she could not do gym because she had a cold. No sooner had she handed the note over when she gave an enormous sneeze, and wiped her nose on the sleeve of her blouse.

'Dorothy Clark!' thundered Miss Spurgeon. 'If you *must* sneeze, do so into your handkerchief *if you please!* Remember, "*Coughs and sneezes spread diseases! Trap the germs in your handkerchief!*" Please remember also that *nice* little girls do *not* wipe their noses on the sleeves of their blouses!'

'Yes, Miss Spurgeon, 'm sorry, Miss Spurgeon,' said Dotty. 'Please, Miss Spurgeon, I haven't got a hanky, Miss Spurgeon.' She sneezed again, twice.

'I would have preferred that you had stayed at home, Dorothy,' said Miss Spurgeon, 'Rather than spread your germs to the entire school! It's not fair to risk spreading your cold to the rest of the form. You're excused lessons for today. Go and put on your coat and hat, then go home and ask mummy to put you to bed.' But Dotty just stood there gazing at Miss Spurgeon. 'Well, go *on,* don't just *stand* there looking gormless! Go and put on your hat and coat, and go home.' Dotty stood, rivetted to the spot. 'Go on, girl!' Miss Spurgeon was getting impatient.

'P—p—please, Miss Sp—Spurgeon,' stammered Dotty, 'I c—*can't*.'

'Of *course* you can, Dorothy. Don't be silly.'

Dotty began to cry. 'B—but, M—miss Spurgeon, M—mummy's gone t—to w—work and I c—can't g—g—g—g—get in.' She wiped her eyes on her other sleeve.

'Oh, Dotty, what are we going to do with you? You'd better go to Matron and ask her if she can put you in the sick bay until dinner-time.'

'Yes, Miss Sp—Spurgeon.' But Dotty stayed as if glued to the spot.

'Off you pop then; there's a good girl.'

'I c—can't.'

'Of course you can, a big strong girl like you.'

'P—please Miss Sp—Spurgeon, I've f—f—forgotten where M—m—m—matron's room is.'

'For Heaven's *sake*, Dorothy!' Miss Spurgeon exploded. 'You're enough to drive a saint crazy. Somebody take this half-wit to Matron before I lose patience completely.'

Dotty wailed louder than ever.

'I'll be taking her, Miss,' said Paddy, getting up from her desk. 'Come along, Dotty, I'll show you the way.'

'Thank you, Patricia,' said Miss Spurgeon, 'Explain to Matron will you—And say I'm sorry to have to inflict Dorothy on her.'

'I will, Miss Spurgeon,' replied Paddy, leading Dotty out of the room.

'I'm sorry about that girls. I don't often get ratty. Now get out your dictation books and find a new page.'

From behind my desk lid, I glanced out of the window. It was raining cats and dogs, and I just knew it was going to be *one of those mornings*.

After that nothing really went smoothly. In Algebra it was obvious from the start that Miss Parrot was in a really foul mood. The bottoms of both Maggot and Weevil felt the weight of her gym-shoe. Maggot had equipped herself with some books as padding and this only led Polly into an even worse rage. She insisted that Maggot remove them in front of the whole class and then sent her to Miss Plenderleith. While Maggot was away, Weevil had to stand in the corner. A very sad and weepy Maggot came back about ten minutes later. Miss Parrot refused to have her in the room and sent her to stand outside.

We were all relieved when break came, even though we had to stay indoors because of the rain. Of Maggot and Weevil there was no sign. As we drank our milk in the passage next to the eatery, Harry and I were talking over our ideas about hospital visiting with Nicky, Rob Roy and Jen-Pen. I had paused to take another sip of milk, when Nicky touched my hand.

'Don't look now, Ally,' she said, 'but Queen Julie-Ann's gazing at you like an adoring puppy-dog. From the look in his eyes he's really cracked on you.'

'Help!' I said. 'It must be because I bashed up Kenneth Duncan after choir practise last night. Let's get away from here, somewhere where Julian can't follow us.'

'You bashed-up Pam Duncan's revolting little brother?' said Jenny.

'Yes, Ally gave him a nose-bleed and made him cry,' Harry said. 'How about our changing room, Julie-Ann won't be able to follow us in there. We've got gym after break, so we can get changed early. Are you coming, Jen-Pen?'

'No, but well *done*, Ally,' she replied. 'I'll waylay Julie-Ann for you.'

'Thanks Jen-Pen,' I said. 'You're a pal.'

'Julie-Ann would've been much happier if he'd been born a girl,' said Rob Roy.

"You mean his silly *mother* would have been much happier if he'd been born a little girl,' said Jen-Pen sagely.

*

We enjoyed gym after break, but during history Griff-Bug lost her temper with Lucy Parker, who had left her homework at home. Lucy always left her homework behind when she had not finished it, and Mrs. Griffiths told her that if she ever left it behind again, she would be sent to Miss Plenderleith.

It was a relief when the bell rang for the end of morning lessons, and Harry and I were glad we were going hospital visiting that afternoon.

We never discovered what The Beak said to Maggot. Apart from gating her until the end of term, Maggot wouldn't say. Whatever it was, it certainly struck home. She was a very timid, subdued Maggot for some time afterwards. She was very different in class too—serious, hard-working and from then on, consistently earning high marks.

CHAPTER NINETEEN

Consequences

THE FISH AND CHIPS at lunch time was scrummy, and what had been a rather horrid morning was soon forgotten. Poor Maggot was still very red-eyed and subdued, and obviously finding it very painful to sit down. Scottie, sensing that the normally carefree and boisterous Maggot was being decidedly un-Maggotty, tried hard to help her regain some of her old bounce. But it was to no avail, and after lunch she left the eatery with an arm round Maggot's shoulder, the poor girl still in great distress.

During break, Scottie had told us that the Beak had agreed we could visit the hospital again, and thought the idea of regular visits by six or so girls at a time was splendid. After lunch, Harry and I went to Scottie's room. She had Maggot sitting on her knee, still very upset.

Scottie asked us to wait with Maggot, because she needed to do one or two "wee jobs" before we went out. While she was away, we did our best to comfort poor Maggot. Gradually her sobbing eased.

'I've been g—g—g—gated,' she sobbed. 'Un—t—til th—th—the end of t—t—ter—err—erm.'

Harry frowned. 'I say, that's a bit unfair. What you did was not *that* bad, for goodness sake—'

'No,' I agreed, 'But maybe she thought you'd played tricks on Polly once too often.'

Scottie returned about ten minutes later. 'Maggot, I've been to see The Beak on your behalf and told her that I thought gating you to the end of term was rather harsh. I told her that you were still crying. She said she was having second thoughts about your gating, and agreed that you shall come with us to the hospital with us this afternoon. We both think it will do you good to see how some children have been made suffer by this war.'

Maggot put her arms round Scottie and hugged her, bursting into tears at the same time. 'Thank you, Scottie, I promise I'll turn over a new leaf from now on.'

'There, there, my poor wee lamb, dry your eyes,' Scottie said gently, stroking her head. 'You'll run out of tears soon and you will end up as a wee spot of grease on my carpet. You're spouting almost as much water as the fountain in front of the Pavillion Theatre.' Maggot grinned a Maggotty grin at last. 'Now, off you pop and wash those tear stains off your cheeks and make your eyes look a little less puffed up. Then put on your hat, coat and gumboots, and meet us in the hall in five minutes. And don't forget your gas-masks, girls.'

*

The rain was still bucketing down as we set out for the bus stop. Scottie had brought an enormous black umbrella. I had never seen such a big one, it was even bigger than the golf umbrellas I had seen in 1974.

'What a huge brolly,' said Harry. 'I hope you didn't pinch it from outside some Parisian café.'

'And who has ever seen a black brolly outside a Parisian café, or any other café for that matter?' retorted Scottie.

'I thought you might've dyed it black,' said Harry, already dancing away from the playful swipe she knew Scottie would pretend to aim at her. Maggot grinned, and looked much more her old self.

Standing at the bus stop, all of us, Scottie, Goody, Maggot, Harry and I were sheltered by that brolly, and there was still room for two more. We had just missed a bus, so we had to wait for about a quarter of an hour for the next one. When we arrived at the hospital, The Ogress in the Dark Green Dress gave us an even more withering glare than she had the first time, complaining in her loud and disapproving voice about 'Little girls making puddles all over the nice clean floor!'

We made our way to the ward and were welcomed by Sister Tranter. She showed us where to hang our hats and coats and change into shoes, while she and Scottie had a chat.

'Scottie's told me your idea about regular visits to cheer up my patients,' said Sister. 'I think it's a splendid idea. Matron will be along in a few minutes to meet you, so we thought you would like to tell her about your idea yourselves.'

'How is old *Droopy Drawers* these days?' asked Scottie. 'I've not seen her since last Christmas. D'you remember, Emily, how dreadful she was to us when we were staff nurses and she was ward sister?' Goody giggled and Maggot looked astonished. Harry explained to her about Matron's name which brought a delighted giggle from Maggot. I caught Scottie's eye and she winked.

'Can we go and see Caroline while we wait?' I asked.

'Off you go,' said Sister; 'But try not to be noisy. There's a little lad behind those screens who's rather poorly.'

Harry led the way to Caroline's bed. She couldn't see us coming because the bed next to her had screens round it. As soon as we passed it she looked up and smiled. Her head was no longer bandaged, and her hair looked as though it had been cut with a pair of garden shears.

'Golly!' she said, beaming.'Four visitors, what a lovely surprise!'

'Where's your turban?' asked Harry. 'And what did they do to your lovely long hair?'

'Mr. Mac said I didn't need my turban any more, and they cut off my hair in the operating place 'cos it was all bloody, and got in the way of the stitches.' She put her hand to her mouth. 'Oops!—Sorry—! Mummy says I shouldn't say that, 'cos it's terribly rude!'

'What's rude, Caroline?' asked Scottie.

'She said they had to cut off her hair because it was all bloody,' said Harry.

'It's not rude if you say it that way, my lamb,' said Scottie. 'How are you feeling today. How's your poorly leg, I hope it's not hurting so much.'

'It's ever so much better, thank you, Scottie,' she said, and grinned. 'See, I remembered to call you Scottie and not Matron.'

'And what do you think you are doing, Staff Nurse Scott?' said a loud voice from behind us. We turned round and saw a large, cottage-loaf-shaped lady, in a dark blue uniform with a hat like a cake frill perched ridiculously on top of her grey hair. She was advancing down the ward like a galleon under full sail! 'And why are all these schoolgels cluttering up my nice tidy ward?' She smiled a very friendly smile.

'Dru,' said Scottie. 'How are you? Still the same old battleaxe?' They put their arms round each other and hugged.

'Overworked, short staffed and going to an early grave,' replied Matron. ''Tis good to see you. Sister says your gels have something to ask me.'

'Let me introduce them,' said Scottie. 'The one with the boyish haircut is Harry Gordon.'

Harry held out her right hand to Matron. 'How d'you do, Matron,' she said politely, shaking matron's hand.

'Hello, Harry,' said Matron, and turning to me asked; 'And what's your name, young lady?'

'Alex Muir, Matron,' I said, shaking hands with her.

'That's a good firm handshake, young Alex. Do all your gels have boy's names, Scottie?'

'No, thank goodness,' laughed Scottie. 'This is Margot Burton with the red hair, who answers to Maggot, and finally Barbara Goodbody, whom we call Goody-Two-Shoes or Goody for short.'

Matron shook hands all round. 'Now what's all this I hear about an idea you've had?'

'It was Alex's idea, Dru,' said Scottie.

'Why don't you tell me all about it then, Alex?' said Matron, smiling at me.

'Well!' I said. 'When Harry and I were here last time, we saw all the children with nobody visiting them, I thought we could talk to them and cheer them up. When we told Scottie, she thought some of the other girls might like to come too. There's not much we, as schoolgirls, can do towards helping with the war, but this just might be something, 'specially if the children had lost their mothers and fathers.'

'Well, Alex,' said Matron, 'I think it is a topping idea, isn't it, Sister?'

'Yes, Matron, I agree, it *is* a splendid idea,' replied Sister. 'I think they should start right now if they'd like to.'

'Indeed, Sister, no time like the present,' said Matron. 'Scottie, you know your gels; would you like to introduce them to some of our patients. Sister knows who would like a visitor.'

'As Harry and Alex came to see Caroline,' said Scottie, 'One of them should stay with her for a bit, and the rest of us will spread ourselves round, won't we girls?'

'Let Harry stay with Caroline,' I said. 'I'll talk to someone else and see her later. After all Harry's known her longer than any of us. Sister? Who's that with the bandages and just a nose and mouth showing? May I talk to her, or is she a he?'

'Of course you may, Alex,' replied Sister. 'I shall introduce you. *He* is called Alex too, so you've got something to talk about straight away. His home was bombed, and his eyes were hurt and one of his legs broken.' She led me down the ward to where the boy with just a nose and mouth showing beneath the bandages was lying silently on his bed. 'Alex, I've brought someone to talk to you. Her name's Alex too. I'll get a chair so she can sit by you. Or she could sit on the edge of your bed. It's against the rules really, but I won't report you to myself!'

The mouth smiled. 'Are you really a girl called Alex?' asked the boy in bandages. 'My eyes have gone funny, so I can't see you unless you sit close enough for me to touch you.'

'Yes I'm Alex too,' I said. 'I'll sit on your right hand side. One of my best friend's chums is here, Caroline. She goes to our school.' He stretched out a hand to me. I took hold of it and squeezed it. He smiled, and when I was sitting on the bed beside him, he moved his hand up my arm. He stopped when he came to the buttons on the shoulder of my tunic.

'You're wearing school uniform,' he said. 'My sister wears a gymslip like—.' He went silent for a moment. 'I mean she *used* to wear a gymslip like yours; the bomb killed her, and Mummy. Dad's away in the army, somewhere overseas.'

'Oh, I'm sorry,' was all I could think of saying. 'My dad was killed in an aeroplane crash.'

'Was he a fighter-pilot?' he asked eagerly. Fighter pilots were everyone's heroes.

'No, it was before the war. He was a test pilot,' I replied.

His hand moved from my shoulder up to my ear. He felt my face, and then my hair. 'You look nice, and you've got a kind face. It's a pity you've got plaits; you'd look nicer without them. How old are you?'

'I'm ten and a half,' I replied. 'How old are you?'

'I'll be twelve next birthday. You're about the same age as Monica, my sister, was.'

'How long have you been in here?'

''bout ten weeks, I *think*—I'm not sure. Not being able to see makes it hard to know when it's day and when it's night. They say I might get sight back in one eye, if I'm lucky. I'm learning to read Braille just in case.' He put his hand on mine and squeezed. 'I like you, Alex, it's good to have someone new to talk to. You've not once said how awful it must be for me. Some old ladies visit us sometimes, and all they say is; "Deary me, poor little chap, how brave!" and barmy things like that. Then they pat me on the head like a pet Pekinese. You're the first person of my own age who's visited me, and talked properly. Of course I chat with the other kids in the ward, but most of them have to stay in their beds. D'you live at home, or are you a boarder?"

'We're all boarders,' I replied. 'I've only been one for a week. I was on a train going to London, and it got bombed. I wasn't hurt, thank goodness, but I could easily have ended up in hospital. Then, while I was in London with Mummy, there was an air-raid and Buckingham Palace was bombed. That's why I arrived at school so late.'

'What does your mother do?' he asked.

'I don't really know, but it's something to do with when she was a girl and lived in France. She speaks French, you see. All I know is that it's ever so hush-hush.'

'Perhaps she's a secret agent. Or a spy;' he said. 'I bet you worry about her.'

'Yes, I do, but I say prayers for her every night, and my best friend's mummy too; they work together. I'll say prayers for you too, and your Dad, Alex, if you'd like me to.'

'Would you? I'd like that. May I pray for your mother and your friend's mother?'

'That'd be great,' I said. 'If they're doing what you think, they'll need all the prayers they can get. Here comes Harry, *she's* my best friend; I'll introduce you.'

'Crikey, two girls, and *both* with boys' names!' he laughed, but not for very long as I saw him wince. It must hurt him to laugh. 'All we need now is a boy with a girl's name!'

'Harry, come and say hello to another Alex. He thinks that being called Harry you should a boy. Come and sit where he can see you're a girl.' I made a sign to her that he 'saw' by touch. 'I'll get down now, Alex, and you can look at Harry.' I slipped off the bed, and she took my place.

She took his hand. 'Hello,' she said, 'How d' you like my best friend Alex, Alex?'

'She's jolly nice,' he replied. 'You sound Scotch.'

'Aye, I am so,' she replied, emphasising her slight accent. 'But we say *Scots*. Scotch is whisky!'

The bandage-swathed mouth smiled. 'It's jolly nice to have someone decent to talk to f'ra change. I was telling Alex that we get old ladies coming in and telling us all how brave we've been! They only make us feel worse most of the time.' His hand had reached Harry's shoulder, and the buttons on the shoulder of her tunic. 'You're wearing a gymslip too.'

'Well, you'd have got a frightful shock if I'd not been wearing it,' she replied. He grinned at her and his hand reached up to her face, touching all round and stroking her hair.

'You've got a nice smile,' he said. 'But why's your hair cut short like a boy's. You're pretty, but you'd look much nicer if your hair was longer. Like a proper girl.'

'It's a long story,' she said. 'I don't have nits or anything like that! Before I came here I went to a boys' school in Scotland. I wasn't pretending I was a boy or anything—well, not ALL the time anyhow—so it was easier for me to look like all the other chaps, 'specially when I played footer for the school. Our opponents'd've had fifty thousand fits if they'd known a *girl* was playing in the St Mungo's eleven.'

'But what about clothes? Did you have to wear boy's clothes?'

'In a *sort* of a way I s'pose,' said Harry. 'In Scotland boys often wear kilts to school, and so that's what I wore.'

'Golly, what a lark,' said Alex. He was holding her hand now. 'You're both jolly nice. Are you still there, Alex? I wish they hadn't put bandages over my ears as well; I have to rely on my ears a lot at the moment.'

'Still here,' I replied. 'I must just go and say "hello" to Caroline. Have a chat with Harry and I'll come and see you again before we go.' I turned away and went back to Caroline. 'Hello, Caroline, how're you today? 'Have you still got that piece of shrapnel?'

'Yes,' she replied, 'And look, I've got more writing on my plaster. Goody and Maggot have written things on it.' I looked round the ward. Maggot was by the boy with both legs in plaster, they were getting on like a house on fire, and Goody was holding an earnest conversation with the girl in the neck support. 'I saw you talking to Alex. He's ever so nice. He'll probably be blind for ever. He does things awf'ly well, just by feel. And,' she pulled me closer, put her mouth next to my ear and whispered; 'And, he tells terribly rude stories when Sister's not here.'

'*Does* he? What fun! Hilary sends his love, by the way.'

'Yes, his mummy brought him to see me after school yesterday. It was ever so nice to see him.' She smiled, and took hold of my hand. 'Poor Hilary, he was so frightened when he came, and he cried so much. He said you and Harry have been looking after him. I told him I hoped I'd soon be well enough to leave hospital. I'm getting some crutches tomorrow, so I'll be able to get out of bed and go and talk to Alex. Isn't it funny that you're both called Alex. He's ever so nice isn't he?'

'Yes, jolly nice, I'd like to come and see him again.'

'Harry says you're going to be in the choir at church.'

'Yes, me with all those boys! Isn't it bang on?' I said. 'I'll be singing for the first time on Sunday. I'm jolly well looking forward to it.'

'Is it true what Harry said, that you bashed up Kenneth Duncan after choir practice?' she gave a little giggle.

''Fraid so,' I admitted. 'Wasn't I a naughty girl? But I had to show I wasn't scared of him. Here's Scottie coming back.'

'She's probably going to take you all away again,' Caroline said. 'Scottie, you can't make them go before we've had tea.'

'Of course not, my wee pet,' Scottie said. 'I was just coming to say that Sister has arranged for a little tea party again.'

*

On the bus going home, we compared notes about the children we had visited.

'George was ever so nice,' said Maggot. 'It took them over twelve hours to find him. He was trapped under a door that had fallen on top of his bed. He says if it hadn't he'd be dead. His legs hurt a lot still—'

'Gwendolyn, the girl with a broken neck,' said Goody, 'Can't feel her legs;

they're paralysed as well. D'you know? We were both born on the same day. Isn't that a coincidence?'

'I liked Alex,' said Harry. 'He said that the old ladies who visit sometimes keep saying how brave he is, and it makes him feel worse. He likes *Just William* stories, so I said we'd bring one next time and read to him. It must be awful being blind.'

'Yes,' I said, 'and he's so cheerful. I'm sure if I was hurt like him I'd feel terrible. Isn't he clever the way he sees with his hands?'

'Yes,' said Harry, 'and he told me I must let my hair grow so I'd look like a proper girl. I told him I *was* growing it, 'cos *you'd* told me to, Ally!'

When we got back to school the other girls were already at Prep. In spite of running to try to catch it, we just missed a number 22 bus in Boscombe, so had to wait for another one. At least the rain had stopped, so we didn't mind waiting at the stop for the next trolleybus that was going our way.

We took off our hats and raincoats, and Scottie came with us to our form-room so that we wouldn't be given lateness marks by the prefect on duty who, that evening, was Bren-Gun. Maggot sat next to Weevil, grinned at her, and settled down to her prep. Weevil kept trying to distract Maggot, so I touched Harry's arm and nodded in Weevil's direction. Harry whispered that we should have words with Weevil afterwards.

Our history prep was an essay about the causes of the English Civil War, such as the King demanding payment of unpopular taxes like Ship Money, and his attempt to arrest five leading members of Parliament. Then there was the puritans' dislike of the Church of England with its "Popish" rituals, and Queen Henrietta Maria being a Roman Catholic. As we had been five minutes late, we decided to stay behind for five minutes at the end. When the bell rang for the end of prep, instead of closing our books and slamming our desk tops, Maggot, Harry and I kept on working. Weevil began larking around, trying to disturb Maggot, pestering her to go and play outside. When she jogged Maggot's right elbow, causing her pen to scratch across the work that she had done, Harry was just about to tell Weevil off when Maggot saved her the trouble. She turned on her best friend and punched her hard in the tummy.

'If you're so keen to go and play, why don't you go and play with the *babies* in the remove?' Maggot told Weevil. 'I'm trying to make a decent job of my prep, and you've spoilt it jogging my elbow, making my pen blob ink all over the place. You're nothing but a *pest*. I'm *fed* up with you getting me into trouble. Why don't you act your age for a change?' Weevil gave an anguished wail, burst into tears and rushed out screeching; 'I hate you! I *hate* you!' We worked on in silence for about ten minutes, then I looked up at the clock.

'Well!' I said, blotting the last line of my essay, 'I hope Grif-bug likes that.'

'I've finished too,' said Maggot returning her exercise book to her desk and taking her pen out of the ink-well. 'I'm hopping mad with Weevil for mucking up my essay. I'll write it out again over the week-end, 'cos I want to show the staff that I really *can* do decent work and behave properly.'

'Well *said*, Maggot,' said Harry. 'I was going to tell Weevil off myself, but you saved me the trouble. Well *done!* She needs taking down a peg or two. It was fun helping those children in hospital wasn't it?'

'Yes,' replied Maggot, 'I'd like to do it again. When I first saw them—I—I wanted to hide my eyes and not look at them. My first feeling was "how *terrible,* such things *can't* happen." But I saw they *had.* Then, when I saw little Caroline, all chirpy and pleased to see us, with her leg in plaster and her hair chopped off roughly, I realised that after the next air-raid it could be me lying there with both legs broken, blinded and paralysed.'

'Maggot, after high tea we're going to Scottie's room to write out a notice to put up in the common rooms,' I said. 'D'you want to come and help?'

'Rather!' she said. 'I hope Scottie'll let me go next time. It's a chiz my being gated, otherwise I'd have liked to go again tomorrow after lunch. I'd like to take some sweets to George, he was such a nice boy.'

At that moment The Beak came in.

'Did I hear right?' she said. 'Was Margot Burton actually saying she would like to give some of her sweets ration to a boy in hospital?' Maggot blushed. 'I see my ears weren't deceiving me. I have just seen Weevil in floods of tears, Maggot, saying she hates you. What have you done to upset her?'

Maggot frowned, she didn't approve of sneaking so she kept mum.

'Please, Miss Plenderleith,' said Harry, 'Maggot won't sneak, any more than I will, other than say that Weevil got what she deserved—she'd been asking for it. She was being a pest while we were trying to finish our prep.'

'I see. Thank you, Harry,' said the Beak. 'If you want to visit your friend in hospital tomorrow afternoon, Maggot, you may do so, as long as Harry and Alex go with you. Scottie told me what a good job you all did this afternoon, and I think I may have misjudged you, Maggot. I'm very pleased with you, *all* of you.'

'Oh, Miss Plenderleith, you're an angel,' said Maggot. 'I'm awf'ly sorry I've been such a nuisance. I *will* try to behave better from now on. But I *won't* promise not to throw horse doings at St. Aloysius' boys any more. Some of them are so bumptious they need taking down a peg.'

'Well, so long as it's not reported to me,' said the Beak, smiling. 'I'll admit that I was secretly rather pleased when I heard about it, but as they had made an official complaint, I had to punish you. If you *must* do it again, *don't do it when a master's watching,* so if a boy sneaks on you I can say he was only doing it to get you into trouble, as I know you'd never *dare* do such a thing again, would you Maggot?' She winked at Maggot and gave her shoulder an affectionate squeeze.

'Oh *no-oh,* Miss Plenderleith,' said Maggot putting on the most innocent and angelic look. 'I *do* think you're a ripper, Miss Plenderleith.'

And that, from Maggot, was praise indeed.

'Now, go and make it up with Weevil,' said the Beak. 'I hate to see anyone looking miserable. I'm going to ask Scottie to take her to the hospital next week, but not at the same time as you, Maggot, the two of you together would be more than the hospital could stand. And I'm glad you can sit down again—believe me, it hurts me far more than it hurts you. Your gating ends tomorrow night, but you may visit the hospital in the afternoon.'

'Gosh, thanks, Miss Plenderleith, you really *are* top-hole!'

'Now, you two,' said the Beak looking at Harry and me. 'Are you willing to go to the hospital with Maggot tomorrow?'

'Yes, Miss Plenderleith,' we replied in unison.

'Good,' she said, and left the room.

'I'd better go and make it up with Weevil,' said Maggot. 'The Beak's absolutely topping, isn't she?'

'Yes. D'you want us to come with you to see Weevil?' I asked.

'Would you?' said Maggot. 'We *must* tell her no more larks in lessons.'

*

After high tea, we met up with Maggot in Scottie's room. Goody came along too, and we spent some of the time chatting about the afternoon's visit. Miss Plenderleith had already been to Scottie and related the conversation we'd had in our form-room after prep. She was delighted we had decided to give up our free time on Saturday afternoon, and said she would trust us to go on our own if we wanted to.

'Miss Plenderleith told me she was very touched when she overheard you saying you would give your sweets ration to the boy in hospital, Maggot,' said Scottie. 'She admits she was all wrong about you.'

'I hope I can live up to all this saintliness,' said Maggot, grimacing.

'I am sure you can. I'd better ring Dru in the morning,' said Scottie, 'just to warn her to expect another invasion.'

'Scottie?' said Harry, 'Puddles and Rob Roy said they'd like to come too.'

'And Jen-Pen,' said Goody.

'Let me see,' said Scottie, 'that would be seven of you. I don't suppose you'll manage to wreak havoc in the hospital with only seven of you! Alex, go and see if those three can spare us ten minutes, will you?'

'Okay, Scottie, I'll be back in half a tick.'

Puddles and Rob Roy were in the JCR playing snakes and ladders with some of the babies. Jen-Pen couldn't come because she was just going into second Prep.

It didn't take long to decide what to do, and we agreed that we'd meet outside the Beak's study at five to two next afternoon.

*

There was another long air-raid that night. It was the longest I had experienced, starting just before ten o'clock. It was after four o'clock in the morning when we were finally tucked up in our beds again.

CHAPTER TWENTY

Wet Start to the Weekend

It was raining cats and dogs, again, on Saturday morning, so our lacrosse practice was cancelled. Instead, Bendy Wendy decided to give us some indoor netball coaching. The Bombardier was prevailed upon to rig up a spare set of goal posts in the gym, so we could have a practice game of sorts, even though the court was a bit small. Because the weather was so terrible, only two of the day-girls who usually came to play lacrosse on Saturday turned up; Peggy Frost and Judy White, both of them sports mad. Judy was still mourning her father, but she said she felt much happier when she was at school where the activities took her mind off sad things, and she was able to relax and enjoy herself.

Although netball was not an official sport at Seabourne, Bendy Wendy was rather keen to get it going, as she had been netball captain at The Convent School of Saints Helena and Cathleen, and still played for the old girls' team, known very unofficially, and rather irreverently, as *The Hell-Cats!* First of all, she explained the basic rules to us. Her enthusiasm for the game quickly rubbed off on us and soon we were bounding round the gym, passing the ball from one to the other, making high leaping catches and shooting at goal. After a bit of practice, Bren-Gun and Jacko each picked a team so we could try playing properly. Harry and I were in Bren's team, playing Goal Attack and Wing Attack respectively. Also in our team were Nicky as Goal Shooter, Bren as Centre, Judy as Wing Defence, Paddy as Goal Defence and Maggot as Goal Keeper. What we found most difficult to start with was keeping to our particular playing areas. The game ended in a draw. Lunch was steak and kidney pie, with not a lot of steak and even less kidney, but there were lots of carrots and potatoes to mash up in the gravy. The pudding was really nice, Bakewell tart and custard.

*

We got to the hospital by a quarter to three. The rain had eased to a fine drizzle, but everything dripped fine droplets on us. On the way, we stopped at Fishermans Walk to buy our sweets ration from Mr Pitcher, then caught the next bus to Ashley Road. When we were inside the hospital, The-Ogress-in-the-Dark-Green-Dress must have got used to us, because she actually smiled welcomingly this time.

'How nice to see you again, girls,' said The Ogress. 'Matron's told me how much you are cheering up our patients. Go straight upstairs, my dears, Sister's expecting you.'

'I bet old Droopy Drawers told her to be nice to us,' Harry whispered in my ear as we began to climb the stairs. We reached the first floor, and as we went along the corridor towards the ward, Matron rushed out of one of the other wards and nearly knocked us over.

'I'm so *sorry*, my dears,' she said. 'I'm a naughty gel who should look where she's going. It would never do for me to squash one of you, because I haven't got a spare bed to put you in!' She laughed at her own joke and Maggot giggled, which pleased Matron tremendously, giving her a happy smile. 'I'll be along to see you all later on.' And with that she rushed off down the corridor as if the devil was on her tail.

Sister Tranter welcomed us with a beaming smile. We introduced her to Jen-Pen, Puddles, Nicky and Rob Roy, then spread ourselves among the patients. Harry went to see Caroline, and was surprised to find her bed empty. A couple of minutes later the door opened and Caroline came in, swinging herself along between a pair of crutches, her injured leg still in the plaster with all our get-well messages on it. I went to Alex, said; 'Hiya, Boy-Alex,' and stood close to him so he could look at me with his hands.

'Hiya, Girl-Alex,' he said instantly. 'You look ever-so much nicer with your hair like that.' Scottie had suggested that I wear my hair loose for the visit, as she had heard Alex scolding me about my pigtails last time. She had found a broad ribbon that she tied over the front and under my hair at the back, like Alice in Wonderland.

'I wondered if you'd recognise me with my hair loose. I think you're jolly clever to know me just by touching my face.'

'Well, I cheated a bit,' he said, 'Because I knew it would be either you or Harry, and I can't mistake her because she looks like a boy and sounds Scotch. What colour's your hair? I meant to ask yesterday, but I forgot.'

'Sort of light brown,' I replied. 'What colour's yours?'

'Sort of reddy brown, what colour are your eyes?'

'Blue,' I told him. 'I've brought a *Just William* book to read to you.' I smiled at him, and when he touched my mouth he smiled back at me. It was such a cheerful, friendly smile, I wondered what he looked like without all the bandages.

'You've got a nice smile,' he said. 'You make me feel happy. Come and sit on the bed while you read.' He moved over to make room beside him.

'I'll just take my shoes off so I don't make your bed dirty,' As soon as I was sitting by him he put an arm around my waist.

'Just to stop you falling off,' he said. 'I thought you might be wearing a dress today, as it's Saturday, but I see you've got school uniform on again.'

'We've got to wear it when we go out on Saturdays,' I replied. 'I don't often wear dresses, I look silly in them.'

'Never!' he exclaimed. 'You'd look jolly nice. What's the book you've brought called?'

'*William the Conqueror*,' I replied, opened it at the first chapter, called *Enter the Sweep*, and began to read.

After about half an hour, Harry came to find out how we were getting along. With her came Caroline on her crutches.

'Are you two having a cuddle?' asked Caroline, seeing Alex's arm round my waist.

'No, Caroline, 'course not,' laughed Alex, 'I'm just holding on to her so she doesn't fall off the bed on to the floor.'

'You're doing jolly well with your crutches, Caroline,' I said. 'Did Harry tell you we tried netball in the gym this morning instead of getting wet playing lax?'

'Lax?' queried Alex. 'Isn't that a sort of chocolate they give you to make you do number twos!' Caroline gave a spluttering giggle.

'That's *Ex-Lax*, dumb cluck,' guffawed Harry. 'It's *lacrosse* we're talking about.'

'Talking of chocolate,' I said, 'Would you like a Smartie, Alex?'

'Can you spare one?' he said, 'You shouldn't give away your sweets ration, you know.'

'You can have a jelly-baby if you'd rather,' I told him. 'Have both, I'd like you to.' I guided his hand to the bag of jelly babies. He picked one out.

'What colour is it?' he asked.

'Green,' I replied.

'Oh *goody!* he said, and bit its head off. 'My favourite!'

'Did somebody call me?' said Goody-Two-Shoes, who was telling a fairy story to the little girl in the next bed.

'I think Alex was swearing, Goody,' replied Harry with a grin.

'You haven't met our Goody-Two-Shoes yet, have you, Alex?' I said. 'Her name's Barbara Goodbody, actually, but we call her Goody for short.'

'I say, Alex,' said Nicky, joining our group round Alex's bed. 'You look jolly comfy there.'

'Which Alex do you mean? Me or her?'

'Are you *both* called Alex?' asked Nicky.

'Boy-Alex, meet Nicky,' said Harry.

'Acksherly my name's Sarah Nickerson, but I *detest* Sarah so my chums usually call me Sally or Nicky.' She was standing on the other side of the bed, and took Alex's hand and shook it.

'Let me look at you,' said Alex, taking his arm from round me and using both hands explored Nicky's face. 'You're jolly pretty too,' he said, 'I like your hair, Nicky, I told Harry yesterday that she should let her hair grow so she won't look like a boy. Come here, Harry, I want to see how it's getting on.'

'Give it a chance, Alex, old chap,' said Harry. 'It won't have grown much since yesterday—' She went to stand beside him. His hands scanned her face.

'It's definitely an improvement,' he laughed. His hands stopped by her eyes. 'Gosh, what lovely long eyelashes you've got. I reckon you're going to grow up into a really pretty lady. We won't be able to call you Harry then! D'you have another name?'

'My middle name's Catriona,' said Harry, blushing. 'It's the Gaelic for Katharine.'

'You're a naughty boy, Alex,' I joked. 'You've made my best friend blush.'

'Good!. It proves she's a real girl. Harry, I'd like to call you Kate; I hope you don't mind,' he said. 'Do *you* have another name, Alex?'

'Frances,' I replied, adding, 'and don't you *dare* call me Fanny, it sounds like a dotty or prim old aunt! You may call me Ally, like Harry does, if you like.'

'Okay, Ally, I'd like that,' he said. 'I think I can hear the tea trolley coming; I'm starving! You don't mind if I share your name for her, do you, Kate?'

''Fcourse not,' replied Harry, as the double doors were pushed open by the tea trolley, closely followed by Matron.

*

It was a very jolly tea party with Sister and Matron as joint "mummies," and we girls acting as waitresses, passing round the sandwiches and cakes. All the patients were able to join in and Brian, the boy who had been so poorly the day before, was out of danger and had been having a long talk with Rob Roy. Maggot—who had almost patched up her differences with Weevil—had been telling George some of her more daring exploits, and he was delighted to hear the horse manure episode, as Saint Aloysius was his school's most deadly rival.

Jen-Pen had been chatting with Gwendolyn, an evacuee from London. It was rather ironical that she had been sent away from home to escape the bombing, only to have the place she had been evacuated to bombed one night.

'It musta' bin a mistyke,' she told us cheerfully, in her cockney accent. 'The village was miles from anywhere. The A.R.P. bloke finks the Jerry plyne 'ad gort lorst, and dropped 'is bombs jus' anywhere, b'fore flyin' back ter Germ'ny. Ma says I gotta gow back ter the smoke when me neck's bet'er.'

Eevie Green, the little girl who Goody had been with, was the youngest patient in the ward. Her mother was a patient too, and Matron had arranged for her to be brought down in a wheelchair to visit us during the 'tea party'. She had broken a leg and her collar bone as well, and it was the first time that she had visited Eevie, it being much easier for Eevie to visit her.

'I think it's everso kind of you little girls to give your time to come and cheer up our kiddies,' said Mrs. Green. 'Reely Christian of you, I call it. Have you had a nice time, Eevie?'

'Oh yeth, Mummy,' replied Eevie. 'She'th called Goody-Two-Thyooth, aren't you?'

'That's what my chums call me, Eevie,' said Goody.

When everything had been eaten, Matron said that we ought to be going back to school, as she had promised Scottie that we would be back in good time. She thanked us all and said it had been a great success. We went round the ward, saying goodbye to our friends and telling them we would be back soon. I left Alex till last.

'Cheerio, Alex,' I said, taking his hand to shake it. 'I hate saying goodbye, cheerio's much nicer. I'll come and see you again soon.'

'Thanks, Ally,' he said, giving my hand a squeeze. 'It's been wizard seeing you again. I hope I'll be able to see you properly, soon, not just with my hands. Come again soon, Ally. See you.'

*

When we arrived back at school, Scottie was waiting for us, anxious to hear how our visit had gone. No sooner had we hung up our hats and coats, than the banshee wailing of the siren on top of the water-tower down Tuckton Road started up. A daylight air-raid, the first I had experienced. We put our coats on again, grabbed our gas-masks and headed for the shelter. As soon as we got outside, I looked up to see if I could spot the approaching bombers. I could hear the anti-aircraft guns pounding away in the distance, and thought of our walk last Sunday when we saw them shooting at the towed target, which I had since learned was called a drogue.

Half a dozen Spitfires flew over, on their way to intercept the Jerry bombers. I knew all about Spitfires, having seen a couple of them flying, and being allowed to sit in one of them, at an air display during the last school holidays. I was about to tell Harry about it, when I remembered that she didn't know that I was from the future. I only just stopped myself in time.

It was Scottie who checked us into the shelter this time. She looked terribly funny in The Beak's tin hat. It was much too big for her, and every time she looked down to tick off a girl's name, it fell forward over her eyes and she had to push it up with the end of her pencil. By the time it was our turn to have our names ticked off, Harry and I were in fits of uncontrollable giggles.

'What are you two giggling about?' she asked, pushing the tin hat up again with her pencil. 'You're worse than the Willises!'

'I'm sorry, Scottie,' Harry chuckled. 'It's just that you look so *funny* in Miss Plenderleith's tin hat, and the way it keeps falling over your eyes, and you keep pushing it up again with your pencil. Where is Miss Plenderleith this afternoon?'

'She's away out just now,' Scottie replied. 'She went to have tea with an old school friend.'

'I can't imagine The Beak ath a thchoolgirl,' announced a voice in the queue behind us.

'And who told you you could call the headmistress that, Amanda Hardy. Her name is *Miss Plenderleith*,' said Scottie frostily. 'And why, pray, can't you imagine her as a schoolgirl?'

'I dunno, Thcottie,' replied Amanda going very red.

'I do not know, *Matron*,' said Scottie, tetchily. 'How many times have you been told not to use sloppy, guttersnipe speech?'

'I dunno, Matwon,' said the ever reddening Amanda.

'Really, Amanda! Don't you ever listen to a word I say?' Scottie said, getting ratty. 'Consider yourself lucky not to have been given a misconduct mark, my girl.'

Amanda burst into tears, but her wails were drowned by more Spitfires flying over. Harry and I were well on our way down to the shelter, not wishing to do anything that might put us in Scottie's bad books. Down in the shelter, Maggot was trying to make Weevil understand why she should try to turn over a new leaf.

'It's not going to be *fun* any more, if you're going to be a goody-goody,' complained Weevil, sullenly. 'And, you've been to visit the children in hospital *twice,* and I haven't been *once*. S'not *fair!*'

'I've had to promise I'll work hard from now on, Weevil,' Maggot told her. 'When I saw those poor children in hospital with legs, necks, and arms broken, one boy blinded by a bomb, I realised how lucky we are.' Weevil frowned. 'I was scared to go the first time,' Maggot continued. 'I thought I wouldn't be able to look at them, let alone talk to them. George's had both his legs broken, and he might still lose one. He's ever so brave, they all are, yet they don't like being told that they are. George is only nine, and talking to him, made me see how I'd been behaving like a silly baby. I gave him my sweets ration today. It made him so happy he hugged me. I wanted to hide myself away and cry. It's the first time I've ever made someone happy like that.'

'D'you think Scottie'd let *me* go too?' asked Weevil.

'Ask her. She's coming in now.'

'But I'm scared I couldn't *help* them,' said Weevil.

''Fcourse you could,' replied Maggot. 'She *could*, couldn't she, Ally? Cheer up the children in hospital, I mean.'

'Yes,' I replied. 'You'd be jolly good at it, Weevil.'

'But I wouldn't know what to *say*.'

'Just talk to them,' said Harry, 'Like you do to Maggot, or me, or Ally.'

'You'll soon find something to talk about,' I added, 'George thought your horse manure stunt was tremendous, didn't he Maggot?'

'Yes,' said Maggot, blushing. 'He'd have done a dance if he could. He goes to Holmlea, and the Saint Ali's Wash-House lot are their most deadly enemies. He said if I ever did it again, he wanted to join in!'

'Now, Maggot!' said Scottie, grinning. 'Remember what Miss Plenderleith said!'

'Oh *yes*, Scottie,' replied Maggot. 'I'll make sure there are none of their sneaky masters about before I throw a single nugget!'

'And I'll nugget you in a minute, lassie,' said Scottie, trying hard to keep her face straight.

'Scottie?' asked Weevil, timidly.

Scottie sat beside her, and put an arm round her. 'Yes, my wee Weevil,' she said. 'Have you forgiven Maggot yet? She was only cross with you for your own good, you know.'

'We-*ell*,' said Weevil, '*al*most.'

'Give her a hug and make up,' said Scottie, 'Because I've something to ask you, and I refuse to ask an evil Weevil.'

'Oh, Scottie,' said Weevil, hugging her.

'No! I want you to hug Maggot, not me, you silly wee goose.'

'I'm ever so sorry I punched you, Weevil,' said Maggot.

''Twas my *own* fault, I c'n see that now. I didn't mean to spoil your essay. Sorry, M—M—Maggot,' said Weevil, bursting into tears and flinging herself on her best friend and hugging her.

Scottie glanced at Harry and me and winked.

'I think Weevil's just taken the first step towards growing up,' Harry whispered in my ear. Scottie must have heard, because she put a finger to her lips. Maggot groped in her knickers for her hanky and wiped away Weevil's tears. They grinned happily at each other, held hands and turned to Scottie.

'What did you want to ask me, Scottie,' asked Weevil.

'Are you my own wee Weevil again?' asked Scottie.

Weevil nodded, put her arms round Scottie and grinned at her.

'Good girl. Would you like to join our team of hospital visitors?'

'Ooh, yes, *please*, Scottie,' she replied. Then she frowned; 'But I'm a bit scared I wouldn't know what to say to them.'

'I think you'll manage all right,' Scottie told her. 'Don't you think so, Ally?'

'The kids would adore to hear about some of your pranks,' I replied. 'And you're always so jolly and cheerful.'

'Except when I ruin M–M–Maggot's history prep,' said Weevil. 'I wish I could make it better. She worked so hard at it and I had to go—had to go—go and sp-spoil—' She began to cry again and buried her head in Scottie's bosom.

'Perhaps you'd like to write it out for Maggot,' Scottie suggested. 'I'm sure Mrs. Griffiths would understand if you told her why. Would you like her to write it out for you Maggot?'

''T's all right, I'll do it,' replied Maggot. 'I've forgiven her now. But you may help me if you like, Weevil.'

'Oh, Maggot! *May* I? Thank you,' said Weevil, managing a smile. 'When shall we do it?'

'How about after church tomorrow?' suggested Maggot, putting an arm round her.

'All right,' replied Weevil giving her friend a broad grin.

The all-clear sounded about ten minutes later. We trooped back into the school and waited in the common room for the high tea bell to ring.

CHAPTER TWENTY-ONE

Super Sunday—Misery Monday

On Sunday morning I awoke with giant butterflies doing a war-dance in my tummy. I had washed, and started to dress, but I could get no further than my vest and knickers before I had to sit down on my bed; I was in a blue funk. When Harry came into my cubicle she found me still sitting there, gazing vacantly at the floor.

'What's the matter, Ally?' She sat beside me and put an arm round my shoulders. 'Got the colleywobbles?'

I nodded.

'It's your big day, so it's only to be expected. You can't just sit there in your undies; you must get dressed or you'll be late for brekker. It's boiled eggs and Marmite toast today.'

'I'm scared, Harry. I don't think I can do it.'

'Yes, you *can*! And you're going to sing *brilliantly*—I *know* you are.' She picked up my blouse and held it out for me. I put one arm in, then the other, and she buttoned it up for me. 'Come on, Ally. I want to be proud of you today, all of us do.' I tied my tie. Scottie had told us to wear stockings now it was colder. I had never worn stockings before, and was not sure how to put them on. Harry passed one to me. It was mid-brown, thick cotton lisle like I had seen old ladies wearing. I pushed my foot into it and tried to pull it up like a sock. 'What're you doing, Ally? You'll ladder it if you're not careful——'

'I've never had long stockings before,' I confessed. 'I don't know what to do.'

'Let me help,' she said, and showed me how to put them on and attach them to the suspender tapes on my liberty bodice. She even put my shoes on for me. Then she dropped my tunic over my head, tightened the girdle round my waist, plaited my hair and marched me down to brekker.

'Thanks, Harry. What'd I do without you?'

'What would *I* do without *you*?' she replied. 'Don't worry, you're bound to feel nervous, aft'r'all you've not sung in a church choir before.'

I wished I could tell her that I had, but as a boy, thirty four years in the future, and it was because of that, that I might somehow give myself away like I had with the descant on the previous Sunday. At least I knew that there were no descants being sung today, and I would have a hymn book with the music in it for me to go by.

'Harry?' I said, after Grace had been said and we were sitting down. 'Harry, I'm going to ask if I can leave for church earlier than the main croc. I always like to get there early, so I can be in the right mood. Would you come with me if I asked

The Beak or Scottie?' Suddenly I realised that I had said more than I should have done, or meant to; I should never have said *always!*

''F course I will,' she replied. 'It's what best friends are for, isn't it?' She put her hand on my arm and squeezed. She appeared not to have noticed, and I felt better because I would not have to make jolly conversation with all and sundry on the walk to church. After that I was able to enjoy my egg.

I went to find Scottie as soon as I had done my dormitory chores.

'Can I leave for church early, please, Scottie?' I asked: 'And can Harry come with me, please?'

'I was going to suggest it to you,' she replied. 'How are you feeling?'

'I've got huge butterflies doing a war-dance in my tummy,' I confessed. 'Harry had to help me dress this morning. I felt I wanted to hide away or be ill so I wouldn't have to go.'

'Och, my poor wee lamb,' she said, putting an arm round me. 'It's what actors and actresses call "first-night nerves". It's only natural you should feel nervous.'

We set off a good twenty minutes before the others. The weather was fine, but there was a chilly wind. Scottie had said that we need not wear raincoats, as the weather was going to be dry and sunny, but blustery. It was certainly windy, but not as bad as it had been on the previous Sunday, but quite a bit colder.

'I'm glad Scottie made us wear our bullet-proofs,' Harry said, and seeing me frown, added; 'You know, long stockings! The wind's jolly chilly.' She had linked her arm through mine. 'How're you feeling now? Still got the colleywobbles?'

'Bit better now,' I replied. 'Scottie told me it was what actors and actresses call "first-night nerves", only in my case I s'pose it's "first-morning nerves!"' I grinned at her, and she squeezed my hand.

'That's more like my old Ally,' she said and grinned back at me.

We passed where Southbourne Grove forked right towards Fishermans Walk, and were passing the end of Arnewood Road, when somebody called my name. I looked round, and recognised Derrick Ackroyd riding his bike.

'Hiya, Derrick!,' I said. 'Do you know my best friend, Harry?'

'Yes 'fcourse,' replied Derrick, 'My little sister introduced us at your sports day last term. Your hair's grown quite a lot since then. You almost look like a girl now!'

Harry laughed, stuck out her tongue at him and tried to knock him off his bike. 'That's right, you asked me why I was wearing a dress, because you thought that having short hair and being called Harry, I was a boy!'

'Was your hair was even shorter than it is now?' I asked.

'Gosh, yes, the barber made a mistake and cut it much too short.' She giggled. ' 'Cos he actually thought that I really *was* a boy, and even called me *sonny!*'

'Serve you right!' Derrick chuckled and turned to me; 'How are you feeling, Alex?'

'Bit nervous—' I replied.

'Good, you'll sing well then,' he told me. 'Although after the way you dealt with

Kenneth Duncan on Thursday, I wouldn't have thought you were scared of anything. Did you hear about it, Harry?'

'Yes, she told me about it when she got back to school,' she replied. 'I wish I'd been there to see it. I've had a few fights myself, but I've never given anyone a nose-bleed.'

'You're not jealous, are you, Harry?' I asked, and danced away from her to avoid the playful retaliation that I was sure would come.

*

Harry came down to the vestry with me. ('*To protect you from the boys—*' she had said and then changed it; '*No! To protect the boys from you!*') Mr Grubb was there, and Peg-leg Pugh beamed when we entered. Several of the boys had arrived already, and John Spender and Alan Fraser came to welcome me. I was glad that, of Julian Quinn, there was no sign; we heard later that he had a "tiny sniffle" and his mummy would not let him out of her sight. I was surprised when Kenneth Duncan came and shook my hand.

'Alex, I want to say sorry about the other night,' he said. 'Pam, my big sister, said it served me right for attacking a girl. Where did you learn to fight like that?'

'I've got a twin brother,' I fibbed. 'He taught me. I really didn't mean to give you a nose-bleed, so I'm sorry too. No hard feelings, eh?'

'No hard feelings,' said Kenneth, grinning sheepishly, and shaking my hand again. 'The best man won!'

'Ah! There you are, Alex,' said Mr Grubb. 'Hello, Harry, are you going to join us too?' His eyes twinkled at her. 'You can help Alex robe up if you like.'

Harry found a peg labelled "Alex Muir" and hung my school hat and blazer on it. I found my robes and Harry buttoned the ruff round my neck, then held up my cassock for me to put my arms in. Lastly she dropped my surplice over my head.

'There!' she said. 'Every inch a choirboy!'

"Cept for my pigtails," I grinned sheepishly. We talked for a few minutes about this and that. Mr. Grubb had gone to the organ loft and was playing quietly while the congregation took their seats.

Derrick came to check I was all right. 'Five minutes to go,' he said. 'You'd better scram to your pew, Harry, or you'll be in trouble for being late.'

'Gosh, yes! Good luck, Ally,' she said. 'I'll keep my fingers crossed for you.' She gave my arm a squeeze, winked and went to join the others.

We assembled ready to climb the stairs to the church. The Vicar cleared his throat and said; 'Let us pray.' I shut my eyes tightly as he said, 'The Lord be with you.' We replied, 'And with thy spirit.' Then he said, 'May the Lord open our lips, that we may sing forth His praise,' and we answered '*Amen.*'

The vicar told us, 'The processional hymn is number three hundred and ninety-one.' I found it in my hymn book, and saw it was *Onward, Christian Soldiers*. We climbed the stairs and assembled ready for the procession, waiting as Mr Grubb finished his voluntary. After a brief pause while he changed the music in front of him, he played the last two lines of *Saint Gertrud*, Sir Arthur Sullivan's wonderfully stirring tune for *Onward, Christian Soldiers*. As we began to sing and process down the south aisle the butterflies in my tummy flew away and it was just as if I was back in my own time again with the choir of which I was a regular member. I walked as I had been taught, placing one foot directly in front of the other so as not to wobble. As we progressed up the aisle I glanced towards my school-mates standing in their usual pews; Harry winked at me which made me smirk and it took me all my strength not to giggle. We sang the last verse standing in the choirstalls, then the vicar said; '*The sacrifices of God are a broken spirit: a broken and a contrite heart, O God thou wilt not despise. Dearly beloved brethren, the Scripture moveth us in sundry places...*' After that we knelt for the General Confession and the vicar pronounced the Absolution. Then we said the Lord's Prayer and sang the Versicles and Responses. For all the prayers, except the Creed, for which we stood facing the altar, we shuffled forward so that our knees rested on the kneeler in front, while our bottoms perched on the front edge of the seat.

We sang the *Venite*, Psalm 81, *Exultate Deo* to the chants by Dr. Hiles and T. Kelway, the *Te Deum* and the *Benedictus*. The hymns were *Holy Father in Thy mercy, Hear our anxious prayer* (a hymn for absent friends, very appropriate for war-time), *The Church's one foundation*, and *Eternal Father strong to save*.

Peg-leg Pugh gave a stirring sermon in which he told us how important it was that we should all pull together to help defeat the Germans; how anything we could do, however small, to assist our fellow human beings would all help towards that end. The time seemed to fly by, and in no time at all we were heading back to the vestry. The vicar blessed us, then we disrobed and, looking like ordinary children again, left the church.

Outside, Miss Plenderleith, Scottie, Miss Bendall, Harry and the girls were all waiting for me. 'Well done, Alex!' said the Beak. 'You sang beautifully, didn't she Scottie?'

'Indeed she did, the wee soul,' replied Scottie, giving my shoulder a squeeze. 'She really looked the part too.'

'Well *done*, Ally,' said Harry. 'I thought you were going to giggle when I caught your eye in the procession.'

'I nearly did, you *rotter!*' I replied, aiming a kick at her behind.

'Naah—naah—na—na—naah—' she chanted, dancing out of the way. Just as we were forming our crocodile to march back to school, Julian Quinn came over. He gazed at me through adoring puppy-dog eyes and offered me an apple.

'I bwought thith for you, Alecthandwa,' he lisped. 'It'th fwom one of the apple tweeth in our garden.'

'Thank you, Julian,' I said, feeling very embarrassed. 'It's very kind of you.'

'Come along, darling,' called his mother. 'It's time to go home now. You mustn't stand around in the cold when you've got a tiny sniffle.'

'Coming, Mumthee. 'Bye-bye, Alecthandwa, 'bye-bye, Henwietta.' He waved, skipped over to her and they set off, holding hands, with him hopping and skipping happily beside her.

'When he didn't turn up to sing, I hoped I'd escaped his hero worship for today,' I told Harry, as we started back to school.

'Never mind, Ally, you got an apple out of being his crack,' said Harry. 'What he needs is to get away from his awful mother, and have his hair cut! I say, fancy Kenneth Duncan saying sorry like that. I loved the way he said the best *man* won!' She guffawed. 'He *did*, didn't *she!*'

*

As soon as we were back at school, we went to the common room to write our weekly letters to our parents. Neither Harry nor I had received a letter from our mums yet. Harry was worried that something had happened to them, but I said that if they were in France, as we suspected, it would be jolly hard to send us letters from there. We had an address in London to send ours to, and supposed they would be sent on to them somehow.

Our big news was our "contribution to the war effort," the hospital visiting— I wrote all about Alex, and how he had been blinded in one eye and possibly the other one as well. I also told her about Caroline and her mummy. Then there was the choir, and Harry of course. I didn't write about bashing-up Kenneth, because from what I could remember of what Gran had told me about my Aunt Alexandra, she was a sweet, timid little girl who could never have said boo to a goose.

Harry thought I should have written about the Kenneth episode, but I said that as the Beak probably checked our letters for bad spelling and grammar, it would be best not.

Lunch was roast mutton with carrots and roast potatoes. What meat there was, was rather fatty and the gravy watery, but there were plenty of carrots and roast potatoes which I enjoyed. The pudding was one of my favourites—jam roly-poly and custard.

We went for another walk along the cliff top with Bendy Wendy in the afternoon. It was bracing on the cliff-top, but the sun took the bite off the cold wind. Of the "errand boys" there was no sign, much to Bendy Wendy's relief, but once again we found the Home Guard doing their stuff at the bandstand.

'A'ternoon, girls,' said Mr Evans. 'Not so windy as last week, is it? You're looking pretty today, Wendy.'

'Oh, golly-gosh, Mr Evans—Thanks,' she replied, blushing and looking coyly at the ground and rocking from one foot to the other and flapping her hands, as if unsure what to do with them. 'D'you really think so?'

'I'd not say it if I didn't mean it,' he said, and turning to me; 'Did I see this young lady being a choirboy this morning? The Missus was flabbergasted, I c'n tell you.' He winked at me.

'Yes,' I said. 'I really enjoyed it.'

'Actually, I think she's a boy in disguise,' Harry told him. 'Her name's Alex, you know, and she sings just like a boy, so why shouldn't she be in the choir? We're all jolly proud of her.'

'Quite right too,' said Mr Evans. 'The Missus said she could hear you and you made quite a difference. And she's a singing teacher, so she knows what she's talking about.'

'Gosh, really?' was all I could reply. I felt myself blushing, and lowered my gaze, not so much because of Mr Evans' praise, but because Harry's remark came dangerously near the truth. Bendy Wendy said we should press on, so we said 'Cheerio,' and returned to school in good time for tea.

*

There was yet another air-raid that night, and at prayers on Monday morning, Miss Plenderleith announced that Mrs. Baxter, Caroline's mother had died of her injuries during the night.

The news of Mrs. Baxter's death shocked everybody. A lot of tears were shed that morning, particularly amongst those of us who had visited Caroline in hospital. For several days afterwards, a pall of gloom spread over the whole school, and when we next visited the hospital, we found a very subdued, weepy and forlorn Caroline. We did our best to cheer her up by telling her all about what had been going on at school, and reading stories to her, but we always sensed that tears were not very far away.

The doctors were pleased with her progress, saying that she would soon be fit enough to be released. But with no mother, and no home, for the bomb had destroyed it completely, her future had a large question mark hanging over it. Her father, a captain in the Merchant Navy, had visited her one day while his ship was loading in Southampton. Afterwards he came to see us, and thanked us for what we had done for her.

When visiting her a week or so later, we met Mrs. Logan, her Granny, who lived in Brockenhurst. She said Caroline was going to live with her but she would like to stay at school as a boarder. By that time Caroline was dashing round on crutches and her hair covered the scar where the shrapnel had so nearly embedded itself in her brain.

Scottie had a long talk with Mrs. Logan, who afterwards, called at the school to see Miss Plenderleith before catching the train back to Brockenhurst. If all went according to plan, Caroline would return to school after half term, as a boarder.

Boy-Alex was also getting better. The bandages had been taken off, and we were delighted when he said he could still see with his right eye. He was wearing a black patch over his left one, and I told him it made him look like a pirate—Harry said she thought he looked more like Lord Nelson.

CHAPTER TWENTY-TWO

Confession

During the following weeks, Harry and I stuck to one another like glue. Her hair was getting longer, and she was beginning to look pretty in a girlish way, rather than boyishly handsome. I sang in the church choir every Sunday, and at weddings on Saturdays if the choir was required, which also earned me an extra 3d. pocket money.

One grand wedding we sang for was that of a Seabourne Prep old girl, Ruth Bamber, whose youngest sister Charlotte was in the upper fifth. It was quite a "Seabourne Prep event," with Charlie, Jacko and Harry as bridesmaids. Harry was standing in for a Bamber cousin, who was stuck in another part of the country, and who was the same size as her. They wore white dresses over layers of *frou-frou* petticoats. Harry had never looked so pretty and with her longer hair was undoubtedly Henrietta Catriona that day; tomboy Harry being unable to escape through all those layers of petticoats! She admitted to feeling a bit of a sissy when she had first tried her dress on, but on the day she really enjoyed herself. It was her first time as a bridesmaid, as on both previous occasions she had been asked to be one she had refused, insisting on being a page-boy instead!

The Bambers had asked for the choir to sing Mendelssohn's motet, *Hear my Prayer* during the signing of the register. Derrick was ill, so Mr Grubb asked me to sing the treble solo because he knew I was familiar with it, having sung part of it for my voice test in class on my first Tuesday. I felt honoured to be asked and with his coaching, I think I sang okay. Afterwards, Mr. and Mrs. Bamber thanked me, and asked me to the reception. Scottie and The Beak said I could go, and asked if I minded that I was wearing my tunic instead of a party frock. I replied that I didn't mind what I was wearing and would even have gone in a grass-skirt and wellington boots if I had had nothing else!

The three-tier wedding cake looked amazing. Harry said it was as good as anything she had seen in peacetime; and that they must have saved up loads of points (ration coupons) to get it. Sadly, it turned out to be made of papier mâché, "iced" with plaster of Paris! and hired from a local baker, who used it as a window display. The real cake was tiny, and hidden in a compartment inside the "fake cake!" We didn't get any, because there was not enough to go round. 'What a swizz!' we said. 'Horrible Hitler!'

*

As day followed day, 1974 receded further and further into the distance, and I began to wonder if I might be stuck in the past for good. I withdrew into myself more and more. I knew Harry was worried about me, and one day, I think it was the 11th October, we had been at the hospital, and were due for our Friday night bath. We had gone upstairs early, as we could not face the merriment in the J.C.R. At the hospital we had seen a girl called Alison, who had terrible injuries; she had been badly burnt, lost a leg, all the fingers of one hand, and an eye. It all seemed so unfair that children, who had done nothing to harm the enemy, should be maimed and killed. Such is the terrible barbarity of all-out war.

I sat on my bed, picked up Edward Bear Esquire, and stared at the pleats of my tunic's skirt covering my knees. Harry came into my cubicle, sat beside me and took my hand. 'Ally, I'm worried about you.' She looked into my eyes. 'Something's wrong, I *know* it is. You've got something on your mind, haven't you? You're a funny girl, I don't mean funny ha-ha, but funny peculiar, not in a *bad* way, I'm not saying you're dotty or anything like that, it's just that I *know* there's something you're hiding from me, or think you can't tell me. It's like a door that let's me come in just so far and not any further. It's as if you've got a dark secret that you're a*shamed* of, or a*fraid* to tell me; like something connected with telling Scottie you were a boy. You often behave as if being a girl's new to you. I watched you in church on that first Sunday. You knew where everything was, and yet you hadn't ever been inside All Saints before. You sang just like a choirboy. You knew all the responses by heart, and all the prayers, without even a glance at the Prayer Book. And there was that amazing descant you sang.

'That first Sunday you sang in the choir; we went together, earlier than the others. You said you *always* liked to get there early so you could get in the right mood. You thought I hadn't noticed the word "*always*," didn't you?' She squeezed my hand as I nodded. 'That told me it was not the first time you'd sung in a church choir. It explained why you're so much at home in the choir; you knew what to do, as if you'd been doing it for ages. In church that morning I kept an eye on you because I was worried about you singing in the choir for the first time. But you were perfectly relaxed. I was the one with colleywobbles in her tummy.

'Also, when we dressed that morning I had to show you how to put your bullet-proofs on. Every girl must have watched her mummy putting her stockings on. And on the trolleybus the first time we went to the hospital, you were so excited about the tickets; it was as if you had never seen bus tickets before, or ridden on a trolleybus for that matter; you behaved just like the boys at St Mungo's Academy. Scottie noticed it too, and said on the bus that you were just like a wee boy.

'Then there was that first choir practice, when you bashed up Kenneth Duncan. Girls just don't *do* that sort of thing, Ally. I couldn't have done it any more than fly over the moon! Even as a tough wee tomboy in a boys' school. Ally, you're a girl, I *know* you are, a jolly nice one, and pretty too. We're best friends, you can trust me; so if there's something you're worried about, or hiding, however dreadful it might be, *please* tell me and let me help you. Best friends are s'posed to help each other. You keep drifting away, as if you were in a trance, shutting me out, and I'm afraid that one of these days you won't come back, and I'll never see you again. Och, Ally, you're the sister I never had.' She took hold of my hand in both of hers. 'Pul-*ease*, Ally?' She buried her face on my shoulder and began to weep.

'Don't cry, Harry,' I said, coming to a decision. 'You're right, there *is* something I've been keeping from you. I've been dreading this moment. I knew it would come one day, and I've been thinking for a while that I would have to tell you in time.' I took out my hanky and dried her eyes. She smiled at me and gave my hand a squeeze. 'It's so hard to explain.' I paused for a moment, then went on; 'It's so utterly unbelievable. I'm not who you think I am; I'm n—not Alexandra!' There was a huge lump in my throat, and I did not know what to say next. I began to cry, the tears running down my cheek and falling on to my skirt. Harry wiped my eyes for me. I took the bull by the horns.

'D'you remember the day we met, it was Friday the thirteenth?'

She nodded, 'How can I forget it? As you said, that was the day you arrived; the day I became a boarder; the day we met.'

'Oh, Harry, you're never going to *believe* this, it's a *nightmare,* like something out of a story-book.' I took a deep breath. 'On Thursday the twelfth, I was a happy, ordinary *boy* called Alexander Francis Muir, living in the year 1974, thirty four years in the future.'

I paused briefly to see her reaction. She was staring at me rather strangely, earnestly, probably wondering what I was going to say next. 'My Gran, Alexandra's mummy, had to go to hospital for an operation. As both my parents (when I was a boy) were dead, I lived with Gran, so we had to find somewhere for me to stay while she was away. In 1974, this building is used as a children's home. (The school closed when the Beak retired in 1964.) I went to bed in what is our sick-bay on the night of the twelfth, just before midnight. Gran had forgotten to pack my pyjamas, and the matron could only find a girl's nightdress to fit me. She made a joke about me having to pretend to be a girl that night!

'Well, I went to sleep in 1974, and when I woke up seven hours later, it was 1940. As soon as I woke, I knew something was wrong; something had happened, but didn't know what. I felt different somehow. The first real clue that I'd changed into a girl was when I discovered that the only clothes I could find were girls' ones. Then, when Scottie made me put on a pair of navy knicks, I realised that something very peculiar must have happened during the night. After Scottie left, a quick look confirmed the awful truth: *I had changed into a girl!* I was horrified and didn't know what to do! I felt horribly frightened and alone. I only realised I'd become my dad's twin sister—Alexandra Frances Muir—when I found her name tape sewn in my shirt. Edward Bear Esquire used to be hers; in my own time he has only one eye and is very moth-eaten, poor old chap. Now he's got both eyes and looks much younger.' I gave him a hug. 'Alexandra died young, and I had been named after her.'

I looked for a reaction, hoping that she might show some sign of understanding, but she just stared at me coldly, in utter disbelief. 'You don't believe me, do you?'

She shook her head. 'But, Harry, I swear on our friendship that it's true. Cross my heart! Please, don't tell a soul about this, will you, Harry, or they might put me in a loony-bin.'

'You're right, they would—' she said coldly. 'How can you expect me to believe a *single* word of it? Coming from the future? Changing from a *boy* into a *girl*? What on earth d'you take me for? Do I *look* like the sort of simpleton who'd *believe* such a fairy-tale? Who d'you think I *am*? *Dotty-Dot?* I thought you were my *friend*, Alexandra!' She turned her back on me and burst into heart-rending tears.

I stood up, tears welling inside me again. 'Harry, listen—*please!* I've not finished yet; there's much worse to come.' I turned her round to make her face me. She turned her head away, refusing to look at me and wrenched herself free.

'Go *away*, Alexandra. Go a-*WAY*—I don't want to hear any more fairy-tales! Go and tell your lies to Dotty Dot! I hate you, I *hate* you!' She rushed to her own cubicle, threw herself on her bed, buried her head in her pillow and wept. I followed her and tried to make her look at me. I was crying too.

'Harry, p—*please* listen. Pul–*ease,*' I took her hand, but she snatched it away again. '*Please,* Harry! ' I sobbed. 'Do you think I'd tell you such a story if it wasn't true? You're my best friend. You asked me to tell you. If you were in trouble I'd do anything to help you, *ANY*thing; I'd even die to save you. There's *one* more thing I *must* tell you.'

She covered her ears with her hands. 'Go a-way—You can't be my best friend any more! Go away, leave me *BE!* I don't want to hear any more lies and fairy-stories!' She howled and sobbed.

I didn't know what to do. I managed to prise one of her hands away from one ear. 'Harry, let me finish, pul–*ease*.Who's shutting whom out now—? Listen, the worst bit's to come—I'm going to die—while I'm still at school—during the war—'

She turned her head towards me staring coldly, still hostile. 'So, you're going to die—*Good!*' she snapped. Then she frowned and added—her voice showing concern; 'How d'you know you're going to die?'

Thankfully I had her attention again—

'Dad told me. He was Alexandra's twin brother, my twin as I am now.—You don't think I'm looking forward to that, do you? We used to put flowers on her grave, my grave, at All Saints, every week. Oh, Harry, *please* be my best friend still. I'm so frightened and unhappy, but with you as my friend I can face it. Without you, I'd be so lonely—I'd *want* to die. Pul-*ease* help me!' Feeling tears welling up again, I turned away, hiding my eyes. 'What if I die before I can get back to my own time? P'raps I never do get back.' Tears poured down my cheeks.

She turned to face me. She had a haunted, forlorn look now. 'Oh, Ally, I d–didn't mean I want you to d–die!' she sobbed, her eyes red and swollen; 'Of c–course I don't; I'm s–sorry I was ratty just now, but how can you expect me to *believe* a tale like that? I shouldn't have called you a liar, but you scared me and I didn't know what to do; I should've let you finish telling me, I want you to be my best friend, of course I do, but look at it from my side. If I told you that I was some sort of queer apparition from the future, what'd *you* think? Could it be some terrible dream you've had?' She sat up, swung her legs round, and patted the bed, bidding me sit beside her. She put an arm round me, and I put my head on her shoulder and cried as I had never cried before. She groped for her hanky again and wiped my eyes, then wiped her own. 'I'm sorry, Ally, but it's not the sort of thing I can believe—just like that—without any proof. P'raps if you tell me some more, and maybe I'll be able to understand better. Please?'

'Oh, Harry! I wish it *was* a dream. I thought I was dreaming when I woke up that first morning; I should never have told you, but it was all bottled up inside, and I had to tell somebody. You're the only person I trust, the only one I dared tell, hoping you'd believe me. Now I've spoilt everything and you hate me!' I buried my face in her clothes and clung to her, frantic for the friendship I had destroyed, convulsing in misery. 'Oh Ha–Har–*reee*, pul–*ease* h–help m–*mee*—' I wailed. 'I can't prove any of it—'

'Poor Ally, I don't hate you, *really*.' She wiped my wet cheeks. 'You see, suddenly you weren't my best pal Ally any more; you were some queer girl telling me she was really a boy.' She put an arm round my shoulders. We stayed like that for a couple of minutes. I wiped away my tears, and when I felt able to go on, I raised my head and looked into the eyes that, only minutes before had been so hard and hostile. Now they were full of grief and tenderness. She pulled out her her hanky again and wiped away more of my tears. 'Let's not quarrel about it. Would you like to tell me some more?'

I thought for a minute. Perhaps if I was to explain about the resistance; that might help. 'You know how I told you about the French resistance?' She nodded. 'The reason I know so much about it is because my Gran, "*Loir*", told me about it. She got captured by the Germans once, and was rescued by another brave British lady, who was working with her. That would probably be your *Maman*— but I'm not sure; you see, there were *three* ladies who went to France together, but only two of them returned to England; one of them was betrayed to the *boche* by a collaborator and was captured, tortured by the Gestapo and then put in front of a firing squad and shot.'

'What *horr*ible things happen to people. Your Granny must have survived the war, because she told you about it.' I nodded. 'But is *Maman* going to be all right?' she asked anxiously. She had taken on that haunted look again.

'I don't *know*,' I replied in anguish, gripping her hand. 'I *wish* I did, then I could tell you. If it's any help, we're going to win the war, eventually.'

'I'm still not sure I can believe you, Ally, but just suppose—' she said, looking into my eyes, '—just suppose all these things you have told me *are* true. D'you *ever* get back to your own time? D'you want to go back to your own time, and how *do* you go back?'

'That's the worst bit of all—I don't *know*.' I gave a long sigh. 'I don't even know how I *got* here, let alone how to get *back*—*if* I could get back; I'd miss you terribly, my best-ever friend, but there's not much future in store for me here, Alexandra's *got* to die, while still a schoolgirl. But the other thing that puzzles me is what has happened to the real Alexandra? Is she being a boy in my place in 1974?'

'I wonder what I'll be doing in 1974,' said Harry. 'I'll be forty-four, older than *Maman* is now, an old lady, almost! Probably with a husband and children of my own. If what you say's true—' her eyes twinkled, more like her usual self, '—and you *do* manage to get back to your own time, wouldn't it be fun to meet? I shall be your *Auntie Harry*, and I'd tell all your little schoolboy chums how I had to teach you how to put on your bullet-proofs and plait your pigtails!' She grinned for the first time since I began telling my awful tale.

'Promise you won't tell anyone what I've told you?'

'I promise I won't tell a soul—cross my heart and swear to die. I hate to think of you dying. And what happens if you go back to your own time and the real Alexandra takes your place? I might not even *like* her!'

'I've seen photos of her,' I said, 'She looks just like me. After all, she is my auntie, so I'm sure you would get on with her. Anyhow, you'd soon find another best friend.'

'I'd never find another like you,' she said; and added in a whisper. *'Alexander!'* which made me cry again.

Moments later we heard the sound of approaching footsteps. We recognised them immediately as Scottie's; she would be coming to tell us it was our bathtime. We quickly dried our eyes, but our faces were still puffed up and tear-stained.

'What's this?' she said when she saw us. *'Why* were my best girls quarrelling? I heard you. What on earth can you have been saying to each other to make you both look so unhappy?'

'It's just that we were upset about something and a wee bit tired,' said Harry, doing her best to cover the traces.

'Well, perhaps these will cheer you up,' she said, giving each of us an little packet with something hard and square in it. I opened mine. It was the photograph; the one of the two of us, standing side by side, the one she had taken for her Rogues' Gallery, in a tiny frame about three inches square.

'Thank you, Scottie,' I said, reaching up so I could kiss her cheek. 'I shall treasure it and keep it by me for ever and ever!'

'So'll I—' said Harry, kissing her other cheek.

'And now, my scallywags,' said Scottie, 'It's your bath-time. And no more squabbles, eh? I don't like it when I hear my best girls quarrelling.' She put an arm round each of us and Harry and I put our other arms round each other, then we both buried our faces in Scottie's clothes, and began to cry again.

CHAPTER TWENTY-THREE

Despatches From The Front

TWO DAYS LATER, on Sunday the thirteenth of October, I had spent a whole month in 1940. After lunch we took our usual walk along the cliff-top and were back in good time for tea, which that day was a bit special, as Gladys had made a chocolate cake. At a quarter past five we crowded round the wireless for Children's Hour to hear Princess Elizabeth making her very first broadcast; a message to the children of the Empire. She was fourteen years old, and at the end she asked her sister, Princess Margaret Rose, to say 'Good Night' with her. Princess Margaret was only ten, the same age as me, and most of the girls in our form.

It was the week before half-term, and boarders who lived within fairly easy reach of the school would be able to spend a few days at home with their parents. The rest, which included Harry and I, would be staying behind because either our homes were too far away, or our parents were involved in vital war work.

It was not a happy week for me. Although outwardly friendly in front of the other girls, Harry was still showing a degree of coolness towards me. No more did Tigger bounce on me in the mornings. No more did we wear each other's clothes. No more did we go for walks together. No more did we have those spontaneous bursts of merriment and if we were alone together she often refused to talk to me. How I wished I had never said anything, and that I could go back to 1974 and get out of her life for ever.

Each week, on Thursday evenings, she had been coming to choir practice with me, (*to protect the boys from me!*) and often joined in, for she had a good voice. I was surprised when she came with me as usual on the Thursday before half-term; I hoped against hope that she was relenting, so our friendship could return to something like normal. We both got on well with the boys, joining in their pranks and jokes. It was as if they had forgotten that we were girls, and I said so to Harry as we walked up Beresford Road to catch the bus at Fishermans Walk, afterwards.

'Even though I can't really believe your story,' she said, 'I do see that it could explain a lot of your strange behaviour. The boys like you because you behave and act so like the boy you say you are inside. I s'pose they must think you're a wild, ferocious tomboy!'

'Like you! I say, I'm jolly glad Julian's not in the choir any more; I only wish he wasn't cracked on me at school. He's always making goo-goo eyes at me in the playground, and giving me apples and sweets. If he was gazing at me across the quire, like a forlorn, love-sick puppy, I'm sure it would make me sing off key!'

'The girls in his form rag him all the time now; even soppy dates like Cynthia Douglas and Pam Vaughan, who were his best friends when he was in the remove.'

'You'll never guess!' I said, changing the subject. 'I had a letter from Mummy today. It had a London postmark, but she wrote it ages ago.'

'Don't you mean *Grandmère?*' she whispered, and touched her lips with one finger. '*Peut-être elle est à Londres?*'

'Not really,' I replied barely above a whisper. 'She *said* she's working with your *Maman* in a dingy government office in Baker Street. In my *own* time, she told me that the only way she could send letters back home from France was to ask one of the couriers who was being picked up to come back to England. They run a terrible risk; if the Jerries should catch them with letters written in English, it could betray the whole group. The letters have to be read by censors at the War Office, to make sure she doesn't give away any secrets.'

'I wish they were safe and sound in England like ordinary mothers,' she said, lowering her voice to a whisper. 'I worry so much about *Maman;* and yet I feel so terribly *proud* of her, I want to shout "*Maman* works for the French resistance" at the top of my voice. I'd like the whole world to know how proud I am of her. But careless talk, walls have ears and all that jazz. I hope she survives. I can't bear to think of her, or your Gran getting hurt.'

'They really are *jolly* brave,' I said. 'Look, here comes the 'bus.'

We got on, and sat downstairs. Everything was very dim because of the blackout. We had met the clippie several times before; her husband had been killed at Dunkirk, but her seventeen-year-old son had come back safely. She asked the driver to stop right outside the school gates for us, so we did not have so far to walk in the dark.

Each week, when we returned from choir practice, we went to see Scottie. She always had mugs of cocoa for us and we used to sit on the hearth rug in front of the fire, warming ourselves. It was the first time we had been in her room since she had given us our photos, so we looked on the table, and saw ours in the middle. She had had it enlarged to postcard size.

'Looking at your picture, are you?' said Scottie. 'And how did choir practice go? Maybe we shall be seeing Harry in the choir one of these Sundays.'

'It went fine, Scottie,' replied Harry. 'But I can't sing anything like Alex—'

'Aye, you've a bonny voice, my wee Alex,' said Scottie, giving my shoulder a squeeze. 'Come away, the pair o' you, and drink your cocoa before it gets cold.'

I sat on the hearth-rug in front of the fire, hugging my knees and enjoying the warmth of the fire on my legs. Harry settled beside me and from time to time we would have a sip of cocoa. We did not talk much, preferring to gaze into the fire, watching the patterns made by the flames dancing like will-o'-the-wisp up the chimney. Every so often we would glance at each other and grin.

We drained the last drops of cocoa from our mugs. Harry put them to one side, and sat by me again. 'I wonder what our mummies…' We began speaking together, with exactly the same words. We looked at each other, joined hands and burst into fits of giggling.

'After you, Madam,' I said, gesturing with my free hand.

'No no, *Sir*, after *you*. I insist,' replied Harry, and we had another spontaneous fit of giggling, wrestled each other and then overbalanced and lay on our backs giggling uncontrollably. When Scottie returned from putting three juniors into their baths, she looked down at us with an amused smile.

'I am glad to see you acting more like your old selves again,' she said. 'I have hardly had a smile from either of you all week. What has brought this on all of a sudden?'

'We began speaking together with exactly the same words and got the giggles,' replied Harry, sitting up and pulling down her skirt so she looked respectable again. 'We were just wondering what our mummies might be doing just now.'

'Sitting in front of a nice warm fire like you, if they've any sense,' she said.

Secretly, I thought of them planting explosives on railway tracks, cutting telephone wires, blowing up bridges, or leading shot-down British airmen to safety, like I had seen in films on television about the resistance.

'Scottie? Are we on the list for hospital tomorrow?' I asked. 'I can't remember if we're down for it or not.'

'Yes, but nobody's going on Saturday because it's half-term,' she replied. 'And there's no school on Monday or Tuesday.'

'Golly, doesn't time fly,' Harry remarked. 'We might go on Saturday anyhow, even though Boy-Alex is going home then.'

'It'll be odd visiting when he's not there; he's become a really good friend,' I said, still lying on my back with my knees bent; I could feel delicious warmth from the fire on my shins and the backs of my thighs. 'He's going to live with his Granny in Christchurch, and she wants us to go to tea one day.'

The bell rang as I was speaking. Harry jumped to her feet and held out her hands to pull me up, but I pulled first and she came down on top of me. Scottie looked on, an indulgent smile on her face as we wrestled for a few seconds.

'Come on now! Enough is as good as a feast,' she said. 'You behave more like two wee boys than girls. Now, I suggest you disentangle yourselves and go and get ready for bed. Goodness only knows what The Beak would say if she was to come in now and find you brawling on my hearth-rug.'

*

There was no air-raid that night, and I woke next morning before the rising bell. I lay warm under the blankets, and realised it was the start of my sixth week in 1940. I wondered how Gran's operation had gone, and what had been happening in 1974 during my five weeks away. Was the real Alexandra going to my school as a boy? If so, what would she make of it all and what would my mates make of her/him? It was hard enough for me going back in time; learning how to behave like a girl was my main problem, for the school work was easy; but poor Alexandra would find that life in a boys' school in the nineteen-seventies was very different to a girls' school in the forties.

I was wide awake when the bell went, and for once I was awake before Harry, so I went and bounced on her for a change. She wasn't expecting me to strip her bedclothes off her seconds after the bell, like she did to me so often. I leapt on her, pinning her down like she did to me and tickled her before she had time to react. She just looked at me and grinned.

'I'm—not—tick—lish, naah—naah—na–na—naaah!' she chanted. She squirmed an arm free and pretended to attack me. 'But—I—know—who—i–is!'

'No, Harry, stop it! Stop it! Stop tickling!' I squealed, beginning to giggle before she had even before she had touched me.

'I haven't touched you! *Yet!*' We wrestled momentarily and then went to wash. Everybody was saying how nice it was not to have had to get up in the middle of the night, and grope our way in the dark to the air-raid shelter. Everybody was talking about the half-term exeat which started, officially, as soon as morning lessons ended. Most of the boarders were going home for the weekend, but Harry and I and eight or nine others who, like us, had parents away on war duties, or whose homes were too far away, would be staying behind at school. Monday and Tuesday were holidays, but boarders had to be back in time for high tea on Tuesday. Scottie told us that The Beak had planned something special, so we would not be wandering round "like poor wee lost souls."

While we queued outside the eatery for brekker Jen-Pen told us that she would be staying behind, so would Puddles, Nicky and Rob Roy. Maggot and Paddy were going to stay with Weevil at her home near Blandford, and the Willis twins would be going home to Winchester. Amanda Hardy was going to visit her Grandmother in the New Forest. We told her to beware of the Big Bad Wolf. 'What big teeth you have, Gwand-mama!' said Harry, mimicking Amanda's silly, squeaky, lisping, little-girl voice exactly.

'All the better to eat you with, my dear!' I added in as gruff a voice as I could manage.

'You're howwid beatht-th! *All* of you,' lisped Amanda, near to tears. 'Ethpethially *you*, Henwietta Gordon and *you*, Alecthandwa Muir. I hate you! *All of you!*' and she dissolved into tears, just as the brekker bell rang and we trooped into the eatery.

'Whoever would have thought that would make her turn on the waterworks,' said Harry, when we had sat down after Grace. 'She's thirteen, you know, yet she acts more like a baby in the kindergarten. At her age she should be in the lower fifth at least, and yet she's only in the fourth.'

'Look,' I said, 'She's going out, I wonder why?'

'She'll be going to the lav.,' said Jen-Pen, 'With Amanda it's always a case of waterworks at both ends! She always has to "go" when she's upset! When she first came, she was always wetting her pants, and her bed; even last term.'

After brekker, while many of the girls were packing their overnight bags, Scottie came looking for Harry and me. She was looking worried, not her usual cheerful self. Harry and I glanced at each other.

'Please would you go and see The Beak before prayers,' said Scottie, and seeing us frown added; 'Don't worry, you're not in hot water. It's just that there's something she has to give out at prayers, and she thinks both of you ought to know first.'

'Okay, Scottie,' I replied. 'We'll go as soon as we've done our chores.' I had a sudden feeling that was foreboding bad news.

'No sooner said than done,' said Harry.

*

'Come away in,' called Miss Plenderleith in answer to our knock. Harry opened the door and we went in. 'Come away in, my dears, it's good of you to come so quickly. Please sit down.' She looked tired and drawn, and I realised that my premonition must have been true. I knew it couldn't be Gran, because she survived the war, but suppose it was Harry's *Maman?* We looked anxiously at each other and held hands as we sat close to each other on the sofa.

'I wanted to tell you this before I announce it to the rest of the school at morning prayers,' she said quietly. I could tell she was upset. 'First, I have letters for you both from your mothers. They came inside a letter for me this morning. You will want to read them as soon as you can. What I am about to tell you must go no further than these four walls. I know you're both sensible girls, and I can rely on your discretion, so that is why I've decided to tell you now.'

'It's about our mums being in France—with the resistance—isn't it?' I said.

'You guessed,' she said. 'When I heard that you often listen to the messages on the BBC foreign broadcasts, I thought you might have put two and two together. Yes, they *are* working for the resistance in the boche-occupied zone. They're doing very brave work, vital to the war effort.

'They parachuted into France one night, a matter of days after you both started boarding here. Three brave women dropped into France that night; three good friends who had been schoolgirls together in Limoges over twenty years ago. Two of them were your mummies; the third member of the team was Yvette Foster, my dear, dear friend from my teaching days in France.' She pulled a hanky from her sleeve and dabbed her eyes. I knew what was coming next, and looked at Harry. She turned to me with a look of anguish, the colour draining from her cheeks. I knew she was thinking about what I told her a week ago, and she too had guessed what The Beak was going to say.

'Yvette was betrayed to the boche by collaborators and taken prisoner after leading a party of our shot-down airmen to safety. After interrogation by the Gestapo, she was shot by a firing squad.'

'Oh no! *no! NO!*' wailed Harry, bursting into tears. '*Pauvre Tante Yvette! Comme c'est affreux! Maman sera desolée!* They were such close friends. She often came to stay with us up in Scotland.'

'*Oui, ma petite*, Annie-Collette had known her much longer than I,' said Miss Plenderleith, 'And Marie-Françoise too, Alex. I don't know if you were told, but the reason you're both here, is because we were all such close friends, and your mothers thought you would be well looked after here. I would've liked to have volunteered also, but I am older, and one of us had to stay behind.'

I put my arms round her. 'Poor Miss Plenderleith, I'm ever so sorry. Is there anything we can do?' Harry wiped her eyes, pushed her hanky away under her tunic and threw her arms round The Beak also. Miss Plenderleith put her hands on our heads and then hugged us close to her.

'What you're doing now is wonderful, my dearest girls. We all have to endure pain and sadness, particularly in wartime. Now, I know you'll want to read your letters, so let's dry our eyes and put on a stiff upper lip, or everyone will think we are a trio of silly sausages!' We looked up at her and saw she was smiling. She hugged us again and we smiled back. 'I grieve that I have lost such a dear, dear friend, but I am so very, very thankful that it was not one of your dear, brave mothers.'

'I think *you're* brave too, Miss Plenderleith,' I said.

'So do I,' said Harry.

'There *is* something you could do for me, Alex,' said The Beak. 'As a very special favour to me.'

'I'll do anything I can.'

'Please, would you sing the twenty-third Psalm, *The Lord's my Shepherd*, to the tune *Crimond*, for us during prayers. I know you never met *Tante Yvette*, but you would have loved her just as much as Harry and I do.'

'Of course I will,' I replied. 'Is there anything else?'

'Yes, one more thing my dears,' she replied. 'When it's just us and Scottie together, as your dear mothers and I are such old, old friends, I feel more like an aunt to you than a headmistress, so I would like you to call me Auntie Vera?'

'Yes, Miss Plenderleith,' I said. Harry gave me a dig in the ribs with her elbow and we both said; 'We mean—Auntie Vera—Miss Plenderleith.'

'You're as good as a tonic.' She managed a wan smile. 'I love you both. Now, off you go and read your letters, and don't you *dare* be late for prayers!' She winked at us.

'*Oui, ma Tante Plenderleith*,' we chorused, and curtsied.

'Away you go, you *awful* little girls,' she said giving us each a friendly pat on our bottoms to propel us towards the door.

Harry wanted a dry hanky, so we went upstairs. Once inside her cubicle, she took my hands in hers and looked me straight in the eye. I had never seen her looking so miserable. 'Och, Ally, can you *ever* forgive me for being so *horrible* to you last Friday? I didn't believe you and accused you of lying. Even though we sort of made friends again, I've still th–thought hateful things about you. Oh, Ally— I'm s–so s–sorry. I'm not worthy to be your b–best f–f–friend any more!' She began to cry again. 'I wanted s–so much to believe you, but I c–couldn't, t-till now. I'm glad you t–told me then, because this *awful* news of *Tante Yvette* proves what you told me is the Gospel truth. Poor you! It must've been *terrible* for you that first morning, when you discovered you'd changed into a girl. When I was at St. Mungo's I longed to be a boy more than anything else; I used to envy my chums so much. But I'd have died of fright if I'd woken up one morning and discovered I'd grown something during the night. Oh, Ally, can you *ever* forgive me? Please, Ally?'

Tears poured down her cheeks. I groped for my hanky and wiped her tears then I put my arms round her so she could cry on my shoulder. 'Don't cry. You *know* I forgive you. I can understand how you must've felt; if you'd told me something like that, *I* wouldn't have believed *you*. You know, when I woke that first morning, I thought it was a horrid, spiteful prank someone was playing on me. It was only when I discovered that I really had changed into a girl, and saw all the other girls, that I finally accepted that something very queer had happened to me and I was very scared. Then I met you, and you made me feel better. I don't know what I'd have done without you!'

'When I saw Auntie Vera looking so unhappy, I thought she was going to say that *Maman* had died. I'm terribly sad about *Tante Yvette*—but I am so *relieved* it wasn't *Maman*. You see—all week—ever since that horrid evening when you—I—we er—' She paused, searching for the right word. I suggested, 'quarrelled?' She looked at me gratefully. 'Yes—well—ever since—then—I've been thinking that *Maman* was going to die—and I would never see her again—and was blaming you—Och, Ally, I'm so *ashamed* of myself! Please forgive me and say we're still best friends; Pul-*ease*, Ally?'

'Of *course* I forgive you, and of course I still want you to be my best friend. I had the same horrid thought, you see, I just didn't *know* if your *Maman* survived; but now we know both our Mums are safe and we shall both see them again!' We threw our arms around each other and bear-hugged each other with all our might.

'Oh, Ally, I'm so glad we're proper best friends again.'

'So'm I,' I replied, giving her an extra hard squeeze.

We never heard Scottie come in, so we were startled when she spoke. 'I thought I'd find you here.' She put her arms round both of us. 'Isn't it *dreadful* news. Your mothers will grieve so much. But we must all be brave, because that's what Yvette would have wished. I'm glad to hear that you're proper best friends again. I hated seeing my best girls squabbling and being so unhappy. Now dry those eyes, wash your faces and come downstairs; the bell will soon be going for prayers.'

'And I've got to sing a solo—and mustn't look all red-eyed and weepy.'

We linked arms, delighted to be proper best friends again, and headed for the bathroom. Much later that day, we wondered just how much Scottie knew about our unhappy quarrel.

CHAPTER TWENTY-FOUR

Half-term Begins

A STUNNED GASP OF HORROR arose at prayers as Auntie Vera broke the news of Yvette Foster's execution at the hands of the Gestapo. It was a great shock to staff and pupils alike, since we had been told she was helping an elderly relative. It never occurred to anyone that the elderly relation was *La Belle France* in her darkest hour.

Many of the girls burst into tears, and I realised that this brave lady had been a much-loved member of the school family. I was sad that I had never had the pleasure of knowing, or of having been taught by her. Harry, who knew her better than anyone present, save Auntie Vera, was dabbing her eyes again, so I linked my arm through hers and gave her hand a squeeze. She turned and smiled, and laid her head upon my shoulder.

Auntie Vera held up her hand, and the hubbub died down. 'The first time I met Yvette was when we were teaching at Lycée Mont Choisis in Limoges. In those days she was still Yvette Bonchoses, for she did not meet Gregory Foster until she came to England for a camping holiday with me in the Lake District. Greg, a captain in the Merchant Navy, pitched his tent next to ours by Coniston Water. He had the use of a sailing dinghy belonging to a friend of his. He took us sailing one day and instantly fell in love with our dear Yvette. I had just founded this school at premises in Seabourne Road, and was delighted when she agreed to come and join me to teach French.

'While we were at the Lycée, as we tramped and camped all over France together, she added to her tremendous knowledge of the highways and by-ways of many regions of France. It was this knowledge that made her the ideal choice to set up an escape line for British airmen who had been shot down over occupied France. I don't know how many of you listen the "personal messages" on the wireless, but those who do, may have heard mention of *La Maîtresse*. I believe that to have been Yvette Foster's code name.

'As far as French lessons this term are concerned, I am afraid you'll have to continue putting up with your crotchety old Beak for the time being, until I can find a new French mistress.' She looked round at all our grave faces and gave a wan smile. 'I am a poor substitute for Yvette, I'm afraid, but the life and work of the school must go on, sadly without dear Yvette who was such a pillar of strength to us all. She was, first and foremost a great patriot; who willingly answered the call of her beloved France, and gave her life for her; so that one day her citizens shall be free of the Nazi tyranny that bears down upon them at this terrible time. *Vive* la France! Vive Yvette!'

'*Vive Yvette!*' replied the assembled pupils and staff.

'In a moment or two, I shall ask you to stand for one minute's silence, then we shall kneel and pray for the soul of Yvette, and all those brave men and women who have fallen in this conflict. Remember also our loved ones in the armed services, and especially those brave men and women who are working for the resistance in France and other occupied countries—working to cripple and disrupt Hitler's relentless war machine. And should the Nazis ever invade *our* shores, I know that every truly patriotic Briton, be they woman, man, girl or boy, will rally to the cause and obstruct the Nazi invaders at *every* turn. You may have heard Mr Churchill's memorable words on the wireless after the miracle of Dunkirk in May. "*We shall defend our Island, whatever the cost may be. We shall fight on the beaches, we shall fight on the landing grounds, we shall fight in the fields and in the streets; we shall fight in the hills. We shall never surrender.*" Girls! Let those be *our* watchwords also! *We shall never surrender!*

'Certainly, we are fortunate indeed that the narrow strip of water we call the English Channel, has proved to be such an obstacle to the invader ever since our beaches were last violated by one William of Normandy, nearly nine centuries ago in 1066. We can only hope and pray that it remains so.'

'Hear! hear!' said Harry, and then the whole assembly, pupils as well as mistresses, echoed to the sound of 'Hear! hear!'

'And now,' said Auntie Vera, 'Will you please stand in silence for one minute, in honour of our dear Yvette.' We stood silently, most of us with our eyes tightly shut. Then Auntie Vera said; '*Let us pray,*' and we all knelt down. '*O Lord hear our prayer.*'

'*And let our cry come unto Thee,*' We responded from habit.

'*Our Father,*' Auntie Vera began, and we all joined in. There were several more prayers, after which Auntie Vera said; 'You may sit down, girls. Before prayers today I asked our very own *choirboy*, Alex Muir,' she paused, smiling in my direction, waiting for the ripple of laughter to die down; 'Our very own church chorister, Alex Muir, if she would sing *The Lord's my Shepherd*, the twenty-third psalm, to that fine old tune *Crimond*, a setting of which Yvette was particularly fond. She agreed readily, for Yvette was a close friend, not only of us here, but also of the mothers of both Alex and Harry. Alex, my dear, would you please come to the front so everyone can see you.'

I stood up and went to stand beside Auntie Vera. 'Do you need a copy of the words?' she asked.

'No, thank you, Miss Plenderleith,' I replied, 'I know it by heart.'

'Are you ready, Alex?' asked Mr Grubb, seated at the piano. 'Would you like me to accompany you, or would you prefer to sing unaccompanied?'

'Unaccompanied, if I may, please, Sir.' It was the first time I had sung in front of the whole school. I felt my tummy churn, but as soon as he gave me the note,

the tension left me, I took a deep breath, and sang;
> 'The Lord's my shepherd, I'll not want,
> He makes me down to lie
> In pastures green; he leadeth me
> The quiet waters by—'

When I had finished singing the last verse there was a deathly silence until Auntie Vera started to clap. That was taken as a signal for everybody. In church nobody would applaud, but I supposed it was different at school. I turned to my new "auntie" and saw tears rolling down her cheeks.

She stood up, put a hand on my shoulder, and held up the other to stop the applause; 'Thank you, Alex. That was beautiful.' ('Hear! Hear!' said Harry.) 'A fitting tribute to our dear, brave Yvette. Ally, my dear, we are very proud of the way you have so successfully invaded that male bastion, the church choir.' ('Hear! Hear!' said Harry.) 'You may return to your place now, thank you so very much, my dear, dear girl.' She gave my shoulder a squeeze and smiled so kindly, it brought a lump to my throat.

As I returned to my place, several of the girls clapped me on the back. Harry was smiling like a proud mother. 'Well done, Alexander, my *boy!*' she whispered in my ear, and put an arm round my waist and squeezed me so tightly to her that I could hardly breathe.

'That's all for prayers this morning,' said Auntie Vera. 'A little longer than usual, and you will be distressed to hear the terrible news that first period will be fifteen minutes shorter this morning.' She smiled and held up her hand. 'Please don't all cheer at once! I am sorry that this has been such an unhappy start to the half-term weekend. However, I will, as usual, say; "Have a lovely time, girls, forget all about school for four days, and come back refreshed and invigorated for the second half of the term up to Christmas." Quiet now please.' She paused. '*The Grace of Our Lord Jesus Christ and the love of God and the fellowship of the Holy Ghost be with us all evermore. Amen.*'

'*Amen,*' echoed the assembly. The staff left and we followed, form by form.

Back in our form-room I was surrounded by "fans," and had to be protected by Harry, Rob Roy and Nicky. I felt embarrassed by all this admiration, and was glad when Miss Spurgeon came in and we had to go to our desks.

She smiled at me and said; 'At the risk of adding to your blushes, Ally, I would like to say how splendidly you sang this morning. I'm sure that our dear Yvette, listening on the other side, was also moved to tears as I and so many of us were. Thank you, my dear.' I felt myself blushing again and Harry gave my hand a squeeze. 'Now, I think it's another morning for a Pooh story instead of boring old dictation, don't you? Alex, you've given all of us the pleasure of hearing you sing, would you like to choose the Pooh story for this morning?'

'Yes pul-*ease,* Miss Spurgeon.' I thought for a moment, and then said, 'I'd like Tigger coming to the forest and having breakfast, please, Miss Spurgeon.'

'D'you have a special reason for that particular one?'
'Yes,' I replied. ''Cos Harry bounces on me like Tigger as soon as the getting-up bell rings in the morning, don't you, Tigger?' This brought a ripple of giggles, particularly from the day-girls.

'Worraworraworraworraworra!' replied Harry, sticking out the tip of her tongue at me. 'She tiggered me this morning, didn't you, Ally?'

'What me?' I said, trying to look innocent. 'Oh, Tigger! How *ever* could you suggest such a thing?'

'Harry coming to the forest it shall be then,' said our form-mistress. 'Don't pick your nose, Dotty, dear! *Nice* little girls don't do that sort of thing.' She found the page and began to read; '*Winnie-the-Pooh woke up suddenly—*' and once more we relaxed as we listened to the story. It helped to ease the sadness that we all felt.

*

It was algebra next. Since Maggot and Weevil had turned over a new leaf, Polly's lessons had been a lot less fraught, and, may I add, not *nearly* as much fun. Not once had she cause to wield her gym-shoe after sending Maggot to Auntie Vera all those weeks ago; the only discords in maths came when poor Dotty Dot was being dimmer than usual. Pretty Polly rarely picked on her these days, as it was clear that algebra was quite beyond our Dotty.

At the start of algebra, Pretty Polly came and told me how angelically I had sung, blaa-blaa-blaa! For a terrible moment I thought she was going to kiss me, with all her fangs protruding! I was spared that. Thank goodness! When, afterwards, I told Harry of my fears, she said it would've been like being kissed by a vampire, as she would surely have gone for my jugular vein!

After break we had gym with Bendy Wendy, and our last lesson until Wednesday was history. Mrs. Griffiths said that instead of learning ancient history, for a change we might prefer to hear about the causes of the war that was affecting all our lives so much.

When the bell rang for the end of lessons, the day-girls, and boarders who were going home for the exeat, almost threw their books into their desks and left the form-room hot on the heels of Mrs. Griffiths, who wished us all a happy half-term.

*

Five minutes later, there was not a day-bug to be seen. For the boarders who were going home by train, there was a coach, or *charabanc*, as many people called them in 1940, to take them to the station. Whilst the nearest station was Pokesdown, it was mostly slow, local trains that stopped there; so the coach was to take them to Bournemouth Central. At twenty to one, a pale yellow Bournemouth Corporation Transport Bedford utility coach with uncomfortable slatted wooden seats, drew into the playground. As soon as it had stopped and the door opened, there was a stampede of girls rushing to get aboard.

'Bagth I the fwont theat,' lisped Amanda Hardy, trying to push her way through the scrum.

'Hard cheese, Amanda Hardy,' said Maggot, 'I baggyed it first, so go away! Come on, Weevil—and you, Paddy—there's room for all three of us!'

The coach was due to leave at ten to one. Girls were rushing hither and thither, looking for things they thought they had lost or forgotten, and trying to remember where they had put their overnight bags. Auntie Vera was ticking names on lists, giving out tickets and journey money, as well as checking that everybody was looking neat and tidy. Meanwhile Scottie was checking everybody had packed hankies, nightgowns and clean underthings in their overnight cases, and Bendy and Jacko were making sure that they all had their gas masks.

As we were staying behind, Nicky, Rob Roy, Puddles, Harry and I were watching the proceedings with some amusement, from the comfort of the garden seat at one side of the playground.

At eleven minutes to one, Miss Bendall boarded the coach and counted heads. Then she got off again, looking flustered. 'There's one missing,' she said. 'Are you sure you checked them all aboard Miss Plenderleith?'

'Yes. Take the list and call the roll again; that's the only way to discover which little lamb has gone astray.'

Miss Bendall boarded the coach again, called the roll, and got off once more. 'It's Amanda *Hardy*, Miss Plenderleith. She was there about three minutes ago but she had to dash indoors.'

'Not her, again!' exploded the Headmistress. 'She'll be late for her own funeral! Go and dig her out, Miss Bendall, or the charabanc will have to leave without her and she'll have to stay *here* over half-term; *not* a prospect I relish!'

'Righty-ho,' said the games mistress, and she strode in the front door, just as the hapless Amanda was coming out.

'And where do you think you have been, young lady?' demanded Auntie Vera with a face like thunder.

'If you pleathe, Mith Plenderleith—' lisped the unfortunate Amanda, 'I had to go and be ecthcuthed.'

'It's time you learnt to control your bladder, Amanda Hardy,' said Auntie Vera. 'I think that for the second half of the term I shall make you wear nappies. Then at least, you won't be forever running off to "be excused" as you call it.' A roar of laughter came from inside the coach. 'Now get on the charabanc this instant, before I decide to keep you here over half-term.'

'I c-can't help it,' wailed Amanda. 'You can't make me wear nappieth—'

'My dear child, I can make you wear anything I wish,' said the Beak stonily. 'If I say you will wear nappies, young woman, you will wear nappies. Is that understood?'

'Yeth, Mith Plenderleith,' said Amanda, blushing deep crimson. 'It'th not fair!' There was a roar of laughter from inside the coach.

Bendy Wendy pushed Amanda on to the coach, got on behind her and closed the door. The driver started the engine and drove down the drive and out of sight.

HALF-TERM BEGINS

Auntie Vera and Scottie came and sat with us. 'That Hardy child'll be the death of me one day,' sighed Auntie Vera.

'Me too,' said Scottie, with a glint in her eye. 'And if you expect me to change her nappies, Vera, you've got another think coming. But, I must say her face was a picture when you suggested it.' She smiled, and we all collapsed into helpless laughter.

*

At lunch, we were just ten girls, Scottie and Auntie Vera. We all sat at the top table, Auntie Vera at one end, with Jacko on her right and Jen-Pen on her left. Scottie, at the other end, had Harry on her right and me on her left. Between Harry and Jen-Pen were Nicky, Rob Roy and Puddles, and between Jacko and me sat Goody with two of her little ones, Greta and Susie.

Auntie Vera beamed at us. 'Well, my dears,' she said, 'peace and quiet at last. You're my family, and we're going to have such fun together. After lunch, I suggest you all go and change out of your tunics. Let me see,' she paused, 'Harry, would you please say Grace?'

We all stood still while Harry recited;
>'O Lord, when hunger pinches sore.
>Do thou stand us in stead,
>And send us from thy bounteous store
>A tup- or wether-head! Amen.'

'*Amen*,' we echoed, and sat down.

'Is that Burns?' said Scottie. 'I seem to remember hearing it once before, at a Burns Supper in—Dumfries, I think.'

'Yes,' Harry replied. 'It's the Grace he wrote for the Globe Tavern there. It makes a change from *Some hae meat—*'

'It's a new one to me,' said Auntie Vera. 'Did you learn it at Saint Mungo's Academy, Harry?'

'Yes. The English master was a Burns fanatic,' she answered. 'He could recite the *Tale of Tam o' Shanter* from beginning to end, by heart. It's two hundred and twenty lines long, you know. I've never been able get beyond the first twelve without having to look at the words.'

'It's a wonderful poem though,' said Auntie Vera. 'I'd like you to recite it to the school one day, Harry. Perhaps you could do it at the end of term concert. Ah, here's Gladys with the soup. What have you managed to find for us today, Gladys?'

'Tomater—seein' as 'ow it's 'arf term,' replied Gladys. 'An' arter that, plaice an' chips. I 'ad ter plead h'on me bended knees ter the man at MacFisheries up Sarfbourne Grove, ter get enough fer all of us.'

'You'll come and eat with us, won't you, Gladys?' said Auntie Vera, 'And we'll all help with the washing up afterwards, won't we, girls. It's half-term after all, and many hands make light work.'

'An' too many cooks spoils the broff an' all,' said Gladys, as she ladled tomato soup into bowls and we passed them round. 'It's not that I ain't grateful fer the offer, but plates is 'ard ter get 'old of these days, wot wiv the war an' all, an' I'd 'ate fer any ter get broke. Perky an' me, we got use to it. Done in a jiffy so it is. Right now, 'as h'everyone got soup?'

'Yes thank you, Gladys,' we replied in unison.

'Well!' said Scottie, 'This makes a nice change, I must say.'

'It's absolutely spiffing soup,' said Harry. 'It's a real treat; tomato's my absolute favourite!'

I thought about my own time; how we took for granted things like tomato soup; and plaice and chips; Gran always kept plaice and chips in the freezer. Perhaps they did not have freezers in 1940?

'It's *brill!*' I agreed. Harry caught my eye from across the table and winked. She must have realised that I had used a 1974 expression. My weeks in 1940 made me realise just how lucky we were in 1974 to live in a time of plenty.

The plaice and chips, to use Harry's words, was 'absolutely gollumptious!' Gladys had managed to get tinned peas instead of the dried ones that had to be soaked overnight. What is more, we each got a whole fillet of plaice with breadcrumbs, instead of the miserable scrap of nondescript fish, battered in more senses than one! For afters Gladys excelled herself again; jam roly-poly with real strawberry jam, and custard. *And* there were seconds, so there were benefits if you had to stay at school over half term. When we had finished, Harry was called to say Grace again.

> 'O Lord, since we have feasted thus,
> Which we so little merit,
> Let Meg now take away the flesh,
> And Jock bring in the spirit. Amen.'

After we had taken our dirty plates and cutlery to the scullery, we rushed upstairs to change out of school uniform for our half-term visit to the hospital.

CHAPTER TWENTY-FIVE

Patients' Progress

HARRY AND I WERE SITTING on her bed, trying to decide what to wear for our trip to the hospital. I thought about Nick and Jackie in 1974, and how they had told me that they, and most of the other girls at their school, wore jeans in their spare time. How I wished I had some jeans with me.

'Harry? D'you ever wear jeans?'

'Wear Jean's what?' she replied. 'I don't think I know anyone called Jean——'

'No-no, you *clot!* They don't belong to anyone called Jean, they're *called* jeans.'

'What're called jeans, Ally? Sorry, I don't understand.'

'Jeans are long trousers made of blue cloth,' I tried hard to explain. 'I think they were invented in America for cowboys.'

'Why would I want to wear cowboy trousers?' she asked. 'I can see why a boy might want to wear them, but why should a girl?'

I looked round to make sure there was nobody who could overhear. 'In my own time,' I whispered, '*Every*body wears them. My cousins, Nick and Jackie, my Auntie Kate's daughters, who I sail with in Christchurch harbour, always wear them at the weekend and in the hols. Most children do, girls as well as boys. Nick and Jackie are at boarding school, and wear them there when they don't have to wear uniform. At some schools, girls are even allowed to wear jeans to lessons.'

'Coo-oo!' exclaimed Harry. 'Fancy not having to wear skirts to school. So what shall we wear now, then? D'you want to borrow my kilt?' We heard footsteps approaching. 'Here's Scottie, let's ask her what she thinks.'

'Let's ask Scottie what she thinks about what?' said Scottie.

'We were wondering what to wear to visit Boy-Alex,' I said. 'He's going home to his grandma's in Christchurch tomorrow.'

'I think he'd like to see you wearing pretty dresses,' Scottie replied. 'You've got that nice warm navy-blue velvet one, Alex, and you've the one made of Black Watch tartan, Harry.'

'I don't like that one very much,' said Harry, 'I wouldn't mind so much if it was my own, Gordon tartan. Would you like to borrow it, Ally? Or my kilt? May I borrow your velvet frock again? I do so like wearing it.'

' 'F course you may, if I may borrow your kilt,' I replied. 'I *do* like wearing that, 'n may I wear my hair loose, please, Scottie?'

'Certainly you may,' replied Scottie. 'Would you like me to brush it for you? I've some tartan ribbon to make a bandeau to keep it out of your eyes. It'll go perfectly with Harry's kilt. Get changed as quickly as you can. We're all going except Goody and her bairns; Greta and Susie are a bit young yet. It might upset them to see how badly some of the children are hurt; so Goody's taking them for a walk down to Tuckton Bridge to see the ducks at Newlyn and Ball's Tea Gardens.'

'Is Auntie Vera coming?' asked Harry.

'Not today, she's busy planning something extra-special for us all tomorrow,' replied Scottie.

'Tell us what it's going to be, Scottie?' I asked. 'Pul–*ease?*'

'I honestly don't know,' she replied, 'And even if I did, I would not be telling you. It's Auntie Vera's secret. I shall be back to see to your hair in five minutes, Ally. We're all meeting under the clock in the hall in about fifteen minutes time.'

*

When we got to the hospital, The Ogress was really-really pleased to see us. 'D'you remember how she used to look at us those first few times we came?' Harry asked, as we climbed the stairs.

'Yes, and we thought she was the horriblest lady we'd ever met. She's quite nice really, isn't she, Scottie?'

'It just shows that you should never judge a person by your first impression,' replied Scottie.

We left our raincoats in the usual place, and went straight to the ward where Sister and Matron were expecting us.

'Well now!' said Sister Tranter, 'Don't you all look pretty this afternoon?'

'It's half-term, and these poor wee lassies have to stay behind at school because home's too far away, or there's nobody there to look after them. So I still have them on my hands, and we thought it would be nice if they wore pretties.'

'It's a hard life, Scottie!' said Matron. 'Go on, gels; go and talk to your friends.'

I looked towards Boy-Alex's bed. It was empty. 'Where's Boy-Alex?' I asked anxiously. 'He hasn't gone home yet, has he?'

'I'm right behind you, Girl-Alex,' he said. I felt his hands on either side of my waist. 'Your hair looks nice.' He turned me round to face him. He was wearing grey flannel shorts, a grey shirt, school tie and a grey pullover. There was not a bandage in sight, save for the piratical black patch over his left eye.

'Golly, I'd never have recognised you,' I said. 'I've not seen you with clothes on before.'

Harry gave a snorting sort of guffaw, Nicky, Jen-Pen, Puddles and Rob Roy sniggered, and Jacko hooted with laughter. Scottie and Sister were both grinning, and so was Boy-Alex. Matron had turned her back to me and I could see her shoulders shaking with laughter. She turned round and peered at me over the top of her little half spectacles.

'Are you sure that's what you meant to say, young lady?' she said, still laughing. 'Perhaps it would be better if you could re-phrase that somewhat, my dear. I really had no idea that my patients had been running round the ward stark naked—'

Then I realised what I had said, and felt myself blushing. I put my hands up to hide my face.

'I didn't recognise you wearing your kilt,' said Alex, grinning cheekily and squeezing my arm. 'We're as bad as each other, aren't we, Ally?'

'It's not my kilt; it's Harry's,' I said. 'She's wearing my best frock.'

'You both look jolly nice,' Alex told us. 'Come over to my bed, and you, Kate, I've got something to ask you both.'

'Have you any news of Caroline, Scottie?' Sister asked.

'Indeed I have,' she replied. 'I spoke to her Gran today. She's just fine now, and coming back to school as a boarder on Tuesday, at the end of half-term.'

'Is she going to have the spare bed in Goody's dorm.,' asked Nicky.

'That's the plan,' said Scottie. 'There are three wee bairns from the remove there already, and Goody will be like a mother to her, as she is with all her bairns. You remember Goody, don't you, Dru? She'll make a marvellous children's nurse one day. She's already decided that's what she wants to do when she grows up. She's a natural with wee ones, and when you consider she'll not be twelve until mid-December, she is remarkably responsible.'

We went with Alex to the bed that had been his home for the last four months or so. He sat between us, an arm round each of our shoulders. I thought back to the first time I had seen him, his head swathed in bandages, only his nose and mouth visible, and a leg in plaster. All the girls who had visited him had signed his plaster. When the bandages were taken off his eyes, he found that he still had sight in his right eye, and was able to read the messages we had written.

'Granny came yesterday,' he told us, 'and said I was to ask you both to come to tea on the Sunday after next. I'd love you both to come because without your help, I'd never have got better so quickly. When I was lying here, in a dark world, having you come to chat and read to me, made me want to get better. I really looked forward to your visits; I prayed like anything that I'd have one good eye, so I'd be able see you properly. '*Please* say you can come?'

'Rather,' I replied. 'We'd love to, wouldn't we, Harry, but we'll have to ask Scottie's permission first.'

'It would be spiffing!' added Harry. 'Try and keep us away!'

'Will you come in what you're wearing now?' he asked. 'You look so much nicer like that than you do in gymslips.'

'If Ally will let me borrow her frock,' said Harry.

'Only if you let me borrow your kilt, and if Scottie lets us,' I replied with a smile. 'You see, Harry and I share everything. Alex.'

'Absolutely everything,' said Harry, then added; 'Even you!'

'Bang on!' he said. 'I've got a letter from Granny to give to Scottie, asking her permission for you to come. Let's ask her now, then I can tell Granny when I she comes for me tomorrow.'

Scottie came over. 'Now you two, one of you should go and see one of the other patients. Boy-Alex, you look tremendous; I hear you're away home tomorrow.'

'Yes, Scottie,' he replied, 'It's all due to Ally and Kate, and you and all the other girls too, of course. Until you all started visiting me, I used to lie here, wishing the bomb had killed me too. Granny would like them both to come to tea on Sunday next week. She asked me to give you this letter asking permission.' He handed her an envelope.

'You'll let us go, won't you, Scottie,' I said, 'Pul–*ease*?'

'Pul–*eeease,* Scottie?' pleaded Harry. 'And please may we wear our home clothes, like we're wearing today?' We both gazed pleadingly up at her.

'I'd need to be a hard, hard woman to refuse when you make eyes at me like that, my wee monkeys,' she replied. 'Though why anyone would want to ask you out to tea, I can't think!'

'Thanks, Scottie,' Harry said, standing up and giving her a hug. 'You're absolutely spiffing, isn't she, Ally?'

'Aye,' I replied, mimicking Harry's Scots intonation, 'Ab-so-*lute*-ly spiffing!'

'You just *watch* it, pal, or I'll bash yous,' said Harry putting on an extra thick accent, then continued in her normal voice; 'As Maggot isn't here, I'll away and chinwag with George for a wee while. He'll be wondering why she's not here. You two Alexes carry on jawing without me.' We watched her cross the ward to George. He beamed when he saw her. She gave him a hug and began to talk to him straight away. Just then Kate Jackson passed by.

'Jacko?' I called.

'Yes, Ally,' she replied, stopping and giving us a smile.

'I'd like you to meet my friend Alex,' I told her. 'Boy-Alex, this is Kate Jackson, our head girl. She lets her friends call her Jacko.'

'Hello, Boy-Alex,' she said, shaking his hand. 'I hear you're going home to your Gran's tomorrow. Bad show your Mummy and little sister going for a Burton.' She took his hands in hers and squeezed. 'It must have been really tough.'

Alex looked at her and smiled. 'Thanks, Jacko. I've got used to it now. At least it was quick, so they felt nothing.'

'When we first saw him,' I said, 'His head was all bandaged, and you could only see his nose and mouth. We couldn't even tell if he was a boy or a girl!'

'It's mainly due to Ally and Kate—er—Harry, that I've got better,' he said. 'They really cheered me up and made me want to get better. I wanted to see what they really looked like; I was so scared I might not be able to see at all. But I'm lucky, I've got one good eye, and I hope to have a glass one on the other side.' He laughed. 'I've just thought, if someone tells me to keep an eye on something, I'll be able to take it out and lay it on whatever it is I'm meant to be minding!' He grinned happily, delighted with his gruesome joke.

'When we first came,' I said, 'He used to look at us with his hands, feeling us all over. He could even tell we were wearing school uniform, and he told Harry she should grow her hair because she looked too much like a boy.'

'So it's *you* who's responsible for the change in Harry. Jolly good s*how,* old chap!' said Jacko. 'Maybe we'll *all* be calling her Kate soon. I must say she looks jolly pretty now, and she actually behaves in a more ladylike way too.'

There was a sudden burst of applause from along the ward. We turned to find out the cause. It was Harry, walking down the ward on her hands.

'Oh dear!' exclaimed the head-girl. 'I spoke too soon! I'm afraid our *Kate's* going to be tomboy Harry quite a while yet! I say, it's a jolly good thing she's wearing her harvest festivals!'

'*Harvest festivals?*' I cast a puzzled look at Jacko.

'Her navy bags, Ally,' replied the head girl. 'It's what my Grandma calls them— *All is safely gathered in!*'

CHAPTER TWENTY-SIX

The Beak Arranges a Treat

WE WERE GLAD we were going to keep in touch with Boy-Alex, as we had both grown fond of him over the weeks; and he would still have Harry as a friend when, or if, I returned to my own time. Harry's high jinks had caused no more than raised eyebrows and a mild ticking off from Scottie, who had not seen Harry walking on her hands before; usually it was a trick she only performed during gym. The only time she had done it "in public" was in the playground, just after she had been told that she was to be a boarder.

'You see, Scottie,' said Harry, when we were on the trolleybus back to Southbourne, 'George bet me I wouldn't dare do it, so you see I couldn't let a dare like that go by without doing something about it. It was like a red rag to a bull!'

'You'll never guess, Scottie,' laughed Jacko, 'I'd just said how much more ladylike Harry's behaviour was these days, and she had to prove me wrong by behaving in a truly Harry-like way!'

'Me? *Lady*like? Me-ee?' Harry guffawed. 'What an ab-so-*lute* giggle! I'm *never* going to be ladylike; NEVER—ever—even when I'm an old, old, old lady!'

'Never mind,' laughed Scottie, putting a hand on Harry's knee and giving it an affectionate squeeze. 'The patients enjoyed it, and that's the main thing. It would not have been nearly so much fun if you'd been ladylike, as Jacko calls it!'

As there was no prep that evening, we had spent more time at the hospital than usual. When we got back Auntie Vera was looking her usual self and said she was, "just fine now," when we asked how she was feeling. She said she would tell us what she had fixed for tomorrow's half-term treat at the end of high tea.

It was my turn to say Grace at the start of high tea. We had baked beans on toast with a sausage. And, there was real strawberry jam, with real strawberries in it, to put on our "bread and scrape."

'Well now, my dears,' said Auntie Vera, when we had finished eating. 'Have another cup of tea if you like, and I'll tell you all about tomorrow afternoon's treat. We are all going to the Pavilion.' She paused to see our reaction. 'Yes, the Pavilion Theatre, to see *Come to the Show*, which is a song and dance revue, and I have heard it is very gay and jolly. I have booked two-shilling seats for us at the matinèe performance, and afterwards we shall have afternoon tea in the restaurant at Beales.'

This was a treat indeed. 'Gosh! Miss Plenderleith, thanks,' said Jacko. 'That's absolutely bang on, good show, wizard prang, isn't it, chaps?' Her father was a fighter pilot, so, inevitably, her speech was full of RAF slang expressions.

'Yes, rather,' Jen-Pen agreed.

'Soo–oo–per,' said Rob Roy.

'Abso–*lute*–ly!' said Harry, glancing at me.

'*Brill*–iant!' we said together, grinning at each other.

'And tea at Beales,' said Nicky. 'That'll be stupendous. You get toasted tea cakes or crumpets, and dainty little sandwiches, and they have the most gorgeous cream cakes. Gosh! I hope they still have them now it's wartime.'

'We'll just have to wait and see, won't we?' said Auntie Vera. 'I'm pretty sure they do. May I take it that the arrangements meet with your approval?'

'Ye–*esss!*' came the unanimous reply.

'Rather,' I said. 'Ab–so–*lute*–ly—'

'—Spiffing,' added Harry, Rob Roy and Puddles together.

*

After high tea, Harry and I stayed in the common room until we had to go upstairs for our baths. Jacko, Jenny, Puddles and Goody, who would normally inhabit the Senior common room, decided it would be more fun with us, so we all played Monopoly. When Harry and I had to go upstairs, we were both doing quite well, but would not have won. We cashed in our hands and found that we had each made a small profit.

'Ally,' said Harry, as we were undressing. 'Isn't it wonderfully quiet and peaceful without those silly Willises galumphing and giggling around?'

'Ra*ther!*' I replied. 'We've got the whole school to ourselves and our good friends until Tuesday high tea.'

'I wonder if we'll have an air-raid tonight,' said Harry.

Scottie was waiting for us in the bathroom, running our baths to the 'regulation' depth. 'Would you like me to wash your hair for you?' she asked. 'As there are only a few of us, I can do it and you can dry it in front of my fire afterwards. Then everyone except the two wee ones, who are asleep already, will be joining us for my half-term cocoa party.'

'Yes, please, Scottie,' replied Harry. 'I love having my hair washed by someone else, don't you Ally?'

'Ra*ther,*' I replied for the second time in as many minutes. 'That'd be brill, thank you, Scottie. You spoil us.'

'Well,' said Scottie, 'It is only fair that you poor wee orphan lambs should be a wee bit spoiled, because you have to stay here instead of going home for half-term. I shall do yours first, Ally; it's longer than Harry's so it will take longer to dry. I'll just away and fetch the shampoo.'

I lay back in the bath wetting my hair, waiting for Scottie to come back. My hair had grown a good bit longer since I arrived in 1940, and now fell well below my shoulders. I wondered what Nick and Jackie would say if they could see me now? Nick would certainly have something witty to say. I suddenly thought how like Harry she was, even to the dark hair, hazel eyes and long eyelashes; and when Harry's hair had grown a bit more, there would be an even greater likeness. Maybe that was why I got on so well with Harry; she was so like Nick. Just then, Scottie came back with the shampoo.

*

We had heard that Scottie's half-term cocoa party was one of the traditions of Seabourne Prep. According to Jacko and Jen-Pen, they had been lavish affairs before the war, with sausage rolls, dainty little sandwiches, cream cakes, and all sorts of other fancies. But wartime rationing had put paid to such luxuries, so we had to make do with a few biscuits and some fairy cakes that Gladys had managed to find the ingredients for.

When we got out of our baths, Scottie wrapped huge bath-towels round us and rubbed us dry. 'I know you can dry yourselves,' she said, 'But I like to do things for my best girls at half-term.'

We put on our nightclothes, and went to her room. She wanted us to get our hair as dry as possible before the party started.

'Shouldn't we get dressed again?' asked Harry.

'And why should you want to be doing that?' replied Scottie. 'Everyone comes in their nightclothes, even Auntie Vera.'

'Gosh! is she coming too?' I said.

'Of course,' said Scottie, 'She always comes. She wouldn't miss it for the world. Now, come and sit on the rug in front of the fire, while I dry your hair with fresh towels.' Suddenly I wondered if they had electric hair dryers in 1940.

Scottie had almost finished drying Harry's hair, when there was a timid tapping at the door. Scottie called her usual, 'Come away in,' but nobody did. Then the timid tapping came again so Scottie went to the door and opened it.

Outside stood two small girls in their nighties, Susan Morgan, tears streaming down her cheeks, with Margretta Ransom holding her hand, and trying to comfort her. 'Sc—sc—ottie, I h—h—had a nasty dweam,' sobbed Susie. 'I'm s—sowwy to b—bother you, but I was f—f—fwightened.'

'My poor wee lamb,' said Scottie, lifting her up and carrying her into the room. 'Come and sit by the fire with Alex and Harry; you too Greta. You ought to have put on your "goonies;" you will catch your deaths of cold like that. Alex, be a kind lassie and give Susie a cuddle while I pop and get their "goonies".'

She put her down by me. 'Come on, Susie,' I said, putting an arm round her. Only seven, she was small for her age, it was her first term as a boarder, and she must be very homesick. We went to the sofa and she climbed on my lap. She flung her arms round my neck, tears running down her cheeks.

'What are all these tears for?' I asked. 'Tell Auntie Alex all about it.' She looked up at me. 'Do you feel better now?' She nodded. 'Got a hanky?' She shook her head, so I found mine.

Harry was grinning broadly, all over her face. 'You'd better come and sit on Auntie Harry's lap,' she told Greta. When Scottie returned with their dressing gowns, Goody came with her.

'Come on, my wains,' said Scottie. 'Let me help you into your "goonies", then you can have more cuddles with Alex and Harry.'

'D'you want to tell me about your dream?' I asked Susie, as she sat beside me again. She shook her head, and hid her face in my dressing gown. A few moments later she looked up.

'It was about Germans doing howwid things to Daddy,' she said shyly. 'He's been taken pwis'ner, you know.' Then I remembered; her father had been shot down on a raid over Germany. At least he was alive. A solitary tear rolled down her cheek.

'If your Daddy's a prisoner of war,' I said, 'At least we know he's alive.' I turned to Scottie. 'They don't have to go back to bed straight away, do they, Scottie? Surely they can stay up for a little while.'

'Of course they can,' she replied. 'Goody, why don't you go and get changed, the others will be here any moment now. Your bairns are in good hands.'

About ten minutes later everyone else arrived. Gladys and Scottie had just started to fill the mugs with cocoa, when the party was interrupted by the wailing of the siren.

We went straight to the dormitory to fetch our gas-masks, and put on a few more layers of clothes. Just in case the school got a direct hit, I gathered up Edward Bear Esquire and the photo Scottie had taken of Harry and me, which I slipped into my dressing-gown pocket, before taking the rug from my bed and falling in with the others for roll-call. In just a few minutes from hearing the siren, we were safely in the shelter and continuing the party there.

*

The air-raid was a long one, and we had to spend most of that night in the shelter. After the jollity of the party, most of us managed to sleep stretched out on the benches, but it was uncomfortable and not very warm, so we were glad when, at about ten to six, the all-clear sounded and we were able to return safely to our dormitories.

We were allowed to sleep in until nine o'clock that morning. Scottie told us to put on home clothes when we dressed; I wore Harry's kilt as she wanted to wear my velvet frock again. In spite of the long lie-in we were still half asleep when we assembled in the eatery for brekker. It was bacon and egg and fried bread, an unheard of treat for us.

'I say, Gladys!' exclaimed Jacko, 'This is a real wizard prang brekker. Have you got a boyfriend in the black market or what?'

'No not me, it's bad enough 'avin' Perky as a 'usband, wivout 'avin' boyfrien's as well!' laughed Gladys. 'An' yer won't catch me doin' no business wiv them spivs. Nah, Perky's got some more 'ens, and we 'ad a few heggs goin' spare, so we fought you'd like a breakfuss treat for 'arf-term.'

'Thank you, Gladys,' said Auntie Vera, 'How sweet of you both. You'll be sure to thank the Bombardier for us, won't you? It really is a treat for us, isn't it, girls?'

There were enthusiastic murmurings of 'Yes, Rather! Thanks! Absolutely Spiffing! Wizard Prang! Bang on! and Smash-ing!' as we showed our appreciation. It really was a great treat, even for me. It was now over six weeks since I had last tasted bacon and egg together, and it must have been a great deal longer for most of the other girls.

Brekker did a lot to revive our spirits, and after we had done our usual morning chores, Harry and I went to the common room to read for a while. There would be no lacrosse that morning, because Bendy Wendy was spending half-term with her mother, who was on her own, as father Bendall was a Major in the 8th Army, fighting in the North African desert.

During the morning, Harry suggested we ask Auntie Vera if we could have Boy-Alex to tea, the Sunday after we went to tea with him at his grandmother's.

'Come away in,' came the answer to our knock. I opened the door, and we went in. Auntie Vera was rummaging through a pile of papers on her desk. As we closed the door behind us she looked up and smiled. 'Harry, and Ally, to what do I owe the honour of a visit from my nieces?'

'Auntie Vera? You know we've been invited to go to tea with Boy-Alex next Sunday?' said Harry.

'Yes, my dear,' said Auntie Vera, still rummaging. 'Ah! here it is. Let me just make one telephone call, and you'll have my full attention after that.' She picked up the telephone receiver and waited for the operator to answer. 'Bournemouth one,' she said in reply to the operator's 'Number please?' She waited while the operator made the connection.

'Hello!' said Auntie Vera. 'Is that Beales?... Can you connect me to the restaurant please?...' She covered the mouthpiece with her hand. 'I'm phoning to confirm the booking for our tea this afternoon.' She took her hand away, 'Hello, Hello, is that the restaurant?... This is Miss Plenderleith, headmistress of Seabourne Preparatory School. I am just confirming my booking for afternoon tea this afternoon... Yes, that's correct. There will be twelve of us in the party... That's right, two adults and ten girls... We'll be with you by a quarter to five... Thank you so much, that's very kind of you. Goodbye.'

She replaced the receiver in its cradle and looked up at us. 'Now, my dears, what were you saying about Boy-Alex. He does have a surname, I take it?'

'Yes, Drummond,' replied Harry. 'As in *Bulldog!* We were wondering if we might ask him to Sunday tea, here, the weekend after we go to tea with him at Christchurch?'

'I don't see why not,' replied Auntie Vera. 'I shall ask Gladys if she could do something a bit special, if you like.'

'That would be spiffing, Auntie Vera,' said Harry, 'Wouldn't it, Ally?'

'Absolutely spiffing,' I replied.

'I'll give you spiffing, my young scamps,' laughed Auntie Vera. 'By the way, you know it's school uniform for the theatre this afternoon, don't you? Pass the word round will you? I didn't know you had a kilt, Alex; I must say you suit it.'

'It's Harry's,' I replied. 'I like wearing it; it's so lovely and warm. Anyhow, she's got my best frock on. When I'm at home, I wear Rory's kilt sometimes; he has to have one for school. Harry and I often wear each other's things. She had to borrow a pair of my socks last week, because all hers were religious.'

'Religious socks?' queried Auntie Vera, raising her eyebrows and peering over her pince-nez at me. 'What on *earth* are relgious socks, when they're at home?'

'They have lots of holes in them,' explained Harry, 'So they are "holey" socks!'

'Oh dear,' groaned Auntie Vera. 'I fell for that one, good and proper. Go away, you awful, awful little girls—before you inflict any more of your terrible jokes on me! The two of you are worse than schoolboys!'

'Yes, Auntie Plenderleith,' we said, trying to look innocent and keep our faces straight while we curtsied. 'Thank you, Auntie Plenderleith.'

'Don't try that "butter wouldn't melt" act on me, my young scallywags. Off you go! Shoo!' she laughed, and propelled us towards the door. 'I'll see you both at lunch. We shall be having it fifteen minutes early today, to give you time to change immediately afterwards. Tell the others for me, will you?' As we left, she began rummaging through the papers on her desk again.

'It's jolly unfair,' I said, closing the door behind us, 'She scolds us like mad when our desks are untidy, and yet hers is ten times worse than Weevil's *ever* is!'

'When she said we were like schoolboys, Auntie Vera was nearer the truth than she imagined, eh, *Alex, mon gars?*'

'*Attention à ça que tu dis ici—les murs ont des oreilles—*' I whispered, putting a finger to my lips.

CHAPTER TWENTY-SEVEN

The Outing

Our conversation over lunch was all about the afternoon ahead. A trip to the theatre and then tea at Beales, was more than a consolation for not going home for half-term.

Jen-Pen and Rob Roy had changed into tunics before lunch, so as soon as lunch was over, Harry and I dashed upstairs to change into ours. She asked me to undo the buttons at the back of her frock, and afterwards I sat on her bed and we nattered while she changed. Then she came into my cubie and cuddled Edward Bear Esquire while I changed. We were so looking forward to the outing, and Harry had the same look of excited anticipation that I had seen so often on Nick's face.

'You're so like my cousin Nick—in my *own* time, that is. You're so alike that if I could bring her here, you'd almost look like sisters.'

'What's Nick short for? Nicola?'

'No, Nicole,' I replied.

'That's one of *Grandmère's* names; she's Henriette Nicole.' Suddenly she looked haunted. '*J'espére que tous va bien avec Grand-mère Henriette?* I wonder if *Maman* has managed to see her?'

'You know a lot of French, don't you,' I remarked. 'Gran has taught me quite a bit, but you sound the same as Gran when you speak it, with a proper French accent.'

'That's because *Maman* spoke to me in both French and English from the start, so I grew up speaking both languages. Your accent's pretty good too, you know. When Daddy died, I started to call *Maman* Mummy, and she spoke to me mostly in English after that, but we've kept our French up by always speaking it at mealtimes. D'you want me to do your plaits?'

'Yes, please,' I replied. 'I still haven't got the knack.'

'I s'pose if you go back to being a boy, you won't need to be able to plait your own hair,' she said, 'unless boys go round with long hair—like girls.'

'Some do in 1974. Quite a lot of boys have hair much longer than mine is now,' I said. 'But they don't have plaits—as far as I know!"

'You could start a whole new fashion,' she said, adding with a grin; 'I say, wouldn't it be jolly confusing if you wore a kilt?'

'No more so than you wearing a frock with your boy's hair!' I retorted, with a grin. 'Don't forget what Derrick Ackroyd said to you on sports day.'

She looked up at me and stuck out her tongue.

*

Curtain-up at the Pavilion was at a quarter to three, so we were waiting at the bus-stop by five to two, well wrapped up against the chilly wind. We were really looking forward to our half-term treat.

I had been to the Pavilion twice in my own time; both times to see the Christmas Pantomime. The first time was with Mummy and Dad, about three months before they were killed; Nick and Jackie, Auntie Kate and Uncle Dougal, her husband (Mummy's brother), all came. We went to see Father Christmas at Beales in the morning, and then had lunch in the restaurant. I had Bombay curry and rice, and apple crumble and ice cream for pudding. That was about thirty years ahead, in peace-time. I remember watching the fountains in the Pavilion forecourt with coloured lights changing the colours of the water jets as they cascaded into the pools.

We only had a few minutes to wait for the trolleybus. While we waited at the bus-stop, my thoughts wandered back to my own time again. I could just remember the trolleybuses before they were replaced by diesels. Seeing them in 1940, somehow they looked different. It wasn't just the headlamp hoods, fitted so as not to attract the attention of enemy aircraft, but something else. As a number 21 from Christchurch whispered round the corner, I realised what it was; the roof! In peacetime the buses were yellow all over with a reddy-brown band under the windows of both decks. In wartime the roofs were dark coloured, I supposed for the same reason as the headlamps were hooded. I felt happier when I had solved that mystery.

As the trolleybus drew to a halt, Harry tugged one of my pigtails. 'Wakey-wakey, Ally! You're doing it again, aren't you?'

I smiled. 'Tell you later," I said, and squeezed her hand. She realised I could say no more, as the other girls didn't know I was anything other than what I appeared to be, an ordinary ten-year-old schoolgirl.

We clambered aboard the bus and stampeded upstairs to bag the long front seat only to find that it was occupied by three big boys and one smaller one, all smoking cigarettes. I thought I recognised the smaller one, and when he turned round and stared at us, my hunch proved to be true; it was Kenneth Duncan. Auntie Vera gave him a hard stare, and he turned very red and guiltily tried to hide the cigarette he was smoking. I nudged Harry, and nodded in Kenneth's direction. She grinned, because we both knew that even though he had shaken hands with me in the vestry that Sunday, he really wanted to get even with me.

Auntie Vera murmured something to Scottie. I just heard mention of "Mrs. Duncan", so I guessed that Kenneth's mother would soon hear of her wayward son's misdemeanour.

The conductress came up the front stairs and made her way back to us. 'Fares please *HI* thang-you!' she sang out, steadying herself by grabbing one of the seat-backs as the driver braked a bit harder than usual. We stopped to let on more passengers, and the conductress stared back at the round curved mirror on the corner of the staircase, so she could see what was happening on the rear platform. When she saw that everybody had got on safely, she sang out; 'Hold-very-tight-please, *Hi* thang-you!' and pressed the bell button twice.

She returned to us; 'Fares please, *Hi* thang-you!'

'Two and ten halves to Westover Road please,' said Scottie.

'Two and ten 'alves to Westover Road, I thangou,' repeated the conductress, pulling two yellow and ten blue tickets from her ticket rack, inserting each one into her punching machine in turn. It went 'ting' each time she pushed the lever down to punch a ticket. 'Two 'n thruppence, please, 'um, *Hi* thang-you!' She passed Scottie the tickets and taking the half-crown offered in payment said, '*Hi* thang-you!' again. She put the half-crown in her money pouch, gave Scottie a threepenny bit as change and went on to take the fares of the next passengers. 'Fares please, *Hi* thang-you!'

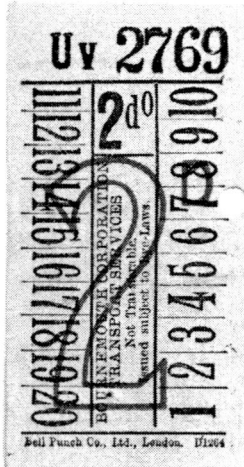

'I suppose you want the tickets again, Ally,' said Scottie. 'Although, why a wee girl should want to collect bus tickets is beyond my ken.' She held out the tickets for me.

'Thanks, Scottie,' I replied, taking them.

'I think she wants to be a bus conductress when she grows up,' said Harry, giving me a playful dig with her elbow. I replied by showing her the tip of my tongue

When the trolleybus turned left at Pokesdown Station, Kenneth and the big boys got up and went downstairs. The big boys were wearing long trousers, whereas Kenneth, being only eleven, would be wearing shorts for at least another three or four years.

'I bet they're going to the pictures,' said Harry, as we passed the cinema. '*The Case of the Frightened Lady*,' she added. 'It must be a detective story; and It's Certificate A—so *that's* why Kenneth was with those big boys. The cinema wouldn't let him in unless he was with somebody over sixteen. I didn't much like the look of them, did you, Ally?'

'No,' I replied. 'They looked like yobs to me.'

'Rather like those *errand-boys* who whistled at poor Miss Bendall, when the wind caught her dress that Sunday,' said Harry.

'Pamela's wee brother seems to be getting into bad company,' said Scottie. 'I recognised George Waters was one of them—he's been in Borstal twice that I know of. Mind you, the whole Waters bunch are a bad lot. The father's always in and out of prison, and somehow has dodged the call-up. He's a right spiv, that one, and it wouldn't surprise me if he's involved in the black market. I saw Mrs. Waters the other week, flaunting her silk stockings and fine clothes, and as for her daughter, Gloria, she's only fourteen, and yet I saw her hanging on the arm of a sailor who must have been thirty if he was a day.'

'I am glad I decided we were "full" when they wanted to send Gloria to us as a pupil,' said Auntie Vera. 'A girl like that would have done nothing for our good reputation as a school for *nice* little girls.' She lowered her voice, and continued; 'Of course Mr. Waters isn't her real father, you know.'

'I didn't,' replied Scottie, 'But I can't say I'm surprised.'

Harry nudged me and grinned. 'Now, young Harry, just because we enjoy a gossip as much as anybody, you mustn't go round telling everyone what we said.'

'Yes, Scottie,' said Harry, 'or do I mean no, Scottie?'

'I'll "no Scottie" you, you saucy young scallywag!' she said good-humouredly, her bright eyes twinkling.

We had passed through Boscombe, and were going down the hill just before Lyndon Hall Hydro, a big hotel with its own swimming pool, where Auntie Kate taught me to swim, with Nick and Jackie.

'Could we go to the baths for a swim, sometime, Scottie,' I asked. 'I love swimming.' Harry nudged me frowning furiously. Of course, I was not supposed to know there was a pool there because this was supposed to be the first time I had ever been to Bournemouth; which I suppose it was, in actual fact, because I would not be born for another twenty-four years.

'Well, my Alex,' said Scottie, seeming not to have noticed my *faux pas*. 'It would be nice, but I'm afraid we can't, because all the swimming baths have been commandeered by the forces, for training their men.'

We stopped opposite Lyndon Hall, with Boscombe Chine on our left. I glanced across the road at the familiar building. Even though the sun was shining, it looked drab and run down, shabby somehow, and dirty. I barely recognised it, even though I knew it well. I supposed it must be something to do with what grown-ups called "the ravages of war."

The trolleybus set off again, climbing the hill, Christchurch Road bearing gently right before the long straight run to Landsdowne. On the left as we approached, was the Odeon Cinema, which was showing "The Last Outpost", starring Cary Grant. I had seen a film of his on TV in the last week of the summer holiday. It couldn't have been very old, because the cars looked no more than two years old (in 1974). I thought that if Cary Grant was in films during the war, he must be absolutely ancient in 1974! I badly wanted to tell Harry, but knew I would have to be patient and tell her when we could not be eavesdropped. On one corner of the Landsdowne roundabout stood the Metropole Hotel, which would be destroyed by enemy bombing later in the war. Then the trolleybus took us down Bath Road, and straight after passing the Royal Bath Hotel, turned right into Westover Road. On our right, the Ice-Rink looked very shut up. On the left was our destination, the Pavilion Theatre, but the fountains were dry; I supposed it must be because of the war.

'Westover Road, The Square. *H'all* change—*Hi* thang-you!' sang out the clippie, and, just to make sure; 'Hall change *'fyou* please! *Hi* thang-you!' We waited for the bus to stop, then stood up, went down the front stairs and out on to the pavement.

Out of the warm bus, there was quite a nip in the air. 'It's a bit chilly, isn't it?' I said.

'Aye,' Harry agreed, 'I wish I'd put on bullet-proofs instead of knee-socks. *Hi thang-you!*'

'Same here, *Hi thang-you!*' I replied, and we both giggled.

Scottie counted our heads; 'All present and correct, Vera,' she announced. 'All got your gas masks?' We waved our boxes in the air to show her we had them.

'At least we haven't that Hardy creature with us,' said Auntie Vera; 'Asking to spend a penny and locking herself in the lavatory every five minutes!'

'Jacko?' said Harry. She nudged me with her elbow and grinned mischievously.

'Yes, Harry,' replied Jacko, who was walking in front of us.

'Is it true that you're drawing up a rota for changing Amanda Hardy's nappies?'

I glanced at Harry. She managed to keep a perfect poker face until Nicky, Puddles and Rob Roy exploded into the giggles, and Goody's two little charges, Susie and Greta, sniggered as if Harry had said something terribly rude. Jen-Pen and Jacko guffawed, and even Scottie and Auntie Vera allowed themselves a smile.

'That's an excellent idea, Harry,' said Scottie. 'Make sure Harry does the first week, Jacko! Don't forget she has to wash the dirty nappies too. I'll issue a box of talcum powder, and a jar of zinc and castor oil ointment in case Amanda gets nappy rash.'

'Wilco, Scottie,' said Jacko. 'No sooner said than done.'

With an anxious expression Harry glanced at Scottie, who looked deadly serious. As soon as Harry looked away, Scottie winked at me.

'You'd better put me down for the second week, Jacko,' I said, 'Then Harry and I can take it in turns for the first two weeks.' I tried to keep a straight face, but I couldn't and my laugh came out as a sort of spluttery raspberry, as I tried to keep my lips clamped tightly together, and then I snorted.

That set Harry off, and she threw back her head and gave a cackling guffaw. 'You rotters!' she cried. You ab-so-lute rotters! Just you wait, Ally Muir, and you, Jacko, I'll get even with yous yins yet! Grrrrr!'

We quickly walked the hundred yards back to the Pavilion, and after leaving our hats and coats in the cloakroom, we were shown to our seats in the stalls by a uniformed usherette. Scottie and Auntie Vera each bought a programme, so we would know who the artistes were. We settled in our seats, and waited in bubbling anticipation for the curtain to rise.

The show was brilliant; there were comic sketches, witty and serious songs, and slick dancing by eight chorus girls. The music was played by a section of the Bournemouth Municipal Orchestra, conducted by Len Trevor.

We all enjoyed ourselves tremendously, as did the rest of the audience. After their distress at the death of Tante Yvette, it was good to see Auntie Vera, Scottie and Harry relaxing, roaring with laughter at the jokes and tapping their feet to the music. Harry kept glancing at me, grinning and squeezing my hand. We were all sorry when the curtain was rung down for the last time after two extra curtain calls for the performers. We waited for a minute or so before joining the queue to leave the auditorium. Another curtain, with the words "Safety Curtain" painted on a scenic background depicting the Isle of Wight as seen from Bournemouth, came down over the red plush curtain that was used during the performance.

*

As soon as we had fetched our coats and hats from the cloakroom, we left the theatre for the short walk to Beales. I had never seen this Beales, as it would be bombed one Sunday in May 1943. I knew the store that had been built—after the war—to replace it very well, for I often went there with Gran for lunch when we had been shopping. We walked to the lift and were whisked up to the restaurant in next to no time. We were greeted by a tall lady in a smart black suit. I supposed she was the manageress.

'Good afternoon, Miss Plenderleith, good afternoon, girls,' the manageress said. 'Did you all enjoy the theatre?'

There was a chorus of, 'Rather—Absolutely—Brilliant—Spiffing—Excellent—First class—Tophole—Wizard prang—Bang-on—'

'That's good,' laughed the manageress. 'Everything's ready for you. If you'd walk this way, please.' She led the way with short mincing steps and her bottom wiggled inside her tight skirt. I had to stop Harry imitating her—

'Well, she did say "walk this way",' she hissed, 'I was only being a good wee girl and doing as I was told.'

The restaurant was quite full, and the manageress, I can't remember her name, led us between the tables with people having tea, to a long table with twelve places set; one at each end, and five along each side. Each place had a card with a name on. When we had each found our own place, we stood by our chairs until Auntie Vera and Scottie told us to sit down. Also at each place was a paper hat, and as soon as we had we sat down, we put on our party hats and spread our napkins on our knees. Then two waitresses brought huge silver dishes, from which they served us each with a hot-buttered toasted teacake, using spoon and fork in one hand like a pair of tongs. We were told to help ourselves to jam (it had real strawberries in it). After that came dainty egg and cress sandwiches with the crusts cut off, then bread and butter and more jam if we wanted it, then cakes and jelly and ice-cream. They really did us proud.

All too soon it was over. We thanked the manageress and the waitresses for a gorgeous tea. Then we put on our hats and coats, went down in the lift and out into Old Christchurch Road to catch a trolleybus back to Southbourne.

Gladys had high tea waiting for us when we got back, but it was only a small one. She had been warned that we would probably be rather full of the best that Beales could offer. We went to bed happy that night, and were glad that there was no air-raid to disturb us.

CHAPTER TWENTY-EIGHT

Harry's Sunday Shock

AFTER THE EXCITEMENTS OF SATURDAY, we were quite glad that Sunday was more normal. We went to church as usual although there were only a handful of us. Half-term had depleted choir numbers also, as several of the boys were spending the weekend away.

At the last minute, Derrick and Sarah Ackroyd had gone to spend half-term with their grandparents in Wareham, leaving the Decani without a leader.

'You can lead the Decani today, Alex,' Mr Grubb told me.

'Shouldn't one of the boys do it, Sir?' I replied. I was honoured to be asked but didn't want to upset any of the boys. I knew it must be hard enough for them having a girl sing solos regularly, without her as acting leader when the head chorister was away.

'I think you will give the best lead,' replied Mr Grubb; 'and Christopher agrees with me.'

I glanced at Chris Hickingbottom, leader of the Cantoris. 'Go on, Alex,' he said. 'We all want you to do it.'

'Okay, Chris,' I said. 'If you want me to. I'll do my best.'

Mr Grubb smiled. Harry had come down to the vestry with me as usual, and had watched my protests with great glee. However, her grin changed to a look of utter horror when Mr Grubb told her to take off her raincoat and blazer and robe up in place of Kenneth Duncan, whose mother had sent a note saying that he was "confined to barracks" (or "grounded" in nineteen-seventies parlance) at weekends, until the end of term.

'Please, Sir, may I nip and tell Miss Plenderleith?' she asked. 'She'll be expecting me to join them in the congregation.'

Mr Grubb glanced at his watch, then over his specs at Harry. 'No time. She'll know soon enough that you have been "press-ganged," and are not cutting the service. You can process behind Alex; I'm sure Alan won't mind this once.' He gave her a cassock, a ruff and a surplice. 'You'll help her robe up, won't you, Alex?'

A minute or so later she looked the perfect choirboy, much more so than I did, because even though her hair was longer, it was still short enough to make look like a boy.

'Remember, when you're walking in procession,' I told her; 'place one foot directly in front of the other, as if you were walking a tightrope. Then you won't wobble or roll like a drunken sailor.'

Alan Fraser, who was usually on my right, came and wished us luck. He had a fine voice and was excited because he had just heard that he had been accepted for one of the Cathedral Choir Schools, where he would start next term. He was to become one of the best choristers in the country. His youngest son, Brian, was my leader in the 1974 choir.

Peg-Leg Pugh hurried into the vestry looking rather more flustered than usual. 'Good morning, everyone,' he said. When he saw Harry robed up, he beamed. 'I see we have a new boy this morning, Mr Grubb!'

'That's right, Mr Pugh. Harry Gordon,' replied the choir master with a twinkle, winking at Harry and me. Then he went off to play the pre-service voluntary.

Mr Pugh came and shook hands with Harry; 'You are most welcome, Master Gordon. Thank you for swelling our numbers.'

'Thank you, Sir,' she replied. As we formed up for the procession, she whispered in my ear; 'He didn't recognise me. He thinks I'm a boy. He *actually* thinks I'm a *boy*——'

Mr Pugh, satisfied with our turnout said; 'Let us pray.' We closed our eyes and bowed our heads. '*The Lord be with you.*'

'*And with thy spirit,*' we replied.

'*May the Lord open our lips so that we may sing forth his praise,*' prayed the vicar.

We replied; '*Amen,*' and then climbed the stairs and waited with our hymn books open, ready for the processional hymn.

When the organ voluntary finished, Mr Pugh announced; 'Hymn number 601, *The God of Abraham praise Who reigns enthroned above.*' There was a general rustling and shuffling as the congregation stood while Mr Grubb played the first two lines. We came in together, and began processing behind Mr Ramsay who carried the cross in front of us.

As we turned into the nave, Rob Roy, with Harry's place empty beside her, looked round anxiously. When she saw Harry processing behind me, her jaw dropped and she elbowed Puddles in the ribs. When we reached the choir-stalls, I glanced towards Auntie Vera, Scottie and the girls in time to see Scottie, a proud smile on her face, nudge Auntie Vera and nod in our direction.

The service seemed to pass quite quickly. We had one minute's silence remembering those members of the congregation who had lost their lives in battle, or as a result of the war, during the previous week. Among those names was that of Yvette Foster.

*

In the vestry after the service, Harry and I were hanging up our robes, when Mr Grubb came looking for us.

'Well done, girls,' he said; 'And thank you for standing in at such short notice, Harry. Good job you came to choir practise, eh? It wasn't too nerve-racking, was it?'

'I enjoyed myself, Sir,' Harry replied. 'It was fine once we'd got going, but I had terrible butterflies in my tummy before the procession. D'you *know*, even though he teaches me scripture twice a week, Mr Pugh called me *Master Gordon?* I think he *actually* thought I was a *boy!*'

'He probably did, young lady, and he was very flustered, poor man. How would you both like to sing at evensong this afternoon?' he asked. 'I'll clear it with Miss Plenderleith, if you like.'

'We looked at each other and shrugged.

'We haven't anything special on, have we, Ally,' said Harry. 'I'll do it if you will, so long as Auntie Vera says we can.'

'Yes, Mr Grubb, we'll do it; I like evensong.'

Out in the churchyard Scottie, Auntie Vera and the girls were waiting for us. 'So *there* you are, Harry,' said Auntie Vera. 'We wondered why you cut church this morning, didn't we, girls?'

Harry frowned, and was about to say something when Scottie, a grave expression on her face said; 'Yes, it's such a shame, you missed seeing Alex leading the choir, and a new choirboy we'd never seen before.'

'That's right,' said Auntie Vera. 'He reminded me so much of a girl I know, but I can't put a name to her just now!' She broke into a smile. 'Well done, Harry, it's a shame to tease you.'

'Mr Pugh didn't recognise her,' I giggled. 'He really thought she was a boy, and called her "*Master Gordon*".'

'Yes, and he's taught me scripture twice a week for two terms,' Harry added with a grin.

'Mr Pugh's always been rather vague,' said Auntie Vera. 'Here's Mr Grubb. I see you had the press-gang out today, Mr Grubb.'

'Yes indeed, Miss Plenderleith,' he replied. 'I was wondering if err—I might err—press them into *service*, ha-ha-ha,' he chuckled at his little joke, 'For err—Evensong this afternoon?'

'Yes of course, if they would like to,' replied Auntie Vera.

*

After lunch we went for a tramp up on the cliffs with Rob Roy, Puddles and Nicky. The Home Guard were mustered at the band-stand as usual. On our walks with Bendy Wendy, a chinwag with the Home Guard was now a regular thing. Seeing us coming, Mr Evans, who we thought was a bit sweet on Bendy, gave us a cheery wave.

'Hello, girls! Where's Wendy today?' he asked. 'I hope she's not poorly.'

'Och, *no*, Mr Evans,' Harry replied. 'It's half term so she's away to visit her mother. Her father's fighting somewhere in North Af—'

'Sssh! Remember the posters.' Mr Evans put a finger to his lips. '*Be like dad! Keep mum!* Did I see you in the choir this morning, young Harry?'

'Aye, they were a few bods short, so Mr. Grubb press-ganged me.'

'The missus said to me; "Look! There's a new choirboy!" I told 'er you were a girl, but she wouldn't believe me until she saw you outside afterwards in your gymslip.'

'The vicar thought I was a boy too,' said Harry, grinning. 'He even called me

Master Gordon. And, last term, *loads* of people asked why I was wearing girls' things; up home in Scotland I went to a boys' school, so anybody who didn't know me just thought I was a boy like all the other chaps.'

'She wore a kilt,' I explained. 'And played football in their second eleven!'

'What? Wearing a kilt?' said Mr Evans, winking at her.

'No. But I wore it for lessons. Lots of the boys wore them.'

'Good for you, young Harry,' said Mr Evans. 'The missus'll be tickled to death when I tell 'er.'

We watched them drill for a few minutes and then went on our way, pausing at the cliff-lift for a few minutes before we turned back and returned to school. During the war, evensong was held early in winter because of the virtual impossibility of blacking out the church windows. Gladys had been warned and had an early tea ready for us as soon as we returned from our walk.

We took the trolleybus to Fishermans Walk like we did when we went to choir practise. I had always enjoyed singing at Evensong, and never more so than when we sang *Walmisley's Mag and Nunc in D minor*. Harry enjoyed herself and said she could get used to being a choirboy! She was full of it on the bus afterwards.

We arrived back at school about ten minutes before high tea, and dashed up to change into home clothes. How I wished I could rush back to 1974 to get a couple of pairs of my jeans; one for Harry and the other for me. We quickly got out of

our school uniform and put on warm things. Harry said she would like to wear my velvet frock again, so I wore her kilt and a jumper.

'I like wearing your kilt.' I glanced round to check we were alone. 'If I ever get back to my own time, I'm going to ask Gran to buy me one,' I said as I buttoned her up at the back. 'Why d'you like borrowing my frock so much?'

'Because it's yours, and you're my best friend; it makes me feel close to you.'

'Same here,' I said, and we grinned at each other. 'I *wish* I could stay here with you for ever.'

'I wish you could too,' she said, 'But not if you're going to die like you said. I just hope you manage to get back to 1974, and then I'll come and look for you. Tell you what, I'll keep my kilt for you; it'll be too wee for me then! You'll have to call me Auntie Harry. Hey, if we hurry up we might hear the messages on the wireless. Let's go to Auntie Vera, she's sure to be listening in.'

We knocked on the study door. 'Come away in,' we heard her call. We went in, she was sitting in her easy chair, and the wireless was on. She put a finger to her lips and pointed to the sofa.

We sat down. We had arrived just in time to hear the last few messages. Last of all the announcer said; '*The Big Bad Wolf ate La Maîtresse for his breakfast.*'

'*Pauvre Tante Yvette,*' said Harry.

Auntie Vera leaned across and switched off the wireless. 'Well, my little songbirds, how was evensong?'

'Fab—ulous!' replied Harry. 'I'm jolly glad I went to choir practice with Ally. I think I could enjoy being a choirboy. It was a nice service, wasn't it, Ally?'

'Yes it was,' I replied. 'You should have come too, Auntie Vera.'

'Perhaps another time,' she said. 'I must say, you look the part, Harry, in your cassock and surplice. Now tell me, have you two planned anything for tomorrow?'

'Nothing yet,' replied Harry. 'We thought we might go the the hospital.'

'Well, before you make up your minds,' said Auntie Vera, 'Maybe this might interest you. As you know, Caroline Baxter's returning as a boarder for the rest of the term.'

'Yes, on Tuesday—' interrupted Harry.

'Well, that *was* the plan,' said Auntie Vera, peering over her spectacles at Harry and making her blush. 'But her grandma rang me to ask if Caroline could come tomorrow, a day early. Mrs. Logan's got to go somewhere early Tuesday morning, so she won't be able to put Caroline on the school train on Tuesday afternoon.' She paused to look at something on her desk. 'So, how would you two like to take a train to Brockenhurst tomorrow morning? Mrs. Logan and Caroline will meet you there for a picnic lunch. Afterwards, you escort Caroline back on the next available train.'

'All by ourselves' I asked.

'Naturally,' came the reply. 'After all you came on the train all alone from London, didn't you, Ally?'

'Yes, but that was different.'

'Not really, in fact it was a much longer journey, and more difficult.'

I looked at Harry; 'Shall we?'

'Rather,' she replied. 'What do we do about tickets, Auntie Vera?'

'I shall lend you money to buy return tickets,' she replied. 'Mrs. Logan says that she will gladly pay for you, on account of all your good work helping Caroline to mend and get over the shock of losing her poor mother. If you tell her how much they were she will give you the money to give back to me.'

'What about her trunk?' I asked. 'We couldn't carry that; it'ud be much too heavy.'

'It's here already,' said Auntie Vera. 'It arrived on Friday by Carter Paterson, so there's only her little overnight case.'

'In that case it's dead easy,' I said. 'We'd love to do it. Do we catch the train in Bournemouth or Christchurch?'

'Pokesdown; all the local trains stop there, and it's handy for the trolleybus. I knew I could count on you. On Tuesday you can help Caroline settle in before the nomad hoards return. Put on tunics when you get dressed in the morning.'

'*Oui, ma Tante Plenderleith,*' said Harry, a Cheshire-cat-like grin spreading from ear to ear, as she performed a very low curtsy, one knee touching the floor. She was wobbling a bit and I couldn't resist giving her a nudge so she toppled over.

'That'll teach you to be so clever, Henrietta Gordon,' laughed Auntie Vera. 'All right, you rapscallions, go and see Scottie, and she'll fill in the details for you. She'll meet you off the train at Pokesdown on the way back. By the way, Ally, Miss Spurgeon has told me that you got top marks for the last two weeks, so you'll be form captain for the second half of the term. The notice has been posted on the school notice board. Well done, keep it up. It was a close thing—you beat Harry by just one mark and Maggot by three.' Then she pinned a red form captain badge on my jumper. 'Remember to pin it on your tunic, won't you.'

'I will. Thank you, Auntie Vera,' I said, rather overwhelmed.

'I'll see she does it, Auntie Vera,' said Harry, bear-hugging me and lifting me off my feet. 'You clever wee Ally, you, Well done.'

CHAPTER TWENTY-NINE

By Train to Brockenhurst

AFTER HIGH TEA, Harry and I went to our form-room to write our letters. We never said "writing home" like the others, because we had no parents at home. Our letters went to an address in London s.w.3., that was a "mailbox" for the secret government office our mothers worked for. I explained this to Harry, swearing her to secrecy, because in 1940 it was "Most Secret."

When we had finished, we went to the common room to find our friends. There was a fire in the JCR, so Jacko, Puddles and Jen-Pen were slumming it with us juniors again. Over half term, the ten of us who had stayed behind had become knitted together like a family, from the youngest, Susie Morgan, to the oldest, Kate Jackson, with Scottie and Auntie Vera trying to make up for our not being able to go home to see our parents.

'Where have you two been hiding?' asked Jacko. 'We wondered where you'd got to.' She was wearing a royal blue frock and was sitting cross-legged on the floor playing cats' cradles with Susie and Greta.

'Writing our letters in the third form,' I replied. 'It's quiet there.'

'And it's easier sitting at a desk,' added Harry, "specially if you use a dip-pen. We don't all have fancy fountain pens like Ally.' She stuck her tongue out at me.

'I see congrats are in order, Ally,' said Jacko, who now used Harry's pet name for me, pointing to my new form-captain badge. 'Top of the form eh? Jolly good show, wizard prang and all that! It's your first time, isn't it?'

'Aye,' replied Harry proudly, 'She's my clever wee lassie.'

'Not really,' I said, 'You know The Beak said I had only one mark more than you, and three more than Maggot.'

'I'll just have to work harder then,' said Harry. 'And I'll have to watch out for Maggot. It just shows what she can do when she tries.'

We sat on the floor and joined in the cats' cradles game for about fifteen minutes. We were just beginning a game of Snakes and Ladders when Scottie invited us all up to her room for "cocoa and bickies".

We had another undisturbed night, the second night running that there had been no air-raid warning, so we awoke feeling fresh and ready for anything. *Tigger* came and bounced on me as usual; it had become a regular morning ritual, after which we put on our dressing gowns and went to the bathroom together.

After our morning chores, we went to Scottie to get our final instructions for *"Operation Caroline"*. She gave us a slip of paper with all the train times written on it and small but strong paper bag with coins in. It was blue, with *"National Provincial Bank"* printed on it in one line and underneath *"£5 sixpences"*.

'Here's the money for your tickets,' she said, 'And some pennies in case you have to go to the lav. or use the telephone. D'you both know how to use a telephone box? You ask the operator for the number you want, and she'll tell you to put in your tuppence, and when you hear somebody answering, you press BUTTON A so they can hear you speaking. If there's no reply, you press BUTTON B to get your tuppence back. Our telephone number, Southbourne 1635, is written on the same piece of paper as the train times and I've also put down Mrs. Logan's 'phone number in Brockenhurst, just in case. Is all that clear?'

'Yes, Scottie,' replied Harry. 'What about money for something to eat?'

'You won't need any,' came the reply, 'Gladys is making some sandwiches for you, but there's enough money for a cuppa from the station buffet—if there is one, which I doubt—if you want a drink. Did you remember clean hankies?' We both nodded our heads. 'Any other questions?' We both shook our heads. 'Right then, who's going to take charge of the money?'

'*She* is,' we said together, pointing at each other, making us all laugh.

'I shall give it to the form captain,' Scottie said, putting an arm round me. 'Well done, my clever Ally. I'm glad you remembered to pin your form captain badge on your tunic. As you're going to be away all day on your own, you'd better take your National Identity Cards with you.'

She took a pile of buff-coloured cards from her desk drawer, and glancing inside them, selected two and gave one to each of us. I looked inside mine; it showed my National Registration number and said I was "Muir, Alexandra F." and that I lived at 9 Paradise Street, Cambridge. I never knew until that moment where Alexandra had lived before coming to Seabourne Prep. How lucky nobody had asked me where I lived! My Identity Card had been signed on my behalf by *Marie-F. Muir*, my mother. I put it away safely in the inside pocket of my blazer, and watched as Harry did the same with hers.

'Keep them safe and don't show them to anyone but a policeman or an army officer, and then *only* if you are asked for them. And *please* remember, whatever you do, *stay together!* Don't talk to strange men, and don't go wandering off on your own, even if you go to spend a penny. Make sure you both spend one here before you leave, because the ladies' lavs at stations are always disgusting. (*'So are gents' ones!' I thought to myself.*) Take some lavatory paper with you, just in case; there's never any when you need it! Also, don't stick your head out of the window when the train is moving, in case you get a smut in your eye.' She gave me the blue money bag and watched me put it in my blazer pocket. 'One more thing; look for a non-smoking compartment on the train, and it would be nicer for you in one marked *"ladies only"*; then you won't be bothered by strange men. Right, lassies, off you pop, and I'll meet you at Pokesdown this afternoon. Don't forget to take your gas-masks, or to collect your sandwiches from Gladys. Have a lovely time now.' She gave us each a hug, and *"Operation Caroline"* was under way.

*

We didn't have long to wait for a trolleybus. It was our friendly conductress again, and she gave us a cheerful smile when we bought our tickets before going upstairs.

'You're reely nice kids,' she said, 'Thinkin' of me poor ol' legs like that. All this standin' about and runnin' up and down stairs don't do me poor ol' varicose veins no good. Where's you orf to t'day, somewhere nice?'

'We're going to Brockenhurst to fetch one of the younger girls,' said Harry. 'She lost her mummy when their house was bombed at the beginning of term. She was hurt too, and when she was let out of the hospital, she went to stay with her grandma.' We decided against going upstairs, and sat on the seat just inside the bus, next to the rear platform.

'Was she one of the kiddies what you visited in 'ospital?' asked the clippie. 'There was a bit in the *Echo* last week, 'bout 'ow you've bin visitin' the injured kiddies in Boscombe 'ospital reg'lar like. Reel Christian of you, I calls it. The matron said it made all the difference to the kiddies, partic'ly the young ones, to 'ave someone visit 'em reg'lar. 'Scuse me a mo.' She turned to look upstairs and bellowed; 'Grand Avenue next stop, *I thang-you*,' and pressed the bell once to tell the driver someone wanted to get off.

The bus stopped and a man came down the front stairs got off. Our clippie-friend helped a frail old lady with a walking stick get on, and we stood up to allow her to sit where we had been. She smiled sweetly at us.

'What nice polite little girls you are,' she said. 'So thoughtful. My poor old legs are not what they used to be. Thank you,' she said as the conductress helped her to sit down.

'Hold on tightly now, Madam,' said the clippie, and she pressed the bell twice for the driver to start.

'I see you girls go to Seabourne Preparatory,' the old lady said. She had a slightly foreign accent, and said her 'Rs' in the back of her throat. 'My grand-daughter, Hannah Dürnberg, started there zis term, perhaps you haff met her already.'

'Yes,' I replied. 'She's in our form, isn't she, Harry?'

'Rather,' said Harry. 'She's jolly good at games, and good at lessons too.'

'So *you're* ze famous Harry,' said Mrs. Dürnberg. 'And you, my dear, must be Alex; Hannah has told me of you. I hear you haff been singing in ze church choir and I am most interested zat you both haff boys' names.'

'Not really,' I said, 'you see, we both have names that are a bit long, so they got shortened. My name's Alexandra, actually.'

'And mine's Henrietta,' added Harry.

'I think zey are much nicer than your short names, and much more feminine,' Mrs. Dürnberg told us. 'I think it is such a pity zat girls try to imitate boys. I haff always liked Henrietta as a name. It is so very pretty.'

'I was named after my French granny,' said Harry.

'I hope zat she is not in France now, my dear.'

'I'm afraid she is,' said Harry, grimly. 'She lives in a village called Oradour-sur-Glâne, near Limoges. Although Oradour is in Vichy France, I haven't heard from her since June, or seen her since before the war. Mummy and I went to see her in August last year. We got back just three days before war broke out.'

'Goot gracious! You were lucky to get out when you did, you might have got stuck there. And your fathers, are they in the forces?'

'Both our fathers are dead,' I said.

'Before the war,' added Harry.

'I am so sorry,' said Mrs. Dürnberg, 'How very distressing for you both. Hannah's father, my son, is also dead.' She patted my knee. 'And your mothers?'

Harry looked as if she was about to say something, so I gave an almost imperceptible frown.

'Oh, they're *nurses*,' I replied hurriedly. *(This could be true, because they were members of the F.A.N.Y., the First Aid Nursing Yeomanry, many of whose women were seconded, like our mothers, to S.O.E., the Special Operations Executive.)*

'Pokesdown next stop, girls,' the clippie told us. 'You can get off at the back if you like. Mind how you go now!'

'We will. Thank you very much,' said Harry. 'Goodbye, Mrs. Dürnberg.'

'Gootbye, Henrietta, gootbye, Alexandra.' replied Mrs. Dürnberg. 'It has been so very interesting talking to you both.'

We watched the trolleybus turn left at the junction, then crossed the road to the Station. The first thing was to buy our tickets at the booking office.

'Two half third-class returns to Brockenhurst please,' I asked the lady behind the ticket window. Her hair was in curlers with a gaudy scarf tied over them. She had a cigarette hanging from one corner of her mouth and was reading a magazine.

She put down her magazine. 'When're yer comin' back, ducky?' she asked, in a bored, flat voice.

'This afternoon, please, Miss,' I replied, hoping I was being polite.

'Missus ac-chewly,' said the bored voice, taking a ticket from the rack. She stamped the date on each end, and with a pair of scissors, cut the ticket in half diagonally. 'That'll be two an' eightpensaypenny, ducky.' As she talked, the cigarette that was stuck to her lower lip wiggled up and down, as if it was beating time to her words.

I took two florins from the bank-bag Scottie had given us and pushed them through the arch-shaped cut-out in the ticket window and said; 'Four shillings.'

'I c'n see it's four bob, ducky, I ain't blind. There you are, ducky, one an' thre'pensaypenny chynge.' She counted the change on to the counter, a shilling, a threepenny bit, and a ha'penny, and pushed it and the two half-tickets towards me.

'Thank you very much,' I said. 'Where do we get the train to Brockenhurst?'

'Over the bridge and down the other side, ducky. Platform one.'

'Thank you very much,' I said again.

'You're welcome I'm sure, ducky,' she said as she picked up her magazine and continued reading.

We moved away from the ticket office towards the stairs down to the platforms. As soon as we were out of sight of the ticket window, Harry took my arm.

'Come along, ducky,' she said, imitating the booking clerk's bored voice, and we dissolved into fits of giggles.

'Quack-wack,' I replied. 'I thought that old Mrs. Dung-bug on the bus was a bit nosy. Did you hear her accent? She sounded like a *boche* to me.'

'So *that's* why you said about our mummies being nurses,' said Harry, 'I had a feeling about her, too. She's jewish, you know, and Hannah's daddy was killed by the Nazis in Germany about four years ago. I see why you were being careful.'

'I just thought about the posters. You know; *"Careless talk costs lives"* and *"Be Like Dad! Keep Mum!"*. We don't actually *know* she's Hannah Dung-bug's granny; she could easily be a fifth columnist—a *boche* spy! I don't think she approved of our boys' names either.'

'She's just old-fashioned,' Harry said. '*Maman* would disagree with her.'

'Here we are, platform one, down these stairs.'

'How long have we got till the train comes?' asked Harry as we reached the platform.

I looked round for a clock, but couldn't see one. I could see one of the station name boards. The name had been painted over. I pointed it out to Harry.

'It's so the *boche* won't know where they are if they invade us by train!' she said. 'Well, it's to make it hard for them to find their way. It's been done all along the south coast. Almost all the sign-posts on the roads have been taken down, or turned round to confuse the enemy.'

'How do we know when we get to Brockenhurst?' I asked.

'Ask the guard to tell yer,' said a loud voice behind us. We swung round and there was a large, tough-looking lady wearing a porter's hat, trousers and a waistcoat with long sleeves.

'Thank you very much,' I replied. I could hear the sound of an approaching train. Looking down the track I saw a magnificent beast, smoke billowing from it's chimney—a steam locomotive! It was well worth coming back to 1940 to see it, let alone ride behind it. As it clanked in, I felt a waft of hot air, and a smell that I had smelled just once before, at a traction engine rally. The unmistakable smell of steam and oil and coal smoke all mixed together. The engine was painted green with the word "SOUTHERN" in golden yellow letters along its side, and behind it were several coaches painted in the same green.

'This is yer train now,' said the "porteress" as the train drew to a halt with a squealing of brakes. '*POKES*-down, this is *POKES*-down,' she bellowed.

I spotted a third class compartment with "Ladies Only" and "No Smoking" labels, on the window. I looked in. It was empty, so I opened the door and we got in. The "porteress" slammed the door behind us and we sat down. There was the sound of other doors slamming, then the blast of a whistle, and I heard the engine go; *"woooof... wooof... woof... woof..."* and then *"woof... chuff-chuff-chuff-chuff"* as the wheels slipped on the greasy rails before finding its feet again and resuming its slow, steady, regular beat. As they crossed each joint in the rails, the wheels of our carriage had their own song to sing; *"taa-taa, taa-taa.. ta-taa, ta-taa..."* slowly speeding up; *"ta-ta ta-taa... ta-ta ta-taa... ta-ta-ta-taa... tatatataa... tatatataa..."* like the "V for Victory" in Morse Code at the beginning and end of the special messages on the wireless.

I was bubbling with excitement. 'D'you know, this is the very *first* time I've *ever* been on a *real* steam train.'

'D'you mean there aren't any trains in your time, m' boy?' she said, giving my hand a squeeze and smiling.

'Not *steam* ones. They finished when I was three or four. They're all diesel or electric after that. The only place you can see steam trains working is in special museums. Auntie Kate's promised to take me to one of them at Didcot with Nick and Jackie.'

'You're everso fond of your Auntie Kate, aren't you?' said Harry. 'Is she a real auntie or a friend-auntie?'

'A real auntie—I s'pose. Yes, she must be, 'cos she's married to Mum's brother, Uncle Dougal; I mean she's going to marry—Oh! it's so *complicated* having two lives. It seems so long ago that I was a boy, I've almost forgotten what it was like. I s'pose I shouldn't *really* be in a *"Ladies Only"* compartment!'

She put an arm round me; 'Poor wee Ally! I won't tell them that you're a boy wearing a gymmer! If you didn't have to die, would you like to stay as a girl and grow up with me as your friend?'

'I don't know about growing up,' I said, 'But I'd love to be able to stay with you. I wish we could stay together, just as we are now, for ever and ever and ever and ever.'

She put a hand on my knee and squeezed. 'Like Peter Pan girls—*Petronella Pans*,' she said. 'I'd like that too. Grown-ups say that these are the happiest days of our lives, when we're children.'

I let my head rest on her shoulder. Behind the seats on the other side of the compartment was a map of the Southern Railway, and some pictures of places like Bognor Regis, Eastbourne and the Isle of Wight, all served by the Southern Railway. Suddenly, I had a thought.

'Harry? You know how they've painted out all the names of the stations? Well, don't you think it's a bit stupid leaving maps showing the south of England in every carriage? If old Hitler invades or if there are ever any Jerry prisoners of war over here, they could easily use them to help them escape.'

'So they could—clever Ally—I'm surprised nobody's thought of it before.'

The train slowed down for the next station. I let the window down to see where we were. '*CHRIST*church, Christ*church,* this is *Christchurch!*' croaked a very ancient looking porter. Several people got off. Doors slammed. The guard blew his whistle, waved his green flag, and we started off again. One less station to call at before we arrived at our destination.

The train had got up quite a good speed and we were gazing out of the window, when the door to the corridor opened; '*All* tickets please!' It was the guard. I took our tickets out of my purse and gave them to him. 'Thank you, my sweet,' he said.

I felt myself blushing. 'Please will you tell us when we get there? The station names all seem to be painted over.'

'That's so *Mister'itler* won't know where 'e is when 'e invades us,' said the guard. 'I'll come and tell you soon as we've left Sway—that's the station before Brocken'urst. It's the third stop from 'ere—New Milton first, Sway next, and then Brocken'urst.' He punched our tickets and gave them back to me.

'Thank you very much,' I said.

'You're welcome, sweet'eart,' he said, smiling as he closed the door behind him. I felt myself blushing again.

'I'm *not* his sweetheart,' I protested. 'I *do* wish people wouldn't call me *soppy* things like that. It's so jolly *embarrassing.*'

'You should've got used to it by now,' said Harry, 'you've been a girl for almost six weeks now! Anyway, it's your own silly fault for changing into a girl, and being so pretty!'

'But I couldn't *help* changing into a girl! I don't even know how it happened,' I said. 'And anyway what's six weeks when the previous ten and a half years have been spent being a boy?' Our eyes met and we grinned sheepishly. 'It's *brill* being together on our own, isn't it?'

'"Tis, isn't it?' she replied, squeezing my hand. '*Absolutely* brill.'

*

There was much screeching of brakes as the train jerked to a halt at Brockenhurst station. Harry un-hooked the leather window strap and lowered the window so she could open the door using the outside handle. 'Got everything?' she asked, as she stepped down on the platform. I grinned and felt myself all over.

'Yes, have you?' I replied. She stuck out the tip of her tongue. I got off the train, slammed the door and turned the handle horizontal to fasten it shut. We turned to look for the way out, when a whirlwind in the shape of Caroline rushed up to us, nearly knocking us flat.

'Harry! Alex!' she squealed, throwing herself first at Harry, and hugging her, and then at me. As she hugged me I lifted her off her feet and we twirled round. 'Look at me,' she said as I put her down. 'All my plaster's gone. Come and meet Gramma.' She tugged us up the platform, Harry on her right and me on her left, to the barrier where we showed our tickets to the man. Mrs. Logan was waiting on the other side.

'Hello, Harry, hello, Alex,' she said. 'Well met. Caroline's so excited that you've both come to take her back to school, aren't you, my precious?' Hearing those words gave me a moment's anxiety. She sounded so like Gran—my own Gran. (How I longed to know that her operation had been successful.)

'Good morning, Mrs. Logan,' said Harry, shaking hands. 'We hope you're keeping well?'

'Yes, good morning, Mrs. Logan,' I echoed and followed Harry's example. 'It's lovely to see you again. Caroline looks so much better now, doesn't she.' I turned to the younger girl and ruffled her hair slightly; 'And your hair's grown an awful lot.'

'So's Harry's,' said Caroline. 'You look much nicer with it hiding your ears, Harry.'

'D'you mean my ears are ugly?' said Harry, winking at Caroline and squeezing her hand.

'No, 'f course not! I mean you look *everso* much nicer, and much prettier too,' said Caroline. 'Doesn't she look prettier, Alex?'

'Yes,' I agreed, grinning at Harry. 'Not like a boy wearing a gymmer any more!' and stuck out the tip of my tongue at her.

CHAPTER THIRTY

"Operation Lollipop"

'WE'RE GOING TO HAVE A PICNIC,' said Caroline, as we walked away from the station. Brockenhurst Station was situated on the edge of the little New Forest town, so we didn't have far to go to find a suitable place for our picnic lunch.

'We've brought Spam sandwiches,' said Harry. 'Gladys, our cook made them for us.'

'That was kind of her,' said Mrs. Logan. 'I've brought a treat for you both.'

'Gramma digs for victory in her 'lotment. She grows potatoes, cabbages, beans, carrots, onions, peas and lots of things. And we have hens to make eggs for us, don't we Gramma?'

'That's right, my precious,' said Mrs. Logan. 'We'll pool our picnics together, then we can all have a bit of everything.' We came to a stile where a footpath crossed a field. 'We'll go into this field. Climb over the stile, precious.' Mrs. Logan waited for us girls to climb over, then she passed her picnic basket to us and climbed over too.

'Isn't it lucky it's fine, Mrs. Logan,' I said.

'It is, isn't it?' said Mrs. Logan. 'I think "Mrs. Logan" sounds a bit starchy, don't you? Why don't you call me "Gramma" like Caroline? Then you can all be my schoolgirl grand-daughters!'

'That makes you my big sisters,' said Caroline. 'I've always wanted to have a brother or sister, haven't I, Gramma?'

'Yes, my precious, and such pretty sisters too.' Gramma smiled sweetly. She was quite a small lady, just over five foot, only an inch or so taller than Harry and I, who were quite tall for our age. Her hair had been ginger, but now it had faded to a greyish blonde, and she wore it neatly permed. Once over the stile, she led the way to a sunny corner, where we could have our picnic.

'Now, my dears,' said Gramma; 'We'll take off our coats so we can sit on them; the grass is damp and we don't want catch chills, do we?' We laid our raincoats on the grass while Gramma spread a checked table-cloth on the grass and we helped her to lay out red plastic plates, cups and saucers. All the food was wrapped in greaseproof paper. (Not a polythene bag in sight, so I wondered if polythene had been invented in 1940.)

'And now—' said Gramma, taking a tin sandwich box out of the picnic basket. 'Now for our treat!' There were two greaseproof paper parcels inside. From one there came four hard-boiled eggs, and from the other, four pieces of cold chicken.

'Chicken!' exclaimed Harry. 'Where on earth did you get that, Gramma?'

'It's one of my poor old hens who'd gone off the lay,' replied Gramma, sadly. 'I feel a bit like a cannibal eating a dear old friend, but the war's brought such shortages; so I pretend it's a fowl I got from the butcher instead of poor Mrs. Chuckle-Cluck.' She put a piece of Mrs. Chuckle-Cluck on each plate with a hard boiled egg, a lettuce leaf, half a tomato, a couple of spring onions, and a some cucumber.

'Gramma grew all the salad,' said Caroline proudly, 'Didn't you, Gramma?'

'Yes, my precious,' replied Gramma, 'and you helped me pick them. I'm afraid this is almost the end of the tomatoes, but I made some green tomato chutney with the ones that didn't ripen.' She took out a jam-jar covered with a piece of clear cellophane held on by a rubber band. 'Who would like some?'

'Yes, *please*,' Harry and I replied together.

'And who'd like some orange to drink?' asked Gramma.

'Yes, *please*,' we all said together. She took out a bottle, the same shape as the medicine bottles from which Scottie dosed us. The label had a blue Ministry of Food symbol on it, and from it Gramma poured a small dollop of thick, sticky, orange-coloured syrup into each of our cups and then topped it up with water from a Thermos flask. She stirred it well, and passed the cups round.

'It's impossible to get proper orange squash these days,' she told us, 'But this Ministry of Food stuff that they supply for Caroline isn't *too* awful. At least it's got extra vitamins. Tuck in now, my dears, I don't want to see anything left over.'

Gramma had divided the Spam sandwiches that Gladys had made, between the four of us, and Harry and I ate those first, saving the treats till last. I no longer gobbled my food down as I had back in September; I had learned to make it last longer by taking smaller bites. I recognised the taste of the orange squash; it was the same as we were given at our weekend lunches. Between mouthfuls we chatted away, telling Caroline what had been happening at school since we last saw her, about our half-term treat with Scottie and Auntie Vera. Caroline was sorry she had missed the tea-party at Beales, but thought it sounded a jolly good outing.

'Now that you're a boarder, Caroline,' said Harry, 'We must find you a nickname. I s'pose we could call you Carrie, but it's not very exciting. D'you have another Christian name?'

'Laura,' replied the seven-year-old.

'Laurie?' I suggested.

'No,' said Harry, 'it sounds too much like a motor van, and it also sounds like an awful boy called Lawrence at St Mungo's. How about Lolly?'

'Short for lollipop,' giggled Caroline gleefully.

'Lollipop it shall be,' said Harry. 'Now you sound like a *real* boarder. From now on, we're on *"Operation Lollipop!"*

'Do you like that, Lollipop?' asked Gramma, suddenly sneezing twice, very loudly. 'Pardon, Mrs. Vardon,' she said.

'What *are* you doing in my *garden*?' chanted Lollipop, happily.

Soon there was nothing left; we had eaten it all. Gramma had made raspberry elly for "afters". When we had cleared the picnic things, she gave us each a carrier bag containing a fruit cake and some apples for us to take back to school with us. After that we went to talk to some New Forest ponies grazing nearby. Then we returned to the station to collect Lolly's overnight case from the left luggage office, thanked and said goodbye to Gramma and caught the train back to Pokesdown. We found a *ladies only* compartment again and settled in. A lady guard who came along to punch our tickets didn't call me anything embarrassing.

*

Scottie was waiting for us on the platform when the train pulled into Pokesdown station. Lolly had been very brave when she said goodbye to Gramma, and a cuddle from us had soon driven away any tears.

'Welcome back, my wee pet,' said Scottie, bending down to give her a kiss. 'My! Don't you look well! Did you have a good journey?'

'Yes,' replied Lolly, 'the train had a lady guard. And Gramma took us for a picnic in a field where there were New Forest ponies.'

'You must have had a lovely time,' said Scottie. 'What's in your carrier-bags?'

'Tuck,' replied Harry. 'Lolly's grandma has made a fruit cake for each of us.'

'Lolly?' queried Scottie.

'*That's* my new nickname,' said Lolly, 'Harry says it's short for Laura. Sometimes they call me Lollipop.'

'Of course, Lollipop,' said Scottie, smiling. 'How silly of me not to realise.'

She took Lolly's overnight case from me, and we climbed the stairs. After giving our tickets to the large porter-lady at the barrier, we left the station and walked to the bus stop outside the Fire Station and opposite the British Restaurant.

On the trolleybus we told Scottie about our journey, and the picnic with cold chicken and a hard-boiled egg. We were talking so much that we nearly forgot to get off the bus at our stop, and if it hadn't been for the conductress, we would have sailed past the school and down Belle View Road towards Crossroads—

*

There was quite a reception committee waiting for us as we walked through the front door. Susie Morgan rushed up to Lolly and gave her a hug before she had even had time to put down her carrier bag.

'Hello, Cawoline,' said Susie, 'Are you feeling better now?'

'Yes thank you, Susie,' replied Lolly. 'Much better, but the doctor says I mustn't do gym for a few more weeks.'

'She's got a nickname now,' I said, 'Haven't you, Lollipop?'

Lolly nodded and blushed with pride. Auntie Vera took hold of one of her hands. 'That's a jolly good nickname, Lollipop,' she said. 'I bet Harry thought of it.'

'Yes,' said Lolly. 'She says Lolly's short for Laura.'

'I thought it might be,' replied Auntie Vera. She gave Lolly's hand a squeeze. 'Now, Lollipop. Go with Scottie and Goody to your dormitory; Susie and Greta, you go too. Harry and Alex, go and change into home clothes and we'll all meet again for high tea.'

We didn't take long to change. Harry decided to keep her white school blouse on and wear her kilt with it. I thought I would wear my own navy-blue frock for a change.

'If I had my sporran,' said Harry as she buttoned me up at the back, 'I'd almost be wearing my old St. Mungo's uniform.'

'Are you going to leave your tie on?'

'No, I'll take it off and put on a jumper. Ally? You know the fruit cakes Gramma gave us? I've decided to share mine with the other girls who didn't have the treat we did.'

'I was thinking about that, too. Let's get two plates from Gladys, then we can put them on the table for high tea. If we wait till tomorrow, all the girls who've been home will be back, and there won't be enough to go round.'

We looked into Merlin dormitory to see how Lolly was settling in. Scottie was helping her into a bottle-green frock.

'That's a pretty frock, Lollipopkins,' said Harry.

'Yes, Gramma made it for me. You look nice in your kilt, Harry.'

'We've come to take you to the common room,' I told her. 'That's where we spend our spare time, reading, listening to the wireless, or playing games. Are you any good at snakes and ladders?'

Caroline nodded.

'By the way, Scottie,' said Harry, 'Ally and I want to share our fruit cakes with all the others who've spent half term at school. We've had a lovely treat today, so it's only fair that they should get something out of it.'

Scottie smiled; 'That's my best girls, always thinking of others. There, my wee Lollipop, you look as pretty as a picture.'

'Prettier,' I said. 'Come on, Lollipop, we'll take you to the common room.'

*

At high tea, we sat at two tables, so we would not be thirteen at the one table. Scottie, Goody and the three juniors sat at one table, while Auntie Vera sat with the rest of us at the next table. We thought Lolly might be a bit weepy, but she was as happy as a sandboy to be with us. I suppose the shock of losing her mother and her stay in hospital had something to do with it. At school, she was with friends, and we all did our best to make her feel "one of the family."

Gramma's fruit cakes were scrumptious, with lots of sultanas, raisins, cherries and mixed peel. Everybody thought they were *wizard prang*! The girls insisted that Harry and I have two pieces each, as we had shared our "treasure" with them. We all ate it very slowly, savouring each mouthful, and leaving our favourite morsel to be a "last mouthful" fit for a king.

We went to the gym after high tea, for a "family gathering," or *"cèilidh"* as Scottie and Harry called it. We each had to do our party-piece, and we played party games, danced and sang songs. Scottie surprised us all by bringing a concertina, and she played some Scottish tunes. Harry took off her shoes and socks and danced the Highland Fling and the sword dance barefoot. Her kilt whisked about her knees in time to the music as she danced around the crossed swords, never once touching them with her bare toes. Then Puddles and Rob Roy danced the sailor's hornpipe, and Scottie had to play the Highland Fling music again so all three could dance it together. Harry tried to teach me the steps, but I got terribly muddled. Jacko amazed us all by singing some jazz songs, accompanying herself on the piano. We particularly enjoyed one called *The Darktown Strutters' Ball*. Jen-Pen played a tune on her flute, and I sang *Early one morning*, and *The Miller of Dee*, two traditional English folk songs, with Auntie Vera accompanying me on the piano.

Goody baffled us with some conjuring tricks and Nicky did some juggling and acrobatics. Lolly played her party piece on the piano, and Greta and Susie each recited poems; Greta recited *Fairies* by Rose Fyleman which begins, '*There are fairies at the Bottom of our Garden*,' and Susie's poem was *Someone Came Knocking at My Wee Small Door*, by Walter de la Mare. We were wondering who would do the next turn, when Harry started singing a French folk song, "*Chevaliers de la Table Ronde*," which Auntie Vera joined in at the piano, leading us all in the chorus with great gusto.

Then we all joined in singing some of our favourite "air-raid shelter songs" including *Run, Rabbit, Run* and *It's A Long Long Way to Tipparary*. It was a very jolly party, and it ended with Gladys bringing cocoa and biscuits.

Finally, Scottie played *Auld Lang Syne*, and we were packed off to bed after a quick dance around while Scottie played *We're no' awa' tae bide awa'*, an old Scots song that translates as; "We're not going away to stay away;" a jolly way of saying *au revoir*. We thanked the grown-ups for a wonderful evening and called, 'Goodnight' to each other as we went to our dormitories. 'I hope we don't have an air-raid tonight,' Rob Roy said, as she went into her cubicle.

'Same here,' replied Jen-Pen.

'Aye,' said Harry, 'If I had to sing any more tonight, I'd go hoarse.'

'Whee-hee-hee-hee-hee-hee,' I replied, doing a very bad imitation of a horse whinnying.

CHAPTER THIRTY-ONE

Half-Term Ends—

TUESDAY THE TWENTY-SECOND of October dawned fine. We had had yet another quiet night with no air-raid, and I cannot remember hearing the rising bell; I was woken by Tigger bouncing on me. She dragged me half-asleep to the bathroom, filled a basin for me and even threatened to wash me!

We spent a quiet morning, and after lunch went for a walk with Lolly. She wanted to see the ruins of her house, which was only a short distance away, but Scottie said she should wait for a week or two, until she had got used to being a boarder. Scottie promised that we could take her as soon as she felt Lolly was up to it. Lolly said she would wait, saying she was quite glad not to go just yet. So we took her for a walk on the cliffs like we did on Sunday afternoons. Being Tuesday, the Home Guard were not at the bandstand; they were at their ordinary jobs in shops, offices, factories, hospitals, or any of a multitude of jobs, all vital to the war effort of keeping *"His Majesty's Ship Great Britain"* afloat and going full steam ahead towards victory.

Some of the girls who had been home for the exeat began drifting back before lunch. Unlike 1974, when most pupils at schools like Seabourne Prep. would be driven back by car, wartime petrol rationing and the fact that very few families owned a car, made this out of the question for all but a tiny number of people. So the girls all had to rely on trains and buses.

Trains from London ran very erratically. Newspapers and the news bulletins on the wireless told us that London had been bombed every single night since 7th September. Papers, and magazines like *Picture Post*, showed pictures of Londoners queueing every evening for places in air-raid shelters or Underground stations. Pictures that showed entire families camped out on the platforms, cooking meals, relaxing, having sing-songs and children being undressed and put to bed, just as if they were in their own bedrooms at home. Nearer to us, Southampton had been taking a hammering and all the trains from London came through Southampton.

Just before tea-time the siren wailed, so we all went to the shelter. To me, daylight air-raids were not as scary as those at night, because we could see more of what was going on. On our way to the shelter, we could hear ack-ack guns, and saw a squadron of Spitfires flying overhead, but no Jerry bombers.

There was still no sign of Bendy Wendy and the girls who had gone to London and stations on the line to Waterloo. Compartments on the train had been reserved for the school party, and girls could catch the train at stations on the way. The incessant bombing frequently scored direct hits on the railways, causing terrible disruption to the running of the trains.

Scottie and Auntie Vera were beginning to look anxious, in case something awful had happened. Maggot, Weevil and Paddy had got to Bournemouth Central from Blandford, and found the coach waiting for Bendy and company. After waiting in the coach for half an hour, Maggot tried to find out when the train was due; but nobody knew; she phoned Auntie Vera who told them to catch a trolleybus.

At about six o'clock, Harry and I were with Auntie Vera in her study, when the telephone rang. She picked up the receiver.

'Seabourne Preparatory School,' she said, and paused for a few seconds. 'This is Miss Plenderleith speaking... Oh, Good evening, Mrs. Willis,... The train still not got to Winchester. Dear me! Have the railway people said when it's likely to arrive?... Oh! You've not asked! Is there a local they could catch?... You think there is? Good!... Yes, Mrs. Willis, that would be fine; put Dilys and Emily on it and tell them to get off at Pokesdown and catch a trolleybus... Oh, Brenda Gunn's there too. Good! She can take charge of them, she'll know exactly what to do.' She covered the mouthpiece and turned to us; 'Which is more than I can say about Mrs. Willis's bird-brained flibbertigibbets!... Yes, it *is* very worrying, *isn't* it, Mrs. Willis.' She raised her eyebrows, and shrugged in exasperation. 'No, Mrs. Willis, I won't... Thank you for letting me know, Mrs. Willis,... Goodbye, Mrs. Willis. Yes, of course I will, I've got your number in my card index... Goodbye, Mrs. Willis.' She put the receiver back on its cradle. 'Haa-ah dear!' she sighed. 'That was Mrs. Willis having a right flapdoodle. Honestly!' She sighed again. 'No wonder the twins are so scatterbrained. I thought she was *never* going to ring off, she said everything at *least* three times! Apparently she and the twins had been sitting on the platform at Winchester station for more than three and a half hours! Harry, be a dear and pop and ask Gladys to come and see me.'

'Certainly, Auntie Vera,' replied Harry, disappearing.

'Hasn't the train got to Winchester yet then?' I asked.

'Apparently not,' replied Auntie Vera. 'Mrs. Willis watched two local trains leave before she even asked when the train from London was due. I'll phone Bournemouth Central to find out.'

She reached for the telephone receiver just as it rang again. 'Seabourne Preparatory School...Yes, I'll accept the charges.... *Wendy!* At *last!* Thank *goodness!* We've been worried sick. Where *are* you? I didn't quite catch what the operator said...Where's that?...Oh! *North* of Winchester... Line blocked you say?... Oh, so they're getting buses to take you to Winchester... Oh, Wendy, before you ring off, Mrs. Willis and the twins have been sitting at Winchester station for three and a half hours and let a couple of locals leave. She's putting the twins on the next local... No, Bren Gunn's with them; she has to change at Winchester on her way from Abingdon.... All right, Wendy, I'll let the bus people know... Are the girls in good spirits?... I bet they are; still it's all an adventure for them, isn't it?... Good girl, Wendy, so long as you all keep your chins up. I'll expect you when I see you, take care now... *Au revoir*.' She replaced the receiver. 'That was Miss Bendall.

She's somewhere north of Winchester.' There was a knock at the door. 'Come away in.' Gladys entered, followed by Harry. 'Ah! Gladys, there you are! I've just had Miss Bendall on the 'phone. There's a bomb on the line and they're stuck north of Winchester, and Lord only knows when they'll get back. Have you cooked all the high teas yet?'

'No, Miss P. It's soup an' then toad in the 'ole, an' I purposely di'n't cook it all, on h'account of 'ow late they woz comin' back las' term. I was on me way t' see yer, when I bumped into young 'Arry 'ere.'

'That's a relief, Gladys,' said Auntie Vera. 'Food's *so* scarce these days, I hate to think of it going to the *Squander-Bug*.'

'No more'n I do, Miss P.,' said Gladys. 'Any h'idea what time they'll get back?'

'Not yet I'm afraid, but Wendy says she'll try to ring just before they catch a train at Winchester.'

'Yer'll let me know then,' said Gladys.

'Yes, of course.'

Gladys returned to the kitchen, and Auntie Vera turned to us. As far as I can make out,' she said, 'There's an unexploded land mine lodged up against a railway bridge north of Winchester. It's not actually on the line, but the bomb disposal chaps are worried that vibrations from passing trains might set it off.'

'Crikey!' exclaimed Harry. 'So what're they going to do?'

'Until the bomb's been rendered harmless, there's not much they *can* do. All trains in both directions have been stopped; evidently there's quite a queue. The Southern Railway people are having to reverse them to a station where passengers who need to reach their destination urgently, can be transferred to buses. The school train had got back to the station, and they were waiting for a bus to take them to Winchester, where they'll be able to catch a local train back here.'

'Poor things,' I said. 'It could take them *ages* to get back—and it's dark, too.'

'It's a nuisance, but it can't be helped,' sighed Auntie Vera. 'It's the sort of thing that often happens in wartime. I'll make an announcement at high tea, in case any of the girls are worried about their chums. By the by, how's Caroline, is it *Lolly* you call her? How's she settling in? I know you're both keeping an eye on her.'

'She's just fine,' replied Harry. 'Since tea, she's been in the common room playing snakes and ladders with Greta, Susie and Freddie. She's as happy as a sandboy.'

'*Splendid!*' said Auntie Vera. 'Keep me posted. I'll just ring the bus company. They probably don't know what's happened.'

The phone rang and Auntie Vera answered it; 'Seabourne Preparatory School… This is Miss Plenderleith speaking… Oh, good afternoon Mrs. Morgan… Yes, Susan's doing fine, but she worries about her father a bit… Well, that's wonderful news! I'll send for her and tell her straight away… Goodbye, Mrs Morgan. I'm so happy for you, and Susie will be delighted and so will all the other girls.'

'That was Mrs Morgan,' said Auntie Vera. 'Susie Morgan's father's escaped from his P.O.W. camp in Germany and has managed to get back to England.'

'That's wonderful news,' said Harry.

'Susie'll be thrilled,' I added, as the bell for high tea rang; we stood up.

'Will you send Susie to see me, please,' said Auntie Vera. 'Don't say anything to her; I'll break the news gently. And ask Gladys to send some tea here for her, will you. She can have high tea with me. And don't tell anyone the news, will you?'

We saw Susie coming out of the common room with Lolly. 'Susie,' said Harry, 'Miss Plenderleith wants to see you before high tea.' Susie frowned. 'It's all right, Susie, you're not in trouble. I'm sure you'll like what she's going to tell you.'

Susie went and knocked on the study door and Lolly joined us as we went to wash our hands and tidy ourselves.

Near the eatery we met Maggot, Weevil and Paddy, who had just got back. They were about to go upstairs, when Jacko saw them. 'Dump your kit in the hall, girls,' she said. 'Then spend a penny if you need to, wash your hands and come straight into high tea.'

*

When Susie came into the JCR after high tea and she was a different girl—happy, smiling and bubbling with excitement. 'Daddy's escaped from Germ'ny,' she squealed. 'He's in London, and Mummy's going to see him tomorrow. And they're going to come and see me soon.'

'How lovely, Susie,' said Lolly. 'How clever of him to escape?'

'Yes, wasn't it?' said Susie. 'I wonder how he did it.'

'Perhaps he dug a tunnel under the wire fence round the camp and got out that way,' I suggested.

'I'll ask him when I see him,' said Susie.

'Anyway, it's one in the eye for horrid old Hitler, isn't it?' said Harry.

*

Brenda Gunn and the Willis twins arrived twenty minutes before the bed-time bell, and were immediately hustled into the eatery by Jacko. Harry and I had been sent to the kitchen by Scottie with the message that Bendy and the London girls hoped to arrive at about half past nine. Leaving the kitchen, after telling Gladys, we heard her stumping around muttering, '*Blinkin'* 'itler, upsettin' everybody's arrangements. *I'd* give 'im *what for*, if ever *I* lays 'ands on the *so'n'so*.'

'I bet she *would* too,' I said. 'Hitler wouldn't stand a chance against Glad.'

'I say, Ally,' said Harry, 'she could be the new British secret weapon—Shall we write to Mr Churchill about her?' She grinned, just as the bedtime bell rang.

As we undressed, we talked about the unexploded bomb, lying menacingly close to the railway. 'It could have been really awful,' said Harry, as we returned from the bathroom with Rob Roy. 'S'pose the bomb hadn't been spotted, and went off just as the train with Bendy Wendy and the girls on it was going past?'

'I was thinking that,' said Rob Roy. '*Blinkin'* 'itler! as Glad would say.' We giggled, even though it was not really a laughing matter. I suppose we made jokes about the war and Hitler, looking for the funny side of things because it was so serious. If we hadn't done that, we would've gone around with faces a yard long, being miserable all the time. I suppose it was what became known in later years as "*The Dunkirk Spirit.*"

When we got back to the dormitory, Jen-Pen and the Willis twins were there.

'It was *awful* waiting for the train, *wasn't* it?' said Dilly.

'It was a *frightful* bore, we just sat there doing absolutely *nothing*,' added Milly.

'There weren't even any *girls'* books on the bookstall,' said Dilly.

'I'm sure it was terrible for you both,' said Jenny, a little irritably. 'Just get undressed, and go and wash, or Scottie will be giving you both a "miss".'

'Yes, Jen-Pen,' said Dilly.

'Straight away, Jen-Pen,' said Milly. 'Where's Nancy?'

'Somewhere the other side of Winchester, when we last heard,' replied Jenny; 'With Bendy Wendy and the Londoners. Nancy will have caught the train in Basingstoke.'

'Oooh! Was their train delayed too?' asked Milly.

'Of course it was, you pathetic moon calf,' said Harry. 'They are on the train that *you* were supposed to catch.'

'Come *on*, you two,' said Jenny impatiently, 'Stop *dawdling.*'

'Yes, Jen-Pen,' said Milly-Willy.

'Straight away, Jen-Pen,' said her twin.

*

We never heard Nancy come in. She must have been as quiet as a mouse, because when there was an air-raid warning at about half past eleven, she came out of her cubicle and went to the shelter with us. Once in the shelter, we asked about their adventure.

'Actually, there's not much to tell,' she told us. 'We'd passed Micheldever Station, and were going quite well. The train was packed—it was jolly lucky we had reserved compartments 'cos there were people standing all along the corridors, and if we wanted to go to the lav, we literally had to *climb* over the bodies. It was jolly crowded in our compartment, and for part of the time we put Puppy up in the luggage rack.'

'What was it like, Puppy?' I asked.

'A bit like being in a hammock,' Puppy replied. 'Ever-so comfy, much comfier than the beds in our dormies!'

'That's not difficult,' chuckled Harry. 'Go on, Nancy.'

'Well we were going quite well,' she continued, 'until we had to stop in the middle of a field. Well, Peg-Leg, who has a brother who's dotty about trains, come to think of it she's just as bad, well, she let down the window and had a dekko. She said the signal was against us. That was at about half past *two*, and at *five* o'clock we were *still* there; we hadn't moved an inch!'

'In the *name* o' the wee *man!*' exclaimed Harry. 'What on earth did you do all that time?'

'Well, we started by playing I-spy-with-my-little-eye. And when we had spied absolutely everything, inside and outside the train that there was to spy we—Hey! Peg-Leg, what did we do after I-Spy? You know, on the train this after'.'

'Charades,' said Peg-Leg. 'D'you remember, Nancy? Bendy had us in fits when she tried to do Queen Elizabeth stepping on Sir Walter Raleigh's cloak. Then we had a sing-song.'

'And then we started going *backwards*,' giggled Puppy. 'It was rather funny, we thought the engine driver had made a mistake!'

'I was jolly glad we were moving again,' said Peg-Leg. 'I mean, we were sitting ducks if there'd been an air-raid. A jerry fighter could easily have flown along the train machine-gunning us.'

'We had to go back to Micheldever,' said Nancy, 'Where there were buses to take us to Winchester to catch another train.'

'When we got on the train at Winchester,' said Mag-Bags, 'It was dark, so we were a bit scared there might be an air-raid while we were on the train, like you had, Ally. If we hadn't been delayed, we'd have run slap-bang into a raid at New Milton. A lady who got on there said an orphanage at Milford-on-Sea was bombed while the children were having tea. Two of the nuns were injured and had to go to hospital.'

'That must have been the same raid we had here at tea-time,' said Lolly. 'I'm jolly glad you came and fetched me yesterday.'

'So'm I,' said Harry. 'It must have been quite an adventure for you all.'

'It certainly was!' replied Mag-Bags.

'Well, thank goodness you all got back safely,' said Auntie Vera. 'At least you have something interesting to put in your letters home next Sunday.'

*

We were in the shelter just over an hour; the "all-clear" sounded at about a quarter to one. We trooped back to beds which had gone cold while we had been out in the air-raid shelter.

'I'm going to leave my socks and pants on,' said Harry. 'At least until my bed warms up again.'

'Me too,' said Rob Roy. 'Hey! It's Wednesday and we've got art first period.'

'Aye, and arithmetic with Pretty Polly after that,' said Harry. 'How *ugsome!*'

'Oh, I don't know,' I said. 'Her lessons have been okay since Maggot and Weevil started behaving themselves.'

'It's all right for *you*, Ally,' said Harry; '*You're* wizard at maths.'

'Och, Harry! Your maths is jolly good.'

'Hey! Did you hear her, Rob?' said Harry. 'She *actually* said "*och!*" Her Scots ancestry is beginning to surface at long *last!* The only reason I'm any good at maths is because you explain it to me, Ally, ma wee hen!'

CHAPTER THIRTY-TWO

—and the Rest of the Term Begins

THE REST OF THE WEEK following half-term passed in a flash. Lessons were much the same as usual, but being form captain meant I had to set an example to the other girls, as well as leading them into prayers every morning. There was only one night that we had to make the cold trip out to the air-raid shelter.

The week-end was spiffing, as Harry would say. The high spot of Saturday was our Lacrosse match, when our under-twelves beat Dean Park School's under-twelves by seven goals to two, on their ground. Harry scored, so did Jen-Pen, Rob Roy, Nicky and I did too! We had a charabanc to take us there, so there was room for a few of the girls to come along to cheer for us, and a good number of the day-bugs made their own way there. But best of all for Harry and I, was seeing Boy-Alex and his Granny bellowing 'Play up, Seabourne,' at the tops of their voices.

On Mondays, Tuesdays, and Wednesdays, after lessons, Mr Grubb began giving me some extra singing coaching. I was to sing Henry Purcell's Evening Hymn at Evensong on Remembrance Sunday. It is a beautiful but difficult piece with many long runs and long notes, needing careful breath control. I would be singing solo with just organ accompaniment, so I had to be note- and word-perfect. I felt honoured to be asked to sing it, and worked hard to please him.

As soon as lunch was over on the last Sunday in October, Harry and I rushed upstairs to change for going to tea with Boy-Alex. We had been given permission to wear home clothes, because Alex's Gran had asked Scottie specially.

At around two o'clock, we caught a Christchurch-bound, number 21 trolleybus. We went upstairs and sat in the front. As we passed the school, we could see over the fence into the grounds. The bus swung right into Belle View Road and headed towards Crossroads, where the number 22 trolleybuses terminated. The clippie had to get off and pull the chain to change the "points" on the trolley-wires so we could bear left down the hill to Tuckton. On the right before Tuckton Bridge were Newlyn and Ball's Tea Gardens; between them and the bridge, a track led to the creek where, in 1974, Nick and Jackie kept their sailing-dinghy *Puffin*.

On the opposite bank of the River Stour, the boatyard was full of laid-up boats, and we could see into the boat-sheds where they built and repaired all sorts of boats. In front was the pontoon from where the pleasure boats used to leave in peacetime, taking trippers down to Mudeford for picnics. Several boats from Tuckton and Christchurch took part in the rescue of our men from the Dunkirk beaches about three months before I arrived in 1940. We crossed Barrack Road, and carried on down Stour Road past Christchurch Station, until we came to

Bargate, where we turned right towards the centre of the town.

Alex was going to meet us at the terminus, in a short side street on the right off the High Street. As the trolleybus turned into the terminus, we saw him looking for us. I waved and he waved back. As we got off the bus he ran over to greet us.

'Ally! Kate! You made it! Wizard prang! Have you seen how the trolleybuses are turned round here? They drive it on the turntable and push it round by hand. I often help them.'

There were three clunks as the six-wheeled trolleybus drew forward on to the turn-table. Then the conductress used a long pole to pull the trolley poles off the wires and hitch them under two hooks at the rear end of the roof. The driver got down from his cab, and seeing us, pointed to the bus, and the three of us pushed it round on the turn-table. It took hardly any strength, and once it had begun to turn it almost went on its own. After replacing the trolley poles on the wires, the driver climbed aboard again and pulled the bus forward, ready for the return trip.

'Gosh,' said Harry, 'I never thought it'd turn as easily as that.'

'Come on,' said Alex, 'I'll show you the Quay. You could have come across the Wick Ferry if I'd thought. If you'd come by bike it would have been the quickest way. The ferry is a punt which is poled across the river by an old man of about ninety. Not as old as that really, he just looks it! He's a retired fisherman, and he took a thirty-foot open motor boat all the way to Dunkirk and brought about forty soldiers back safely.'

'Golly,' said Harry, 'That was brave. What happened to the ferry while he was away?'

'His wife took over,' said Alex. 'Loads of small boats from here took part in the evacuation of Dunkirk. I bet old Hitler was hopping mad, eh?' He smiled. 'I remember hearing Mr. Churchill on the wireless just afterwards. He said all about fighting on the beaches and never surrendering.' Suddenly, he looked very sad. 'I listened to it with Mum and Monica.' He took a handkerchief from his trouser pocket, wiped a solitary tear from his one eye and blew his nose.

'Gosh, aren't I lucky having two nice girls to look after me?' he said with a grin. 'You know the snag with having only one eye is that I can't wink any more!' Then placing himself between us, an arm round each of our shoulders, me on his right and Harry on his left, we strolled down to the quay before going to his Grandma's little house overlooking the River Stour.

There was some time before tea, and after we said "hello" to Mrs. Drummond, we went up to Alex's bedroom, where his Hornby 'O' Gauge clockwork train set was laid out on the carpet. He had four engines; one, named "Eton", was a model of a Southern Railway 'Schools' class, like the one that pulled our train to Brockenhurst at half term. We had a brilliant time on our hands and knees, playing trains for at least an hour and a half, much to Mrs. Drummond's amusement. She said she had never met girls who liked playing trains before.

Harry winked at me and said; 'You see, Mrs. Drummond, we're not really girls at all. In Scotland I went to a boys' school, and when Ally woke up on her first morning here, she kept telling Scottie that she was a boy!'

'And they both played football for their last schools in teams where all the others were boys,' said Alex.

'So *that's* why you both have boys' names!' she said. 'I must say I *did* wonder!'

She made a great fuss of us and the tea was gorgeous, with a home-made chocolate cake, jam tarts and lemon flavoured junket. She asked us about our families, and hearing that our mothers were both members of the FANYs, the First Aid Nursing Yeomanry, she said how proud we must be of them.

'Ally, d'you remember that letter you wrote to Dad for me,' asked Alex, 'When I was bandaged up like King Tutankamen? Well I've just had a reply from him. It went to the hospital and they sent it on. There's a bit I'd like you to hear. "*Your news,*"' he read, ' "*came as a great shock, and you must feel very lonely and frightened, but remember that I am always thinking of you. Mum was a wonderful person, and it seems ironic, that I am far away dodging the bullets that Jerry keeps aiming at me, and you, Mum and Monica get on the wrong end of a direct hit by one of Hitler's eggs. It has stunned me, I can tell you. I give thanks to Our Lord that you have survived.*

"*You seem to have found two wonderful friends in the girls with boys' names; fancy one being called Alex, like you. And she's singing in the choir at All Saints; I bet it's put some of the boys' noses out of joint! I hope I have a chance to meet both of them one day when this awful war is over and I can come home. I think your idea about their mothers being spies sounds spot on for two such plucky and kind girls. Please thank them for me, and give Gran my love. I shall pray every night that the sight in your right eye will be spared. God be with you, my son, and keep your chin up. All my love, Dad. P.S. Don't forget to include* me *in your prayers.*"'

'So your dad's in the army,' I said.

'Only during the war,' replied Alex. 'I never told you, did I? He's a parson, chaplain to a regiment in North Africa—I think. I've nearly finished a letter to him, so I'll tell him you've come to tea, and you've invited me to tea next week.'

'Send him our love,' said Harry. She glanced at the clock on the mantelpiece. 'Crikey! Is that the time? We'll have to go. We promised we'd be back in time for high tea, and that's in twenty minutes time, and we don't know the times of the buses!'

'Don't worry, you've *loads* of time,' laughed Alex. 'It's Gran's clock! It's always thirty-five minutes fast. She says if it's put right, she never knows what the time is!'

*

At the beginning of November, I had been in 1940 for eight weeks, and was getting worried about returning to 1974. What if I still had not returned by the time the Christmas holidays came round. Where would I go? What was happening in 1974 while I'd been away? I would have been quite happy to stay in the past and get back to 1974 in thirty four years, along with Harry and the rest of my 1940 school friends. But there was a snag; I would be living twice at the same time, as a grown-up woman, probably a mother with children, and as a boy of ten!

The first Sunday of the month, the third of November, was special in more ways than one way. First of all, we celebrated All Saints Day at church. It was a glorious service, with some more of my favourite hymns, specially *For all the Saints who from their labours rest*, in which I sang verse four solo.

Second, it was the nearest Sunday to Jen-Pen's twelfth birthday, and it was also the day that Boy-Alex was coming to tea. Scottie and Auntie Vera put their heads together and suggested that the tea party could serve a dual purpose. They also thought it would be a good idea for us to entertain our gentleman guest in Scottie's room. We thought it was a brilliant idea, and all the regular hospital visitors, Rob Roy, Nicky, Puddles, Maggot, Weevil, and Goody were invited to come, as well as Lolly as a fellow ex-patient, and Mag-Bags who was Jen-Pen's best friend.

We telephoned Boy-Alex to tell him it was going to be Jenny's birthday party as well as our return invitation to him. He thought it was a wizzo idea.

We wanted to buy a birthday present for Jenny, so Scottie made a collection; then she and Mag-Bags went to buy it on the Friday afternoon. They found a pretty little brooch in the shape of a girl playing a flute. When Alex arrived, he gave Jenny a birthday card and told us he'd never been inside a girls' boarding school before.

Gladys created a minor miracle in the form of a birthday cake, and the rest of food was delicious. The party was a great success and Alex said he enjoyed meeting so many friends. He thought Caroline's new nickname, Lolly, suited her perfectly.

*

After tea a few days later, Harry and I were strolling in a part of the grounds where we could be alone, shuffling in the fallen leaves, and making a wonderful rustling sound. I was lost in my own thoughts, unanswered questions churning round and round in my head. I was vaguely aware of Harry speaking, but was oblivious to her words until I felt her tugging at my hand.

'Al-*leee*! You're doing it *again!* I thought you'd stopped shutting me out, because you haven't done it since that awful day we quarrelled. What's wrong? Please tell me. You know your secrets are safe with me. Let me try to help.' She turned me to face her, and gripped my elbows.

I felt I was going to cry. I tried not to, but could not keep the tears back. 'W-what am I going to do, Harry? I don't want to die. What's going to happen if I'm still here when the Christmas hols start? I've got nowhere to go; I'm marooned in a girl's body and you're the only one I can talk to about it. *What's* going to happen to me? *How* do I get back to my own time? *Why* has it happened to me?' It came out in a rush. '*Help* me, Harry.' I put my head on her shoulder and cried. I felt her stroking my head.

'Poor Ally,' she said. 'It must be horrid for you, and you're being so brave. I wish I could help you find a way back to your own time, even though I don't want you to go, 'cause I'd miss you terribly. I wouldn't be the only one either. You've become so much part of the school, and everyone likes and admires you. If it hadn't been for you, we'd never have started the hospital visiting. Ally, I'm sure it'll work out all right in the end. Come and sit down.' I wasn't sobbing so much now, and she led me to a fallen tree trunk and we sat down. She dried my eyes, and I managed a smile.

'That's more like it,' she said, 'If you're still around at Christmas, that's easy; you can spend Christmas with me at Auntie Louisa's house, near Wantage.'

'Could I?' I said, feeling chirpier. 'That would be brilliant. I wish I could get out of dying. It has to happen, I've seen the grave, but I never noticed the date, so I don't know when it's going to happen. I'd love to stay with you and reach my own time at the same time as you do, but there's a problem. There would be two of me, one a grown up lady, probably married with children, and the other a boy. I'd be living two lives at once. That's impossible, even in fairy stories. They always start "Once upon a time".'

'Well yours could start; "Twice upon a time, there was a boy called Alex who was also a girl called Ally."' I laughed, and she smiled reassuringly at me. We heard the prep bell ringing so we went back indoors. She helped me wash off the tear stains, and we went to do our prep, which was French because it was Thursday.

CHAPTER THIRTY-THREE

November—into December

I FELT A LOT BETTER having shared my worries with Harry. She said that if I had to die or go back to my own time, we had to make the most of our time together. Every time she caught me withdrawing into my shell, she would "winkle me out" again, as she put it, and make me tell her what was the matter.

I was also anxious about Gran. Had her operation been successful? What was happening in 1974? Had Alexandra taken my place, as I had taken hers?

From time to time, Scottie remarked that I was not my usual chirpy self, and told me I could confide in her if I was worried about anything. How much I wished I could, but she would never have believed me. The memory of how I had so nearly lost Harry's friendship made me decide to tell Scottie that I was worried about Mummy. This was actually true, but not for the reason Scottie would think. She accepted this explanation, and after that, whenever she saw me looking a bit glum, she would give me a cuddle and do her best to comfort and reassure me.

Remembrance Sunday fell on 10th November. The news on the wireless and the newspapers that morning, told us that Mr Chamberlain, who had been prime minister before Mr Churchill, had died on the previous day at the age of 71.

'No wonder he was such an awful prime minister,' Jacko said. 'If he was that old, he was obviously gaga!'

The church was packed. Absolutely everybody wore a poppy, and many of the older folk were proudly wearing the medals awarded to them in the Great War (1914-1918), and earlier conflicts such as the Boer War. Members of the local branch of the British Legion, all wearing medals, and standards flying, marched to the church. There was a party of ex-servicemen from Douglas House Hospital, many of whom had been gassed during the Great War, and of course the Home Guard was on parade.

During the service, the names of those members of the congregation who had given their lives in action during the present war were read out; names that had been added to the Roll of Honour.

Harry, a regular member of the choir now, was in her place by me in the Decani. Just before eleven o'clock, we stood in silence as one of the old soldiers declaimed:

'*They grow not old, as we that are left grow old.*
Age shall not weary them, nor the years condemn.
At the going down of the sun, and in the morning,
We will remember them.'

The congregation repeated; '*We will remember them.*' Then we stood for the two minutes' silence. You could have heard a pin drop. Mr Grubb even turned off the blower of the organ, lest it should break the silence. Even though I had never met either of them, I thought specially about Yvette Foster, and Judy White's dad who had been shot down over the Channel the day before I arrived in 1940; also Lolly's mother, and Boy-Alex's mother and sister, killed by German bombs. And I couldn't help thinking about Gran and Harry's *Maman,* both in such peril behind enemy lines in France. I knew Harry was thinking the same, because about halfway through the two minutes' silence her hand grasped mine and squeezed. I glanced at her as I squeezed back, and saw her cheeks wet with silent tears. She was not alone in her tears that day; at least three of the boys in the choir, whom I knew had lost fathers, uncles or elder brothers recently, were weeping also.

I felt very honoured to be allowed to be part of this act of remembrance. I knew that from now on, especially if I got back to my own time, Armistice Day would always have a special meaning for me. We sang some glorious hymns including *Soldiers of Christ arise,* and *O God our help in ages past.* The recessional hymn at the end was *Onward Christian Soldiers,* which all but raised the roof. But best of all for me was Thomas Tallis's anthem, *O Lord Give Thy Holy Spirit.* We sang it twice while the congregation took Communion, the second time unaccompanied. When the service was over, the poppy wreaths were laid at the war memorial in the church-yard. Judy White was chosen to lay a wreath on behalf of all the children whose fathers had lost their lives in combat during the Battle of Britain.

After we had disrobed, we went outside and were met by Alex, wearing his black leather eye-patch as proudly as any of the old warriors wore their medals. Instead of going the short distance to the Priory, he and his Gran had come all the way from Christchurch to be with us at All Saints.

'It was a lovely service,' said Mrs. Drummond, 'And I thought you two *choirboys* sang beautifully. I'm so sorry I shan't hear your solo at Evensong, Ally. Alex asked me to stay, but I've promised to visit an old friend who's bed-ridden.'

'That's all right,' I said, 'I'll sing it for you at some other time.'

'I shall look forward to it,' she replied. 'And now I must go to catch my bus.'

Alex came back to school with us, as Auntie Vera had invited him to lunch with us. Afterwards he joined us on our usual Sunday afternoon stroll with Bendy Wendy. He and Lolly had a long chat as they hadn't seen each other since Jenny's birthday party. Then it was back for an early tea before returning to church.

At evensong we sang Stanford's *Magnificat in G,* with Derrick singing the soaring treble solo. He sang really brilliantly. My solo, Purcell's Evening Hymn, came just before the sermon. Harry, at my side, grinned and squeezed my knee as I sat down and Derrick gave me the thumbs-up. In the vestry afterwards, Mr Grubb was delighted with us. Outside, Auntie Vera, Scottie, Lolly, Alex and some of the girls had been joined by Derrick's mother and sister Sarah who was in our form. Derrick and Sarah introduced Harry and me to their mother, who invited us to tea later in the term. It had been quite a day—a Remembrance Day that I would remember always.

*

There had been a number of nightly air raids lately and these continued during the week following Remembrance Day. On Thursday the 14th, Harry and I were walking through the school gate after choir practice when the siren atop the watertower wailed. The other girls would just about be finishing high tea, so we rushed straight to the shelter where Auntie Vera was waiting with her list of names.

'That was well-timed,' she told us. 'I wouldn't have liked your being out during an air-raid.'

'They're early,' said Harry, looking up for any sign of enemy bombers. 'I wonder what their target is tonight.'

'Somewhere in the Midlands probably,' said Auntie Vera. 'the Bombardier said Jerry bombers have been flying north over us for the past few nights and many factories in the Birmingham and Coventry areas have been badly damaged.'

'Coventry,' I thought, and remembered it had been virtually flattened by the *Luftwaffe* one night, but didn't know when. I had been to the new Cathedral with Gran, Auntie Kate, Nick and Jackie and seen photos of the terrible bomb damage.

We spent a long time in the shelter that night and were were told later the next day that Coventry had been virtually razed to the ground that night.

*

As November drew to a close, I was still worried about being stuck in the past. Harry did all she could to keep me cheerful, but the "death sentence" hanging over me prayed on my mind. If I died in 1940, would I escape back to 1974 and carry on living normally?

Sunday the first of December was the first Sunday in Advent, and the hymns were getting Christmassy. At choir practice that week we began rehearing some of the carols we would be singing over the festive season.

Harry and I sang at both Mattins and Evensong each Sunday now. However on the eighth December, ten days before the end of term, we were excused Evensong, as we had been invited, with Lolly, to tea at Judy White's. Judy had become part of our close circle of friends, even though she was a daybug. Mrs. White was one of those lovely ladies for whom nothing was too much trouble. In spite of her grief, she usually managed a cheerful smile and would buckle down to help anybody in trouble. Harry told me that during the summer term, all Judy's classmates were made to feel welcome any time they called, and Mrs. White always found a cake or a jam tart, 'To fill the space in a growing girl's tummy!'

Since the death of Judy's father, Mrs. White had not felt like having hoards of schoolgirl-visitors—in fact we were the first to be invited to tea since the tragedy three months earlier.

It had been a fine morning, but during lunch it clouded over. It looked like it might rain later, so Scottie insisted we wore raincoats when we went to Judy's. Lolly had settled into life as a boarder really well, and both Scottie and Auntie Vera were pleased with her progress.

The Whites lived only about ten minutes walk away, and we set out at about half past two. We would pass quite close to Lolly's bombed out home, and Scottie had said we could go and look at the ruins on our way back if we really wanted to.

The front door of Judy's house was hidden from view by a thick wall made of pale grey brick. I had noticed that several houses had these walls, and asked Harry about it. It was Lolly who answered me.

'Gosh, Ally, don't you know what it's for? You are a dimwit. It's a blast wall so that your door and hall windows don't get blown down if a bomb lands near the house.'

'Come along, Dimwit!' laughed Harry, 'Lolly's shown you up good and proper.' She walked through the narrow gap between the wall and the front door and rapped on the knocker.

The door was opened by Judy. Knowing the rule that boarders had to wear school uniform when going out to tea, she was wearing her tunic so we wouldn't feel different. 'Come in, everybody,' she said, and then called out; 'Mummy! Harry, Alex and Lolly have arrived.'

'Just coming, darling,' we heard Mrs. White replying from somewhere out of sight. 'Help them off with their coats, and hang them up in the cupboard under the stairs.'

I looked very solemnly at Judy. 'You can't do that,' I said. 'We haven't got loops sewn to the backs of our necks to hang us up by!'

Harry looked at the back of Lolly's neck, and trying to keep a straight face said; 'You're right, Ally. Lolly's been sent out of the factory without one. But you're all right, Ally, we can tie your pigtails together and hang you up by them!'

'Oh, Ally! Honest-*ly*!' giggled Judy. 'Mummy didn't mean hang *you* up under the stairs. She meant your coats.'

By this time we were all laughing, and Mrs. White, drying her hands on her apron, came out of the kitchen to greet us. 'That's what I like to hear, happy laughter. May I share your joke?

'Oh, Mummy! It was so funny!' giggled Judy. 'Ally thought you wanted me to hang them up in the cupboard under the stairs, instead of their coats.' We had taken our coats off and now we passed them to Judy to hang up.

'I knew having you to tea was a good idea,' said Mrs. White. 'I haven't heard Judy laugh like that for ages. Well done, Ally. May I call you that?'

'Yes, of course, Mrs. White,' I said, smiling at her. 'It was Harry who started calling me that, and now all my close friends do. Now Harry's hair is longer and she doesn't look so much like a boy, we even call her Kate sometimes.'

'You can talk!' said Harry. 'Who was it who tried to persuade Scottie she was a boy when she woke up on her first morning?'

'Did you, Ally?' asked Judy in amazement. '*Really?*'

''Fraid so,' I admitted, feeling myself blushing.

'I think she had a dream about being a boy in another life.' said Harry, winking at me. 'That's it, isn't it, Ally?'

'Oh yes,' I replied, 'Abso-lute-ly.' I looked at Mrs. White and grinned sheepishly.

'You'll do, Ally,' she said, squeezing my arm. 'It's so good to hear happy voices in the house again. No wonder you have such a good effect on the kiddies in hospital. Judy tells me that the visiting was all your idea, Ally.'

'Not *just* me; it was Harry's idea just as much as mine.'

'But it was *you* that said I should visit Lolly,' Harry said. 'I only did it because you came with me to hold my hand.'

'You see, Lollipop,' I said. 'It's all your fault!'

'Now, Judy,' said Mrs. White, 'Why don't you take your guests up to your room to play, while I finish off getting the tea.'

'Lead on, MacDuff,' Harry told Judy, who started up the stairs. On a half-landing three quarters the way up, a window partly covered by a black roller-blind, overlooked the front garden; four more stairs led up to the landing proper.

'That's Mummy's room,' explained Judy pointing at a door on the left. Straight ahead were two doors. The right hand one was ajar, revealing the bathroom. Judy opened the one on the left. 'Here's the lav. if you need it.' She opened another, next to the lav., 'This is the spare room, where Mummy does her dressmaking.' We went in. Against one wall was a bed, with several almost-finished children's frocks laid out on it. In front of the window was a treadle sewing machine and next to it was a tailor's dummy wearing a partly-made wedding dress. Judy picked up one of the children's frocks and held it against me.

'These are bridesmaids' dresses for Alison Ball's wedding,' she said, 'You know Norma in the lower fifth? Alison's her eldest sister. They're going to have pink sashes round the waist tied in big bows at the back. Aren't they pretty? They're lucky to get them; Mummy bought the material before the war.'

'Does your mummy do lots of dressmaking?' asked Lolly.

'Rather!' replied Judy. 'She made Ruth Bamber's wedding dress and all the bridesmaids dresses too, didn't she, Harry? D'you remember how you blushed when you saw yourself in the mirror that time you came to try it on?'

'Did you, Harry?' I asked.

''Fraid so,' she replied. 'You see it was the first time I'd ever worn such a fancy frock, and all those frilly petticoats made me feel a bit of a sissy. That's why I didn't want you to come to the fitting with me. I thought you might laugh at me.'

'I'd never have done that,' I said. 'You looked jolly pretty in it; you *really* were Kate that day, wasn't she, Judy?'

'Rather!' replied Judy. 'Come on let's go to my room to play.' She led the way across the landing. As soon as she opened the door, we could see an enormous dolls' house, and Lolly's eyes lit up.

CHAPTER THIRTY-FOUR

Bomb-site!

JUDY'S ROOM WAS LIGHT AND AIRY. In one corner was her bed, where a large persian ginger cat lay sleeping, curled up with its exceedingly fluffy tail draped elegantly over its nose.

'Oh, Judy! What a gorgeous cat,' I exclaimed, going straight to the bed and sitting on the edge. 'What's she called?'

'Nutkin,' replied Judy, 'and *she*, is a *boy!*'

'Hello, Nutkin,' I said softly, stroking his head. He looked up at me, yawned and then stretched, had a sniff at my hand and, deciding that I was nice to know, climbed on my lap and curled up with his head close by my tummy.

'Careful, Ally,' said Judy, 'He'll shed hairs all over your gymmer.'

'I don't mind, he's sweet, aren't you Nutkin?' I replied, picking him up kissing the top of his head and putting him back on my lap. 'I can feel him purring against my tummy.'

Harry and Lolly both kneeled on the floor in front of me and stroked him. His purring grew louder.

'Why's he called Nutkin?' asked Lolly.

'When he was a kitten,' replied Judy, 'His bushy tail reminded us of a Squirrel.' I tickled him under his chin and he stretched his neck out and seemed to be smiling with pleasure.

'We had a pussy,' said Lolly, 'But I think she was killed by the bomb. Poor Neenee, she was so sweet. I miss her an awful lot. She was white with black and ginger patches, sort of piebald. P'raps she's with Mummy in heaven.'

Harry put an arm round her. 'I'm sure she is,' she said. 'You can always get another one. I'm sure Gramma would buy a kitten if you asked her. Let's go and look at Judy's dolls' house.' She got to her feet and with Lolly went over to the dolls' house. 'Judy, it's huge, how long have you had it?'

'As long as I can remember,' replied Judy, ''twas Mummy's when she was a girl.'

I put Nutkin back on the bed and stroked him to make him settle, but he preferred the comfort of my lap, so I had to stay where I was and look at the dolls' house from the bed.

Judy lifted a catch at one side and the whole front swung open. Lolly and Harry gasped as the interior was revealed, complete to the tiniest detail. On the ground floor there was a sitting room with perfect armchairs and a sofa. On a table at one side of the fireplace was a wireless set, and there was a table lamp on the table on the other side. There were pictures on the walls, carpets on the floors; a grandfather clock, made by Judy's dad using an old watch, really worked.

On the other side was the dining room, with a dining table and chairs, laid up with tiny knives and forks. Against one wall, a dresser with willow pattern plates on its shelves, had a joint of beef waiting to be carved. There was a serving hatch through which we could see the kitchen. Upstairs were two bedrooms, the bathroom and a lav., complete with a chain that could be pulled and even a tiny roll of "botty-paper!"

'Look!' squealed Lolly with delight. 'There's even a potty under the bed.'

'Gosh, Judy,' said Harry, 'It's absolutely spiffing! It's the first dolls' house I've ever seen that I would like to own—'

The door opened and Mrs. White came in. 'Did I hear right? Did *Master* Harry Gordon actually admit she'd like to have a *spiffing* dolls' house?' she said, winking at my best friend.

'It's the sort of thing I'd like to build myself,' Harry added quickly. 'I was jolly good at carpentry at St Mungo's.'

'Well I hope you're all jolly good at eating tea,' said Mrs. White. She looked at me. 'I see you've been adopted by Nutty, Ally. You *are* honoured—he doesn't do that to many people—' She bent over to pick him off my knee. He gave a complaining yowl and clung to my gymmer with his claws, lifting it as Mrs. White picked him up.

'Really, Nutkin! You're a very naughty pussy, Nutkin,' giggled Lolly. 'Don't you know it's rude to lift up girls' skirts?'

Mrs. White laughed as she unhooked his claws. 'You'd better get up before I put him down again,' she said. 'Judy, darling, get a clothes brush and brush Nutty's hairs off Ally's tunic for her—and then all of you pop into the bathroom to wash your hands and then come downstairs for tea.' She went over to the window and looked out. 'Gracious me, look at those clouds; it looks like the heavens are about to open at any minute.'

*

The tea exceeded all our expectations. How Mrs. White was able to make such a wonderful spread from the tiny rations that were available is beyond belief. When the time came for us to leave, we were all feeling very full.

The weather was even more glowering, but as yet not a drop of rain had fallen. It seemed to be waiting for us to start the walk back to school.

'Thank you very much for having me, Mrs. White,' I said, as she brushed the last of Nutkin's hairs off my tunic. 'The tea was gigantically gorgeous!'

'What a sweet little girl you are, Ally darling,' she said, putting an arm round me and giving me a hug. She made me feel so safe and secure, that I put my arms round her neck and kissed her. She gave me another hug, kissed me and squeezed my hand. I had already decided that Mrs. White was a very kind and loving lady.

'It was absolutely gollumptious and spiffing,' said Harry. 'Thank you so much, Mrs. White. It's been a *gorgeous* party.'

'Yes, thank you for having me,' added Lolly, 'And thank you for letting me play with your lovely dolls' house.'

'You're all very welcome,' replied Mrs. White, giving each of us a hug and a kiss in turn. 'It's been splendid having you girls here; and it's been absolutely marvellous to hear happy voices in the house again.'

'Yes, it's been *spiffing* having you,' said Judy. 'I hope you'll come again soon.'

'Rather!' replied Harry. 'We'd love to—if Mrs. White can put up with us.'

'Of course I can,' laughed Mrs. White, opening the front door. 'Bye-bye, girls. I hope you get back before the rain starts.'

''Bye, Mrs. White, and thank you again for the lovely tea.'

''Bye, Judy, see you at school tomorrow.'

At the gate, we turned and waved, and they waved back.

*

We didn't take the shortest route back to school, but took a short detour, because we'd promised Lolly we would go back past her bombed-out home. It was not far out of our way, and would add only a few minutes to our walk. As we turned into the road where Lolly's house had been, large drops of rain began to fall.

'*Botheration!*' Harry exclaimed loudly. 'We'll get soaked—'

'—Never mind,' I said. 'We've not got far to go from here.'

We soon arrived at Lolly's house—or what was left of it! One side was just a crater and a heap of rubble, while the other side still had a bit of roof, and the stairs hung precariously over the crater.

'Crikey!' exclaimed Lolly. 'The shelter where I used to sleep must be under that big pile of bricks.'

We walked into the garden to take a closer look. Suddenly there was a flash of lightening and a white cat with black and ginger patches shot past us and bolted up the stairs into the room that still had part of its roof over it.

'It's *Neenee!*' cried Lolly. 'I must go and *get* her!'

'No you don't, Lollipopkins!' said Harry, grabbing the collar of her raincoat. 'You stay where you are. I'll try to get her for you.'

There was a rumble of thunder. The rain was pelting down now, and our raincoats were wet on the outside, but we were still dry underneath. Harry picked her way round the heap of bricks to the stairs and began to climb one step at a time, using her hands like fore-paws.

'Do be careful, Harry,' I called. 'It doesn't look very safe.'

'It's all right,' she called back, 'I'm being everso careful. It seems to be quite solid. Neenee, *come* along, Neenee, puss-puss-puss-*puss!* Neenee-Neenee-Neenee, *come* on, Neenee, come on—*Good* puss!' She reached the top of the stairs, and steadying herself against the wall, went into the room.

'That used to be Mummy's bedroom,' explained Lolly.

'Oh, do be *careful,* Harry!' I called out, anxiously.

There was another rumble of thunder, nearer this time.

'Sssh,' I heard her say. 'You're frightening Neenee. Come on, Neenee, come to

Auntie Harry—There's a good puss! There, there. That's better! You're a wee bit thin, old puss and you could do with a saucer of milk, couldn't you—There, there, come with Auntie Harry. I do believe you're trying to purr.'

Lolly and I waited anxiously. She was clinging to me as we watched for Harry to re-appear. After I'd put on my raincoat, I had left my pigtails inside it, and now I could feel water dripping down my neck and running down my back under my clothes. Silently, I cursed my clottishness, shivered, and hugged Lolly closer to me. After what seemed like half a lifetime, Harry re-appeared at the top of the stairs with Neenee in her arms.

She started to come downstairs carefully, step by step, feeling with each foot, not being able to see where she was going, because Neenee was in the way.

Suddenly, there was a fearsome, crackling flash of lightning at the same time as an almighty crash of thunder. In fright Neenee struggled free from Harry's grasp, making her foot slip on the greasy wood of the stair. She fell backwards, and then there was a splintering noise, and the whole staircase collapsed, crashing to the ground taking Harry with it. Lolly and I screamed as we watched her being buried under a pile of timber.

Lolly managed to catch Neenee and picked her up.

'Look after Neenee,' I told her. 'I'm going to help Harry. Take Neenee and go straight to Scottie and tell her what's happened. *Quick* as you can! Harry will probably be hurt. Have you a hanky I can borrow in case Harry needs a bandage?'

'Yes. But you'll have to get it out 'cause I mustn't let go of Neenee. It's pushed up the right leg of my knickers—'

I found it and she ran off in the direction of the school, clasping Neenee to her. I picked my way over the rubble. 'Harry?' I called anxiously, 'Harry, are you all right?'

There was no reply.

'*HARRY!*' I screeched at the top of my voice. I could feel tears welling up inside me. 'Harry—where *are* you? *Answer* me, Har-*REEE!*'

Still no reply came!

Then I saw her. She was lying on her back, very still, her head and shoulders poking out of the pile of timber that had been the staircase. She was lying so still I thought she was dead! The rain was pelting down harder than ever as I made my way gingerly to my stricken best friend.

'O Lord,' I prayed, '*please don't let Harry die!*'

As I knelt beside her, I felt a sharp pain in my knee. I looked and saw there was a tin-tack sticking into it. I pulled it out and blood seeped through my stocking— I bent over her—her hat had come off. I put my ear by her mouth. She was breathing. She was alive.

'Thank you, God,' I said stroking her hair, being careful not to move her head, in case her neck was injured. I was glad I'd passed my first-aiders badge in the

Cubs. Luckily there was not as much timber on top of her as it had looked at first glance. I worked feverishly, clearing it off her. There was no time for tears as I pulled the wreckage away from her and threw it aside. I talked to her all the time, hoping my voice would help to bring her back to consciousness.

Then I saw her left hand. It was covered in blood. I took out my own hanky and wiped it away as best I could. The blood was gushing quickly from a cut on her wrist. I was already sopping wet underneath my raincoat, so I took it off and laid it over her to keep her warm and looked at the wound on her wrist again; the blood was gushing from it freely.

'I must *stop* it,' I told myself aloud. 'I need a tourniquet! But what can I make one from? Hanky? No! Not big enough.'

I undid one sleeve of my shirt, and gave it a hard tug, trying to rip the seam. It gave way at the third try. All the time I was calling her name. I tore my sleeve off at the shoulder, wrapped it round her arm twice, just above the elbow, and knotted it. There was a convenient length of wood about three-quarters-of-an-inch square nearby. I pushed it under the sleeve I had tied round her arm, and then began to twist it to tighten this make-shift tourniquet—the blood flow from the wound slowed down.

She made a weak whimpering sound. I was worried about her legs, and while holding the tourniquet with one hand tried to pull the last few pieces of timber off her. There was one piece I couldn't shift without letting go of the tourniquet, or risking bringing down more debris, possibly burying us both. Luckily it did not seem to be pressing on her too heavily.

One of her legs was doubled under her. In the fading light I saw no sign of bleeding, but couldn't be absolutely sure. It was getting darker and darker, due as much as to the storm as to the approaching night, and the rain was now pelting down harder than ever.

Another huge flash of lightening lit up the scene momentarily. The crash of thunder came barely two seconds later. I re-arranged my raincoat over her to keep her warm, then spat on Lolly's hanky and began to wipe the wound on her wrist clean. It was quite small. Thank goodness! How long before help would come? I heard myself praying; 'O Lord, *please* don't let her die!'

She must have heard me, because she groaned. Holding the tourniquet with one hand, I stroked her hair with the other. 'Harry, it's me, Ally. You're going to be okay, Lolly's gone to get Scottie. She'll be here soon. Speak to me, Harry, if you can hear me—' I put my face close to hers, and I could just feel her warm breath on my cheek. Her eyelids gave a twitch and slowly they opened—

'Hello, Ally,' she said in a quiet voice. 'What happened? My left foot's gone to sleep. I'm sorry, I let Neenee go. Is Lolly very upset?'

'Don't worry, Lolly's caught her safely,' I said. 'Just stay quiet. You've cut your left wrist a bit and I'm trying to stop the bleeding.'

'Where did you learn first aid?' she tried to smile.

'In the Cubs. I'm a sixer.'

'If *Scottie* asks you,' she murmured, 'You'd better make sure that you say it was in the *Brownies*.' Her voice was getting stronger and she even managed a little giggle. She was shivering—from shock I thought.

'Don't talk,' I said, stroking her cheek. 'We'll soon get you back to school.'

'Your gymmer's soaked, Ally. And you're shivering. Where's your coat, and what's happened to your blouse?' She moved her leg and winced. 'Ouch!'

'Stay still, Harry, darling. Don't worry about *me*. I used my sleeve to make a tourniquet. Keep still till Scottie gets here.'

'You're my boy scout doing his good deed for the day,' she took my free hand and squeezed it.

'I'm just going to release the pressure on your arm for a few seconds—your hand's going a bit blue.' I unwound the stick a few turns, and, just in case the bleeding re-started, after a few seconds, I tightened it up again.

'You certainly know about first aid,' she said, giving a much more Harryish smile. 'What d'you want to be when you grow up?'

'Well, I thought about being an engine driver,' I said, unable to keep my face straight. 'The trouble is when I'm grown up there won't be any steam trains left.'

'Och, *you*!'

'Actually, I've always wanted to be a doctor.'

'You'll make a jolly good one, Ally.'

I thought I heard voices, so I turned. Three cowled torches were coming through the gate. 'Ally?' It was Scottie's voice. 'Where are you? Have you got her free?'

'Over here, Scottie,' I called back. 'She's almost free. Who's with you?'

'Miss Bendall, Jacko, Jen-Pen and Bren Gunn.' The beam of her torch shone in my eyes for a second.

'Mind how you go,' I called. 'I've almost got her free, all but one plank that I was scared to move. Also I didn't want to let go of the tourniquet.'

'Is she bleeding *badly*?' asked Scottie. I could just make her out, picking her way across the rubble. She was wearing an oilskin coat and a sou'wester. 'Let me have a look at her. Bren, bring my first aid kit over, and a blanket for Ally; the poor wee mite's soaked to the skin. Have you released the tourniquet at all, Ally?'

'Yes. Just before you came. It's almost stopped bleeding. It's only a small cut, but it was gushing out so I reckon something must have nicked a vein.'

'And where did you learn about tourniquets?' she asked.

'In the Boy Scouts, of course,' Harry told her, 'where did you think she learned about them?'

'You just pipe down and hold your huisht, my wee Harry,' said Scottie. 'Is the Bombardier here yet, Bren?'

'Not yet, but Dr. Hall's just arrived.'

'Good,' Scottie said. 'Wendy, will you wrap Ally in that blanket; the poor wee mite's soaked to the skin and she's shivering. It's all right, Ally, I've got the tourniquet now. You go with Wendy.'

I let go of the tourniquet, and as I stood up I saw my stocking was all bloody where I had knelt on the tin-tack. Bendy wrapped the blanket round me, and cuddled me.

'Jacko, Jenny, and Bren,' called Scottie, like a general ordering troops. 'See if you can move that baulk of timber that's trapping Harry, without bringing the rest of the house down on us. We're over here, Doctor.'

'Coming, Scottie.' There was another flash of lightening, and I saw a tall man carrying a Gladstone bag. 'How's the patient?'

'In remarkably good shape, thanks to young Alex here,' Scottie replied. 'She tore up her own sleeve to make a tourniquet, and has stopped the bleeding completely. She needs to get warm though, she's soaked to the skin and shivering, the poor wee mite.'

'Wendy,' said Dr Hall. 'Take Alex and put her in my car, then come back to help us get Harry out. There's another blanket in my car, wrap that round Alex; it's dry and will be warmer.'

'Come on, Ally,' said Bendy Wendy. 'It seems you've been a bit of a heroine, what? Jolly good *show!*' She lifted me easily, and carried me, picking her way over the rubble, to Dr Hall's car. It was a huge Daimler, with loads of room in the back. I stood shivering, while Bendy opened the back door and spread another blanket on the back seat for me. I got in and she wrapped the dry blanket round me and then put the other one on top. 'You just sit there and get warm. The Bombardier's helping the Doc lift Harry out now.' She took another rug from the front seat and spread it on the seat beside me. 'That's for Harry.'

'Did Lolly get her pussy-cat back to school all right?'

'Yes, fine. Susie and Greta took charge of her, while Goody put Lolly straight into a hot bath.'

'Thanks for carrying me out, Bendy.'

'Don't mensh, old chap—here comes the Doc with Harry. We'll soon have you both back safe and in nice hot baths.' She went round the other side of the car and opened the door so Harry could be lifted in. As they wrapped her in a dry blanket, she grinned at me.

'I've sprained my stupid ankle,' she said, giving my hand a squeeze. 'Thanks for the boy-scout bit, you really are the best friend a girl ever had.'

Suddenly the horror of the whole episode hit me. I burst into tears and I buried my face in Harry's blanket.

CHAPTER THIRTY-FIVE

Safe Once More

WHILE DR. HALL DROVE US back to school, Scottie sat between us, with an arm round each of us, like a mother hen protecting her chicks with her wings. Bren, and Jacko managed to squeeze in too, and Bendy Wendy sat in the front next to the doctor, with Jen-Pen on her lap.

As soon as we were inside the school, we were whisked upstairs to a hot bath. Harry's ankle was swollen, and painful to walk on, but Dr Hall and Scottie were sure it was only a sprain. Compared to me, Harry was relatively dry, so Scottie quickly took me in hand, as I stood shivering in front her.

'Look at you, you poor wee drookit mite. You're sopping wet! Arms up! Skin a rabbit!' She pulled my sopping tunic over my head. 'Look at your poor blouse. You're a plucky wee lass, no mistake,' she said as she helped me out of it. When she pulled off my stockings, she noticed the congealed mixture of mud and the blood on my knee.

'You've cut your knee,' she said. 'How did you do that?'

'Oh, I kneeled on a tin-tack while I was helping Harry. It's all right, I was able to pull it out straight away. Look, it's stopped bleeding.'

'As I just said, you're a plucky wee girl,' Scottie told me. 'I ought to put some antiseptic on it; I don't want you to get blood poisoning. It's a warm bed for a day or two for you, young woman. You and Harry can keep each other company in the sick-bay.'

I glanced towards the door as Harry came in, supported by Jacko. Scottie helped me into the bath. It was wonderful to feel the hot water wrapping me in a cocoon of warmth.

'Where do you want the walking wounded, Scottie?' asked Jacko. I sat up again to watch my best friend.

'Over here, Jacko. They're best friends so they can share the same bath! Lie down, Ally, and get warm. I'll wash your hair as you got it so wet. Come along Harry, let's get those damp things off you. Jacko, bring that stool over so she can take the weight off her ankle. Arms up, Harry.'

'I can manage,' she insisted, untying her girdle. She tried to pull off her tunic over her head and winced. 'Ooooh, ouch!'

'Let me do it, you stubborn young, stubborn young, *Harry,* you—Grrrrr!' Scottie growled and eased Harry's tunic off over her head. 'Now sit on the stool and let me take those stockings off. You can undo your tie.'

'Oh, I'm *much* too ill, Scottie,' said Harry, putting the back of her hand on her forehead and raising her eyes heavenwards as if she was about to swoon, like the heroine of a Victorian melodrama.

'Now I *know* you're all right,' laughed Scottie. She finished undressing her and helped her into the bath, the other end from me. We looked at each other and grinned.

' 'M sorry I blubbed like that in the car,' I said. 'But I was so happy you were all right.'

'Don't be a silly sausage,' said Harry, splashing water at me. 'I felt like crying too, but the tears wouldn't come. Thanks for rescuing me.' She smiled and held out her right hand. I took it in my right hand and shook it solemnly. Scottie smiled, Jacko hooted with laughter and we exploded into happy giggles.

'I'll go and get your nighties,' said Scottie, when she had finished washing our hair, and had wrapped our heads with turban-towels. 'I've asked Gladys to send your high tea to my room so you can have it in front of the fire.'

'You're not going to spoil us, are you, Scottie?' said Harry.

'As if I'd ever do such a thing!' she chided us. 'I just don't want my best girls to come to any harm.' She stood up, dried her hands, and left us on our own.

'She's jolly nice—such a kind lady.'

'Yes,'' I replied, 'she is. Just like a mummy.'

'Ally?' said Harry, taking my hand. 'I'll never, *ever*, be able to repay what you did for me this afternoon.'

'Don't *you* be a silly sausage! If it'd been me you'd have done just the same; 't'swhat best friends are for.'

Scottie returned, followed by Jenny with our nighties and dressing gowns.

'Right, young Ally,' said Scottie. 'Out you get, so I can dry you.' She wrapped a hot towel round me. It felt wonderfully soft and warm against my skin and I felt cosy and safe as she gently rubbed me dry. 'I want you both to wear underclothes in bed tonight. I don't want either of you catching cold.' She held out a clean, dry pair of pants for me, being careful they didn't touch the puddle of bath-water on the floor. 'The last time I did this for you, you insisted you were a boy!'

'But she *is*, Scottie,' said Harry. 'Didn't you *know?*'

'Yes, and *I'm* the Lord Mayor of London,' Scottie and I said together, laughing. She pretended to box my ears.

'Arms up,' she said and pulled my liberty bodice over my head and tucked it in. 'And again.' I raised my arms for my nightie. 'Now let me look at that knee. It looks quite clean, but it's best we make sure. She produced a small brown-coloured bottle labelled *Tincture of Iodine*, and took out the cork. Then she put a small wad of cotton-wool over the top, up-ended the bottle for a second or two and dabbed the wound on my knee.

'Ouch! That *stings!*' She put an Elastoplast on it, and went out, leaving me to put on my dressing gown.

She soon returned with a hot towel for Harry. When she was dry and in her nightie, Scottie put a clean dressing on her wrist and strapped up her ankle with a crepe bandage; 'That'll stop it swelling, and give it some support.'

'Thank you, Scottie,' said Harry, hobbling over to me.

'Come on, use me as a crutch. How's the ankle?'

'Throbbing a bit,' she said looking at me, her eyes watery. 'Oh, Ally! Thank you! Thank you!' She flung her arms round me and gave me a huge bear-hug. 'What would have happened if you hadn't been there?' I hugged her and wanted to cry again. The bell rang.

'Come along, my scallywags,' said Scottie. 'That's the high tea bell and Gladys will be sending up yours any moment. Can you make it to my room?'

'Come on, *crutch*,' said Harry, 'let me lean on you.' She put her left arm round my neck and I walked, she hopped, to Scottie's room. 'By the way, Scottie, how's Lollipopkins; and did she get Neenee back safely?'

'Mother and daughter are doing just fine,' replied Scottie. 'You'll be able to see them both later.'

'I'm glad we rescued Neenee,' said Harry, 'She'll be someone for Lolly to love.'

'You ran a terrible risk, young lady,' said Scottie, as she made us sit down in front of the fire. 'That fall could easily have injured you seriously or even killed you. You were very lucky.'

'I had Ally. She's my boy scout and guardian angel who saved me from getting badly hurt.' Suddenly she looked deadly serious. 'Scottie?'

'Yes, my pet.'

'Ally knowing about first aid was useful, wasn't it?'

'Aye, she did a fine job,' said Scottie. 'Why?'

'Would you teach *me* first aid?' she asked. 'I'm sure several of the others would be interested too.'

'Of course I will. Find out who else would like to learn, and I'll teach you, and you can take the St. John's Ambulance test.'

There was a knock on the door. 'Come away in.'

The door opened, and Jacko and Bren Gunn came in, carrying a tray each. Jacko asked, 'Where shall we put them, Scottie?'

'On the table please, Jacko, I'll just clear those papers away. At least I'm not as untidy as The Beak.' She winked at Jacko and Bren and they grinned. Harry and I giggled, but my giggle ended in a loud sneeze. It caught me by surprise, and I couldn't get my hanky out of my dressing-gown pocket in time. Scottie watched me while I blew my nose. 'I hope you've not caught a cold, Ally, pet.'

' 'Msorry, Scottie,' I said, 'I didn't mean to sneeze over everybody; it took me by surprise and I couldn't get my hanky out in time.'

'I wasn't being cross, you funny wee soul,' she said, putting a hand on my shoulder. 'I was only worried that you were going to be poorly.'

'How's the ankle, Harry?' asked Jacko.

'Still there—Throbbing a bit, but not too bad. Scottie says I must stay in bed for a day or two, worst luck. Thanks for helping to dig me out.'

'Will she be fit for the lax match next Saturday?' asked Bren Gunn anxiously.

'I doubt it,' said Scottie. 'She must rest that ankle for a few days. You can't count on Ally either, not if she's getting a cold.'

'Och, Scotteee!' anguished Harry.

'It's no good "och, Scottie-ing" me, young woman! After today's wee escapade you're both going to have a few days in bed—Scottie's orders!'

'Yes, Scottie,' replied Harry meekly. She knew only too well than once Scottie had come to a decision, no amount of argument would make her change her mind.

'Now eat your suppers before they get cold, there's my good girls,' Scottie told us, ruffling Harry's hair. 'There's lovely milky Ovaltine for you instead of tea. Thank Gladys for me will you, Jacko?'

'I will, Scottie,' replied Jacko, who as she reached the door, turned and looked at us. 'And you terrible twins must do *exactly* what Scottie says, or I'll give you— a hundred misconduct marks—each!'

'Aye-aye, Sir! Thank Gladys for us too,' said Harry, and we sat down to our high tea. It was Spam fritters, which were one of my favourites, but I only managed to eat about half and didn't want any more.

'Harry?'

'Yes, my terrible twin?'

'Would you like the rest of my Spam fritter?'

'But they're your favourite. Are you sure?'

'Yes, I know they are. I just don't feel very hungry.'

'Pass it over then. Are you sure you don't want it?'

'Absolutely.' I passed it over to her.

'Thanks, Ally.'

Scottie must have been looking in my direction, for she came over. 'What's the matter, Ally, pet? Are you feeling poorly?' She felt my forehead. 'You don't seem to have a temperature.'

'No. It's just that I'm not very hungry.' I could feel a huge lump in my throat. 'Oh, Scottie, when Harry didn't answer me when she was lying there, I was so scared she was going to die.' I clung to her, hiding my face in her cardigan, and cried again.

'There-there,' said Scottie softly, stroking my head. 'It's all over now, my wee one. You'll feel better for a good cry.'

Harry came and cuddled me too. Scottie cuddled both of us, and said soothing things. Gradually my tears subsided and I took out my hanky and wiped my eyes.

I looked at Scottie and smiled. She took my hanky, dried my eyes properly, and kissed me on the forehead. I looked at Harry. Her cheeks were wet with tears too. I smiled and she gave me one of her bear-hugs. It made me feel much better, and I thought how lucky I was to have such a wonderful friend.

'Now,' said Scottie, 'How about some Marmite toast? Would you like to make the toast? I've got a toasting fork and there's bread on your tray.' I nodded, and knelt down on the hearth rug. Scottie speared one of my pieces of grey war-time bread with her toasting fork, and gave it to me to hold in front of the fire. 'Don't hold it too close, or it'll burn.' Then she opened the door of her medicine cupboard, and took out a jar of Marmite.

When Harry smelled my hot-buttered—well—marged actually!—toast, she decided to have some too. We were kneeling in front of the fire making toast when there was a knock on the door and Auntie Vera came in.

'What's all this I hear?' she asked. 'Rescuing cats and nearly killing yourselves in the process! One of these days your good deeds are really going to get you into difficulty.'

'We couldn't not rescue Neenee, Auntie Vera,' said Harry. 'We did it for Lolly. You see, she thought Neenee had been killed by the bomb, then we saw her and Lolly wanted to rescue her herself. The only way I could stop her was to do it myself. If there hadn't been that huge thunder-clap when I was carrying Neenee down the stairs, she wouldn't have struggled free, and I wouldn't have slipped and fallen. It was my falling on the stairs made them collapse. Anyhow, I've only sprained my silly old ankle.'

'I heard you'd cut your wrist badly,' said Auntie Vera.

'Ally ripped the sleeve off her blouse, and with a stick made it into a tourniquet,' said Harry, proudly. 'She was absolutely brilliant.' She put an arm round my neck and gave me another hug, which made me want to cry again.

'Ally knew exactly what to do,' added Scottie, 'And went about it in a cool and calm manner. Her only thought was for Harry. When we got there, the wee mite was soaked to the skin. She'd taken off her raincoat to keep Harry warm. I'm going to keep them both in bed for the next few days.'

'You're plainly your mothers' daughters,' said Auntie Vera. 'You both have their spunk and determination, and I expect they'll be very proud of you both—as I am. Do just as Scottie says, or I'll—' I interrupted her with a sneeze.

'What'll you do, Auntie Vera?' asked Harry. 'Expel us? Jacko's already threatened us with a hundred "misses" each!'

'Quite right too,' laughed Auntie Vera. 'After the cat-o'-nine-tails, of course! Good night, my dear nieces.' Then she gave each of us a kiss, and left us with Scottie.

'Now finish off your toast and Ovaltine,' said Scottie, 'And be off to the sick bay, or I'll give you the cat-o'-*ten*-tails!'

'Scottie, please may I fetch something from the dorm. on the way?' I asked.

'If you're quick. I don't want you catching cold.'

As we passed our dormitory, I dashed in and picked up Edward Bear Esquire, and the photo of us both. I had no pocket on my nightie, but it was just small enough to fit into the hanky pocket of my navy bags.

Not long after Scottie had tucked us up in the sick-bay, Lolly came to see us with Neenee, who looked much better, purring happily in Lolly's arms. Lolly looked better too; she was a much happier girl now, and it was obvious that having her pet back made all the difference.

The news of our adventure spread like wildfire, and we had a constant trail of visitors that evening. In the end, Scottie had to limit us to two visitors at any one time, and then for a maximum of five minutes. It was Maggot and Weevil who touched us most. They wanted us to have their entire sweets ration for that week. We told them that we still hadn't touched our own, and they mustn't deprive themselves for us. But they insisted we have something, so we each took a bull's-eye and a toffee.

Scottie came back. 'Is there anything you want before I put your light out?' she asked.

'I'd like to spend a penny, please, Scottie,' I replied.

'All right; put on your dressing gown and slippers and be as quick as you can,' she told me. 'How about you, Harry?'

'I'd like to go too, please, Scottie. Wait for me, *crutch!*'

'All right, quick as you can.'

We were not long, and when we got back, Scottie was not there. About two minutes after we had got back into bed, Scottie came in with two chamber pots.

'Och, look, Ally,' exclaimed Harry chirpily. 'It's that well-known Welsh lady, Scottie-the-Potty!'

'Any more of that, young woman,' replied Scottie, trying to look severe, 'and I'll give you Scottie-the-Potty on your botty!'

Harry let out one of her sniggering snorts and I giggled. Scottie, kept her severe expression for a moment, then, unable to keep a straight face any longer, laughed with us.

'No, no,' said Harry, 'my botty goes on the potty, Scottie, not the potty on my botty, Scottie!' We laughed so much, it brought tears to our eyes, and Goody, who was passing our door on her way to tuck up her "babies", looked in on us to find out what all the hilarity was all about. Harry was delighted to give a repeat performance.

'All right, Harry,' said Scottie, regaining her composure. 'All right, my Harry, enough is as good as a feast. Settle down now. Would either of you like a glass of milk before I put your lights out?'

'Yes, please, Scottie,' we replied, and she went to fetch it for us.

After she had brought the milk to us, she left us for about ten minutes, before she came back say 'Good-night', and put our lights out. When she had shut the door behind her, we said, 'Good Night, see you in the morning,' to each other, and snuggled down.

I waited for sleep to overtake me. For the first time in weeks I wondered whether it would be 1940 or 1974 when I woke up in the morning.

CHAPTER THIRTY-SIX

Friday the Thirteenth—Again

WHEN I WOKE UP ON MONDAY MORNING my throat was sore and I had a runny nose. I sneezed, and blew my nose, to be answered by nose-blowing from the bed next to me. It was still dark, as the blackout blind was covering the window. I felt through my nightie to check that the photo was still there.

'Ally, are you still there?' came Harry's anxious voice.

'Yes.'

'I'm *so* glad, I'd a horrid feeling you *might* have gone back to the future'

'I wondered too. Maybe I'm not *meant* to go back.'

'I *hope* you stay. It wouldn't be the same without you. Ca-vee! I think I can hear Scottie-the-Potty coming. Aaah–*chooo!* The door opened, and Scottie came in.

'And how are my scallywags this morning?' she asked. 'Did I hear one of you sneezing just now?'

'I did,' we replied together.

She came over and put her hand on my forehead. '*Hmmm!*' was all she said. She put on her specs and took a thermometer from her top pocket. She peered at it, gave it six or so energetic shakes, squinted at it again and stuck it in my mouth. Then she felt the inside of my wrist with the tips of her fingers, and looked at her watch. After half a minute she let go of my wrist, took the thermometer from my mouth and looked at it again.

'Have I got a temperature, Scottie?' I asked.

'Just a wee one, ninety-eight point eight. Not enough to worry about. By the way, your heart's still beating. Now, Harry, your turn,' she said, producing another thermometer and sticking it in Harry's mouth. 'You're normal,' she told her, after taking her pulse and reading the thermometer.

'Oh, Scottie!' said Harry, 'What *wonderful* news! Does that mean I'm *not* an imbecile and *won't* have to go to the loony-bin after all?'

'Och well,' she replied, looking at Harry over the top of her spectacles, 'We'll have to see about that. How's that ankle this morning?'

'It feels just fine the noo,' Harry replied, 'But I've no' tried walking on it yet.'

'What about you, Ally?' Scottie asked.

'I've got a bit of a sore throat,' I replied, 'And my nose is a bit stuffed up.'

'You're probably starting a chill. Have you been to the lav. this morning?'

'I used the potty in the night, but I want to go again now.'

'Off you go then.'

When I got back, Scottie was not there. As I climbed into bed, she returned carrying a big bottle and a desert spoon. The bottle was labelled: "*Matron's Nasty*

Jalap." She poured some into the spoon, and gave it to Harry.

'*UGH!*' said Harry pulling a face, 'That was *UG*some!'

'This'll make it better,' said Scottie, taking a sweet from her pocket. Then she came to me, and poured me a dose. I held my nose, opened my mouth, and waited for her to put the spoon in. It was revolting. I pulled a face. '*Ugh*! *Scottie!* That was absolutely the *horrible*-est, *disgusting*est medicine I've *ever* had! I'd rather *die* than have to take any more of that!'

'Here's a sweetie for you, for being such a good wee lassie,' she said, taking a sweet from her pocket and popping it into my mouth. 'Your brekkers will be coming up soon. Is there anything else either of you want before I go?'

'No thank you, Scottie,' I said.

'I'm just fine, thanks, Scottie,' said Harry.

Our brekker was brought by Rob Roy and Puddles. Rob Roy put her tray in front of Harry, and Puddles gave me mine.

'Thanks, Rob. It's gorgeous to be waited on hand and foot like this, isn't it, Ally?'

'Rather. Thanks, Puddles, how's everybody today?'

'They're fine and send their love to you both,' she replied. 'If there's anything you want from the common room, let us know when we come back for your trays.'

'Give them our love,' said Harry, 'And tell them we'd love to have some visitors.'

'Okay,' said Rob Roy. 'We must dash, or we'll get what for! Come on, Puddles.'

I looked at my tray. The porridge had more milk and sugar on it than we got in the eatery. I took a spoonful, and it slipped down my sore throat without difficulty.

'*Ugh!*' said Harry. 'Mine's got *sugar* on it!' She tried a tiny bit. 'Actually it's not too bad for a change. I could get used to having it the Sasannach way.' We grinned at each other.

I found the toast difficult to swallow with my sore throat, and anyhow I was not feeling much like eating. Scottie came to see how we were doing.

'What's up, Ally? Don't you want any more, pet?'

'Sorry, Scottie. The toast's hard to swallow, even chewing and chewing and chewing and chewing it.'

'Never mind, would you like some more porridge?' she asked.

'No, thanks,' I replied. 'I've had enough. Really. D'you think I could have a glass of milk, please?'

'I'll see what I can do. Harry, would you like to finish up Ally's toast?'

'Yes please, Scottie. Thanks, Ally.'

Our trays were collected afterwards by Nicky and Nancy, and before school we were visited by Miss Spurgeon. 'Hello, you young heroines,' she said. 'What's all this I hear about rescuing pussy-cats from bomb-sites and demolishing the rest of the house on top of you?'

'I *had* to do it, Miss Spurgeon,' said Harry. 'Poor wee Lolly would've been broken-hearted if I hadn't rescued Neenee for her. She wanted to do it herself, but

I wouldn't let her—'

'Quite right, but you should have thought of the risk—I hear you cut your wrist badly. That could have been dangerous.'

'But Ally made a tourniquet, Miss Spurgeon.'

'And got soaked to the skin in the process, I hear. It was a very selfless act on your part, Ally. Your joint exploits are the talk of the school. Everyone is terribly impressed.'

'I only did what I had to do for my best friend,' I replied, feeling myself blushing. 'She'd have done the same for me.'

'Harry might, I agree,' said our form mistress. 'But there are precious few girls in this school who would have done what you did, even for their best friends. Most of them wouldn't have known what to do.' She gripped my shoulder, and then Harry's. 'I thought you'd like these jig-saws. I always find they are fun to do when I'm poorly. They've got rather boyish pictures, I'm afraid, but they'll help to pass the time.' She took one of them from her carrier bag and gave it to me.

'THE CORNISH RIVIERA EXPRESS! Brilliant! I adore trains, so does Harry. We played with Boy-Alex's Hornby train set all afternoon when we went to tea. Gosh, thanks, Miss Spurgeon.' I gave her one of my best smiles. 'What've you got Harry?'

'THE CHELTENHAM FLYER! Absolutely wizard! Thanks.'

'You two are well named,' laughed Miss Spurgeon. 'You're more like boys than most of the *boys* I've known.'

'Well, actually, Miss Spurgeon,' said Harry, 'I think Ally *is* a boy really, but the doctor made a mistake and told his mummy he was a girl.'

'Look who's talking,' chuckled Spug-Bug. 'Although, now your hair's longer, you're beginning to *look* like a girl—at *long* last!' Harry blushed and lowered her eyes, showing her long eyelashes.

'I'll soon be able to call her Kate all the time, won't I, Miss Spurgeon?' Harry turned towards me and stuck out the tip of her tongue. The bell rang downstairs.

'There's the bell for prayers,' said Spug-Bug. 'I must fly, or The Beak'll be giving me a lateness mark. Chin up! Is there anyone you'd like to see during break.'

'We'd like to see Judy, wouldn't we, Harry?'

'Yes, that would be nice,' agreed Harry. 'We were on our way back from having tea at her house when—when—er—*IT*—happened.'

'All right, I'll tell her,' replied Miss Spurgeon. 'Be good, and do everything Scottie tells you.'

'We will,' said Harry. 'Thanks for the jig-saws, Miss Spurgeon.'

*

A short time after Miss Spurgeon left, Scottie brought a tray for us to do the jig-saws on. Harry said it would be much more fun if we worked on a puzzle together, and suggested I got into bed with her, then we could have the tray on our laps. It was quite a difficult puzzle, and we decided it would be more fun if we tried to do it without looking at the picture on the lid of the box. Four hundred and eighty pieces made up the picture, so it was going to take a while to finish.

By break-time, we had completed the four sides made up of the pieces with one straight edge, and had begun to build up the picture inside. Just after we heard the bell, Scottie came to see how we were getting on.

'I've brought you your mid-morning milk,' she said, 'And two visitors.' We looked up, and Judy was there with Sue Spender, her best friend. 'Now you *won't* tire my patients out, *will* you?'

'No, Matron, we won't,' said Judy.

'Hiya, Judy—hiya, Sue,' said Harry cheerfully.

'Is there anything you want before I go?' Scottie asked us.

'No thanks, Scottie, we're fine. Thanks for bringing our milk.'

'Sit on the bed, you two,' said Harry, when Scottie had gone.

'Golly, doesn't she mind you calling her Scottie?' asked Sue.

'Boarders' privilege, Garters,' replied Harry. 'She likes us to call her that—*unless* we've been naughty—then it *has* to be *Matron*. Just before lights out last night,' she lowered her voice and began to chuckle, 'I called her Scottie-the-Potty—'

'You *didn't!*' gasped Sue.

'She did *so!*' I said, and told them what had happened.

'Golly!' said Judy, 'I'd never have thought Matron was nice like that.'

'She's one of the kindest, dearest people ever,' I said. 'Just like a mummy to us. Last night she gave us our high tea in front of the fire in her room, then gave us a cuddle because we were feeling a bit miserable.'

'She even dried us with hot towels after our bath, didn't she, Ally?'

'Tell us exactly what happened,' said Judy. 'All The Beak said was that you'd had an accident, Harry, and Ally had rescued you.'

'You remember Lolly saying she thought her cat had been killed in the air-raid?' said Harry. 'Well—' She told them the whole story; from seeing Neenee, right up to the staircase collapsing under her, and I had to take up the story after that.

'Gosh, Ally,' said Garters, 'How *ever* did you know what to do? I'd have gone all wobbly at the knees and panicked.'

'She learnt first aid in the cubs,' said Harry, grinning.

'Don't you mean the *Brownies?*' asked Judy.

'No,' I said. 'Harry's right, I used to go to cubs in place of my twin brother sometimes.'

'And she used to take his place in the choir when he wanted to go fishing, didn't you, Ally?' Harry added. I grinned and nodded.

'But what about your *pig*tails?' asked Garters.

'My hair was shorter then, a bit like Harry's is now.'

'No wonder you two get on so well,' said Judy. 'I can see you as a boy, Ally.'

After they had left I had to go to the lav. again; it was the third time that morning. Harry told me I was getting worse than Amanda Hardy.

*

We completed the jig-saw during the afternoon. Bendy Wendy, wearing her tunic, came to see us just after she had taken the third for gym. 'Hello, chaps,' she said, standing on one leg, entwining the other round it and wringing her hands. 'I've got a few minutes to spare so I thought I'd just pop in and see you and find out how you are. You were sorely missed in gym. Scottie tells me you're "off games" until your ankle's fully better, Harry. It's a shame, because we're playing Talbot Woods on Saturday and the team needs you both. Still it can't be helped I s'pose—I say—what a wizzo jig-saw! I love doing them.'

She sat cross-legged at the foot of the bed—as if she was our big sister. I think she really enjoyed being 'girls together' with us. She picked up a piece. 'Look, I think this bit goes there.' It fitted perfectly. 'There.'

'Jolly dee, Bendy,' said Harry. 'We're sorry we're off games just now. It's all my silly fault for being such a dumb-cluck—but it wouldn't have done for Lolly to have gone up there.'

'True,' Bendy found where two more pieces fitted and the bell rang again. She got off the bed. 'Look, I must dash! I've got the remove next period. If there's anything you want, just ask.'

'Thanks, Bendy,' I replied. 'We will.'

'Good show, try not to be miz, eh? Chins up, chaps, chests out, toodle-oo.'

''Bye, Bendy, thanks for coming,' I said, and then coughed.

Harry looked at me, frowning. 'That didn't sound very good. I hope you're not getting something nasty, Ally.'

'No, it's just what Gran would call a tickle. Nothing to worry about. Hey look! This piece fits here and this one here, and this one goes he—Oh—it doesn't. What a chizz!'

'*This* bit fits there, Ally, look! And this one goes in there. Now we've only this wee space to fill and we've finished it.'

I turned my head away and coughed again; into my hanky this time. I looked at Harry. She was watching me anxiously, her brow furrowed. She touched my cheek, and put her hand on my forehead.

'I don't like the sound of that cough, Ally,' she said. 'I've never heard you cough like that before. Your brow's a bit warm.'

'I'm all right, really,' I replied, trying to reassure her. In truth, I was not feeling too grand and could sense a stinking cold coming on.

*

As soon a she heard me coughing, Scottie gave me a dose of cough mixture. It tasted much nicer than "*Matron's Nasty Jalap*". Afterwards, she took my temperature again.

'You've still got a slight temperature,' she said, 'But it's no worse than it was this morning. You've got a nasty chill. Are you still going to the lav. a lot?'

I nodded. 'Yes, lots and lots.'

'And you're having plenty to drink?'

I nodded again and croaked, 'Yes, Scottie.'

'You left most of your lunch. You *must* to try to eat some more. Have you still got a sore throat, my poor wee lamb?'

'Yes, it hurts when I swallow. But I managed the treacle pudding and custard. And the porridge at brekker.'

'I'll have a word with Gladys,' said Scottie, 'And see if she can cook you something soft that will slip down easily.' She was just leaving when Harry sneezed. 'Don't say you're getting a cold as well?'

By lights-out we both had streaming noses. There was an air-raid warning that night and we had to go to the shelter. We were put in a corner, well cocooned in blankets, as far away as possible from the others, so they'd not catch our germs. Fortunately, the air-raid warning turned out to be a false alarm and we were soon back in our warm beds.

The next morning my temperature had risen to over a hundred and Scottie said that if it went up any further, she would have to send for Dr Hall. My cough was worse that morning. Harry was still full of cold, but her ankle was a lot better, and she was able to put some weight on it again. The wound on her wrist was healing well too.

Scottie brought the *Echo* for us to read. The main story was about a Spitfire shooting down a Junkers 88 dive-bomber over Poole. It crashed in flames, with the crew still aboard.

It occurred to me that being back in the room in which my time journey had taken place, it could well be that my return would take place within the next few days. I was not sure whether or not I should mention it to Harry. I didn't want to leave her, we were such close friends, and I knew I would miss her terribly, and even though she would be grown up, and more than old enough to be my mother, I was determined to search her out when, *or if ever*, I returned to being a boy again in 1974.

I was feeling pretty awful on the Wednesday morning, and when Scottie took my temperature it was nearly a hundred and four, so she called in Dr. Hall. She gave me a beaker to spit any phlegm I coughed up into. While we waited for him to come, Harry sat by my side, holding my hand and looking unhappy.

'Oh, Ally,' she cried, tears streaming down her cheeks. 'It's all *my* fault. If *only* I hadn't been so *stupid*, you wouldn't have got wet and caught whatever it is you've got. Darling Ally, you're my dearest, bestest, friend ever; pul-*ease* get better.' She put her arms round me, and her head on my shoulder and burst into tears.

'Don't cry, Harry, *please*.' I ruffled her hair and she clung to me even more tightly.

'It's the thirteenth on Friday, and I think you're going to leave me and go back to your own time. I don't know what I'm going to do without you. I love you like I would my own sister or brother. I'll miss you *so* terribly!'

'I'll miss *you* terribly too, but we don't *know* that I'll go back. If I *do*, will you look after Edward Bear Esquire for me? He'll look after you for me, and then I'll know that we've *got* to meet again in the future. 1974 seems an awful long way away now, and I've got used to being a girl and quite enjoy being one. I've almost forgotten what it was like to be a boy.'

She looked at me and grinned in that happy, cheeky manner of hers. 'You'll be able to stand up when you go wee-wees!'

'You great *mooncalf!*' I laughed and aimed a punch at her, glad that she was more her normal chirpy self. Laughing made me cough again.

'Suppose you didn't change back into a *boy?*' she said. 'That could be a bit awkward. What would your school-friends say? What school is it, by the way?'

'Saint Ali's Wash-House,' I said, grinning. 'I could hardly go back *there* if I was a girl. I suppose I'd go to Southbourne High. I don't know what my tomboy cousins, Nick and Jackie would say! I s'pose I could go to *their* boarding school.'

'You're a tomboy too—so you'd still be one' she said. 'They'd still love you just the same; I would, whatever you were, even if you were a complete loony!'

'*I am, I am,*' I said, pulling a hideous face. 'Totally starkers feeble bonkers! Didn't you know?' We laughed; it made me cough again and I spat some more phlegm into "*Ally's Spit-Pot*", as Harry had labelled it! She had that round-eyed haunted look again. I hated to see her looking like that.

Dr. Hall came during the afternoon. He made me stick out my tongue, then listened to my chest with his stethoscope, made me say '*Aa-ah!*' and used his pen-torch to peer at my throat. He took my temperature and looked serious as he spoke quietly to Scottie.

I thought I heard the word "*pneumonia*" and realised that I might never see Christmas 1940. After he had seen me, Dr Hall examined Harry's ankle and wrist, both of which were still bandaged. He listened to her chest, made her stick out her tongue and looked down her throat.

'You'll live, young Harry,' he said. 'Nothing a few more days in bed won't cure. Look after your best friend.'

'I will, Dr. Hall. I *promise.*'

The next couple of days are all a bit of a blur. Scottie was really kind, doing her best to make me comfy. I had the treasured photo in my pocket, and Edward Bear Esquire shared my pillow. Harry was at my side constantly, doing her best to comfort me and cheer me up, but seeing me so poorly upset her terribly. At lunch on Friday, I spilled some soup on my nightie, and Scottie brought me a clean one to put on; it was the pink one that had been lent to me by the Matron at Colvin. It was then I realised it was Friday the thirteenth again——

I was hot and feverish and feeling so tired I slept a lot. Harry did her best to keep me cheerful, but I could see she was worried about me. I remember smiling at her when she put Edward Bear Esquire in my arms. I smiled at her and ruffled her hair. She kissed my cheek, and taking my hand, squeezed it gently as I gradually drifted off to sleep.

CHAPTER THIRTY-SEVEN

Saturday the Fourteenth

As I wakened I became aware of a bright light. I felt unreal, like you do when you leave the cinema after a very dramatic film. I half-opened my eyes and became aware of sunshine coming through pale blue curtains. Where was the blackout— The other bed was empty—Where was Harry? A lady was leaning over me.

'He's coming round——'

"He?" Did she really say *"He?"* Had it all been a dream? I took a look under the sheets—I was still wearing Girl-Alex's pink nightie and navy-blue knickers, and there was still an Elastoplast on my knee. A swift check confirmed I really was a boy again, and I could feel the little picture frame was still in the pocket where I had put it. I took it out and peered at it through bleary eyes—Harry and Ally grinned back at me. Beside me on the pillow was a shabby, moth-eaten, one-eyed Edward Bear Esquire. I was back!

I opened my eyes fully, looked at the photo again and then at the lady leaning over me. She was plump and jolly looking, and there was another lady standing beside her who was slender, pretty and elegant. 'Hello, Goody-two-shoes,' I said to the plump lady.

'Hello, Alex,' she replied. 'I'm glad you got back safely. How're you feeling?'

'A bit sleepy still,' I answered. Then I saw the other lady clearly and knew her at once. '*Harry*—!' I screeched. 'How *spiffing* to see you! I was so scared I'd lose you for ever. What's today's date?' I swung my legs out of bed, stood up, and buried my face in her bosom, hugging her as tightly as I could.

'Welcome home, Ally, darling. It's Saturday the fourteenth of December 1974,' said Auntie Kate, hugging and kissing me. 'You've been away for three whole months; but I've had to wait much longer than that to thank my best friend for saving my life. When you died in 1940 I cried and cried and cried. But Edward Bear Esquire comforted me, sharing my pillow for many years; often getting *very* soggy with my tears. I loved you *such* a lot. I was inconsolable for ages—blaming myself for your death.'

'I loved *you* just as much,' I replied, 'and still do. I'm glad you had Edward Bear Esquire to look after you. But it wasn't your fault that I died. Alexandra *had* to die. Remember, her grave's in All Saints churchyard.'

'I know,' she said, 'But I was scared *YOU* might die, as you had taken Alexandra's place. How I've longed for this moment, it seemed a lifetime away. I met your Dad at Alexandra's funeral, and we became firm friends. When you were born I was so happy when they called you Alexander Francis. I had just had Nick, and your Mum and I used to take turns to look after and feed each others' babies. It was almost as if we had both had the same twins!

'Your Mum and Dad never knew about your "adventure". Gran and I decided it wouldn't be fair to tell them. It was only Gran, Goody, myself and one or two others knew you'd have to go back on that Friday in September. We worried about letting you go, but if you hadn't, the whole sequence would have gone wrong. We were so afraid you might not get back safely. While you've been away, we've been biting our finger-nails down to the quick!'

'Where *is* Gran?' I felt a sudden pang of anxiety. 'Why isn't she *here?* Did her operation go okay—?'

'Her operation went *fine*, but she's needed a long convalescence, due in part to her worrying about you,' replied Harry. 'She sends her love, and says I've to give you a kiss from her. She'll be coming out of the nursing home soon, so you're going to stay with us for a few nights. You don't mind sharing a room with Nick do you?'

'Not if she doesn't mind. How is she? She's at school, isn't she—Jackie, too?'

'No, I wanted them both to be here to welcome you home; they'd normally have broken up next Tuesday, but they were given special leave to break up early, yesterday. I've told them about what's been happening you, and they're longing to welcome their *time-travelling Auntie Ally* home! You were so right about Nick being like me. I can't understand why you never worked out that Harry in 1940 would grow up to be Auntie Kate in 1974. It was staring you in the face all the time.' She went to the door. 'Come in, my darlings——'

Nick, looking anxious, came straight to me. Her dark hair had been cut in a boyishly short crop—like Harry's had been, and she was wearing what I was sure had been *my* navy-blue velvet frock, with white collar and cuffs, which I had last seen Harry wearing a week ago, the previous Saturday evening—in 1940. Nick gazed at me through Harry's eyes from under Harry's long eyelashes—so like her mum only last night in 1940. How had I never realised the truth?

'Hiya, Nick, it's spiffing to see you,' I suddenly realised I was using 1940's words. 'Isn't that my frock you're wearing? You look just like your mum when she wore it it last Saturday.'

'Hello, Auntie Alexandra!' said Nick, grinning Harry's grin as she gave me a bear-hug. 'It's *brill* to see you again. I'm really-*really* glad you're back safe.' She pointed at the Elastoplast. 'What've you done to your knee?'

'Not much! Knelt on a tin-tack at a bomb-site in 1940'

'While she was saving my life,' added Harry.

'Ouch!' Nick drew in a sharp breath. 'Mummy called you "she". What are you, a girl or a boy? You look very girlie to me!'

'I'm a boy, so I hope you're not going to go on calling me *Auntie Alexandra!*'

She giggled. 'No, I'll just call you *Auntie!* Till you get your hair cut anyhow. Golly! It's so lovely and *long*; it makes you look really-*really* pretty, much more girlie than *I* do. *And* you've got a *PINK NIGHTIE* on! I wear p'jamas in bed, so *there!*' she added archly, sticking out the tip of her tongue, just like I had seen her mother do so often in 1940. 'I hope you don't mind me wearing your best frock. You don't want it back, do you? 'cos you won't want to wear it now you're a boy again—' She frowned, looking uncertain. 'Will you?'

'I'd love you to have it and think you look brill in it and I'd like to see you wearing it sometimes.' We hugged again; it was like hugging young Harry again.

'It really *is* your frock, Ally,' Harry said. 'After you'd left us, Gran gave it to me as a keepsake. I often wore it after that and felt you close to me still. I've treasured it ever since; it even has your name-tape in it still. I knew you'd like to see how like me, my sweet Nicky looks in it.' She hugged us both. Jackie, hovering in the background, watched me warily. Her hair was still in a longish bob and she was wearing a frock of Black Watch tartan which I recognised instantly. Harry beckoned her. 'Come on, poppet, Ally's not going to bite you. I know his hair's rather long, and in his nightie he looks like a little girl, but it really *is* him.'

I held out a hand to her; 'I've been looking forward to seeing you again, Jackie.'

She came forward hesitantly and shyly shook my hand. 'Did-you-really-really-change-into-a-girl-and-go-to-school-with-Mummy?' came all in a rush.

'Yes, really-*really!* Look!' I showed her the photo. 'That's your Mum and me in our uniform. We were best friends and did everything together; lessons, gym, lacrosse, even our cubies were next to each other in our dormitory. We even used to have a bath together sometimes.'

'What! You and *Mummy*—? *Bare*—? Without any clothes on? In the same bath?' exclaimed Jackie, looking terribly shocked.

'Yes, my angel, of course,' said Harry. 'Just like you and Nick often do. We weren't any different from you, just two ordinary little girls in the same bath.'

'You mean he really-really became a *real* girl?' asked Jackie, wide-eyed.

'Yes, my angel.' said Harry. 'She was just as real a little girl as I was or as you and Nick are, and she often wore that frock you're wearing, didn't you, Ally?'

'Yes, I did; I liked it better than my own, that Nick's got on.'

'It suited you well,' said Harry, 'And my kilt; I've kept it for you as I promised. It's waiting for you at home.'

'Thank you, Auntie Harry,' I giggled. 'D'you remember you said I'd have to call you that if we ever met in my proper time.'

'Hey! Auntie Ally, look at me!' called Nick. She was re-enacting Harry's half-term exploit at the hospital, walking on her hands.

'I told her about my *performance* in Boscombe Hospital,' said Harry, 'and how Scottie ticked me off good and proper for showing my pants to all and sundry. Nick's been practising it specially for your benefit.'

'She's a chip off the old block, isn't she, Harry?' The new voice was a surprise because I hadn't heard the door open. I swung round and saw an elderly lady with twinkling eyes and grey hair done up in a bun. 'How's my wee Alexander? How's my best *boy*? I'm glad you're safe and have got the photo. I wondered where it had vanished to. My copy's still in pride of place in rogues' gallery.

'I'm sorry I didn't believe you when you said you were a boy. Yet how could I? On the outside you were just an ordinary wee girl. Yet all the time, there was a boy hiding inside the kind, thoughtful and brave wee lassie I was so fond of. It explains a lot I must say; like collecting bus tickets, and giving Kenneth Duncan a bloody nose after choir practise. Hardly what I would expect of a ten-year-old girl, even a tomboy like Harry.

'When you were taken from us everybody missed you tremendously; the whole school was miserable for the rest of term. I'm so thankful you've come back safely. Welcome home, laddie. Harry (or Kate as we called her by then) told me your secret when she came to us as French mistress in 1951. I'm proud to know you, Ally, but I'll always remember you best as the plucky wee girl you were for those few short months in 1940; one of my own two very special girls, either of whom I'd have been proud to call my own daughter.' She stooped and gave me a kiss.

'Scottie!' I sobbed, flung my arms round her, buried my face in her jumper and burst into tears.

*

After a wash at the basin, Harry and Scottie helped me to dress. Scottie took delight in holding my Y-Fronts out for me. 'This is to make up for my not believing you in 1940—' she said, her eyes twinkling as I stepped into them. I took off Alexandra's nightie and liberty bodice for the last time, dropped them on top of her already-discarded knickers, put on my own vest and shirt, pulled on my jeans, and began to feel more like a boy again.

'Ally, d'you remember asking me if I wore jeans?' asked Harry, 'and I replied "Jean's what?" and that I didn't know anybody called Jean!' Nick gave an explosive guffaw, just like the young Harry used to, and Jackie giggled.

I nodded. 'Don't forget it was only a few weeks ago for me.'

'I suppose so,' sighed Harry. '1940 seems so far away and remote now—'

Then Scottie brushed my hair for me, as vigorously as she ever did. 'D'you want me to plait it for you?' she teased with a twinkle in her eye, 'or tie it up with a pretty ribbon?'

'*No–oo!*' I wailed in anguish, while Nick grinned oafishly and Jackie sniggered. So it was left loose covering my shoulders.

Then we went to Scottie's old room, which was now occupied by Goody, where I had brekker. It was bacon, egg, sausage, tomato and fried bread, with toast, butter and marmalade to follow. After almost three months of wartime rationing, it was truly a breakfast to remember. Funnily enough, I had returned to a bread shortage, due to a bakers' strike.

On the way back to Harry's house, I sat in the back of her Renault 16TX, with Nick and Jackie on either side. My jeans felt tight, restricting and quite uncomfortable after being used to the looseness and freedom of my gymmer. Scottie sat in front with Harry. I noticed that most of the shops we passed were ablaze with Christmas lights. What a change from war-time!

'Auntie Kate, you don't mind if I go on calling you Harry, do you?'

'Of course not, poppet, it's still my name and I hope we'll still be best friends. We can be, can't we?'

'Ra*THER!*'

As soon as we were inside the house, Nick took me up to her room to show me where I was to sleep. Harry's kilt was laid out on my bed, and on the pillow were my pyjamas. I asked Edward Bear Esquire to guard them, in case they went walkies before bedtime. Nick picked up the kilt and held it in front of me.

'Why don't you wear it *now*, Ally?' she said. 'I'm going to put my jeans on 'cos I don't want to spoil *our* dress. Will you undo me at the back, please? I find it rather difficult to unfasten buttons when they're round the back.'

'They *are* a bit hard to reach, aren't they? And rather fiddly. Harry and I always used to do them for each other. Are you *sure* you don't mind a *boy* undoing your buttons for you? I don't think *I'd* have let a boy to undo *my* buttons when *I* was a girl!' I grinned at her sheepishly.

She giggled. 'Don't be silly, Ally. You're still my auntie until Mummy cuts your hair; then you can be my brother. Anyhow, you didn't mind me and Jackie watching while you got dressed at Auntie Goody's.'

I did as she asked, and she wriggled "our dress" off her shoulders and stepped out of it. In her vest and navy knicks she could so easily have been that leggy girl I had met for the first time during gym on my first morning in 1940. Now I realised why I never made the connection! *Her hair!* Until now, I had never seen Nick with Harry's boyish short-back-and-sides haircut. I had only seen her with longer, bobbed, hair—covering her ears and neck. She sat beside me on the bed and reached out to touch my hair.

'Your hair's really-really pretty, Ally,' she said, stroking it. 'It seems *such* a shame to cut it. I think you should keep it long.'

'Maybe if I was a girl; but it's far too long now I'm a boy again—and much too difficult to look after and keep clean and tidy.'

'You could have a *pony*-tail!' She giggled, and drew my hair back tightly into one with her hands. 'Or *bunches*—or *PIGTAILS!* Would you have liked to stay being a girl, Ally, or are you glad to be a boy again?'

'I'm glad I'm back as a boy, but I'm sure there'll always be a bit of me that is Girl-Ally. It was fun being a girl for a change, once I'd got used to it! It was a horrid shock when I discovered I really was one.' I grinned. 'D'you know, my first thought was, *"How do I do a wee?"* Oh, Nick, how I *wished* you'd been there to tell me what to do. I knew you'd have giggled like mad. Then I met your Mum during gym and we became best friends next day. She was *such* a help, even though I couldn't tell her my secret until much later. I could never have managed without her help. We were like twin sisters, sharing and doing everything together. She bossed me about like anything, but I didn't mind. You really are *awf'ly* like her. I used to tell her how like you she was, never dreaming she'd grow up to be your Mum. I can see now that it was staring me in the face all the time, and yet I never twigged—'

She squeezed my hand. 'I'm glad you're a boy again too, but I wouldn't have minded if you'd come back as a girl—you could've come to our school. I'm everso glad you're safe.' We never heard Harry come in, and both started when she spoke.

'So *that's* where you both are. Nicky, darling, be a good girl and put on your jeans and a woolly; you'll catch your death hanging around half dressed.'

'We were just coming, Mummy,' said Nick, pushing one leg into her jeans. 'But Ally's been telling me how you taught him to behave like a good little schoolgirl.'

'I hope you weren't giving away any of our *private* secrets, Ally?'

'What *me?*' I said, trying to look innocent.

'Yes, *you!*' laughed Harry. 'Downstairs, *tous les deux. Toute de suite!*'

Scottie and Jackie were in the kitchen, Jackie still wearing Harry's Black Watch frock. Outside it was pouring with rain, so we sat round the table and chatted, while Harry cooked lunch.

'What happened to the rest?' I asked. 'What about Maggot and Weevil?'

'Well,' said Harry, 'Eventually Maggot became head girl. After you left us we became best friends, never as close as you and I were, Ally, but not far off. Weevil became very holy and pi, which irked Maggot intensely. When she was head girl, I was games captain. We both went on to Cranbourne, then Somerville College, Oxford. She read English and History, and I read French and History. Her first teaching job was at Seabourne too, taking over history when Mrs. Griffiths retired. Now she's headmistress of Spettisbury Manor which, as you know, is where Nick and Jackie are at school. I often see her now the girls are there. It's due to her kindness that they're here now to welcome you home.'

'We call her *The Maggot*,' giggled Jackie, 'don't we, Nick? But not to her *face*— we wouldn't *dare!* When no one else is around, she lets us call her Auntie Margot.'

'Why don't you come with me when I take them back next term. I know Maggot would adore to see you again.'

'I hope she won't throw horse-manure at me, now I'm a boy again—' I said. Jackie giggled with delight, earning a hug from Harry, and Nick guffawed in a very Harry-like manner.

'I think she's given up that sort of thing now,' chuckled Scottie, 'But she still enjoys a good joke.'

'What about Lolly?' I asked.

'When the war was over, her father retired from the Merchant Navy and joined the Coastguard Service. After Seabourne, she went to Talbot Heath as a day-girl. Eventually she married Boy-Alex, who had become a vicar like his Dad. They have twins, a girl and a boy, the same age as you and Nick. Now they live in Swanage, where Alex has the living. His dad, who's retired now, lives with them and helps in the parish.

'And Auntie Vera?' I asked. 'Is she still alive?'

'Indeed she is,' said Scottie. 'I visited her only last week. Since retiring she's lived in Wareham and spends her time writing children's books. Your Gran visited her a few weeks before going into hospital, to remind her about your adventure. When I said we were hoping you'd come back today, she sent her love and said she'd adore to see you again. When Harry returned to Seabourne as French mistress and deputy head we often used to talk about you. Vera was terribly fond of you, as were we all.'

'And what happened to Weevil?' I asked.

'She went into nursing,' said Harry, 'then became a nun. Now she runs a mission hospital somewhere in darkest Africa. Maggot's still in touch and gives us regular news of her.'

We carried on talking about 1940 right up to lunch-time, with Nick and Jackie asking loads of questions. I knew how hard it must be for them to visualise life as it had been then. Looking back, although it had been a terrible shock for me at the time, I'm glad it happened. It made me realise how lucky I was to live in peacetime, but, sadly, the comradeship that drew everyone together as we faced our ruthless enemy no longer existed.

For lunch Harry had made a steak and kidney pie, and there was chocolate ice-cream for pudding. Afterwards Harry said she'd cut my hair, but not before Nick had plaited it, to an accompaniment of delighted giggles from Jackie (who wanted me to put on the navy-blue frock). Nick thought I should wear her gymmer, but I said '*No!* *very firmly,* to both ideas. In the end Harry suggested I wear her kilt, and when Scottie saw me with pigtails, wearing it again, she beamed and gave me the hugest hug. Nick rushed upstairs to change into *our frock* again so Harry could take a photo of Ally and Harry II to add to "rogues' gallery." Then she took another of us with Jackie, *Auntie Ally and her two nieces,* but Nick said we actually looked more like three sisters. Then Nick took one of me with Scottie and Harry.

Then Harry cut my hair, and cut it much the same as Nick's. Inspecting myself in the mirror I was glad that, at long last, I looked like a proper boy again. Harry tied three locks of Girl-Ally's hair with tartan ribbon, one each for Gran, Scottie, and herself. Then, leaving the girls with Scottie, she took me to visit Gran.

When we arrived, she was dressed and sitting in an armchair, reading *Woman's Journal.* She looked up and I went straight to her and gave her a kiss. 'Are you feeling all right now, Gran?' I asked. 'Harry—Auntie Kate—says your operation went okay, and you're coming home next week.'

'Hello, my precious. I'm fine now; especially now I know you're back safe and sound,' she said, putting an arm round my waist and kissing me. It's strange, but I didn't mind her calling me "precious" any more. I flung both my arms round her and gave her an enormous hug. 'I'm *so* relieved you've come home safely, precious. And *my!* Don't you look smart in that kilt?'

'It's Harry's—the one she used to lend me at school. She's given it to me.'

'How kind of you, Kate, darling,' said Gran, and turning to me again, added, 'We've been thinking about you such a lot, haven't we, Kate?' Harry nodded. 'Tell me, my precious, how did you like being a little girl at boarding school in 1940?'

'It was okay, but I'd have been lost without my best friend.' I glanced at Harry, who squeezed my hand and smiled. 'I didn't think much of the food. How did you manage to stand it for the rest of the war, Harry?'

'We didn't have any choice, Ally, darling, and rationing lasted a long time after the war was over. We still had ration books when I became French mistress at Seabourne in 1952. By the way, *Tante Marie*, what do you think of Ally's haircut?'

'Very smart,' replied Gran. 'I thought you might bring him along with pigtails, wearing that navy-blue frock *you* were so fond of, Kate.' She winked at me. 'I always wanted to see what "Alexandra's twin sister" looked like.'

I took the little picture out of my sporran and passed it to her. 'Here's a snap that Scottie took of Harry and me together.'

'Bless my soul!' exclaimed Gran. 'I've got a copy of this at home; Vera sent it to me. I always thought it was your poor Auntie Alex.'

'No, it's definitely Ally,' Harry told her. 'I never met the *real* Alexandra. Oh, Ally, don't forget you've brought something for Gran.'

I gave her the envelope in which Harry had put the lock of Girl-Ally's hair. She opened it. 'Thank you, my darling,' she said, wiping a tear from her cheek. 'What a lovely thought.'

'It was Harry's idea, ' I said. 'And Nick plaited my hair before she'd allow Harry to cut it, and we all had our photos taken. Nick put on my dark blue frock and looked just like Harry when she wore it last weekend—I mean in 1940!'

'Nick's just like you used to be, isn't she, Kate?' said Gran. 'And in your kilt, my precious, you look exactly like your dear father when he was your age.'

We chatted for an hour before going back to Harry's for tea. It had been lovely seeing Gran again, looking so well. After tea, Harry ran Scottie home, but not before she'd made me promise to have tea with her soon. While they were gone Nick, Jackie and I watched television—the first I had seen for three months.

After Harry returned, we all played *Cluedo* until supper-time. We had sardines on toast, and then watched a bit more television.

'Would you like to have a bath, Ally?' Harry asked, as it got close to bedtime.

'Yes please,' I replied eagerly. 'I haven't had one since that one we had together after your accident.'

'Then I should think you *need* one by now,' chuckled Harry. 'That was thirty-four years ago last Sunday—!'

The End

믿음의 흔적을 찾아
한국의 기독교 유적

한국기독교역사연구소 편

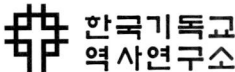

간행사

한국 기독교인들이 오랫동안 기다렸던 책이 간행되어 기쁘다. 그동안 우리 연구소는 기독교 유적지의 답사에 필요한 안내서를 출판해달라는 요청을 부단히 받았다. 그러나 유적이 있는 지역들에 대한 연구가 부족해 이를 미루고 있다가 2009년에야 이 책의 집필에 착수하게 되었다.

이미 출판된 기독교 유적지 안내서들이 유적지 일부를 소개하는 답사기 형태의 글들이라면, 이 책은 전국의 기독교 유적지를 소개하고 그것의 역사적 배경과 의미를 객관적으로 설명하는 점에서 다른 책들과 크게 구별된다. 이 책의 필자들은 한국교회사뿐만 아니라 한국종교사, 한국사 분야에서 훈련받은 전문가들이라서 이들이 제공하는 풍부한 역사적 정보는 신뢰해도 좋다. 다만 남한 지역의 유적지만을 소개하는 점이 아쉬움으로 남는다. 조국통일의 그 날이 어서 오기를 기대하는 마음 간절하다.

『믿음의 흔적을 찾아: 한국의 기독교 유적』을 펴내면서 이 책이 기독교인들의 유적지 순례에 도움이 되고 선진들의 믿음의 흔적을 되살리는데 기여하기를 두 손 모아 기도한다.

2011년 10월
한국기독교역사연구소
소장 김흥수

책을 내면서

일반적으로 '기독교 유적'이란 서구 기독교 신앙과 문화의 도입으로 형성된 건물 및 시설물 형태의 문화재를 가리키는 것으로 여기에는 개항 이후 6·25전쟁 전후까지의 기간에 축조된 예배당·병원·학교·선교사 주거지 등이 포함된다. 한국기독교역사연구소는 국내 기독교 유적지에 대한 교계의 관심 증가 및 답사 수요의 팽창에 부응하여 한층 깊이 있고 대중적인 종합안내서를 제공한다는 목적을 갖고 지난 2009년부터 이 책의 발간을 준비해 왔다. 시중에 나와 있는 기존의 이야기식 답사 안내서들을 좀 더 보완하여 전문성과 전국성을 두루 갖춘 핸드북을 만들어보자는 문제의식도 갖고 출발했다.

우리 집필진은 "1950년대 이전에 지어진 기독교 건물 및 시설물로서 현재 가시적으로 남아있는 건축물"을 '기독교 유적'으로 선정, 집필한다는 원칙을 세웠다. 여기에 덧붙여 스테이션(mission station) 유적지와 잘 알려진 순교 유적지 그리고 역사성을 갖고 있는 선교 유적지는 건축물의 현존 유무를 불문하고 그 대상에 포함시키기로 하였다.

한말·일제강점기에 서구 선교사들에 의해 집중적으로 조성된 전국 주요 도시의 스테이션은 해당 지역 복음화의 전진기지였다는 점에서 역사적으로 높은 가치를 지니고 있다. 한국 기독교 유적지 가운데 가장 큰 비중을 차지하는 것도 스테이션 유적이다. 한국 선교를 주도했던 장로교·감리교 등 주류 교단 선교부는 예외 없이 선교 거점 도시에 대규모의 스테이션을 설치하고 그곳을 중심으로 선교 활동을 벌여 나갔기 때문이다. 스테이션 안에는 거액의 자금을 들여 지은 여러 채의 서양식 주택과 남·여 중등학교, 병원, 그리고 스테이션 직할교회가 세워져 있었고, 그 건물들의 일부가 오늘날까지 전해오고 있다. 다만 호주장로교의 진주, 마산, 통영, 거창스테이션과 남장로교의 군산스테이션은 남아있는 건물이 전혀 없어서 문제가 되었지만 그곳들도 해당 지역 기독교 전파의 발상지였다는 점에서 기독교 유적지로 간주하여 그 현재 상태를 추적해 보았다. 순교 유적지로는 최근 답사 코스로 부상하고 있는 논산의 병촌성결교회와 영광 염산·야월교회, 신안 증도의 문준경 전도사 순교지 등이 선택되었고, 선교 유적지로는 최초의 개신교 선교사 귀츨라프가 머물었던 보령의 고대도와 성경이 최초로 전달되었던 서천 마량진 등이 포함되었다. 이 지역들은 당시 상황을 알려주는 가시적 유적/유물을 지니고 있지 않지만 한국 기독교의 기원과 관련해서 역사적 의미가 남다른 곳들이기에 포함시킨 것이다.

이 책은 몇 가지 특징을 지니고 있다. 먼저 각 지역의 기독교 유적지를 소개하기에 앞서 각 지역(광역자치단체 수준)의 기독교 전래 과정을 개관하고 해당 도시의 지역교회사를 서술하였다. 개별 기독교 유적의 조성 과정을 파악하고 그것들이 갖고 있는 배경과 정신을 알기 위해서는 지역교회의 역사에 대한 선이해가 필수적으로 요청된다고 보았기 때문이다. 한 지역의 기독교 유적지는 그 지역 교회공동체의 산물이자 신앙의 외적 표현이다. 그러므로 이 책은 우리 연구소가 갖고 있는 강점을 십분 살려 해당 지역교회의 역사를 충실하게 담으려고 하였다. 둘째 기독교 유적지가 소재해 있는 해당 도시의 역사·문화와 일반 유적지를 소개하였다. 건축물은 여러 가지 배경을 간직한 사회·문화 현상이기 때문에 해당 종교뿐 아니라 지역사회의 역사와 문화를 함께 알아두는 것이 필요하다. 일반 유적지는 해당 기독교 유적지와 인접해 있어서 함께 둘러볼 수 있는 곳을 중심으로 선정하였다. 이 책의 또 하나의 특징은 한 권의 책에 전국의 기독교 유적지를 망라했다는 점이다. 이 책 하나만 갖고서도 전국 기독교 유적지 답사가 가능하도록 꾸몄다. 개별 기독교 유적에 대한 설명은 핵심 내용을 쉽게 전달하려고 노력했고, 사진은 최소한으로 줄이는 대신 풍부한 역사 정보를 제공하는데 주안점을 두었다. 또 최근 지리정보시스템의 확산 추세에 맞추어 모든 기독교 유적지에 주소를 표기함으로써 독자들이 쉽게 해당 유적지에 접근하도록 배려하였다.

본서의 발간을 위해 기획 단계에서부터 줄곧 필자들을 격려하고 지원한 연구소의 김홍수 소장에게 우선 감사를 드린다. 이덕주 교수의 『한국 기독교 문화유산을 찾아서』 시리즈가 본서를 집필하는데 큰 도움이 되었다. 연구소의 운영위원들은 다양한 의견을 제시하여 집필 방향과 서술 과정에 큰 도움을 주었다. 이 책의 집필진은 모두 3명으로, 송현강 박사는 충청-호남-영남 지역을 담당했고, 서울-경기-강원 지역은 이진구 박사가 담당하였다. 이순자 박사는 한국근대사와 관련된 일반유적지와 사진 작업 부분을 맡아 수고하였다. 이 외에 홍승표 목사가 사진의 일부를 제공해주었다. 우리 집필진은 지난 2년 동안 긴밀하게 의견을 주고받으며 원고의 완성도를 높이기 위해 노력하였다. 하지만 필자가 아닌 독자의 눈으로 보면 여전히 누락된 유적이나 서술과정에 부족한 점이 있을 것이다. 미진한 부분은 앞으로 계속 보완할 것을 약속드리며, 부디 이 한권의 책이 오늘을 사는 우리의 믿음의 흔적을 찾아 나아가는 귀한 길잡이가 되길 소망한다.

2011년 9월
집필자 일동

차 례

간행사 iii
책을 내면서 v

CHAPTER 1 서울지역 ·· 2

❈ 서울 소개 2 / ❈ 서울 기독교의 전래 4

❈ 서울 기독교 유적지

첫번째, **정동**

정동 북장로회 스테이션터 5 | 새문안교회 7 | 시병원터 8 | 배재학당터 9 |
이화학당터 10 | 정동제일교회 12 | 성공회서울대성당 13 |
옛 구세군사관학교 14

두번째, **종로**

승동교회 15 | 대동서시터 16 | 중앙교회터(가우처예배당터) 17 |
태화여자관터 18 | YMCA 19 | 배화여학교 20 | 종교교회와 자교교회 21 |
남감리회 스테이션터 23 | 연지동 북장로회 스테이션터 24 | 연동교회 25 |
정신여학교 세브란스관 25 | 경신학교터 26 | 안동교회 27 | 동대문교회 28 |
복음교회터 28

세번째, **서대문**

감리교신학대학교 29 | 이화여자대학교 30 | 연세대학교 30 |
경성성서학원터 32 | 아현감리교회 33

네번째. **남대문**
　🚗 상동교회 34 | 남대문교회 35

다섯 번째. **기타**
　🚗 양화진외국인선교사묘원 35 | 숭실대 한국기독교박물관 37 | 국립 서울현충원 37

✲ 서울 일반 유적지
　🚗 옛 러시아 공사관 38 | 경운궁(덕수궁) 40 | 경성 부민관 폭탄 의거지 41 | 서대문 독립공원 42

CHAPTER 2 인천·경기지역 ·········· 44

1. 인천지역

첫번째. **인천광역시**

✲ 인천 소개 44 / ✲ 인천 기독교 전래 46

✲ 인천 기독교 유적지
　🚗 내리교회 47 | 창영사회복지관(인천기독교사회복지관) 47 | 영화초등학교(인천영화학교) 48 | 성공회내동성당(내동교회) 49 | 한국기독교100주년기념탑 50 | 인천기독병원 50 | 국제성서박물관 51 | 한국선교역사기념관 52

✲ 인천 일반 유적지
　🚗 인천우체국 52 | 일본 18은행 인천지점 53 | 인천 개항박물관 54 | 한국이민사박물관 54 | 인천자유공원 55 | 인천외국인묘지 55

두번째. **강화**

✲ 강화 소개 56 / ✲ 강화 기독교 전래 57

✲ 강화도 기독교 유적지
　🚗 강화읍성공회성당 58 | 온수리성공회성당 59 | 교산교회 60 | 홍의교회 61 | 길직교회(현 강화초대교회) 62 | 교동읍교회 62 | 강화중앙교회와 합일초등학교 63 | 강화 서도중앙교회(진촌교회) 65 | 백령도중화동교회 65

2. 경기도 지역

첫번째. 수원

❋ 수원 소개 66 / ❋ 수원 기독교 전래 67

❋ 수원 기독교 유적지
🚗 수원종로교회 67 | 매향학교와 삼일중학교 본관 68 | 동신교회 69

❋ 수원 일반 유적지
🚗 수원화성 71 | 화성행궁 72

두번째. 화성
🚗 화성 제암교회와 수촌교회 73

세번째. 용인
🚗 소래교회 75 | 한국기독교순교자기념관 76 |
용인 성공회 성당(대한성공회용인교회) 77

네번째. 안산
🚗 안산 샘골교회와 최용신기념관 78

다섯 번째. 이천
🚗 이천중앙교회와 구연영전도사순국추모비 79 | 이천한국기독교역사박물관 81

여섯 번째. 기타
🚗 김포제일교회 81 | 고양감리교회 82 | 가나안농군학교 82

CHAPTER 3 강원지역 ················· 84

❋ 강원도 기독교 역사 84

첫번째. 철원

❋ 철원 소개 86 / ❋ 철원 기독교 전래 86

❋ 철원지역 기독교 유적지
🚗 철원제일교회터 87 | 장흥교회와 서기훈목사순교기념비 87 |

지경교회터와 새술막교회터 88 | 대한수도원 89

두번째. 원주

✽ 원주 기독교 전래 89

✽ 원주 기독교 유적지
🚗 원주제일교회와 원주기독병원(서미감병원) 90

세번째. 춘천

✽ 춘천 소개 92 / ✽ 춘천 기독교 전래 93

✽ 춘천 기독교 유적지
🚗 춘천중앙교회 94

네번째. 기타

🚗 홍천한서교회, 남궁억기념관, 무궁화동산 95 | 동해 최인규권사 순교기념비와 천곡교회 97 | 화진포 선교사휴양지 98 | 예수원 99

CHAPTER 4 충북지역 100

✽ 충북 기독교의 시작 100

첫번째. 청주

✽ 청주 소개 102 / ✽ 청주 기독교 전래 103

✽ 청주 기독교 유적지
🚗 일신여고 구내 청주 스테이션 유적지 104 | 청주제일교회 107 | 신대교회 109 | 대한성공회 청주수동교회 110

✽ 청주 일반 유적지
🚗 흥덕사지 및 고인쇄박물관 111 | 망선루 112 | 청주 중앙공원 113 | 청주 삼일공원 114

두번째. 진천 · 음성

🚗 대한성공회 진천교회 115 | 대한성공회 음성교회 116

xii 믿음의 흔적을 찾아: 한국의 기독교 유적

CHAPTER 5 대전·충남지역 118

1. 대전지역 118

✱ 대전·충남 기독교의 시작 118

첫번째. **대전광역시**

✱ 대전 소개 120 / ✱ 대전 기독교 전래 120

✱ 대전 기독교 유적지
　🚗 한남대 인돈기념관과 오정동 선교사촌 121 ｜ 국립 대전현충원 123

2. 충남지역

첫번째. **공주**

✱ 공주 소개 125 / ✱ 공주 기독교 전래 126

✱ 공주 기독교 유적지
　🚗 아멘트기념관 127 ｜ 공주 선교사 묘지 128 ｜ 공주제일교회 129

✱ 공주 일반 유적지
　🚗 우금치전적지 및 동학혁명군위령탑 129 ｜ 공주 송산리고분군 130 ｜
　공주 중동성당 131 ｜ 김옥균 선생 유허 132

두번째. **천안**

　🚗 매봉교회와 유관순 열사 생가 134 ｜ 대한성공회 부대동교회 134

세번째. **강경**

✱ 강경 기독교 전래 135

✱ 강경 기독교 유적지
　🚗 옥녀봉 침례교 최초 예배지 136 ｜ 옛 강경성결교회당(구 북옥감리교회당) 137 ｜
　강경제일감리교회와 만동학교터 138 ｜ 강경성결교회 최초 신사참배 거부 선도 기념비
　138 ｜ 병촌성결교회 139

✱ 강경 일반 유적지
　🚗 구 남일당한약방 140 ｜ 구 한일은행 강경지점 140 ｜ 연산역 급수탑 141

차례   xiii

네번째. **서천과 보령**
  🚗 서천(마량진) 142 | 보령(고대도) 144

CHAPTER 6 대구·경북지역 ······ 146

1. 대구지역

✱ 대구·경북 기독교의 시작   146

첫번째. **대구광역시**

✱ 대구 소개 148 / ✱ 대구 기독교 전래 149

✱ 대구 기독교 유적지
  🚗 대구제일교회 구 예배당 150 | 계명대학교 동산의료원 151 | 계성중학교 154

✱ 대구 일반 유적지
  🚗 관덕정순교기념관 156 | 계산성당 156 | 국채보상운동기념공원 157 |
  대구 시민 만세운동 기념비 158 | 우재 이시영 선생 순국기념탑 159 |
  이상화 고택 160 | 서상돈 고택 161 | 약령시 한의약문화관 162

2. 경북지역

첫번째. **안동시**

✱ 안동 소개 163 / ✱ 안동 기독교 전래 163

✱ 안동 기독교 유적지
  🚗 안동교회 164 | 경안고등학교 165 | 성소병원 166

✱ 안동 일반 유적지
  🚗 안동독립운동기념관 167 | 병산서원 168 | 안동 하회마을 169

두번째. **기타**
  🚗 영천자천교회 170 | 봉화 척곡교회 172 | 군위성결교회 173 |
  울진 행곡교회와 용장교회 173

CHAPTER 7 부산·경남지역 ·········· 176

1. 부산지역 176

❋ 부산·경남 기독교의 시작 176

첫번째. **부산광역시**

❋ 부산 소개 178 / ❋ 부산 기독교 전래 179

❋ 부산 기독교 유적지

　부산진교회와 부산진일신여학교 건물 그리고 일신기독병원 180 | 초량교회 182 |
　부산 복병산 유실 묘역 182 | 대한성공회 부산주교좌성당 183

❋ 부산 일반 유적지

　🚗 부산근대역사관 184 | 40계단 기념관 185 | 백산기념관 185 |
　　　박차정 의사 생가 186 | 임시수도기념관 187

2. 경남지역

첫번째. **진주**

❋ 진주 소개 188 / ❋ 진주 기독교 전래 189

❋ 진주 기독교 유적지

　🚗 진주교회 190 | 배돈병원 자리 191 | 광림학교와 시원여학교 자리 192

❋ 진주 일반 유적지

　🚗 진주성 192 | 형평운동 70주년 기념탑 194

두번째. **마산**

❋ 마산 소개 195 / ❋ 마산 기독교 전래 195

❋ 마산 기독교 유적지

　🚗 제일문창교회와 마산 스테이션 자리 그리고 창신학교터 196 |
　　　경남선교 120주년 기념관과 순직 호주 선교사묘원 197

❋ 마산 일반 유적지

　🚗 국립 3·15민주묘지 199 | 마산시립박물관 200 | 마산문학관 200

세번째. 통영

✿ 통영 소개 201 / ✿ 통영 기독교 전래 201

✿ 통영 기독교 유적지
   🚗 충무교회와 통영 스테이션터 202

네번째. 거창

✿ 거창 소개 203 / ✿ 거창 기독교 전래 203

✿ 거창 기독교 유적지
   🚗 거창교회와 거창 스테이션 터 204

CHAPTER 8 전북지역 ········ 206

✿ 전북 기독교의 시작 206

첫번째. 전주시

✿ 전주소개 208 / ✿ 전주 기독교 전래 209

✿ 전주 기독교 유적지
   🚗 전주 예수병원 210 | 전주 신흥고등학교 212 | 전주서문교회 213

✿ 전주 일반 유적지
   🚗 전주 한옥마을 214 | 풍남문 215 | 전동성당 216

두번째. 군산

✿ 군산 소개 216 / ✿ 군산 기독교 전래 217

✿ 군산 기독교 유적지
   🚗 구암교회 218

세번째. 익산시

   🚗 남전교회 219 | 익산 두동교회 220

네번째. 김제시

   🚗 금산교회 222

CHAPTER 9 광주·전남지역 224

1. 광주지역

❈ 광주·전남 기독교의 시작　224

첫번째. **광주광역시**

❈ 광주소개　226　/　❈ 광주 기독교 전래　227

❈ 광주 기독교 유적지

🚗 오웬기념각과 호남신학대학　229 | 광주 수피아여고　233

❈ 광주 일반 유적지

🚗 전남도청 본관　236 | 국립 5·18묘지　236 | 5·18 자유공원　237 |
광주학생운동기념탑　238

2. 전남지역

첫번째. **목포**

❈ 목포 기독교 전래　238

❈ 목포 기독교 유적지

🚗 정명여중 구내 목포스테이션 유적지　240 | 목포양동교회　242

두번째. **순천**

❈ 순천 기독교 전래　243

❈ 순천 기독교 유적지

🚗 매산중학교와 매산여고　244

세번째. **여수**

🚗 여수 애양원　247 | 여수 장천교회　249

네번째. **기타**

🚗 지리산 선교사 유적지　250 | 신안 증도 문준경 전도사 순교지　252

다섯 번째. **영광**

🚗 야월교회　254 | 염산교회　255

차례　xvii

CHAPTER 10 제주지역 256

✽ 제주 소개 256 / ✽ 제주 기독교 전래 258

✽ 제주 기독교 유적지
  🚗 대정교회 259 | 금성교회 260 | 강병대교회 261 | 이기풍선교기념관 261

✽ 제주 일반 유적지
  🚗 제주4.3평화공원 262 | 제주 하멜기념비 263

믿음의 흔적을 찾아
한국의 기독교 유적

CHAPTER 1
서울지역

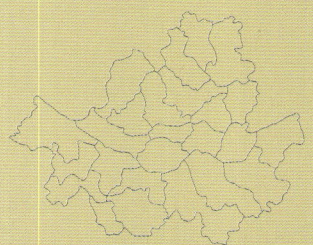

정동지역 → 종로지역 → 서대문지역 → 남대문지역 → 기타 → 일반 유적지

✽ 서울 소개

　서울은 대한민국의 수도로서 정치 경제 사회 문화의 중심지이다. 민족의 젖줄인 한강이 흐르고 있는 서울은 산세와 경관이 뛰어날 뿐만 아니라 한반도의 남과 북의 경계지대에 위치하고 있어 예로부터 전략적 요충지였다. 삼국시대에는 고구려, 백제, 신라가 한강 유역의 주도권을 차지하기 위해 치열하게 다투었다. 오랫동안 백제의 도읍이었던 서울지역은 6세기 중반 신라에 의해 점령되었으며 통일신라 시대에는 한양군으로 개칭되었다. 고려초기에는 양주楊洲로 불리다가 11세기 중반부터 남경南京으로 승격되었다.
　조선의 건국과 함께 서울은 한반도의 수도로 다시 자리 잡으며 역사의 중심으로 재등장하였다. 고려의 수도였던 개경으로부터 도읍을 옮긴 조선왕조는 새 도읍지를 한성漢城이라 부르고 통치에 필요한 기반 시설을 구축하였다. 새로운 왕실의 권위를 상징하는 궁궐로서 경복궁을 창건하고 창덕궁과 창경궁을 별궁으로 건립하였다. 이 세 궁은 임진왜란 때 거의 불타 없어졌고 현존하는 건물들은 그 뒤 중수重修한 것이다. 한성을 관할하는 관청으로 한성부를 설치하고 최고책임자로 정2품에 해당하는 판윤判尹을 두었다. 하부 행정구역으로 오부五部와 방坊, 계契, 동洞을 두고, 정치권력의 주요 거점이 되는 육조六曹와 중추부, 사헌부 등의 관청을 경복궁 남쪽 대로에 설치하였다. 군사와 치

서울지역

양화진외국인선교사묘원

안의 필요에 따라 수도 주변에 높이 8.5 m, 둘레 18 km의 도성을 축조하였으며 도성의 안과 밖을 연락하기 위해 4대문과 4소문을 뚫었다.

조선왕조는 국가의 정신적 토대가 되는 종묘와 사직을 현재의 위치에 건설하였다. 억불숭유 정책에 따라 도성 안에 사찰의 건립을 금하고 불교 승려의 도성출입을 금했다. 도성 안에 승려가 다시 출입할 수 있게 된 것은 개항 이후 일본 승려의 건의에 의해서이다. 건국 초에 국가 기관의 하나로 설치된 도교사원 소격서昭格署도 임진왜란 이후 완전히 폐지하였다. 유학의 진흥을 위해 최고 교육기관인 성균관을 비롯하여 사부학당四部學堂을 도성 안에 두었다.

19세기 말 개항 이후 서울은 서구 문물을 본격적으로 받아들이며 한국사회 근대화의 견인차 역할을 하였다. 서구 열강의 외교관, 군인, 상인, 선교사 등이 서울에 밀집하고 각국의 공사관이 설치되면서 서울은 근대적 도시로 변모하였다. 근대 문물의 상징인 전신, 전화, 전차, 철도 등이 서울에서 먼저 개통되고 근대식 병원, 학교, 공원, 호텔 등도 서울을 중심으로 설립되었다. 최초의 근대식 병원인 광혜원, 최초의 관립학교인 육영공원, 최초의 서구식 공원인 탑골공원 등이 서울에 세워진 대표적인 근대적 시설이다.

1910년 조선총독부는 한성부를 '경성부京城府'로 바꾸었으며 1945년 광복과 함께 서울로 개칭하였다. 1948년 정부수립과 함께 서울은 수도로 결정되었고 1949년 '서울특별시'로 지정되어 오늘에 이르고 있다. 이처럼 서울은 예로부터 한반도의 중심지였고 백제와 조선왕조의 도읍지로서 오랜 역사를 지녀 왔기 때문에 많은 유물과 유적을 간직하고 있다.

✻ 서울 기독교의 전래

기독교의 복음이 한국에 처음 들어올 무렵 서울은 조선왕조의 수도였기 때문에 거의 모든 선교부는 서울을 선교활동의 출발지로 삼았다. 서울에 들어온 최초의 방문 선교사는 일본 주재 미국 북감리회 선교사로서 일본 선교를 책임지고 있던 매클레이Robert S. MacLay, 맥리가였다. 그는 미국 북감리회로부터 한국선교 개척의 임무를 부여받아 1884년 6월 24일 부인과 함께 서울에 도착하여 2주 동안 체류하였다. 그 동안 개화파 인사 김옥균을 통해 고종으로부터 학교와 병원 사업에 대한 허가를 얻었으며 미국 공사관 옆에 선교부지를 마련하고 귀국하였다.

이 무렵 미국 북장로회는 중국에서 의료선교사로 활동하던 알렌Horace N. Allen, 안련을 한국 주재 선교사로 임명하였다. 1884년 9월 22일 서울에 도착한 알렌은 미국 공사관의 의사로 봉직하면서 한국 최초의 정착선교사가 되었다. 1885년 4월 5일 북장로회의 언더우드Horace G. Underwood, 원두우와 북감리회의 아펜젤러Henry G. Appenzeller, 아편설라 부부가 인천 제물포항에 도착하였다. 당시는 갑신정변의 여파로 외국인의 서울 거주가 위험하였기 때문에 아펜젤러 부부는 일본으로 돌아갔다. 하지만 언더우드는 서울로 들어와 알렌의 제중원 교사로 활동을 시작했다. 1885년 5월과 6월, 북감리회 선교사 스크랜턴William B. Scranton, 시란돈 부부와 그의 모친 스크랜턴Mary F. Scranton 대부인, 아펜젤러 부부, 그리고 북장로회의 헤론John W. Heron, 혜론 부부가 서울로 들어왔다. 이로써 미북감리회와 북장로회는 미국 공사관 근처의 정동에 기지를 마련하고 선교에 착수할 수 있었다.

1892년 미국 남장로회 선교부가 한국선교를 시작하였다. 언더우드와 윤치호가 미국에서 행한 한국선교의 필요성에 관한 강연에 감동을 받은 테이트Lewis B. Tate, 최의덕, 레이놀즈William D. Reynolds, 이눌서 등 젊은 신학생들이 선교사로 임명을 받고 그해 11월 3일 한국에 도착했다. 서울에 도착한 선교사들은 강화나 평양 등으로 순회여행을 떠나면서 선교지를 물색하였지만, 1893년 장로교공의회에서 남장로회의 선교지역이 호남지역으로 정해짐으로서 남장로회는 서울과는 직접적 관련을 맺지 않게 되었다.

미국 남감리회의 한국선교는 1895년에 시작되었다. 한국 최초의 남감리회 교인이 된 윤치호의 선교 요청으로 1895년 10월 13일 남감리회의 헨드릭스Eugene R. Hendrix 감독과 중국에서 활동하던 리드Clarence F. Reid, 이덕 선교사가 내한하였다. 이들은 서울에 1주일간 체류하면서 선교 가능성을 탐색하였다. 헨드릭스 감독은 리드를 한국 개척선교사로 임명하고 남대문 안 상동에 선교부지를 마련하였다.

성결교의 경우 선교사가 아니라 한국인에 의해 복음 전파가 시작되었다. 1907년 동양선교회에 의해 창설된 일본 도쿄 성서학원을 졸업한 김상준金相濬과 정빈鄭彬이 귀국하여 서울 종로 염곡에서 '동양선교회 복음전도관'이라는 간판을 붙이고 전도를 하기 시작하였다. 처음에는 교파나 교회를 조직하지 않고 순수 복음전도에만 종사했으나 1921년부터 '성결교회'라는 명칭을 사용하면서 정식 교회조직을 갖추었다.

성공회와 구세군은 영국 선교사들에 의해 시작되었다. 영국 캔터베리 대주교로부터 주교 서품을 받은 코르프Charles J. Corfe, 고요한 신부가 1890년 9월 29일 인천에 도착함으로써 성공회의 한국선교를 시작하였다. 성공회는 초기에는 인천과 강화지역을 중심으로 선교하였지만 점차 서울을 비롯하여 전국으로 선교활동을 확산시켰다. 1908년 10월 1일 영국 구세군 창설자 부드William Booth의 임명을 받은 호가드Robert Hoggard, 허가두가 내한함으로써 구세군의 한국선교도 시작되었다. 호가드는 종로구 평동平洞 76-9번지에 선교부지를 마련하였으며 야주개현 종로구 신문로에 있는 '흥화 경매소' 건물을 임대하여 첫 번째 영문營門을 설립하였다.

러시아정교회의 한국선교는 1897년 6월 러시아 황제 니콜라이 2세의 한국선교 명령, 1898년 1차 선교단의 입국 시도와 암브로시우스 구드코Ambrosius Gudko 대신부의 입국 실패, 1900년 2차 선교단의 내한으로 시작되었다. 선교단은 서울 정동에 있는 러시아 공사관 안에 교당을 설치하고 1900년 2월 17일 공식 예배를 드렸다. 그러나 러일전쟁 이후 러시아인들이 축출되면서 러시아정교회의 한국선교는 약화되었다. 플리머드형제단Plymouth Brethren의 한국선교는 1896년에 시작되었다. 일본인 전도자 노리마츠乘松雅休가 개인 자격으로 내한하여 서울, 경기 지방을 중심으로 전도활동을 하였으며 1898년 브랜드Herbert G. Brand가 내한하여 서울 서소문에 선교부를 개설하고 본격적인 선교를 시작하였다.

✽ 서울 기독교 유적지

첫번째. 정동

정동 북장로회 스테이션터

북장로회 스테이션은 정동 소재 미국 공사관 서쪽 5천여 평의 부지에서 시작되었다. 알렌, 언더우드, 마펫Samuel A. Moffet, 마포삼열 등 초기 북장로회 선교사들의 사택을 비롯하여 경신학교와 정신여학교, 새문안교회가 모두 이곳에서 시작되었다. 1895년 북장로회 선교부가 연지동으로 이전함으로써 정동 스테이션은

10여년의 역사를 마감하게 되었다. 지금은 당시 선교부 관련 건물이 거의 남아 있지 않고 흔적만 남아 있다.

덕수궁길에서 정동극장을 끼고 골목 안으로 들어가면 새로 복원된 2층 건물 중명전(중구 정동 1-11)이 보인다. 1983년 서울시 유형문화재 제53호로 지정된 중명전重明殿은 원래 북장로회 최초의 의료선교사 알렌의 사택이 있던 곳이다. 1884년 9월 미국 공사관 부속 의사로 들어온 알렌은 공사관과 붙어 있는 한옥을 구입하여 사택으로 사용하였다. 1887년 알렌이 선교사직을 사임하고 본국으로 귀환하자 독신 여선교사 엘러스Annie Ellers, 호튼Lillias H. Horton, 헤이든Mary E. Hayden, 도티Susan A. Doty 등이 입주하였다. 1887년 6월 엘러스가 여자 아이 한 명을 가르치면서 정동여학당(정신여자중고등학교의 전신)이 시작되었다. 1897년 정부가 이 집을 사들여 중명전을 건립하였고 1905년 이곳에서 '을사조약'이 체결되었다. 1969년 이방자李方子 여사가 구입하였고 1976년 주식회사 경한실업으로 소유권이 넘어갔다. 2006년 문화재청이 정동극장으로부터 중명전의 소유권을 인수받아 원형복원 사업을 시작하였고 2010년 8월 근대 역사교육 및 체험의 장으로 개방하였다.

중명전 옆에 위치한 예원학교 운동장은 언더우드 사택이 있던 곳이다. 1885년 4월 5일 내한한 언더우드는 알렌의 집과 붙은 곳(정동 13-1번지 일대)에 기와집 세 채가 딸린 900여 평의 한옥을 구입하였다. 1886년 5월 16일 이 집 사랑채에서 고아 한 명을 가르쳤는데 이것이 경신중고등학교의 시작이다. 대한성서공회의 전신인 '성서번역상임위원회', 한국 장로교 최초의 조직교회인 새문안교회, 대한기독교서회의 전신인 '조선성교서회'도 모두 이곳에서 시작되었다. 그후 이 터는 여러 차례 소유권과 용도가 변경되었다. 1902년 정부에서 구입하여 덕수궁 소유가 되었다가 미

언더우드 사택 사랑채터(철봉대 부근)

국 감리회 여선교부가 독신 여선교사 사택용으로 매입하였다. '그레이 하우스' Gray House로 불리기도 한 이 집은 1971년 이화학원이 매입하여 현재 예원학교 운동장으로 사용하고 있다.

예원학교 교사가 들어서 있는 곳은 마펫 선교사의 초기 사택이 있던 곳이다. 1890년 1월 내한한 마펫은 언더우드 사택의 북쪽(정동 1-45번지 일대)에 가옥을 마련하였는데 3년 만에 평양 주재 선교사로 떠났다. 그후 이 집은 덕수궁에서 구입하여 황화사皇華舍를 설치하였다. 1953년 이화학원에서 매입, 1963년 5층 건물을 지어 예원학교 교사로 사용하고 있다. 예원학교와 접하고 있는 미국대사관저 일부(정동 1-9번지 일대)도 선교사 사택이 있던 곳이다. 1885년 6월 북장로회 선교사로 내한한 헤론J.W. Heron의 사택이 이곳에 있었는데 그가 1890년 7월 별세하자 선교사 빈튼C.C. Vinton, 빈돈이 입주하였다. 1902년 이 집은 덕수궁 소유로 넘어갔다가 해방후 미국 대사관 부지로 편입되었다.

새문안교회

 서울시 종로구 신문로1가 42번지

한국 최초의 조직교회인 새문안교회는 1887년 9월 27일 정동 언더우드의 사택에서 14명의 한국인과 언더우드 목사, 로스 John Ross, 나약한 목사가 첫 예배를 드림으로써 시작되었다. 당시 참석자 중 3인의 한국인이 세례를 받았으며 2명의 장로가 선출되었다. 1895년 서대문안, 경희궁 건너편 옛 피어선 성서학원 바로 아래(현재의 신문로 2가 시티은행이 있는 곳)에 한옥 예배당을 마련하여 교회를 이전하였다. 이때부터 '정동교회'란 명칭 외에 '서대문교회West Gate Church'와 '새문안교회 Saemoonan Church'라는 명칭이 혼용되다가 점차

새문안교회(1972년 신축 이전의 벽돌 예배당)

새문안교회로 정착되었다. 교인이 늘어나자 1910년 현재의 위치에 서양식 벽돌 건물을 짓고 교회를 이전하였다. 당시 건축비는 일화 4,000여 원이나 되었으며 건물은 1,200여 명을 수용할 수 있는 규모였다. 1949년 교회당 좌우측에 종탑을 세웠으며 1957년에는 예배당 전면하단에 굴다리형 계단을 증축하였다. 1972년 교회 신축으로 예배당이 철거되어 옛 모습을 볼 수 없게 되었지만 본관 입구 계단 옆에 있는 종탑이 옛 교회의 흔적을 보여주고 있다. 교회 앞뜰에는 1927년 장로회 총회가 건립한 언더우드 목사의 기념비가 서 있다. 그 옆에는 김영주金英珠 목사 순교기념비가 서 있다. 김영주 목사는 새문안교회 3대 담임목사를 역임하다 6.25전쟁시 납북되었다. 기념관 3층에 마련된 교회사료관에서는 새문안교회의 역사와 한국교회사에 관한 풍부한 문헌 및 사진자료를 볼 수 있다.

시병원터

서울시 중구 정동 34번지

현재 정동제일교회 문화재예배당 부근은 감리교 최초의 병원인 시병원施病院이 자리하고 있었다. 1885년 5월 북감리회 의료선교사로 내한한 스크랜턴W.B. Scranton은 덕수궁 서쪽 성벽 아래의 한옥을 선교사 사택으로 매입하였는데 이 집은 사랑채와 헛간이 딸린 두 채의 가옥으로 이루어져 있었다. 아펜젤러 부부가 성벽과 붙은 서쪽 집에 살고 스크랜턴 가족은 동쪽 집에 살았다. 스크랜턴은 처음에는 사랑채에서 진료를 시작하였지만 동쪽으로 붙은 집을 하나 더 구입하여 1886년 6월 15일 정식으로 병원을 열었다. 이 병원에서 첫 번째 치료를 받은 환자는 풍토병에 걸려 성벽 밑에 버려져 있던 모녀였다. 3주 만에 회복한 여인은 패티Pattie라는 세례명을 받고 선교사 집일을 도왔으며 네 살짜리 '별단이'도 이화학당을 졸업하고 간호사가 되었다. 이 병원은 찾아오는 사람들에게 빈 병에 약을 담아 나누어 주었기 때문에 '시약소施藥所'로 불렸다. 1887년 정부에서 '시병원施病院'이라는 이름을 내려주자 스크랜턴은 출입문 양쪽에 'AMERICAN DOCTOR's DISPENSARY, 미국의원 시병원, 美國醫院 施病院'이라는 3개국어

간판을 붙였다. 그리고 간판에는 영어와 한글로 "남녀노소를 막론하고 병 있는 사람은 누구나 어느 날이든지 낮 10시에 빈 병을 가지고 와서 미국의원에게 보이시오"라고 썼다. 빈 병을 가져오게 한 이유는 환자들이 약병을 한 번 가져가면 안 가져 왔기 때문이다. 10여 년 뒤 스크랜턴은 가난한 사람들이 많이 거주하는 남대문 부근의 상동으로 병원을 옮겨 빈민 치료에 힘썼고, 병원이 떠난 이 자리 부근에 감리교 최초의 예배당인 정동교회가 세워졌다.

배재학당터

서울시 중구 정동 34-35번지

현재 배재공원과 러시아대사관이 위치한 장소는 우리나라 최초의 서양식 근대 교육기관인 배재학당이 있던 곳이다. 선교사 아펜젤러는 자신의 집에서 학생들을 가르치다가 서소문 언덕에 7천여 평의 부지를 마련하고 1886년 6월 학교를 열었다. 1887년 고종이 '배재학당培材學堂'이라는 학교명을 지어주었다. 학생이 급증하자 100여 평의 단층 르네상스식 벽돌 건물을 짓고 강의실, 도서실, 예배실로 사용하였다. 학생들이 일하면서 돈을 벌수 있도록 반지하에 작업실도 마련하였다. 이 작업실에서는 한글, 한문, 영어 3개국의 활자판을 갖추고 책을 인쇄하였기 때문에 '삼국문자인쇄관Tri-lingual Press', '삼문三文출판사', '미이미美以美출판사' 등으로 불렸다. 이 출판사는 학당 옆에 독자적 건물을 갖추고 '감리교출판사'로 발전하여 기독교 관련 서적을 출판하였다. 1932년 1,500명을 수용할 수 있는 강당이 들어서면서 이 두 건물은 헐렸다. 1984년 배재중고등학교가 고덕동으로 옮겨간 후 이 강당은 임대사무실 등으로 사용되다가, 2001년 배재정동빌딩이 들어서면서 헐렸다.

현재 이곳에 남아 있는 배재학당 시절의 유일한 건물은 '동관東館'이다. 이 건물은 1914년부터 3년에 걸쳐 지은 2층짜리 르네상스식 붉은 벽돌 건물로서 지금은 배재학당 역사박물관으로 사용하고 있다. 2001년 서울시가 기념물 제16호로 지정하였다. 이 건물과 똑같이 생긴 '서관西館'이 현재 고덕동 배재중고등학교 교정에 서 있다. 배재학당은 1923년 동관 건너편에 쌍둥이 건물로 '서관'을 건립하였는데 고덕동 교사로 이전할 때 원형 그대로 옮긴 것이다. 동관 옆에는 15 m 정도의 향나무 한 그루가 서 있는데 수령 500년이 넘은 것으로 추정된다. 이 나무의 돋통 중간 부분에 손가락만한 굵기의 쇠못이 박혀 있는데 임진왜란 당시 이곳에 주둔하고 있던 일본군대의 장수 가토 기요마사加藤淸正가 말을 매어 두기 위해 박은 못이라고 한다. 현재 이 향나무는 보호수로 지정되어 있다.

이화학당터

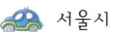 서울시 중구 정동 32번지

현재 이화여고 교정은 감리교 최초의 여선교사 스크랜턴M.F. Scranton 대부인이 세운 이화학당의 터에 자리잡고 있다. 스크랜턴 대부인은 1885년 10월 북쪽 성벽과 연결된 언덕정동 32번지에 1천여 평의 땅을 학교 부지로 구입하고 200여 칸 되는 'ㄷ자형' 기와집을 지었다. 1887년 10월 내한한 여선교사 로드와일러 Louisa C. Rothweiler는 이화학당 일을 도왔고, 여의사 하워드Meta Howard는 시병원 북쪽에 여성 전용 병원을 설립하였다. 1887년 정부는 여학교에 '이화학당梨花學堂'이라는 이름을 하사하였고, 1889년에는 하워드의 여성 병원에 '보구여관保救女館'이라는 이름을 하사하였다. 스크랜턴 대부인은 1897년 기존의 기와집을 헐고 그곳에 붉은 벽돌로 된 2층 양관 '메인홀Main Hall'을 지었다. 'T 자형'으로 된 이 건물은 전형적인 르네상스식 건물이었지만 6.25전쟁 중 폭격당했다. 이 자리에는 현재 '한국여성 신문화의 발상지'라는 글이 새겨진 기념석과 스크랜턴 대부인의 흉상이 서 있다.

이화여고 교정 동문 쪽 공터 입구에 '손탁호텔터'라는 표지석이 보인다. 이곳은 본래 북장로회 선교사 기포드Daniel L. Gifford, 기보의 집이었는데 북장로회 정동선교부가 연지동으로 이전할 때 독일 출신 여성사업가 손탁Sontag에게 넘어갔다. 그녀는 이곳에 2층짜리 르네상스식 건물을 지었는데 이 호텔은 한말 외교관과 서양인의 사교 공간으로 각광을 받았다. 1920년 이화학당에서 매입하여 기숙사로 사용하다가 1922년 그 자리에 붉은 벽돌식 3층짜리 '프라이홀Frey Hall'을 신축하였다. 1975년 화재로 이 건물은 사라지고 현재 공터로 남아 있다.

초기 이화학당 건물로서 유일하게 보존되고 있는 것은 심슨홀Simpson Memorial Hall이다. 공터에서 남쪽으로 약간 떨어진 곳에 위치한 붉은 색 3층 벽돌 건물이다. 이곳은 원래 언더우드가 '예수교학당' 교사로 사용하던 장소이다. 언더우드는 자신의 사랑채에서 시작한 고아원이 비좁아 기포드의 집과 붙어 있던 이곳에 넓은 집을 구입하여 학교로 사용하였던 것이다. 1897년 정부가 이 건물을 구입하여 덕수궁 관리들을 위한 '시종원侍從院'으로 사용하였는데 1910년에 폐쇄되었다. 이화학당에서 이 터를 매입하여 1915년 심슨홀을 지었다. 이 건물은 1922년과 1960년 두 차례의 증축 과정에서 원형이 많이 훼손되었기 때문에 현재 문화재청의 지원을 받아 복원 공사를 하고 있다.

이화여고 남쪽 담 너머에 있는 정동제일교회의 사무실은 감리교 최초의 여성전용 병원 보구여관이 있던 자리다. 1900년대 초 보구여관이 동대문부인병원으로 합류하면서 이 건물은 이화학당 교실과 기숙사로 사용되었다. 1921년 이 건물을 헐고 에드가 후퍼 기념관Mrs. Ralph Edgar Hooper Memorial Kindergarten Building을 세워 이화유치원과 이화보육학원으로 사용하였다. 그후 정동제일교회에서 이 자리에 1960년 '젠센 기념관'을 세워 운영하다가 1979년 '100주년 기념예배당'을 신축하였다.

이화여고 본관 서쪽 언덕 아래에는 오래된 우물이 하나 있다. 그 옆에 '유관순 열사가 빨래하던 우물'이라는 표지판이 있지만 원래 이 우물은 이화학당이 자리잡기 전부터 그 지역에 살던 부인들이 빨래를 하던 곳이라고 한다. 이화여고 동문 왼쪽에는 또 하나의 문이 있는데 1923년에 세운 이화학당의 정문으로서 사주문四柱門 형태로 되어 있다. 지금의 대문은 2000년에 해체하였다가 다시 복원한 것이다.

정동제일교회

서울시 중구 정동 34번지

정동 사거리에 위치한 정동제일교회는 한국 최초의 감리교회로서 1887년 10월 9일을 창립일로 삼고 있다. 두 개의 교회 건물 중 뒤편에 있는 것이 '100주년 기념예배당'이고 앞쪽에 있는 오래된 건물이 사적 256호로 지정되어 있는 '문화재예배당'이다. 문화재예배당은 1897년 12월 26일 봉헌되었지만 정동교회는 그보다 10년 전에 '벧엘교회당'이라는 이름으로 시작하였다. 아펜젤러에 의해 시작된 벧엘교회당은 정동이 아니라 상동지역, 현재의 남대문로 3가 한국은행 부근에 있었던 것으로 추정된다. 아펜젤러는 교인이 늘어나자 시병원施病院 근처, 현재의 문화재예배당 부지에 1897년 새 예배당을 세워 교회를 이전하였다. 이 건물의 외부는 중세 가톨릭교회의 고딕풍을 취하고 있지만 내부는 설교 중심의 단순한 형태를 특징으로 하는 개신교회 예배당의 전통을 따르고 있다. 예배당 남쪽 뜨락에는 조선선교 50주년 기념비가 보이는데 '한국감리교 선교 약사'가

정동제일교회 문화재예배당

국한문과 영문으로 새겨져 있다. 이 기념비 좌우에는 아펜젤러Henry G. Appenzeller 의 흉상과 최병헌催炳憲의 흉상이 자리잡고 있다. 종탑에는 '경세종警世鐘'으로 불리는 종이 걸려 있었는데 1902년 순직한 아펜젤러를 기념하여 미국에서 제작하여 들여온 것이다. 현재의 문화재예배당은 내부 구조가 매우 낡아 2000년부터 1년 동안 원형을 유지하면서 해체, 복원한 것이다. 교회 서쪽에 있는 사회교육관 5층에는 '만곤도서실'이 있고 그 안에 '만곤기독교역사자료실'이 마련되어 있다. 여기에는 최병헌의 친필 원고와 저서, 아펜젤러가 사용한 성찬기, 벧엘예배당 머릿돌에 들어 있던 한문성경 등을 비롯한 정동교회 및 한국기독교사 관련 귀중한 사료들이 비치되어 있다.

성공회서울대성당

 서울시 중구 정동 3번지

1889년 영국 옥스퍼드 출신의 코르프C.J. Corfe 신부가 한국 주교로 서품을 받으면서 한국 성공회의 역사는 시작되었다. 코르프 주교는 트롤로프Mark N. Trollope, 조마가 신부를 비롯한 사제와 신학생, 의사와 인쇄기술자로 구성된 선교진을 이끌고 1890년 9월 인천항에 도착하였다. 성공회의 초기 선교부는 낙동과 정동 두 곳이었다. 현재 대연각 빌딩 자리(중구 충무로 1가 25-5)에 있던 낙동 선교부에는 선교사 사택과 인쇄소, 남성병원(성마태병원)이 있었고, 일본인 교회와 한국인 교회(부활성당)가 그곳에서 시작되었다. 러일전쟁시 이곳이 일본군 병참기지로 사용되면서 선교부는 철수하였다. 정동 선교부는 영국 공사관 옆에서 미국과 캐나다 선교사 소유이던 집 두 채를 빌려 교회와 시약소를 열었다. 러일전쟁 이후 낙동 선교부에 있던 부활성당이 정동으

성공회서울대성당

로 옮겨와 여자 병원인 성베드로병원 건물을 사용하였다. 교인이 계속해서 늘어나자 성당 신축의 필요성이 제기되고 1926년 서울대성당을 건축하였다.

영국대사관 옆에 위치한 로마네스크 양식의 성공회 서울대성당(중구 정동 3번지)은 서울시 지방유형문화재 78호로 지정되어 있다. 이 성당은 70년에 걸쳐 완공된 건물이다. 1890년 12월 21일 영국 공사관 옆 초가에서 초대 주교 코르프가 미사를 드리면서 이 성당의 모체인 '장림성당'이 시작되었다. 2대 주교로 부임한 터너Arthur B. Turner, 단아덕가 성당 건축을 위한 모금운동을 시작하고 급환으로 별세하자 1911년 3대 주교로 부임한 트롤로프가 성당 건축계획을 발표하였다. 그는 '앵글로 가톨릭 의회Anglo-Catholic Congress'로부터 건축비를 지원받아 1923년 '터너 주교 기념 성전'으로 명명된 지하성당을 완공하고, 1926년 '성모 마리아와 성 니콜라 대성당'으로 명명된 본당 축성식을 거행하였다. 그러나 이때 축성된 성당은 건축비의 한계로 처음 구상한 규모의 반에도 미치지 못하는 '미완성' 성당이었다. 한국 성공회가 관구로 독립한 이후 성당건축을 본격화하여 1996년 지금 모습의 성당으로 완성되었다. 지하성전 마룻바닥 중앙에는 황금색 동판이 부착되어 있고 그 아래 트롤로프 주교의 시신이 안장되어 있다. 대성당 바깥에는 성가수녀원, 옛 주교관 건물, '영빈당迎賓堂'으로 불리는 교구 사무실이 있다. 이 건물들은 모두 전통 한옥으로 되어 있으며 특히 영빈당은 왕실의 자제를 가르치던 '수학원修學院' 건물로서 덕수궁 소유였는데 1920년대에 옮겨 지은 것이다.

옛 구세군사관학교

🚗 서울시 중구 정동 1-23

정동사거리에서 덕수궁과 미국대사관저 사이의 언덕길을 따라가면 덕수초등학교 못미쳐 오른편에 르네상스풍 건물이 보인다. 1985년 과천 캠퍼스로 이전하기 전까지 구세군사관학교가 사용하던 건물이다. 1910년 평동에서 시작한 구세군사관학교는 이곳에 있던 옛 선원전璿源展 부속건물을 헐고 220여 평 규모의 2층 붉은 벽돌건물을 건립하여 입주했다. 이 건물은 1926년 칠순을 맞은 만국본

영 2대 사령관 브람웰 부드Bramwell Booth 대장을 기념하여 조직한 한국 구세군 '미주순회단'이 미국과 캐나다를 순방하여 모금해 온 7만 원으로 지었다. 1928년 완공된 이 건물은 영국 구세군 건물 클랩톤 콩그레스 홀Clapton Congress Hall을 모델로 하였는데 당시 서울 장안의 10대 서양식 건물 가운데 하나였다. 2002년 서울시 기념물 제20호로 지정되었으며 현재는 구세군역사박물관으로 사용하고 있다. 2011년 2월 박물관을 리모델링하여 1층은 100주년기념관, 2층은 자료전시실로 확장하였다.

두번째. 종로

승동교회

 서울시 종로구 인사동 137

승동교회

승동교회는 1893년 3월 19일 미국 선교사 무어Samuel F. Moore, 모삼열가 지금의 롯데호텔 자리인 곤당골의 한 가정집에서 16명으로 첫 예배를 드리면서 시작하였다. 무어 목사는 백정 등 천민을 대상으로 복음을 전해 곤당골교회는 '백정교회'로 불리기도 했다. 1895년 양반이 천민과 함께 예배드릴 수 없다고 하면서 양반 출신 신자들이 길 건너 홍문섯골에 독자적인 예배당을 마련하고 나갔다. 1898년 곤당골교회에서 화재가 나자 곤당골교회와 홍문섯골교회는 통합하였으며 교회의 명칭을 '홍문섯골교회'로 하였다.

1905년 미국 교인 컨버즈J.H. Converse의 도움을 받아 '절골寺洞'로 불린 현재의 자리에 한옥 예배당을 마련하였다. 교회 명칭은 '중앙교회'로 바꾸었으며 승동勝洞교회로도 불렸다. 1913년 한옥 예배당을 헐고 그 자리에 100평 규모의 서양

서울지역 15

식 벽돌예배당을 지었다. 건축에 조예가 깊었던 선교사 클라크Charles A. Clark 곽안련가 설계하고 중국인 모문서毛文序가 공사를 맡은 새 예배당은 지하층을 갖춘 단층 건물이었지만 지상 건물이 2층 높이로 되어 있어 멀리서 보면 3층 건물로 보였다. 건물 외형은 고딕 양식에 충실한 반면 내부는 칸막이나 기둥이 없는 단순한 양식으로 1천여 명을 수용할 수 있었다. 1958년 부분 증축을 하였지만 예배당의 원형이 잘 보존되어 있다. 2001년 서울시 유형문화재 제130호로 지정되었다.

승동교회는 문화재로서의 가치만이 아니라 교회사적으로 매우 의미 있는 사건을 지닌 교회이기도 하다. 승동소학교 교사로 사용된 교회 지하층은 3.1운동 당시 연희전문학교 학생이자 승동교회 면려청년회장이던 김원벽金元璧이 서울 시내 학생대표들과 만세 시위를 모의한 곳이다. 1940년에는 승동교회 장로 김대현金大鉉이 이곳에서 조선신학교(한신대학교의 전신)를 시작하였다. 1959년 장로교가 WCC 가입문제로 분열될 당시 '승동측'으로 불린 예장(합동측)이 탄생한 장소이기도 하다. 승동교회 앞뜰에는 서울시에서 세운 '3.1운동 발상지' 표지석과 교회에서 세운 '3.1운동 안내판'이 있다.

대동서시터

🚗 서울시 종로 2가 84-9번지

2002년 폐업 직전까지 종로서적이 있던 곳은 대동서시大東書市의 옛터이다. 1890년 1월 아펜젤러는 종로 선교를 위해 종로통 육의전六矣廛 거리에 서점 용도의 집을 사서 최병헌崔炳憲에게 운영을 맡겼다. 최병헌은 '대동서시'라는 간판을 걸고 문서선교 사업을 하였으나 1900년대 접어들어 중단하였다. 1907년 대영성서공회(현재의 대한성서공회)가 대동서시 터를 매입하여 성경출판 및 판매 사업을 하였다. 1905년 예수교서회(현재의 대한기독교서회)가 대동서시터 바로 옆집(종로 2가 84-8)을 사서 문서선교 사업을 하였다. 1980년대 중반까지 이곳에서 나란히 기독교 문서선교를 하던 이 두 기관은 그후 강남으로 이전하였다.

대한성서공회는 1985년 서초동으로 옮겨갔고 대한기독교서회도 1987년 삼성동으로 옮겨갔다.

중앙교회터(가우처예배당터)

 서울시 종로구 인사동 246번지

120년이 넘는 역사를 지닌 감리교 중앙교회는 현재 종로구 인사동 하나로빌딩 안에 있다. '가우처기념예배당Goucher Memorial Church'이라고 불렸던 중앙교회의 발상지는 현재의 위치에서 남서쪽으로 100 m 정도 떨어진 곳에 있다. 고려대학교 동창회관 건너편에 있는 낡고 허름한 붉은 벽돌 창고건물이 옛 중앙교회 예배당이다. 1890년 1월 '종로교회'라는 이름으로 시작한 이 예배당은 이조집리吏曹執吏 오상연의 저택이었는데 아펜젤러가 구입하여 예배를 시작했다. 1923년 미국 감리회 한국연회는 미국 감리교 해외선교 백주년을 기념하여 가우처기념예배당을 이 자리에 짓기로 하였다. 가우처J.F. Goucher는 1883년 워싱턴행 기차 안에서 보빙사절단으로 미국을 방문중이던 민영익閔泳翊을 만난 것을 계기로 한국 선교 기금을 내고 매클레이R.S. MacLay의 방한을 주선했던 인물이다. 처음에

중앙교회터(가우처예배당터)

는 남감리회와 연합으로 3천여 명을 수용할 수 있는 예배당을 짓기로 하였으나 뜻대로 되지 않아 북감리회 단독으로 3백 명 수용 규모의 건물을 지었다. 1975년 중앙교회가 태화기독교사회복지관 자리로 옮겨가면서 이 예배당을 성지사라고 하는 출판사에 팔았고, 현재 이 건물은 창고로 사용되고 있다.

태화여자관터

 서울시 종로구 인사동 194번지

현재 12층 태화빌딩이 자리잡고 있는 곳은 3·1운동 당시 민족대표가 독립선언서를 낭독한 역사적 장소이다. 이 건물은 원래 이완용李完用의 소유였으나 안순환安淳煥이 임대하여 태화관泰華館이라는 요리집으로 사용하고 있었다. 태화관 후원에 위치한 '별유천지 6호실'에서 독립선언문이 낭독되었다. 3·1운동 이후 이완용이 이 저택을 매물로 내놓았을 때 남감리회 여선교부가 매입하였다. 남감리회 여선교부는 미국 남감리회 선교부에서 보내준 20만 원의 '선교 백주년기금'으로 매입 자금을 충당하였다. 여선교부는 옛 건물을 다소 손질하여 1921년 '태화여자관'이라는 사회사업 기관을 개관하였다. 이때 '태화'라는 명칭은 그대로 사용하였지만 한자는 '태화泰和'로 바꾸었다. 태화관은 유치원, 탁아소, 여자성경학원, 요리 및 재봉 교육, 영어 교육 등 매우 다양한 활동을 펼쳤다. 1939년 11월 옛 건물을 헐고 그 자리에 연건평 718평 규모의 3층짜리 석조 건물을 지었다. 새 건물의 외양은 서구 르네상스 양식이었지만 '팔작 지붕'에 겹처마 양식을 취하는 등 한국적인 멋을 가미하였다. 특히 3층 예배실의 지붕과 벽면 모서리의 목조 트러스와 바닥의 긴 의자 옆 막개에 태극 문양을 새겨 넣었다. 1978년 서울시의 재개발 계획에 의해 이 석조건물은 헐리고 12층짜리 태화빌딩이 들어섰다. 옛 건물 해체시 기둥머리 지붕돌과 정초석, 태극 문양이 새겨진 예배실 의자 몇 개는 수거하여 1996년 수서로 이전한 태화기독교사회복지관에서 보관하고 있다. 인사동 태화빌딩 오른쪽에 '삼일독립선언유적지' 표지석이 있으며 빌딩 로비에는 독립선언 역사화가 걸려 있고 독립선언서 부조가 새겨져 있다.

YMCA

서울시 종로구 종로 2가 9번지

    종로 한복판에 위치한 서울 YMCA는 황성皇城기독교청년회를 모태로 한다. 1899년 개화사상을 지닌 조선 청년 150명이 세계 YMCA 연맹에 한국 YMCA 창립을 건의하였고 1903년 황성기독교청년회가 창설되었다. 초기의 회원은 선교사와 외국인 중심이었으나 한성감옥에 정치범으로 투옥되었다가 '옥중 개종'을 한 개화파 지식인이 대거 들어왔다. 이상재, 이원긍, 이승만, 신흥우, 김정식, 홍재기, 안국선, 유성준 등이 대표적 인사들이었다. 창립 당시에는 향정동(현재 인사동) 감리교 중앙교회의 한옥 예배당을 빌려 회관으로 사용했다. 독자적 활동 공간이 필요해 졌을 때 개화파 지식인 현흥택이 24칸 기와집과 대지 1,200여 평을 제공하였고 미국의 백화점 왕 워너메이커J. Wanamaker가 4만 달러를 보냈다. 여기에 국내외의 모금을 보태 1907년 5월 상량식을 거행하였다. 이 행사에는

1908년 준공 당시 황성기독교청년회

현재 YMCA

정부 고관을 비롯하여 영친왕英親王도 참석하였다. 영친왕은 정초석에 새길 글씨 '일천구백칠년'을 썼고, 청년회는 이 글씨를 화강암에 새겨 회관 정문 오른쪽 벽 아래에 부착하였다. 1908년 12월 완공된 이 건물은 해리 장Harry Chang이라는 중국인 기술자가 감독을 맡았으며 전형적인 르네상스 양식으로 3층짜리 붉은 벽돌 건물이었다. 그러나 6.25전쟁으로 이 건물은 완전히 파괴되었으며 1967년 현재의 7층짜리 새 건물이 들어섰다. 새 건물은 호텔과 사무실 기능을 중심으로 하고 있다. 6.25 전쟁시 잔존한 영친왕의 글씨가 새겨진 정초석을 새로 지은 회관 중앙 출입구 오른쪽 벽면에 그대로 부착하였다. 정초석의 유래를 새긴 작은 동판 글씨는 원곡原谷 김기승金基昇이 썼다. 6.25의 폐허 속에서 찾아낸 정문 돌기둥은 지금 현관 건물 뒤편 한 귀퉁이에 있다. 현재 회관에는 토착 성화 몇 점이 걸려 있다. 회관 2층 회장실에 걸려 있는 그림은 이당以堂 김은호金殷鎬 화백의 '부활후'라는 작품으로서 토착적 그리스도상을 보여주고 있으며, 1층 로비에 걸려 있는 장운상張雲祥 화백의 '동심'이란 작품1963은 '갓 쓴 예수'가 '한복 입은 아이들'에 의해 둘러싸여 있는 그림이다.

배화여학교

 서울시 종로구 필운동 12번지

배화여자중고등학교는 현재 종로구 필운동에 위치하고 있지만 학교가 처음 시작한 곳은 경복궁 부근의 고간동, 지금 서울경찰청 자리(내자동 75번지)이다. 1898년 남감리회 선교부는 미국 침례교 계통 엘라딩기념선교회Ella Thing Memorial Mission로부터 1,000여 평의 땅과 그곳에 있던 집들을 구입하여 여선교부 부지로 삼고, 여선교사 캠벨Josephine P. Campbell, 강모인은 이곳에서 여학생 6명으로 기숙학교를 시작하였다. 이것이 배화여학교의 출발이다. 1900년 여선교부는 2층 벽돌 건물 두 처를 지어 교사校舍와 선교사 주택으로 사용하였다. 학교 이름은 캐롤라이나 학당Carolina Institute이었지만 한국인들은 동네 이름을 따라 '잣골학교'로 불렀다. 1903년 학부 인가를 받았으며 윤치호가 '배화培花'라는 이름을 지어 주었다. 선교사들은 학교 운영과 함께 교회도 개척하였는데 1901년 학교 구내에 '루이스워커 예배당Louis Walker Chapel'을 지어 교회로 사용하였다.

1913년 남감리회는 공간 부족과 위생상의 이유로 선교부를 사직단 뒤쪽으로 이전하였다. 이곳은 백사白沙 이항복李恒福의 생가가 있던 필운대 아래(누하동 149번지)쪽으로서 부지가 4천여 평에 이르렀다. 선교부는 이곳에 100여 평 규모의 여선교사 사택과 160여 평 규모의 학교를 각각 2층 벽돌 건물로 지었다. 1926년에는 학교 건물 바로 위쪽에 연건평 620평에 달하는 2층 건물을 올렸다. 이것이 '캠벨 기념관Campbell Memorial Hall'이라 불린 고등학교 전용 건물로서 지금도 교실로 사용하고 있다. 옛 교사는 보통학교와 유치원이 함께 사용하였다.

현재의 배화여자고등학교 정문으로 들어가면 운동장 건너편에 1914년에 건축한 옛 건물이 눈에 들어온다. 여러 차례의 수리와 증축 과정을 거쳤지만 원형이 남아 있다. 실용적이면서 견고한 르네상스 양식으로 된 이 건물은 지금도 고등학교 과학관 및 유치원 교실로 사용하고 있다. 운동장 바로 위쪽으로는 독신 여선교사들이 살던 사택이 남아 있다. 지하실을 갖춘 2층 주택 건물로 역시 르네상스 양식인데 전통 한옥의 팔작 지붕에 조선식 기와를 올린 것이 특징이다. 해방후 선교사들이 떠난 뒤 생활관으로 사용하다 지금은 동창회관으로 사용하고 있다. 동창회관 위쪽 언덕에는 리드C.F. Reid 선교사 내한 100주년 기념비와 캠벨 부인 흉상이 건립되어 있다. 본관 서쪽에 4층 별관이 있고 바로 뒤에 절벽이 있는데 이것이 필운대이다. 거기에는 백사 이항복의 집터임을 알리는 안내 표지석이 있고 암벽에는 이항복이 새겼다는 '필운대弼雲臺'라는 글씨가 보인다.

종교교회와 자교교회

종교교회: 서울시 종로구 도렴동 32번지 / **자교교회**: 서울시 종로구 창성동 156번지

세종로 정부종합청사 뒤편에 위치한 종교宗橋교회는 1900년 4월 15일 여선교사 캠벨J.P. Campbell에 의해 배화학당 구내(내자동 75번지, 지금의 경찰청 자리)에서 '잣골교회'로 시작되었다. 1901년 그곳에 2층 예배당을 신축하였는데 헌

금한 두 사람을 기념하여 루이스워커 기념예배당Louis Walker Chapel이라고 불렀다. 1908년 현재의 자리로 옮겼으며 이때부터 '종교교회'로 불렸다. '종교'라는 이름은 그 동네에 있던 '종침교琮琛橋'라는 다리 이름에서 유래하였다. '종침교'가 '종교'로 되고 '옥구슬 종琮'자도 '마루 종宗'자로 바뀌어 '종교'라는 이름이 생겼다고 한다. 1910년 한옥 예배당을 헐고 80여 평 규모의 고딕 양식 교회를 신축하였는데 '십자형' 벽돌 예배당의 모습을 취했다. 이 예배당에서 담임 목사였던 오화영吳華英 목사와 설교 강사로 왔던 정춘수鄭春洙 목사가 3.1운동에 대한 모의를 시작하였고, 이 교회 담임을 지냈고 한국 감리교 초대 총리사를 지낸 양주삼梁柱三 목사가 이 교회당에서 공산군에 체포되어 북으로 끌려갔다. 1959년 '총리사 양주삼 목사 기념' 석조 예배당을 지으면서 이 건물은 헐렸고, 1999년 '100주년 기념' 예배당을 지으면서 이 석조 예배당도 헐렸다. 그렇지만 교회측에서는 교회를 신축하면서 1910년에 지은 교회 건물의 벽돌과 1959년에 지은 양주삼 목사 기념 예배당의 벽돌을 교회의 외벽에 나란히 설치해 과거의 흔적을 남겼다. 또 교회 안에 역사자료 박물관을 설치하여 종교교회의 역사를 한 눈에 살펴볼 수 있게 하였다.

경복궁역에서 하차하여 3번 출구로 나와 자하문터널 방향으로 600 m 정도 북진하면 오른쪽에 붉은색 벽돌의 아담한 교회당이 눈에 들어온다. 종교교회와 한 뿌리를 지닌 자교교회이다. 1908년 고간동 잣골교회에서 도렴동으로 교회를 옮길 때 일부 교인은 그곳에 그대로 남았다. 하류계층으로 추정되는 이 교인들은 1910년 경 현재의 위치에 작은 한옥(195평)을 구입하여 교회를 시작하였는데 자교교회로 불렸다. 1922년 5월 남감리회 선교부로부터 일부 기금을 지원받아 40평 규모의 아담한 2층 벽돌 예배당을 건축하였다. 자교紫橋라는 교회 이름은 부근에 있는 자하문紫霞門의 자紫와 자수교慈壽橋의 교橋를 따서 지은 것이다. 해방후 교회 건물을 여러 차례 증축, 개축하였기 때문에 본래의 모습을 찾기는 어렵지만 1922년에 지은 교회당의 흔적이 일부 남아 있다. 교회 벽을 보면 새로 증축한 예배당의 붉은 벽돌과 중간 허리부분을 차지하고 있는 처음 예배당의 붉은 벽돌의 색이 확연히 구분된다. 2층 복도 한 귀퉁이에는 이 교회에서 오랫동안 사용해 온 낡은 성미함이 보관되어 있으며, 교회 100주년 기념 당시 교육관 1층에 '캠벨관'을 설치하여 교회의 역사 관련 자료를 전시하고 있다.

남감리회 스테이션터

 서울시 종로구 사직동 311번지

1906년 남감리회 선교부는 남송현(현재 한국은행 본점 자리)에 있던 선교부지를 팔고 사직동 언덕마루로 이전하였다. 사직동 311번지 일대 4천여 평의 땅을 매입하여 남성 선교사와 기혼 선교사 가족을 위한 사택을 미국 남부 장원 주택양식의 2층 붉은 벽돌 양옥으로 지었다. 선교부지 안에 있던 기와집들은 선교부에서 일하는 한국인 직원들의 숙소로 활용하였다. 사직동 선교부는 필운동의 배화여학교와 여선교사 사택, 도렴동의 종교교회까지 걸어서 10분 거리에 위치하였다. 태평양전쟁의 여파로 1942년 5월 한국내 미국인 소유 재산 일체가 '적산敵産'으로 처리되면서 선교부 토지와 건물도 일본인이나 정부기관으로 넘어갔다. 해방 이후 선교부 재산을 되찾았으나 새로 내한한 선교사들이 선교부지의 사택을 대대적으로 수리하였다. 6.25전쟁시 인공 치하에서는 공산군이 점령하여 사용하였고 수복 후에는 미군이 HID 본부로 사용하였다. 전쟁이 끝난 후 선교부 부지는 대폭 줄어들었다. 네 채였던 선교부 사택 중 두 채는 한국인에게 넘어가 완전히 변형되었고 언덕 위쪽의 돌집 두채만 남아 선교사 사택으로 사용하고 있다.

사직동 선교부에서 언덕을 내려오면 사직공원 정문 바로 건너편에 서 있는 10층 파크뷰타워(필운동 285)를 볼 수 있다. 원래 이 자리는 감리교 초대 총리사를 지낸 양주삼 목사의 사택이 있던 곳이다. 양주삼 목사는 자신이 흠모하던 이항복의 호를 따서 자신의 호를 '백사당白沙堂'이라 하였고 자신의 2층 양옥집에 '백사당'이라는 당호를 부여하기도 하였다. 6.25전쟁 시 양주삼이 납북된 이후 그의 부인 양매륜梁邁倫이 1980년까지 계속 거주하였다. 그후 그의 조카딸 양정환 장로가 '석연石淵'이라는 한정식 음식점을 경영하였는데 1995년 문을 닫았고, 1998년 파크뷰타워가 세워졌다.

연지동 북장로회 스테이션터

🚗 서울시 종로구 연지동 136번지

북장로회 스테이션은 원래 정동에 있었으나 낙후된 선교사 사택 수리 문제, 길 건너 북감리회와의 관계, 정부의 덕수궁 확장 시도 등의 요인에 의해 1894년경부터 폐쇄하는 쪽으로 방향을 잡았다. 정동 스테이션의 재산을 매각한 북장로회 선교부는 1903년 연지동 136번지 일대 13,000여 평 대지를 구입하고 선교사 사택 7채를 건축하였다. 남자 선교사로는 기포드D.L. Gifford를 비롯하여 게일James S. Gale, 기일, 빈턴C.C. Vinton 등의 북장로회 선교사들이 들어와 살았으며 여자 선교사로는 정신여학교 교장을 역임한 도티S.A. Doty를 비롯하여 여러 명의 선교사가 살았다. 기혼 선교사 가족들은 주로 연동교회 남쪽과 경신학교 서쪽의 사택에 거주한 반면, 정신여학교와 세브란스 병원에 근무하던 독신 여성 선교사들은 정신여학교 뒤쪽 언덕 위의 사택에서 살았다. 한편 세브란스 병원이나 예수교서회와 같은 연합기관에서 활동하던 남장로회 선교사들을 위해 경신학교 서쪽에 '딕시Dixie'라 불린 사택 1채를 마련하였다. 이중 현재까지 남아 있는 유일한 사택은 1997년부터 장로교출판사가 사무실로 사용하고 있는 건물이다.

8채의 선교사 사택, 정신여학교와 경신학교, 연동교회로 이루어져 '양관洋館 동네'로 불리기도 한 연지동 북장로회 스테이션의 토지는 23,000평에 이른 적도 있을 정도로 광대하였다. 지금까지도 이 일대는 기독교 관련 단체들이 매우 많아 '기독교 동네'로 알려져 있다. 1960년대에 10층 건물로 세워진 기독교회관에는 한국기독교교회협의회NCCK를 비롯하여 한국기독학생총연맹KSCF, 한국기독교청년협의회EYC, 기독교연합봉사회 등 에큐메니칼 단체들이 들어서 있고, 기독교방송CBS도 목동 사옥으로 이전하는 1992년까지는 이곳에 있었다. 예장(통합)과 기장 총회 및 산하기관들도 입주해 있다. 기독교회관 북쪽으로는 연동교회, 한국교회100주년기념관, 여전도회관이 있고, 기독교회관 뒤쪽으로는 기독교

연합회관이 들어서 있다.

연동교회

 서울시 종로구 연지동 136-12

종로5가 전철역에서 대학로를 따라 300 m 정도 북쪽으로 직진하면 왼편에 붉은 벽돌로 지은 연동교회가 보인다. 연동교회는 1894년 기포드D.L. Gifford와 서상륜徐相崙의 주선으로 언더우드 사랑방에서 모이던 장로교인 몇 명이 연지동 136-17번지(현재 연동교회 입구)에 초가 한 채를 마련하고 예배를 드리면서 시작되었다. 교인이 늘자 기포드는 지금의 연동교회 자리로 주택을 옮기고 20평 규모의 사랑채를 예배당으로 개조하여 예배를 드렸다. 러일전쟁 후 교인이 급증하자 연지동 136-13에 한옥 한 채를 더 구입하고 '애린당愛隣堂'이라는 간판을 걸고 주일학교와 연동소학교 교사로 사용하였다. 1907년 효제동 47번지(현재 이화회관 뒤편), 옛 어의궁於義宮터 바로 뒤쪽에 300평 대지를 마련하고 133평 규모의 단층 목조 건물을 지었는데 동양과 서양의 양식을 혼합한 건축양식이었다. 1942년 교회 건물과 부지를 남선전기주식회사에 넘겨주고 애린당 옆 전도실에서 예배를 드리다 1954년 기포드 사택이 있던 두번째 예배당 자리에 100평 규모의 2층 벽돌 예배당을 마련하였다. 1978년 기존 건물을 헐고 지하 1층, 지상 3층에 1천여 명을 수용할 수 있는 400평 규모의 현재 예배당을 지었다.

정신여학교 세브란스관

 서울시 종로구 연지동 136-5

연동교회 뒤편에는 붉은 벽돌로 된 3층짜리 르네상스 양식의 건물이 보인다. 1978년 정신여학교가 강남으로 이사가기 전까지 본관으로 사용하던 세브란스관이다. 정신여학교는 1887년 옛 알렌 사택(현재 중명전 자리)에서 출발하였는데 1895년 10월 연동교회 옆 한옥 세 채를 구입하여 교실과 기숙사로 개조해

정신여학교 세브란스관

사용하였다. 처음에는 '연동여학교'로 불리다가 1909년부터 '정신여학교'로 불렸다. 1906년 연동교회 뒤쪽 언덕에 2층 벽돌양옥 건물을 짓고 기숙사 겸 교사로 사용하였다. 1910년에는 언덕 서쪽 기슭에 670평 규모(지하 1층, 지상 3층)의 본관을 지었다. 르네상스 양식을 한 이 건물의 벽은 붉은 벽돌이고, 지붕은 양철 지붕에 도머창domer window을 내었다. 세브란스 병원의 건축 기금을 낸 세브란스가 건축비를 내었기 때문에 건물 이름을 세브란스관으로 지었다. 일제하 민족운동에서 중요한 역할을 한 김마리아를 비롯한 많은 교회 여성이 이 건물에서 가르치고 배웠다. 세브란스관 왼쪽에는 1958년에 지은 과학관(루이스관)이 남아 있다. 현재 세브란스관과 과학관은 대호흥산이라는 업체에 소유권이 넘어가 있다.

경신학교터

 서울시 종로구 적선동 66번지

연동교회에서 대학로를 따라 북쪽으로 올라가면 쌍둥이 고층 빌딩이 눈에 들어온다. 2010년 3월 입주한 현대그룹 신사옥으로서 동관 15층, 서관 18층으로 된 최신식 건물이다. 이 부지는 원래 경신儆新학교가 있던 곳이다. 1886년 언더우드에 의해 정동에서 시작된 경신학교는 처음에는 '언더우드학당', '민로아학당' 등으로 불리며 10여 년을 지내다 폐쇄되었는데, 1901년 게일이 지금의 연지동에서 중학교로 다시 개교하였다. 처음에는 연동교회의 첫 번째 예배당에서 가르쳤지만 1902년 연지동 1번지에 한옥 두 채를 구입, 개조하여 교사와 기숙사로 삼았다. 이때는 '예수교중학교'로 불렸지만 1905년부터 '경신학교'로 불렸다. 1906년 미국인 웰즈John D. Wells의 기금으로 50여 평 규모의 건물(지하 1층 지상 2층)을 짓고 '존 디 웰즈 기념관'이라 불렀다. 1912년에는 연건동 195-10(현재 이화예식장 자리)에 수공부手工部 건물을 지었는데 이곳에서는 미국에서 직물 기계를 들여와 학생들이 직접 양복을 제작하기도 하였다. 1925년에는 웰즈 기념관 오른쪽에 115평 규모의 강당을 건축하였는데 기금을 제공한 미국인 포스트James S. Post의 이름을 따 '포스트 기념당'으로 불렀다. 일제 말엽 신사참배 거부로 인해 선교사들이 운영하는 학교들이 대거 폐쇄되었는데 경신학교 역시 문을 닫게 되었다. 이때 선교부는 경신학교의 교명 변경과 학교 부지 이전을 조건으로 학교 건물과 부지를 한국인에게 매도하였다. 경신학교를 인수한 안악의 김씨 문중은 이 학교부지와 건물을 총독부 산하 체신국에 매도하고 정릉에 새 교사를 짓고 '경신'이라는 이름을 유지한 채 학교를 운영하였다. 경신학교는 1957년 혜화동으로 학교를 옮겨 오늘에 이르고 있다.

안동교회

서울시 종로구 안국동 27번지

지하철 3호선 안국역 1번 출구에서 스타벅스가 있는 골목을 따라 200 m 정도 직진하면 안동安洞교회가 나온다. 안동교회는 1909년 3월 유성준兪星濬과 박승봉朴勝鳳이 김창제金昶濟의 집에서 창립예배를 드림으로써 시작되었다. 김창제의 집은 양반 동네로 알려진 북촌北村에 있었고 이들은 모두 양반 출신이었기에 안동교회는 '양반교회'로 불렸다. 박승봉은 소안동에 예배처소를 마련하고 평양신학교 최초의 졸업생인 한석진韓錫晉을 청빙하여 전도목사로 삼았다. 1911년 박승봉이 장로로 장립되면서 한석진 목사와 함께 당회를 구성하였다. 이처럼 안동교회는 한국인이 중심이 되어 당회를 구성하였을 뿐만 아니라 1912년에는 붉은 벽돌로 된 웅장한 2층 예배당을 자체의 힘으로 건립하였다. 이 예배당은 1979년 교회 신축 때 헐렸고 그 자리에 현재의 현대식 건물이 들어서 있다.

동대문교회

 서울시 종로6가 65번지

동대문사거리에서 옛 이대부속병원쪽으로 직진하면 도로 옆 언덕 위에 현대식으로 지은 동대문감리교회가 보인다. 동대문교회는 한국 최초의 여성병원인 보구여관保救女館의 동대문분원에서 시작되었다. 1890년 스크랜턴 선교사가 이 병원에서 예배를 드리면서 교회가 시작된 것이다. 1892년 미 선교부 총무 볼드윈 부인의 기부금에 의해 새 예배실을 짓고 볼드윈채플Baldwin Chapel이라고 이름지었다. 이곳에서 한국 감리교회 최초로 남녀가 함께 예배를 드렸다고 한다. 교인이 증가하자 볼드윈채플을 헐고 1909년 붉은 벽돌로 된 2층 예배당을 지었으며, 1973년 이 건물을 다시 헐고 현재의 교회를 신축하였다.

복음교회터

 서울시 종로구 종로6가 210-1

현재 기독교대한복음교회 총회사무국 및 서울복음교회가 자리잡고 있는 곳은 이 교단의 전신인 기독교조선복음교회가 시작된 터이다. 복음교회는 1936년 당시 이곳에 있던 부활사 건물을 매입하여 교단 본부로 삼았다. 당시 건물의 흔적은 찾아볼 수 없지만 이곳은 복음교회의 출발지라는 역사적 의미를 지니고 있다. 교회 안으로 들어가면 복음교회의 창설자 최태용의 흉상이 보이는데 교단창립 70주년을 맞이하여 최근에 설치한 것이다. 복음교회는 1935년 12월 22일 최태용과 백남용이 중심이 되어 '기독교조선복음교회'라는 이름으로 중구 소격동의 한옥주택에서 창립되었다. 이들은 당시 조선교회가 서구 선교사에 의해 정치적, 경제적, 문화적으로 종속되어 있다고 비판하면서 조선인에 의한 주체적 신앙과 자주적 교회의 필요성을 설파하였다. 이러한 신앙갱신 운동이 기성교회로부터 '이단'으로 정죄당하자 이들은 1935년 독자적 교회를 설립하였는데 창립 당시 교회는 16개소였다.

세 번째. 서대문

감리교신학대학교

서울시 서대문구 냉천동 31번지

미감리회 선교부는 현지인 목회자 양성을 위한 목적으로 1887년 신학교육을 최초로 실시하였으며 1907년 남감리회와 함께 협성協成신학교를 설립하였다. 처음에는 건물이 없어 이동 수업을 하였지만 1910년 독립문 서편 산록에 있는 전 규장각 소유 대지 5천 평과 기와집 건물을 구입하여 임시 교사로 사용했다. 1915년 갬블Gamble 부인이 건축비를 제공하여 양옥 3층 건물을 세워 새 교사로 활용하였다. 이 건물은 후원자를 기념하여 '갬블기념관'이라 불렸다. 1918년 화재로 교사가 불타자 1921년 새 교사를 지었다. 1959년 웰치Herbert Welch, 월취 감독이 주선해준 건축비로 새 강당을 건축하고 '웰치기념관'이라 불렸는데, 이 건물은 2003년 웨슬리 채플이 들어서면서 철거되었다. 현재 남아 있는 비교적 오래된 건물로는 1956년 준공된 교수회관(현재 교수연구실)과 1960년 준공된 청암기념관(현재 대학원 건물)이 있다. 감리교신학대학교는 개교 120주년을 기념하여 2007년 역사박물관을 개관하였는데 감리교 및 감리교신학대학과 관련된 1만여 점의 귀중한 자료를 소장하고 있다.

이화여자대학교

 서울시 서대문구 이화여대길 52

1886년 정동에서 출발한 이화학당은 점차 발전하여 1934년 신촌에 대학캠퍼스를 마련하였다. 구황실舊皇室 능터인 이곳에 대지를 구입하고 화강암으로 된 고딕양식의 건물들을 지었는데 아직도 몇 건물이 남아 있다. 캠퍼스 중앙에 위치한 석조고딕 본관은 1935년 완공된 것으로서 건물 전면 위편에 십자가 조각을 하여 기독교 대학을 상징했다. 이 건물은 6·25전쟁 전까지 전교생이 수업을 받았던 곳으로 2002년 등록문화재로 지정되었다. 함석지붕으로 된 석조건물인 대학원관은 1935년 지상 3층으로 건축되었으나 1948년 4층으로 증축되면서 현재의 모습을 갖추게 되었다. 이 건물은 미국 남감리회 부인선교부 총무 사라 에스터 케이스 여사의 업적을 기념하여 케이스홀로 명명하였다. 초기에는 음대에서 사용했으나 현재는 학술원 전용 공간으로 사용하고 있다. 대학원관과 붙어 있는 중강당은 대학원관과 함께 건축된 것으로서 에머슨 부인이 기금을 제공하여 500여 석 규모로 지었으며 에머슨 채플Emerson Chapel로 불렸다. 대학원관 앞쪽에 있는 대학원별관은 3층 고딕석조 건물로 1936년에 완공되었다. 2006년 창립 120주년 기념으로 세워진 이화역사관은 지하 1층 지상 1층의 목조건물로 이화학당 최초의 한옥교사를 복원한 것이다. 이 건물은 이화의 역사와 비전을 주제로 한 상설전시관과 기획전시관 등을 운영하고 있다.

연세대학교

 서울시 서대문구 신촌동 134번지

연세대학교 교문에 들어서 백양로를 따라 직진하면 캠퍼스 한 가운데 언더우드 동상이 나타난다. 동상을 배경으로 담쟁이로 덮인 오래된 건물들이 배열되어 있는데 뒤편에 언더우드관, 좌편에 스팀슨관, 우편에 아펜젤러관이 각각 위치해 있다. 스팀슨관은 미국 로스앤젤레스의 스팀슨Charles M. Stimson의 기부금에 의해

1920년에 건축된 석조 2층 건물(문화재사적 275호)로서 연세대 캠퍼스에 세워진 최초의 건물이다. 언더우드관은 연세대학의 창설자인 언더우드를 기념하기 위해 그의 형이었던 존 언더우드John T. Underwood의 기부금에 의해 1924년 세워진 석조 4층 건물(문화재사적 276호)이다. 아펜젤러관은 미국 매사추세츠주 피츠월드 제일감리교회의 기부금에 의해 1924년에 준공된 석조 3층 건물(문화재사적 277호)이다. 언더우드관 뒤쪽으로 100 m 정도 떨어진 곳에 담쟁이로 덮인 연희관이 있다. 이 건물은 1956년 미 제5공군과 연세대학교의 지원에 의해 건축한 5층 석조건물이다.

캠퍼스 서쪽에 위치한 삼성관(생활과학대학 및 생활환경대학원)에서 북쪽으로 약간 올라가면 담쟁이넝쿨로 덮인 언더우드가家 기념관이 나타난다. 이 건물은 연세대 설립자인 언더우드 선교사와 그의 후손을 기념하기 위해 2003년 그들이 기거했던 연희동 사택을 새롭게 조성해 개관한 것이다. 기념관 내부의 전시실은 생활 재현 공간인 '언더우드의 삶', 유품을 전시한 '한국과 언더우드', 언더우드 관련 정보를 제공하는 '문헌자료실'로 구분되어 있다. '언더우드의 삶' 전시실은 언더우드 1세, 아들 원한경, 손자 원일한이 저술한 책과 가족사진 등을 비치하고 있고, '한국과 언더우드' 전시실은 언더우드 선교사가 직접 편찬한 한영사전, 친필편지, 타자기, 2차세계대전과 한국전쟁에 참전한 원일한 박사의 군장물 등을 전시하고 있다.

백주년기념관과 학생회관 사이 길로 접어들면 복원된 광혜원廣惠院이 나타난다. 광혜원은 1885년 2월 29일 고종이 미국 선교사 알렌Horace N. Allen의 건의를 받아들여 서울 재동齋洞에 설립한 한국 최초의 근대식 병원이다. 알렌은 갑신정변 당시 칼을 맞아 중상을 입은 민영익閔泳翊을 치료해 준 것이 인연이 되어 왕실의 시의관侍醫官으로 임명되었다. 그는 고종에게 근대식 병원의 설립을 건의하였고, 고종이 이를 윤허하여 설립된 것이 광혜원이다. 광혜원은 개원 12일만인 3월 12일 통리교섭통상사무아문統理交涉通商事務衙門의 계啓에 따라 제중원濟衆院으로 이름을 바꾸었다. 광혜원은 종로구 재동(현 헌법재판소 자리)에 있었으나 이듬해 정부의 후원으로 홍영식洪英植의 집(현 을지로입구 외환은행 본점)으로 옮겼다.

연세대학교 캠퍼스에 복원된 광혜원 건물이 서 있는 곳은 영조의 후궁 영빈 이씨의 묘가 있던 '옛 수경원 터'이다. 1961년 영빈의 묘가 서오릉 터로 옮겨가고 연세대학교 교회가 그 자리에 섰다. 1985년 연세대창립100주년기념사업의 일환으로 광혜원 복원 사업이 추진되어 교회가 다른 곳으로 옮겨가고, 1987년 그 자리에 본래의 것과 같은 모양과 크기로 복원한 것이다. 이 건물은 단층의 화강석 기단 위에 사각형 초석을 받치고 있으며 정면 5칸, 측면 3칸 규모에 팔작지붕을 하고 있다. 현재 이 건물은 연세사료관으로 사용하고 있는데 광혜원의 설립자 알렌 자료와 연세대학교의 역사 및 언더우드에 관한 자료를 구비하고 있다.

대운동장 옆에 있는 제2공학관 건물은 연희전문 시절 치원관致遠館이 있던 곳이다. 1919년 3월 1일 오전 11시 연희전문 학생청년회YMCA 회원 약 40명은 치원관 강당에 모여 월례회를 마친 뒤, 특별회를 개최하여 학생단 독립운동을 주도할 연희전문의 대표자로 김원벽을 추대하고, 60여 명의 학교 생도 모두가 체포될 때까지 독립운동에 매진할 것을 결의하였다. 이 자리에서 김원벽은 당일 오후 2시 탑골공원에서 독립선언식이 있을 예정이라는 사실을 회원들에게 통지하였다. 3.1운동 당일 개별 학교 차원에서의 거사 준비과정을 보여주는 대표적인 사례로 역사적 의미는 있으나, 당시의 원형이 전혀 남아 있지 않아 아쉬움이 남는데 관련 내용을 담은 표지석이라도 마련되었으면 한다.

경성성서학원터

🚗 서울시 서대문구 충정로 3가 35번지

아현성결교회 부지 안에 있는 옛 경성성서학원 교사는 성결교단 내에서 가장 오래된 건물이다. 1921년 미국 선교사 카우만Charles E. Cowman과 킬보른Ernest A. Kilbourne, 길보륜이 중심이 되어 세웠다. 이 교사는 똑같이 생긴 5층짜리 붉은 벽돌 건물 두 개가 서로 연결되어 있는 쌍둥이 건물로서 400여명이 앉을 수 있는 강당과 80여명을 수용할 수 있는 기숙사와 식당을 갖추고 있었다. 1920년대 초에는 명동성당, 종로 YMCA 건물과 함께 서울의 3대 건축물로 꼽혔다고 한다. 경성성

옛 경성성서학원 건물에 세워진 성결어린이집

서학원은 1940년 경성신학교, 1945년 서울신학교, 1959년 서울신학대학으로 개칭되었다. 1974년 서울신학대학이 부천으로 이전하면서 이 건물은 명지병원에 매도되었다. 1997년 아현성결교회가 다시 매입하여 예배홀, 기숙사, 어린이집으로 사용해 왔다. 아현성결교회가 100주년 기념예배당 건축을 준비하면서 2010년 10월 20일 이 건물을 철거하였다. 경성성서학원에서 출발한 서울신학대학교는 역사기념관을 마련하여 이 건물의 벽돌과 돌계단을 건물 미니어처와 함께 전시하기로 했다고 한다.

아현감리교회

 서울시 서대문구 북아현동 950번지

지하철 2호선 아현역 2번 출구에서 신촌로를 따라 충정로역 방면으로 200m 정도 직진하면 왼쪽으로 아현감리교회가 보인다. 아현감리교회는 감리교 초기 교회의 하나이다. 1888년 가을 스크랜턴W.B. Scranton 선교사는 서대문 밖 애오개에 집 한 채를 마련하고 12월부터 시약소施藥所 형태로 의료사업을 시작하였다. 이곳은 조선시대 전염병 환자들을 격리 수용하던 '서활인서西活人署'가 있던 곳이고 가까운 언덕에 공동묘지가 있어 가난하고 버림받은 사람들이 살던 곳이었다. 이곳에 진료소가 세워지자 환자들이 몰려들었으며 1889년부터는 의사 먹길William B. McGill, 맥우원이 진료하였다. 이 시약소는 환자와 주민을 대상으로 한 전도활동도 실시하였는데 이것이 아현교회의 시작이다. 1890년 시약소가 폐쇄되었지만 애오개지역의 선교는 중단되지 않았다. 선교사 올린저Franklin Ohlinger, 두림길가 애오개를 왕래하며 복음을 전하였고 스크랜턴M.F. Scranton 대부인도 나와서 여인들을 전도하였다. 올린저의 뒤를 이어 노블William A. Noble, 노보을 부부가 2년간 '애오개 집회'를 인도했는데 노블 부인의 '오르간 연주'가 동네 주민에게 큰 인기를 끌었다고 한다. 이로써 정식 교회는 아니지만 '기도처' 형태의 아현교회가 시작되었다. 올린저, 노블 선교사 등이 다른 지역으로 옮겨가면서 애오개 집회는 자주 중단되었지만 여성 교인들의 간절한 요청에 의해 1898년 애오개에 '매일학교'가 설립되었다. 이 학생들을 지도하기 위해 배재학당과 이화학당 출신 교사들이 파송되었으며 이때부터 교인들이 증가하였다. 1909년 애오개 교인들은 '서문밖구역'으로 독립 구역을 조직하게 되었다.

네번째. 남대문

상동교회

서울시 중구 남창동 1번지

숭례문오거리에서 남대문로를 따라 한국은행 방향으로 300 m 정도 직진하면 오른쪽에 새로나빌딩이 보이는데 그 건물 안에 상동교회가 있다. 상동교회는 스크랜턴 선교사가 정동 施병원에 이어 이곳에 세운 진료소에서 시작되었다. 1888년 창립예배가 있었고 1893년 정식 교회가 조직되어 스크랜턴이 1대 담임목사로 취임하였다. 1902년 붉은 벽돌 예배당을 봉헌하여 사용하였으나 1944년 일제의 강압에 의해 문을 닫았다. 해방 후 교회 재건이 추진되었으며 1976년 현재의 예배당을 신축하였다. 1977년 이 건물에 새로나 백화점을 개설하여 수익 사업을 하였으나 1998년 경영난으로 폐업하였다. 상동교회는 한말 민족운동에서 매우 중요한 역할을 한 '상동파'의 근거지로 유명하다. 특히 상동교회 6대 담임목사를 역임한 전덕기全德基 목사는 구국기도회, 을사조약 무효상소운동, 을사오적 암살기도사건, 헤이그밀사사건, 비밀결사 신민회의 창설에 깊숙이 관련되어 있었으며 공옥攻玉학교와 상동청년학원을 설립하여 민족교육에 힘썼다.

남대문교회

서울시 남대문로 5가 544번지

　서울역 앞 옛 대우센터빌딩(현 서울스퀘어)과 밀레니엄서울힐튼호텔 사이의 언덕에 위치한 남대문교회는 초기 장로교회의 하나이다. 남대문교회의 출발은 한국 최초의 서양식 병원인 제중원과 밀접한 관련을 맺고 있다. 한국 최초의 장로교 의료선교사 알렌H.N. Allen은 제중원 소속 의사로 일하면서 1885년부터 선교사들과 함께 제중원에서 공식예배를 드렸다. 남대문교회는 이 예배를 기점으로 교회가 창설되었다고 보고 남대문교회의 창립 연대를 1885년으로 삼고 있다. 1887년 제중원이 구리개(을지로 입구, 현 외환은행 본점 자리)로 이전하면서 한국인들과 함께하는 예배가 시작되었고, 1904년 다시 남대문 밖(현재 세브란스 센터빌딩)으로 이전하면서 교회가 병원에서 분리되었다. 이때부터 제중원은 세브란스 병원으로 이름이 바뀌었고 교회는 남문밖교회, 남대문밖교회, 남문외교회, 남문밖제중원교회 등으로 불렸다. 1910년 세브란스 병원 옆 부지에 독자적인 교회당을 세웠는데 6.25전쟁시 파괴되었다. 현재의 예배당은 1955년 현재의 위치에 짓기 시작하여 1969년 완공된 건물이다. 초기 교회당의 모습은 현재 교육관으로 사용하는 '알렌기념관' 역사자료실에서 사진으로 볼 수 있다.

다섯 번째. 기타

양화진외국인선교사묘원

 서울시 마포구 합정동 145-8

　전철 2호선 합정역 7번 출구로 나와 양화진길로 200 m 정도 가면 깔끔하게 단정된 외국인 공동묘지가 보인다. 묘지의 총 면적은 13,224 m² 이다. 여기에 안

양화진외국인선교사묘원

장된 외국인은 417명이며 그중 선교사(가족 포함)는 145명이다. 이 묘지는 미국 북장로회 의료선교사로 내한하여 헌신적으로 활동하다 전염성 이질에 걸려 죽은 헤론John W. Heron이 1890년 7월 이곳에 묻히면서 시작되었다. 헤론이 죽자 당시 서울의 외국인들은 묘지를 요구하였고 조선 정부는 이곳 약 280평을 매입하여 외국인묘역으로 조성하였다. 일제 말 선교사의 강제 출국으로 묘역이 방치되었다. 6·25전쟁을 거치면서 묘비에 총탄 자국이 생겨 비문 판독이 불가능할 정도로 묘역은 더욱 황폐화되었다. 1985년 '100주년기념사업협의회'가 이곳을 대대적으로 정비하면서 성역으로 재탄생하였다. 이 묘역의 명칭은 양화진외인묘지楊花津外人墓地, 경성구미인묘지京城歐美人墓地, 서울외국인묘지공원 등으로 변경되다가 2006년 5월 현재의 명칭으로 최종 확정되었다. 묘역 안에는 2005년 100주년기념교회가 설립되어 묘역 관리 및 운영을 맡고 있다. 그 옆에 세워진 홍보전시관과 양화진홀은 선교사의 입국 과정과 활동에 관한 다양한 자료를 전시하고 있다.

숭실대 한국기독교박물관

 서울시 동작구 사당로 19

　숭실대학교 캠퍼스안에 위치한 한국기독교박물관은 장로교 목사이자 고고학자인 김양선金良善 교수가 1948년 서울 남산 조선신궁朝鮮神宮터에 '기독교박물관'과 '매산고고미술관'을 개관한 것에서 비롯되었다. 1950년 한국전쟁을 거치면서 많은 자료가 분실되고 박물관 자리가 국회의사당 부지로 결정됨에 따라 김양선 교수는 자택으로 유물을 옮겨 보관하였다. 타계 직전 그는 소장 자료 3,600여 점을 모교인 숭실대학교에 기증하였다. 숭실대학교는 웨스트민스터 채플에 일시 보관하다 1976년 단독건물을 지어 개관하였다. 2003년에는 현대적 전시시설을 갖추고 과학적 수장 공간을 구비한 현재의 건물을 신축하였다. 그리고 그간의 소장유물과 발굴유물을 재정리하여 2004년 '숭실대학교 한국기독교박물관'으로 재출발하였다. 지하 1·2층에는 박물관 사무 및 수장 공간이 마련되어 있고, 지상 1·2·3층에는 한국기독교역사실, 숭실역사실, 근대화와 민족운동실, 고고미술실 등의 상설전시실이 마련되어 있다. 특히 한국기독교역사실에는 통일신라 시대의 것으로 추정되는 돌십자가를 비롯한 고대 경교景敎 관련 유물을 비롯하여 천주교의 성장과 박해, 개신교의 수용과 발전과정 등을 보여주는 다양한 유물이 전시되어 있다.

국립 서울현충원

 서울시 동작구 현충로 210

　1954년 국군묘지로 시작된 현재의 국립서울현충원에는 약 17만기의 묘가 있다. 129만m²(43만 평)의 넓이를 지닌 이곳은 국가원수묘소, 임시정부요인묘소, 애국지사묘역, 무후선열제단, 국가유공자묘역, 장병묘역, 경찰묘역으로 구분되어 있다. 이곳에 안장된 기독교인의 정확한 숫자는 알 수 없지만 상당수가 포함되어 있다. 국가원수묘소에는 정동교회 장로였던 이승만 초대 대통령이 안장되어 있다. 임시정부요인묘소에는 순국선열 18분이 안장되어 있는데 정동제일교회에서 목회하였던 손정도 목사와 전주서문교회에서 사역한 김인전 목사가 있다. 이 두 사람은 모두 의정원장을 역임했다.

애국지사묘역에는 한말, 일제하에 독립운동을 하던 순국선열과 애국지사 214인이 안장되어 있는데 기독교인 상당수가 포함되어 있다. 대표적인 인물로는 제3대 총독 사이토 부임시 서울역에서 폭탄을 던졌던 강우규 의사, 한국정부의 친일 외교고문 미국인 스티븐스를 암살한 장인환과 전명운 의사, 3·1운동 민족대표였던 이필주·신석구·유여대 목사, 독립협회를 창설한 서재필 박사, 신사참배에 반대하다 순교한 주기철 목사, 그리고 캐나다인으로서 3·1운동 당시 일제의 만행을 해외에 알리는데 중요한 역할을 한 스코필드 박사가 있다. 무후선열제단은 순국하였으나 유해도 찾지 못하고 후손도 없는 순국선열 133분을 위패로 봉안하고 있다. 이곳에 모셔진 대표적 기독교인으로는 한말 독립운동의 거점 역할을 했던 상동교회의 전덕기 목사를 비롯하여 김규식, 유관순, 이상설, 이위종, 김마리아, 이동휘, 오화용 등이 있다. 국가유공자 묘역은 제1묘역, 제2묘역, 제3묘역으로 구분하여 총 62위를 안장하고 있는데 제2묘역에 안장된 한글학자 주시경 선생과 일제하의 민족지도자 조만식 선생이 대표적 기독교인이다.

✱ 서울 일반 유적지

옛 러시아 공사관

🚗 서울시 중구 정동 15-3

덕수궁 정동길을 걷다 보면 이화여고 맞은편에 사적 제253호로 지정된 옛 러시아 공사관 탑이 보인다. 이곳은 1896년 2월 11일 아관파천 이후 1897년 2월 20일 경운궁으로 이어하기까지 고종이 머무르며 국사를 보았던 곳으로 한국 근대사의 한 자락을 차지하는 곳이다.

명성황후가 일본 낭인들에게 시해 당한 후 고종은 일본과 친일내각에 포위된 채 경복궁에서 불안한 나날을 보내야 했다. 그러자 친미·친러 세력은 이를 기회로 고종을 궁 밖으로 탈출시켜 친일정권을 타도할 계획을 세웠다. 하지만 1895년 11월 28일(음력 10월 12일)의 '춘생문사건'은 사전에 발각되어 실패하고 말았다. 이후 고종 측근의 이범진과 이완용·이윤용 등은 러시아 공사 베베르K. I. Waeber 등과 모의하여 국왕을 탈출시킬 계획을

옛 러시아 공사관의 탑

다시 세우고 고종의 윤허를 받았다. 그리고 1896년 2월 11일 새벽 전국적인 의병 봉기를 진압하기 위해 중앙의 친위대 병력까지 동원된 틈을 타 러시아공사관으로 파천을 단행하였다.

궁녀들이 타는 가마에 몸을 감추고 경복궁을 빠져나온 고종은 러시아공사관에 도착한 뒤 경무관 안환을 불러들여 김홍집을 비롯한 친일내각 대신들에 대한 포살령을 내리고, 새 정부를 발족시켰다. 이후 고종은 1897년 2월 20일 경운궁으로 이어하기까지 1년 동안 러시아공사관에 머무르며 국사를 처리하였다.

아관파천의 역사 현장인 러시아공사관은 1890년에 건립한 르네상스풍의 2층 벽돌 건물로 러시아인 사바틴H. N. Sabatin이 설계를 했다. 해방 후에는 소련 영사관으로 사용했으며, 한국전쟁 때 크게 파손되어 탑옥 부분과 지하 2층만 남았다. 1973년에 현재의 모습대로 복원하고 1981년에 다시 주변의 조경과 보수공사를 실시하여 현재는 시민들이 쉬어 갈 수 있는 공원시설을 함께 마련해 두었다.

경운궁(덕수궁)

🚗 서울시 중구 정동 5-1

경운궁(덕수궁)은 사적 제124호로 지정되어 있다. 1897년 2월 고종이 러시아 공사관에서 환궁한 이래 1919년 1월 승하할 때까지 머물렀던 경운궁은 원래는 성종의 형 월산대군의 사저로, 임진왜란 때 의주까지 피난갔다 돌아온 선조의 임시 거처로 사용되면서 정릉동 행궁으로 불려졌다. 그뒤 선조의 뒤를 이어 즉위한 광해군이 1611년(광해군3) 복구공사가 마무리된 창덕궁으로 이어하면서 경운궁으로 이름을 바꾸었다.

인조반정 후 즉조당, 석어당과 왕비의 궁방인 명례궁 건물만 남아 있다가, 1897년 2월 고종이 러시아공사관에서 옮겨오면서 비로소 궁궐다운 모습을 갖추게 되었다. 전성기 때의 경운궁은 현재 넓이의 3배에 달하는 큰 궁궐이었다. 현재의 미국대사관저 건너편 서쪽의 중명전을 비롯해 황실 생활을 위한 전각들이 있었고, 북쪽에는 역대 임금들을 제사 지내는 선원전이 있었으며, 동쪽에는 하늘에 제사지내는 환구단을 설치하여 대한제국의 위세를 과시하였다.

정전인 중화전中和殿과 역대 임금의 영정을 모신 진전眞殿 등이 세워졌고, 정관헌靜觀軒과 돈덕전惇德殿 같은 서양식 건물도 들어섰다. 1904년의 화재로 다수의 전각이 불타는 재난을 겪었는데, 이때 궁궐 남쪽에 있던 인화문 대신에 동쪽의 대안문大安門을 대한문大漢門으로 이름을 바꿔 정문으로 삼았다. 고종은 1907년 일제의 강압으로 순종에게 황위를 넘겨준 이후에도 1919년 승하할 때까지 계속 경운궁에 머물렀는데, 이때 궁호가 덕수궁德壽宮으로 바뀌었다. 고종이 승하한 뒤 1920년부터 일제가 선원전과 중명전 일대를 매각하여 궁역이 크게 줄어들었으며, 1933년에는 많은 전각들을 철거하고 공원으로 조성하여 일반에 공개했다.

경성 부민관 폭탄 의거지

서울시 중구 태평로1가 60-1(현재 서울특별시의회 건물)

경성 부민관 폭탄 의거지는 현재 문화재청 등록문화재 제11호로 지정되어 있다. 성공회 서울대성당 옆에 있는 이곳은 1945년 7월 24일 일어난 경성부민관 폭탄의거 현장이다. 1935년 1,486평 부지에 부립극장으로 건립된 경성부민관은 지하 1층, 지상 3층에 대강당, 중강당, 소강당, 담화실 등을 갖춘 다목적 회관이었다. 경성부민관은 당시로는 드물게 냉난방 시설과 조명, 음향시설을 갖추어 각종 극단의 공연은 물론 전시총동원체제하 각종 관변 집회의 장소로 널리 이용되었다.

경성부민관 폭탄의거를 주도한 조문기, 유만수, 우동학, 강윤국 등 당시 20세 안팎의 열혈청년들은 1945년 5월 서울 관수동 13번지 유만수의 집에서 대한애국청년당을 결성하고 항일투쟁의 기회를 엿보았다. 1945년 7월 24일 저녁 경성부민관에서 친일파 거두인 박춘금 일당이 주최하는 아세아민족분격대회가 열린다는 보도가 나오자, 이들은 비밀회합을 갖고 대회장을 폭파할 계획을 세웠다. 그들은 사제 폭탄 두 개를 만들어 대회 전날 밤 대회장 뒤편 화장실 쪽에 설치하였다. 폭탄은 대회 당일인 7월 24일 밤 9시 경 박춘금이 시국강연을 위해 등단한 얼마 뒤에 터졌고, 그것으로 대회는 중단되고 말았다.

해방 직후 이 건물은 미군정에서 사용하다가 1949년 서울특별시 소유로 넘어갔으며, 1950년부터 국회의사당으로 사용, 1975년 9월 국회의사당이 여의도로 이전한 뒤 시민회관이 되었다. 1976년 세종문화회관이 세워지면서 그 별관으로 사용되다가 1991년부터 서울특별시의회 건물로 사용되고 있다. 현재 기념표석이 서울특별시회관 입구에 설치되어 있다.

서대문 독립공원

서울시 서대문구 현저동 101번지 일대

　서대문 독립공원은 3호선 독립문역에서 내려 4번이나 5번 출구를 이용해 밖으로 나가면 보인다. 1992년 8월 15일 개원한 독립공원은 조국의 독립을 위해 항거하다 옥고를 치렀던 애국지사의 자주독립 정신을 후손에게 기억시키기 위해서 만들어졌다. 2007년 4월부터 추진한 독립공원 재조성 사업을 통해 2009년 10월 재개장하여 독립문, 역사관, 독립관, 순국선열추념탑 등을 유기적으로 연결함과 동시에 노후한 공원시설을 정비하여 공원을 방문하는 시민들의 편의를 최대화하였다. 특히, 독립문은 그동안 시민들의 접근을 제한하였으나, 서대문독립공원 재조성 사업으로 112년 만에 시민들에게 개방하였다. 공원 내에는 순국선열 추념탑, 3.1독립선언 기념탑, 서재필 선생 동상, 독립문(사적 제32호), 독립관, 영은문주초(사적 제33호), 서대문형무소역사관(사적 제324호) 등이 마련되어 있다.

　독립관은 본래 영은문을 통해 들어온 중국 사신에게 연회를 베푸는 모화관으로 사용되던 사대외교의 상징적 건물이었는데, 조선정부가 청으로부터 자주독립을 선언한 이후 사용하지 않아 방치된 채로 있었다. 이에 독립협회는 모화관을 개수해 사무실 겸 집회장소로 사용하기로 하고 약 2천 원의 경비를 들여 공사를 마무리한 뒤 1897년 5월 23일 현판식을 거행하였다. 현판은 당시 왕태자였던 순종이 한글로 '독립관'이라고 썼다. 독립협회는 개관 초기 독립관에서 매주 일요일 오후 강연회를 개최하였다. 그러나 강연회가 큰 성과를 거두지 못하자 독립협회는 8월부터 강연회 대신 토론회를 조직하기로 하고 8월 29일 첫 토론회를 열었다. 토론회는 학생과 시민들의 커다란 호응 속에 회를 거듭하며 성황을 이루었다. 그에 따라 독립협회는 개화, 개혁의 여론을 조성하는 민중계몽단체로 자리를 잡아 나갔고, 독립관은 공론을 형성하는 토론마당으로 시민사회의 형성에 커다란 역할을 하였다.

　사적 제32호로 지정된 독립문은 청일전쟁 이후 청으로부터 자주독립한 사실을 내외에 알리기 위해 중국사신을 영접하던 사대외교의 표상인 영은문을 헐고 그 자리에 세운 기념물이다. 1896년 7월 서재필의 발의로 창립된 독립협회의 주도하에 왕실과 관료, 그리고 일반의 기부를 받아 같은 해 11월 21일 정초식을 거행하고 1년 뒤인 1897년 11월 20일 완공하였다.

 높이 14.28 m, 너비 11.48 m로 화강석을 쌓아 만들었는데, 가운데 홍예문이 있고 내부 왼쪽에 옥상으로 통하는 돌층계가 있으며, 꼭대기에는 돌난간이 둘러져 있다. 홍예문 가운데 이맛돌에는 대한제국 황실의 상징인 오얏꽃무늬가 새겨져 있고, 그 위 앞뒤에는 한글과 한자로 쓴 '독립문'이라는 글씨 양옆에 태극기를 새긴 현판석이 자리하고 있다. 프랑스 파리의 개선문을 본떠 만들었다고 하는데, 문 앞에 사적 제33호로 지정된 영은문 주춧돌 2개를 그대로 남겨두어 사대와 독립의 의미를 대비시키는 상징조작을 시도하였다. 도로 행정의 편의를 위해 원래 위치에서 옮겨져 있기에 역사적 의미를 찾는다는 취지에서는 아쉬움이 있다.

 서대문형무소는 3.1운동 당시 시위관련자 1,600여 명이 수감된 것을 비롯해 의병장 허위와 유관순 열사, 강우규 의사 등 수많은 애국지사들이 순국한 민족수난의 현장이다. 정미7조약으로 대한제국의 사법권이 일본으로 넘어간 뒤인 1908년 10월 21일 일본인 건축가 시텐노 가즈마 四天王要馬의 설계에 의해 독립문 근처 금계동에 한국 최초의 근대식 감옥인 '경성감옥'으로 준공되었다. 신축 감옥은 480평 규모의 감방과 80평 정도의 부속시설에 수감인원이 500여 명 정도였는데, 이후 여러 차례 증축되었다. 마포 공덕동에 또 다른 감옥이 지어지면서 1912년 9월 서대문감옥으로, 1923년 5월 서대문형무소로 다시 이름이 바뀌었다. 1945년 8월 15일 해방을 맞기까지 수많은 애국지사들이 처형 또는 투옥되어 고초를 겪은 민족수난의 현장이다. 1945년 11월 서울형무소로, 1961년 12월 서울교도소로, 1967년 7월 서울구치소로 바뀌었는데, 1987년 11월 구치소가 경기도 의왕시로 옮겨간 뒤 1992년 8월 15일에 '서대문독립공원'으로 개원하였다. 1995년 서대문구에서 사적지 성역화사업을 시작하여 새롭게 단장하고, 1998년 11월 '서대문형무소 역사관'으로 개관하였다. 역사관에는 옥사 7개동과 사형장, 보안과 청사가 원형대로 보존되어 있는데, 그 중에서 제10, 11, 12 옥사와 사형장은 1988년 2월 사적 제324호로 지정되었다.

CHAPTER 2

인천·경기 지역

인천 → 강화 → 수원 → 화성 → 안산 → 용인 → 이천 → 기타

1. 인천지역

첫번째. 인천광역시

❋ 인천 소개

　　인천지역은 지리적으로 한반도의 북부지방과 남부지방의 중간적 위치일 뿐 아니라, 옹진반도와 태안반도 사이에 형성된 경기만 연안에 자리 잡고 있어 육지와 해양의 중간적 위치이기도 하다. 따라서 인천은 육상교통과 해상교통을 이어주는 요충지일 뿐만 아니라 서울의 중요한 관문 역할을 맡아 왔다. 산업의 측면에서 보면 인천지역에는 제당, 제분, 제철, 정유, 제재 및 가구 등과 같은 공업이 발달하고 있다. 또 바다와 천연의 자연을 많이 볼 수 있는 연안의 섬들은 중요한 관광자원으로 각광받고 있다.

　　인천의 최초 명칭은 미추홀彌鄒忽이다. 미추홀 지역이 하나의 행정구역으로 등장하는 것은 고구려 장수왕 때의 매소홀현買召忽縣이고 신라가 삼국을 통일한 후에는 한자식으로 바뀌어 소성현邵城縣이 되었다. 고려 숙종 때 경원군慶源郡으로 개칭, 승격되었다가 인종때에 인주仁州로 승격되었다. 공양왕 2년에 다시 경원부慶源府로 환원되었다. 조선왕조가 개창되면서 인천은 다시 인주로 강등되

인천·경기 지역

인천여선교사숙소(인천창영사회복지관)

었으나 태종 13년 인천군仁川郡으로 탄생하였다.

고려시대의 인천은 해상교통의 거점으로서 중요한 역할을 하였다. 대외관계에서 매우 개방적이었던 고려왕조가 개성에 도읍을 정하면서 인천의 역할은 더욱 강화되었다. 고려 왕실은 개성에 이르는 수로 예성강 입구에 위치한 강화, 교동, 자연도 등을 중심으로 대외교통의 거점을 개발, 정비하는 한편, 이를 군사적 경제적으로 지원하면서 수도 개성의 남방지역을 방어할 안남도호부安南都護府를 수주樹州, 현재의 부평에 설치하였다. 안남도호부에는 인천의 출발지 소성현과 시흥, 양천, 통진, 김포 등이 예속되었다.

조선왕조는 쇄국정책을 취했기 때문에 조선시대 동안 인천의 지정학적 중요성은 감소되었고 이로 인해 인천은 평범한 농어촌으로 존재하였다. 그러나 19세기말 개항과 더불어 중요한 지역으로 다시 부상하였다. 제물포조약 이후 제물포에는 인천해관海關과 인천감리서監理署가 설치되고, 각국

영사관과 전관조계專管租界 및 공동조계共同租界가 들어섰으며, 이들을 중심으로 하여 각국의 상공업 시설과 종교, 교육, 문화시설도 빠르게 설립되어 갔다. 황해를 통한 외국과의 해상교통이 폐쇄된 지 500년 만에 다시 인천지역이 국제적 도시로 탈바꿈하기 시작한 것이다.

✱ 인천 기독교 전래

1885년 4월 5일 부활절, 미국 북감리회 아펜젤러H.G. Appenzeller 부부와 북장로회 언더우드 H.G. Underwood 선교사가 제물포에 도착하여 개신교 선교의 시작을 알렸다. 그러나 당시는 갑신정변이 일어난 직후라 서울은 정세가 불안하여 외국인 여성이 자유롭게 생활하기 곤란한 상황이었다. 독신 선교사 언더우드는 서울로 올라가 광혜원을 운영하던 알렌의 집에서 머물렀으나, 아펜젤러 부부는 인천에서 1주일간 머물다 일본으로 돌아갔다. 아펜젤러 부부는 6월 20일 재입항하여 7월 19일 서울로 들어갈 때까지 인천 내리의 초가에서 38일간 머물며 한국어를 배우고 직접 혹은 간접으로 선교사역을 했다. 그해 7월 7일 증기선으로 오르간이 도착했는데, 이때 아펜젤러 부부가 찬송가를 부르며 예배를 드린 것이 인천에서의 첫 공식예배로 기록된다.

같은 해 5월 3일 미감리회 선교사 스크랜턴W.B. Scranton도 제물포를 통해 입국하여 20여 일 체류하였다. 스크랜턴은 가톨릭의 성당부지 매입 추진 등 적극적인 인천 선교 준비과정을 보며 개신교도 서둘러 인천지역 선교에 힘써야 함을 주장했다. 이에 아펜젤러는 노병일盧秉日을 인천지역 관리자로 파송하였다. 노병일은 싸리재에 있던 두 채의 초가를 팔고 내동內洞으로 거처를 옮겼다. 그 뒤 1887년 12월 말 아펜젤러의 요청으로 온 올린저F. Ohlinger 선교사가 노병일과 함께 인천선교를 위해 2년 반 동안 뛰었다. 노병일은 1891년 6칸의 예배당을 건축하였는데 이것이 후일 내리교회로 발전하였다. 1891년 6월 내한한 굿셀Daniel A. Goodsell 감독은 한국선교회를 서울구역과 인천구역으로 나누고 아펜젤러를 인천구역의 담당자로 파송하였다. 이때부터 아펜젤러는 매주 토요일 말을 타고 7시간 걸려 인천에 내려가 주일을 지킨 후 월요일에 서울로 올라와 배재학당에서 학생을 가르치는 힘든 일을 했다.

1892년 봄, 아펜젤러의 후임으로 존스Gorge H. Jones, 조원시 선교사가 부임하였다. 존스는 자신의 한국어 선생으로 배재학당에서 일하고 있던 강재형 부부와 함께 교육선교를 시작하였다. 존스는 1893년 강화 교산교회 개척을 필두로 담방리교회(현 만수교회), 강화 홍의교회, 강화 상도교회, 강화 고비교회, 부평 굴제교회 등을 차례로 개척하였다. 또한 이화학당에서 음악교사로 일하던 마거릿 벤젤Margaret J. Bengel이 인천에 정착하여 여자 어린이 교육을 시작하였는데, 이것이 영화학당의 시작이다. 벤젤은 존스 목사와 결혼하여 '존스 부인'으로 불렸다. 영화학당은 1892년 8월에 내리교회 안에 설립되어 초등교육기관으로 자리를 잡았다.

✱ 인천 기독교 유적지

내리교회

 인천시 중구 내동 29번지

　1891년 아펜젤러는 현 위치에서 웨슬리기념교회라는 이름으로 예배당을 처음 지었는데 이 예배당은 6칸으로 된 단층 건물이었다. 바깥은 하얗게 칠하고 지붕은 일본식으로 꾸몄다. 방을 두 개 만들었고 바닥에는 매트를 깔았으며 설교자를 위해 방석 한 개와 작은 강대상을 올려놓았다. 1901년 웨슬리기념교회는 십자 모양을 지닌 서구식 건물로 거듭 태어났다. 그러나 1958년 교회를 신축하면서 그 교회의 원형이 사라져버렸다. 현재의 교회 건물은 1987년에 신축한 '선교100주년기념성전'이다. 최근 내리교회는 역사적 유적으로서의 가치를 지닌 웨슬리기념예배당 복원을 위해 현 교회 옆에 부지를 마련하여 공사에 들어갔다. 내리교회 2층 입구에는 초대 담임목사 아펜젤러, 2대 담임목사 존스, 그리고 한국인 최초의 목사이자 3대 담임목사를 역임한 김기범金箕範의 흉상이 나란히 세워져 있다. 정원에는 '하와이 이민100주년 기념비', 한국선교120주년기념비, 1901년에 만들어진 종鐘이 전시되어 있다. 내리교회 3층 로비에 마련된 역사전시관에서는 교회역사를 한눈에 살펴볼 수 있는 유물과 사진들을 볼 수 있다.

창영사회복지관(인천기독교사회복지관)

 인천시 동구 창영동 42-3

　영화초등학교에서 동남쪽으로 100 m 정도 떨어진 곳에 인천기독교사회복지관이 있다. 이 건물은 19세기 말 미국 감리교회가 파견한 여선교사들이 합숙소로 사용했던 사택이다. 1894년 건축될 당시 이 건물은 'Gamblee Home'으로 불렸다고 한다. 당시에는 이 건물 외에도 현재 복지관 동쪽 인천세무소 부지에 남자선교사들을 위한 부지가 있었고 그 주변에 아펜젤러 사택도 있었다고 한다.

여선교사 숙소로 사용되던 이 건물은 1949년 미 감리교 선교사 헬렌 보일즈에 의하여 '인천기독교사회관'으로 개명되고 6.25전쟁 동안에는 폐쇄되었다. 1956년부터 기독교사회복지관으로 다시 사용하였다. 2003년 4월 사회복지법인 감리회사회복지관재단이 인천시 서구 심곡동으로 이전하면서 이 건물은 매각되었다. 이 건물 바로 옆에 있던 창영교회가 인수하여 현재는 창영사회복지관이라는 이름으로 독자 운영하고 있다.

이 건물은 양철(함석)지붕으로 구조가 독특하며 벽체는 빨간 벽돌로 쌓았다. 창호窓戶는 조선시대 서원이나 승방僧房 등에서 사용하던 방법을 빌어, '쓸 용用' 자 모양으로 꾸몄고, 가장자리는 빗살 모양으로 짜 넣었다. 내부는 목조로 되어 있으며, 2층 가로축에 지하로 드나들 수 있는 통로를 마련하였다. 비교적 원형을 잘 보존하고 있는 근세 르네상스 양식의 이 건물은 1993년 인천광역시 유형문화재 제18호로 지정되었다.

영화초등학교(인천영화학교)

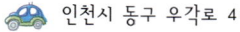 인천시 동구 우각로 44

창영사회복지관과 100 m 정도 떨어진 곳에 영화永化초등학교가 있다. 영화초등학교 건물과 영화여자정보고등학교 건물 사이에는 문화재로 지정된 영화학교 본관동이 있다. 인천영화학교는 한국 최초의 근대식 초등교육기관인 사립학교 영화학당의 후신이며 현재 영화초등학교의 모체이다. 1892년 이화학당에서 음악 교사로 일하던 마거릿 벤젤Margaret Bengel이 인천에 정착하여 내리교회에서 여자 어린이 교육을 시작한 것이 영화학당의 시작이다. 내리교회 제2대 담임인 존스G.H. Jones 목사와 결혼하여 '존스 부인'으로 불린 벤젤은 교육에서 배제되어 온 여자 어린이를 열심히 가르쳤다. 학교 이름은 '영생永生'과 '교화敎化'의 합성어로서 기독교적 의미를 지니고 있다. 서울의 이화학당과 배재학당이 중등교육기관으로 발전한데 반하여 영화초등학교는 초등교육기관으로 자리를 잡았다. 한국 여성계의 선구자인 김활란, 서은숙, 김애마, 김영의가 모두 영화학당 출신

이다. 1904년 존스 선교사가 미국의 자선사업가인 콜린스로부터 1천 달러를 기부받아 그해 11월 인천시 중구 경동 싸리재에 벽돌로 된 단층짜리 교사를 신축하였으나 1911년 지금의 자리인 창영동 36번지에 2층 벽돌집 교사를 신축하여 이전하였다. 당시 건립된 영화초등학교 본관동이 현재까지 보존되고 있으며 인천시 유형문화재 제39호로 지정되어 있다. 이 건물은 반지하 1층, 지상 3층으로 구성된 맞배지붕 구조이며 3층 발코니는 인자人字 형태로 내부에 서까래를 노출시켰으며 3층 예배실은 십자형 평면으로 계획하여 종교적 의미를 가미하였다.

성공회내동성당(내동교회)

 인천시 중구 내동 3번지

내리교회에서 서쪽으로 100 m 정도 가면 인천성공회 내동교회가 나온다. 인천 최초의 성공회 성당인 이 건물은 의료선교사 랜디스E.B. Landis에 의해 시작되었다. 랜디스는 현재의 자리에서 성누가병원을 개설하고 의료구호사업을 전개하였다. 그는 1865년 미국 펜실바니아에서 출생하였으며 1888년 펜실바니아 의과대학에서 박사학위를 받았다. 1890년 코르프C.J. Corfe 주교와 함께 인천 선교사로 부임하여 병원을 짓고 진료를 시작하였다. 이 건물은 1902년 6개월간 러시아영사관으로 사용되었고 1904년 제물포해전 당시에는 일본 적십자병원이 설치되기도 하였다. 6.25전쟁때 일부 파괴된 것을 수리하여 1955년까지 중학교 교사로 사용하였다. 현재의 건물은 1956년에 중건된 것으로 지붕의 목조트러스를 제외한 외벽을 화강암으로 견고하게 쌓아 올린 중세풍의 석조이나 한국의 전통적인 목구조 처마양식을 가미하였다. 성당 뜨락에는 랜디스 기념비와 '영국병원'이라는 글씨가 새겨진 비석이 세워져 있다. 2000년 12월 23일 인천광역시 유형문화재 제51호로 지정되었다.

한국기독교100주년기념탑

🚗 인천시 중구 중앙동1가 18

　　인천항이 바라보이는 작은 언덕에 '한국기독교100주년기념탑'이 세워져 있다. 이 탑은 한국 교계가 1986년 기독교선교 100주년을 맞아 아펜젤러와 언더우드 선교사가 제물포항에 내린 것을 기념하기 위해 세운 조형물이다. 약 50평의 대지 위에 17 m 높이로 세워져 있는데 교회에서 전통적으로 사용해 온 종을 본뜬 세 개의 탑신塔身이 하늘을 향하고 있는 모양이다. 탑 중앙에 아펜젤러 부부와 언더우드를 상징하는 높이 2.7 m의 3인 청동상이 세워져 있고 그 밑에는 아펜젤러 선교사가 제물포항에 내리면서 드렸던 기도문이 새겨져 있다.

인천기독병원

🚗 인천시 중구 율목동 237

　　인천 배다리사거리에서 개항로를 따라 서쪽으로 걷다 보면 큰우물로와 교차하는 곳에 예지장례식장이 나타나고 그 뒤편에 인천기독병원이 자리잡고 있다. 1932년 미국 감리회 선교부에서 율목동 70여 평의 부지에 진료소를 세운 것이 인천기독병원의 출발이다. 일제 말엽에는 술집 접대부의 검진소로 주로 사용되었기 때문에 부인병원으로 불렸다. 해방 후 명맥을 이어가던 이 병원은 6.25전쟁 중이던 1950년 감리교 총회에서 인천에 병원을 세우기로 하면서 새롭게 발전하였다. 당시 감리교 유형기 감독과 사회국 문창모 위원장, 김응태, 조영제, 김관우, 강치안, 박완규 등이 병원 설립에 주도적 역할을 했으며 미국 선교사 사우어Charles A. Sauer, 사월 부자와 빌링슬리Allice M. Billingsley, 변연사 등 11명의 선교사가 큰 도움을 주었다. 전쟁 중인 1952년 개원한 이 병원은 건물의 낙후와 의료기자재 및 약품의 부족으로 애를 먹었지만 이후 각계의 성원과 기독교인 의료진의 활동으로 발전하였다. 1963년 미국감리교 선교부의 원조로 현재의 서관에 1,485 m^2의 병동과 419 m^2의 부속건물을 신축하였다. 또 1972년 인천간호전문대학을

한국기독교100주년기념탑

설립하여 많은 간호사를 배출하기도 하였는데 안산시에 있는 안산1대학의 전신이다. 현재는 학교법인 새빛학원이 기독병원을 운영하고 있다.

국제성서박물관

 인천시 남구 경인북2길 8번지

　인천주안교회 교육관 5층에 마련된 국제성서박물관은 세계 최대의 성서 박물관이다. 미국의 유명한 성서 수집가 웨이커필드David Wakefield 박사가 전 세계에서 수집하여 기증한 희귀성서 1만여 점과 주안교회 담임 목사를 역임한 한경수 감독이 55년간 90여 국가를 돌며 수집한 7천여 점을 합쳐 총 17,000여 권의 성서가 500여 평의 박물관에 분류, 전시되어 있다. 1947년 쿰란동굴에서 발굴된 사해사본 복사본 두루마리성경(길이 9 m)을 비롯하여 구텐베르크 성경(1456년), 그

로싸 오디너리아 성경(1462년), 포리그랏 성경(1517년), 루터 성경(1526년), 감독성경(1539년), 제네바성경(1560년), 시리아 성경(1571년), 킹제임스 성경(1611년) 등과 같은 희귀본만이 아니라, 한국 선교에 중요한 역할을 담당한 스코틀랜드 선교사 로스John Ross와 매킨타이어John MacIntyre, 마륵태가 서상륜徐相崙의 도움을 받아 번역한 『예수성교젼서』(1887년)도 전시되어 있다. 이 박물관에는 성서 이외에도 다양한 성물이 전시되어 있다.

한국선교역사기념관

 인천시 부평구 갈산동 5-12번지 일대

부평순복음교회 옆에 위치한 한국선교역사기념관은 한국 기독교의 역사를 생생하게 체험할 수 있도록 재현한 기념관이다. 부평순복음교회가 대지를 제공하고 정부와 인천시의 지원을 받아 2008년 12월 개관한 이 기념관은 총 면적 4,575㎡에 지하 1층, 지상 4층 규모를 지니고 있다. 1층 '성서역사관'은 하나님의 언약, 모세의 출애굽, 예수의 공생애, 기독교의 성장 순으로 신구약의 주요사건들을 재현하고, 2층 '한국기독교관 I'은 한국 기독교의 전래와 수용, 대부흥운동과 기독교민족운동, 사회운동 등 해방 이전까지 기독교의 활동을 재현하고 있다. 3층 '한국기독교관 II'은 6.25전쟁과 기독교의 수난, 기독교의 재건과 폭발적 성장, 기독교의 영성운동과 선교활동 등을 재현하고 있다.

✻ 인천 일반 유적지

인천우체국

 인천시 중구 항동 6가 1번지

인천우체국은 인천광역시 유형문화재 제8호로 지정되어 있다. 인천의 우체사郵遞史는 우리나라 우정郵政 역사와 그 궤를 같이 한다. 갑신정변이 일어난 해인

1884년에 우정총국이 설립됐고 그 해 11월 17일에 우정총국 인천분국이 개원되었다. 서울보다 먼저 우편업무가 개시되면서 인천우체국은 사실상 우리나라 우정업무의 효시가 된다. 인천우체국은 1923년에 신축되었는데 1982년 인천시 유형문화재 제8호로 지정될 만큼 서양과 동양의 건축양식이 절묘한 조화를 이루고 있는 소중한 문화유산이다.

일본 18은행 인천지점

🚗 인천시 중구 중앙로2가 24-1

일본 18은행 인천지점

일본 18은행 인천지점은 인천광역시 유형문화재 제50호로 지정되어 있다. 일제가 한국 금융지배를 위해 설립한 일본 나가사키 18은행 인천지점이었던 이 건물은 1890년 준공되어 그 해 10월에 개점하였다. 18은행뿐만 아니라 이 당시에 세워진 일본은행들은 모두 한국 금융계를 식민지화하려는 목적으로 설립되었다. 천일은행을 제외한 7개의 은행과 13곳의 보험사 소유자는 모두 일본인이었다는 것이 이를 증명하고 있다. 건물은 전반적으로 절충주의 양식을 취하고 있으며 단층으로 이루어져 있다. 조적조 구조 위에 몰타르 마감이며 기둥과 기단 부위는 돌로 마감되어 있다. 출입구의 석주 장식은 아주 정교하게 시공되어 있으며 지붕은 모임지붕 형태로 목조 트러스 위에 일식기와를 얹었다. 1954년 상공은행과 신탁은행의 합병으로 발족한 한국흥업은행으로 사용된 이후, 1992년까지는 카페, 그 후에는 중고가구 도매상이 임대하여 사용하였다. 현재는 내부를 부분적으로 보수하여 인천광역시 인천개항장 근대건축전시관으로 사용하고 있다.

인천 개항박물관

 인천시 중구 중앙동 1가 9-2

인천 개항박물관은 구(舊)일본제1은행(대지면적 677.7㎡, 건물 연면적 428.05 ㎡)이다. 1899년 축조된 이 석조건물은 르네상스풍의 돔이 설치된 절충주의 양식을 취하고 있으며 인천시 유형문화재 제7호로 지정되어 있다. 2006년 중구청이 이 건물을 매입한 후 근대건축물로서의 가치를 훼손하지 않으면서도 전시가 가능한 박물관을 조성하였다. 2010년 개관한 이 박물관은 4개의 전시실을 두고 있다. 제1전시실은 박물관의 주전시실로 최초의 갑문식 도크에 대한 영상 자료, 최초의 해관 자료, 대한제국의 경비함 광제호의 태극기 등 희귀한 관련 자료를 전시하고 있으며, 제2전시실은 한국철도사와 관련된 자료를 전시하는 공간으로 한국 최초의 경인철도 관련 유물과 자료를 소개하고 있다. 제3전시실은 개항 당시 인천 개항장 일대 각 조계지의 입체 거리 모형과 시청각 자료를 구비하고 있으며, 제4전시실은 은행으로 사용될 당시의 금고를 활용한 전시실로 개항기 금융기관 관련 자료와 유물을 전시하고 있다.

한국이민사박물관

 인천시 중구 월미로 329(북성동1가)

한국이민사박물관은 2008년 개관한 우리나라 최초의 이민사박물관이다. 2003년 미주 이민 100주년을 맞아 인천광역시 시민들과 해외동포들이 뜻을 모아 건립을 추진한 이 박물관은 100여 년의 한인 이민역사를 체계적으로 보여주고 있다. 지하 1층, 지상 3층으로 된 이 박물관에는 4개의 상설 전시실이 마련되어 있다. 제1전시실은 개항 당시의 인천을 소개하고 첫 공식 이민이 이루어지기까지의 국내 정세 및 하와이 상황을 자세하게 보여주고 있다. 당시의 황성신문 기사와 이민 모집 광고, 이민을 담당한 유민원에서 발행한 최초의 공식 여권인 집조, 이민자들을 싣고 하와이로 떠난 첫 선박인 갤릭호 모형 등이 전시되어 있다. 제2전시실은 하와이에 정착한 한인들의 애환과 미국 전역에 뿌리를 내린 한인들의 발자취 등을 담은 사진자료 및 유물을 전시하고 있다. 제3전시실은 중남미로 떠난 한인들의 삶과 조국의 광복을 위해 몸을 바쳤던 선열의 활약상을 보여주고 있다. 제4전시실에는 세계 각국으로 진출한 7백만 해외동포의 근황에 관한 다양한 자료를 전시하고 있다.

인천자유공원

 인천시 중구 송학동1가 11번지 일대

인천자유공원은 대한민국 최초의 서구식 공원이다. 1889년 인천 외국인 거류지에 외국인을 위한 공원으로서 만국공원萬國公園이라는 이름을 달고 개설되었다. 일제 강점기에는 서공원西公園으로 불리다가 해방 후에 원래 이름인 만국공원으로 불렸지만, 1957년 자유공원으로 다시 이름이 바뀌었다. 1957년 인천상륙작전을 기념하기 위해 UN군 사령관이었던 맥아더의 동상을 공원 동편에 건립했다. 공원 안에는 한미수교백주년기념탑, 6.25 학도의용대 위령탑, 제물포구락부(옛 인천문화원), 인천기상대, 석정루, 연오정 등의 시설도 있다.

인천외국인묘지

 인천시 연수구 청학동 산 53번지

인천외국인묘지는 인천 개항 이후 우리나라에 들어와 활동하다 사망한 외교관, 통역관, 선교사, 선원, 의사 등 외국인들이 안장된 공동묘지이다. 묘지 면적 1만 362 m²를 포함하여 총 면적은 1만 9,008 m²이다. 인천의 외국인 묘지는 1883년 중구 북성동에 설치된 뒤 1887년 7월 첫 매장이 이루어졌고, 이후 북성동을 비롯하여 중구 율목동과 남구 도화동 등지에 외국인 무덤이 조성되었다. 1965년 5월 25일 지역 개발에 따라 여러 곳에 산재한 외국인 묘를 현재의 장소로 이장하였다. 미국인 묘 17기, 독일인 묘 11기, 영국인 묘 9기, 러시아인 묘 5

기, 이탈리아인 묘 3기, 오스트레일리아인과 네덜란드인 묘 각 2기, 프랑스인·캐나다인·스페인인·폴란드인·체코인·중국인 묘 각 1기와 국적 불명의 11기 등 모두 66기가 있다. 현재 이 묘지는 관리가 제대로 되지 않고 있다. 담장의 상당 부분이 녹슬어 있고 심지어 구멍까지 생겼다. 묘지의 둘레석과 철근이 파손된 것은 물론 비석의 일부는 떨어져 나갔다.

두번째. 강화

❋ 강화 소개

한강 하류에 위치한 강화도는 산지와 평탄한 충적지가 함께 발달하고 해양성 기후를 지녀 거주지로서는 매우 적합한 환경을 지니고 있다. 구석기시대의 유물과 신석기시대의 토기가 출토되었고 유네스코 세계문화유산으로 등재된 70여 점의 고인돌을 비롯한 청동기 유물이 다수 발굴되었다. 삼국시대에는 백제와 고구려의 중요한 전략적 요충지였으며 장수왕의 남하정책 이후 고구려에 편입되었다. 고구려 시기에는 혈구穴口 혹은 갑비고차甲比古次, 신라 시대에는 해구海口로 불리다가 고려시대에 강화로 개칭되었다. 몽골의 침입시 임시 수도가 되면서 궁궐과 왕릉이 축조되었고 국난 극복을 위해 강화 선원사지에서 고려대장경을 제작하였다.

조선시대에는 외적의 침략을 막기 위해 성, 진, 보, 돈대, 포대 등의 방어기지를 곳곳에 설치하였다. 그리고 정족산鼎足山 사고史庫를 설치하여 국가의 귀중한 사료인 왕실의 족보와 실록을 보관하였으며 외규장각外奎章閣도 설치하였다. 한편 강화도에서는 조선 중기 이후 하곡霞谷 정제두鄭齊斗를 중심으로 하는 양명학파陽明學派가 등장하여 성리학과 대조되는 하나의 학풍을 이루었다.

개항기에 접어들어 강화도는 다시 한번 역사의 중심 무대로 등장하였다. 프랑스 함대와의 전쟁인 병인양요(1866)와 미국 군대와의 전쟁인 신미양요(1871)를 연이어 거치면서 조선 정부는 마침내 서구 열강에게 문호를 개방하는 최초의 근대적 조약인 병자수호조약(1876)을 강화도에서 체결하였다. 이후 강화도에는 우리나라 최초의 근대적 해군사관학교인 통제영학당統制營學堂이 설립되고 서구의 여러 종교도 유입되었다.

강화 기독교 전래

강화도 지역의 기독교는 감리교와 성공회에 의해 시작되었다. 1892년 가을, 제물포구역 책임자로 있던 감리교 선교사 존스G.H.Jones가 강화선교를 위해 강화읍 갑곶나루에 상륙하였다. 그는 강화성江華城에 들어가 복음을 전하려고 하였으나 강화유수留守의 입성入城 금지에 의해 인천으로 되돌아갔다. 1893년 제물포교회(현 내리교회)를 다니던 강화 서사면 시루미(현 양사면 고산리 송산마을) 출신 이승환이 고향에 돌아와 복음을 전하면서 강화 선교의 발판이 마련되었다. 존스는 제물포 교인 이명숙李明淑을 강화전도인으로 파송하고 이승환의 집을 선교의 거점으로 삼기 함으로써 강화의 첫 감리교 신앙공동체가 탄생하였다. 강화 최초의 교회는 교항마을의 초시 김상임金商壬과 그의 가족이 기독교로 개종하면서 설립한 교항교회이다. 1896년에 송해면 상도리 홍의마을의 한학자 박능일朴能一이 서당학생 20여 명 및 종순일, 권신일과 함께 자기 집에서 홍의교회를 설립하여 강화의 두 번째 교회가 탄생하였다. 1900년 9월, 홍의교회에 출석하던 주선일, 박성일, 허진일, 김봉일 등 몇몇 교인이 강화읍 천교하川橋下, 현 강화읍 신문리에 초가집을 마련하고 첫 예배를 드림으로써 오늘날 강화중앙교회의 모체가 설립되었다. 다음해 4월 존스 선교사의 협조로 기와집 25칸, 초가집 16칸을 구입하여 교회를 현 위치로 옮겼다. 이때 소요된 건축비는 존스 선교사의 주선으로 미국 오하이오주 매리에타Marietta에 살고 있던 찰스 오토Charles Otto가 보내 준 기금에 의해 충당되었다. 이로써 8년 전 존스가 강화성에 입성하려던 꿈은 강화 토착인들에 의해 이루어지게 되었다.

강화도에 처음 온 성공회 선교사는 워너Leonard O. Warner, 왕란도이다. 그는 1893년 7월 강화 외성外城 진해루鎭海樓 근처에 집을 한 채 사서 기도처로 정하고 '성 니콜라스' 회당이라 이름지었다. 성공회 신부들이 성안으로 들어간 것은 1897년부터이다. 워너 신부의 후임으로 강화에 온 트롤로프M.N. Trollope 신부는 조선수사해방학당朝鮮水師海防學堂 교관들이 살던 관청리 집을 구입하였으며, 1899년 견자산 산마루에 있는 강화 내성內城 성터 3천여 평을 구입하여 성당 부지로 삼았다.

1900년 어간에는 온수리에도 성공회가 들어왔다. 1896년 트롤로프 신부와 힐라리 신부F.R. Hillary, 길강준, 평신도 로스Arthur F. Laws, 노인산 등 세 선교사가 강화에 부임하였다. 의사인 로스는 1900년 무렵 온수리 초입인 난저골에 집 한 채를 사서 진료소를 차렸다. 간호사로 들어와 있던 마가레타Margaretta, 알마, 로다 수녀도 난저골 진료소로 내려와 일을 도왔다. 로스는 한해에 3,400여명을 진료하면서 널리 알려졌다. 로스의 진료소가 좋은 반응을 얻자 강화읍에 있던 힐라리 신부도 이곳으로 옮겨와 교회와 진명학교를 시작하였다. 특히 온수리에서 유력한 집안이던 광산김씨 집안의 김영선金永善, 김영지金永志 형제가 성당에 나오면서 성공회의 교세가 급증하였다. 1906년 난저골에 15칸 규모의 성당을 건축하였으나 곧 비좁게 되어 5년만에 그보다 1 km 남쪽에 위치한 지금의 위치에 3천 평 부지를 마련하고 27칸 규모의 온수리성당을 짓게 되었다.

강화도 기독교 유적지

강화읍성공회성당

🚗 인천시 강화군 강화읍 관청리 422

서울에서 48번 국도를 타고 강화대교를 지나 4 km 정도 직진하면 강화읍 고려당삼거리가 나오고, 우회전하면 김상용(金尙容)선생순절비가 보인다. 기념비 옆 골목으로 난 오르막길을 100 m 쯤 오르면 사찰처럼 보이는 강화읍성공회성당이 나타난다. 1900년 한옥식 건물로 지어진 이 성당은 동양과 서양의 조화를 보여주고 있다. 전체 성당의 모습은 배 모양을 취하고 있으며 성당 내부는 전형적인 바실리카 양식이다.

건물은 넓이 4칸, 길이 10칸의 장방형이며 출입문은 전통 사찰처럼 3개의 문을 거쳐 본당 안으로 들어가게 되어 있다. 3칸 솟을지붕으로 된 대문에는 태극원에 십자가 문양이 그려져 있고 홍살로 장식된 토담벽이 둘러 있다. 두 번째 문 역시 3칸에 단층 팔작지붕으로 되어 있는데 종각으로 쓰고 있다. 성당이 처음 완공되었을 때에는 대문과 종각이 없었지만 1914년 영국에서 주조된 종이 들어오면서 종각과 대문을 만들었다. 이 종은 '신종(神鐘)'이라 불릴만큼 종소리가 맑으나 일제말 징발되어 사라졌고 1993년 새로 주조한 것이다. 종과 함께 공출되었던 정문 난간은 최근 복원되었다. 2010년 11월 일본 성공회가 한일강제병합 100주년을 맞이하여 과거 일제 침략전쟁을 참회하면서 난간을 복원한 것이다.

성당 뜰 안에는 영국 수녀 알마 기념비가 서 있다. 그녀는 1896년 내한하여 강화 온수리병원에서 간호사로 일하다 1906년 전염병에 감염되어 목숨을 잃었다. 강화 교인들이 그녀를 기리기 위해 화강암 비석을 세운 것이다. 본당 뒤쪽에는 전통 한옥으로 된 사제관이 있다. 본당 내부는 사방이 유리로 된 고창층 창문으로 빛이 잘 들어오며 천장은 들보와 서까래를 그대로 드러내고 하얀 회벽으로 처리하여 고풍스러운 멋이 난다. 실내 공간은 4 m가 넘는 20개 기둥이 영역을 갈라놓고 있으며 양쪽으로 8개씩 세운 사각 모양의 나무 기둥들은 복도와 회중

강화읍성공회성당

석을 구분하고 있다. 동쪽의 8개 격자 기둥들은 제단과 회중석을 구분하고 있다. 이 성당은 1981년 경기도 지방유형문화재 111호로 지정되었다. 그러나 강화군이 인천광역시로 편입되면서 인천지방유형문화재로 변경되었다가 2001년 1월 국가사적 424호로 지정되었다.

온수리성공회성당

🚗 인천시 강화군 강화읍 길상면 온수리 505-3

    강화읍에서 전등사 표지판을 따라 온수리로 들어가면 오른쪽 정족산 산자락에 붉은 벽돌로 지은 온수감리교회가 나오는데 길 건너편 마을 한 가운데 온수리성공회 성당이 있다. 성당으로 들어가는 입구에 한옥 사제관이 두어 채 있고 야트막한 고갯길을 오르면 정문에 이른다. 성당 정문은 솟을대문 형태를 취하고 있으며 지붕 아래 영국 해군이 기증한 종을 매달아 놓았었으나 일제말 징발되어

1989년 전통양식의 종을 새로 제작하여 달았다. 온수리성당은 정면 3칸, 측면 9칸으로 된 일자형 전통 한옥이며 지붕은 단층 팔작지붕이다. 지붕 용마루 양쪽 치미鴟尾에 십자가 장식이 있고 지붕 양쪽 끝 합각 벽면에도 십자 장식을 새겨 놓았다. 성당 내부는 바실리카 양식으로 열두 사도를 상징하는 열두 개의 기둥으로 회중석과 지성소를 구분하고 있다. 측랑은 없고 회중석 가운데 복도가 남녀석을 구분하고 있다. 안드레성당으로 불리는 이 성당은 2003년 10월 인천광역시 유형문화재 제52호로 지정되었으며, 한옥 사제관은 인천광역시 유형문화재 41호로 지정되어 있다. 현재는 성당 뒤편에 로마네스크 양식으로 건축된 새 성당을 본당으로 사용하고 있다.

교산교회

인천시 강화군 양사면 교산리 201

강화읍에서 48번 국도를 따라 인화리 방면으로 가다가 우측의 산이포 방향으로 언덕길을 넘으면 '강화 교산교회'라는 팻말이 보인다. 교산교회는 강화도 서북쪽 해안 마을에 위치한 교회로서 강화도 감리교회의 모교회이다. 1892년 가을, 제물포구역 책임자로 있던 존스G.H. Jones 선교사가 강화 남문을 통하여 강화성江華城에 들어가 복음을 전파하려 하였으나 강화유수의 완강한 거절로 입성하지 못하였다. 다음해 양사면 시루미 마을 출신으로 제물포에서 주막을 운영하던 이승환이 존스 목사를 만나면서 복음이 들어오는 계기가 마련되었다. 존스는 이승환의 모친에게 선상에서 세례를 주고 인천에서 활동하던 전도인 이명숙과 전도부인 백헬렌을 시루미로 파송하여 이승환의 집에서 예배가 시작되었다. 시루미가 천민 출신이 많은 마을인 반면 거기서 좀 떨어진 다리목은 양반 동네였다. 다리목에 살던 '김초시'로 불린 김상임金商壬이 존스 목사로부터 세례를 받으면서 마을 전체가 개종하였다. 김상임이 1894년 자기집 앞마당에 초가 12칸을 구입하여 예배당을 마련하자 시루미 마을의 교인들이 옮겨와 함께 예배를 드리게 되었다. 교산교회라고 하는 이름은 다리목의 한자어인 교항橋項의 '교' 자와 시루미의 한자어인 증산甑山의 '산' 자의 결합에서 나온 것이다. 김상임은 초기 감리교 교역자 양성과정인 신학회를 졸업하고 목사 안수를 받기 직전 1902년 4월 별세하였다. 교산교회에는 강화기독교백주년기념사업회에서 세운 김상임의 공덕비가 서 있다.

현재의 교산교회는 해방 이후 자리를 옮긴 것으로 시루미와 다리목 중간에 있다. 김상임이 지었던 12칸짜리 교회는 지금 텃밭으로 바뀌어 흔적을 찾을 수 없지만, 김상임이 살던 집은 지붕만 바뀐채 그대로 있다. 집을 끼고 야트막한 언덕을 오르면 김상임의 가족 무덤이 보인다. 김상임 전도사 부부와 손자 부부의 묘를 비롯하여 10기 이상의 봉분이 있는데 특히 김상임의 손녀 며느리는 강화의 '찬송 할머니'로 유명한 김리브가 부인이다. 그녀는 찬송가에는 수록되지 않았지만 교인들 사이에 입으로 전해지던 상당수의 찬송가를 <노래집>으로 남겼다.

홍의교회

인천시 강화군 송해면 상도리 943

홍의교회는 교산교회와 강화읍 중간에 위치하고 있으며 강화도에서 두 번째로 생긴 감리교회이다. 홍의 마을에 감리교가 들어온 것은 1896년이다. 이 마을 서당훈장이던 박능일朴能一이 교산교회의 김상임金商壬을 만나고 돌아와 자기 집에서 예배를 드리면서 시작되었다. 불과 1년 만에 교인수가 80명이 넘었으며 선교사의 도움 없이 토담집 예배당을 건축하고 인천에서 오는 전도사의 생활비도 부담하였다. 서당도 학교로 바꾸어 신식 교육을 시작하였다. 홍의교회의 교인들은 실용적이지 못한 흰 옷에 물을 들여 검은 옷을 일제히 입었다. 같은 신앙공동체의 일원이라는 정체성의 표현으로서 이름도 통일적으로 바꾸었다. 각자의 성姓은 바꾸지 않되 끝자를 '일一'자로 통일하고 가운데 글자만 선택하여 이름을 지었다. '일'자는 "처음 믿었다" 혹은 "한 가족이다"라는 의미로 돌림자가 되었다고 한다. 홍의 마을의 첫 교인 박능일도 이러한 식으로 이름을 바꾼 것이다. 이러한 개명 운동은 강화도의 다른 지역에도 영향을 미쳐 초기 강화 교인 중 '일' 자로 끝나는 이름을 지닌 인물이 60여 명으로 조사되고 있다. 바다 건너 교동에서는 '신信' 자를 돌림자로 했다. 현재의 홍의교회는 도로변에 자리잡고 있으며 흔히 볼 수 있는 붉은 벽돌 예배당으로서 옛날 토담집 예배당과는 전혀 다른 분위기를 보여주고 있다. 다만 교회 왼쪽에 묘지동산이 보이는데 '본처전도사'로 평생 교회를 지킨 김경일 전도사의 묘비가 있다.

길직교회(현 강화초대교회)

🚗 인천시 강화군 길상면 길직리 782-3

길직교회는 강화초대교회의 전신이다. 1919년 3월 18일 일어난 강화의 만세운동을 모의하던 길직교회의 터는 그대로이나 교회 건물은 신축되었다. 1919년 3월 9일 오후 3시경 길직리 예수교회당에서 길직리의 조종환, 장명순, 장동원, 장상용, 장삼수, 장흥환 등과 선두리의 황유부, 황도문, 염성오, 유희철, 온수리의 유봉진, 상방리의 이진형 목사 등이 회합하였다. 이들은 주로 길직교회와 선두교회의 지도급 인사들이었다. 이 자리에서 서울의 만세운동에 참가하고 돌아온 황도문과 조종환은 서울에서의 만세운동에 관한 상황을 전하고 강화에서도 만세운동을 할 것을 제안하였다. 이에 돌아오는 장날 가운데 여건이 좋은 날을 정해 이진형 목사가 부내면 신문리의 잠두교회와 의논하여 거사를 일으킬 것을 결의하였다. 이후 여러 번의 논의를 통해 18일 장날을 거사일로 정해 대대적인 만세운동이 일어나게 되었다. 현재 교회 마당에는 3·1독립만세운동기념비가 세워져 있다.

교동읍교회

🚗 인천시 강화군 교동면 상용리 777-2

강화도 창후리 선착장에서 배를 타고 30분 정도 가면 교동도에 상륙할 수 있다. 현재 강화도와 교동도를 연결하는 다리 공사가 한창이다. 교동도 선착장에 내리면 1990년에 새로 지은 교동교회 건물이 눈에 들어온다. 교동교회에서 오른편으로 나 있는 좁은 길로 접어들면 상룡리 옛 교동교회를 만날 수 있다. 옛 교동교회는 인적이 드문 곳에 위치하고 있어서 보존 상태가 양호하다. 예배당 앞에 서 있는 종탑은 옛 모습을 그대로 간직하고 있는데, 이 종은 일제말 전쟁 물자로 공출하려고 배에 싣고 가다가 큰 파도로 인해 다시 제자리에 걸어놓았다고 한다. 예배당은 처음 지을 때 초가였던 지붕을 1970년대에 푸른색 양철지붕으로 바꾼 것 외에는 옛 모습 그대로다. 실내는 신발을 벗고 들어가게 돼 있고, 드리워진 커튼을 걷으면 햇빛이 잘 들어와 조명이 필요 없다. 예전부터 쓰던 오래된 풍금과 재봉틀을 변형해 만든 테이블도 있다.

예배당 맞은 편에는 '마라 쓴물 온천장'이 있다. 교동교회 박용호 권사가 1991년 양어장을 만들 계획으로 시추했던 곳에서 뜨거운 온천이 쏟아져 나왔고, 그 물이 신경통과 관절염 환자에 효험이 있다는 것이 밝혀져 온천장으로 개발했다. 처음에는 베데스다 온천이라고 명명했으나 물맛이 짜고 써서 출애굽기에 나오는 '마라의 쓴물출 15:23'이라는 명칭을 1994년부터 사용했다. '마라 쓴물 온천장'은 2000년 강화도의 창후리로 옮겨갔다. 교통이 불편하고 밀려오는 손님을 감당하기에는 이곳의 시설이 너무 열악해 창후리에 현대적 시설의 온천장을 새로 만든 것이다. 현재 교동도에 있는 원래 '마라 쓴물 온천장'은 영업을 하지 않고 있으며, 하루 한번씩 물만 길어 강화도로 나르고 있다.

강화중앙교회와 합일초등학교

강화중앙교회: 인천시 강화군 강화읍 신문리 549 / **합일초등학교**: 인천시 강화군 강화읍 신문리 452

강화대교를 건너 48번 국도를 따라 4 km 정도 직진, 신문사거리에 못 미쳐 좌측으로 보면 언덕위에 우람한 강화중앙교회가 보인다. 1900년 9월 1일 상도리 교회에 다니던 주선일 등 10여명이 강화읍 천교하에 6칸짜리 가옥을 매입하여

기도처로 삼으면서 창립된 교회이다. 1901년 선교사 존스의 도움으로 현 위치에 기와집 25칸과 초가집 16칸을 사서 '잠두교회'라는 이름의 한옥예배당을 세웠다. 교인이 빠른 속도로 늘어나자 1914년에는 교인들의 헌금과 미국 선교회의 도움으로 서양식 교회를 신축하였다. 이 교회당은 여러 차례 개축하며 사용하다가 2000년에 헐고 1,800명을 수용할 수 있는 "선교100주년 기념성전"을 건축하였다.

강화중앙교회는 1901년 4월 잠두의숙蠶頭義塾을 설립하고, 1902년 합일여학교를 설립하여 기독교 신앙에 바탕을 둔 민중교육을 시작하였는데 이후 두 학교는 통합되어 합일초등학교로 발전하였다. 이 학교는 민족운동과 개화운동의 산실이 되었다. 강화진위대장을 지낸 민족운동가 이동휘李東輝(임시정부 초대 국무총리)는 이 교회 출신 권사로서 보창학교를 설립했으며, 독립운동가 유경근도 이 교회 속장이었다. 1907년 정미의병운동이 일어났을 때 이 교회 신도였던 김동수 권사와 동생 김남수 권사, 그의 사촌 김영구는 일제에 의해 더리미 해안에서 처형되었다. 이들의 죽음을 기리기 위해 2003년 교회 앞에 삼형제 순국추모비를 건립하였다. 교회 현관에는 역사전시관을 설치하여 강화중앙교회의 역사만이 아니라 강화 기독교의 역사에 관한 자료를 제공하고 있다.

강화중앙교회에서 동쪽으로 100 m 정도 떨어진 곳에 4층으로 된 합일초등학교가 있다. 학교 본관 오른쪽에 최상현 선생 동상과 기념비가 보인다. 이 학교는 선교사에 의해 시작되었지만 일제의 방해로 학교 운영이 어려워지자 지역 유지였던 최상현이 인수하여 운영하였다. 최상현은 자신의 전답 18만 평을 지역 농민들에게 거의 무상으로 임대하여 생계를 유지하게 하였을 뿐만 아니라 사후에는 전답 전체를 학교에 기증하였다. 1933년 그의 사망 후에 농민들이 뜻을 모아 시혜비施惠碑를 세웠는데 그 동안 방치되었던 것을 2000년에 현재의 동상 옆으로 이전하였다.

강화 서도중앙교회(진촌교회)

 인천시 강화군 서도면 주문도리 718번지

강화도 외포리 선착장에서 배를 타고 1시간 정도 서쪽으로 가면 주굿도에 도착한다. 이 섬의 한 가운데 있는 교회가 서도중앙교회이다. 1902년 감리교 전도사 윤정일이 복음을 전하기 위해 이 섬으로 들어오면서 교회가 세워졌다. 1923년 개보수한 예배당이 현재의 진촌교회라는 간판을 달고 있는 한옥예배당이다. 1978년 '서도중앙교회'로 이름을 바꾸었으며 현재는 이 예배당 위쪽어 새로 지은 건물에서 예배를 드리고 있다. 한옥예배당의 지붕은 옆에서 볼 때 여덟 팔八자 모양의 팔작지붕이며 홑처마집이다. 건물 안은 중세 전기의 서양교회 양식을 하고 있으나 매우 단순하여 예배실로 쓰이는 좁은 신랑과 측랑, 중앙의 강단으로 구성되어 있다. 전통 목조건물의 가구형식을 바탕으로 서양교회를 지었다는 특징을 지니고 있다. 이 예배당은 1997년 인천광역시 문화재자료 14호로 지정되었다.

백령도중화동교회

 인천시 옹진군 백령면 연화리 335

백령도 서남쪽에 위치한 중화동교회는 백령도에서 가장 오래된 교회이다. 현재의 교회 건물은 신축한 것으로 역사적 가치는 없지만 앞뜰에 있는 백주년 기념비와 비문, 오래된 향나무와 놋쇠로 만든 종이 교회가 오랜 역사를 지녔음을 증명하고 있다. 칼 구츨라프Karl F.A. Gutzlaff 목사를 필두로 여러 선교사들이 조선에 입국하기 전 백령도에 임시 정박하여 선교활동을 펼쳤다는 기록이 있지만 교회가 정식으로 설립된 것은 1896년이다. 백령도 진의 첨사 자문역으로 참사 벼슬을 지냈던 허득이 그곳에 유배되어온 김성진, 황학성, 장지영 등과 함께 한문서당에서 중화동교회를 설립하였다. 창립예배에는 한국 최초의 자생교회인 소래교회의 서경조徐景祚 장로가 참석하였으며 초대 당회장은 언더우드였다. 교회 옆 백령기독교역사관이 백령도 교회의 역사를 잘 보여주고 있다. 백령기독교역사관은 군비를 들여 지은 역사박물관으로서 30평 규모의 현대식 건물이다. 내부에는 초기 중화동교회의 모습, 백령도에 처음 복음이 전파되는 장면, 서양선교사의 성경 전달 모습, 토마스 선교사의 방문 모습, 언더우드 선교사의 세례 집례 장면 등이 재현되어 있으며, 이외에도 중화동교회의 설립 역사, 역대 목회자의 사진, 언더우드 목사의 기념비 등이 전시되어 있다.

2. 경기도 지역

첫번째. 수원

✱ 수원 소개

경기도 남서쿠에 위치한 수원은 동쪽으로 용인, 서쪽으로 안산, 남쪽으로 화성, 북쪽으로 의왕과 접하고 있으며 현재 경기도의 도청 소재지다. 선사 시대의 유적이 다수 출토된 것으로 보아 오래전부터 마을이 형성되었던 것을 알 수 있다. 삼국시대 초기에는 백제의 영토였지만 장수왕의 남하정책시 고구려의 영토로 편입되었는데, 당시 지명은 '매홀買忽'이었다. 매홀은 물고을이라는 발음의 표기로 추정되며, 여기에서 한자식 지명인 수원水原이 유래한 것으로 보인다.

신라가 삼국을 통일한 이후에는 9주 5소경의 설치에 따라 수원은 한산주漢山州에 속하였는데, 757년(경덕왕 16)에 전국의 지명을 한자漢字로 바꿀 때 한주漢州 소속의 수성군水城郡이 되었다. 고려시대에는 수주水州라 하였고, 1271년(원종 12)에 수원도호부水原都護府가 되어 '수원水原'이라는 명칭이 처음 등장하였다. 이후 수주목으로 승격되었다가 수원부, 수원군, 수원부 등으로 변화를 거듭하였다. 조선시대에 들어서는 1789년(정조 13) 사도세자의 묘 현륭원이 수원부내로 옮겨지면서 수원의 읍치는 화산 아래에서 팔달산 아래로 이전되었다. 1790년에는 수원의 이름을 화성華城으로 바꾸고 수원부사를 유수겸장용외사행궁정리사로 삼고 판관 1명이 화성유수를 보좌하도록 하였다. 1794년에 성을 쌓는 공사가 시작되어 1796년 화성이 완성되었다. 정조의 정치적 이상이 녹아있는 화성유수부는 정조 사후 겨우 명맥을 유지하다가 1896년 경기도의 도청소재지가 되었다.

✻ 수원 기독교 전래

미감리회는 1880년대까지는 인천과 서울을 근거로 선교활동을 펼쳤지만 1890년대부터는 평양, 원산과 함께 수원에서도 선교활동을 시작하였다. 미감리회는 서울 이남 지역을 관할하는 수원순회 구역을 조직하였는데 여기에는 수원, 시흥, 오산, 이천, 광주 등의 지역이 포함되었다. 1890년대에 이미 오산이나 광주 등지에서는 여러 신앙공동체가 생겨났지만 수원은 외세에 대한 반감이 강해 성 안으로의 진출이 어려웠다.

서울 이남 지역의 선교가 활성화되기 위해서는 수원 성안에 교두보를 확보하는 것이 급선무였다. 1901년 미감리회 선교사 스크랜턴W.B. Scranton은 신실한 신앙을 지닌 김동현金東鉉을 통해 화성 안에 가옥을 구입하고자 하였다. 그러나 구입하려는 가옥이 화령전華寧殿과 너무 가까웠기 때문에 화성 유수의 반발을 초래하였다. 화성유수는 기독교의 교당을 짓는 것을 신성모독으로 여기며 가옥 구입을 허용하지 않았다. 이 일로 인해 김동현은 감옥에 갇혔으며 거래를 취소한 이후에야 풀려났다. 화성유 수는 화령전 부근 이외의 장소는 허용한다고 하면서 성안의 몇 군데를 추천하였다. 따라서 수원 및 공주 순회구역장이었던 스웨어러Wilbur C. Swearer, 서보는 김동현 대신 이명숙李明淑을 통해 북문 안 보시동의 13칸짜리 초가를 구입하였다. 이로써 수원 성안에 선교 근거지가 마련되었다. 1902년 2월 17일 남자 3명과 여자 4명이 신자로 등록하면서 수원 성안의 최초 교회당인 수원읍교회, 오늘의 수원종로교회가 탄생한 것이다. 그리고 베크S.A. Beck, 백서암의 도움으로 15명으로 매일학교를 개설하였는데 이것이 지금의 삼일학교와 매향학교의 시작이다. 교회가 급속도로 성장하면서 1908년 수원 종로교회를 중심으로 '수원지방'이 조직되어 1912년에는 수원지역 뿐만 아니라 제천, 음성을 포함한 충북지역과 여주, 이천 등의 경기 동부, 그리고 남양, 안산 등 경기 서부를 관할하게 되었다.

✻ 수원 기독교 유적지

수원종로교회

🚗 경기도 수원시 팔달구 북수동 386번지

수원종로교회는 수원읍교회로 출발하였다. 1899년 미감리회 스크랜턴 선교사가 수원에 스테이션을 세우고자 서울에서 영향력 있는 신자 몇 가정을 이주시키면서 교회가 시작되었다. 1900년 선교사 스웨어러W.C. Swearer 부부가 북문안 보시동에 기와집 10여 칸을 매입하여 복음 전파를 시작하였다. 1901년 선교부의 파송을 받은 이명숙 전도사가 북문 안에 13칸짜리 초가를 구입, 개축하고 가족을 이주시켰다. 이로써 정착 선교가 가능해졌다. 1902년 스크랜턴 대부인이

여학교(현 매향여자중학교 및 매향여자정보고등학교)를 세우고 1903년에는 교회 안에 사숙私塾(현 삼일학교)을 설립하였다. 1907년 교회를 보시동(북수동) 116번지에서 북수동 386번지 현재 위치로 이전하였다. 1913년 예배당을 새로 건축하였다. 미국 뱁콕 부인Mrs. Althera Babcocks Teither이 자기 모친을 위해 기념 예배당을 지으라고 150달러300원를 버딕George M. Burdick, 변조진 선교사에게 주었는데 이 돈과 보시동교회를 매각한 돈을 합쳐 함석지붕의 예배당 40평을 신축한 것이다. 이 예배당터는 본래 관가의 소유로서 천주교인들을 처형하던 곳이었다고 한다. 1923년, 1932년 두 번에 걸쳐 교회 증축과 개축을 하였으며 1969년 현재의 예배당을 신축하였다.

매향학교와 삼일중학교 본관

🚗 **매향학교**: 경기도 수원시 팔달구 수원천로 350번지 / **삼일중학교 본관**: 경기도 수원시 팔달구 수원천로 342번지

수원천변 화홍문華虹門 근처 110번지 일대에는 매향중학교, 매향여자정보고등학교, 삼일중학교, 삼일상업고등학교, 삼일고등공업학교 등 여러 학교가 몰려 있다. 이 학교들은 모두 북감리회의 미션스쿨로 시작한 학교들이다. 1902년 6월 미국 북감리회 여선교부의 선교사 메리 스크랜턴Mary F. Scranton이 여학생 3명의 삼일소학당으로 개교하였고, 1910년 3월 제1회 졸업생 3명을 배출하였다. 1937년 30년간 교장으로 봉직한 밀러Lula A. Miller, 미라 선교사가 퇴직하여 귀국한 이후 4년간 교장 없이 지내면서 학교의 존립이 위태로워졌다. 그러나 수원의 유지였던 차준담이 1941년 학교를 인수하고 수원여자매향학교로 인가를 받은 뒤 수년간 1천만 환 이상의 사비를 들여 학교를 운영하였다. 초기 학교의 건물은 그 흔적을 찾아볼 수 없지만 2002년 개교100주년을 맞이하여 마련한 '매향역사실'을 통하여 매향학교의 역사의 편린을 찾아볼 수 있다. '매향역사실'에는 개항기 선교사들이 예배에 사용한 것으로 추정되는 악기인 양금이 전시되어 있고, 사진류로는 삼일학당 시절의 교사와 학생, 체육대회 사진 등이 전시되어 있다. 현재 매향정보

고등학교 정문 앞을 흐르는 수원천변에 있는 아담한 다리는 유서 깊은 역사를 지닌 다리이다. 원래 이 자리에 있던 다리가 홍수로 인해 자주 유실되자 1926년 매향학교 교장이었던 선교사 밀러가 사비 1,400원을 들이고, 3·1운동에 가담하여 매향학교 교감직에서 쫓겨나 있던 김세환 선생이 감독하여 만든 것이다. 당시에 삼일교로 불리던 이 다리를 1992년 새롭게 단장한 것이 현재의 다리다.

매향학교(현 매향중학교, 매향여자정보고등학교)와 붙어 있는 학교가 삼일학교(현 삼일중학교)이다. 삼일학교 현관은 2001년 1월 16일 경기도 기념물 제175호로 지정되었다. 이 건물은 1923년에 건립된 삼일학원의 교사校舍로서 미국 아담스교회의 도움을 받아서 아담스기념관이라는 이름이 붙여졌다. 삼일학원은 1903년 선교사 스웨어러W. Swearer가 15명의 소년을 모아 시작한 교회부설학교로, 처음에는 자체 건물 없이 중포산中布山 기슭의 교회 건물을 빌려 사용했다. 수원지방 감리사 노블W.A. Noble이 이 사정을 미국 아담스교회에 알려 교인들로부터 건립기금 2만 엔을 기부 받아 건물을 지었다. 미국 아담스교회 선교부에서 설계하고, 공사는 중국인 왕영덕王永德이 맡았다. 우진각지붕의 2층 벽돌조 양옥으로 현관은 건물 한쪽으로 치우쳐 있다. 지하층은 거칠게 다듬은 돌로 쌓았고 1층과 2층은 적벽돌로 벽체를 쌓았으며 층간에 목조 마루틀을 설치하여 바닥을 꾸몄다. 지붕은 벽체 위에 목조 트러스를 올리고 널판을 깔아 함석판을 올렸다. 1940년 고 최태영 기념관이 새로 건립되어 교사를 옮기기 전까지 교실과 사무실로 사용하였으며, 이후에는 삼일중학교의 본관, 교장실과 교무실, 예배실, 기도실 등으로 사용하였다. 1988년 현관과 1층 내부를 수리하고 보강하였다. 현재 1층은 미술과 특별교실, 방송실, 창고 등으로 쓰고 있으며, 2층은 재단사무실로 사용하고 있다.

동신교회

경기도 수원시 팔달구 매향동 116번지

수원시 화홍문에서 천변을 따라 남쪽으로 조금 내려오면 무형문화재 전수회

노리마츠 기념비

관 옆에 조그마한 교회가 보인다. 동신교회는 그리 널리 알려져 있지 않은 교회이지만 1830년경 영국에서 일어난 플리머드 형제운동에 그 기원을 두고 있다. 플리머드 형제단 소속의 영국인 선교사 브랜드H.G. Brand가 1888년 일본에서 선교를 시작하자 이에 동참했던 노리마츠 마사야스乘松雅休가 한국에 전도하면서 비롯되었다. 일본 메이지학원대학 신학부를 다니던 노리마츠는 1896년 명성황후가 무참히 살해된 사실을 알게 된 뒤 조선선교를 결심했다. 그는 조선인들에게 사죄하고 희망을 잃은 조선인들을 기독교 신앙으로 돌보고자 그해 12월 23일 인천항에 도착했다. 노리마츠는 서울에 도착하여 한 여인숙에서 주인의 도움으로 청년 조덕성을 소개받고 1897년 1월부터 한글을 배우며 노방전도를 시작하였다. 1898년 브랜드가 내한하여 서울 지역을 맡자 그는 수원 장안동으로 이주하여 1900년 9월 자신이 살고 있는 집을 '성서강론소聖書講論所'로 삼아 선교활동을 펼쳤다. 1909년 8월 김태정金泰貞이 수원천변 토지를 기부하자 신자들의 헌금과 협력으로 한옥 집회소를 지어 '수원 성서강당' 이라 하였다. 1917년 일제 당국의 요청에 따라 '기독동신회基督同信會'로 종교단체 등록을 하였다. 노리마츠는 한복을 입고 식기와 집도 한국식으로 생활하면서 아들에게도 한국어를 할 수 있게 할만큼 한국을 사랑한 일본 기독교인이었다. 그는 경상북도와 충청북도 등지에 38개 교회를 개척하는 등 열정적으로 사역을 펼쳤으나 건강의 악화로 1921년 2월 조선에 뼈를 묻어달라는 유언을 남기고 고향 오다하라에서 생을 마감했다. 1922년 동신회 수원교회 성도들은 그의 유골을 가져와 수원교회 뜰에 무덤과 기념비를 세웠다.

✱ 수원 일반 유적지

수원화성

 경기도 수원시 팔달구 행궁길 185번지

사적 제3호로 지정 관리되고 있으며 소장 문화재로 팔달문(보물 제402호), 화서문(보물 제403호), 장안문, 공심돈 등이 있다. 수원화성은 1997년 12월 유네스코 세계문화유산으로 등록되었다. 수원화성은 정조의 효심이 축성의 근본이 되었을 뿐만 아니라 당쟁에 의한 당파정치 근절과 강력한 왕도정치의 실현을 위한 원대한 정치적 포부가 담긴 정치구상의 중심지로 지어진 것이며 수도 남쪽의 국방요새로 활용하기 위한 것이었다.

수원화성은 규장각 문신 정약용이 동서양의 기술서를 참고하여 만든 『성화주략』(1793년)을 지침서로 하여, 채제공의 총괄 아래 조심태의 지휘로 1794년 1월에 착공에 들어가 1796년 9월에 완공하였다. 축성시에 거중기, 녹로 등 신기재를 특수하게 고안·사용하여 장대한 석재 등을 옮기며 쌓는데 이용하였다. 수원화성 축성과 함께 부속시설물로 화성행궁, 중포사, 내포사, 사직단 등 많은 시설물을 건립하였으나 전란으로 소멸되고 현재 화성행궁의 일부인 낙남헌만 남아 있다.

수원화성은 축조 이후 일제 강점기를 지나 한국전쟁을 겪으면서 성곽의 일부가 파손·손실되었으나 1975~1979년까지 축성직후 발간된 『화성성역의궤』에 의거하여 대부분 축성 당시 모습대로 보수·복원하여 현재에 이르고 있다.

수원화성은 축성시의 성곽이 거의 원형대로 보존되어 있을 뿐 아니라, 북수문(화홍문)을 통해 흐르던 수원천이 현재에도 그대로 흐르고 있고, 팔달문과 장안문, 화성행궁과 창룡문을 잇는 가로망이 현재에도 도시 내부 가로망 구성의 주요 골격을 유지하고 있는 등 200년전 성의 골격이 그대로 현존하고 있다. 축성의 동기가 군사적 목적보다는 정치·경제적 측면과 부모에 대한 효심으로 성곽 자체가 "효"사상이라는 동양의 철학을 담고 있어 문화적 가치외에 정신적, 철학적 가치를 가지는 성으로 이와 관련된 문화재가 잘 보존되어 있다.

수원화성은 중국, 일본 등지에서 찾아볼 수 없는 평산성의 형태로 군사적 방어기능과 상업적 기능을 함께 보유하고 있으며 시설의 기능이 가장 과학적이고 합리적이며, 실용적인 구조로 되어 있다. 또한 약 6 km에 달하는 성벽 안에는 4개의 성문이 있으며 모든 건조물이 각기 모양과 디자인이 다른 다양성을 지니고 있어 동양 성곽의 백미라 할 수 있다.

축성 후 1801년에 발간된 『화성성역의궤』에는 축성계획, 제도, 법식뿐 아니라 동원된 인력의 인적사항, 재료의 출처 및 용도, 예산 및 임금계산, 시공기계, 재료가공법, 공사일지 등이 상세히 기록되어 있어 성곽축성 등 건축사에 큰 발자취를 남기고 있을 뿐만 아니라 그 기록으로서의 역사적 가치가 큰 것으로 평가되고 있다.

화성행궁

화성행궁은 정조가 현륭원에 전배展拜하기 위하여 행행幸行 때에 머물던 임시처소로서, 평상시에는 부사뒤에는 留守가 집무하는 부아䕃衙로도 활용하였다. 뿐만 아니라 정조가 승하한 뒤 순조 1년(1801) 행궁 곁에 화령전華寧殿을 건립하여 정조의 진영眞影을 봉안하였는데, 그뒤 순조·헌종·고종 등 역대 왕들이 화성행궁을 찾아 이곳에 머물렀다. 따라서 이 행궁은 조선시대에 건립된 수많은 행궁 중 그 규모나 능행면에서 단연 으뜸이 될 만큼 건축물의 규모뿐만 아니라 성곽과 더불어 정치적·군사적 면에서 큰 의미를 갖고 있다.

정조 때 최대의 역사였던 화성 성역은 1차적으로 화산의 현륭원 호위와 함께 팔달산 정상 바로 아래 성내 중심부에 건립된 행궁을 둘러싸면서 이를 수호하는 것을 주요 목적으로 설립되었다. 화성행궁은 성곽과 더불어 단순한 건축조형물이 아니라, 개혁적인 계몽군주 정조가 지향하던 왕권강화정책의 상징물로서 정치적·군사적인 큰 의미를 지닌다.

화성행궁은 처음부터 별도의 독립된 건물로 일시에 건축된 것이 아니라 행궁과 수원부 신읍치의 관아건물을 확장·증축하는 가운데 조성되었다. 정조 14년

간행된 『수원신읍영건공해간수성책』에 의하면 수원 신읍치에 건립된 건물은 크게 공해와 객사, 향교 및 군영으로 구분된다. 먼저 공해에는 장남헌壯南軒을 비롯하여 득중정得中亭 · 은약헌隱若軒 · 내아內衙 · 비장청裨將廳과 정문인 진남루鎭南樓 등이 포함되어 있다. 객사는 원래 그 안에 전패殿牌를 봉안하고 한달에 두 차례씩 왕께 배례하며, 때로는 손님을 모시는 곳으로 수원 신읍치의 객사에는 벽대청과 동서헌東西軒 등이 있었다. 향교는 성전聖殿을 중심으로 전사청典祀廳과 동 · 서무, 동 · 서재東西齋가 마련되어 있었다. 끝으로 편의상 군영과 기타 건물로 구분된 건물로는 강무당을 비롯하여 군기대청 · 군향고대청 · 초관청哨官廳 등이다. 당시 군영 건물은 장용영이 성립된 초기였던 만큼, 정조 17년 신읍치에 장용외영이 설치되고, 정조 19년과 정조 22년 군영의 일대 개편에 따라 그 건물도 늘어난 지휘자와 병력수에 따라 그 수용을 위한 신 · 증축을 거듭했을 것으로 추측된다. 화성행궁은 화성축조가 완공되는 것과 때를 같이하여 576칸 규모의 웅장한 건물이 되었다. 행궁은 평상시에는 외관인 수원부사(뒤에 유수)가 집무하는 지방행정의 관아로 사용하다가 왕의 원행시에는 왕의 거처로 이용되었다. 정조 13년에서 24년까지 왕의 현륭원 차배가 정례화된 화성행궁은 특히 서울 경복궁景福宮 다음의 부궁이라 할 정도로 다른 지방의 행궁보다 그 규모나 건축구조 · 기능면에서 단연 뛰어나고 웅장하게 건축된 것이 특징이다.

두 번째. 화성

화성 제암교회와 수촌교회

제암교회: 경기도 화성시 향남읍 제암리 16 / **수촌교회**: 경기도 화성시 장안면 수촌리 674

서해안고속도로 발안IC를 빠져 나와 발안IC삼거리에서 좌회전하여 괄안천을 따라 700 m 정도 직진, 제암리로 들어서면 사적 제299호로 지정된 3·1운동 관

화성 제암교회

제암교회 3·1운동순국기념탑

련 유적지가 나타난다. 이곳은 3·1운동 당시 가장 격렬한 시위운동이 일어난 곳이며 일제에 의해 집단학살이 행해진 비극적 장소이다. 1919년 4월 15일, 일본 육군중위 아리타 도시오 有田俊夫가 이끄는 일본군이 제암리에 들이닥쳐 주민들을 제암교회에 몰아넣고 방화와 함께 무차별 사격을 가해 23명이 희생되었던 것이다. 당시 스코필드 Frank W. Scofield, 석호필를 비롯한 선교사들에 의해 이 만행이 전세계로 알려졌다. 현재 이곳에는 제암교회, 합장묘역, 제암리3·1운동순국기념관, 3·1운동순국기념탑 등이 있다. 제암교회는 1905년 감리교인 안종후의 사랑채에서 시작되었다. 처음 예배당은 제암리학살 사건 당시 불타 없어졌으나 1938년 기와집 예배당으로 다시 지었다. 1970년 일본 기독교계와 양심적 사회단체 등이 보내온 1천만 엔의 성금으로 새로 건축했으나 2001년 정부가 이 일대를 순국유적지로 지정하면서 지금의 현대식 건물로 다시 지었다. 옛 초가 예배당과 일본인의 성금으로 지어진 옛 건물은 순국기념관 전시관에 마련된 모형으로 볼 수 있다. 제암교회 뒤편 언덕에 있는 묘역은 제암리 학살 사건 당시 학살된 23인의 유해가 발굴됨으로써 1982년 합장묘역으로 조성된 것이다. 2001년 정부는 제암교회 자리에 교회와 함께 3·1운동순국기념관을 세워 이 일대를 공원형태의 성역으로 조성하였다. 순국기념관 제1전시관은 제암리에서 일어난 3·1운동의 역사적 자료를 총 10가지 주제로 나누어 전시하고 있으며 제2전시관은 경기도와 전국의 3·1운동에 관한 자료를 8가지 주제로 나누어 전시하고 있다.

제암리 옆 마을인 수촌리에서도 3·1운동 당시 격렬한 만세운동이 일어났고 일제는 이 마을의 가옥에 불을 질렀고 이때 수촌교회도 전소되었다. 수촌교회는 1905년 김응태의 주도로 정창하의 집에서 7명이 예배를 본 것을 시작으로 1907년 초가 15칸을 매입하여 예배당으로 사용하였다. 1922년 선교사의 도움으로 초가 8칸을 건립하여 예배당으로 사용하였고, 1932년 수촌리의 현재 위치로 이전하였다. 현재 교회로 사용하는 건물은 1965년 미국인의 후원으로 건립된 것이며, 그 옆에 1986년 화성시 향토유적 제9호로 지정된 원래의 초가 교회가 있다. 초가 교회는 1974년 지붕을 양식 기와로 개량하였다가 1987년 원래의 초가 형태로 복원하였다.

세번째. 용인

소래교회

 경기도 용인시 양지면 제일리 산 41-11

영동고속도로 양지 톨게이트를 빠져 나와 북동쪽 방향으로 1 km 정도 가면 총신대학교 양지 캠퍼스가 나오고, 교문 안으로 들어서면 좌측에 있는 기숙사동 뒤쪽 나지막한 언덕 위에 복원된 소래교회가 보인다. 원래 소래교회는 선교사들이 들어오기 이전인 1883년 5월 서상륜徐相崙, 서경조徐景祚 형제에 의해 황해도 장연군 대구면 솔래松川里에 세워진 한국 최초의 자생교회이다. 처음에는 초가였지만 1895년과 1896년 두 차례에 걸쳐 증축하여 총 16칸 32평의 기와집 교회로

소래교회

되었다. 소래교회는 한국 개신교 초기 역사에서 두드러진 역할을 했다. 언더우드가 본격적인 선교 활동을 시작했을 때 처음 세례를 받은 사람은 대부분 소래교회 신자였고 장로교 최초의 조직교회인 새문안교회가 세워졌을 때 주축이 된 것도 소래교회 출신들이었다. 한국에 새로 오는 선교사들은 소래교회에서 한국의 전통과 선교 방법을 익혔다. 북한에 공산정권이 들어선 후 교회 신자들이 대거 월남하면서 문을 닫게 되었는데 1988년 황해노회가 중심이 되어 총신대 구내에 지금의 모습으로 복원하였다. 복원된 소래교회는 1896년 증축된 예배당의 모습으로서 팔작지붕을 지닌 'ㄱ'자 형태의 한옥이다. 교회 마당에는 '예수천당'으로 유명한 최권능崔權能 목사의 기념비, 소래교회의 설립자인 서상륜의 기념비, 그리고 한국교회의 선각자인 이수정李樹廷의 기념비가 세워져 있다.

한국기독교순교자기념관

 경기도 용인시 양지면 추계리 산 84-1

영동고속도로 양지IC를 빠져나와 양지IC사거리에서 이천방향으로 좌회전, 42번 국도를 따라 3 km 정도 직진, 선일자동냉장 앞 신호등에서 추계리마을 방향으로 좌회전하여 2 km 정도 직진하면 한국기독교순교자기념관이 나온다. 총신대 양지캠퍼스 뒤쪽으로 1 km 정도 떨어진 야산에 위치해 있다. 기념관 입구 가까이에 있는 500 m 정도의 길을 따라가면 순교자들의 이름과 성경구절을 새겨 놓은 자연석들이 늘어서 있는 것을 볼 수 있다. 기념관은 1989년 한국기독교100주년기념사업회가 한국 교회 순교자들의 신앙과 정신을 기리고 한국기독교백주년을 기념하여 개관한 것이다. 기념관(건평 336평)은 3층 건물로 전체적으로 직사각형이며 가운데 원통형의 공간이 있고 각 층이 나선형 계단으로 연결되어 있다. 1층 로비와 계단에는 한국교회사를 한 눈에 볼 수 있는 역사화 40여 점이 전시되어 있다. 2층에는 회의실과 예배실이 있으며 예배실에는 초기 한국교회와 사회상을 담은 사진 120여점이 전시되어 있다. 3층에는 순교자들의 존영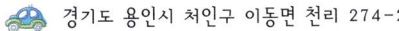과 유품이 전시되어 있다. 한국교회사학계에 의하면 한국 기독교 순교자는 2,600여 명에 달하는데 이중 600여 명의 순교자 명단이 이 기념관에 헌정되어 있다.

용인 성공회 성당(대한성공회용인교회)

경기도 용인시 처인구 이동면 천리 274-2

성공회 용인성당은 아담한 한옥으로 지어진 단층 건물이다. 1908년 성공회 수원교회가 용인을 경기 남부 지역의 선교 거점으로 설정했고 1937년 현재의 터에 천리교회라는 이름의 성당을 건축하였다. 이 성당이 세워진 자리에는 원래 한천서원(1865년 대원군에 의해 철폐)이 있었는데 이 건물을 매입하여 교회로 삼은 것이다. 그러나 상주하는 성직자가 없어 교회는 평신도 중심으로 운영되었다. 1940년 이후 1980년까지 40여 년간 박안토니오(수덕) 신도가 회장을 맡았고, 그 이후 1992년까지는 이베드로(남산) 신도 회장이 교회의 명맥을 유지하였다. 1992년 수원교회의 배려로 성직자가 처음 부임하여 상주하여 오늘에 이르고 있다. 최근에는 옛 성당건물을 마당에 둔 채 새 건물을 건축하여 예배를 드리고 있다.

네번째. 안산

안산 샘골교회와 최용신기념관

 경기도 안산시 상록구 본오3동 879-4

　서울에서 4호선 오이도행 전철을 타고 상록수역에서 내려 남서쪽으로 500 m 정도 가면 상록수공원을 만난다. 최근 안산시는 상록수역에서 상록수공원에 이르는 길을 최용신崔容信의 삶을 이야기 형태로 한 테마거리로 조성하였기 때문에 이 길을 따라가면 어느 새 공원에 도달한다. 신도시 개발로 인해 현재 아파트촌으로 둘러싸인 이 작은 공원 안에는 일제시대의 농촌계몽가로 널리 알려진 최용신의 생애를 기억하게 하는 몇가지 기념물이 잘 보존되어 있다. 그의 농촌활동의 기반 역할을 한 샘골교회(천곡교회)와 샘골강습소터(천곡학원), 최용신기념관과 그의 묘역, 샘골강습소의 주춧돌 15개와 건축 당시 심었던 향나무 몇 그루, 그리고 심훈문학기념비와 표석 등이 눈에 띈다. 1907년 홍원삼, 홍순호 형제에 의해 사리교회라는 이름으로 시작된 샘골교회는 오랫동안 천곡교회로 불리다가 최근 샘골교회로 다시 이름을 바꾸었다. 현재의 건물은 여러 차례 증축을 거듭하였기 때문에 초기 교회의 흔적을 찾아보기 힘들다. 교회를 마주 보고 있는 최용신기념관은 2007년 최용신의 생애를 기리기 위해 연면적 545.5 m^{2}에 지하1층, 지상1층의 한옥 형태로 신축한 건물이다. 지하층에는 전시실과 영상실이 있고 지상층에는 교육실과 사무실이 있다. 전시실에는 옛날 샘골강습소의 풍경을 재현한 디오라마, 당시 사용하던 교가 악보와 국어 교재, 심훈의 『상록수』 초판본 등과 생존한 제자의 인터뷰 등을 담은 영상물이 구비되어 있다.
　최용신은 함경도 원산에 위치한 루씨여자보통학교와 루씨여자고등보통학교를 마치고 여자협성신학교(현재 감리교신학대학교)에 다니다가 1931년 조선여자기독교청년회연합회YWCA에 의해 농촌계몽가로 샘골로 파견되었다. 그는 처음에는 샘골교회 건물을 빌려 가르쳤지만 늘어나는 학생들로 인해 공간이 비좁아지자 1933년 마을 사람들과 YWCA의 지원으로 샘골강습소(천곡학원)를 신축

최용신기념관

하였다. 1934년 새로운 지식을 배우기 위해 일본 고베여자신학교神戶女子神學敎로 유학을 가서 공부하였지만 건강이 좋지 않아 귀국하였다가 다음 해 수원도립병원에서 장중첩증으로 사망하였다. 그의 유언에 따라 학교의 종소리가 들리는 부근(일리 공동묘지, 현 일동 818번지 일원)에 묻혔다가 현재의 묘역으로 이장되었다. 1995년 정부는 그의 공훈을 기려 건국훈장 애족장을 추서하였다. 향토유적 18호로 지정된 그의 무덤 옆에는 약혼자였던 김학준金學俊의 묘가 나란히 있다.

다섯 번째. 이천

이천중앙교회와 구연영전도사순국추모비

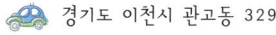 경기도 이천시 관고동 329-4

경기도립의료원인 이천병원에서 경충대로를 따라 이천경찰서 방향으로 500m 정도 직진하면 오른쪽에 위용을 자랑하는 교회가 보인다. 2006년 현대식으로 신

축한 이천중앙교회이다. 이 교회는 1902년 8월 13일 문경호 전도사에 의해 창전리 153번지(구 읍사무소 자리)에서 시작된 유서 깊은 교회이지만 1914년 이천읍 중리 현위치로 이전, 6.25전쟁 당시 폭격과 유엔한국재건단의 지원에 의한 신축, 1986년 재건축을 거쳐 2006년 현재의 모습으로 바뀌었다. 따라서 현재의 교회 건물은 유적지로서 가치는 없지만 교회 앞 주차장 옆에 세워진 비석에서 이 교회의 역사를 읽을 수 있다. 1979년 제작된 구연영具然英 구정서具禎書 전도사 부자父子 순국추모비가 그것이다.

   1864년 서울에서 출생한 구연영은 1895년 1,000명의 의병으로 이천창의소를 조직하였으며 1896년 1월 넓고개에서 일본군 수비대와 첫 전투를 벌여 대승을 거두었다. 그후 이현전투와 남한산성 전투를 비롯한 의병투쟁을 앞장서서 지휘하던 그는 1897년 2월 스크랜턴 선교사를 찾아가 기독교인이 되었다. 그는 상동교회 전덕기全德基 목사가 이끄는 엡윗청년운동에 적극 참여하여 민족운동에 힘쓰다가 1905년 이천읍교회(현 이천중앙교회) 3대 담임전도사로 부임하였다. 구연영은 이천읍 교회를 비롯한 9개 교회 교인을 돌보았는데 칼 대신 성경을 들고 십자가의 구원을 외치며 이천, 광주, 장호원, 여주지방을 순회하였고, 자신의 집 앞에다 장대 끝에 십자가를 매달아 세워놓고 예배를 드리면서 의병활동과 선교활동, 애국계몽활동을 병행하였다. 일본 측으로부터 주목을 받아 오던 중 일진회의 밀고로 아들 정서와 함께 체포되었다. 구연영 부자는 함께 당시의 관아 서편 작은 언덕(창전동 365번지)에서 총살당하였다. 정부에서는 1963년 구연영 전도사에게 건국공로훈장 단장을 추서하였으며 아들 정서에게는 1991년 건국공로훈장 애국장이 추서되었다. 교회에서 조금 떨어진 창전동 개나리공원에는 구연영, 구정서 부자 순국기념비가

구연영·구정서 전도사 순국추모비

세워져 있는데 2007년 8월 구연영 의사 순국 100주년 추모행사 추진위원회가 그들이 순국한 곳에 설치한 것이다.

이천한국기독교역사박물관

경기도 이천시 대월면 초지리 474-2

경기도 이천IC에서 남쪽으로 빠져나와 대월면사무소를 지나 초지리에 이르면 노인요양원인 한나원 옆에 3층 벽돌건물 한국기독교역사박물관이 보인다. 이 기독교역사박물관은 2001년 11월 한영제 장로가 사재를 털어 개관한 사립박물관으로서 10만 여점의 기독교역사 관련 자료를 갖추고 있다. 한영제 장로는 50여 년 간 기독교 출판 및 서점을 운영하면서 모은 방대한 자료를 한국교회와 공유하기 위해 역사박물관을 세웠다고 한다. 소장 자료는 초기기독교 잡지와 갖가지 희귀한 출판간행물이 주류를 이루고 있다. 박물관에는 5개의 상설전시장이 있어 역사의 전개에 따라 기독교의 변천사를 한 눈에 알아보게 하고 있다. 소장 자료에 비해 공간이 협소해 주제별로 특별 기획전시를 열기도 한다. 박물관 한쪽에는 평양장대현교회를 1/5크기로 축소한 모형을 전시하고 있는데 이는 평양대부흥운동의 실상을 직접 체험할 수 있는 체험학습의 장으로 활용되고 있다.

여섯 번째. 기타

김포제일교회

 경기도 김포시 북변동 264

김포제일교회는 김포 최초의 교회이다. 1894년 3월 김포 걸포리 304번지 유공심의 집에서 창립예배를 드렸다. 그후 두 차례 예배장소를 옮기다 1905년 4월 언더우드 선교사가 인쇄기를 팔아 교회대지 3,500평을 기증하여, 현 위치에 700원의 헌금으로 33평 예배당을 건축했다. 그후 몇 차례의 증축 과정을 거쳤기 때문에 초기 교회의 원형은 찾아볼 수 없다. 그렇지만 이 교회는 새문안교회가 설립한 10개 교회 중 하나로서 언더우드가 초대 당회장으로 재직하였다. 현재 언더우드 선교사의 친필 당회록(1912년)을 보관하고 있다.

고양감리교회

 경기도 고양시 덕양구 고양동 51-1

고양감리교회는 미국 남감리교회에서 세운 한국 최초의 교회이다. 이 지역은 예로부터 한성과 개성을 잇는 교통의 요지로서 근처에 벽제관터가 남아 있다. 옛 교회 건물은 사라져 그 흔적조차 찾아볼 수 없지만 교회 한쪽에 '고양교회 100주년기념비'가 남감리회 최초의 교회임을 증거하고 있다. 1897년 5월 2일 남감리회의 첫 선교사인 리드C.F. Reid가 이곳에서 어른 24명과 아이 3명에게 세례를 주었고 속장과 유사有司도 1명씩 임명하였다. 이 교회의 탄생 과정에는 리드 선교사만이 아니라 토착 전도인과 윤치호尹致昊의 역할이 지대하였다. 리드는 미감리회 선교사 스크랜턴으로부터 상동교회 출신 김주현金周鉉과 김흥순金興順을 소개받아 매서인으로 채용하였는데 이들이 고양, 벽제 지역에서 1여 년간 책을 팔며 전도한 결과 세례 후보자들이 생겨난 것이다. 윤치호는 새로 형성된 교회가 건물이 없어 어려움을 겪는 것을 보고 건물과 부지 구입 비용으로 사비 30원을 제공하였다. 김주현의 전도로 개종을 한 후 개성 지방에서 '맹인 전도자'로 이름을 날린 백사겸도 이 교회 출신이다.

가나안농군학교

 경기도 하남시 풍산동 산 52-2

가나안농군학교는 1962년 김용기金容基에 의해 설립된 농민교육기관이다.

1909년 경기도 양주에서 태어난 김용기는 광동廣東학교를 졸업하고 기독교 정신에 입각한 농촌운동을 전개하였다. 그는 일제하에서 봉안奉安교회 및 이상촌 건설운동을 통한 민족운동을 전개하였으며 해방후에도 여러 곳에 교회와 농장을 건설하는 방식으로 기독교 농촌운동을 지속적으로 전개하였다. 경기도 삼각산 농장, 에덴농장, 가나안농장 등이 대표적이다. 보다 체계적인 농민지도자 교육을 위해 1962년 현재의 위치에 제1가나안농군학교를 설립하였고, 1973년에는 강원도 원주에 제2가나안농군학교를 세웠다. 김용기의 농민운동은 1970년대 정부 주도로 추진된 '새마을운동'에도 깊은 영향을 미친 것으로 평가되고 있다.

CHAPTER 3

강원 지역

철원 → 원주 → 춘천 → 기타

❋ 강원도 기독교 역사

    강원도 지역의 선교는 초기에는 미북장로회, 캐나다장로회, 미감리회 등이 진출하였으나 여러 차례에 걸친 선교지 협정으로 미감리회와 남감리회의 관할 구역으로 최종 확정되었다. 1909년 당시 미감리회는 원주, 횡성, 평창, 영월, 정선, 강릉, 삼척, 울진, 평해 등을 관할하고, 남감리회는 춘천, 철원, 양구, 이천, 지경대 등을 맡았다.

    1888년 8월 미감리회 소속 아펜젤러 목사와 존스 목사가 지역 순방을 위해 처음 강원도 땅을 밟았지만 강원도 선교 사업에 제일 먼저 착수한 사람은 하디Robert A. Hardie, 하리영 선교사였다. 캐나다장로회 소속이었던 하디 선교사는 1898년 5월 남감리회 선교부로 이적하여 원산에 거주하면서 강원도 지역을 다니며 전도활동을 하였다. 그는 1901년 3월 강원도 김화군 지경터에서 장년 15명에게 세례를 주었는데 이것이 강원도 최초의 교회인 지경터교회의 시작이다. 하디가 강원도 지역을 선교할 당시 매서인 겸 전도인 역할을 한 사람은 1896년 리드C.F. Reid 선교사에게서 세례를 받은 윤성근이다. 지경터교회는 초기에는 침체되었으나 1903년 원산부흥운동을 계기로 활성화되었다.

강원 지역

철원제일교회 터

1908년 춘천 스테이션이 설치되어 무스 선교사Rev. and Mrs. J.R. Moose 부부가 파송되었다. 그해 9월 송도에서 열린 제12회 선교연회에서 지방회가 처음으로 서울-송도, 원산, 춘천으로 분할되었다. 1909년 10월 미감리회 서울본부는 북장로회로부터 원주 지역을 이관받자 즉시 데밍 Charles S. Deming, 도이명을 파송하여 지방 전체를 답사하게 하였다. 1910년에는 노블W.A. Noble, 1911년에는 레퍼트R.R. Reppert, 유부수를 파송하여 원주, 강릉 지역을 수시로 순회하도록 하였다. 1912년 원주읍과 강릉읍 두 모교회에 권신일 전도사와 이동식 목사를 각각 다송하였다. 같은 해 목사 박원백을 원주 및 강릉 겸임 감리사로 임명하였다. 1920년 7월 철원 스테이션이 설치되고 앤더슨 부부Dr. and Mrs. E.W. Anderson와 코델리아 어윈Cordelia Erwin, 어윈이 파송되었다.

첫번째. 철원

❋ 철원 소개

강원도 북서부에 위치한 철원은 내륙지방이면서도 고도가 높아 기온차가 큰 대륙성 기후를 띠고 있으며 바람받이 지역이 형성되어 지형성 강우가 야기되기도 한다. 동북방은 1,000 m 내외의 고봉으로 연결되어 있고 중부와 서남방은 언덕과 평야를 이루어 곡창지대로 널리 알려져 있다. 이 지역은 고구려 시대에는 철원 또는 모을동비라고 불렸으나 통일신라 경순왕 시대에 철성鐵城으로 개칭되었다. 901년 궁예가 풍천원(현 철원군 북면 홍원리)에 도읍을 정하고 국호를 마진摩震으로 하여 (911년 태봉으로 개칭) 18년간 통치하였다. 918년 궁예를 몰아내고 고려를 세운 왕건王建은 옛 지명을 계승한다는 의미에서 철원으로 개칭하였으나 다음해 개성으로 도읍을 옮기면서 다시 동주東州로 개명하였다. 조선시대에는 도호부를 두었고 한말과 일제시대에 몇차례 행정구역 개편이 있었다. 해방 직후 남북분단으로 철원군 전역이 공산치하에 들어갔으나 6.25전쟁시 국군의 북진에 따라 일부 지역이 남한 땅으로 편입되었다.

❋ 철원 기독교 전래

철원지역에는 1900년대 접어들어 교회가 세워지기 시작하였다. 1901년 지경터교회와 새술막교회가 연이어 세워졌다. 선교사가 거주하기 이전에는 원산 지역의 여선교사 쿠퍼Sallie K. Cooper, 거포계가 왕래하며 여성 신자들을 관리하였다. 철원지역의 여성 기독교인들은 1918년 6월 25일부터 7월 2일까지 거최된 제1회 남감리회 전도부인대회에 참석한 이후 철원에 여선교회를 조직하였다. 이 전도대회 이후 철원지역에는 여성 신입교인이 130명으로 증가하였으며 10명이 세례를 받고 사경회 1년 과정을 35명이 이수하였다. 그리고 15개의 여선교회가 조직되었다.

철원지역의 선교활동이 본 궤도에 오른 것은 1920년부터이다. 이 해 5월 철원지방에서는 최초로 붉은 벽돌 건물로 철원읍교회가 낙성되었으며, 7월에 선교사 주재소가 신설되고 의료선교사 앤더슨E.W. Anderson 부부와 여선교사 어윈Cordelia Erwin이 상주하게 되었다. 1930년 기독교조선감리회가 조직된 이후 철원지역에서는 사회복지 사업이 활성화되었다. 세브란스를 졸업하고 동경의 성누가병원에서 공중보건 관련 훈련을 받은 간호사들이 유아진료소, 어머니교실, 가정방문간호사업, 기타 공중보건사업을 추진하였다. 1938년경 철원복지관의 유아위탁양육 사례는 제조유를 통한 유아건강사업의 효과를 잘 보여주고 있다. 생후 1년 반이 되었는데도 몸무게가 9파운드밖에 나가지 않는 아기를 어머니의 동의하에 철원복지관이 맡아서 1개월간 우유로 양육한 결과 몸무게가 2배로 늘었다. 이처럼 철원은 강원 북부 지역의 선교거점으로서 중요한 역할을 담당했다.

✳ 철원지역 기독교 유적지

철원제일교회터

🚗 강원도 철원군 철원읍 관전리 100-2

철원읍에서 87번 도로를 타고 3 km 가량 북진, 월하삼거리에서 다시 좌회전하여 1 km 정도 지나면 오른쪽에 폐허가 된 철원제일교회터가 보인다. 6.25전쟁 당시 폭격으로 전면 출입구, 벽과 바닥 일부의 잔해만 남은 이 교회는 원래 지상 3층 지하 1층의 웅장한 석조건물이었다. 철원제일교회는 1905년 웰번Arthur G. Welbon, 오월번 선교사에 의해 장로교회로 시작되었지만 선교지 분할 협정에 의해 1907년 감리교회로 되었다. 1920년 붉은 벽돌로 지은 교회당을 1937년 재건축하였는데 당시 유명한 설계사인 보리스W. M. Voris가 설계를 담당하여 1년여 만에 완공하였다. 가로 24 m, 세로 12.2 m로 현무암과 화강암을 쌓아 만든 이 건물의 1층은 소예배실(교육관)과 10개의 분반공부방, 2층은 대예배실로 사용하였다. 총 공사비 27,200원 중에서 선교부가 15,850원을 보조하였다. 이 교회는 공산 치하에서 기독청년들의 반공 투쟁 거점으로 사용되었지만, 6.25 당시에는 북한군의 병동으로 사용되고 교회 지하실에서는 양민 학살이 행해졌다. 전쟁 당시 북한 병력이 숨어 있다고 하여 미 연합군의 폭격을 받았다. 2002년 근대문화유산 국가지정문화재 23호로 지정되었다. 최근 일본 오사카예술대학 박물관에서 보리스의 설계도면이 발견되었으며 2008년 범 감리교단 차원에서 복원기공예배를 드렸다.

장흥교회와 서기훈목사순교기념비

🚗 강원도 철원군 동송읍 장흥리 577-1

장흥교회는 철원제일교회를 모태로 하는데 교회 왼편에 서기훈목사순교기념비가 있다. 서기훈 목사는 1925년 목사 안수를 받고, 주로 동부연회 원산 지방과 철원 비장에서 목회자로 사역했다. 6.25 전쟁 당시 장흥교회 담임목사로 있던 서기훈 목사는 반공활동의 전위대인 대한청년단의 고문으로도 활동했다. 당시 장흥교회 청년들이 퇴각하는 인민군을 사살한 것에 대한 책임으로 인민군 대열 정치 보위에 수감되었다. 1951년 1월 8일 인민군의 총에 의해 70세로 순교했는데 그의 비문에는 유언이 이렇게 쓰여 있다. "죽을 때를 당하여 죽는 것은 참 죽음이 아니요 살면서 생을 구하는 것은 참 생이 아니다 死於當死 非當死 生而求生 不是生". 교회 뒤편 동산으로 올라가면 6.25전쟁 때 순교한 자들을 기리는 충혼탑이 서 있는데 여기에는 사연이 있다. 탑을 건축한 이들은 전쟁 당시 이 마을에서 공산당원 활동에 앞장섰던 이들의 후손이었다. 그들은 사죄하는 뜻에서 탑을 세웠지만, 공산당의 일에 앞장섰던 자신들의 할아버지와 아버지의 이름도 새겨 넣었다. 제막식 당일에 이 사실을 알게 된 마을 사람들이 그들의 이름이 새겨진 부분만 떼어내고 비문 명단을 고쳤다고 한다.

지경교회터와 새술막교회터

자경교회터: 강원도 철원군 갈말읍 지경리 / **새술막교회터**: 강원도 철원군 김화읍 학사리 274

현재 지경장로교회가 있는 곳에서 50미터 인근에 감리교회인 지경터교회가 있었던 것으로 추정된다. 지경터교회는 원산으로 파송받은 남감리회의 하디R.A. Hardie 선교사가 1901년 철원지역에 세운 최초의 감리교회이다. 1903년 지경터 지방회가 조직되어 산하에 철원구역, 금화구역, 회양구역, 안변구역을 가지고 있었으며, 1908년 춘천지방과 원산동지방, 원산서지방이 생겨 감리교회가 부흥했다. 1912년에는 지경터지방회가 강원 서지방으로 바뀌어 철원지역이 춘천과 함께 강원도의 선교 거점으로 자리 잡기 시작했다. 1956년 아무 것도 남겨져 있지 않은 이곳에 군 선교차원에서 군목 파송제 형태로 장로교회를 세워 현재에 이르고 있다.

지경장로교회에서 10리 정도 떨어진 곳에는 현재 김화교회가 자리잡고 있다. 김화교회의 전신은 김화읍교회이고 김화읍교회의 전신이 새술막교회이다. 새술막교회는 지경터교회와 거의 비슷한 시기에 하디에 의해서 설립되었는데 현재는 그 지역이 논바닥으로 변해 정확한 위치를 찾을 수 없다.

대한수도원

 강원도 철원군 갈말읍 군탄리 706-7

대한수도원은 남한의 최북단 한탄강변 순담계곡에 자리잡고 있다. 일제 강점기인 1938년 10월 장흥교회 박경룡 목사를 주축으로 한 항일 비밀기도모임이 모태가 돼 '조선기도원'이란 이름으로 설립되었다. 초대 원장은 일본에서 귀국한 유재헌 목사였고 1946년 원산중앙교회 전도사로 있던 전진이 2대 원장으로 취임하였으며, 1973년부터는 최조영 목사가 맡고 있다. 이 수도원의 특징은 흰 저고리에 검은 치마를 입은 제단지기 여성들이 집회에 참여한 일반 교인들 앞에서 정기적으로 '성령춤'을 추는 것이다. 이 춤은 전진 전도사가 일제하 루씨신학교 교수였던 백남주白南柱가 운영하던 원산신학산에서 배운 것이며, 백남주의 제자였던 김백문金百文이 이스라엘수도원에서 성탄절 축하행사의 하나로 행한 것이라고 한다. 현재 대한수도원은 초교파적으로 운영되고 있으며 가장 오래된 건물은 소성전이다.

두번째. 원주

❋ 원주 기독교 전래

원주에 처음 기독교가 들어온 것은 1905년 무렵이다. 1905년 4월 15일 미국 남감리교회 무스 J. Robert Moose, 무아각 선교사가 상동리(현 일산동)에서 4칸 반의 초가에서 처음 교회를 시작하였다. 원주읍교회로 출발한 지금의 원주제일교회는 장의원, 한치선, 김봉규, 안인혁 등 5,6명의 교인이 열심히 전도하면서 점차 확장되었다. 무스 선교사는 미 캐롤라이나주에서 출생하였고, 6세때

부모를 잃고 고아로 자랐으며, 1892년에 트리니티 전문학교를 졸업하고 목사가 되었다. 1899년 9월 내한하여 주로 서울과 개성에서 사역을 하였으며, 1908년부터는 강원도 중남부를 순회전도하다가 아예 춘천에 머물면서 많은 사역을 하였다. 무스 선교사에 이어 1897년 한국에 온 콜리어 Charles T. Collyer, 고영복 선교사가 1907년부터 순회전도사로서 교회를 이어받았으며, 김용덕 목사는 원주읍교회가 배출한 첫 번째 목회자이다.

원주 기독교 유적지

원주제일교회와 원주기독병원(서미감병원)

강원도 원주시 일산동 114번지

원주제일교회의 마당에는 해외선교사의 기념비 두 개가 세워져 있다. 하나는 모리스Charles D. Morris, 모리시 선교사의 기념비이고 다른 하나는 레어드Esther J. Laird, 라애시덕 선교사 기념비이다. 조그마한 흰 돌로 되어 있는 모리스 선교사 기념비는 한국에서 26년간 선교사역을 하다가 1927년 1월 18일에 소천한 모리스의 공덕을 기리기 위해 1928년에 세워졌다. 1900년 드루신학교를 졸업한 모리스는 그해 목사 안수를 받고 1901년 미국 감리교 해외선교부 파송을 받아 내한하였다. 1903년 루이스O. Louis와 결혼하고 평양에 거주하면서 영변, 해주 지역까지 순회전도 활동을 하였다. 1916년 원주 선교부로 전임되어 원주와 강릉에서 주로 선교하였다. 1926년 11월 강원도 동해안 일대의 전도여행길에 건강이 악화되어 1927년 1월 18일 세브란스 병원에서 사망하였다. 모리스 선교사의 부인 루이스는 남편의 죽음 이후에도 강릉유치원 등을 운영하며 강릉과 원주 지역에서 교육과 전도사업을 계속하였다. 1928년 7월 15일 원주제일교회(당시 원주읍교회)는 모리스 선교사의 죽음을 기념하여 기념비를 세웠다.

레어드는 1926년 미감리회 여선교사로 내한하여 원주에서 전도 및 교육활동을 하였다. 그녀는 모리스 부인과 함께 1931년 원주기독여자관을 세웠으며 여자 야학, 유치원, 부녀자 생활 개선 등에 힘썼다. 일제 말엽 선교사 철수령에 의해 귀국하였다가 해방 후 다시 내한하여 원주에서 결핵요양원, 소녀 클럽, 재봉소 운영 등 여러 사회사업 활동을 하였다. 6.25전쟁으로 잠시 귀국하였다가 다시 내한하였으며 1953년부터는 대전으로 선교지역을 옮겨 대전사회관과 대전 결핵요양원을 건립하여 운영하였다. 1983년 11월 27일 추수감사주일에 레어드 선교사를 기억하는 많은 사람들이 뜻을 모아 원주제일교회에 기념비를 세웠다.

원주제일교회로부터 약 100 m 떨어진 곳에 자리잡고 있는 원주기독병원의 모체는 서미감병원이다. 1913년 의료선교사 앤더슨A.G. Anderson 선교사 내외가 일산동 116번지에 120평 규모의 붉은 벽돌 건물 2층 병원을 시공하여 17병상의 현대식 병원을 개원하였다. 이 병원의 총 투자액은 6,600달러로 기금의 대부분은 미국 감리회 선교부에서 출연하였으며 그 중 일부를 스웨덴 감리교회에서 기부하였으므로 병원의 이름을 "스웨든 감리병원"The Swedish Methodist Hospital으로 불렀다. 한자로는 스웨덴의 '서', 미국의 '미', 감리교회의 '감'을 따 '서미감瑞美監' 병원으로 표기하였다. 그러나 1933년 선교부 사정으로 문을 닫았다. 그후 미감리회 선교부가 병원복원 계획을 추진하던 중 캐나다연합교회와 공동으로 1959년 종합병원을 건립하였는데 이 병원이 현재의 원주기독병원이다. 1976년

서미감병원 소속 의료선교사 숙소 건물

부터는 연세대학교 의과대학 부속 원주기독병원으로 합병되어 지금에 이르고 있다.

서미감병원 건물은 6.25전쟁 당시 소실되었다. 현재 기독병원 본관 뒤에 붉은 벽돌로 된 양옥집이 있는데 이 건물은 서미감병원과 거의 같은 시기에 건립되고 건물 형태도 거의 같은 모양을 하고 있다. 당시에 이 건물은 의료선교사들의 거처로 사용되었는데 현재는 연세대 의대 동문회 사무실로 쓰이고 있다. 이 건물은 의료선교의 본거지로 활용되었을 뿐만 아니라 서미감병원을 연상시키는 건물 외양, 그리고 당시 건물 양식을 알아 볼 수 있는 건축문화 자료로 활용될 수 있다. 서미감병원과 함께 강원도 최초의 서구식 건물로 추정되는 이 건물의 건평은 약 200 m²이며 붉은 색 벽돌면에 유리창을 지니고 있다.

세번째. 춘천

✱ 춘천 소개

한반도의 중심부에 위치한 춘천은 산과 강으로 둘러싸인 아름다운 도시이다. 전면적의 76% 이상이 산악지대에 속하며 평지가 극소한 관계로 도처에 산수가 수려하며 명산인 삼악산, 등선폭포, 구성폭포등 자연경관이 뛰어나다. 이중환의 「택리지擇里志」에는 우리나라에서 사람 살기에 가장 좋은 곳으로 평양 외성 다음으로 춘천을 꼽고 있을 정도이다. 금강산에서 발원한 북한강이 화천을 거쳐 춘천에 이르고 오대산에서 발원한 소양강은 인제를 거쳐 춘천에서 북한강과 합류한다. 시내 한 가운데로는 제법 넓은 공지천이 흐른다. 해방 후 북한강과 소양강에 집중적인 댐 건설이 이루어져 1965년 춘천댐, 1967년 의암댐, 1973년 소양댐이 건설되면서 춘천호, 의암호, 소양호 등 인공호수가 생겼고 그때부터 춘천은 '호반의 도시'로 불리게 되었다.

춘천은 고대 부족국가인 맥국貊國의 수도로 알려져 있지만 행정구역의 단위로 처음 등장하는 것은 삼국시대이다. 삼국시대 초기에는 고구려의 영토였지만 신라 영토로 편입된 이후 선덕여왕 6년 (637년) 우수주牛首州 혹은 우두주牛頭州가 설치되어 군주軍主가 통치하였다. 통일신라시대에는 수약주首若州, 삭주朔州, 광해주光海州 등의 이름으로 계속 변천하였다. 고려를 세운 왕건은 개국공신 신숭겸申崇謙를 배출한 이 지역의 위상을 높여 태조 23년(940) 춘주春州로 개칭하였다. 조선 태종 3년 (1403) 현재의 이름인 춘천春川이 등장하고 행정구역상 춘천군으로 편제되었다. 고종 25년(1888)

유수부留守府로 승격되면서 경기에 예속되었고, 당시 춘천유수 민두호閔斗鎬가 왕명으로 현재 봉의산 아래 강원도청 자리에 이궁離宮을 건축하였다. 이는 조정이 위급할 때 피난처로 삼기 위한 것이었다. 1896년 13도제로 행정구역이 개편될 때 다시 춘천군으로 편제되었다. 해방 이후 1949년 지방자치법이 시행됨에 따라 춘천시로 개편되어 현재에 이르고 있다.

기독교의 복음이 들어오기 이전 춘천에는 전통적 종교문화인 유교와 불교가 공존하고 있었다. 봉의산 동편 산기슭에 자리잡은 춘천향교는 유교의 상징이다. 일제에 의해 국권이 침탈되던 19세기 말 20세기 초, 의암毅菴 유인석柳麟錫을 중심으로 하는 유생 의병들은 춘천향교를 거점으로 의병항쟁에 나섰다. 조선조의 숭유억불 정책에 의해 불교는 약화되어 있었지만 청평산의 청평사는 19세기 말까지 '221간' 건물을 보유할 정도로 상당한 기반을 지니고 있었다. 개항 이후에는 동학의 2세교주 최시형이 관의 탄압을 피해 강원도 산악지역으로 피신하면서 춘천지역에도 동학교도가 생겨났고 3·1운동 시기에는 천도교가 춘천지역의 만세운동을 주도하였다. 일제의 침략과 더불어 일본불교의 사찰과 일본의 고유종교인 신도神道의 신사神社도 건립되었다.

✼ 춘천 기독교 전래

1897년 12월 8일 미국 남감리회 한국선교부 제1차 연회가 강원도 선교를 결정하면서 춘천지역 기독교의 역사가 시작되었다. 1898년 4월 서울교회(현 광희문교회)의 교인이었던 나봉식羅奉植과 정동렬이 춘천지역에 파송되어 선교활동이 시작되었으며 퇴송골(현 퇴계동 남춘천파출소 자리)이 첫 예배를 드린 장소로 알려져 있다. 1901년 4월 무스J. Robert Moose 선교사가 춘천 퇴송골에 첫 속회를 조직한 이후 춘천지역의 교세는 매년 성장하였다. 1905년에서 1907년 사이에 교세가 급속도로 성장하였다. 2년 사이에 학습인 수가 30배 이상 증가하였고 세례인은 약 5배, 예배처는 약 10배 증가하였다. 이러한 교세증가를 반영하여 춘천의 위상은 점차 높아지기 시작하였다. 1904년 남감리회는 춘천을 서울구역에서 분리하여 독자적인 '춘천구역circuit'으로 설정하였고, 1908년에는 남감리회 한국지방회가 셋으로 분리될 때 춘천지역을 하나의 독자적 '지방회district'로 독립시켰다. 이러한 과정에서 선교부지가 마련되었다. 1907년말 무스 선교사는 전도인 이덕수의 도움을 받아 춘천 중심부, 조선시대 강원도 관찰부와 춘천부가 있던 아동리衙洞里와 대판리大板里 일대 3만5천여 평을 확보했다. 이 선교부지에는 병원, 학교, 예배당, 선교사 사택이 점차적으로 들어섰다. 병원 건물이 완공되자 1908년 9월 무스 선교사는 춘천지방회 감리사의 자격으로 가족과 함께 이주하여 복음 전파에 힘썼다. 무스 선교사의 부인은 여러 여성 모임과 기도회를 만들어 4명의 전도부인들과 함께 복음을 전파하였다. 1909년 춘천지방은 춘천구역과 양구구역으로 분화되고 1910년에는 홍천구역이 추가되었으며, 1912년에는 가평, 인제, 화천 구역이 춘천지방회에 포함되었다.

✱ 춘천 기독교 유적지

춘천중앙교회

🚗 강원도 춘천시 퇴계동 202번지

　1898년 나봉식과 정동렬이 춘천에서 선교를 시작하고 교인들이 퇴송골(현 퇴송동 남춘천파출소 자리)에서 첫 예배를 드리면서 춘천중앙교회의 역사가 시작되었다. 1902년 경기도에서 사역을 하던 이덕수 전도사가 아동리(현 봉의동)에 다섯 칸짜리 초가를 마련하여 예배를 드렸으며 그해 10월에 대관리(현 조양동)로 확장, 이전하였다. 1925년 여선교사 마이어스Mamie D. Myers, 마의시는 미국 남감리회의 주선으로 허문리(현재 강원일보 건너편 자리인 요선동)에 'ㄱ'자 모양의 2층 선교관을 세웠다. 1층은 유치원, 2층은 요리강습소, 성경공부실, 양재 교육실 등으로 이용하고 밤에는 야학 교실을 열었다. 이 건물은 춘천 최초의 근대식 건물로 남자와 여자의 자리가 엄격하게 분리되어 있었는데 6.25전쟁으로 파괴되어 현재는 사진으로만 볼 수 있다.

　춘천중앙교회는 1955년 미 감리회 선교부 병원으로 사용되던 벽돌건물(옥천동 소재)을 인수하여 본당으로 사용하였다. 1971년 아폴로 우주선 모양으로 설계된 254평의 현대식 건물을 그 옆에 세워 본당으로 사용하고 벽돌건물은 교육관으로 사용하였다. 붉은 벽돌로 된 이 건물은 춘천중앙교회의 가장 오래된 건물로서 오래 동안 교육관으로 사용하다가 교회 이전시에 춘천시에 매각하였다. 춘천시는 교회측의 간곡한 부탁을 받아들여 이 건물을 훼손하지 않고 현재 시립미술관(옥천동 73-2)으로 사용하고 있다. 춘천중앙교회는 1982년 쥬디 기념관, 1987년 오월기도원을 각각 준공하였다. 1998년 '교회창립 100주년 기념성전'을 짓기 시작하여 2001년 현재의 퇴계동 소재 건물로 이전하였다.

네번째. 기타

홍천한서교회, 남궁억기념관, 무궁화동산

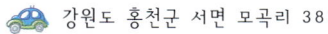 강원도 홍천군 서면 모곡리 387

　홍천군 서면에 있는 한서교회 진입로에 들어서면 오른편에 한서교회, 왼편에 한서 남궁억 기념관, 중앙에 새로 복원된 예배당, 그리고 교회 앞엔 80여 종의 무궁화를 2,000여 그루를 심어 놓은 '무궁화동산'이 조성되어 있다. 이러한 유적지는 모두 한서 남궁억 翰西 南宮檍 선생에 의해 세워지거나 관련된 것이다. 문화관광부는 독립운동가이자 교육자이며, 황성신문을 창간하고 무궁화보급운동을 전개한 남궁억 선생을 2000년 1월의 문화인물로 선정하였다.

　한서교회의 원래 명칭은 동네 명칭을 딴 모곡교회였는데 남궁억 선생의 호를 따서 한서교회로 바꾸었다. 한서교회 앞에는 신축 당시 없었던 종탑이 높게 서 있다. 남궁 선생의 정신을 받들었던 어느 교인의 신앙유산을 기린 유자녀들이 기증한 것이라고 한다.

　교회 부근 무궁화동산은 한서 선생이 일제에 맞서 무궁화 묘목 30단 그루를 심어 전국에 퍼뜨리기 위해 만든 무궁화 묘목장이다. 한서 선생은 '을사조약'이 체결되자 무궁화를 통한 애국심의 함양과 여권의 신장에 온 힘을 기울였다. 이 때문에 그는 교단을 떠나야했고 모곡리 고향 마을에 교회를 짓고 주일학교를 시작하였다. 학교 뒤뜰에 무궁화 밭을 일구어 7만이나 되는 많은 무궁화 묘목을 길러서 몰래 나눠 주었으며, 무궁화 노래를 지어 널리 퍼뜨려 민족정신을 일깨웠다. 홍천읍 연봉리에는 남궁억 선생의 무궁화보급 운동을 기념하기 위해 별도로 '무궁화공원'이 조성되어 있다.

　교회 앞에는 남궁억 선생 기념관이 서 있다. 2004년 6월 29일 충의문화유적 관광벨트 조성사업으로 건립된 것이다. 기념관에는 무궁화십자가당사건 취조장면, 보리올 모곡학교 모형, 남궁억 선생의 붓글씨와 저서, 무궁화십자가당사건 재판기록(20권), 독립신문 영인본, 황성신문 영인본, 무궁화 자수지도 등이 전시

남궁억기념관

되어 있으며 그가 작사한 노래 중 10여곡을 청취할 수 있는 코너도 있다.

　남궁억 선생 기념관 옆에는 말끔히 복원된 옛 모곡교회당 건물이 있다. 1933년 11월 '무궁화사건'으로 일제에 의하여 강제로 뜯겨 폐교된 것을 옛 모습 그대로 복원한 것이다. 이 건물 안에는 당시의 모습을 재현하기 위해 강대상을 비롯하여 다양한 유물이 전시되어 있는데, 특히 가운데 흰 천을 중심으로 남녀가 따로 앉아 예배를 드리던 모습을 인형으로 재현하고 있다.

　남궁억 선생은 "죽거든 무덤을 만들지 말고 과수나무 밑에 심어 거름이 되게 하라"라고 유언했지만 후손들은 무덤을 만들었다. 한서교회 뒤쪽에 있는 한서초등학교(홍천군 서면 모곡리 492-1)의 정문을 끼고 왼편으로 돌면 무덤이 나온다. 선생의 묘에는 둥글게 호석이 둘러져 있고 봉분 앞에는 제사음식을 올려놓을 수 있는 상석이 있다. 상석의 오른쪽에는 '정삼품통정대부칠곡부사'라고 표기된 묘비가 있고 그 앞쪽으로 망주석 1쌍이 배치되어 있으며 묘역의 입구에는 돌계단이 마련되어 있다. 300여개의 돌계단을 올라가면 선생이 매일 새벽기도를 하던 유리봉 정상이 나오는데 거기에는 기도하는 자세로 조각된 남궁억 선생의 기념동상이 있다. 이 묘역은 1977년 홍천군에서 조성한 것으로서 강원도기념물 제77호로 지정되어 있다.

동해 최인규권사 순교기념비와 천곡교회

 강원도 동해시 천곡동 1081-8

동해시 시청 로터리에서 천곡로를 따라 500 m 정도 서진하면 천곡아파트 부근에 천곡교회가 나온다. 천곡교회는 신사참배를 거부하고 순교한 최인규의 모교회로 교회 입구에 순교기념비가 건립되어 있다. 감리교 권사 최인규는 1881년 11월 5일 북평읍 송정리에서 태어나 1921년부터 북평교회에 출석하며 신앙생활을 하였다. 1933년 전 재산을 천곡교회에 헌납하고 복음 전파에 힘쓰다 일제 말 신사참배 거부로 검속되었다. 대전형무소에서 옥고를 치르던 그는 1942년 63세로 순교하였다. 그의 구속으로 교회 건물은 폐쇄되고 교인들은 흩어졌다. 해방 후인 1946년 3월 강릉지방 삼척구역 7개 교회가 삼척제일교회 교정에 그의 유

최인규권사 순교기념비

해를 안장하는 동시에 순교기념비를 세웠다. 1950년 교인들이 샘실(현 동해시청 앞)에 '최인규 기념예배당'을 마련하였지만 도시 계획으로 사라졌다. 1982년 현 위치에 천곡교회가 들어선 뒤 1986년 최인규권사순교기념비를 세웠는데 이 때 삼척제일교회에 안장되어 있던 유해를 옮겨와 기념비 밑에 안장했다. 순교비는 최인규 권사가 사용하던 강대상을 본따 만들었는데 상하 2단으로 되어 있다. 전면에 십자가 문양이 새겨져 있고 좌우면과 후면에는 그의 순교를 기리는 내용과 성경 구절 등이 새겨져 있다.

화진포 선교사휴양지

🚗 강원도 등해시 고성군 거진읍 봉평리

화진포 이승만 별장

화진포는 빼어난 자연경관으로 유명하다. 호수 옆에 돌로 지은 이기붕 별장이 있는데 이 건물은 원래 1920년대 영국 선교사들이 지어 사용하던 것이다. 6·25전쟁 이전에는 북한군의 간부 휴양소로 사용되다가 휴전 이후 이기붕의 부인 박마리아가 개인 별장으로 사용하였다. 별장 옆에 고인돌이 있고 부근에 선교사들이 사용하던 미니 골프 시설이 있어 당시 선교사들의 일상을 엿보게 한다.

이기붕 별장의 맞은 편, 해안가 쪽으로는 '화진포의 성'이라 불리는 김일성 별장이 있다. 이 건물은 중일전쟁 당시 일본이 원산에 있던 외국인 휴양촌을 강제 이전시키면서 지은 것이라고 한다. 당시 독일인 건축가 베버Weber가 지은 것인데 1945년부터 북한이 귀빈휴양소로 활용하였다. 김일성 가족이 이곳에서 여름 휴가를 보내면서부터 '김일성 별장'으로 불렸다. 6.25전쟁 이후 원래의 건물이 훼손되어 1964년 재건축하였다. 1995년 개보수하여 장병휴양시설로 사용해 왔으며 1999년부터 현재와 같이 운영하고 있다.

호수가에는 이승만 별장이 있고 그보다 약간 높은 곳에 이승만기념관이 있다. 별장은 1956년에 지어졌는데 1960년 이승만 대통령의 하야 이후 철거되었다. 1999년 육군본부에서 현재의 위치에 복원하고 이승만 대통령의 역사적 자료와 유품을 전시하였다. 그가 사용하던 책상과 걸상, 성경, 배재학당 시절 및 한성감옥에서 찍은 사진, 미국 유학 당시의 자료 등이 보존되어 있다. 이승만기념관은 원래 별장 자리였는데 육군관사로 사용하다가 2007년 기념관으로 전환하였다. 시기별로 이승만의 약력이 전시되어 있다.

예수원

강원도 태백시 하사미동 산 7번지

예수원은 1965년 대천덕Reuben A Torrey III, 戴天德 신부의 주도하에 세워진 성공회 계통의 수도원이다. 1918년 중국 산동성에서 태어난 대천덕은 평양외국인학교, 중국 연경대학, 미국 프린스턴 대학 등지에서 공부하고 1946년 성공회 사제로 서품을 받았다. 그는 건축기사노조활동, 흑인해방운동과 같은 사회운동에 적극 참여하다 1957년 내한하여 성미가엘신학원(현 성공회대학교의 전신)을 재건하였다. 1965년 강원도 산골 현 위치에 예수원을 세우고 2002년 생애를 마칠 때까지 다양한 활동을 하였다. 예수원은 노동과 기도의 삶을 중시하는 신앙공동체로 영성 훈련, 생태 교육, 기술교육 등 다양한 프로그램을 전개하고 있다.

CHAPTER 4

충북지역

청주시 ➔ 진천·음성

✲ 충북 기독교의 시작

　초기 충북 선교는 미국 북감리회, 북장로회, 남감리회 등 모두 세 교단 선교부에 의해 시작되었다. 먼저 북감리회선교부가 한강 이남 선교를 계획한 것은 1892년이었다. 서울의 감리교 공동체가 어느 정도 자리를 잡게 되자 이제 그 선교사들은 수원과 공주 등 남부 지역으로 시야를 넓히기 시작했던 것이다. 그리고 감리교 전도인들의 발걸음이 경기도를 지나 충북 땅에 다달은 때는 대개 1901년 무렵이었다. 이천 덕들교회에서 세례를 받은 박해숙은 그 어간에 목천을 거쳐 진천과 충주, 청주 등지를 돌며 전도했다. 그 후 1903년 공주에 스테이션이 설치되면서 북감리회의 충청도 선교가 본격화되었다. 스웨어러Wilbur C. Swearer, 서원보와 샤프Robert A. Sharp 선교사는 그때부터 1909년까지 한국인 전도인들과 함께 청주, 보은, 영동, 진천, 충주 등지를 순행하며 이곳에 감리교의 공동체들을 조직하였다.
　북장로회선교부의 충북 선교는 그보다 먼저 충청도 선교에 나섰던 침례교 계통 엘라딩기념선교회가 1901년 인력과 재정난으로 일시 철수하자 그 공백을 메우는 차원에서 진행되었다. 이미 경기도 남부 지역에서 활동하고 있던 북장로회 선교사 밀러Frederick S. Miller, 민로아는 그때부터 자신의 선교 영역을 차령산맥 이남의 충청도까지 확장시켰다. 1905년 청주로 이주한 밀러는 그 후 보

충북지역

일신여고 포사이드 기념관

은, 괴산, 영동, 조치원, 옥산 등지를 두루 순회하며 신앙공동체의 조직에 나섰다. 장로교 전도인들의 활동은 멀리 충주까지 이어졌다.

충북 제천지역은 원래 남감리회 춘천구역에 포함되어 있었다. 그러니까 남감리회도 초기 충북 선교의 일원으로 보아야 할 것이다. 하지만 1907년 강원도에 대한 남감리회와 북장로회의 선교지역 분할협상에서 제천은 북장로회의 선교 구역으로 조정되었고, 그 2년 후인 1909년 다시 북감리회의 영역으로 재구획된 사연을 갖고 있다.

20세기 초 충북지역에 대한 북감리회와 북장로회의 공격적인 선교는 당연히 선교 지역 중복이라는 문제를 야기시켰다. 한 도시에 감리교회와 장로교회가 나란히 세워졌다. 이른바 선교 혼재 상황이 빚어진 것이다. 그러자 북감리회와 북장로회의 선교사들은 이를 타개하기 위해 1908년부터 충북에 대한 선교지역 분할협상을 시작하였다. 처음에는 서로의 협상안을 가지고 제안과 역제안으로 맞서며 쉽게 합의에 도달하지 못했다. 양 교단의 본국 선교 스탭들은 이 문제들을 둘러싸고 미국의 뉴욕에서도 협상을 진행하였다. 결국 1909년 9월 두 선교부는 충청북도를 반으로 나누어 진천, 음성, 충주, 제천, 청풍, 영춘, 단양, 괴산 등 북부지역은 북감리회가 맡고, 연풍, 청주, 문의, 영동,

회인, 청산, 보은, 옥천, 황간 등 충북 남부 지역은 북장로회가 담당하는 것으로 협상을 매듭지었다. 이때 많은 수의 교회들이 각기 자신의 교파적 정체성을 감리교에서 장로교로(충북 남부의 경우), 또는 장로교에서 감리교로(충북 북부의 경우) 바꾸게 되었다. 그리고 1909년의 협정으로 형성된 충북의 기독교 지형은 1936년 선교지 경계가 철폐될 때 까지 거의 변함없이 지속되었다.

첫번째. 청주

✽ 청주 소개

마한의 옛 땅인 청주는 백제 때에는 상당현으로 불렸다. 그 뒤에 한 때 고구려의 영역이기도 하였지만 신라 진평왕 때 신라 땅으로 확정되었다. 통일신라 경덕왕 때에는 서원경으로 이름을 바꾸었다가 고려시대부터 청주라고 부르기 시작했다. 조선 세조 때 도호부가 설치되었고, 선조가 청주목으로 승격시켜 2군 9현을 관할하게 하였다. 1896년(고종 33) 지방제도가 개정되면서 전국을 13개도로 개편함에 따라 충청도가 남북으로 분리되어 우선 충주에 관찰사가 배치되었다. 조선시대에는 수운이 발달한 충주가 교통의 요지로 부각되었기 때문이다. 하지만 1905년의 경부선 철도 개통은 이러한 관계를 역전시켰다. 1908년 충북도청이 청주로 옮겨오게 된 것이다. 그 후 청주는 충북 행정의 중심지가 되었고, 1920년 충북선 철도의 개설과 이후의 연장 증설(1923년 증평, 1928년 충주)로 청주는 더욱 빠르게 발전할 수 있었다. 1931년에는 청주면이 청주읍으로 승격되었고, 1946년에는 청주부로, 그리고 1949년부터는 청주시가 되었다. 1983년에는 청원군 강서면, 낭성면 등의 3개리, 1987년에는 청원군 북일면 주중리 등 14개리를 편입시켜 그 영역을 크게 확장했다. 청주시가 커감에 따라 1995년 청주 중심부를 흐르고 있는 무심천을 경계로 서쪽의 상당구와 동쪽의 흥덕구 등 2개구를 신설하였다.

청주시가지 동쪽에 위치한 우암산은 소가 누운 모습과 비슷하다 하여 와우산臥牛山이라 불리는 청주의 진산鎭山이다. 해발 353.2 m의 우암산 정상에 오르면 청주시가지가 한 눈에 들어오는데, 1904년 조성을 시작한 북장로회의 청주 스테이션 유적지 역시 이 산의 남쪽 끝자락에 위치해 있다. 우암산은 상당산성에 이르는 동서의 능선에 토성土城의 흔적이 뚜렷이 남아있고 계곡마다 사찰을 품고 있어 경주의 남산처럼 불교유적의 보고寶庫로 불리기도 한다. 토정 이지함이 천하의 명당이라 예견한 우복동牛腹洞 전설을 간직한 우암산은 침엽수와 활엽수가 울창하여 등산로와 산책로로 손색이 없다. 또 산자락에 청주향교, 국립청주박물관, 청주대학교, 3·1공원을 품고 있기도 하다.

청주의 젖줄 무심천은 청주를 동(상당구)과 서(흥덕구)로 나누며 남에서 북으로 흐르고 있다. 청원군 낭성면 추정리에서 발원하여 미호천에 이르는 지방 하천으로 물줄기가 80여리에 이른다. 우암산과 함께 청주의 거의 모든 학교 교가校歌마다에 들어가 있는 청주의 상징 무심천은 선사시대로부터 삶의 터전을 이루어 문화를 꽃 피워 온 청주 역사문화의 뿌리이다. 물줄기를 따라 양 옆으로 남석교를 비롯 용화사 석불군, 정북토성 등 중요 유적들이 줄지어 있으며, 흥덕사에서 찍어낸 금속활자본 '직지'와도 깊은 연관이 있다. 또 청주의 관문인 진입로 가로수길은 경부고속도로 인터체인지에서 시내 입구까지 6km에 걸쳐 플라타너스 터널로서 청주를 찾는 이들에게 싱그러움을 안겨준다. 1950년대부터 조성되기 시작한 가로수길은 1,500여 그루의 나무들이 4열로 늘어서 있어 계절마다 다른 분위기를 자아내고 있다. 가로수길은 현재 8차선 확장공사가 진행 중에 있다.

✲ 청주 기독교 전래

청주에는 20세기 초 복음이 전래되었다. 먼저 경기도 이천에서 예수를 믿은 감리교 전도인 박해숙의 순회 전도가 있었고, 북감리회 선교사 스웨어러Wilbur C. Swearer, 서원보 역시 청주를 방문하여 공주 스테이션과 연결된 이곳의 감리교공동체와 접촉한 바 있다. 장로교 역시 비슷한 시기에 청주에 들어왔다. 1901년 설립된 것으로 추정되는 신대교회(청주시 흥덕구 신대동)는 당시 청원군 강서면 신대리에 살던 오천보, 문성심, 오삼근 등이 1902년 1월 개최된 경기도 죽산군 둔병리 사경회에 참석한 이후 지속적인 성장이 이루어졌다.

그 후 본격적인 청주 선교는 북장로회 선교사 밀러Frederick S. Miller, 민로아가 주도하였다. 1901년 9월 북장로회선교부로부터 충청도 선교책임자로 임명받은 밀러는 한국인 전도인 김흥경과 함께 청주를 돌며 전도하였다. 곧 청주의 지역유지와 젊은이들이 예수를 믿기 시작하였다. 그들은 김원배, 방흥근, 이영준, 김재호, 이범준 등이었다. 밀러는 이들을 중심으로 1904년 남문밖에 초가집 한 채를 마련하여 청주읍교회(현 청주제일교회)를 시작하였다. 또한 교회와 함께 방흥근의 집에서 청남학교도 시작하였다. 초기 청주 기독교인들의 이러한 행적은 19세기말 20세기초 한강 이남 기독교의 초기 전파 과정에서 흔히 관찰되는, 지역사회 내부에서 기독교 수용을 주도하는 인사들의 전형적인 모습이다. 즉 구체제에 대한 미련은 없으면서, 어느 정도의 경제력과 교양을 갖추어 지역민들의 신망을 받는 한편, 유교적 공동체의 기능이 파괴된 향촌사회의 정신적·도덕적 긍백 상태를 기독교의 교회와 새로운 학교 환경을 통해 개선하려는 의지를 갖고 있던 사람들이었다. 그들은 성리학주의 대신에 이른바 "문명개화론"을 받아들여 자신이 속한 지역사회에 교회와 학교의 설립을 병행하고 있었다. 당연히 그들은 자신들이 세운 교회와 학교의 유력한 후원자들이었다.

1901년 밀러를 충청도에 파송한 북장로회선교부는, 다시 1903년 청주에 스테이션을 설치하기로 결정하였다. 이것은 청주를 중심으로 충북 선교에 주력하겠다는 북장로회의 의지를 드러낸 것이기도 하다. 그 후 1904년 가을 탑동 청주 스테이션 부지 매입이 시작되었고 이듬해에는 밀러가 가족들과 함께 청주로 이주하였다. 밀러는 스테이션 조성 공사에 박차를 가하는 한편 후임 선교사들과 힘을 합하여 전도와 교육 그리고 의료 사업 중심의 유기적인 선교 활동을 벌여 나갔다. 밀러 이후 청주에 부임한 선교사들로는 우선 1907년 가을에 온 카긴Edwin H. Kagin, 계군이 있고 그 다음 1908년 임지에 도착한 의사 퍼비안스Walter C. Purviance, 부반서 부부와 쿡Welling T. Cook, 국유치 부부 그리고 여선교사 도리스Anna S. Doriss, 도신녀가 있다. 이듬해인 1909년에는 여선교사 데이비스Grace L. Davis와 로간J. V. Logan부인도 청주 선교에 가세하였다. 이로써 청주 스테이션의 진용이 어느 정도 갖추어졌다. 이후 청주에서 활동한 대표적인 선교사로는 솔타우Theodore S. Soltau, 소열도, 퍼디Jason G. Purdy, 부례선, 로위Dewitt S. Lowe, 노두의 등이 있다.

✳ 청주 기독교 유적지

일신여고 구내 청주 스테이션 유적지

🚗 충북 청주시 상당구 탑동 185-1번지

　1904년 10월 밀러 선교사의 한국인 대리인이었던 김흥경에 의해 매입이 시작된 청주 탑동 스테이션 부지는 그 후 15차례에 걸쳐 확산되었다. 그곳은 청주읍성에서 약 1/3마일 떨어진 우암산 자락 남쪽 언덕으로, 도성都城을 조망할 수 있는 위치였다. 근처의 풍광이 수려했음은 물론이다. 당시 선교사들은 자신들의 안전과 쾌적한 환경을 위하여 한국인들이 밀집해 살고 있는 읍성邑城에서 조금 떨어진 곳의 구릉지를 넓게 확보하고자 했는데, 청주 역시 예외가 아니었다.

　1905년 청주로 이주한 밀러는 잠시 초가집을 거쳐 그 해 여름 선교 구내에 두 채의 기와집을 지어 자신의 임시거처로 삼았다. 서양식 주택을 건축하기 위한

일신여고 선교사 묘지 동산

예비 행동이었다. 지방에 내려온 선교사들의 주거 방식은, 우선 전래 한옥을 매입·개조해서 살다가 그 후 한양절충韓洋折衷의 건물을 짓게 되는데, 청주 스테이션 역시 그러한 전형을 보인다.

그리고 밀러가 시카고의 포사이드H. M. Forsyth의 기부금으로 1906년 여름 완공한 건물이 바로 '포사이드기념관'(제4호 양관, 충북유형문화재 133-4호)이다. 청주에 지어진 최초의 서양식 주택으로 짐작되는 이 건물은, 일신여고(충북 청주시 상당구 탑동 185-1번지) 본관을 지나 학교 중앙 언덕에 자리하고 있다. 적갈색 벽돌과 한식기와를 사용한 전형적인 한양절충식의 반지하 단층으로, 청주읍성을 가장 잘 조망할 수 있는 곳에 위치해 있었다. 포사이드기념관은 완공이 임박했던 1906년 여름 청주의 큰 물난리로 인해 언덕 위의 선교 구내로 대피한 수재민 200여 명에게 숙식을 제공한 선교사들의 구호활동은 그 후 청주사람들에게 좋은 인상을 남겼다.

포사이드기념관 앞에는 모두 3개의 묘비와 1개의 기념비가 나란히 서 있는 묘지 동산이 있다. 그 작은 동산의 맨 왼쪽에 있는 묘비가 바로 청주 선교의 개척자 밀러의 것이고, 그 다음에는 퍼디Jason G. Purdy, 부례선 선교사의 무덤이 있다. 1923년 청주에 부임한 퍼디는 보은, 옥천, 영동 등 충북 남부 지방을 중심으로 활동하다가 1926년 황간에서 전염병에 걸려 순직하였다. 당시 그의 나이 29세였다. 세 번째의 작은 묘비는 1918년부터 1937년까지 20년 간 충북 선고에 헌신한 솔타우Theodore S. Soltau, 소열도 선교사의 아들 데오도라Theodora G. Soltau의 것이다. 그 아이는 1922년 두 살의 나이로 청주에서 사망했다. 본래 이 무덤들은 금천동 앞산에 있었으나 1984년 충북노회가 한국 기독교 선교 100주년을 맞이하여 현재의 위치로 옮겼다. 맨 오른쪽의 '민노아 부례선 선교사 기념비'는 그때 함께 세운 것이다.

1908년 미국의 북장로회 선교본부는 청주 스테이션에 병원과 두 개의 주택을 더 짓도록 하였다. 계속 선교사들이 늘어나는데다가 의료선교사 퍼비안스Walter C. Purviance, 부반서의 진료활동을 위한 병원시설이 필요했기 때문이다. 그리하여 1911년에 '던컨기념관'(제6호 양관/소민병원, 충북유형문화재 133-6호)과 '로

일신여고 던컨기념관

위기념관'(제5호 양관/노두의기념관, 충북유형문화재 133-5호) 그리고 '밀러기념관'(제3호 양관/민노아기념관, 충북유형문화재 133-3호)이 새로 지어졌다. 일신여고 본관 뒤편에 있는 던컨기념관은 1908년 던컨J. P. Duncan 부인이 보낸 기부금으로 1911년 세워진, 한식기와지붕에 지하 1층 지상 2층 붉은 벽돌의 병원 건물이었다. 일신여고 정문에 들어서서 정면에 보이는 로위기념관은 1910년 캔자스주 매클렁J. S. McClung의 지원으로 건축된 성경학원 건물이었으나 얼마 지나지 않아 선교사들의 주택으로 사용되었다. 이 집에서 가장 오래 산 사람은 1929년부터 1959년까지 활동한 로위DeWitt S. Lowe, 노두의 선교사였다. 그와 동시에 건축된 밀러기념관은 포사이드기념관 뒤에 자리하고 있는데, 화강석 석재의 기초부에, 적갈색 조적조組積造: 벽돌 등을 쌓아 올려서 벽을 만드는 건축 구조의 벽체부, 한식기와를 얹은 지하 1층 지상 2층의 건물이라는 점에서 로위기념관과 유사하다. 다만 밀러기념관은 들보가 7개인데 비해 로위기념관은 5개이다.

청주 스테이션 자리에 남아 있는 나머지 두 채의 건물은 1930년대에 지어진 '솔타우기념관'(제1호 양관/소열도선교사기념관, 충북유형문화재 133-1호)과 '퍼디기념관'(제2호 양관/부례선목사기념성경학교, 충북유형문화재 133-2호)이

퍼디기념관

다. 일신여고를 벗어나 뒤편 주택가에 자리한 솔타우기념관은 1930년경에 건축된 것으로 보이는데, 한식기와를 사용했지만 다른 건물들과는 달리 전형적인 미국식 주택이라는 특징을 갖고 있다. 역시 이 집에서 오래 거주하며 활동한 이는 솔타우Theodore S. Soltau, 소열도 선교사였다. 또 일신여고 뒤쪽 길건너에 있는 퍼디기념관은 영동 지역에서 활동하다가 장티프스로 순직한 선교사 퍼디Jason G. Purdy, 부례선를 기리기 위하여 미국의 가족들과 지인들 또 미국 전역의 주일학생들이 보낸 성금으로 1932년 지은, 지하 1층 지상 3층의 함석지붕 성경학원 건물이다.

청주제일교회

충북 청주시 상당구 남문로 1가 154번지

청주 스테이션의 직할교회였던 청주제일교회(1935년까지는 청주읍교회로 불림)는 1904년 남문밖의 한 초가집에서 시작되었다. 그 후 청주제일교회는 청주영장관사淸州營將官舍 터에 1백석 규모의 한옥기와집을 지었고, 1913년에는 그 자리에 다시 목조예배당을 세웠다. 현재 청주제일교회가 사용하고 있는 2층 규

청주제일교회

모의 서양식 고딕형 벽돌예배당은 1939년 처음 건축된 후 다시 1951년 증축된 것으로, 첨탑 지붕의 중앙 종탑 좌우로 출입구를 냈으며 외부에서 바로 2층 예배실로 올라 갈 수 있도록 계단을 설치했다. 예배당 2층 전면 중앙에는 예서체로 "淸州第一敎會禮拜堂"이라 새긴 돌판을 부착했다.

청주제일교회 마당의 '창립100주년기념비'(1904~2004) 옆에는 청주에서 가장 오래된 한글 비석으로 알려진 '로간부인긔렴비'가 있다. 1921년 세워진 이 비석은 1919년 사망한 여선교사 로간Mary L. Logan을 기념해서 건립된 것이다. 로간 부인은 1856년 9월 17일 미국 켄터키주에서 태어났다. 남편은 미국 남장로회 대학이었던 켄터키센트럴대학 학장이었으며, 로간 부인도 센트럴대학 YMCA와 YWCA를 지도하였다. 남장로회 선교사로 목포와 광주에서 활동했던 유진 벨Eugene Bell, 배유지이 바로 그녀의 지도를 받은 학생이었다. 그런 이유로 해외 선교에 관심을 갖던 중, 1908년 남편이 죽자 한국선교를 자원하여 1909년 3월 내한하였다. 그 때 나이 53세였다. 선교부의 봉급을 받지 않는 '자비량선교사'로서 로간 부인은 그 후 10년 동안 청주지역 여성 선교를 전담하였다. 탑동에 있던 그녀의 방문 앞에는 적게는 열 켤레, 많을 때는 마흔 켤레 이상의 짚신이 놓여 있었다고 한다. 청주의 여성 교인들에게 로간 부인은 언제나 찾아가 만날 수 있는 '자애로운 어머니'였던 것이다. 지금 청주에는 로간 부인이 살던 집(로위기념관)이 남아 있고, 서울 양화진(제2묘역 가-6)에 그 무덤이 있다.

신대교회

충북 청주시 신대동 426번지

　미호천변 뚝방길을 달려 조용한 농촌마을 신대동에 들어서서 신대교회쪽으로 가다보면 먼저 '기독교전래기념비'가 눈에 들어온다. 1985년 한국기독교선교100주년기념사업회 충청북도협의회가 충북에 기독교가 전래된 것을 기념하여 세운 것이다. 그 뒷면에는 1901년 신대리교인들이 첫 교회를 설립한 내력과 이곳에서 복음이 충북 전체로 퍼져 나간 역사가 새겨져 있다.

　1970년대에 건축된 붉은 벽돌 예배당의 신대교회 마당에는 '李春成傳道婦人功德碑'(이춘성 전도부인 공덕비)와 '吳乙錫長老追念碑'(오을석 장로 추념비)가 나란히 서있다. 이춘성은 신대교회 설립자였던 오천보의 부인으로 교회 부흥의 선두에 섰을 뿐만 아니라 충청도 전역을 무대로 복음을 전했던 전설적인 전도부인이었다. 1945년 10월 장로가 된 오을석은 해방 후의 혼란기에 교회를 지켜 교인들의 존경을 받았다.

이춘성 전도부인 공덕비와 오을석 장로 추념비

대한성공회 청주수동교회

대한성공회 청주수동교회

🚗 충북 청주시 상당구 수동 202번지

　원래 성공회 충청도 선교의 중심은 진천이었다. 성공회 선교사들은 1907년 진천에 스테이션을 설치하고 음성, 충주, 청주, 천안, 병천 등지로 그 세를 확장시켜 나갔다. 그런데 1920년 청주의 도시화가 진행되면서 성공회 지도부는 충북 선교의 거점을 진천에서 청주로 옮길 것을 결정한다. 그리하여 1935년 9월 완공된 '청주 수동교회 성당'(충북유형문화재 149호)은 청주를 한 눈에 내려다 볼 수 있는 우암산 서편 언덕에 자리하게 되었다. 구내에 신학교 시설까지 갖춘 새로운 스테이션이었다. 건축비는 영국 버밍햄의 성그레고리교회 St. Gregory Church 교인들의 지원이 있었다. 이 건물은 전체적으로 한국 전통기와집의 형태이지만, 서양식의 개구부 開口部와 붉은 벽돌의 사용 그리고 주춧돌의 형태 등에서 근대적인 분위기를 느낄 수 있다. 성당 내부는 9개의 들보와 서까래가 그대로 노출된 천장이 주는 자연스러움이 돋보인다.

❋ 청주 일반 유적지

흥덕사지 및 고인쇄박물관

🚗 충북 청주시 상당구 수동 202번지

사적 제315호로 지정된 청주시 흥덕구 운천동 옛 연당리에 있는 흥덕사지興德寺址는 1985년에 운천지구택지개발사업중 많은 유물이 출토되어 공사를 중단하고 청주대학교 박물관에 의하여 발굴된 고사지古寺址이다.

사찰 창건 연대와 규모는 알 수 없으나, 현존하는 세계 최고의 금속활자본인 『백운화상 초록불조직지심체요절』하권에 고려 우왕 3년(1377)에 청주 흥덕사에서 금속활자로 책을 인쇄하였음을 명기하고 있는데, 이것은 독일의 구텐베르크 성경인쇄보다 70여 년이나 앞선 것으로 1972년 "세계 도서의 해"에 세계 최고의 금속활자본으로 인정된 것이다.

그동안 흥덕사의 정확한 위치를 확인할 수 없던 중 발굴조사 결과 출토된 청동금구와 청동 불발에 "흥덕사"라는 명문이 음각되어 있어 그 위치를 입증하게 되었다고 한다. 발굴결과 흥덕사는 신라 전통 양식인 단탑가람식으로 밝혀졌으며, 명와明瓦가 출토되어 신라 문성왕 11년(849)에 이미 이곳에 불사가 이루어지고 있었음을 시사하고 있다.

1987년부터 1991년까지 5개년에 걸쳐 12,400평의 부지위에 우리나라 인쇄문화의 발달과정을 살필 수 있는 고인쇄박물관과 정면 5칸, 측면 3칸 겹처마 팔작지붕의 금당과 3층석탑을 복원하고 1992년 3월 17일 개관하였다. 고서, 인쇄기구, 흥덕사 출토유물 등 총 1,100여점의 유물을 소장하고 있다.

망선루

🚗 충북 청주시 상당구 남문로2가 92-6

망선루望仙樓는 도지정 유형문화재 제110호로 본래 취경루聚景樓라 하였다. 고려시대에 관아의 부속 누정으로 창건되었다고 하나 정확한 건축 연대와 사용 용도는 알 수 없는, 청주에서 가장 오래된 건축물이다. 『신증동국여지승람』의 기록에 의하면, 고려 공민왕 10년(1361) 홍건족의 침입 때 왕이 안동으로 파천하였다가 그 해 11월 청주에서 수개월 피신하고, 난이 평정되자 기뻐하여 청주에서 문과와 감시를 행하고 합격자의 방을 이곳에 붙였다고 한다. 조선 세조 7년(1461)에 목사 이백상이 새로 중수하고 한명회가 편액을 고쳐서 망선루라 하였고 그 후 몇 차례 중수를 거듭했으며, 1922년 일제의 무덕전 신축으로 망선루가 헐리게 되자 청주청년회 회장이던 김태희를 중심으로 망선루 보존운동을 전개하여 1923년 제일교회(당시 청주읍교회)에 이건하였다. 이는 민간단체에 의한 최초의 시민운동이었다. 이전된 망선루는 청주지역 최초의 근대적 교육기관인 청남학교와 청산여학교, 상당유치원 등 민족교육운동과 한글강습, 각종 집회 및 강연장으로 활용되었고, 해방 후에는 세광중·고등학교가 이곳에서 탄생하는 등 육영의 장소로 많은 인재를 배출하였다. 근자에 망선루의 노후로 붕괴위험이 있어 원래의 자리에 옛 모습 그대로 복원하고자 하였으나 아쉽게 그 뜻을 이루지 못하고, 1999년 10월 이 건물을 해체하여 2000년 12월 청주시민이 가장 많이 이용하는 중앙공원으로 옮겨 세웠다.

망선루(望仙樓)

청주 중앙공원

충북 청주시 상당구 남문로2가

　청주 중앙공원은 천년 고도의 숨결이 고스란히 담겨 있는 곳으로 충청병마절도사영이 있던 옛 관아터로 청주역사의 산 증인이다. 철 당간과 동헌을 이웃하고 있는 이 공원에는 임진왜란 당시 청주성 탈환의 주역이었던 선봉장 조헌적장기적비와 척화비, 서원향약비, 의병장 한봉수 송공비 등 50여기의 비석들이 숲을 이루고 있어 비림공원碑林公園이라고도 한다. 그 외에도 고려말 충신들을 구해낸 전설이 서려 있는 수령 9백여 년을 자랑하는 압각수(도 기념물), 고려시대 관아 부속건물이던 망선루(도 유형문화재), 충청병마절도사영문(도 유형문화재) 등 문화재 5점이 있다.

　나뭇잎이 오리발처럼 생겨서 붙여진 압각수鴨脚樹 은행나무에는 다음과 같은 전설이 전해지고 있다. 고려말 공양왕 때 윤이와 이초가 이성계 일파를 없애기 위해 중국 명나라로 가서 이성계가 공양왕과 함께 명나라를 치려 한다고 거짓말을 하였다. 이 때문에 이색, 정지, 이승인, 권근 등이 청주옥에 갇히고 문초를 받자 갑자기 하늘에서 폭우가 쏟아져 성안에 홍수가 났다. 이때 근처에 나무가 있어 죄수들이 올라가 목숨을 건졌는데 그 나무가 바로 압각수이다. 원래 이 나무가 있는 곳은 청주 객사의 마당이었는데, 일제시대 충북도청이 이곳에 있다가 이전하면서 공원이 되었다.

　또한 충청도병마절도사영문은 충북 유형문화재 제15호로 이 건물은 청주읍성 앞에 있던 충청도 병마절도사영의 출입문이었다. 정면 3칸, 측면 2칸의 1층 가운데에 대문을 달아 출입을 하도록 하였다. 조선후기 병영의 출입문 형식을 잘 보여주는 건물로 지붕의 추녀곡선 등이 아주 정교하고 세련된 아름다운 전통 목조건축물의 진수를 보여주고 있다.

이 외에도 흥선대원군이 서양 세력이 침략하는 것을 경계하기 위해 고종 8년 (1871)에 서울을 비롯하여 전국 각지에 세운 척화비 중 하나가 남아 있다. 이 척화비는 버려져 석교동 하수도 뚜껑으로 쓰이던 것을 1976년에 지금의 자리로 옮겨 온 것이다.

청주 삼일공원

충북 청주시 상당구 수동 159-1

삼일공원은 청주 시내를 한눈에 내려다 볼 수 있는 우암산 기슭에 3.1운동 '민족대표' 33인중 충북 출신 손병희, 권동진, 권병덕, 신홍식, 신석구, 정춘수 등 6명의 동상을 세우고 조경과 편의시설을 새롭게 하여 1980년에 조성하였다. 그러나 그 가운데 정춘수는 3.1운동 후 변절하여 민족지도자로서의 품위를 잃어 1996년 2월 시민단체에 의해 동상이 철거되었다.

청주 삼일공원 내 민족대표 동상

두번째. 진천 · 음성

대한성공회 진천교회

 충북 진천군 교성리 63-9번지

  충북 진천군은 삼국시대에 고구려가 차지했을 때에는 금물노군이었다가 그 뒤 신라의 영토가 된 뒤에는 만노군으로 불렸다는 기록이 있다. 고려 초에는 강주, 그 후에는 진주라고 했고, 조선시대에 들어서 진천현이 되었다. 진천군에는 바로 이곳에서 태어난 신라 장수 김유신과 관련된 유적이 많다. 그의 위패를 모신 길상사가 있고, 그가 태어난 뒤에 태를 묻었다는 태령산도 있다. 또 김유신이 들어가 몸과 마음을 닦았다는 장수굴, 그의 덕을 기려 세웠다는 높이 7.5 m의 송덕 불상, 그의 아버지가 놓았다는 농다리가 그러하다.

  지난 1890년 한국 선교를 시작한 성공회의 선교사들이 서울 · 강화 · 수원을

대한성공회 진천교회

충북지역 115

거쳐 충청도에 당도한 것은 1907년 무렵이었다. 그 해 11월 성공회의 거니 Wilfred N. Gurney, 김우일 선교사는 진천군 북변면 상리(현 읍내리) 일대 3천여 평을 매입하고 곧바로 교회를 지어 1908년 2월 완공하였다. 뿐만 아니라 강화에 있던 의료선교사 로스Arthur F. Laws, 노인산가 1909년 2월 진천으로 와서 애인병원愛人病院을 짓고 진료를 시작한데 이어 휼렛George H. Hewlett, 유신덕 선교사도 신명학교信明學校를 출범시켰다. 진천 스테이션은 성공회의 충북지역 선교거점이었던 것이다. 현재 진천군 교성리에 있는 한옥교회(등록문화재 8호)는 1923년 건축된 교회당에 뿌리를 두고 있다. 거니 선교사가 지은 교회당이 1920년 소실되자 진천교회는 1923년 다시 붉은 벽돌에 단층 팔작 목조 기와로 된 전통 한옥의 교회 건물을 짓게 된다. 이 예배당은 1970년대 이건移建되면서 일부 훼손되기도 하였지만, 진천교회(충북 진천군 교성리 63-9번지)가 현재의 교성리로 옮기면서 처음 모습으로 복원되었다.

대한성공회 음성교회

🚗 충북 음성군 음성읍 읍내리 640-3번지

충북 음성은 삼국시대 초기 백제의 영토였다. 그러다가 고구려의 영역이 되면서 잉홀현으로 부르게 되었다. 음성이라는 지명은 통일신라 경덕왕 때 붙여져 오늘날까지 이어지고 있다. 이름난 산은 없으나 소백산맥 줄기인 가섭산(710 m), 부용산(644 m), 수리산(505 m), 수레의산(679 m), 오갑산(609 m) 등 자연생태계가 잘 보존되어 있는 아름다운 산을 지니고 있다. 음성군은 전통적인 농업 지역으로 비옥한 땅과 풍부한 수원을 바탕으로 청결고추, 인삼, 미백복숭아, 사과, 수박, 참외, 포도 등 전국적인 지명도를 갖고 있는 농특산물이 생산되고 있기도 하다. 가볼만한 곳으로는 6·25전쟁 때 최초로 공산군을 물리친 무극국민관광지가 있고, 금왕읍의 삼형제 저수지는 낚시 동호인들에게 인기가 높다.

성공회 충북선교의 또 다른 축은 음성교회 였다. 1900년대 말에 설립된 것으로 보이는 음성교회는 1915년부터 교세가 확장되자 1923년 교회당을 지었다.

대한성공회 음성교회

역시 전통한옥의 팔작 목조와가八作木造瓦家였다. 당시 음성의 갑부였던 현씨 집안에서 철거한 목재들을 가져다 지은 것이라고 한다. 이 건물은 기존 한옥을 개조해서 사용하던 선교 초기의 모습을 여실히 보여준다는 점에서 의미가 크다.

그 밖에 음성에는 두 개의 성공회 교회가 더 있다. 1934년 건축된 것으로 추정되는 대소교회 예배당(음성군 대소면 오산리)과 1938년 지어진 매일교회 예배당(음성군 삼성면 상곡리)이다. 전자는 팔작지붕에 겹처마가 나온 것이 특징이며, 후자는 통칸 구조에 마룻바닥이 특이하지만 두 곳 모두 원형이 훼손된 채 사택으로 사용되거나 방치된 상태에 있다.

CHAPTER 5

대전·충남 지역

대전광역시 → 공주 → 천안 → 강경 → 서천(마량진)과 보령(고대도)

1. 대전지역

❋ 대전·충남 기독교의 시작

　대전·충남 지역은 침례교, 감리교, 장로교, 성결교, 성공회 등 다양한 교파의 선교사들이 동시에 사역했던 대표적인 선교혼재지역이다.
　충남에는 먼저 침례교가 들어 왔다. 1896년부터 1901년까지 강경과 공주 그리고 부여 임천의 칠산을 중심으로 금강 연안의 마을을 두루 다니며 선교 사업을 벌여 이 지역 기독교의 효시가 되었던 침례교 계통 '엘라딩기념선교회'의 활동은 다시 대한기독교회(한국 침례교의 전신)로 이어져, 부여와 예산, 연기군으로 확대되었다. 1906년부터 1915년까지 열 차례에 걸쳐 열렸던 대한기독교회의 대화회大和會: 총회 개최 장소를 살펴보면 그 중 일곱 번은 강경, 공주, 임천, 익산(강경구역)에서 열렸는데, 이것은 대한기독교회와 충남 지역과의 관계를 다시 한 번 나타내는 것이다.
　미국 북감리회와 남장로교의 충남 선교는 1901년 4월 재정 압박으로 엘라딩기념선교회가 일시 철수하면서 본격화되었다. 북감리회의 공주 스테이션 설치(1903년 여름)와 군산 주재 남장로교 선교사 불William F. Bull, 부위렴의 서천 방문(1903년 봄)은 비슷한 시기에 이루어졌다. 북감리회는 선교사 샤프Robert A. Sharp와 스웨어러Wilbur C. Swearer, 서원보를 연달아 파견하여 공주를 중심

대전·충남 지역

아멘트기념관

으로 홍성과 천안 등지로 빠르게 진출했다. 남장로교 선교사 불의 발길은 금강을 출발하여 멀리 안면도에 이르고 있었다. 그 결과 북감리회와 남장로교는 충남의 강경-부여-홍산-임천-남포를 경계로 대치하게 되었다. 결국 1907년 북감리회는 남장로교의 충남 서남부 지역의 기득권을 인정하면서 충남에 대한 선교지역 분할 협정을 매듭짓게 되는데, 오늘의 서천, 금산, 보령의 절반과 논산 일부를 제외한 나머지 충남의 10개 군은 이때 북감리회의 선교 구역이 되었다.

  1912년에 세워진 충남 부여의 규암전도관(현 규암성결교회)은 동양선교회(한국 성결교회의 전신)가 한국에 다섯 번째로 세운 공동체로서, 서울 이남에서는 최초로 설립된 성결교회이다. 그리고 머지않아 충남의 은산과 홍산, 강경 그리고 대전에 연달아 성결교회들이 세워졌다. 1927년도의 통계에 의하면 당시 조선예수교 동양선교회 성결교회는 총 6개의 '지방'(성결교의 지역 조직)을 두고 있었는데, 충남 '지방'은 교인 총수가 555명으로 경기 '지방'에 이어 두 번째의 규모를 지니고 있었다. 그리고 그 숫자는 1938년 1,916명으로 눈에 띄게 증가하고 있었다.

첫 번째. 대전광역시

✱ 대전 소개

오늘의 대전은 조선시대 회덕현, 진잠현, 공주목 유성의 영역이었다. 대전의 근대사를 얘기할 때 빼놓을 수 없는 것은 회덕의 한가운데를 관통하며 지나간 경부선 철도 부설 공사와 관련된 지역사회의 변화된 모습이다. 20세기 초의 대전은 전통과 근대가 미묘하게 만나는 또 하나의 진열장이었다. 1904년에 세워진 대전역을 경계로 하여 북쪽인 회덕이 전통의 중심이었다면, 남쪽의 대전은 뭔가 다른 일이 벌어지고 있는 새로움의 현장이었다. 회덕은 구체제의 패러다임을 못내 아쉬워하면서 변화에 저항했고, 대전은 갑자기 자신들에게 다가온 새로운 삶의 방식을 불안하게 경험하고 있었다. 같은 공간이면서도 회덕과 대전은 매우 다른 모습을 띠게 되었다.

사실 충남의 내륙 깊숙한 곳에 연이어 있던 회덕과 진잠과 유성은 개화의 흐름과는 별 관련이 없던 곳이다. 금강 하구에 있던 충남의 다른 도시들 같이 상업적 유통이 활발하다거나, 홍주나 공주처럼 사람과 물자들이 몰려들었던 지방 행정의 중심지도 아니었다. 또 이곳은 17세기를 풍미했던 호서사림의 성리학적 전통이 위정척사의 모습으로 간직되고 있던 곳이기도 하다. 그런데 바로 이곳 회덕의 남쪽인 산내면 대전리에 대전역이 들어섰다. 대구에서 인구 밀집 지역인 논산-공주로 우회하지 않고 바로 북쪽으로 뻗어야 적은 비용으로 공기를 단축시킬 수 있다는 1900년 실측의 결과였다. 대전역이 들어선 산내면은 1895년 공주군의 영역에서 회덕군으로 편입된 5개면 가운데 하나로 그 때의 대전리는 회덕군의 남쪽에 위치하고 있었던 대전천변의 "갈대가 무성하고 황량한 한촌"에 불과했다.

경부선 철도공사와 대전역의 등장에 뒤이은 식민도시 대전의 눈부신 발전은 회덕의 주민 집단이 일찍이 경험하지 못한 매우 중대한 사건이었다. 그 후 회덕의 구성원들은 어떤 방식으로든지 새로운 도시가 뿜어내는 근대성에 반응하고 또 적응해야 했다. 대전의 일본인 거주는 1904년 경부선 철도공사가 회덕군 경내에서 진행되면서 시작되었다. 최초의 일본인 188명은 대부분 철도 공사장에서 일했던 품팔이꾼들로 노역장에서 받은 월급으로 대전역전의 논밭을 사들였다. 그리고 1905년 11월 경부선과 관부關釜 연락선이 연결됨에 따라 일본인의 대전 거주 인구는 날로 증가하여 1909년에는 2,487명에 달하였다. 이들 일본인 거류민들이 황무지였던 대전역을 중심으로 시가지를 건설하여 도시화를 이루어가고 있는 반면에 회덕의 주민들이 예전의 경제구조와 생활모습을 간직한 채 살아가는 상황은 이제 더욱 뚜렷한 대비를 이루게 되었다. 이제 회덕은 대전의 강력한 자장磁場의 영향을 받게 되었다. 결국 회덕군청을 비롯한 공공기관들이 대전으로 이전되었다. 1908년 시작된 대전의 개신교 역시 회덕이 아니라 대전의 대동리에서 시작되었다. 행정구역 개편과 지역 정보 등 국내의 상황에 민감했던 미국 선교사들이 대전을 염두에 두었기 때문이다.

✱ 대전 기독교 전래

지난 2007년은 대전지역에 기독교가 전래된 지 100년이 되는 해였다. 한국 중남부 대부분의 지역이 그러했던 것처럼 20세기 초 이곳 대전에도 선교사들의 방문이 시작되었다. 그리고 향촌사회 새로운 리더들의 노력으로 먼저 대전에 감리교 계통의 신앙공동체(현 대전제일감리교회)가 형성되었다. 대전이 감리교의 공식선교구역에 포함된 것도 그 즈음이었다. 그런데 다시 1920년이 되면 이번에는 성결교의 신자집단(현 대전중앙성결교회)이 대전에 그 모습을 드러냈다. 대전의 성결교회는 공격적인 전도활동을 통해 대전 사람들에게 널리 알려졌다. 또 1937년에는 구세군 대전영문(현 대전중앙영문), 1938년에는 장로교회(현 대전제일장로교회)가 각각 대전에 설립되었다. 해방 이전 대전지역에는 이렇게 모두 4개소의 교회에 수 백 명의 교인이 있었던 것으로 추산된다. 당시 대전의 인구(7만여 명) 대비 기독교인 비율은 대개 0.1% 미만으로 전국 평균(0.5%)에 한참 못 미치는 수준이었다. 일제강점기 대전지역의 기독교는 그 상징성에도 불구하고 인구학적으로나 종교적으로 소수세력에 지나지 않았던 것이다.

그런데 해방 후 불과 10여 년 만에 대전의 종교지형에 큰 변화가 일어났다. 우선 교회 수가 1952년의 14개를 거쳐 1960년에는 모두 58개로 늘었고, 교인 수도 1960년에 이르러서는 1만여 명(5%)으로 급증했다. 이러한 증가세는 당시 비슷한 규모의 도시들 가운데 가장 높은 것이다.

뿐만 아니라 그 사이 새롭게 대전에 진출한 미국 선교사들에 의해 집중적으로 설립된 여러 개의 교육·사회사업기관들은 이 지역에서 기독교의 사회적 위치와 영향력을 결정적으로 강화시켰다. 1950년대 대전지역에 세워진 감리교대전신학교(1954년: 미국 감리교, 현 목원대), 침례회신학교(1954년: 미국 남침례교, 현 침례신학대), 대전보육대학(1956년: 미국 감리교, 현 배재대), 대전기독학관(1956년: 미국 남장로교, 현 한남대)은, 당시 이 지역의 기독교계가 지방정부(1952년 도립 충남대학)를 포함한 지역사회의 어떤 부문에 비해서도 많은 숫자의 고등교육기관을 운영했음을 보여준다. 또 지난 1949년 북장로회 등 한국에 진출한 북미의 5개 교파 선교부가 연합하여 대전에 설치했던 '기독교연합봉사회Union Christian Service Center'의 농민학원·영아원·후생학원 운영과 수족절단자 교도사업 등의 구제 사업은 당시 대전 지역 기독교가 수행했던 사회사업의 규모와 수준을 잘 보여준다. 사회복지의 측면에서 대전지역 기독교의 활약은 분단과 전쟁으로 야기된 지역사회의 절박한 요구에 가장 잘 부응하는 것이었다. 해방 이후 한국전쟁을 거치면서 기독교는 이렇게 대전 지역사회에서 자신의 영역을 급속도로 확장해 갔던 것이다.

✱ 대전 기독교 유적지

한남대 인도기념관과 오정동 선교사촌

🚗 대전시 대덕구 오정동 133번지

해방 이후 한국전쟁을 거치면서 인구 증가와 도시화가 신속하게 진행되고 있던 대전의 새로운 가능성에 주목한 집단은 바로 선교사들이었다. 해방 이전까지 호남 선교에 집중했던 미국 남장로교 한국선교부는 1949년 대전에 새로운 스테이션을 설치하기로 하고 대덕군 회덕면 오정리(현 대전광역시 대덕구 오정동) 일대의 땅을 집중적으로 매입하였다. 전쟁으로 일시 중단되었던 그 사업은 1954년 대전에 스테이션과 아울러 대학(한남대)을 세우는 것으로 급진전되었다. 그 결과 1955년 오정리 선교 지구에 선교사 주택 3채를 비롯하여 대학 본관 건축공사가 시작되었다.

이 때 조성된 '오정동 선교사촌'(대전 문화재자료 44호)은 현재 한남대학이 관리하고 있는데, 그 안의 주택 세 채는 모두 똑같이 한국식 팔작기와지붕에 서양식 조적조의 단층 'ㄷ'자형으로 지어졌다. 들어가면서 첫 번째 집이 남장로교 선교사 린튼William A. Linton, 인돈이 살았던 '린튼하우스'이다. 1912년 22살의 젊은 나이로 독포에 도착한 린튼은 그 후 48년 동안 전주신흥학교와 한남대를 중심으로 남장로교의 교육선교사업에 헌신했다. 그는 레이놀즈William D. Reynolds에 이어 남장로교 한국선교부를 대표하는 인물이었다. '서머빌하우스'로 부르는 두 번째 집은 1954년 내한하여 1994년까지 주로 한남대 교수로 사역했던 서머

서머빌하우스

빌John N. Somerville, 서의필 선교사가 살았다. 서머빌은 안동 권씨 족보 연구로 1974년 미국 하버드대학에서 박사학위를 받은 한국학 전문가였다. 서머빌하우스는 현재 한남대 인돈학술원으로 사용되고 있다. 나머지 한 채인 '크림하우스'는 1952년 남장로교 선교사로 파송되어 1966년까지 한남대와 장신대에서 가르쳤던 유명한 구약학자 크림Keith R. Crim, 김기수의 집이다. 미국 브릿지워터 대학과 버지니아 유니온신학교를 나온 그는, 미국으로 돌아가 존낙스 출판사 편집장, 미국성서공회 굿뉴스바이블 번역위원, 컴먼웰스 대학교 교수, 웨스트민스터 출판사 편집장 등으로 활약하면서 미국 성서학 분야에서 매우 활발하게 활동했다.

또 1956년 5월 1일 착공하여 1957년 9월 30일 준공된 한남대 '인돈기념관'(본관)은, 미국 앨라배마 버밍햄의 건축가 데이비스C. S. Davis의 설계로 지어진, 지하 1층 지상 3층의 라멘조(철근이나 철골이 뼈대가 되는 구조) 슬라브 지붕 건물이다. 특히 붉은 벽돌의 외벽면에 십자가 무늬를 부조 형식으로 처리함으로써 건물의 종교적 의미를 강조하고 있다.

국립 대전현충원

대전광역시 유성구 갑동 산 23-1번지

지난 1979년 국립묘지관리소 대전분소로 문을 연 대전현충원에는 모두 3개의 애국지사묘역이 있다. 애국지사묘역은 항일투쟁 및 독립운동에 헌신하신 분들을 안장하는 곳인데, 현재 조성된 약 1,760여 기의 애국지사 묘지 중 228명이 기독교인이었던 것으로 파악되고 있다. 그 상황을 자세히 살펴보면 애국지사 제1묘역(총 456명)의 기독교인은 44명, 제2묘역(980명)은 137명, 제3묘역(약 330명)은 47명에 이른다. 대상자가 많으므로 여기서는 세 분만을 소개하기로 한다.

애국지사 제2묘역-393의 주남선 목사는 1888년 경남 거창 출신으로 1909년 거창읍교회 설립의 주역이었다. 그는 진주의 경남성경학원을 졸업한 뒤 1919년 거창읍교회 교인들과 함께 3·1 만세운동을 벌였다. 그 해 12월 장로 장립을 받고 경남노회의 추천으로 1920년 평양 장로회신학교에 입학하였으나 뒤늦게 거

국립 대전현충원 주남선 묘

창지방 독립운동 사실이 발각되어 옥고를 치러야 했다. 1930년 신학교를 졸업한 그는 1931년 거창읍교회 목사로 부임하여 이후 평생을 그 교회에서 목회하였다. 1938년 신사참배 문제가 발생하자 주 목사는 반대운동을 활발히 전개하여 결국 1940년 검속되고 말았다. 그는 일제의 압력에 굴하지 않고 신앙을 지킨 한국교회의 존경받는 지도자였다.

애국지사 제2묘역-1015의 엄주신 장로는 1890년 경남 함안군 칠원면 구성리에서 태어났다. 1910년 칠원교회 방명원 조사助事로부터 학습을 받았고, 1913년 세례를 받았다. 1914년부터 한의사로 일했는데, 그 후 아주 용하다고 소문이 나 서부 경남의 환자들이 몰렸다. 1919년 3월 30세의 그는, 손종일 장로(손양원 목사 부친) 등과 함께 독립만세운동을 계획하고 약봉지를 만든다는 핑계로 문종이를 대량 구입하여 칠원면 용산리의 깊은 산중 가장정佳藏亭에서 태극기를 제작, 칠원읍 장터에서 시위를 주도하였다. 그 일로 그는 징역 8개월의 옥고를 치러야 했다. 그 후 엄 장로는 1924년 칠원교회당을 지을 때 옛날에 심어놓은 아름드리 버드나무 40주를 교회에 바쳐 성전 재목으로 사용하게 했다. 또 1933년 장로 장립 이후에는 한학자로 주일 성경공부를 오랫동안 인도하였다. 그의 성경공부 시간에는 교인들로 예배당이 가득 찼다고 한다. 그렇게 40여 년간 교회를 위해 헌신하던 엄 장로는 1973년 8월 28일 소천하였다. 그의 유해는 지난 2002년 대전현충원으로 이장되었다.

애국지사 제3묘역-187의 현석칠 목사는 1880년 평남 용강에서 출생했다. 어려서부터 유학을 공부하다가 18세 되던 해 우연히 성경을 구해 읽고 개종했다. 1905년부터 성서공회 매서인이 되어 평안도와 황해도에서 복음을 전하고, 1909년 해주읍교회에서 전도사로 목회를 시작하였다. 1911년 감리교 협성신학교를 졸업하고 목사안수를 받은 그는, 그 후 서울 동대문교회, 평양 남산현교회, 공주읍교회, 영변읍교회, 신창읍교회 등지에서 목회했다. 현 목사는 1919년 3·1운동 때 공주읍교회를 담임하고 있었다. 그는 공주 영명학교 교사와 학생 그리고 졸업생들과 함께 만세 시위를 모의한 후 4월 1일 공주 장날을 기해 대대적인 군중 시위를 주도했다. 그 일로 현 목사는 4개월간 옥고를 치러야 했다. 풀려난 후에도 상해임시정부와 연락을 취하며 독립운동을 하던 애국부인회, 애국단 등을 지원하다가 체포되어 다시 4개월 간 투옥되었다. 1938년 일제의 신사참배 강요가 노골화되자 현 목사는 만주로 건너갔고 1943년 소천하였다. 그의 유해는 60년 만에 북간도 용정에서 발견되어 지난 2005년 대전현충원에 모셔졌다.

2. 충남지역

첫번째. 공주

✱ 공주 소개

기원을 전후한 시기에 금강 일대는 삼한의 하나인 마한의 소국이 자리 잡았다가, 4세기 중반 백제가 마한지역을 병합하면서 백제세력권에 포함되었다. 5세기 무렵 백제가 금강 유역으로 이동하면서, 이 일대는 2백여 년간 웅진(공주), 사비(부여)시대의 본거지가 되었다. 이 시기에 백제는 중국과 활발한 교류를 통하여 특유의 세련된 문화를 꽃피웠다.

이 시기에 축조된 공주 무령왕릉은 백제 중흥의 상징으로 남아 있다. 1971년 도굴되지 않은 온전한 상태로 발굴된 무령왕릉에서는 웅진시대 백제문화를 한 눈에 볼 수 있는 2,600여 점의 유물이 쏟아졌다. 또 송산리 고분군 유적은 무령왕릉을 포함하여 모두 7기가 보존되어 있는데, 그 중 송산리 5호분은 둥근 돔식 천장을 설치한 굴식돌방무덤이며, 6호분과 무령왕릉은 벽돌로 석실을 쌓고 터널식 천장으로 마무리한 벽돌무덤이다. 이것은 중국 남조의 무덤 양식을 모델로 한 것이다.

통일신라시대에는 충남지역의 대부분이 속한 웅천주가 충청지역의 13개 군과 29개 현을 통괄했는데 그 치소治所가 공주에 있었다. 고려 성종 2년(983) 전국에 12목이 설치될 때 충남지역에서는 유일하게 공주목이 설치되어 충청지역 행정중심지로서의 전통을 인정받았다. 임진왜란 직후인 1602년에는 충청감영이 충주에서 공주로 이전되면서 명실공히 충청도 54개 고을의 중심지가 되었다. 그 후로도 오랜 세월 공주는 행정과 교통, 상업의 요지로서 지역을 대표하고 있었고, 한말까지 금강을 이용한 내륙 수운의 발달로 도시 발전의 속도도 빨랐다. 그러나 일제시대 공주에 있던 충남

도청이 대전으로 이전하면서 그 발전은 지체될 수밖에 없었다. 1931년 3월 공주 사람들은 도청 이전을 반대하는 격렬한 시위를 벌였다. 횃불이 켜졌고, 투석전이 있었다. 일제는 경찰 3백명을 동원, 가담자 50명을 구속하는 강경책을 폈다. 공주 사람들의 거센 반대에도 불구하고 도청 이전은 신속하게 진행되었다. 그 한 달 뒤인 4월에는 도청 이전 계획이 일본 귀족원의 승인을 받았다. 결국 1932년 9월 도청은 대전 선화동으로 옮겨 갔다.

✲ 공주 기독교 전래

공주에는 먼저 침례교가 들어 왔다. 미국 보스턴의 클라렌돈 스트리트 침례교회The Clarendon Baptist Church가 설립한 엘라딩기념선교회The Ella Thing Memorial Mission는 1895년 한국에 폴링E. C. Pauling 부부와 가데린Amanda Gardeline 등 3명의 선교사를 파송하였다. 그들은 곧 충청도로 진출할 계획을 세우고 1896년 초 서울에서 240 km 떨어진 은진 강경포로 내려왔다. 그리고 뒤이어 엘라딩기념선교회 소속 선교사 2진이 도착했다. 스테드맨F. W. Steadman과 두 사람의 여선교사Sadie Ackles & Arma Ellmer였다. 스테드맨 일행은 강경에서 조금 떨어진 충남 공주의 반죽동에 자신들의 거처를 정하였다. 그러나 강경에서 전도하였던 폴링 선교사가 얼마 후에 철수하자 스테드맨 선교사는 공주를 떠나 강경으로 그의 선교 거점을 옮겼다.

북감리회의 한강 이남 지역에 대한 선교계획은 1892년의 선교부연례회의에서 대구와 수원 그리고 공주를 언급함으로 시작되었다. 당시 감리사로서 감리교의 한강 이남 선교 책임을 맡게 된 선교사 스크랜턴William B. Scranton, 시란돈은 우선 한국인 사역자 유치겸을 배치해서 이 지역에 대한 선교 기반을 조성하게끔 했다. 유치겸은 스크랜턴의 공주 순방을 염두에 두고 두 번이나 그곳에 다녀왔지만, 결국 그 해 스크랜턴의 공주 답사는 이루어지지 않았다. 아직 한강 이남으로 진출하기에는 선교부의 여력이 부족했기 때문에, 스크랜턴은 두 번이나 짐을 꾸렸다가 포기하고 말았다고 술회하고 있다. 여기서 우리는 남쪽의 도시들 가운데 지리적으로 서울과 가까운 공주가 그들의 우선적인 목표였음을 알 수 있다.

이어서 북감리회 한국선교부는 1898년 8월의 연례회의에서 그 해 4월 내한한 선교사 스웨어러Wilbur S. Swearer 서원보를 수원·공주 구역의 책임자로 임명하였다. 1898년 5월 이 구역을 광범위하게 순회한 스웨어러는 그 회의에서 매우 넓게 퍼져있는 이 지역을 한 사람이 감당하기에는 너무 벅차다고 토로한 바 있다. 스웨어러는 다시 1898년 가을과 1899년 봄 두 차례에 걸쳐 자신의 구역을 순방하며 공주 진출을 준비하였다. 그리고 결국 북감리회 한국선교부는 1902년 가을 공주에 좋은 위치의 선교부지와 선교사 사택을 매입하고, 우선 한국인 사역자를 파견할 수 있었다.

1903년 봄 공주에 머물면서 실제로 그곳의 현장을 경험한 스웨어러는 그 해의 선교부 연례회의에서 공주의 중요성을 강조하며 의료선교사 1명과 일반 선교사 1명을 각각 파송할 것을 주장하였다. 그의 언급처럼 공주는 당시 충청남도의 도읍으로 행정과 교통의 중심지였다. 감리교선교부가 공주에 스테이션을 개설한 것은 그들이 향후 충남에서 선교의 주도권을 행사하겠다는 의지를 드러낸 것이다. 이미 그들은 서울과 평양 그리고 제물포에 강력한 스테이션을 건설하고 있었다. 스웨어러의 주장은 상당한 공감을 불러 일으켰던 것으로 추정된다. 벌써 의료선교사 맥길William B. McGill, 맥우원은 이용주와 함께 1903년 7월 공주에 도착하여, 그 해의 여름을 그곳에서 보내고 있었다. 그리고 공주읍내에 교회를 세우려는 그들의 노력으로 새로운 신자들이 생겨나게 되었다. 공주읍교회는 이렇게 시작되었다.

1903년 공주 스테이션 개설 이후 이곳에서 활동한 대표적인 선교사들로는 맥길과 샤프Robert A. Sharp, 1904~1906를 필두로 1906년과 1907년 각각 공주와 인연을 맺게 된 교육선교사 윌리엄스Frank E. C. Williams, 우리암, 1906~1940와 선교사 테일러Corwin Taylor, 대리오, 1907~1922 그리고 샤프의 미망인으로 남편 사망 이후 계속 공주에서 활동했던 앨리스Alice J. Hammond, 사애리시, 1908~1940가 있다. 또 1919년부터 공주에서 사역하기 시작한 아멘트Charles C. Amendt, 안명도, 1919~1940는 오랜 기간 이곳에 머물면서 충남의 감리교회 형성에 큰 영향을 미쳤다. 의료선교사 반 버스커크James Dale Van Buskirk, 반복기, 1909~1913 역시 공주의 의료사업을 제 궤도에 올려놓았다고 평가된다.

✱ 공주 기독교 유적지

아멘트기념관

🚗 충남 공주시 중학동 9-1번지

1903년 의료선교사 맥길William B. McGill, 맥우원을 공주에 보내 하리동 언덕 위에 스테이션을 개설한 북감리회는, 그 후 선교사 샤프Robert A. Sharp와 스웨어러Wilbur S. Swearer, 서원보를 연달아 파견, 그곳을 중심으로 충청도 선교에 전념하도록 하였다. 일제강점기 공주 스테이션은 선교사들의 주거 공간과 함께 공주읍교회와 영명학교, 공주중앙영아관, 시약소施藥所, dispensary가 갖추어져 있었는데, 지금 공주시 중학동 9-1번지에 남아있는 '아멘트기념관'(등록문화재 제233호)은 바로 1917년부터 공주에서 활동한 아멘트Charles C. Amendt, 안명도가 살던 집이다. 1921년 10월 23일 건립된 이 건물은 지하 1층 지상 3층의 붉은 벽돌 조적조 함석 지붕으로 되어 있다. 이 집은 아니지만 그 16년 전 샤프 선교사가 공주 스테이션 구내에 처음 2층짜리 서양식 주택을 지었을 때, 그것을 구경하러 온 공주 사람들은 "목사 당신은 천당에 갈 필요가 없겠소" "우리는 돼지 같이 사는데, 여기는 얼마나 깨끗한가"라고 말했다. 공주 스테이션의 선교사 주택은 이 지역의 명물이었고 또 한국인들에게는 어떤 동경의 대상이었던 것이다.

공주 선교사 묘지

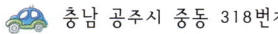 충남 공주시 중동 318번지

공주 영명고등학교 강당 뒤편 산 중턱에 조성되어 있는 공주 선교사 묘지에는 모두 5개의 묘비를 만나 볼 수 있다. 그 중 가장 큰 것이 샤프Robert A. Sharp의 무덤이다. 1903년 내한한 샤프 선교사는 먼저 배재학당과 정동교회에서 일하였는데 그 사이에 여선교사 앨리스Allice J. Hammond, 사애리시와 결혼했다. 1904년 충청구역 책임자로 임명된 그는 1905년 공주로 내려와 공주 최초의 양옥집을 짓고 이주하였다. 하지만 1906년 2월 논산지방을 순회 전도하다가 발진티프스에 감염되어 순직하였다. 악천후를 피해 잠깐 머물렀던 곳이 바로 상여집이었는데 그 상여를 만진 것이 감염의 원인이 되었던 것이다. 부인의 정성어린 간호에도 불구하고 샤프는 1906년 3월 15일 34세의 젊은 나이로 운명하여, 이곳에 묻혔다.

샤프의 묘지 외에 나머지는 선교사 2세의 무덤들이다. 샤프의 묘비 앞 쪽에는 오랫동안 영명학교 교장을 지냈던 윌리엄스Frank E. C. Williams, 우리암의 두 아들, 올리브Olive Williams, 1902~1917와 조지George Z. Williams, 우광복, 1907~1994의 무덤이 나란히 놓여 있다. 해방 이후 해군 대령의 신분으로 영명학교 재건 작업을 지원했던 조지는 자신이 태어난 곳이자 형의 무덤이 있는 공주에 묻히기를 소원했다고 한다. 다시 그 아래에는 테일러Corwin Taylor, 대리오 선교사의 딸 에스터Ester M. Tayior, 1911~1916와 아멘트Charles C. Amendt, 안명도의 아들 로저Roger Amendt, 1927~1929의 무덤이 있다. 선교지의 열악한 환경에 적응하지 못하고 희생된 어린 아이들이었다.

공주 선교사 묘지

공주제일교회

🚗 충남 공주시 봉황동 10번지

1903년 맥길William B. McGill 선교사에 의해
설립된 공주읍교회(현 공주제일감리교회)는
원래 선교 구내에 있었지만, 1930년 시내의
중심부인 상반정에 고딕 양식의 붉은 벽돌
예배당을 짓고 이전하였다. 그런데 그 건물은
6·25전쟁 때 폭격으로 파괴되었고, 현재의
교회당은 1956년 11월 재건되었는데, 전면
중앙에만 종탑을 배치한 양식이다. 교회 마당
에 있는 '고 양두현 지루두 기념비故梁斗炫池累

공주제일교회

斗紀念碑'는 1939년 5월 건립된 것으로 부부 사이였던 그들은 당시 논 1만8천여 평과 밭 2천7백여 평을 바쳐 교회 자립의 기반을 제공했다고 한다. 이 건물은 지난 2012년 등록문화재 472호로 지정되어 현재 공주기독교역사박물관으로 운영하고 있다.

✱ 공주 일반 유적지

우금치전적지 및 동학혁명군위령탑

공주에서 부여로 가는 40번 국도 작은 고갯마루에는 우리 근대사에서 가장 가슴 아픈 이야기를 담고 있는 곳이 있다. 바로 1894년에 관리들의 폭정과 수탈에 견디다 못해 '보국안민 제폭구민'을 기치로 떨쳐 일어선 농민군이 마지막 치열한 전투를 벌였지만 패배를 당했던 우금치이다.

우금치 고개는 1894년 동학농민군이 관군과 일본군의 연합군을 상대로 최후

의 격전을 벌인 장소이다. 공주에서 부여로 넘어가는 견준산 기슭의 고개로 우금고개, 우금재 또는 비우금 고개라고도 부른다.

1894년 9월, 전봉준이 이끄는 동학농민군은 일본군의 경복궁 침범과 경제적 약탈을 규탄하며 반봉건·반외세의 기치를 내걸고 재봉기를 했다. 이곳 우금치를 장악하면 중부지역의 거점인 공주 점령의 기선을 잡을 수 있는 중요한 곳이었다. 공주를 중심으로 향후 전쟁을 이끌어 나가려던 동학농민군은 죽검으로 총에 맞서 싸우다 결국 거의 전멸하게 되었다. 우금치 싸움 후, 재기를 노리던 전봉준이 체포되어 이듬해 3월 처형됨으로써 1년 동안 전개된 동학농민전쟁은 막을 내리게 되었다.

동학군의 넋을 달래기 위해 1973년에 이 고개의 동학혁명군위령탑이 세워졌으며, 동학농민전쟁 100년이 지난 1994년에 이르러 우금치는 사적(제387호)으로 지정되었다. 우금치는 동학농민군이 반봉건·반외세 기치를 걸고 마지막 항전을 이루어냈던 장소로, 한국 근대사의 한 고비를 이루는 무대가 된 뜻깊은 장소이다.

공주 송산리고분군

충남 공주시 금성동과 웅진동에 위치한 사적 제13호 송산리고분군은 백제 웅진시대 왕들의 무덤이 모여 있는 곳이다. 무령왕릉을 포함한 이 일대의 고분들은 모두 7기가 전해지는데, 송산을 주산主山으로 뻗은 구릉 중턱의 남쪽 경사면에 위치한다. 계곡을 사이에 두고 서쪽에는 무령왕릉과 5·6호분이 있고 동북쪽에는 1~4호분이 있다. 1~6호분은 일제시대에 조사되어 고분의 구조와 형식이 밝혀졌고, 무령왕릉은 1971년 5·6호분의 보수공사 때 발견되었다.

먼저 1~5호분은 모두 굴식 돌방무덤(횡혈식 석실분)으로, 무덤 입구에서 시신이 안치되어 있는 널방(현실)에 이르는 널길이 널방 동쪽벽에 붙어 있는 것이 특징이다. 1~4호분은 바닥에 냇자갈을 깔아 널받침(관대)을 만들었는데, 5호분은 벽돌을 이용하였다. 이처럼 같은 양식의 무덤이면서 구조와 규모에서 약간의 차이가 나는 것은 시기 차이가 반영된 것으로 보인다. 5호분은 원형으로 남아 있으나, 1~4호분은 조사되기 전에 이미 도굴되었다. 이외에 벽돌무덤(전축분)으로 송산리벽화고분이라고도 불리는 6호분과 무령왕릉이 있다.

6호분은 활모양 천장으로 된 이중 널길과 긴 네모형의 널방으로 되어 있는데, 오수전五銖錢이 새겨진 벽돌로 정연하게 쌓았다. 널방 벽에는 7개의 등자리와 사신도·일월도 등의 벽화가 그려져 있다. 무령왕릉도 6호분과 같이 연꽃무늬 벽돌로 가로쌓기와 세로쌓기를 반복하여 벽을 쌓았다. 벽에는 5개의 등자리가 있고, 무덤주인을 알 수 있게 해주는 지석 등 많은 유물이 출토되었다.

6호분과 무령왕릉은 현재 남아 있는 백제의 벽돌무덤으로, 이러한 형식의 벽돌무덤은 중국의 영향을 받은 것이며, 벽화는 고구려의 영향을 받은 것으로 보인다. 특히 무령왕릉의 경우 확실한 연대를 알 수 있어, 백제사회의 사회·문화상을 연구하는 데 귀중한 자료로 평가되고 있다.

공주 중동성당

 충남 공주시 중동 31-2번지

중동성당은 국고개로 불리던 언덕 위에 자리한 서양 중세 때 유행하던 고딕건축 양식의 천주교 성당으로 5백여 명의 신자를 수용할 수 있는 규모이다.

평면이 약간 변형된 라틴식 십자가형으로, 두 단의 화강석 위에 외벽을 구축하였는데 외관이 붉은 벽돌로 되어 있다. 중앙 현관의 꼭대기에는 높은 종탑이 있고, 현관 출입구와 창의 윗부분은 끝이 뾰족한 아치로 장식되어 있다. 엷은 황색의 내부는 중앙에 여러 사람이 앉을 수 있는 긴 의자를 놓고 그 양쪽에 복도를 둔 형식이다. 중앙의 넓은 공간과 복도 사이에는 6개의 돌기둥이 있는데, 단면이 6각형을 이루고 있다.

최종철 신부(1890~1945)가 설계했고, 1934년에 착공하여 1936년에 완공한 것으로, 1997년 원형을 살려서 개수되었으며, 현재 비교적 원형을 잘 간직하고 있어 전통적인 목조건물에서 현대 건축으로 넘어가는 과도기의 모습을 엿볼 수 있다.

김옥균 선생 유허

🚗 충남 공주시 정안면 광정리 38번지

김옥균 선생 유허는 충남기념물 13호 지정되어 있다. 이곳은 한말의 정치가이자 개화사상가인 김옥균이 6세까지 살던 생가터로, 김옥균 생애비가 있는 곳이다. 예전에는 김옥균의 생가를 비롯하여 8~9호의 민가가 작은 마을을 이루고 있었으나, 화재로 모두 없어졌다.

김옥균은 수구파 자객 홍종우에게 암살당한 후 처음에는 일본 동경의 청산 외인무덤에 묻혔는데, 1914년 아산군수였던 그의 양자 김영진이 충청남도 아산시 영인면 아산리로 옮겨와 부인 유씨와 합장하였다.

생가터는 정안면에서 동북쪽으로 500 m 가량 떨어진 지점인데 터는 없어지고 넓은 밭 가운데 감나무만 서 있다. 그 자리에 1989년 2월 22일 공주군 주관으로 대지 2,473 m²에 생가터를 다듬고 바로 앞에 추모비를 세웠다. 묘는 아산시에 있으며, 묘역에는 석등·석양石羊·망주석望柱石·문인석文人石·비 등이 세워져 있다.

두번째. 천안

매봉교회와 3·1운동

천안 병천(아우내)의 만세운동은 목천군 이동면 용두리교회의 존재와 밀접하게 관련되어 있다. 그래서 아우내의 3·1운동을 '매봉교회(용두리교회의 새 이름)의 독립운동'으로 보는 시각이 있을 정도이다. 감리교 선교사 스웨어러Wilbur C. Swearer, 서원보는 1899년 3월 경기도 이천에서 한 남자와 그 가족에게 세례를 주게 되는데, 그가 바로 이천 덕들교회의 박해숙이었다. 그리고 그의 전도활동의 결과로 1901년경 목천과 진천에 교회가 설립되었다. 그러니까 천안은 천안읍

(1915년)보다 그 주변에 복음이 먼저 전래된 것이다. 이 때 목천의 교회는 사자골에 있었던 것으로 추정된다. 그리고 얼마 뒤에 그곳에서 몇 리 떨어진 충남 목천군 이동면 지령리(후에 용두리로 바뀜)에도 교회가 세워졌다. 지령리교회는 1907년 8월 '대지령야소교당大芝靈耶蘇敎堂'의 이름으로 국채보상운동에 참가하였는데, 그 때 동참한 교인이 82명에 달하였다.

그런데 당시 지령리교회가 있던 목천군 일대는 의병 운동이 성했던 곳이다. 당시 신문들은 그곳에서 몇 차례 있었던 일본군수비대와 의병의 충돌 소식을 전하고 있다. 그리고 1907년 11월 일본군은 목천의 사자골교회 신자 3명을 총살한데 이어, 지령리교회당에 불을 질러 건물을 전소시켰다. 이것은 지령리교회의 상당수 교인들이 국채보상운동에 참여할 만큼 항일적인 성향을 지니고 있었던데 대한 일본군의 보복으로 보인다. 지령리교회는 항일운동이라는 지역의 정서와 문명개화라고 하는 시대의 흐름이 잘 녹아있던 정신적인 공동체였다.

그리고 지령리교회의 이같은 흐름은 교회의 재건을 통해서 계승되고 있다. 예배당이 불에 타면서 해산됐던 교회를 1908년 다시 재건한 주역들은 내내 1907년 국채보상운동에 참여했던 지령리의 교인들이었다. 유관순의 일가였던 유빈기와 숙부 유중무는 케이블Elmer M. Cable, 기이부 선교사의 지원을 얻어 지령리교회를 다시 세웠다. 3·1운동 당시 용두리(1914년 지령리에서 행정구역 변경)교회의 속장이었던 조인원도 이때부터 교회에 가담한 것으로 보인다. 조인원은 자신의 사랑채를 사경회 장소로 개방하고, 케이블 선교사의 권유에 따라 아들 조병옥을 공주영명학교에 입학시켰다. 또 유빈기가 매서인으로 떠난 후 용두리교회의 지방 사역자로 활약했던 유중무의 조카 유우석과 유관순은 각각 공주 영명학교와 이화학당의 학생이 되었다. 유관순의 오빠인 유우석은 이미 1907년 국채보상의연금 납부자의 일원이었다. 그리고 1919년 유중무와 조인원어 의해 주도되고 있었던 용두리교회는 독립만세운동의 격랑에 빠지게 된다.

매봉교회와 유관순 열사 생가

 충남 천안시 동남구 병천면 용두리 338-6번지

경부고속도로의 목천IC를 나오면 바로 독립기념관으로 가는 길이 나오는데, 중간에 우회전하여 병천을 지나면 곧바로 매봉산 밑에 유관순열사기념관과 추모각이 나타나고 약간 위로 오르면 초혼묘와 봉화탑이 보인다.

그리고 다시 기념관에서 왼쪽 길로 1 km쯤 가면 유관순 열사의 생가와 매봉교회가 나온다. 지난 1991년 복원된 유관순열사 생가는 'ㄱ'자형 한옥 초가집으로 꾸며져 있다. 유관순열사는 1904년 바로 이곳에서 태어났다. 생가 바로 옆에 있는 매봉교회는 바로 3·1운동 당시 용두리교회의 전통을 계승하고 있다고 할 수 있다. 교회의 지하 전시실에는 연보年譜, 수형기록표, 재판기록 등 유관순열사의 생애와 행적에 관한 자료들이 전시되어 있다. 지금의 매봉교회 건물은 지난 1998년 새롭게 지은 것이다.

대한성공회 부대동교회

충남 천안시 서북구 부대동 118번지

성공회 천안 부대동교회가 처음 초가집 교회당을 마련한 것은 1907년 11월의 일이었다. 1905년 이후 수원에서 남쪽으로 영역을 넓히고 있던 브라이들G. A. Bridle 선교사의 활동 때문이었다. 이 교회는 1908년 북일학교를 세우게 된다. 그 후 교인이 늘자 부대동교회는 새로운 교회당을 지었는데, 1921년 11월 4일 완공되어 현재도 교육관으로 사용하고 있는 바로 그 단층 한옥 건물이다. 생김새는 장방형의 팔작지붕에 바실리카식 평면 형태를 취하고 있으며, 화강암 기초석 위의 붉은 벽돌로 쌓은 벽과 격자무늬 창문이 인상적이다.

세번째. 강경

✽ 강경 기독교 전래

19세기 금강 유역의 대표적 포구였던 강경은 당시 전국 3대 시장의 하나로 온 나라의 상선이 모이는 원격지 교역의 창구이자 넓은 강경평야를 배후에 가진 곡창이었다. 뿐만 아니라 일제 강점 이후에는 충남 제2의 일본인 거주지로서 식민행정의 중심지이기도 했다.

강경의 기독교는 1896년 침례교 계통 선교사들에 의해 시작되었다. 그들은 한국인 사역자 지병석의 집이 있던 북옥리북정 137번지 부근의 옥녀봉 일대 7천여 평을 매입하여 충청도 선교의 전진기지로 삼았다. 비록 재정적인 문제로 말미암아 그 선교사들은 얼마 뒤 철수하였지만 강경과 인근 칠산의 침례교회는 1901년 여름 4~50명의 신자들이 주일마다 함께 모여 독자적으로 집회를 갖고 있었다. 그 후 강경침례교회(당시는 봉대교회)는 또 다른 선교사 펜윅M. C. Fenwick, 편위익의 인도를 받으며 한국 침례교의 전신인 "대한기독교회"의 유력한 교회 가운데 하나가 되었다.

강경 지역 기독교 전래와 관련하여 한 가지 주목할 점은 당시 강경 남쪽 황산포에 있었던 황산교회의 존재이다. 그 때 황산은 전북 여산군 북일면 지역으로 남장로교 군산 스테이션의 선교 구역이었다. 황산교회가 설립된 시점은 1905년에서 1906년 무렵으로 추정된다. 그 교인들은 하루 16시간씩 돗자리를 짜면서 생활하는 영세한 사람들이었지만 자력으로 예배처소를 구입할 수 있었다. 그런데 황산교회는 설립 7~8년 만인 1913년 그곳의 행정구역이 바뀌면서 선교사들의 양해 아래 강경의 감리교회와 통합되었다.

강경의 기독교는 19세기 말 침례교 계통 선교사들에 의해 시작되지만 그 후 강경 선고를 주도한 교파는 감리교였다. 1903년 공주에 스테이션을 설치한 북감리회 선교사들은 그곳을 근거지로 하여 점차 영역을 넓혀갔고 그 사역자들의 발걸음은 곧 논산을 거쳐 강경에 이르렀다. 강경감리교회(현 강경제일감리교회)는 그 전에 이미 존재하고 있던 기독교 지향의 공동체를 기반으로 하여 대개 1907년 무렵 조직된 것으로 보인다. 이는 1908년 3월 연회年會에서 강경포구역을 신설하고 이용주 전도인을 파견한 사실을 통해 알 수 있다. 여기서 하나의 구역이 설치되었다는 것은 그 구역 안에 1개 이상의 신앙공동체가 있었다는 것을 뜻하며, 북감리회 선교 담당자들의 총회였던 연회는 보통 전년도의 상황을 근거로 자신들의 조직을 개편했으므로 강경에는 1907년에 이미 선교사들이 인정하고 있는 신자 집단이 있었다고 생각하면 된다. 당시 공주에서 교육선교사로 활동하고 있던 윌리엄스Frank E. C. Williams, 우리암 역시 1907년 무렵 강경교회가 시작되었음을 강하게 암시하고 있다. 그리고 강경감리교회는 조직된 지 불과 1년 만인 1908년에 만동학교를 설립하게 된다.

강경성결교회는 1918년 경성성서학원현 서울신학대학을 졸업한 정달성의 활동으로 시작되었다. 정달성의 강경 목회는 처음부터 난관에 봉착했다. 어느 정도 기반이 갖추어진 상태에서 시작되었던 부여의 다른 성결교회들과는 달리 강경성결교회는 먼저 목회자가 파견되어 개척하는 형식을 취했기 때문이었다. 그래서 강경성결교회의 첫 신자는 여학생 한 명이었다. 또 그 후에 들어온 교인들도 남편 또는 아버지의 반대로 고통을 당하고 있었다. 또 모임 장소도 퍽 비좁았다. 강경성결교회가 안정을 찾기 시작한 것은 매일 새벽 두 시 반부터 남녀 교우 40여 명이 기도회로 모여 큰 은혜를 받은

1922년 겨울 이후였다. 그리하여 이듬해인 1923년에는 새로운 예배당의 필요성이 제기되어 결국 건축을 하게 되었다.

✽ 강경 기독교 유적지

옥녀봉 침례교 최초 예배지

🚗 충남 논산군 강경읍 북옥리 137번지

한국 침례교의 발상지인 강경의 옥녀봉에는 침례교 선교사들이 처음 선교를 시작한 건물이 아직 남아 있다. 1895년 서울에 도착한 '엘라딩기념선교회' 소속 선교사들은 곧 충청도 선교를 계획하고 선교 거점으로 강경을 선택하였다. 1896년 초 은진 강경포로 내려온 그들은 강경 사람 지병석의 집에 머물며 그곳을 예배 장소로 삼아 활동하기 시작했는데, 바로 그곳이 강경읍 북옥리 137번지 한옥으로, 후에 선교사들이 그 주변의 땅과 함께 선교의 전진기지로 매입함으로써 한국 침례교의 출발점이 되었다. 북옥리 옥녀봉에 위치한 이 집은 목조 기둥에 함석지붕이며 부분 변형되어 있는 상태로 있다가 2013년 새롭게 복원되었다.

옥녀봉 침례교 최초 예배지

그런데 옥녀봉에는 침례교 유적 외에 기독교 관련 기념비가 하나 서있다. 바로 1974년 세워진 강경중앙감리교회 안득순 권사 순교기념비이다. 안득순 권사는 6·25전쟁 때인 1950년 7월 17일 소복을 입은 채 공산군에게 끌려가 최후 기도를 하고 대한민국 만세삼창을 한 후 총살당했다고 한다.

옛 강경성결교회당(구 북옥감리교회당)

🚗 충남 논산군 강경읍 북옥리 96번지

옛 강경성결교회당(등록문화재 42호)은 1953년 강경 북옥감리교회가 매입해 예배당으로 사용하다가 최근 다시 원래의 주인인 성결교회 측에서 사들였다고 한다. 강경성결교회는 1918년 경성성서학원을 졸업한 정달성 전도사가 시작하였다. 당시 부여의 규암과 은산, 홍산에는 강력한 성결교의 공동체들이 세워져 있었다. 강경성결교회는 그 후 우원식, 이인범 목사를 거치면서 교인이 늘어났고, 1924년에는 바로 현재 우리가 보는 예배당을 건립할 수 있었다. 강경성결교회의 건축은 미국 교인들의 지원 덕분이었다. 당시 교회를 짓는 데는 500불에서

옛 강경성결교회당(구 북옥감리교회)

2,000불 가량 들었다. 헌당식은 1924년 9월 선교사 헤인즈Paul E. Haines, 허인수의 집례로 거행되었다. 이 예배당은 함석 팔작지붕의 겹처마 목조 건물로 한옥교회의 특징을 유감없이 보여준다.

강경제일감리교회와 만동학교터

충남 논산군 강경읍 대흥리 10-206번지

1907년 무렵 시작된 강경제일감리교회는 창립 100주년을 맞아 역사전시실을 새롭게 단장했다. 그 안에 전시된 사진 자료들은 강경교회의 지난 100년을 압축해 보여 준다. 또 지난 1919년 건축되었던 옛 황산교회 시절 예배당의 창틀 일부가 거기에 보존되어 있다. 처음 강경교회는 고정된 예배당이 없어 지역 유지들의 지원 속에 덕유정 등에서 모이다가 1913년 남장로교의 황산교회와 통합하면서 황산리 죽림서원竹林書院 언덕 위에 정착하였다. 그 후 교회가 성장하면서 1918년과 1919년 잇달아 학교(만동학교, 황산리 102번지)와 예배당(황산리 107번지)을 지었다. 지금 그곳에 가면 당시 강경교회가 심혈을 기울여 운영했던 만동학교의 흔적을 발견할 수 있다.

강경성결교회 최초 신사참배 거부 선도 기념비

충남 논산군 강경읍 홍교리 129

강경성결교회의 '최초 신사참배 거부 선도 기념비'는 1924년 강경성결교회 주일학생 57명이 신사참배를 거부한 일을 기념하여 세운 것이다. 이 사건은 한국교회사에서 최초의 신사참배거부운동으로 기록되고 있다. 1922년 강경성결교회에 부임한 백신영 전도사는 1919년 상해 임시정부의 군자금 모금과 관련된 애국부인회 사건의 주역으로 투옥되었던 독립운동가였다. 그리고 백신영 전도사의 주일학교 교육은 당연히 그 교회의 학생들에게 깊은 영향을 주었다. 당시 일제는 강경 옥녀봉에 신사를 세우고 학교 학생들을 동원하여 참배를 강요했다.

그런데 유독 강경성결교회 주일학교에 다니던 학생들은 신사참배를 거부했던 것이다. 이 사건은 그 지역뿐 아니라 총독부까지 개입된 전국적인 사건으로 발전하였고 결국 그 학생들은 퇴학당했다.

병촌성결교회

 충남 논산군 성동면 개척리 228번지

강경 인근의 성동면 병촌성결교회는 1935년경 창립된 것으로 보인다. 충남의 성결교회는 1912년 부여 규암에서 시작해 은산, 홍산, 강경, 대전, 홍성 금당리, 조치원을 거쳐 대개 1930년대 논산 지역으로 확산되었다. 병촌교회는 1943년 12월 일제에 의해 성결교단이 강제 해산되면서 없어졌다가 해방 후 유제학, 김주옥 집사 등에 의해 재건되었다. 그런데 당시 성동면 일대는 사상 분쟁이 치열하게 전개되고 있던 지역이었다. 그리고 6·25전쟁이 발발하자 기독교인에 대한 박해가 시작되었다. 급기야 인천상륙작전 이후 1950년 9월 27-28일 이틀간 공산군들이 후퇴하는 과정에서 병촌교회 교인 16세대 66명(남 27, 여 39)이 학살되었다. 그 중 다섯 가정은 가족 전체가 몰살당했고, 교회적으로는 직원 1명, 세례교인 14명, 학습인 12명, 원입인 8명, 학생 및 유아 31명 등이 목숨을 잃었다.

병촌성결교회

병촌성결교회는 1956년 현 위치에 52평의 순교자기념예배당을 신축하고, 1989년에는 66인 순교기념탑을 건립하였다. 이 교회는 기독교대한성결교회 순교사적 제1호로 지정되어 있다.

✳ 강경 일반 유적지

구 남일당한약방

🚘 충남 논산군 강경읍 중앙리 88-1

구 남일당한약방

구 남일당한약방은 지상 2층 규모의 한식 목조건물, 우진각 기와지붕으로 1923년에 건축되었으며, 등록문화재 제10호로 지정되어 있다.

지붕내부의 상량문 癸亥年 八月 五日 酉時 立柱上梁을 통해 1923년에 준공된 것을 확인할 수 있는 이 건물은 강경의 하시장 下市場을 중심으로 했던 번성시기에 시장 중심에 위치하여 호황을 누리기도 하였으며, 1920년대 촬영되어진 강경시장 전경사진 속의 건물들 중에서 현존하는 유일한 건물로 건축 당시 '남일당 南一堂 한약방'으로 사용되던 것을 건축주가 바뀌면서 '연수당 건재 대약방 延壽堂 乾材 大藥房'으로 상호를 변경, 현재 후대 자손이 관리하고 있다.

구 한일은행 강경지점

🚘 충남 논산군 강경읍 서창리 51-1

구 한일은행 강경지점 건물은 등록문화재 제324호로 붉은 벽돌조의 단층건물로 대지면적은 978.83 m²이고, 대지 중앙에 르네상스풍 절충양식의 본관 건물이 전면 도로와 면해서 위치하고, 좌측은 공터, 우측은 부속동과 증축된 상가건물과 연접하여 재래시장과 맞닿아 있으며, 본관 뒤쪽으로 단층 주택이 본관과 연결되어 있다.

기능과 관련된 연혁을 보면 한일은행 강경지점 → 동일은행 강경지점 → 조흥은행 강경지점 → 충청은행 → 사유건물(중앙도서관) → 젓갈창고 → 논산시 매입으로 공공시설물로 활용되고 있다.

연산역 급수탑

 충남 논산군 연산면 청동리 127-74

연산역 급수탑은 등록문화재 제48호로 1911년 호남선의 개통과 함께 증기기관차의 물을 공급하기 위해 같은 해 12월 30일에 설치되어 1970년대까지 약 60여 년간 사용되었다.

전체 높이는 16.2 m, 지면부의 바깥지름은 5.28 m이며, 최상단부 철제 물탱크의 바깥지름이 4.1 m인 총 용량 30톤 규모의 원기둥형 급수탑으로 하단부에는 출입구와 창을 두어 사람이 출입할 수 있도록 하였다. 급수탑 옆에 위치하고 있는 우물은 폭이 2.8 m, 깊이 6 m의 크기로 급수탑의 급수용으로 축조하였다.

남아 있는 급수탑 가운데 연대가 가장 오래된 것으로 상단부의 급수탱크에는 외부에 철제 사다리를 설치하여 최상단 강판 지붕으로 올라갈 수 있도록 하고, 전체 높이의 2/3정도를 차지하고 있는 하단은 화강석으로 축조하고, 상단에 철제 물탱크를 올려놓은 형태로 몸체의 경우, 비교적 거칠게 다듬은 화강석을 주로 사용하고, 외곽선은 보다 정교하게 다듬은 돌을 사용하였으며, 출입구를 아치로 마감하고, 키스톤을 둠으로서 조형감을 더해주고 있다. 열차의 발전과 함께 기능을 상실한 채 남아 있던 이 급수탑은 근대 산업시설물로의 역사성과 희소한 조형적 가치를 지니고 있다.

네번째. 서천과 보령

서천(마량진)

🚗 충남 서천군 서면 마량리

충남 서천 마량진은 서해안고속도로 춘장대IC에서 쉽게 접근이 가능하다. 마량진 포구 옆에는 커다란 기념비 두 개가 나란히 세워져 있다. 하나는 '한국최초성경전래지'라는 돌비이고 다른 하나는 아펜젤러 선교사의 순직 104주년 기념비('하늘이여 바다여 파도여!')이다. 1902년 당시 아펜젤러Henry G. Appenzeller, 아편설라는 레이놀즈William D. Reynolds, 이눌서, 게일James S. Gale, 기일 선교사와 함께 성경 공인번역위원회의 위원으로 레이놀즈가 있던 목포로 가서 공동작업을 하기 위해 여객선 구마가와마루호球磨川丸를 탔다가 어청도 부근 해상에서 선박충돌 사고로 침몰하는 와중에 순직하고 말았다. 6월 11일 밤 11시 경의 일이었다. 서천군기독교연합회와 감리교 충청연회는 아펜젤러의 순직을 기려 이 기념비를 세운 것이다.

'한국최초성경전래지' 돌비는 1816년 9월 5일 성경이 최초로 전래된 것을 기념하여 건립되었다. 영국 순양함 알세스트Alceste호와 리라Lyla호가 현재의 충남 서천군 서면 마량리 앞바다에 나타난 것은 1816년 9월 4일 오후 3시경이었다. 당시 알세스트호의 함장은 맥스웰이었고, 지원함 리라호의 선장은 바실 홀Basil Hall이었다. 그 해 2월 영국을 떠나 6개월의 항해 끝에 중국 천진天津에 도착한 그들은, 암허스트Amherst경을 단장으로 하는 중국사절단 일행을 내려놓은 후 다시 해도 작성을 위하여 조선 서해안에 내항來航했던 것이다. 당시 마량진 갈곶에 정박한 알세스트호의 맥스웰 일행은 다시 보트를 타고 해안으로 이동하던 중 문정問情을 위해 군졸들을 거느리고 출동한 노대관老大官을 해상에서 만났다. 이렇게 마량진 앞바다에서 맥스웰 일행과 조우하여 리라호에 오른 노대관은 당시 마량진 첨사 조대복이었다. 첨사 조대복은 비인 현감 이승렬과 함께 이양선에 올라 문정問情을 시도했지만 언어의 불통으로 특별한 정보를 얻지는 못했던 것 같다. 이어서 조대복은 다시 알세스트호에 승선해서 재차 문정을 시도했으나 결과는 마찬가지였다. 그 날 밤 마량진으로 돌아온 첨사는 곧 이양선 출현을 충청 수영水營에 알렸고, 충청 수사水使 이재홍李載弘은 즉시 이 사실을 상부에 보고하는 한편 그 후속 조치에 대한 조정의 답신을 기다렸다.

다음 날인 9월 5일 아침 조대복과 이승렬은 재차 리라호에 승선했다. 그들은 리라호를 실측하고 승무원들의 숫자를 조사했다. 또 배 안에 머물면서 함께 식사하고, 현감 이승렬은 리라호의 군의관에게 진찰을 받기도 했다. 그 과정에서 현감 이승렬이 맥스웰 일행에게서 책을 선물로 받게 되었다. 이승렬에 이어 첨사 조대복이 성경을 선물로 받은 것은 그 날 정오 무렵이었다. 맥스웰 일행의 육지 상륙 시도를 완강하게 거부하던 조대복은, 남쪽을 향해 그곳을 떠나려던 알세스트호의 항행을 제지하며 다시 승선하였다. 조정의 명령을 기다리고 있었던 조대복으로서는 맥스웰 일행의 돌연한 출발에 당황하였던 것이다. 그는 경직된 자세를 보였다. 그런데 몸짓을 이용하여 각자의 입장을 표현하면서 좌중의 분위기가 조금 누그러지자 조대복의 관심은 선실의 서적으로 옮겨 갔다. 그리고 이 때 마량진 첨사 조대복은 선물로 성경을 받아가지고 하선했던 것이다. 그리고 알세스트호는 그 곳을 떠났다.

영문판으로 추정되는, 조대복이 받은 이 성경은 그 후에 어떻게 되었을까? 우선 조정은 이양선이 임의로 드나들게 한 책임을 물어 첨사 조대복과 현감 이승렬을 파직시켰다. 그리고 계속해서 이 사건의 후속 조치에 관한 충청수사 이재홍의 보고가 이어진다. 우리는 여기서 조대복이 받은 성서의 행방을 어렴풋하게 알 수 있다. 조대복과 이승렬이 받은 서적들은 일단 상사上使와 병영 그리고 수영에 각각 1권씩 나누어 이관되었다. 그들은 그 책들을 소유하지 않고 즉시 유관 기관에 보낸 것이다. 그리고 다시 이들이 파직된 후 함선에서 그들이 받았던 물건들은 모두 충청수사에게 보내져 결국 서울로 이송된 것으로 보인다. 충청수사의 보고가 그것을 입증한다. 그 후 그 서적들이 어떻게 되었는지에 대해서는 크게 알려진 게 없다.

보령(고대도)

🚗 충남 보령시 오천면 삽시도리

충남 대천항에서 배를 타고 1시간 20분을 가면 고대도에 닿는다. 바로 개신교 선교사로서 한국을 최초로 방문한 이라고 알려진 귀츨라프Karl Friedrich August Gutzlaff, 1803~1851가 1832년 여름 약 20일 간 머물면서 복음을 전했다는 바로 그 섬이다. 그래서 현재 고대도교회는 귀츨라프기념교회라 부르며 2층에 그를 기리는 역사관을 두고 있다. 그런데 귀츨라프가 머문 곳이 고대도가 아니라 인근 원산도일 것이라는 주장도 계속 제기되고 있다. 실제로 원산도에는 이미 지난 1982년에 귀츨라프의 방문을 기념하는 "선교사 카알 귀츨라프 기념비"가 그곳의 한 유지에 의해 세워지기도 했고, 최근에는 원산도 설을 지지하는 책(신호철, 『귀츨라프행전』, 2009, 양화진선교회)도 나와 있다. 여기서는 일단 기존의 견해인 고대도 설에 입각하여 귀츨라프를 소개하기로 한다.

1832년 영국 동인도회사는 린제이H. H. Lindsay를 책임자로 하여, 극동의 새로운 통상지를 개척 탐사하려는 목적으로, 타이완-조선서해안-제주도-오키나와에 이르는 항해를 계획하였다. 그런데 선장 린제이는 중국어에 능통한 의사요 선교사인 귀츨라프 목사를 선의船醫 겸 통역관으로 동승시켰다. 당시 중국에 주재하고 있던 선교사 모리슨R. Morrison은 그에게 한문성서를 주어 반포토록 하였다. 동인도회사가 준비한 암허스트호는 1천 톤급의 군함으로 선장 리스Rees를 포함한 67명의 승무원이 타고 있었다. 이 항해의 목적은 영국과의 통상에 적당한 항구를 조사하고 그 지방 관민의 통상 개시에 관한 관심을 살피는 데에 있었다.

1832년 7월 25일 귀츨라프 일행은 충남 보령군 오천면에 소재한 고대도古代島에 당도하였다. 고대도 도착 다음날인 1832년 7월 26일 귀츨라프 일행은 그 지역의 지방관이었던 홍주 목사 이민회와 수군 장교 김형수의 방문을 받는다. 귀츨라프는 그들에게 자신들이 조선을 방문한 목적이 국왕에게 통상을 정식으로 청원하려는 것임을 밝히고, 조선 관리들이 호의를 보이자 성서 한 질과 전도문서 그리고 유리그릇, 목양목, 모직물, 담요 등과 함께 한문으로 쓴 통상청원서를 그들에게 전달했다.

통상 청원에 대한 조선 정부의 답신을 기다리면서 귀츨라프 일행은 대략 8월 11일까지 고대도에 머물렀다. 7월 27일에는 고대도에 상륙하여 섬 전체를 돌아보고 그들을 방문한 두 명의 조선 사람에게 기독교를 소개했다. 또 그들 중 한사람인 '양이Yang-yih'는 한문으로 된 주기도문을 보여주자 즉석에서 그것을 한글로 번역하기도 하였다. 그러나 그들은 기독교에 대해 별 반응을 보이지는 않았다. 아울러 귀츨라프는 주민들에게 전도문서와 복음서를 나누어주었으며, 성서를 줄 때에는 역사와 지리책도 함께 주었다. 또 7월 30일 오후에는 해변으로 가서 100개가 넘는 감자를 심고, 재배법을 설명한 종이를 땅 주인에게 주었다. 7월 31일에는 주민들에게 포도주와 포도즙 만드는 법을 가르쳐 주었다. 8월 2일에는 노인 감기 환자 60명분의 약을 처방하여 나누어주었다.

홍주 목사로부터 외국 선박의 고대도 정박에 관한 최초의 보고를 받은 승정원에서는 역관譯官 오계순을 파견하여 문정問情한 다음, 우의정 김이교의 명령에 따라 홍주 목사 등이 조정의 사전 허락을 받기도 전에 외국인의 통상 청원서와 진상품을 받은 것은 부당한 처사이므로, 귀츨라프 일행에게 돌려줄 것을 지시한다. 1832년 8월 9일 조정의 특사 자격으로 암허스트호에 승선한 오계순은 통상 청원의 거절과 선물 반환을 통고하였다. 실망한 귀츨라프 일행은 떠날 계획을 세우고 물품을 요청한 후에, 8월 11일 물품이 공급되자 서한과 진상품의 접수를 거절하고는 20여 일간 머물렀던 고대도를 떠났다.

귀츨라프의 충청도 서해안 방문은 오직 조선 선교만을 염두에 두고 이루어진 것이 아니다. 그가 승선했던 암허스트호는 영국 동인도회사의 개척탐사선으로 그 임무는 통상을 위한 항구 조사와 통상에 대한 그 지방 관민의 관심의 정도를 알아보려는 데에 있었다. 귀츨라프의 승선 목적은 조선 방문에만 국한된 것이 아니라 아직 알려지지 않은 극동의 변방 지역을 선교적인 관심을 갖고 광범위하게 탐색하고자 했던 것이다. 충청도의 서해안 고대도에 약 20일간 체류하면서 주민들에게 성경을 나누어 주고 기독교를 소개하는 등 제한적인 접촉을 시도했지만 역시 그의 포교 내용에 관심을 가진 한국인은 없었다. 귀츨라프는 이점을 못내 아쉬워했다. 그의 고대도 전도 활동을 통해 한국인 개종자가 발생하기에는 주어진 시간이 너무도 짧았다.

CHAPTER 6

대구·경북 지역

대구광역시 → 안동시 → 기타

1. 대구지역

✲ 대구·경북 기독교의 시작

　대구·경북 지방은 처음부터 미국 북장로교의 선교구역이었다. 1891년부터 부산에서 활동하기 시작한 북장로교 선교사 베어드William M. Baird, 배위량의 선교 반경은 경상도 전역을 포괄하고 있었다. 1893년 봄 베어드는 43일간에 걸쳐 경남뿐만이 아니라 대구, 상주, 안동, 의성, 영천, 경주 등을 둘러보았다. 경북 내륙 깊숙한 곳까지 그의 발걸음이 미쳤음을 알 수 있다. 그러면서 대구가 베어드의 눈에 들어왔다. 당시 대구는 경상감영이 있던 행정 중심지이자 인구 밀집 지역이었다. 결국 베어드는 1896년 대구로 거처를 옮기게 된다. 그 후 얼마의 준비과정을 거쳐 1899년 5월 북장로교 대구 스테이션이 공식 개설되었다. 북장로교 영남 선교의 축이 부산에서 대구로 전환된 것이다. 이어서 북장로교는 대구·경북에 집중하고자 경남 선교를 호주선교부에 맡기고 부산에서 완전히 철수하였다.

　대구 스테이션의 개척자 베어드는 그 몇 달 뒤 서울로 전임하였고 그의 처남이었던 아담스James E. Adams, 안의와가 의료선교사 존슨Woodbridge O. Johnson, 장인차과 함께 1897년부터 대구·경북 선교를 이어갔다. 그리고 1899년에는 브루엔Henry M. Bruen, 부해리, 1901년에는 바렛William M. Barrett, 박위렴이 합류하였다. 1902년부터 대구 선교사들은 경북을 세 구역으로 나누어 동부의

대구·경북 지역

계명대학교 동산의료원 챔니스 주택

아담스, 안동을 포함한 북부의 바렛, 서부의 브루엔으로 전도사역을 분담하였다. 1906년에는 남부 구역을 신설하여 맥파랜드Edwin F. McFarland, 맹의와가 그곳을 맡았다. 그 외에 대구 스테이션 구내에는 존슨이 세운 제중원(지금 동산의료원) 그리고 계성·신명학교가 연달아 세워져 복음-의료-교육 분야로 이루어지는 삼각 선교 체제가 완성되었다. 경북 기독교는 이러한 과정을 겪으면서 확산의 계기를 마련하였다.

대구에 이어 북장로교 선교사들이 경북 선교의 두 번째 거점으로 삼은 곳은 안동이었다. 대구에서 70마일 거리의 안동은 걸어서 사흘거리의 교통 한계 때문에 순회를 통한 관리가 매우 어려운 지점에 있었다. 그런데 바렛과 맥파랜드 그리고 어드만Walter C. Erdman, 어도만이 번갈아 담당했던 이곳 경북 북부지역의 교인 수가 1903년 12명에서 1906년 200명을 거쳐 1908년에는 1,000명 이상으로 늘었다. 선교사들이 고무되지 않을 리 없었다. 결국 북장로교 선교부는 안동에 스테이션을 설치하기로 하고 소텔Chace C. Sawtell, 사우대에게 개척 임무를 맡겼다. 또 마침 북감리교와의 선교지역분할 협상 결과 북장로교가 원주에서 철수하면서 웰번Arthur G. Welbon, 오월번과 의료선교사 플레쳐Archibald G. Fletcher, 별리추가 안동에 투입되었다. 크로더스John Y. Crothers, 권찬영는 1909년 11월 갑작스레 사망한 소텔의 후임으로 이듬해 안동땅을 밟았다. 그 후 안동의 선교사들은 금곡동 언덕에 4채의 선교사 주택을 지어 생활의 안정성을 확보한 다음 인근에 조성된 같은 선교구내의 안동교회-계명학교-성소병원을 중심으로 본격적인 경북 북부지역 선교에 착수하였다.

북장로교 선교부의 경북 지역 스테이션과 선교구역

스테이션(개설연도)	선교구역
대구(1899)	대구 경산 경주 김천 상주 선산 달성 칠곡 성주 고령 군위
안동(1909)	안동 의성 예천 영양 청송 영주 봉화

첫번째. 대구광역시

✽ 대구 소개

대구에는 금호강과 그 지류로 둘러싸인 들판을 중심으로 선사시대부터 사람들이 많이 모여 살았던 것으로 추정된다. 삼국 통일 이후인 신문왕 때에는 달구벌(대구의 옛 이름)이 천도의 후보지로 부각되기도 했으나, 진골귀족의 반발로 좌절되었다. 그리고 후삼국의 혼란기에 이곳은 후백제와 고려의 각축장이었다. 신라에 대한 주도권을 장악할 수 있는 요충지였기 때문이다. 927년 후백제 견훤이 신라를 침범해오자 왕건이 신라를 도우러 경주로 가던 중 동수(동화사 인근 지역)에서 만나 일대 격전을 벌였다. 이른바 동수대전이다. 이 싸움으로 인해 대구에는 왕건과 관련된 지명이 많이 남아 있다. 즉 왕건의 군사가 크게 패하였다는 파군재破軍峙, 왕건의 탈출로를 비추어 주던 새벽달의 반야월半夜月, 왕건이 혼자 앉아 쉬었다는 독좌암獨坐巖 등이 그것이다.

그 후 고려 말까지 대구는 조그마한 현縣에 불과했다. 당시 경상도의 대표적인 도시는 경주와 상주였다. 경상도라는 도명道名 자체가 그것을 상징한다. 경주와 상주는 조선 전기에도 각각 경상좌도와 우도의 감영소재지였다. 그런데 임진왜란 이후인 1601(선조 34)년 경상감영이 대구로 이전 설치되었다. 조선 왕조 수립 이후 인구와 조세수입의 증가라는 사회경제적 성장과 군사전략상의 중요성이 부각되면서 결국 대구는 영남 지방의 중심지로 발돋움할 수 있었던 것이다. 또한 감영의 이전은 대구의 상업도시로서의 모습을 선명하게 만들었다. 대구에서 장시가 번창한 것은 임진왜란 이후의 전후 복구과정에서 생필품의 수요가 크게 증가한데 기인한 것이다. 거기다가 1678년 상인의 대대적인 활동을 유발시킨 대동법이 경상도에 실시되면서 상설점포가 형성되었다. 대구 약령시藥令市는 1658(효종 9)년에 경상감영의 객사 주변에서 처음 열렸는데, 해를 거듭할수록 번창하여 중국과 일본을 잇는 대규모의 시장조직으로 발전하였다.

국채보상운동은 1907년 대구에서 서상돈, 김광제 등에 의하여 처음 시작되었다. 이 운동은 당시 대한제국 정부가 일본으로부터 들여온 1,300만원의 차관을, 금연을 통한 국민 의연금으로 갚자는 것이었는데, 전국적인 호응을 얻은 바 있다. 또 일제강점기인 1915년에는 윤상태, 서상일 등이 중심이 되어 비밀 항일독립운동단체인 조선국권회복단 중앙총부가 대구(당시 달성군 수성면) 안일암에서 결성되었다. 이들은 3·1운동에 적극 가담하여 지방의 3·1운동을 주도하였을 뿐만 아니라 상해上海 임시정부가 수립되자 각 지방에서 모은 독립운동자금을 송금하기도 하였다. 또한 우림단儒林團이 전개한 파리강화회의에 제출할 독립청원서 작성 운동에도 적극 참여하였다. 그러나 이들의 활동은 끝내 일본경찰에 탐지되어 36명의 단원이 체포되고 조직은 해체되었다.

❋ 대구 기독교 전래

선교사의 신분으로 대구를 처음 방문한 이는 감리교의 아펜젤러Henry G. Appenzeller, 아편설라와 존스George H. Jones, 조원시였다. 그들은 1888년 여름 서울에서 부산으로 가는 전도여행 길에 잠깐 대구를 들렀다고 한다. 이어서 1889년과 1890년에는 캐나다선교사 게일James S. Gale, 기일과 호주선교사 데이비스Joseph H. Davies, 덕배시가 각각 대구를 방문했다. 그들 역시 부산으로 가는 길에 스치듯 대구를 지났다.

선교를 염두에 두고 대구를 방문한 첫 사람은 북장로교 선교사 베어드William M. Baird, 배위량였다. 1890년부터 부산 스테이션을 개척한 그는 1893년 4월 경상도 전역을 순회하던 중 대구를 둘러보았다. 그 후 두어 차례 남부 내륙 지방을 답사한 베어드는 결국 북장로교 선교부 남부 내륙 스테이션을 대구에 설치하기로 하고, 1896년 부산에서 대구 남문안 한옥(현 중구 남성로 50번지 대구제일교회 구예배당 자리)으로 이주했다. 이후로 대구는 북장로교 영남 선교의 중심지가 되었다. 하지만 대구 기독교의 실질적인 출발은 베어드가 아니라 그의 처남인 아담스 선교사에 의해 이루어졌다. 베어드는 부임하던 그 해 가을 서울로 전임하였고, 이듬해인 1897년 가을부터 아담스가 대구 선교를 맡게 되었기 때문이다. 또 그 무렵 의료선교사 존슨이 합류하였다. 그때부터 아담스는 교회(대구제일교회)와 학교(대남소학교)를 시작했고, 존슨은 병원(제중원)을 열었다.

그리고 1899년에는 브루엔, 1901년에는 바렛 선교사가 대구에 부임하였다. 이렇게 어느 정도 선교 인력이 보강되자 대구 선교사들은 1902년부터 경북을 세 구역으로 나누어 동부의 아담스, 북부의 바렛, 서부의 브루엔으로 전도사역을 분담하였다. 1906년에는 남부 구역을 신설하여 맥파랜드Edwin F. McFarland, 맹의와가 그곳을 맡았다. 그 후 바렛이 건강 문제로 귀국하면서 북부구역은 맥파랜드와 어드만(1908) 그리고 그린필드Willis M. Greenfield, 권필두, 1912와 블레어Herbert E. Blair, 방혜법, 1914가 잇달아 담당하였고, 브루엔은 1910년 서부구역의 절반을 탐스John U. Selwyn Toms, 도서원에게 인계하였다. 또 1913년부터는 아담스와 맥파랜드가 서로의 구역을 맞바꾸어 사역하였다.

대구 스테이션의 교육사업은 아담스 선교사가 1900년 대남소학교를 세우면서 시작되었다. 이어서 1901년 여선교사 노어스Miss Sadie Nourse에 의해 형성된 여학생반이 1902년부터 브루엔 부인에 의해 신명여자소학교로 발전하였다. 그 후 이 두 학교는 희원학교와 순도여학교로 이름을 바꾸었다가 1920년대 희도학교로 통합되었다. 그리고 중등학교로는 1906년 아담스에 의해 설립된 계성중학교와 역시 브루엔 부인이 1907년 세운 신명여학교가 있다.

대구 스테이션의 의료선교는 1899년 12월 의사 존슨에 의해 개원된 시약소施藥所, 제중원를 중심으로 전개되었는데, 1900년 여름까지 존슨이 진료한 환자는 모두 1,700명에 달했고, 그 외에 80회의 왕진과 50회의 수술이 이루어졌다. 이처럼 제중원의 존재는 북장로교 대구 선교의 기폭제가 되었다. 그리고 1910년부터는 존슨에 이어 플레처Archibald G. Fletcher, 별리추가 의료 사역을 계승하였고, 간호사로는 카메론Miss Christine Cameron, 캐머런과 맥켄지Miss Mary McKenzie가 활동하였다.

✱ 대구 기독교 유적지

대구제일교회 구 예배당

🚗 대구시 중구 남성로 50번지

대구시 중구 남성로 50번지 약전골목 약령시한약문화관 옆에는 대구제일교회가 1933년 지은 2층 붉은 벽돌 예배당(대구시 유형문화재 30호)이 남아있다. 대구 선교를 위해 베어드가 처음 매입한 한옥 4채의 남문안 선교 부지가 바로 이 터였다. 또 여기는 베어드를 이어 대구에 온 아담스와 존슨이 교회와 학교를 시작한 장소이기도 하다. 그 후 선교사들은 인근의 동산 언덕 2만평의 땅을 매입하여 선교사 주택과 병원, 학교를 지었고, 이곳은 주로 교회당으로 사용되었다. 교인이 차츰 늘어나자 교회는 1907년 이 자리에 함석지붕으로 된 140평의 두 번째 예배당을 지었다. 1919년

대구제일교회 구 예배당

3·1운동 당시 이만집 목사와 김태련 조사 그리고 계성과 신명의 교사, 학생들이 일으킨 대구만세운동은 바로 두 번째 예배당 시절의 일이었다. 그로부터 14년 뒤인 1933년 총공사비 1만 5천원을 들여 건축한 세 번째 예배당을 지금 우리가 보고 있는 것이다. 이 건물은 1937년 벽돌조 5층 높이의 종탑을 세우면서 현재의 모습을 갖게 되었다. 그리고 그 입구 왼쪽에는 '목사안의와선교기념비'가 서있다. 1935년 경북노회가 아담스 선교사의 경북 선교 개척 공로를 후세에 전하기 위하여 건립하였는데, 일제 말기 파괴될 뻔한 것을 교회 뜰에 묻어두었다가 해방 후 발굴하여 지금 위치에 다시 세웠다고 한다. 입구 오른쪽에 있는 것은 '제일교회50주년기념비'이다.

계명대학교 동산의료원

 대구시 중구 달성로 216번지

대구제일교회는 지난 1994년 남성로 구교회당에서 10분 거리인 동산동 3,600평 구 영남신학교 자리 위에 화강암 예배당을 지어 이전했다. 그리고 그 옆에는 지금 동산의료원(대구광역시 중구 달성로 216번지)과 신명고등학교(대구광역시 중구 동산동 206번지)가 자리하고 있는데 1901년부터 선교사들이 조성한 대구 스테이션이 바로 이 일대 '청라언덕'에 들어서 있었다. 1897년 남문안 한옥에서 교회와 병원 사업을 시작한 아담스와 존슨은 대구 선교가 어느 정도 정착되어 가자 곧바로 동산동 언덕 2만평을 사들여 본격적인 선교 구내 건설에 착수하였던 것이다. 그리하여 1901년 3채의 선교사 주택을 시작으로 병원과 학교 등이 들어섰다. 그 후 10여 채 더 지어진 선교사 주택과 함께 숲이 으거진 동산정東山町 대구 스테이션은 일제강점기 도시의 명소로 성가가 높았다.

대구제일교회를 거쳐 동산의료원에 들어서면 왼편에 종탑이 눈에 띈다. 지난 1999년 10월 1일 동산의료원 개원 100주년을 맞아 세운 기념종탑이다. 동산의료원이 그 해 담장 허물기 운동을 시작하면서 병원의 유서 깊은 정문과 중문의 기둥과 담장 일부를 옮겨와 세우고, 그 위에 병원이 초창기에 개척했던 교회의 종을 하나 달아놓았다. 그 앞에는 사과나무 한 그루가 서있는데 여기에는 사연이 있다. 바로 이 병원의 초대 원장이었던 존슨 선교사가 사택 뒤뜰 정원에 심었던 미국 사과나무 가운데 유일하게 남아있는 자손 나무로, 대구시 보호수 1호(2000. 10. 19)로 지정되어있다.

대구선교사묘역인 '은혜의 정원Garden of Mercy'은 100주년기념종탑 맞은편에 위치해 있다. 원래 동산병원 동쪽 지금의 제일교회 담 밑에 방치되어 있었던 것을 이곳으로 옮겨 재정비한 것이다. '은혜의 정원'에는 지금 12개의 묘석墓石이 자리 잡고 있는데, 모두 대구·경북 지방에서 활동한 선교사와 그 자녀들이다. 먼저 앞 줄 맨 왼쪽의 마르다 브루엔Martha S. Bruen, 부마태은 헨리 브루엔Henry M. Bruen, 부해리 선교사의 부인으로 1902년 남편과 함께 대구에 부임하여 신명여학교를 설립하는 등 여성교육과 여성선교에 헌신하다가 1930년 10월 20일 55세를 일기로 운명하였다. 바로 그 옆에는 브루엔 부부의 딸들인 안나Anna Bruen Kierekoper, 1905년 2월 2일생와 해리엇Harriette Bruen Davis, 1910년 10월 2일생의 합장묘비가 있다. 두 자매의 무덤은 지난 2007년 10월 22일 신명학교 개교 100주년을 맞아 이곳으로 이장되었다. 앞줄 가운데 누워 있는 스위츠Martha Switzer, 성마리다는 독신 여성선교사로 1911년 대구에 와서 신명여학교 교사로 활동하다가 1929년 과로로 별세하였다. 그 앞의 도어슨John Dawson 무덤은 이 묘역에서 가장 최근인 2008년 11월 11일에 조성되었다. 1963년부터 1966년까지 동산병원 외과 과장을 지낸 도어슨은 지난 2007년 2월 80세의 나이로 사망하였는데, 고인은 60년 의사 생활 중 한국에서의 시절이 가장 행복했었다고 유언했다. 앞줄 맨 오른쪽의 조엘 헨더슨Joel R. Henderson은 남침례교 선교사 윌리 헨더슨Willie G. Henderson 선교사의 아들로 1964년 6월 2일 태어나서 몇 시간 살지 못하고 사망했다. 그 위의 바바라 챔니스Barbara F. Chamness, 1927는 1925년부터 1941년까지 대구에서 활동한 챔니스O. Vaughan Chamness, 차미수 선교사의 딸로 역시 단명했다. 챔니스 선교사는 대구 스테이션의 나병원癩病院이었던 애락원愛樂園에서 자활사업으로 농사와 축산을 지도했으며, 부원장을 역임하기도 하였다. 그 앞의 헬렌 윈Hellen M. Winn은 북장로교 선교사 윈Roger E. Winn, 인노절의 갓난 딸로 1913년

11월 10일 출생하여 열흘 만에 숨을 거두었다. 로저 윈은 안동 스테이션을 대표하는 선교사였다. 그 옆의 루트 번스틴Ruth Bernsten, 1918. 10. 7~1919. 1. 28은 스웨덴 출신 구세군 선교사 번스틴Brigador A. Bernsten, 변세돈의 딸로 생후 4개월 만에 사망하였다. 당시 구세군 대구지방관으로 사역했던 번스틴은 1931년 귀국했다가 6·25 전쟁 이후 중립국감시위원단 스웨덴 대표로 내한한 바 있다. 그 왼쪽의 버디 헨더슨Buddy Henderson, 1920. 6. 5~1921. 9. 17은 계성학교 4대 교장이었던 해롤드 헨더슨Harold H. Henderson, 현거선 선교사의 아들로 아기 때 숨을 거두었다. 뒷줄 왼쪽의 비석은 스웨덴 출신 구세군 여선교사 퀼러Magda Kholer, 1887~1913의 무덤이 있던 자리에 세워졌다. 1913년 사망한 퀼러의 유해는 이곳 대구에 묻혀 있다가 지난 2000년 10월 2일 서울 양화진으로 이장되었다. 그 옆은 대구스테이션을 개척한 아담스James E. Adams, 안의와 선교사의 부인 넬리 딕Nellie Dick Adams, 탁넬리의 무덤이다. 1866년생인 그녀는 1895년 3개월 된 아들 에드워드Edward A. Adams, 안두화를 안고 태평양을 건너와 남편과 함께 초창기 대구 스테이션의 아동·여성선교에 헌신하였다. 넬리 딕은 1909년 10월 31일 넷째아이 유산 후유증으로 43세의 나이에 운명하여 대구에 묻힌 첫 외국인이 되었다. 마지막으로 소텔Chase C. Sawtell, 사우대 선교사의 묘비가 있다. 1907년 10월 16일 북장로교 의료선교사로 내한한 소텔은 안동 스테이션 개설 책임자로 안동 지역을 순회 전도하다가 장티프스에 걸려 1909년 11월 16일 소천하였다. 그의 나이 스물여덟이었다.

　동산의료원 구내에는 모두 3채의 선교사주택이 남아 있다. 지금 선교박물관(대구시 유형문화재 24호)으로 개방되어 있는 사과나무 옆의 스위츠주택은 지하실을 갖춘 2층 건물로 동서양 절충양식을 취하고 있다. 1910년 무렵 건축된 이 집에서는 스위츠를 비롯 계성학교 교장을 지낸 헨더슨과 계명대 초대 학장인 캠벨Archibald Campbell, 감부열 선교사 등이 살았다고 한다. 현재 1층에는 각종 성경과 선교유물이 있고, 2층에는 성막이 전시되어 있다. 의료박물관(대구시 유형문화재 25호) 건물인 챔니스주택에는 계성학교 2대 교장인 라이너Ralph O. Reiner, 나도래와 챔니스 그리고 1948년부터는 동산의료원을 크게 발전시킨 하워드 마펫Howard F. Moffett, 마포화열이 오랫동안 거주했다. 지금 이곳에는 19세기 말 이후의 많은 동서양 의료기기가 소장되어 있다. '은혜의 정원' 앞에 있는 교육역사박물관(대구시 유형문화재 26호)은 원래 블레어주택이었다. 블레어Herbert E. Blair, 방혜법 선교사는 1914년부터 1941년까지 27년간 대구에서 활동하였다. 이곳은 시대별 교육자료와 대구 3·1운동 관련 자료 등으로 꾸며져 있다.

계성중학교

대구시 중구 대신동 277번지

동산의료원 마당을 가로질러 길 건너편 서문시장 안 대신동 언덕에는 대구 스테이션이 운영하던 계성중학교가 있다. 교문에 들어서서 일직선의 길을 걸으면 50계단이 나오고 다시 그 계단을 오르면 웅장한 모습의 핸더슨관(대구시 유

계성중학교 핸더슨관

형문화재 47호)을 마주하게 된다. 지금도 학교 본관으로 사용하고 있는 이 건물은 당시 교장 핸더슨이 1931년 미국에서 블레어가 모금해온 선교비로 지었다고 한다. 화강암 기단석 위에 붉은 벽돌로 중세유럽의 성채처럼 쌓아올린 핸더슨관은 1964년 한 층을 더 올려 지금은 3층이다. 그리고 핸더슨관 왼쪽에 보이는 아담한 동서양 절충식 건물이 바로 대구시 유형문화재 45호인 아담스관이다. 아담스(안의와) 선교사의 어머니인 낸시 아담스Nancy H. Adams를 기념하는 건물이다. 1906년 남문안 한옥에서 중등과정 계성학교를 시작한 아담스 선교사는 1908년 3월 대신동 언덕에 이 건물을 짓고 학교를 옮겼다. 화강암 기단 위에 붉은 벽돌의 아담스관은 지금 계성중학교 교무실(2층), 방송실, 컴퓨터실(1층)로 사용되고 있다. 특히 지하실은 대구지역 3·1운동 당시 태극기와 독립선언문을 인쇄한 장소로서 역사적으로 중요한 곳이다. 핸더슨관 오른쪽의 맥퍼슨관(대구시 유형문화재 46호)은 계성의 2대 교장 라이너 선교사가 미국의 독지가 맥퍼슨McPherson에게 자금 지원을 받아 1913년 붉은벽돌조 2층으로 건축되었다. 현재는 계성교회와 컴퓨터실로 사용되고 있다.

계성중학교 맥퍼슨관

대구 일반 유적지

관덕정순교기념관

대구시 중구 남산2동 938-19번지

관덕정은 원래 무과시험을 관장했던 곳이며, 무사들이 무예를 연마하던 연병장이 있었던 곳이다. 이 주변 아미산은 국법을 어긴 중죄인을 처형하는 형장이 있었던 곳으로, 경상도 지역 천주교 순교자들이 무고한 생명을 잃은 곳이기도 하다. 따라서 대구대교구는 가톨릭 200주년 기념사업으로 관덕정 순교기념관을 건립해 순교자들의 뜻을 높이 받들었다. 지하 1층, 지상 3층 건물로 지어진 순교기념관 건물 지하엔 성인의 유해를 모신 성당과 생활전시실이, 1층에 흥선대원군의 척화비가, 2층에는 천주교 교우촌과 순교자들의 유물이, 3층에는 대구 유일의 성인인 이윤일 요한 성인의 자료와 누각이 있다.

계산성당

대구시 중구 계산동 2가 71번지

대구지하철 반월당역에서 내려 계산오거리 방향으로 10분 걷다보면 성당이 보인다. 사적 제290호인 계산성당은 처음에는 한식 기와집의 십자형 성당으로 세워졌으나 이듬해인 1901년에 원인모를 화재로 소실되었다. 이에 로베르 신부는 서상돈, 김종학, 정규옥 등의 협력으로 1902년 소실된 장소에 다시 고딕식 벽돌건물로 준공하여 1903년 낙성식을 거행하였다. 이는 우리나라에서 건립된 고딕양식의 성당으로는 서울, 평양에 이어 세 번째이고 영남지방에서는 최초의 것이었다.

그 후 1911년 천주교 대구교구가 설정되어 주교좌성당이 되자 성당을 증축하여 종각을 2배로 높이고 성당 뒤쪽을 확장하여 1918년 12월 비로소 현재의 성당 모습을 갖추게 되었다. 이 성당은 대구지방에 천주교가 토착화되는 과정에서의 고층을 상징하는 건조물이라 할 수 있으며, 동시에 서양의 건축양식이 대구에 도입된 표본이기도 하다.

19세기 초반에 대구에 천주교가 들어왔지만 계속되는 박해로 인해 자유로운 포교활동을 할 수 없어 신나무골, 새방골, 한티마을 등 산간벽지로 그 활동 지역을 옮겨 다녔다. 그 후, 1886년에 체결된 조프조약을 계기로 천주교의 활동은 본격적으로 전개되었다. 바로 그 무렵, 신나무골에서 은신하던 로베르 신부가 세상에 나서면서 계산동 성당이 세워졌다. 건물은 적·흙색 벽돌을 적절히 섞어 고딕양식으로 지었으며, 전체적으로 라틴십자형을 이루고 있다. 서쪽 출입구 좌우에 2기의 종탑을 세우고 그 사이어 장미꽃잎 모양의 창을 내어 단조로움을 피하고 있다.

계산성당

계산동 성당과 도로 하나를 사이에 둔 남산동은 대구 천주교의 발상지로, 가톨릭대학을 비롯해 교구청, 수녀원, 성모당 등이 거대한 가톨릭 타운을 이루고 있다. 특히, 프랑스 루르드 동굴을 본떠서 만들었다는 성모당은 전국적으로 유명한 천주교 성지이다.

국채보상운동기념공원

 대구시 중구 동인동 2가 42번지

대구 중구 국채보상로 종각네거리에는 1907년 대구에서 시작된 대표적 민족운동인 국채보상운동을 기념하기 위한 공원이 조성되어 있다. 1907년(융희 1) 2월에 대구에서 시작된 국권회복운동으로 전 국민이 합심하여 일본에 대한 국채(1,300만 원)를 갚아 경제적으로 독립하자는 운동이었다. 서상돈·김광제·박해령 등 16명이 대구에서 조직한 국채보상기성회國債報償期成會는 곧 서울을 비롯한 전국 각지로 확대되었고, 특히 「대한매일신보」·「황성신문」·「제국신문」·「만세보」 등 언론기관이 자금 모집에 적극 참여하였다. 이를 위하여 단연운동斷煙運動이 전개되었고, 부녀자들은 비녀와 가락지를 팔아서 이에 호응했다. 그 외에도 여성단체인 진명부인회·대한부인회 등에서는 보상금모집소를 설치하여 적극적인 활동을 벌였다. 그리하여 이 운동이 실시된 이후 4월말까지 보상금을 낸 사람은 4만여 명이고, 5월말까지 230만 원 이상이 모아졌다. 이에 대해 일제는 송병준 등 친일파가 지휘하던 매국단체 일진회를 이용하여 방해하고, 통감부에서 국채보상회의 간사인 양기탁을 보상금횡령이라는 누명을 씌워 구속하는 등 적극적으로 탄압했다. 결국 양기탁은 무죄로 석방되었지만 국채보상운동은 더 이상 진전되지 못하고 좌절되고 말았다.

그러나 이 운동은 우리 민족의 강렬하고 자발적인 애국정신이 발휘된 국권회복운동으로 평가되고 있으며, IMF를 맞이하였을 때 금모아 나라 살리기 운동의 '시원'이기도 하였다. 이 공원에는 향토 시인들의 시비, 대형 영상시설물 등이 분수와 정자, 석조물 등 깔끔한 조형물과 어우러져 있다.

대구 시민 만세운동 기념비

대구시 동구 효목1동 234-33번지

기미년 만세소리는 한반도 전체에서 울려 퍼졌고 대구도 예외는 아니었다. 기미년(1919) 3월 8일 서문시장 만세운동과 1919년 3월 10일 남문시장 만세운동 때에 대구 시민들이 참여하였고, 1985년 1월에 이들 선열들의 애국정신을 기리기 위해 만세운동 기념비를 건립하였다.

비문의 내용은 다음과 같다.

"기미년 3월 8일 정오 대구 서문시장에서 사회지도자와 학생들이 주도한 대대적인 독립만세운동이 있었다. 준비된 독립선언문을 낭독하고 대한독립만세를 외치니 이 시위에 호응한 군중이 수천 명에 달하였다. 시위 군중은 일본 기마대와 기관총을 앞세운 대구 주둔 80연대의 저지, 탄압에도 굴하지 않고 동성로까지 진출하였다.

이틀 뒤인 3월 10일에도 남문시장에서 또 한 차례의 만세시위가 있었다. 이 땅, 역사를 위해서 이보다 장하고 자랑스러운 일이 다시 있으랴! 3·1운동의 독립정신을 그 후에도 끊이지 않고, 여러 가지 형태의 광복운동으로 계승·발전되어 마침내 1945년 8월 15일 조국 광복의 날을 맞이할 수 있게 된 것이다.

비록 늦게나마 그 날의 정신을 기리기 위하여 1984년 12월 31일 대구시가 동구 효목1동 산234번지 망우공원 내에 기념비를 세우게 되니 그 뜻이 어찌 무겁지 아니하랴.˝

우재 이시영 선생 순국기념탑

 대구시 남구 대명9동 산 227-1번지

대구 앞산공원에는 우재 이시영 선생 순국기념탑가 세워져 있다. 이시영李始榮 1882~1919은 한말의 항일운동가로 본관은 경주慶州이며 대구출신의 독립운동가로 조선국권회복단, 대한광복회를 조직하여 항일운동에 앞장섰다. 이 비는 이시영 선생을 기리기 위해 1972년 6월 17일 건립하였다.

이시영의 자는 중현仲賢이며 아호는 우재又齋이다. 그의 아버지는 이관준李寬俊이다. 그는 어려서부터 그의 아버지에게 한학을 배웠으나 문약한 선비로만 있지는 않았다. 그는 신체가 건장하여 문무에 모두 능하였으며 말보다 실천이 앞서는 성격이었다고 한다.

그는 을사조약乙巳條約이 체결된 다음 해인 25세 때 기울어가는 국운을 한탄하고 항일운동을 하겠다는 결연한 각오 아래 중국으로 건너가 실력투쟁단이 독립의 길이라고 확신하고 윤상태尹相泰, 서상호徐相鎬, 정운일鄭雲馹 등과 애국단이란 비밀조직을 만들었다.

애국단 조직 후 우선 군자금을 마련하기 위해서 서모라는 당시 대구 부호의 지원을 얻기로 했다. 그의 사돈인 서부자徐富者는 이름난 구두쇠인데다가 민족의식이 없어 말로는 그들의 뜻에 동조하지 않을 것 같아 그의 아들을 애국단에 가입시켜 그가 자발적으로 군자금을 희사하기를 꾀했으나 서부자는 끝내 모른 체했다. 이처럼 군자금 마련이 여의치 않자 최후의 수단으로 서부자의 집에 그의 아들을 앞세우고 침입했다가 정체만 드러낸 채 실패하고 말았다. 이로 인해 일경에 체포되어 강도죄로 2년간의 옥고를 치렀다.

출옥 후 다시 최준崔俊, 안희제安熙濟, 서상일徐相日 등의 동지를 규합하여 광복단을 조직했다. 1914년 다시 고국을 떠나 북경에서 항일운동에 이바지했다. 1918년 귀국 후 이듬해 2월에는 지청천·한용운 등과 함께 영남 유림대표 2백여 명을 서울로 보냈다. 그때, 유림측에서 그에게 민족대표로 서명해달라고 하자 "내 목적은 오직 왜놈과 싸우는 것"이라며 과격한 활동노선을 밝혔다. 그후 임시정부에서 재무장관 서리를 맡아 달라는 것도 거절했는데 역시 같은 이유에서였다.

3·1운동 직후 그는 그를 따르는 한위건韓偉健, 김영호金永浩 등 청년을 데리고 만주로 가서 유하현 삼원포에 신흥무관학교新興武官學敎를 세웠다.

그렇지만, 오랫동안의 방랑생활로 인하여 축적된 과로 탓인지 1919년 7월 9일 젊은 나이로 타계하고 말았다. 그가 타계했다는 소식을 들은 안창호는 "문무 겸전한 우제가 갔으니 또 하나 큰 별을 잃었구나"라며 땅을 치며 통곡했고 성재 이시영省齋 李始榮도 "나라의 큰 별이었는데…"하며 말을 제대로 잇지 못했다고 한다. 1990년 건국훈장 애족장을 추서하였다.

이상화 고택

대구시 중구 계산동 2가 84번지

이상화는 일제강점기 비탄에 빠진 우리 정서를 언어로 끌어 올림으로써 한국 현대시의 이정표를 세운 민족시인으로 "빼앗긴 들에도 봄은 오는가"로 우리에게 잘 알려져 있다. 1901년 대구에서 아버지 이시우, 어머니 김해 김씨 사이에서 4형제 중 둘째로 태어난 이상화는 1918년에 서울 중앙학교(지금의 중앙고등학교)를 수료했고, 열아홉 되던 1919년 대구에서 3·1 운동 거사를 모의하다 주요 인물이 잡혀가자 서울 박태원의 하숙으로 피신하였다.

1921년에 현진건의 소개로 박종화와 만나『백조』동인에 참여했고, 1922년 『백조』1~2호에 시를 발표하면서 문단에 나왔다. 프랑스로 유학을 갈 기회를 얻으려고 일본으로 갔으나 1923년 관동대지진이 나자 귀국하여 1925년에 작문 활동을 활발히 했다. 8월에 카프 발기인으로 참여했다. 1927년 대구로 돌아와 1933년 교남학교(지금의 대륜고등학교)에서 조선어와 영어, 작문 교사로 근무하였고 이듬해 사직하였다. 1937년 큰형인 독립운동가 이상정을 만나러 중국에 3개월간 다녀와 교남학교에 복직하여 교가를 작사했다. 1943년 3월에 위암 진단을 받고 투병하다가 4월 25일 대구 자택에서 숨졌다. 1946년 대구 달성공원 내에 시비가 세워졌다.

　이 고택은 이상화가 말년(1939~1943)을 보낸 역사적 장소로 곳곳에 그의 흔적을 느낄 수 있다. 지역개발로 사라질 뻔한 것을 2002년부터 문화계 인사들과 시민들이 '상화고택보존운동'을 전개하면서 필요한 자금을 모았고, 많은 문인들이 이상화 관련 자료들을 모아 오늘의 모습으로 갖추어 2008년 8월에 개관하였다. 마당에는 이상화의 대표적 시인 "빼앗긴 들에도 봄은 오는가"와 "역천" 등의 시비가 세워져 있다. 특히 이 고택은 보존가치가 있는 자연환경과 문화유산을 후손에게 물려줄 취지로 (사)한국내셔널트리스트와 유한킴벌리가 공동주최한 제7회 한국내셔널트리스트 보존대상지 시민 공모전에서 '2009년 잘 가꾼 자연유산 · 문화유산'으로 선정되었다.

서상돈 고택

　서상돈 고택은 이상화 고택과 사이를 두고 나란히 있다. 이 건축물은 과거 서상돈 선생의 집터에 원형 그대로 복원해 둔 것이다.

　국채보상운동의 거장 서상돈徐相敦, 1851~1913은 서울에서 태어났다. 서상돈과 대구와의 인연은 1871년 대구로 가서 지물행상과 포목상 등을 하며 많은 재산을 모으면서였다. 1898년 독립협회와 만민공동회의 간부로 활동하면서 러시아의 내정간섭을 규탄하고 민권보장 및 참정권 획득 운동을 전개하였다.

1907년 대구의 광문사廣文社의 부사장으로 재직 중 사장인 김광제金光濟와 함께 대구에서 금주와 금연으로 나라의 빚을 갚자는 국채보상회를 조직하고 국채보상운동을 벌였다. 이를 계기로 국채보상운동은 전국적으로 퍼져 나갔다.

이 운동은 비록 일제의 방해로 뜻한 바를 이룰 수 없었으나 일제의 경제침탈과 국권침탈에 관하여 한국인들을 각성시키는 계기가 되었다. 정부에서는 고인의 공훈을 기리어 1999년에 건국훈장 애족장을 추서하였다.

약령시 한의약문화관

이상화 고택에서 나가 대구제일교회를 지나면 또 하나 둘러볼 곳이 있다. 약령시 한의약문화관이다. 입구의 약령문藥令門을 지나면 뜰에는 약탕기 모양의 분수대가 답사객을 맞이한다. 대구광역시 소속 약령시보존회에서 관리하고 있는 대구 약령시장은 1658년(효종 9)에 개장하여 수백년 동안 국내는 물론 일본과 중국, 러시아 등 여러 나라에 한약재를 공급해온 한약 물류유통의 거점이다. 대구시가 1993년에 설립한 '약령시전시관'을 '약령시한의약문화관'으로 이름을 바꾸어 개관한 것은 2009년이다. 이곳은 전시관만이 아니라 한의약 및 약령시의 역사, 문화에 대한 입체적 전시, 영상물과 체험공간 위주로 구성하는 새로운 시설로 변모하였다.

전시실에는 인삼, 녹용, 해마 등 각종 한약재를 비롯하여 『동의보감』·『동의수세보원』 등의 한의서와 약연, 약작두 등의 한방기구 등 한방 관련 용품 수백여 점이 전시되어 있으며, 2층에는 체험공간이 마련되어 있어 다양한 경험을 하도록 해놓았다.

2. 경북 지역

첫번째. 안동시

❋ 안동 소개

안동은 봉화군, 영양군, 청송군, 영풍군, 예천군으로 이루어진 경북 북부지방의 중심지로서, 선비정신으로 상징되는 유교문화의 본고장이며 전통문화의 유산이 밀집된 곳이다. 삼국시다 신라 고타야군이었던 이곳은 통일신라 경덕왕 때 고창군으로 바뀌었다가 고려 초 안동이라는 이름을 얻었다. 안동은 소백산맥의 준령과 낙동강의 상류가 만든 내륙의 분지에 위치하고 있다. 또한 삼국시대에는 신라의 최전방으로서 왕실의 관심과 통제를 계속 받아왔다. 이러한 역사지리적 조건은 안동이 보수적이면서도 진보적인 양면적 문화를 형성하는데 영향을 미쳤다. 삼국통일 후 의상이 부석사를 창건하여 신라 왕실의 지속적인 관심을 가진 이래, 후삼국 시기 이 지역의 호족은 고려 건국의 토대가 되었고, 고려 전 시기 동안 기득권을 유지하면서 공민왕의 남행을 계기로 중앙정계에 진출하였다. 이들은 조선의 국가체제를 확립하는데 공헌하면서 주리론적 유교철학을 제창한 이황을 중심으로 남인의 양반문화를 완성하였다. 특히 학연, 문중 중심의 유교 공동체를 기반으로 형성된 충의 대의는 나라의 어려움을 구하는 중요한 이념으로 작용하였다. 이러한 정서는 식민지시기에도 그대로 나타나, 많은 독립지사를 배출하였다. 보수와 진보가 공존하면서 새로운 사상의 수용에도 앞서 나갔다. 안동의 기독교는 바로 이러한 지역 상황 속에서 시작되었다.

❋ 안동 기독교 전래

안동 선교는 미국 북장로교 선교사들이 개척했다. 1890년대 중반 부산의 베어드William M. Baird, 배위량, 1902년 대구의 아담스James E. Adams, 안의와 등이 지방을 순회하면서 안동을 들른 적이 있고, 1903년부터 대구 스테이션의 바렛William M. Barrett, 박위렴과 브루엔Henry M. Bruen, 부해리이 안동 지방을 순회하면서 전도하였다. 그리고 1908년 11월 브루엔과 소텔Chace C. Sawtell, 사우대, 매서인 김병우 등을 안동읍에 파송하여 서문밖(대석동)에 5칸짜리 초가집을 구입하고 '기독서원'이라는 간판을 내걸었다. 양반문화의 본고장에서 서원書院 간판을 건 책방은 효과적이었다.

바로 이곳에서 1909년 8월 8일 주일부터 예배를 드리기 시작했는데, 이것이 안동교회의 출발이다. 매서인 김병우의 뒤를 이어 황해도 소래교회 출신 김영옥이 1909년 11월 웰번Arthur G. Welbon, 오월번과 함께 들어와 전도하였다. 김영옥은 안동교회 초대 목사가 되었고, 교회는 안동진영 터(광석동)의 초가 예배당을 거쳐, 1913년 현재 위치에 50칸 함석예배당을 짓게 되었다.

안동 선교의 개척자들이었던 소텔과 웰번을 이어 안동에 들어온 선교사들로는 먼저 의료선교사 플레처Archibald G. Fletcher, 별리추와 크로더스John Y. Crothers, 권찬영가 있다. 플레처는 안동 스테이션의 의료사업으로 성소병원을 시작했고, 크로더스는 그 때부터 40여 년간 안동에서 활동한 지역선교의 대부代父로 선교사들은 그를 'Mr. 안동'으로 불렀다. 그 다음으로는 레닉Edwin A. Renich, 여나기, 스미스Roy K. Smith, 심의도, 윈Rodger E. Winn, 인노절, 앤더슨Wallace J. Anderson, 안대선 선교사 등이 안동에 주재했는데, 스미스는 1920년까지 10년 동안 성소병원 의사로 일했고, 1914년 부산 스테이션에서 전임해 온 윈은 크로더스와 함께 성경학교를 세우는 등 폭넓은 선교활동을 펼치다 1922년 2월 풍토병에 걸려 순직하였다. 1917년부터 5년 동안 안동에서 활동했던 앤더슨은 1921년 2월 안동교회에서 전국 최초의 청년면려회(CE)를 조직한 것으로 그 이름이 잘 알려져 있다.

✽ 안동 기독교 유적지

안동교회

🚗 경북 안동시 화성동 151번지

안동시청 옆에 자리한 안동교회는 육중한 화강암을 하나하나 다듬어 지은 석조예배당을 갖고 있다. 1913년 지은 함석예배당이 교인 증가로 비좁게 되자

안동교회

1937년 새로 지은 275평의 2층 건물로 지금도 견고한 옛 모습을 간직하고 있다. 다만 교회 후면부 80평 가량은 지난 1959년 증축한 것이다. 건물을 설계한 사람은 당시 일본에서 교회 건축 전문가로 활동했던 보리스William M. Vories였고, 북장로교선교부에서 건축비의 1/4을 지원하였다. 그런데 이 예배당에는 철탑 형태의 십자가 종탑이 없다. 그 대신 지붕을 완만한 삼각 형태로 쌓은 후 그 꼭지점에 작은 돌십자가를 올려놓았다. 안동교회는 2009년 8월 설립 100주년을 맞아 석조예배당 오른쪽 옆에 100주년기념관을 완공하였다.

경안고등학교

 경북 안동시 금곡동 124

처음 안동의 선교사들은 지금 안동교회 교육관 자리에 있던 몇 채의 가옥을 사서 임시주택으로 삼았다. 그러다가 안동교회가 안정되어 가고 또 지역주민과의 유대가 강화되자 선교사들은 본격적인 스테이션 건설에 착수하였다. 웰번은 1911년 지금의 경안고등학교 일대 금곡동 언덕을 매입하여 거기에 붉은 벽돌의 서양식주택 두 채를 지었다. 준공 시점은 분명하지 않지만 한 채(웰번주택)는 그해 12월 웰번이 입주했고, 다른 한 채(원주택)는 이듬해 5월 레닉이 사용하기 시작했다. 원주택은 레닉이 떠난 후 원이 들어와 줄곧 거기서 생활했다. 웰번주택은 지금 경안고등학교 신관 동편 회의실 앞에 있었는데, 6·25전쟁 이후에는 윌슨Stanton R. Wilson, 우위성 선교사가 살다가 경안고에 인계되어 도서관으로 사용되었고, 지난 1992년 학교 본관 건축 과정에서 철거되었다. 지금 경안고등학교 북쪽 동산 위 어린이놀이터 자리에 있었던 원주택은 해방 이후 반리어럽Peter Van Lierop, 반피득 선교사를 거쳐 성소병원장 사택으로 사용되다가 1988년 매각되었고 결국 1992년 철거되었다. 그 후 안동 주재 선교사들의 수가 늘어나자 1913년 안동 스테이션 구내에는 두 채의 선교사 주택이 더 들어섰다. 여기에는 크로더스와 스미스가 각각 입주하였다. 이 두 집은 1950년 6·25전쟁 때 파괴되어 현재는 남아있지 않다. 금곡동의 안동 스테이션 터는 주로 1954년 개교한 경안고

원선교사 묘비

등학교 땅으로 사용되고 있다. 현재 경안고 본관 뒤의 '경안역사관' 건물은 6·25전쟁 이후 안동으로 와서 경안고등성경학교 교장을 지낸 올가 존슨Olga C. Johason, 조운선 선교사의 사택이었다.

경안고등학교 구내의 안동선교사묘지에는 모두 3기의 선교사, 선교사 자녀 무덤이 조성되어 있다. 묘역 왼쪽에 누워있는 원은 1914년 안동에 부임하여 활동하다가 1922년 11월 22일 풍토병으로 사망하였다. 당시 그의 나이 40세였다. 원의 추도식은 1923년 1월 12일 거행되었는데, 원은 안동에 주재했던 29명의 선교사 가운데 유일하게 이곳에 묻혀있다. 가운데의 도로시 앤더슨Dorothy E. Anderson은 1917년부터 5년간 안동에서 활동했던 앤더슨 선교사의 딸로 1919년 6월 12일 태어나서 채 1년이 안된 1920년 1월 25일 숨을 거두었다. 묘비에는 "With Jejus"라고 적혀있다. 그 옆의 윌리엄 뵐켈William H. Voelkel은 해롤드 뵐켈Harold Voelkel, 옥호열의 아들로 1932년 3월 7일 태어나서 1년 조금 지난 1933년 6월 15일까지 살았다.

성소병원

 경북 안동시 금곡동 177번지

안동 스테이션의 의료사업기관이었던 성소병원은 1909년 의료선교사 플레처에 의해 선교사 임시주택에서 시작되었다. 그리고 2대 병원장 스미스는 1914년 현 위치에 서양식 붉은 벽돌의 '코넬리우스베이커기념병원'Cornelius Baker Memorial Hospital을 신축하였다. 이 건물은 미국 뉴욕의 셔플러A. F. Schuffler 부인이 자기 아버지를 기념하는 선교비 1만불을 보내 준공된 것이다. 당시 북장로교 한국선교부의 병원들 가운데 가장 잘 지어졌다는 평을 들었던 그 건물은 6·25

전쟁 중 파괴되었고, 현재의 성소병원은 1956년 2층으로 다시 지어져 몇 차례 증축 혹은 신축된 것이다.

성소병원 신축 건물 뒤쪽 주차장 위 언덕에는 원래 1925년 준공된 '인노절기념성경학교' 교사校舍가 자리하고 있었다. 원 선교사는 한국인 전도인력 양성을 위해 1920년 4월 금곡동 언덕에 경안성경학교를 세웠다. 그러나 그는 그 얼마 뒤인 1922년 풍토병으로 사망하였다. 그러자 원선교사를 기념하는 성경학교 건축을 위해 지역교인들의 헌금이 시작되었고, 원선교사의 부인Catherine L. Winn도 미국에서 모금하여 1925년 '인노절기념성경학교'를 준공하였다. 이 건물은 이전을 위해 최근 해체되어서 지금 그 자리에는 아무것도 남아있지 않다.

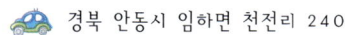
안동 일반 유적지

안동독립운동기념관

경북 안동시 임하면 천전리 240번지

안동독립운동기념관은 안동의 독립운동을 보고 배울 수 있는 공간이다. 전시실은 국내외관으로 나뉘어져 있는데, 국내관은 안동인의 국내독립운동과 독립운동가를 소개하고 있다. 전국 최초로 일어난 1894년 갑오의병부터 1907년 설립된 협동학교, 1910년대 광복회 및 3·1운동, 1920~40년대 대중, 학생운동 등 안동지역과 안동인들의 국내독립운동 51년을 살펴볼 수 있다.

국외관은 국외에서 활약한 안동출신 독립운동가를 소개하고 있다. 1910년 나라가 무너지자 많은 안동인들이 만주로 망명하여 경학사·신흥무관학교 등을 통해 동포사회를 형성하고 독립군을 양성하였다. 나아가 1920~30년대 만주지역 독립운동단체에서 핵심역할을 하였으며, 대한민국임시정부·의열투쟁·한국광복군 등에서도 활약하였다. 이 외에 안동의 독립운동가를 추모하는 영상추모관도 마련되어 있다.

병산서원

🚗 경북 안동시 풍천면 병산리 30번지

사적 제260호로 지정된 풍광이 아름답기로 유명한 병산서원은 조선시대의 대표적인 유교 건축물로서, 서애 류성룡과 그의 셋째아들 류진을 배향한 서원이다. 병산서원의 전신은 풍산현에 있던 풍악서당으로, 고려말부터 사림들의 학문의 전당으로 특히 1572년 류성룡이 지방관으로 역임하던 시절, 현재의 서원 자리로 이건하였다. 그후 임진왜란으로 불탄 서당을 1607년에 다시 중건하였고 1613년 류성룡의 학덕을 기리기 위해 존덕사를 창건하여 위패를 봉안했다. 1850년대 사액서원으로 승격되었으며, 1868년 대원군 서원 철폐령이 내려졌을 때 그 대상에서 제외된 전국 47개, 안동 2개소 중 한 곳이다. 일제강점기에 대대적인 보수가 행해졌으며, 강당은 1921년에 다시 지어졌고 사당은 1937년에 재건되었다. 3월과 9월 초정일初亭日에 향사하고 있다.

병산서원

안동 하회마을

경북 안동시 풍천면 하회리 749-1번지

　중요민속자료 제122호로 지정되어 있는 안동 하회마을은 풍산 류씨가 600여 년간 대대로 살아온 한국의 대표적인 동성마을이며, 현재도 주민이 살고 있는 자연부락으로, 와가瓦家:기와집 초가草家가 오랜 역사 속에서도 잘 보존된 곳이다. 특히 조선시대 유학자인 겸암 류운룡謙菴 柳雲龍과 임진왜란 때 영의정을 지낸 서애 류성룡西厓 柳成龍 형제가 태어난 곳으로도 유명하다.

　마을 이름을 하회河回라 한 것은 낙동강이 'S'자 모양으로 마을을 감싸- 안고 흐르는 데서 유래되었다. 하회마을은 조선시대부터 사람이 살기에 가장 좋은 곳으로도 유명하였다. 마을의 동쪽에 태백산에서 뻗어 나온 해발 271m의 화산花山이 있고, 이 화산의 줄기가 낮은 구릉지를 형성하면서 마을의 서쪽 끝까지 뻗어 있으며, 수령이 600여 년 된 느티나무가 있는 곳이 마을에서 가장 높은 중심부에 해당한다.

　하회마을의 집들은 느티나무를 중심으로 강을 향해 배치되어 있기 때문에 좌향이 일정하지 않다. 한국의 다른 마을의 집들이 정남향 또는 동남향을 하고 있는 것과는 상당히 대조적인 모습이다. 또한 큰 기와집을 중심으로 주변의 초가들이 원형을 이루며 배치되어 있는 것도 특징이라 하겠다. 하회마을에는 서민들이 놀았던 '하회별신굿탈놀이'와 선비들의 풍류놀이였던 '선유줄불놀이'가 현재까지도 전승되고 있고, 우리나라의 전통생활문화와 고건축양식을 잘 보여주는 문화유산들이 잘 보존되어 있다.

　하회마을에 풍산류씨가 들어와 살게 된 데에는 나눔의 정신이 들어 있다. 풍산류씨는 본래 풍산 상리에 살았으므로 본향이 풍산豊山이지만, 제7세 전서典書 류종혜柳從惠 공이 화산에 여러 번(가뭄, 홍수, 평상시) 올라가서 물의 흐름이나 산세며 기후조건 등을 몸소 관찰한 후에 이곳으로 터를 결정했다고 한다. 그리고 집을 건축하려 하였으나 기둥이 세번이나 넘어져 크게 낭패를 당하던 중 꿈에 신령이 현몽하기를 여기에 터를 얻으려면 3년 동안 활만인活萬人을 하라는 계시를 받고 큰 고개 밖에 초막을 짓고 지나가는 행인에게 음식과 노자 및 짚신을 나누어주기도 하고, 참외를 심어 인근에 나누어주기도 하면서 수많은 사람에게 활인活人을 하고서야 하회마을에 터전을 마련할 수 있었다고 한다. 입향 후 풍산 류씨들은 계속된 후손들의 중앙관계에의 진출로 점점 성장하였다.

안동 하회탈과 병산탈, 『징비록』 원고본은 국보로 지정되어 있으며, 양진당, 충효당 등은 보물로 지정되어 그 중요성을 더하고 있으며, 1999년에는 영국여왕 엘리자베스 2세가 하회마을을 다녀갔다. 현재 안동에는 요즘 국내 여행의 트랜드인 고택체험을 할 수 있는 곳이 여러 군데 있어, 고택에 머물면서 옛 조상들의 삶을 잠깐이나마 경험해 볼 수 있다.

두번째. 기타

영천 자천교회

경북 영천시 화북면 자천3리 773번지

대구와 포항을 잇는 고속도로의 영천IC를 나와 쉽게 접근할 수 있는 자천교회에는 오래된 한옥 예배당이 하나 있다. 이 교회의 설립자인 권헌중은 원래 경주의 서당 훈장이었다. 그는 한때 청송군 현서면 수락으로 들어갔다가 1898년 다시 대구로 옮겨갈 것을 결심하고 이주하던 중 영천과 청송의 경계인 노고재에서 당시 대구 주재 선교사 아담스James E. Adams, 안의와와 운명적인 조우를 하게 된다. 아담스와의 만남은 그의 인생을 바꿔놓았다. 권헌중은 대구 이사를 포기하고 인근 보현산 자락 자천리에 초가삼간을 지어 정착하였다. 그는 계속 아담스와 왕래하면서 자신의 사랑방을 서당 겸 예배당으로 이용하였다. 자천교회의 처음 교인들은 권헌중의 문동과 머슴들이었다. 교인이 불어나자 권헌중은 1904년 지금의 예배당을 지었다. 그 후 그 예배당은 여러번 증축되었지만 일자형 한옥 구조의 원형을 지금도 유지하고 있다. 자천교회는 1913년 생도 50명으로 신성학교를 세

영천 자천교회

워 운영하였고, 권헌중은 1922년 조지 원George H. Winn, 위철치 선교사의 집례로 장로가 되었다. 권헌중 장로는 1925년 12월 별세할 때까지 교회를 섬겼다.

지난 2003년 경북 문화재자료 452호로 지정된 자천교회 예배당은 2005년 11월 복원공사를 완료하여 말끔하게 단장되었다. 내부는 남녀가 따로 앉아 예배를 드리도록 나무판으로 분리시켜 놓았다. 교회의 마당에는 독특한 양식의 굴뚝이 있으며 예배당 좌석 뒤편에 사랑방을 만들어 외부 손님이 묵어갈 수 있게 배려하였다. 또 교회 옆에 살던 김부자 댁에서 한옥을 몇 채 기증하여 신성학교로 꾸며 놓았다. 대한예수교장로회(통합)는 자천교회 예배당을 총회 교회사적 2호로 지정해 놓았다.

봉화 척곡교회

경북 봉화군 법전면 척곡1리 833-1번지

척곡교회 예배당은 1909년 무렵 건축된 쌍정방형의 'ㅁ'자형 한옥 건물로 현재 등록문화재 257호(2006. 6. 19), 대한예수교장로회(통합) 총회 교회사적 3호(2006. 10. 18), 영주노회 사적 1호(2005. 10. 4)로 지정되어 있다. 또 예배당 담장 앞에는 교회가 경영했던 명동서숙이 그대로 남아 있는데, 교회 직영 서숙 가운데 국내에서 현재 유일하게 보존되어 있는 건물이라고 한다. 그 외 척곡교회에는 초기 '교적부'(1907년 7월 15일 최재구·우재곡의 학습교인 기록), 초기 '당회록', 1921년 '척곡장로교면려회회록', 1927년 '봉화전도척곡지회회록', 1930년 '척곡교회기본금기성회록' 등 귀중한 교회문서자료들이 남아있다.

척곡교회의 시작은 1906년 강재원에 의해 세워진 영주 내매교회를 배경으로 한다. 봉화 문촌의 강복진 등이 장터의 전도 강연에서 결신하고 내매교회에 출석하다가 문촌교회를 설립하였고, 다시 척곡의 김종숙과 장녹우는 문촌 30리 길

봉화 척곡교회

을 오가며 예수를 믿다가 결국 1907년 척곡교회를 시작하게 되었다. 그리고 그 해 가을 북장로교 선교사들이 척곡에 와서 교인들에게 학습을 주었다.

척곡교회를 시작한 김종숙은 원래 대한제국의 탁지부 관리였다. 서울 새문안 교회에서 언더우드Horace G. Underwood, 원두우의 설교를 들었던 그는 1905년 을사늑약 이후 처가가 있던 경북 봉화로 내려왔다. 그는 먼저 봉화군 상운면 문촌리로 교회를 다니다가 1907년 척곡교회와 아울러 명동서숙을 설립하게 되었다. 그는 1909년 무렵 9칸 규모의 기와집 예배당과 6칸 규모의 초가집 서숙을 지었는데, 바로 그 건물들이 현재 남아 있는 것이다.

군위성결교회

경북 군위군 군위읍 동부리 621-1

지난 2007년 등록문화재 제291호로 지정된 한옥의 군위성결교회 구 예배당은 1937년 무렵 건축되었다. 그런데 여기에는 가슴 아픈 사연이 있다. 이 예배당을 신축하기 위해 1927년 지어진 교회당을 철거하는 과정에서 당시 이종익 담임목사와 노성문 집사 등 두 명이 예기치 못한 사고로 순직했기 때문이다. 그래서 군위성결교회는 교회 마당에 순직기념비를 세워 그들을 기리고 있다.

구 예배당은 연면적 109.56㎡의 1층 건물로 남녀가 따로 사용하도록 양쪽으로 출입구를 배치했으며 출입문에 각각 포치porch: 현관를 설치했다. 원래 내부는 전실 1칸, 예배실 4칸, 목사 사택 2칸이었으나 그 후 전실 1칸에 예배실 6칸으로 바뀌었다고 한다. 하지만 외부는 건립 당시의 원형을 유지하고 있다.

울진 행곡교회와 용장교회

행곡교회: 경북 울진군 근남면 행곡리 102-1번지 / 용장교회: 경북 울진군 죽변면 화성리 274-2번지

울진 행곡교회는 1907년 대한기독교회(한국침례교회의 전신)의 권서순회전

도자 손필환의 방문으로 시작되었다. 캐나다 선교사 말콤 펜윅M. C. Fenwick, 편위익의 오지선교奧地宣敎 이념을 선교 전략으로 갖고 있었던 대한기독교회는 당시 장로교와 감리교 등 주류 선교사들의 발길이 닿지 않았던 경북 내륙 지역 선교를 위해서 손필환을 파송했던 것이다.

등록문화재 제286호로 지정된 'ㅁ'자형의 행곡교회 한옥예배당은 일제강점기에 건립된 것으로 울진읍성의 건물 자재를 활용해서 지었다고 한다. 건물은 정면 4칸 측면 2칸 마룻바닥의 긴 장방형인데, 동쪽에 강단이 설치되어 있으며 또 남녀예배석이 구별되어 있는 등 원형이 잘 보존되어 있다.

행곡교회는 침례교 21명의 순교자 가운데 3명을 배출했다. 3대 감목監牧: 교단 최고 지도자이었던 전치규 목사는 1944년 함흥에서 순교했고, 전병무 목사와 남석천 성도는 1949년 좌익세력들에 의해 학살당했다.

행곡교회의 교세 확장으로 설립된 용장교회 역시 1936년 경 건축된 한옥예배당(등록문화재 제287호)을 갖고 있다. 이 예배당은 팔작지붕에 가로 3칸 세로 2칸의 직사각형 평면구조로 주출입구 오른쪽에 강단이 있으며, 지붕을 제외하고는 건립 당시의 모습을 지니고 있다.

CHAPTER 7

부산·경남
지역

부산광역시 → 진주 → 마산 → 통영과 거창

1. 부산지역

❋ 부산·경남 기독교의 시작

부산·경남 지방은 1890년대부터 미국 북장로교 선교부와 호주 장로교 선교부가 공동으로 선교를 시작하였다. 먼저 호주 장로교는 1890년 데이비스Joseph H. Davies, 덕배시를 부산에 보낸데 이어 다시 1891년 10월 맥케이James H. Mackay, 맥목사 등 5명의 선교사를 파송하여 부산진(좌천동)에 스테이션을 설치하였다. 또 북장로교는 1891년 9월 베어드William M. Baird, 배위량를 부산에 내려 보내 초량 인근 영선현(영주동)에 스테이션을 개설하였다. 그리고 두 선교부는 1893년 1월에 열렸던 '장로교선교부연합공의회'에서 부산·경남지방을 함께 선교하자고 합의하였다.

그 후 10여년이 지난 1903년 양 선교부는 선교지역 분할을 위한 협상에 들어갔다. 선교지역의 중복으로 인한 혼선을 피하고자 한 것이다. 그 결과 경남 지역의 남부와 서부 즉 기장·언양·양산·거제·진해·고성 지역은 호주선교부가 담당하고, 동부와 서부 곧 김해·웅천·밀양·영산·창녕·칠원·창원 등지는 북장로교선교부가 맡기로 하였다. 그리고 인구밀집지역이었던 부산, 동래, 마산은 두 선교부의 공동 선교구역이 되었다. 그 사이 호주선교부는 1905년 진주 스테이션을 조성하였고, 북장로교는 밀양에 소규모의 간이 스테이션sub-station을 두어 해당 지역 복음화의 거점으로 삼았다.

부산·경남 지역

부산진 일신여학교

그런데 당시 북장로교는 서울과 평양 등 중부와 북부지역의 선교에 주력하고 있었으므로 1908년부터 부산·경남 지방 선교를 호주선교부에 맡기고자 하였다. 그래서 우선 1909년의 협의를 통해 북장로교 구역이었던 경남의 동부와 마산 지역을 호주선교부에 이양하였다. 그 대신 초량지역은 북장로교선교부가 전담하도록 하였다. 그 결과 호주선교부는 그 때 부산·경남 150만 인구 가운데 100만명을 선교 대상으로 하게 되었다.

그리고 드디어 북장로교선교부는 1913년의 연례회의에서 부산·경남에서 완전히 철수하기로 결정하였다. 그리하여 1914년부터 부산·경남 지역 선교는 호주선교부가 전담하게 되었다-. 북장로교는 1891년 베어드가 부산 영선현에 스테이션을 개설한 이래 1914년까지 23년 동안 21명의 선교사를 보내어 부산·경남 선교의 일익을 담당하였다. 그 후 호주장로교는 해방될 때까지 모두 78명의 선교사들을 보내어 마산(1911)과 통영(1913), 거창(1913)에 잇달아 스테이션을 조성하는 한편 그곳을 중심으로 교회·학교·병원을 세워 이 지역 복음화에 크게 공헌하였다.

호주선교부의 스테이션과 선교구역

스테이션(개설연도)	선교구역
대구(1899)	대구 경산 경주 김천 상주 선산 달성 칠곡 성주 고령 군위
부산(1891)	부산 초량 동래 김해 밀양 기장 창영 언양 울산 울릉도
진주(1905)	진주 산청 삼가 의령 하동 사천 건양 남해
마산(1911)	마산 함안 창원 웅천
통영(1913)	통영 거제 고성 욕지 진해
거창(1913)	거창 안의 함양 합천 초개

첫번째. 부산광역시

❋ 부산 소개

부산지역의 문화는 오륙도가 상징하는 바와 같이 한반도 남부의 온후한 기후와 동남방으로 펼쳐진 광활한 바다와 영남지방을 관통하여 흐르는 낙동강의 항구라는 자연 조건 속에 형성되었다. 남방의 따뜻한 기후는 안온한 풍속을 만들고, 드넓은 바다는 탁 트인 느낌을 주면서 양질의 해산물을 제공하였다. 또 강과 바다가 만나는 하구는 연안 각 지역의 인구와 물산이 몰려드는 풍성한 도회를 만들었다.

한반도의 남쪽 끝에 위치한 부산은 바다 건너 일본과 대립 융합되는 문화의 접점에 처해 있다. 그러므로 교역과 국방상의 중요성으로 인하여 내륙의 여타 지역과는 다른 특별한 지위를 누렸다. 평화 시에는 외국의 색다른 문물과 접촉하며 교역하는 개방 공간으로, 바다 건너 일본과의 긴장이 고조될 때에는 외침에 대비하는 최전방의 요새가 되었던 것이다. 이런 점들은 부산의 문화 전통을 내륙의 여느 다른 지역과 구별하게 하였던 중요한 요소들이다.

부산이란 지명은 부산포에서 유래된 것이다. 15세기 후반 지금 동구 좌천동에 있는 증산甑山의 모양이 도톰하여 가마솥釜과 같다고 해서 부산釜山이라고 불렀다. 그런데 조선시대의 부산포는 당시 독립된 지방행정구역 단위가 아니라 동래현의 속현(지방관이 파견되지 않은 현)이었던 동평현의 관할 아래에 있었고, 그 후에는 동래도호부의 구역 내에 포함되어 있었다.

조선시대의 부산은 나라의 관문으로서 국방상 요충지였다. 즉 부산의 진산鎭山 금정산의 산성은 그 규모로 볼 때 국내에서 가장 크며, 지금의 부산 수영동에는 경상좌수영이 설치되어 있었다. 동남지방 해양군사거점으로서의 경상좌수영은 다대진에서 울진에 이르는 동남연변의 수군을 통솔하였다. 또 조선 정부는 태종 때부터 부산포에 왜관을 두어 일본인들의 내왕과 교역을 허용하였다. 부산포의 왜관은 조선 전기의 부산포왜관(현 자성대 부근)과 조선 중기의 절영도왜관(현 자성대 부근)·두모포왜관(현 수정시장 일대)을 거쳐 조선 후기 초량왜관(현 용두산과 복병산 일대)으로 이어져 1876년 강화도조약 체결로 부산이 개항될 때까지 지속되었다.

강화도조약 체결 이후 일본은 1877년 1월 동래부사와 〈부산구조계조약釜山口租界條約〉을 체결하여 일본인의 부산 내왕과 통상, 토지임차권, 가옥건축권 등을 확보하였다. 이른바 일본의 침략 기반이 마련되었던 것이다. 또 조선 정부는 그 후속 조치로 1890년대 부산에 감리서(현 봉래초등학교 자리)를 두어 외교·통상 사무를 전담하도록 하였다. 이어서 1883년 영국이 부산에 영사관을 개설한데 이어 1884년에는 청나라가 초량에 영사관과 청관을 조성하였다. 그러나 청일전쟁의 패배로 청관의 토지와 가옥은 일본 영사관에서 접수하였다.

러일전쟁의 승리로 조선에서 독점적인 지위를 갖게 된 일본은 을사늑약의 체결 이후인 1906년 부산에 이사청理事廳을 신설하였다. 그리고 부산의 초량왜관 11만평은 모두 '부산일본제국전관專管거류지'로 설정되었다. 그리고 초량왜관 시절의 제한 조치들이 폐지되면서 부산 일본인 사회를 만들기 위한 제도가 정비되고 시설들이 신속하게 정비되었다. 그리하여 개항 이전 중심이었던 동래와 구별되는 일본인 주도의 식민도시가 형성되었다.

❋ 부산 기독교 전래

19세기말 복음의 파장이 한반도에 미쳤을 때, 중국으로부터 복음을 받아들인 북쪽 관문이 의주였다면 부산은 태평양을 건너 일본을 통해 들어오는 복음의 남쪽 관문이었다. 부산은 서울보다 일찍 복음 전도자가 들어 왔다. 먼저 일본 요코하마 주재 스코틀랜드성서공회 총무 톰슨J. Austin Thomson이 보낸 일본 매서인賣書人 나가사카長坂毅가 1883년 7월 24일 군함을 타고 부산에 도착했다. 그는 그 후 약 2개월 간 부산, 원산 등지를 순회하며 스코틀랜드 선교사 로스John Ross가 만주에서 번역한 〈예수셩교 누가복음젼셔〉와 〈예수셩교 요안나복음젼셔〉를 반포하고 일본으로 돌아갔다. 이것이 부산 선교의 시작이다. 그리고 부산은 일본을 거쳐 내한하는 선교사들의 중간 기착점이기도 했다. 1885년 3월 31일 일본 나가사키를 떠난 감리교의 아펜젤러Henry G. Apperzeller, 아편설라와 장로교의 언더우드Horace G. Underwood, 원두우는 4월 5일 부활절 인천 도착에 앞서 4월 2일 아침 부산항에 기착했다. 그들은 배가 하루 정박하는 사이 반나절 부산을 산책했다고 한다. 그해 11월에는 영국성공회 선교사 울프John R. Wolfe가 중국인 전도자 두 명과 함께 내항하여 전도했다. 다만 이들의 활동은 구체적으로 알려진 바가 없다.

그리고 1889년 8월 서울의 아펜젤러가 존스George H. Jones, 조원시 선교사와 함께 선교 탐색 여행차 원주-문경-대구를 거쳐 8월 31일 부산에 들렀다. 이어서 캐나다 출신의 독립선교사였던 게일James S. Gale, 기일과 하디Robert A. Hardie, 하리영가 각각 1-2년씩 부산에 체류했다. 게일은 최초의 부산 거주 선교사였고, 하디는 부산의 영국세관 전속의사로 일했다.

그 무렵 부산에서 활동하던 울프선교사는 재정 지원 중단으로 부산을 떠나기 앞서 그 안타까운 사정을 글로 써서 호주 교인들에게 알렸다. 그 소식을 접한 데이비스Joseph H. Davies, 덕배시는 호주장로교에 한국 선교를 자원하여 목사 안수를 받은 후 누나인 메리Mary T. Davies와 함께

1889년 10월 내한하였다. 서울에서 5개월가량 한국어를 배운 그는 부산을 선교지로 정하고 육로로 20일 만에 부산에 도착했다. 하지만 그 사이 천연두에 걸려 도착 하루만인 1890년 4월 5일 게일의 집에서 운명하였다. 부산 선교 최초의 희생자인 그의 유해는 복병산 공동묘지(지금 남성여고 주차장 자리)에 묻혔다.

그런데 호주장로교회는 데이비스의 죽음에 충격을 받아 오히려 더욱 한국 선교를 후원하기로 하고 다시 1891년 10월 맥케이James H. Mackay, 맥목사 목사 부부와 3명의 미혼 여선교사 곧 멘지스Belle Menzies, 민지사, 페리Jean Perry, 퍼셋Mary Fawcett, 맥부인 등 모두 5명의 선교사를 파송하였다. 이들은 그 후 부산진 좌천동에 스테이션을 설치하고 본격적으로 부산지역에서 선교하기 시작했다.

북장로교 선교사 베어드는 이보다 약 한 달 앞선 1891년 9월 초량 인근 영주동에 선교부지를 확보한 후 이듬해 4월 선교주택을 짓고 본격적인 선교에 착수했다. 그 결과 베어드는 1893년 6월 4일 자신의 사랑채에서 한국인 신자들과 함께 교회를 시작할 수 있었다. 이렇게 부산 선교를 시작한 베어드는 그 후 평양으로 전임하고 그 뒤를 이어 브라운Hugh M. Brown, 어빈Charles H. Irvin, 어을빈, 아담스James E. Adams, 안의와, 로스Cyril Ross, 노세영, 사이드보탐Richard H. Sidebotham, 사보담, 스미스Walter E. Smith, 심익순, 윈Rodger H. Winn, 인노절 등이 부산을 거점으로 경상도 선교에 나섰다.

부산은 이렇게 선교 처음부터 호주선교부와 북장로교선교부가 함께 선교를 시작했지만 1909년부터 부산을 둘로 나누어 부산진과 고관, 동래 등 동남부지역은 호주선교부가, 초량지역은 북장로교가 선교를 담당하기로 하였다. 그러다가 1913년 말 북장로교선교부가 이곳에서 철수함에 따라 부산은 호주선교부의 전담 선교지역이 되었다. 호주 선교사들은 1892년 매입한 좌천동 686번지 일대의 땅에 교회(부산진교회)와 학교(일신여학교) 그리고 선교사주택을 잇달아 세워 선교의 거점으로 삼은 다음 점차 그 활동 영역을 넓혀 나갔다. 부산의 호주 선교사들로 대표적인 이는 아담슨Andrew Adamson, 손안로, 1894~1909, 엥겔George O. Engel, 왕길지, 1900~1919, 맥켄지James N. McKenzie, 매견시, 1910~1938, 라이트Albert C. Wrigt, 예원배, 1928~1942 등이 있다.

✱ 부산 기독교 유적지

부산진교회와 부산진일신여학교 건물 그리고 일신기독병원

부산진교회: 부산시 동구 좌천동 763라 부산시 동구 좌천동 761-1 / **일신기독병원**: 부산시 동구 좌천동 1-471번지

부산진교회는 부산 지하철 1호선 좌천동역에서 내려 일신기독병원 방향으로 걸어서 5분 거리의 좌천동 골목에 위치하고 있다. 바로 이 일대에 호주선교부의 부산진스테이션이 자리하고 있었다. 부산진교회 건물은 1985년에 지은

800평 규모의 붉은 현대식 예배당과 2007년 지은 '왕길지기념관'으로 이루어져 있어서 옛 모습을 그리기는 어렵지만 교회로비에 마련된 사료실에서 옛날 교적부와 당회록, 제직회록, 선교사 관련 자료들을 만나볼 수 있다. 또 교회 윗마당에는 이 교회 설립자인 멘지스Miss Belle Menzies와 동료 선교사 무어Miss Elizabeth S. Moore를 기념하는 비석('공로긔념 맨지부인 모부인')이 서있다. 1931년 교회 창립 40주년 기념으로 당시 부산진교회 교인들이 세운 것이다. 1891년 미혼 여선교사로 부산에 온 멘지스는 부산진교회와 일신여학교를 시작했을 뿐만 아니라 1924년까지 30여년을 전도와 교육사업에 헌신하여 후배 선교사들로부터 '호주선교부의 어머니' 혹은 '대모代母'라 불리울 만큼 지도적 위치에 있었다. 무어 역시 미혼의 여선교사로 부산에서 20년(1892~1912), 통영에서 5년(1913~1918) 동안 사역하였다. 그리고 교회 정문 오른쪽 옆에는 첫 호주 선교사 데이비스의 기념비(2001년 건립)를 세워놓았다.

부산진교회 바로 앞에는 호주선교부에서 1905년 건축한 부산진일신여학교건물(부산시 동구 좌천동 761-1)이 남아 있다. 지난 2003년 부산시 기념물 제55호로 지정된 대지 385평 2층 벽돌의 이 건물은 국비와 시비를 지원 받아 2006년 원형 복원 공사를 마친 뒤 100년 전 신교육을 받던 여학생들의 생활과 3·1운동 자료, 기독교 자료 등을 전시하는 기념관으로 꾸며졌다. 1919년 3·1운동 때 바로 여기서 공부하던 여학생들이 독립만세를 부르면서 부산지역 만세운동이 시작되었다. 그래서 부산시에서는 지난 1984년 부산진교회 맞은 편에 '부산진일신여학교 만세운동 기념비'를 세웠다. 그 후 일신여학교 고등과는 1925년 동래 복천동으로 옮겨갔다가 일제 말기 호주선교부가 철수하면서 동래여학교로 바뀌었다.

부산진교회 아래에 있는 일신기독병원은 1952년 호주 선교사 헬렌 맥켄지Helen P. Mackenzie, 매혜란와 캐더린 맥켄지Catherine M. Mackenzie, 매혜영 자매에 의해 일신부인병원으로 문을 열었다. 두 자매의 아버지 맥켄지James N. Mackenzie, 매견시는 1910년 내한한 이래 1939년까지 부산 감만동의 상애원相愛園을 중심으로 나환자 사역에 헌신한 선교사였다. 헬렌은 맥켄지의 큰 딸로 평양외국인학교와 멜버른대 의대를 졸업한 산부인과 의사였고, 동생 캐더린은 간호사였다. 두 자매는

6·25전쟁 중 고통당하는 부인들을 위해 부인병원을 열었던 것이다. 지난 1982년 현재의 이름을 갖게 된 일신기독병원 옆에는 2001년 복원된 맥켄지기념비가 있다. 그런데 부산의 나환자들은 1930년 아버지 맥켄지의 한국 선교 20주년을 기념하여 그의 기념비를 좌천동 현재의 병원 옆에 건립한 바 있었지만 그 비석은 1940년대 소실되었다고 한다. 그리고 일신기독병원은 별관인 맥켄지기념관 3층에 '맥켄지선교관'을 두어 선교 자료를 전시하고 있다.

초량교회

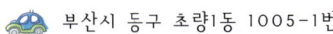 부산시 동구 초량1동 1005-1번지

부산역 지하도를 건너 국민은행쪽으로 10여분 골목길을 오르면 초량파출소가 나온다. 초량교회는 초량초등학교 오른쪽의 언덕배기를 베개 삼아 서있다. 1893년 북장로교 선교사 베어드의 영선현 사랑방(현 코모도호텔 자리)에서 출발한 초량교회는 1922년 초량동 1005번지 현재 위치로 옮겨 여러 차례 예배당을 신축 혹은 증축하였는데 현재 남아있는 400평 규모의 석조예배당은 1967년에 지은 것이다. 그래서 한말이나 일제시대의 흔적을 찾아볼 수는 없다. 하지만 교회 1층의 20평 규모 역사관에는 영선현 시절부터 사용하던 당회록이나 교인명부, 제직회록, 1922년 헌당한 초량교회 건물 사진과 그 건물에 사용된 벽돌 등을 전시하고 있다. 특히 순교자 주기철 목사가 사용했던 강대상과 의자가 눈에 띈다. 평양신학교를 졸업하고 목사 안수를 받은 주 목사는 1926년부터 마산 문창교회로 이임하던 1931년까지 초량교회에 시무했다.

부산 복병산 유실 묘역

 부산시 중구 대청동 1가 10번지

부산 중구 대청동 복병산 언덕에는 1890년 4월 5일 부산 도착 하루 만에 운명한 데이비스의 무덤이 들어선 후 모두 9명의 외국인이 묻혀 있었던 것으로 전해

지는데 현재 신원이 밝혀진 사람은 4명이다. 데이비스에 이어 1892년 1월에는 호주 선교사 맥케이의 부인 사라Sara Mackay가 이곳에 안장되었다. 남편을 따라 1891년 부산에 온 그녀는 임신으로 인한 불면증과 구역질에 폐렴이 겹쳐 도착 3개월 만에 사망하고 말았다. 또 1894년 5월에는 북장로교 부산 선교 개척자 베어드의 두 살 난 딸이 같은 곳에 묻혔다. 이어서 1895년 11월에는 호주 선교사 아담슨 Andrew Adamson의 부인 엘리자Eliza A. Adamson의 묘가 이곳에 마련되었다. 내한 1년 6개월 만에 심장병으로 사망한 것이다. 1935년에는 북장로교 의료 선교사를 역임한 어빈Charles H. Irvin이 복병산에 묻혔다. 1894년 브라운Hugh M. Brown의 뒤를 이어 부산에 온 그는 17년 동안 선교사로 일하다가 부인과 이혼하면서 선교사 직을 사임한 후 1911년부터 동광동 5가 영선현 고개에 '어을빈의원魚乙彬醫院'을 차리고는 계속 부산에서 생활했다. 어빈은 한국여성 양한나와 재혼했다고 한다.

그런데 지금 복병산 선교사 묘역은 유실되어 그 자취를 찾을 수 없다. 1930년대 이 일대가 개발되면서 그 자리에 조선방송국 부산연주소(현 부산KBS)가 들어섰다. 그리고 바로 위 언덕으로 일본인 학교인 미시마고등실업여학교가 있었는데 해방 후 김길창 목사가 인수해서 남성여학교가 되었다. 1972년 부산방송국이 초량동으로 이전하자 남성여고(부산광역시 중구 대청동 1가 10번지)가 그 자리를 사들여 현재 주차장으로 사용하고 있다.

대한성공회 부산주교좌성당

부산시 중구 대청동 2가 18번지

복병산에서 내려와 대청동 시장 입구 좁은 골목에 들어서면 부산에 남아있는 유일한 일제시대 예배당인 대한성공회 부산주교좌성당이 있다. 1924년 지은 고딕 양식의 붉은 벽돌건물로 1960년대 부분 보수한 것을 빼면 옛 모습 그대로다. 이 교회는 1900년 부산에 건너온 일본 성공회 교인들이 설립한 교회로 해방 전까지 일본인들만 다녔다고 하는데 해방 후 한국 교인들이 인수하여 지금은 대한성공회 부산교구 주교좌성당이 되었다.

✱ 부산 일반 유적지

부산근대역사관

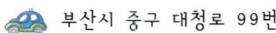 부산시 중구 대청로 99번지

　용두산공원에서 내려와 보수동 방면으로 가는 길에 위치한 부산근대역사관은 일제강점기 대표적인 수탈기구인 (구)동양척식주식회사 부산지점 건물(부산광역시 지정기념물 제49호)을 이용하여 만든 근대사박물관이다. 이 건물은 해방 후인 1949년부터는 미국 해외공보처 부산문화원으로 사용되었으나 부산시민들의 지속적인 반환요구로 미문화원을 철수하고, 1999년 대한민국 정부로 반환된 것을 그 해 6월 부산시가 인수하였다. 이 건물은 일제 침략의 상징이었으나 시민들에게 우리의 아픈 역사를 알릴 수 있는 교육의 공간으로 활용하기 위해 근대역사관으로 조성하였던 것이다. 이는 역사 바로 세우기를 통해 조선총독부 청사를 헐어버린 것과 좋은 대조를 이룬다.

　1920년대 건립된 철근 콘크리트 건물로서 서구 양식이 도입된 당시의 건축 경향을 알 수 있는 몇 안 되는 건물로서 충분히 역사적 자료로서의 가치를 지니고 있다. 역사관의 전시내용은 외세의 침략과 수탈로 형성된 부산의 근현대사를 중심으로 하였다. 개항기 부산, 일제의 부산 수탈, 근대도시 부산, 동양척식주식회사, 근현대 한미관계, 부산의 근대 거리 등으로 구성하였다. 개관시관은 오전 9시부터 오후 6시까지이며 1월 1일과 매주 월요일은 휴관이다(단, 월요일이 공휴일인 경우 다음날 휴관). 관람료는 무료이다.

40계단 기념관

 부산시 중구 동광동 5가 44-3번지

　40계단 기념관은 1950년대 당시 피난민들의 생활과 애환을 기념하기 위해 설립한 교육 전시공간이다. 5층 상설전시실에는 1950년대 피난민들의 힘겨운 생

활상을 담은 사진과 생활용품이 전시되어 있다. 미군 전투식량, 구호 밀가루, 전시의 화폐, 비누, 전쟁 당시 학교 모형이나 교과서, 필기구, 도시락 등을 통해 어렵고 가난한 시절의 향수를 느껴볼 수 있게 전시하였다. 특히 이곳은 지역문화의 전통과 정체성을 살리는 복합역사문화공간으로 부산 시민뿐 아니라 해외 관광객들에게도 유용한 역사 학습장이 되어 주고 있다.

한편 국민은행 중앙동 지점에서부터 40계단을 거쳐 40계단 문화관과 팔성관광에 이르는 거리를 '40계단 문화관광테마거리'로 조성하여 50~60년대 피난민들의 애환과 향수를 재현하여 추억을 회상할 수 있게 함으로써 새로운 관광명소로 육성하고자 조성하여 2004년 6월 부산시 종합평가 최우수거리로 선정되었다. 기념관 관람시간은 평일은 오전 10시-오후 7시까지이고 주말은 오후 5시까지 관람할 수 있다. 동절기에는 오후 6시까지 관람 가능하고 매주 월요일과 국경일, 명절은 휴관이다.

백산기념관

 부산시 중구 동광동 3가 10-2번지

부산우체국과 용두산공원 사이에 위치하고 있는 백산기념관은 1995년 8월 15일, 광복 50주년을 맞이하여 옛 백산상회 자리에 지은 것으로 기념관 내부는 지하 1, 2층의 전시실로 구성되어 있고 입구는 독특하게 피라미드 모양으로 되어 있다. 지하 1층 전시실 입구에는 백산 안희제 선생의 흉상이 있고, 그의 연보와 친필 서한을 비롯한 책과 도장 등의 유품과 독립운동 자료 80여 점이 전시되어 있다. 지하 2층은 독립운동과 관련하여 기획전 형식으로 전시되거나 대관하고 있다.

백산 안희제 선생은 경남 의령 출생으로 양정의숙을 졸업하고, 동래와 의령에 각각 구명학교와 의신학교를 세웠다. 1909년 서상일徐相日·박중화朴重華·신성모申性模 등과 함께 항일비밀결사 대동청년당大東靑年黨을 조직하여 구국운동을 전개하였다. 1911년 북간도와 시베리아를 돌면서 독립군 기지를 돌아보고 3년 후에 귀국, 부산에서 백산상회白山商會를 열고 무역업에 종사하면서 그곳을 국내

독립단체의 연락처로 삼았다. 1925년 중외일보사中外日報社를 인수, 중앙일보사中央日報社로 개칭하여 사장이 된 후 총독정치를 비난하는 글을 발표했다.

1933년 중국 헤이룽장성黑龍江省 둥진청東京城에 발해渤海농장과 발해학교를 세워 교포의 생활안정과 청소년 교육에 힘쓰는 한편, 대종교大倧敎의 총본사전강總本司典講 · 교적간행회장敎籍刊行會長 등을 역임하며 종교를 통하여 민족자주정신을 고취하였다. 1942년 11월 일본경찰에 체포 · 구금된 후 9개월 만에 병보석으로 풀려났으나, 이듬해 1943년 무단강牧丹江병원에서 병사하였다. 1962년 건국훈장 독립장이 추서되었다.

박차정 의사 생가

 부산시 동래구 칠산동 319-1번지

박차정 의사 생가는 1944년 34세의 나이로 순국하기까지 독립운동단체인 근우회, 민족혁명당, 조선의용대 등에서 활동한 대표적인 여성 항일운동가 박차정朴次貞, 1910.5.7~1944.5.27 의사의 애국 · 애족정신을 기리기 위해 건립하였다.

부산 동래 복천동에서 출생한 박차정 의사는 1925년 동래일신여학교(현 동래여자고등학교)을 입학하여 항일 여성운동단체인 근우회槿友會 동래지부 회원, 동래노동조합 조합원, 신간회 동래지회 회원 등으로 활약하였다. 1929년 졸업한 뒤, 근우회 중앙집행위원 · 조사연구부장 · 상무위원 · 선전부장 · 출판부장 등을 맡아 여성 항일운동에 이바지하는 한편, 그 해 12월 근우회를 중심으로 일어난 광주학생운동 동조 시위를 전국적 반일학생운동으로 확대시키다 일본 경찰에 체포되었다.

이듬해 1월 부산방직 파업사건을 주도하다 다시 체포되었으나 병보석으로 풀려난 후, 중국 베이징으로 건너가 의열단 단장 김원봉金元鳳과 결혼해 의열단원으로 활동하였다. 1932년에는 한중 연합 항일투쟁의 일환으로 설립한 조선혁명군사정치간부학교 제1기 여자부 교관으로 임명되어 사관생도 양성에 주력하였다.

그뒤 민족혁명당 부녀부 주임을 거쳐, 1936년 7월 이성실李聖實과 함께 남경 조선부인회를 조직해 부녀자들의 민족의식 고취와 대동단결을 주도하였고, 다음해 11월에는 의열단 한중민족연합전선의 대對 일본 라디오 선전방송을 맡아 활동하였다.

1938년 의열단 기관지 〈조선민족전선〉에 글을 투고해 무장궐기를 촉구하고, 그 해 10월부터 조선의용대 부녀복무단 단장을 맡아 항일 투쟁에 주력하였다. 이듬해 2월 장쑤성 쿤룬산에서 일본군과 교전하다 부상을 입고, 그 후유증으로 고생하다 1944년 5월 사망하였다. 1995년 건국훈장 독립장이 추서되었다.

임시수도기념관

 부산시 서구 대학 2로 43번지

임시수도기념관은 한 때 대통령 관저로 사용되었던 것을 기념하기 위한 곳이다. 일제강점기에 진주에 있던 경상남도청을 부산으로 옮기면서 일제가 건축하였다. 한국전쟁 시 1950년 8월 18일 정부가 부산으로 이전한 뒤 10월 27일 서울로 환도할 때까지, 1.4후퇴로 다시 부산이 임시수도가 된 뒤에 휴전협정으로 환도하기 전까지 이 건물의 본관은 정부청사로, 상무관은 국회의사당으로, 뒤편 경찰국은 군경 합동작전사령부로 쓰였으며, 도지사 관사는 대통령 관저로 사용되었다.

1983년 7월 경남도청이 창원시로 옮겨감에 따라 도지사 관사는 1984년 6월 25일 임시수도 당시의 역사적인 사실과 유물전시를 위하여 임시수도기념관으로 지정되었다. 2층의 붉은 벽돌 건물로 서구식 르네상스 양식이 변형된 양식이다. 시련이 많았던 대한민국의 과거사를 고스란히 간직하고 있는 건물로 가치가 높아 2002년 부산시 기념물 제53호로 지정되었다.

기념관에는 임시수도 당시의 이승만 대통령의 유품을 중심으로 하는 소장품이 1,2층 여섯 개 방에 전시되어 있다. 관람시간은 하절기(3월~10월)는 오전 9

부산 임시수도기념관

시~오후 6시까지, 동절기(11월~2월)는 오전 9시~오후 5시까지이다. 관람료는 무료이며, 매주 월요일은 휴관이다.

2. 경남지역

첫번째. 진주

※ 진주 소개

　진주는 일찍이 경주·상주·안동과 함께 경상도의 대읍大邑으로 특히 경남 서부 지역에 대한 영향력을 행사해 왔다. 먼저 통일신라 때 진주에는 9주의 하나인 강주康州가 설치되어 지방통치의 거점으로 발달하기 시작했다. 당시 강주는 남강을 통해 지리산 동북부와 연결되고, 황강을 통해 낙동강에 나갈 수 있으며, 육로로 하동을 거쳐 호남과 연결되는 교차로에 위치해 있었다. 고려 태조 왕건이 낙동강에 진출하여 내륙으로 북상할 무렵 왕봉규와 윤웅 등 강주의 호족들은 왕건과 교류하기 시작했다. 왕건에게 있어 강주는 남해안 제해권과 관련하여 군사적으로 중요한 지역이었다.

또 이곳은 무인정권 최씨 집안의 오래된 식읍지食邑地였다. 최씨 무인정권은 지리산 일대의 사찰과 깊은 관계를 맺고 있었다. 최우의 큰 아들 만종이 출가한 산청의 단속사를 비롯하여 승주의 송광사, 강진의 백련사 등이 대표적 사찰이다. 조계종이 지리산에서 성립될 수 있었던 것도 최씨 무인정권의 영향력과 무관하지 않다.

조선시대에 들어와 진주는 남명 조식이라는 큰 선비를 배출하면서 한국 유학사에 커다란 획을 그었다. 남명 조식의 사상과 삶은, 실천을 강조한 '경의敬義'와 처사적인 삶으로 특징지을 수 있다. 그는 관직에 나아가지 않았으며, 말년에 지리산 자락의 덕산에 정착하여 후학 양성에 힘을 쏟았다. 남명의 문인들은 16세기 후반 진주를 중심으로 남명학파를 크게 일으켰다. 남명학맥은 진주뿐만 아니라 크게는 경남 지역으로 확산되었으며 호남의 순천·남원 등지로 뻗어갔다. 실천을 강조한 남명학파 인사들은 임진왜란 때 의병의 자취를 뚜렷이 남겼다. 조식은 평소 무예와 병법, 국방문제에 깊은 관심을 보였다. 또한 그는 일찍부터 일본을 경계해야 할 것을 강조한 바 있었다. 때문에 남명의 문인들은 결연히 의병 대열에 합류하였다. 의령의 곽재우, 고령의 김면, 합천의 정인홍, 청도의 박경신 등이 그 대표적 의병장이었다.

19세기 후반 진주는 기존 질서에 대한 저항세력의 중요한 거점이 되었다. 진주의 서북쪽 끝자락, 지리산 남쪽 기슭에 자리잡은 덕산의 장시에서 바로 1862년 농민항쟁이 시작되었기 때문이다. 1870년 이필제는 덕산을 거점으로 해서 변란을 일으키려다 실패하였다. 또 1894년 경남 서부지역 동학조직의 본거지 역시 덕산에 있었다.

조선시대 이래의 진주목은 1895년 지방제도가 개편되면서 진주부가 되어 21개 군을 관할하였다. 당시 경남 땅에는 진주부 말고 동래부가 있었을 뿐이었다. 그리고 그 1년 뒤인 1896년 전국이 8도에서 13도로 나뉘면서 진주는 경상남도의 도청소재지가 되었다. 그런데 부산, 마산이 항구도시로 성장하고, 1925년 경남도청이 부산으로 옮겨가면서 진주의 위상이 달라지기 시작했다. 그 후 진주는 급격한 도시화시대에도 인구이동이 적어 전통적인 사고방식이 많이 남아있는 도시가 되었고, 진주 사람들의 생업도 농업이 적지 않은 비중을 차지하였다. 또 배후지인 남강과 지리산 주변에서 농산물과 임산물이 많이 출하되었다. 근대 상공업 역시 이 지역의 자본과 인력이 많이 참여하는 토착성을 보였다. 최근에는 대전-진주 간 고속도로와 진주-통영 간 고속도로가 개통되어 서울은 3시간 30분, 통영은 30분 거리로 단축되었다. 진주와 중부권, 수도권, 남해안권의 직접적인 연결로 양 지역 간 물류 유통과 관광 교류가 활발해지고 있다.

✱ 진주 기독교 전래

호주선교부가 진주에 공식적으로 스테이션을 개설한 것은 1905년이었다. 하지만 당시 진주는 서부 경남의 중심지일 뿐만 아니라 도청소재지로서 선교사들이 왕래하였으므로 기독교와의 접촉은 그 전부터 시작되었던 것으로 보인다. 진주에 스테이션을 설치하자는 의료선교사 커렐Hugh Currell의 요청을 검토한 호주선교부는 1905년 그를 진주에 파견하였다. 호주선교부 최초의 의료선교사로 1902년 내한한 아일랜드 출신의 커렐은 처음 부산에서 진료하다가 부산에는 이미 북장로교가 운영하는 작은 병원과 일본인 의사들이 있음을 알고 서양의사가 전혀 없었던 진주 근무를 자원했던 것이다. 커렐은 1905년 10월 20일 자신의 조사 박성애 부부와 함께 진주로 이주하였다. 그리고 북문안 초가집(성내동)에 임시로 거주하며 전도와 의료사업을 시작하였다.

당시 이곳 진주의 인구는 약 4만 명으로 추산되는데 전도에 어려움이 있을 것으로 예상했지만 커렐의 의료 시술은 지역민들의 관심을 끌기에 충분했다. 그리고 곧 전도의 결실이 나타나기 시작했다. 커렐은 초신자들을 모아 놓고 예배드리기 시작했다. 지금의 진주교회(옥봉리교회)는 이렇게 시작되었다. 1905년 12월 커렐의 보고서를 보면 그 때 매주일 드리는 예배에 평균 20명의 남자와 7명의 여성이 참석하고 있다고 적혀 있다. 진주에서의 첫 세례식은 1907년 6월 23일 10명의 성인과 3명의 유아에게 베풀어졌다. 또 이 해에 30여 명이 학습을 받음으로 진주교회는 날로 성장해갔다. 박성애는 1915년 진주교회의 장로가 되었고, 다시 평양신학교를 졸업하고 진주지방의 첫 한국인 목사가 되어 진주교회 목사로 시무하였다. 그 뿐만 아니라 커렐 부인은 1906년 박성애 부부의 도움 가운데 남녀학교를 시작하였다. 후일 이 학교들은 시원여학교柴園女學校와 광림학교光林學校로 발전하게 된다. 이어서 커렐은 호주선교부의 지원을 받아 1913년 경남지방 최초의 병원인 배돈병원을 개원하였다.

호주선교사들은 지금의 봉래동(당시 옥봉리) 일대에 진주교회와 그 옆 붉은 벽돌의 배돈병원培敦病院 그리고 광림학교와 시원여학교(수정동)를 차례로 건축하여 제법 규모가 큰 선교 스테이션을 조성하였다. 그리하여 이곳은 서부 경남 지역 복음화의 전진기지가 되었다. 커렐(1905~1915)에 이어 진주에서 사역한 대표적인 선교사들로는 스콜스Miss Nellie R. Scholes, 시교장, 1907~1918, 클러크Francis L. Clerke, 가불란서, 1910~1920, 1922~1934, 매클라렌Charles I. McLaren, 마라연/마찰수 1911~1923, 1939~1941, 커닝햄F. W. Cunningham, 권임함, 1913~1925, 1928~1940, 알렌Arthur W. Allen, 안란, 1915~1927, 네피어Miss Gertrude Napier, 남성진, 1914~1934 등이 있다.

✲ 진주 기독교 유적지

진주교회

🚗 경남 진주시 봉래동 37번지

지금 진주교회가 위치하고 있는 진주시 봉래동 37번지 부근은 1905년 북문안에서 시작한 커렐 선교사의 신앙공동체가 성장을 거듭하면서 1932년 무렵 새롭게 자리 잡은 진주교회의 터전이었다. 또 교회 인근에는 배돈병원과 광림학교, 시원여학교가 포진하고 있었다. 하지만 지금은 그런 옛 모습을 발견할 수 없다. 1933년 지어졌던 벽돌예배당은 6·25전쟁 때 폭격으로 없어졌다. 현재의 교회당은 지난 1997년 건축된 현대식 건물이다. 또 교회 바로 옆의 배돈병원 자리에는 단독주택이 들어서 있고, 선교사 주택이 있었던 자리에는 아파트(삼전빌라)가 섰다. 그리고 교회 뒤편 200 m 부근의 광림학교 자리와, 다시 교회에서 동남쪽으로 3-400 m 떨어진 곳에 있었던 시원여학교 자리 역시 지금은 단독주택가(수정동 1통 2반과 3반)로 변하였다. 그 옛날 진주 스테이션의 흔적을 볼 수 없는 것이 유감이다. 하지만 이렇게 유적지로 소개하는 이유는 바로 이곳이 100여 년 전 신앙의 선조들이 지역 복음화를 위해 집중적으로 헌신했던 역사의 현장이기 때문이다. 다만 진주교회 구내에는 1991년 진주노회가 세운 '선교기념비'와 2012년에 건립된 '진주기미독립만세시위기념종탑'(1919년 3월 18일 진주 장날 만세시위 기념)이 있어 이곳이 역사의 현장임을 말해주고 있다.

배돈병원 자리

 경남 진주시 봉래동 37번지 일대

배돈병원Mrs. Paton Memorial Hospital은 1906년 호주 빅토리아장로교 여전도회가 825파운드를 보낸 이후 호주교회의 계속적인 지원으로 1913년 경남 최초의 병원으로 개원하였다. 호주장로교회가 파송했던 탁월한 선교사 페이튼 여사를 기념하여 이름을 '배돈'이라 한 것이다. 병원설립이 준비되고 있을 때인 1910년 간호사 클러크가 진주로 와서 커렐을 도왔고, 1911년에는 의사 매클라렌이 가담했다. 그는 신경정신과 의사로 나중에 세브란스병원에서 교수로 봉사했다. 1939년도 배돈병원의 통계를 보면 그 해 진료환자는 모두 17,620명으로 그 중 입원환자가 13,753명이었다. 이는 당시 진주 인구가 47,200여명이었음을 볼 때 얼마나 많은 사람들이 배돈병원을 찾았는지 알 수 있다. 그러나 일제말기 병원을 운영하던 호주선교사들이 추방되면서 결국 배돈병원은 문을 닫게 되었다. 병원 건물은 해방 후 해외 귀환동포의 수용시설로 사용되다가 6·25전쟁 때의 폭격으로 완전히 사라지고 말았다.

광림학교와 시원여학교 자리

🚗 경남 진주시 봉래동 37번지 일대

진주 스테이션의 학교 교육은 커렐부인에 의해 1906년 시작되었다. 처음 학교의 이름은 정숙여학교와 안동학교(남학교, 1907년 시작)라 불렀는데, 1909년 배돈병원 뒤편 묘지 빈 터에 건평 30평의 목조기와 1개동을 교사校舍로 건축하면서 두 학교를 합쳐 광림학교라 하였다. 그 후 여학생들이 늘어나자 선교부는 1925년 수정동 광림학교 운동장 부지에 목조 2층 120평짜리 새 교사를 신축하고 광림학교에서 여자부를 떼내어 시원여학교 The Nellie R. Scholes Memorial School로 독립시켰다. 시원柴園이라는 학교 이름은 1907년부터 1919년 4월 사망할 때까지 이 지역 교육선교사로 일한 스콜스 Miss Nellie R. Scholes를 기념하기 위해 명명되었다. 한국인들은 그녀를 시교장柴校長으로 불렀다. 시원여학교는 진주 최초의 근대식 여성 교육기관이었다.

광림학교는 1929년 세계대공황의 여파로 선교비가 줄어들면서 폐교되었다. 이것은 매우 불행한 일이었으나 배돈병원 운영이 더 시급했던 선교부의 고육지책이었다. 그 후 광림학교의 건물은 경남성경학교에서 사용하였다. 시원여학교는 1939년 신사참배 거부로 폐교당했는데, 당시 재학생 303명은 진주공립제2심상소학교 수정분교장(지금의 수정초등학교)으로 모두 편입되었다. 그리고 그 건물은 진주사범학교 기숙사가 되었다. 광림과 시원은 해방 후에도 재개교하지 못하였고 6·25전쟁 중에는 건물들마저 폭격으로 전소되어 자취를 감추었다.

✱ 진주 일반 유적지

진주성

🚗 경남 진주시 남성동, 본성동 일대

사적 제118호인 진주성은 석성(둘레 1,760 m)으로 진주의 역사와 문화가 집약되어 있는 진주의 성지이다. 본래 토성이던 것을 고려 우왕5년(1379)에 석성으로 수축하였다. 임진왜란 때 진주목사 김시민이 왜군을 대파하여 임진왜란 3대첩 중의 하나인 진주대첩을 이룬 곳이며, 왜군과의 2차 전쟁인 1593년 6월, 7만여 명의 민·관·군이 최후까지 항쟁하다 장렬하게 순절하였다. 이때, 논개論介가 적장을 껴안고 남강南江에 투신하여 충절을 다한 곳이다. 이를 기념하기 위해 해마다 이곳에서는 진주남강유등축제를 열고 있다.

특히 진주성이 위치한 남강가 바위벼랑 위에 장엄하게 높이 솟은 촉석루(경남도문화재 자료 제8호)는 영남 제일의 아름다운 누각이다. 고려 고종 28년(1241)에 창건하여 8차례의 중건과 보수를 거쳤다. 이 누각은 장원루壯元樓라고도 하였으며, 전쟁 중에는 진주성을 지키는 지휘본부였고, 평화로운 시절에는 고시장考試場으로 사용되었다. 6.25전쟁으로 소실된 것을 시민들이 힘을 모아 진주고적보존회를 만들어 1960년에 복원하였다.

또한 남강가에는 시도기념물 제235호로 지정된 바위 의암義巖이 있다. 이 바위는 논개가 왜장을 끌어 안고 순국한 바위로 유명한데, 1593년(선조26) 6월 29일, 임진왜란 제2차 진주성전투에서 진주성이 함락되고, 7만 민·관·군이 순절하자, 논개는 나라의 원수를 갚기 위해 왜장을 유인하여 이 바위에서 순국하였다. 이에 논개의 순국정신을 현창하기 위해 영남사람들이 의암이라고 명명하였다.

인조 7년(1629) 진주의 선비 정대륭鄭大隆 : 1599~1661은 바위의 서쪽 벽면에 의암이라는 글자를 전각하였고, 남쪽에는 한몽삼韓夢參 : 1598~1662이 쓴 것으로 전하는 의암이라는 글이 새겨져 있다. 의암 옆의 암벽에는 "한 줄기 긴 강이 띠를 두르고, 의열은 천년의 세월을 흐르리라一帶長江 千秋義烈"는 글이 새겨져 있다.

진주성 내에는 1984년 여섯 번째로 국립박물관인 국립진주박물관이 있다. 개관 당시에는 가야문화를 중심으로 한 박물관이었고, 그후 임진왜란 3대 대첩지였던 진주성이 지닌 역사적 의미를 부각시키기 위해 임진왜란을 주제로 하는 역사박물관으로 1998년에 재개관하였다. 본관 건물은 우리나라 전통 목조탑을 석조건물로 형상화한 것으로 건축가 김수근의 대표적 작품이며, 상설전시실과 기획전시실을 갖추고 있다. 2001년에는 별관이 증축되었으며 이곳에는 재일동포 두암 김용두 선생의 기증 유물 전시실이 마련되었다.

형평운동 70주년 기념탑

경남 진주시 본성동

　진주시 본성동에는 형평운동 70주년 기념탑이 세워져 있다. 형평사衡平社는 말 그대로 '저울처럼 공평한 사회를 만들고자' 만든 단체였다. 1923년 봄, 경남 진주에서 만들어진 형평사는 기본적으로 조선시대 신분 질서 속에서 가장 천한 집단이었던 백정의 차별 관습을 없애고 평등사회를 만든다는 목적을 갖고 많은 사람들이 자발적으로 참여하면서 만든 조직적 사회운동단체였다. '사람 위에 사람 없고, 사람 아래 사람 없다'는 정신으로 시작된 형평운동의 목적은 백정들에 대한 차별 대우를 없애는 것이었지만, 궁극적으로는 모든 사람이 똑같은 권리를 갖고 있다는 점을 일깨워서 평등사회를 건설하자는 것이었다.

　1923년 4월 24일 진주에서 시작된 형평사의 형평운동은 1935년에 이름을 '대동사'로 바꿀 때까지 뜻 깊은 활동을 벌이며, 일제 침략 35년 동안 단일 조직으로 가장 오랫동안 유지된 사회운동단체로 기록된다. 비 백정 출신의 사회운동가들과 백정 공동체 지도자들은 백정들이 겪는 신분차별의 문제를 깊이 인식하고 협력하여 단체를 결성하기로 하였다. 그리하여 1923년 4월 24일 진주 청년회관에서 약 70여 명의 사회운동가들과 백정들이 회합을 갖고 백정들이 직업상 자주 쓰는 저울대형衡과 공평하다는 평平을 혼합하여 형평사로 정하였던 것이다.

　형평사는 진주에 본사를 두고 각 도에 지사, 각 군에 분사를 두어 전국적으로 확산되었다. 우리나라 역사상 최초로 인간 평등을 주장하며, 특정 집단에 대한 차별 관습을 없애려고 활동한 인권단체로 평가된다.

형평운동 70주년 기념탑

두 번째. 마산

✽ 마산 소개

신라시대에 골포라고 불리는 한낱 작은 포구에 지나지 않았던 마산이 역사에 이름을 남기게 된 계기는 1274년 몽고족이 세운 원나라가 일본을 정벌하려고 이곳에 정동행성을 만든 후였다. 마산이 합포라고 불렸던 그 때에 군사들이 물을 마셨다는 몽고정이 지금도 3·15 의거기념탑 옆에 남아 있다. 이곳은 바다를 끼고 있어 수군의 전진기지가 되었는가 하면 조선시대에는 국내 교통의 요지로서 마산포라 이름하였다. 그래서 숙종 8년에는 창원군에 속했던 이 포구에 조창이 들어와 마산 인근에서 세금으로 거둔 대동미를 운반하는 활기를 띠었다.

본격적으로 오늘의 마산을 일으키게 된 것은 1899년 개항 이후였다. 노산 이은상이 '가고파'로 노래한 그 '잔잔한 바다'는 개항 뒤로 풍운의 바다가 되었다. 맨 먼저 1900년 러시아가 일본에 한 발 앞서 얼지 않는 항구를 얻으려고 마산에 왔다. 중국의 여순항과 대련항을 얻은 뒤 이 두 항구와 블라디보스토크를 연결하는 한반도 남해안에 해군기지를 확보하고자 함이었다. 그래서 그들은 1900년 지금의 월영동에 영사관을 마련하고 그 부근에 조계지를 설치했다. 1904년 러–일전쟁에서 패배한 그들은 마산에서 물러났지만 지금도 그곳에는 러시아 영사관 터가 남아있다.

러시아 세력이 물러간 뒤에 일본은 해군기지를 진해에 만들기 시작했고 1909년 마산 개항장을 폐쇄하였다. 일제하에서 마산은 국제항구의 기능은 없어졌지만 대륙침략의 기지로 성장하였다. 1914년에는 지금의 시市를 뜻하는 부府로 승격되어 마산부가 되었으며, 1928년에는 마산 인구의 20%를 차지할 만큼 일본사람들이 많은 도시가 되었다. 당시 어업, 양조업, 미곡거래는 마산 경제를 받쳐주는 기둥이었다.

1960년 3월 15일 부정으로 치러진 정–부통령 선거에 항의하여 거리로 뛰쳐나온 마산 시민과 학생들이 일으킨 3·15 의거는 4·19 혁명의 기폭제가 되었다. 그런 만큼 이 도시는 민주주의를 상징하는 이미지를 갖고 있다. 게다가 3·15의거에서 보여준 마산 사람들의 투철한 정치–사회적 의식은 1970년대 말 이른바 '부마항쟁'을 통해 다시 한 번 확인되었다.

✽ 마산 기독교 전래

호주선교부와 북장로교선교부의 공동 선교 구역이었던 마산은 그래서 두 갈래로 복음이 전래되었다. 먼저 1901년 백도명의 전도로 김마리아와 김인모 등 7명의 여성들에 의해 교회가 시작되었다. 이 교회는 북장로교 로스Cyrill Ross의 지도를 받았다. 또 하나는 호주 선교사 아담슨Andrew Adamson의 영향을 받아 이승규가 세운 교회이다. 1900년 이후 마산지방은 아담슨의 순회구역이었다. 종종 분쟁을 겪던 두 교회는 1903년 결국 하나로 합쳐져 마산포교회가 되었다. 이승규는 1906년 아담슨 선교사의 지원을 받아 성호리에 있던 마산포교회당에 독서숙讀書塾을 세우게 되는데, 이 학교는 1909년 당시 대한제국 학부의 인가를 받아 마산 최초의 근대식 학교인 창신학교昌信

學校로 발전하였다.

　호주선교부는 1910년 마산에 스테이션을 개설하기로 하고 아담슨을 책임자로 지명했다. 아담슨은 그 해 마산으로 이주하여 1911년 상남동 74번지 노비산 언덕 위에 스테이션을 설치하였다. 마산 포교회 역시 상남동 87-1번지로 신축 이전하였다. 창신학교 역시 교회를 따라왔다. 1913년에는 창신에 적을 둔 여학생들로 의신여학교義信女學校를 별도로 세웠다. 그리하여 교회와 남녀학교 그리고 선교사 주택으로 이어지는 선교 기지가 상남동에 마련된 것이다. 아담슨은 창신학교의 초대 교장이자 마산포교회의 당회장으로 있으면서 마산 기독교의 형성에 공헌하였다.

　아담슨(1909~1914)에 이어 진주에서 사역한 대표적인 선교사들로는 라이트Albert C. Wrigt, 예원배, 1912~1914, 맥피Miss Ida McPhee, 미희, 1912-1937, 맥래Fredrick J. L. MacRae, 맹호은, 1916~1940, 알렌Arthur W. Allen, 안란, 1925~1932 등이 있다.

✱ 마산 기독교 유적지

제일문창교회와 마산 스테이션 자리 그리고 창신학교터

🚗 제일문창교회: 경남 창원시 마산합포구 상남동 87-1번지

　1911년 창원시 마산합포구 상남구 87-1번지에 자리 잡았던 마산포교회는 그 후 1919년 길 건너편의 추산동 7번지에 석조예배당을 짓고 이사하였다. 이때 교회 이름도 문창교회로 바꾸었다. 1931년 7월 부임하여 1936년 7월 평양산정현교회로 이임할 때까지 문창교회에서 목회한 주기철 목사의 사역 장소는 바로 이곳 추산동이었다. 그러나 지금은 거기에 다른 건물('놀이터')이 들어서있다. 교회 이전 후 선교사들에 의해 창신학교와 의신유치원으로 사용되었던 상남동 87-1번지 구예배당 자리에는 1970년에 지어진 제일문창교회의 예배당 일부와 최근 신축된 주기철기념관이 자리하고 있다. 주기철기념관 바로 앞에는 이곳이 옛 창신학교 터였다는 것을 알려주는 조그만 비석이 자리잡고 있다. 또 1924년 호주선교부에 의해 교회 북쪽 회원동에 새로이 지어졌던, 그리고 당시 마산에서 가장 크고 높았던 십자형 붉은 2층 벽돌의 창신학교(1925년 호신학교로 개편) 교사 역시 자취를 감추었다. 지금 그 일대는 아파트(회원동 415번지 한효아파트)가 들어서있다. 그리고 선교사들의 생활 공간이었던 상남동 74번지 근처도 아파

마산창신학교 표지석

트(서광아파트)가 세워져있다. '가고파'를 지은 노산 이은상은 마산교회 설립자인 이승규의 아들로 창신학교를 졸업한 바 있다. 그가 동무들과 뛰어놀던 추억의 언덕이 바로 마산 선교사들의 주택이 자리하고 있던 노비산 자락이었다.

경남선교 120주년 기념관과 순직 호주 선교사묘원

경남 창원시 마산합포구 진동면 인곡리 산167-3번지

지난 2010년 10월 문을 연 창원시 창원공원묘원 내 '경남선교 120주년 기념관'에는 부산·경남지역을 중심으로 활동했던 호주 선교사들의 유품이 전시되어 있다. 흰색 바탕의 75평 단층 건물로 지어진 기념관은 외벽을 유리로 마감해 밖에서도 안을 볼 수 있도록 만들었다. 전시 유품으로는 호주 선교사들이 사용했던 성경책과 한영사전(1897년 출간), 그리고 부산진교회 당회록과 라이트 Albert C. Wrigt, 예원배 선교사가 밀양마산교회에 기증했던 교회 종 등이 눈길을 끈다. 또 호주 선교사들이 1960년대 마산 지역의 미망인과 고아들을 돕기 위해 만든 수예품 등도 전시되어 있다.

기념관을 나와 왼쪽으로 가면 '순직 호주 선교사묘원'으로 가는 십자가 통로가 나온다. 양쪽 벽에는 126명 호주 선교사들의 흔적이 담긴 사진이 붙어 있다. 2009년 조성된 묘원에는 모두 8명의 선교사 기념비와 함께 경남 출신의 순교자인 주기철·손양원 목사 기념비도 세워져 있다.

8명의 선교사를 살펴보면 데이비스Joseph H. Davies, 덕배시, 1890, 부산, 맥케이부인 James H. Mackay, 1892, 부산, 아담슨부인Mrs. Andrew Adamson, 1895, 부산, 라이트부인 Mrs. Albert C. Wright, 1927, 진주, 알렌Arthur W. Allen, 안란, 1932, 진주, 네피어Miss Gertrude Napier, 남성진, 1936, 진주, 테일러William Taylor, 위대연, 1938, 진주, 맥피Miss Ida McPhee, 1912, 미희 등이다.

데이비스, 맥케이부인, 아담슨부인은 앞에서 다루었으므로 여기서는 나머지 5명의 선교사들을 소개하고자 한다. 라이트부인은 원래 니븐Alice G. Niven이라는 이름으로 1905년 내한한 미혼 선교사였다. 또 1908년부터 4년 동안 일신여학교 교장으로도 봉직했다. 그 후 니븐은 1913년 4살 연하의 같은 호주 선교사 라이트와 결혼, 마산과 진주에서 남편과 함께 사역하다가 1927년 12월 순직하였다.

호주 멜버른대와 오몬드신학교를 마치고 1913년 내한한 알렌 선교사는 1915년 진주 스테이션에 배속되어 그 때부터 진주 동남쪽 구역-사천·남해·하동-담당 선교사로 지역을 순회하며 교회들을 돌보았다. 또 그는 진주교회 당회장과 광림학교 교장으로도 봉직했고, 1924년에는 진주 남성교회를 설립하였다. 이어서 1925년에는 마산 스테이션으로 전임하여 호신학교 교장을 지냈다. 알렌은 1932년 7월 26일 56세를 일기로 별세하였다.

1872년 스코틀랜드에서 출생한 네피어 선교사는 에든버러간호학교를 마치고 1912년 독신으로 내한했다. 처음 마산 스테이션에 소속되어 모자건강을 위한 진료소Health Center를 운영하다가 1913년 배돈병원이 개원되면서 진주로 전임하여 간호부장으로 사역하였다. 그녀는 1936년 8월 29일 64세를 일기로 운명하였다.

테일러William Taylor 선교사는 1877년 생으로 홍콩의 에든버러의대를 졸업하고 1913년 4월 내한, 통영 스테이션에 배치되었다. 그 후 그는 통영에 방 2개의 진료소를 설치하고 의료사역을 실시하였다. 또 모터보트를 타고 통영·거제·고성·진해·용남의 남해안을 다니며 순회 진료에 나서기도 하였다. 1923년부터는 진주 배돈병원장으로 사역했는데, 그가 재임했던 1928년 배돈병원의 진료 실적은 연인원 12,001명에 달했다. 테일러는 1938년 8월 요코하마에서 풍토병 치료 중 순직하였다.

마지막으로 맥피 선교사는 1911년 내한, 부산진스테이션을 거쳐 창신학교에서 분립된 의신여학교 초대 교장으로 마산에 부임하였다. 처음 의신여학교는 상남동 노비산 언덕 위 선교사 사택 일부를 교사로 사용하였다. 맥피 선교사는 의신여학교 뿐만이 아니라 의신유치원도 함께 돌봤고 진주 시원여학교의 행정 지원업무도 수행하였다. 또 마산지역 기독교면려회운동을 주도하였다. 그녀는 자신의 건강을 돌보지 않고 사역하다가 병을 얻어 1937년 4월 13일 순직하였다.

✽ 마산 일반 유적지

국립 3·15민주묘지

🚗 경남 마산시 구암동 산92번지

국립 3·15민주묘지는 1960년 3월 15일 이승만 자유당 독재 정권의 부정부패와 부정선거에 항거하여 분연히 일어나 싸우다 희생된 영령들의 넋이 잠든 곳이다. 한국현대사에서 중요한 사건인 4.19혁명의 도화선이 되었던 3·15의거의 숭고한 뜻을 기리고 자유·민주·정의를 사랑하는 마산 시민정신을 계승하고자 조성하였다.

최초의 묘역은 1967년 구암동 야산의 3,960 m^2에 지나지 않았으나 1993년 문민정부 출범과 함께 시민 모두가 뜻을 모아 본격적인 성역화 사업을 추진하였다. 1998년 3월 총 부지면적 143,200 m^2규모의 3·15성역공원 조성공사에 착공, 2000년 6월에는 공모를 통해 선정한 상징조형물인 3·15 기념탑과 부조벽을 설치하였으며, 같은 해 12월에는 민주 열사들의 묘를 이장, 묘역조성을 완공하였다.

2002년 8월 1일 3·15성역공원에서 국립 3·15민주묘지로 승격되었으며,

2003년 3월에 준공식을 가짐으로써 애국선열의 거룩한 희생정신을 선양하고 치열했던 민주항쟁의 생생한 모습을 한 눈에 조감할 수 있도록 하였다. 국립 3·15민주묘지는 순국선열의 고귀한 넋을 기리는 추모의 공간이며, 민권 수호의 중심이었던 3·15의거정신을 후대에 길이 전할 민주화의 역사 교육장이다.

마산시립박물관

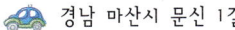 경남 마산시 문신 1길

마산시립박물관은 지역의 특성을 살려 급격한 현대화, 도시화의 물결 속에서 사라져가는 우리의 전통문화 유산을 수집·보존·전시하고자 마산시 개항 100주년기념사업으로 건립되었다. 전시실은 상설전시실과 기획전시실, 야외전시장으로 구성되어 있으며, 상설전시실은 4개의 공간으로 구분하여 주제에 따라 마산의 역사와 문화를 한 눈에 볼 수 있게 각종 전시물이 연출되어 있다.

마산문학관

경남 마산시 상남동 58-8번지

노비산 그린공원 내에 위치한 마산문학관은 근대 마산문학의 흐름을 조망하고 소중한 문학 전통과 자산을 널리 알리기 위해 마련한 문화공간으로 2005년 10월 28일에 개관하였다. 마산지역은 많은 문학인을 배출한 것으로 유명한 지역으로 이 지역 출신 문학가로는 3·1만세 마산의거를 주동한 안확을 비롯하여 이윤재, 이극로, 이은상, 김춘수, 천상병, 이원수 등 근대 문학계의 중요한 인물들에 대한 안내를 받을 수 있다.

세 번째. 통영

❋ 통영 소개

통영의 아름다운 바다 풍경과 고른 날씨는 한려수도가 열리기 훨씬 전 이미 이곳을 찾는 이들을 탄복시켰던 것 같다. "강구안 파래야, 대구, 복장어 쌈아, 날씨 맑고 물 좋은 길을 두고 정승 길이 웬 말이냐." 이 말은 조선시대 오늘날의 통영시에 있던 삼도수군통제영三道水軍統制營에 통제사統制使로 와있던 어떤 이가 정승으로 벼슬이 올라 서울로 떠나기 전 탄식처럼 뱉어 놓은 말이라고 한다.

통영統營이라는 말은 삼도수군통제영을 줄인 말로 조선 선조 37(1604)년 당시 통제사 이경준이 거제 오아포에 있던 통제영을 이곳 두룡포(지금의 통영시)로 옮기면서 지명으로 정착하였다. 그리고 이후 통제사 제도가 없어진 1896년까지 294년 동안 이곳은 조선 수군의 근거지였다. 그 후 대한제국 시대인 1900년까지 고성군의 한 지역이었던 이곳은 1914년 전국적인 행정구역 변경이 이루어지면서 거제군을 병합하여 통영군이라 일컫게 되었다. 그리고 충무시는 1955년 통영읍이 통영군과 분리, 市로 승격되면서 충무공의 시호를 따다 붙인 이름이다. 충무시와 통영군이 통영시로 통합된 것은 지난 1995년이다.

임진왜란 때 이순신 장군은 전라좌수영이 있던 전남 여수에서 한산도 곧 오늘날의 통영시 한산면 두억리로 옮겨 진陣을 친 다음 제승당에서 군대를 양성하는 한편 무기를 만들고 군량을 저축하는 등 모든 군무를 처리하였다. 본래 고성군에 딸린 궁벽한 섬 지방이었던 이곳은 임진왜란을 통해 두각을 나타내게 되었다. 그러므로 현존하는 통영시의 전통문화도 대개 임진왜란과 직·간접적으로 관련되어 있다. 이 가운데 유형문화재로는 착량묘鑿梁廟·세병관洗兵館·충렬사忠烈祠·제승당制勝堂 등이 대표적이며 무형문화재로는 통영오광대統營五廣大와 승전무勝戰舞를 비롯하여 통제영의 병참기지 구실을 하던 12工房에서 제작된 공예품의 전통을 이어가고 있는 기·예능 보유자들을 들 수 있다.

❋ 통영 기독교 전래

통영은 호주선교사 무어Miss Elizabeth S. Moore에 의해 1894년 무렵 복음이 전해졌다. 아마도 이때쯤 통영군 용남면 출신인 김치몽이 예수를 믿게 된 것 같다. 그런데 그는 기독교 신앙으로 인해 주변과 갈등하게 되었고 결국 고향을 떠나 부산에 정착하였다. 그 후 김치몽은 부산 영도에 거주하게 되는데, 1896년 그를 중심으로 세워진 교회가 바로 부산의 세 번째 교회인 영도교회(현재 영도제일교회)이다.

그리고 다시 아담슨의 전도로 1902년 봄 통영군 동항리교회(욕지도)가 세워졌다. 당시 박명출, 박인건, 이영백, 최명언 등 동항리의 초기 교인들은 마을 사람들의 위협에도 불구하고 예배당을 건축했을 뿐만이 아니라 늘어나는 교인들 때문에 머지않아 증축을 해야만 했다. 이어서 통영의 중심지에도 교회가 세워졌다. 1905년의 대화정교회(현 충무교회)이다. 역시 아담슨 선교사의 전도로 권희순이 예수를 믿고 그의 집에서 교회를 시작한 것이다.

호주선교부는 1912년 특별위원회를 열어 통영에 스테이션을 설치하기로 결의하였다. 그리하여 대화정교회 인근 대화정 269번지 산언덕 9,900 m²의 부지에 2층 붉은 벽돌 건물 3개동과 학교 건물 1개동으로 이루어진 선교 구내를 설치하고 여성-복음(교육)-의료선교사로 각각 무어Miss Elizabeth S. Moore와 왓슨Robert D. Watson · 테일러William Taylor 선교사 부부를 배치하였다. 1910년 내한한 왓슨 목사는 통영지방을 순회하던 중 이 지역에 교육기관이 전혀 없음을 알고 스테이션 구내에서 교육사업을 전개하였다. 특히 왓슨 부인은 이 지방 여성교육기관인 진명유치원, 진명야학교, 진명강습소 설립에 크게 기여하였다. 그 외에 통영의 교육선교사들로는 여선교사 커Miss Edith Kerr와 스키너Miss Amy G. M. Skinner 등이 있다. 특히 1914년 9월 내한하여 1940년까지 이곳에서 일한 교육학 전공의 스키너는 지역사회에 큰 영향을 미쳤다.

테일러 의사는 1913년부터 통영에 지금의 보건소와 같은 건강관리소를 설치하고 지역민에게 시약과 치료 등 의료선교를 시작하였다. 특히 섬사람들을 위해 호주의 교인들이 기부한 모터보트를 타고 순회하며 진료하였다. 응급환자나 입원환자는 진주 배돈병원으로 후송하였다. 테일러는 그 후 배돈병원 원장으로 전임되었고 그 뒤를 이어 트루딩거Martin Trudinger 목사와 레인Harold Lane 목사가 통영에서 의료사역을 겸하였다. 이 두 선교사의 부인들은 간호사였다.

✱ 통영 기독교 유적지

충무교회와 통영 스테이션터

🚗 **충무교회**: 경남 통영시 문화동 183번지 / **통영 스테이션 터**: 경남 통영시 문화동 269번지

충무교회는 1905년 아담슨에 의해 건립된 대화정교회의 전통을 계승하고는 있지만 지금 예배당은 1983년 헌당되어 옛 모습을 찾을 수 없다. 다만 충무교회 마당에는 2008년 건립된 '충무교회 설립 및 호주선교100주년 기념탑'이 있어 그 내력을 짐작케 한다. 그런데 충무교회 인근 문화동 269번지 일대에는 통영 스테이션 터가 일부 남아 있다. 그곳은 이순신 장군 사당인 충렬사 앞에 있는 SK 주유소 건너편의 땅이다. 넓었던 스테이션 부지의 대부분이 주택가로 바뀌었지만 현재 산비탈 2,600 m²의 빈 땅 곳곳에 주춧돌과 계단 등의 건물 잔해가 남아 있다. 이 건물들은 당시 통영에는 건축기술자가 없어 중국인들을 데려다가 지었다고 한다. 그 밑 문화빌라가 들어선 곳이 바로 진명학교가 있던 자리이다. 그리고 여기서 작곡가 윤이상, 시인 유치환, 극작가 유치진, 소설가 박경리, 시인 김

춘수 등이 어린 시절을 보냈다. 윤이상은 1930년대 말 대화정교회 성가대를 지휘하며 통영여고, 통영고, 마산고의 교가를 작사하기도 했다. 현재 통영 기독교계는 이곳에 '통영시기독교100주년기념관' 건립을 추진 중이라고 한다.

네번째. 거창

✽ 거창 소개

 삼국시대 대가야연맹체의 일원이었던 거창은 거열居烈, 거타居陀로 불리우다가 통일신라 경덕왕 때(757년) 오늘의 이름을 갖게 되었다. 거창군은 경남의 서쪽 맨 끝에 자리 잡고 있어 전라북도, 경상북도와 맞닿아 있다. 그러면서 한편으로는 대개 일천 미터가 넘는 소백산맥의 봉우리들로 둘러싸여있어 커다란 분지를 이룬다. 거창군을 흘러가는 내 중에 가장 굵은 것이 덕유산에서 발원한 위천천이다. 위천천은 거창읍을 지나 아월천과 합쳐져 황강이 된다. 거창군은 누에치기와 사과 농사로 잘 알려져 있다. 한 때는 거창군 농가의 60%쯤이 누에치기를 겸하고 있었고, 1930년대 일본 사람에 의해 시작된 사과 재배는 이곳 토질과 잘 맞아 지금은 거창읍을 비롯하여 11개 면 모두에 사과밭이 흩어져 있다. 거창사과축제는 지난 1995년부터 시작되었다.
 거창군 위천면 대정리에는 백제의 사신들이 반드시 거쳐 갔던 곳으로 전해지는 너른 반석이 있다. 원래 그 이름은 수심에 차서 송별하는 곳이라는 뜻을 지닌 수송대愁送臺였으나, 퇴계 이황이 수송을 수승搜勝으로 바꾸었다고 한다. 수승대는 위천천 줄기가 흐르는 주변의 경관이 빼어나 사람들이 많이 찾고 있다. 일찍이 퇴계는 이 고장에 반하여 "농사짓는 즐거움, 누에치는 즐거움, 고기 잡는 즐거움, 땔나무하는 즐거움"을 사락四樂이라 하여 시로 읊어 전한다. 그 외에도 거창 주변에는 사적 제238호로 지정되어 있는 남하면 둔마리의 고려시대 고분벽화와 문화재로서의 가치가 빼어난 불상 셋이 전한다. 즉 거창읍 양평동에 있는 석조여래입상(보물 377호)과 거창읍 상동의 석조관음입상(보물 378호) 그리고 위천면 상천리에 있는 기섭암지마애삼존불상(보물 530호) 등이다. 마지막으로 거창군 신원면은 1951년 2월 거창양민학살사건이 발생했던 곳이다.

✽ 거창 기독교 전래

 거창군 기독교의 역사는 1904년 가을 성립된 개명리교회를 시작으로 마상동교회(1906), 대야리 가천교회(1907)로 이어진다. 이 교회들은 모두 당시 부산 주재 북장로교 선교사 스미스Walter E. Smith, 심익순의 전도로 설립되었다. 그리고 그 뒤를 이어 1909년 와룡리교회와 거창읍교회가 세워졌다. 거창읍교회는 오형선, 조재룡, 주남선(주남고) 등에 의해 시작되었는데, 얼마 뒤 진주 주재 호주선교사 맥래Frederick J. L. Macrae, 맹호은의 지도를 받게 되었다. 그 후 오형선은 1918년 거창읍교회 장로가 되었고, 주남선은 평양신학교를 졸업하고 1931년부터 거창읍교회 목사로 시무하게 된다.

거창지방에 스테이션이 설치된 때는 1913년이었다. 호주선교부는 1912년 5월 진주의 맥래를 거창으로 보내 스테이션 개설 업무를 맡겼다. 그 후 1913년 켈리James T. Kelly, 길아각 선교사 부부가 합류하였고, 이어서 1914년 9월에는 미혼 여선교사 스키너Miss Amy G. M. Skinner가 부임하였다. 그녀는 원래 이곳에 보통학교 설립을 계획했으나 일제가 사립학교에서의 종교교육을 금지하자 강습소 형태의 명덕학교를 1915년 거창 죽전리에 세웠다. 이 학교는 비록 비공인교육기관이었지만 교육과정을 비롯한 학사운영은 다른 보통학교와 거의 같았고, 오히려 성경을 자유롭게 가르칠 수 있었다. 스키너 선교사의 후임으로 1916년 거창에 온 미혼 여선교사 스코트Miss Stella M. Scott, 서오성는 그 후 1939년까지 23년간 명덕학교와 유치원, 보육원 등 스테이션의 교육활동을 주도하였다. 그래서 그녀의 별명은 '거창 감독The Bishop of Kuchang'이었다.

1916년 거창 스테이션 관내에는 모두 757명의 교인과 281명의 세례교인이 있었다. 이 수치는 호주선교부가 설치·운영했던 다른 스테이션에 비해 매우 적은 것이다. 하지만 1930년대 거창 일대의 교회들은 놀랍게 성장했다. 1926년 853명이었던 총교인 수는 1937년 3,309명으로 늘었다. 이것은 심지어 같은 시기 통영의 교인 증가(1,697→2,917)를 넘어서는 것이었다. 거창 교회들의 성장은 선교사들의 사역과 아울러 거창 출신으로 영국성서공회 권서勸書, 거창읍교회 장로, 커닝햄 Frank W. Cunningham, 권임함 선교사의 조사助事를 역임했던 거창읍교회 목사 주남선의 지도력에 힘입은 바 크다. 그는 목회자였을 뿐만이 아니라 거창의 3·1운동을 주도하고 일제말기 신사참배 반대로 옥고를 치렀던 항일운동가였다.

거창 스테이션에서 활동했던 대표적인 선교사로는 맥래와 켈리, 스코트 외에 에버리Miss Elizabeth M. Ebery, 이리사백, 1914~1918, 토마스Frederick J. Thomas, 도별익, 1916~1922, 딕슨Miss Ethel V. Dixon, 덕순이, 1922~1925, 1933~1941, 맥카그Miss Jane E. McCague, 맥계익, 1926~1930, 던 Miss Elizabeth W. Dunn, 전은혜, 1929~1940 등이 있다.

❋ 거창 기독교 유적지

거창교회와 거창 스테이션터

🚗 **거창교회**: 경남 거창군 거창읍 중앙리 216번지 / **거창 스테이션 터**: 경남 거창군 거창읍 중앙리 387번지

거창 역시 진주나 마산과 마찬가지로 눈에 들어오는 기독교 유적을 만날 수

없어 아쉽다. 다만 거창읍교회의 역사를 잇는 거창교회는 지난 2006년 붉은 색깔의 기존 예배당 옆에 지상 5층의 '주남선기념관'을 헌당하고 그 지하실에 당회록, 성경책, 강대상, 종 등을 전시하고 있다. 6·25전쟁 때 목회현장을 초연히 지키다가 공산군에게 심한 구타를 당한 후유증으로 1951년 3월 63세의 나이로 소천한 그의 유해는 지금 샛별중학교 위 공동묘지에 묻혔다가 1995년 대전 국립묘지에 안장되었다. 교회 입구에는 '거창교회 약사'와 '목사 주남선 약력'을 적은 돌비석이 서있다.

그리고 거창교회 뒤 시장을 지나 10분쯤 떨어진 거리의 죽전언덕 지금 샛별초등학교(거창읍 중앙리 387번지) 일대가 바로 거창 스테이션이 있던 곳이다. 1950년대 거창고등학교는 호주 선교사들이 쓰던 2층 주택 두 채에서 시작되었는데, 그 집들은 현재 거창고와 같은 재단인 샛별초등학교 건물의 양쪽 옆에 각각 위치해 있었다고 한다. 신사참배 문제로 1938년 명덕학교를 선교사들로부터 인수하여 경영했던 거창읍교회는 전쟁 이후 선교사 주택을 활용하여 새롭게 인문계 고등학교를 세웠고, 다시 1956년 전영창 선생이 교장으로 오면서 자율학교인 오늘의 거창고등학교로 발전하게 되었다. 그리고 그 선교사 사택과 인접해 있었던 명덕학교 교사 역시 지금은 자취를 감추었고, 그 자리에는 송화아파트(거창고 정문 앞)가 들어서있다.

CHAPTER 8

전북지역

전주 → 군산 → 익산과 김제

✼ 전북 기독교의 시작

    1892년 11월 제물포를 거쳐 서울에 온 미남장로회 선교사들은 이듬해인 1893년 1월 기왕의 미북장로회 선교사들과 함께 장로교선교부공의회The Council of Missions Holding the Presbyterian Form of Government를 조직하였다. 또 이 회의에서 남장로회선교부는 자신들의 선교구역으로 전라도를 담당하기로 하였다. 미국 남부 출신인 남장로회 선교사들에게 있어서 한국의 남서부 지역이 그들의 선교지가 된 것은 매우 자연스럽고 친근한 일이었다. 당시 전라도의 인구는 145만이었다.
    1893년 6월 남장로회 선교사 레이놀즈William D. Reynolds, 이눌서의 어학선생인 정해원은 전주 완산 칠봉 아래 은송리에 한 채의 집을 마련했다. 그리고 정해원은 거리에 나가 전도하기 시작했다. 그 해 9월에는 테이트Lewis B. Tate, 최의덕와 전킨William M. Junkin, 전위렴이 2주일간 전주에 머물며 향후 전주 선교를 구상하기도 하였다. 1894년 2월 남장로회선교부는 테이트 선교사 남매를 전주에 파견하기로 결정하였다. 그들은 한 달 뒤인 그 해 3월 전주에 부임하였지만 동학농민봉기로 인해 철수할 수밖에 없었다.
    레이놀즈와 테이트가 다시 전주에 온 것은 동학이 끝난 1895년 2월이었다. 그들은 그 전에 있던

전북지역

전주예수병원

집보다 높은 곳에 있는 초가 두 채를 매입하고 상경하였다. 그리고 그 해 11월 테이트 선교사 남매가 다시 전주로 와서 본격적인 선교 활동을 전개하였다. 곧 전주교회(현 전주서문교회)가 문을 열었다. 1896년 11월에는 새로이 해리슨William B. Harrison, 하위렴 선교사가 부임하여 의료사역에 나섰고, 1897년 6월에는 레이놀즈가 합류하여 전주스테이션의 진용이 갖추어졌다.

그런데 레이놀즈가 전주에 부임한지 얼마 되지 않아 전주 관아와 남장로회 선교사들 사이에 선교부지를 둘러싼 분쟁이 시작되었다. 당시 전주스테이션은 은송리 옆 완산 언덕에 두 처의 건물을 신축하고 있었다. 그런데 당시 전라감사 이완용은 완산이 전주의 주산主山일 뿐만 아니라 조선왕조의 발상지라는 이유를 들어 공사 중지 명령을 내렸다. 이곳은 선교부가 1893년부터 스테이션 건설을 위해 계속해서 토지를 사들였던 지역이었다. 결국 레이놀즈는 주한미국공사관을 통해 정부와 협상을 벌였고, 일단 선교사들이 구입한 땅은 돌려주는 대신, 전주스테이션의 위치를 완산에서 화산華山으로 옮기는 것으로 마무리되었다. 또 조선 정부는 보상금을 지급하기로 했다. 이 때 전주스테이션 이전과 함께 은송리의 교회도 전주성 서문 옆으로 자리를 옮겼다. 지금의 전주서문교회 터와 화산 언덕 일대의 전주스테이션 구내는 이렇게 조성된 것이다.

화산 언덕의 새로운 스테이션 건설 공사는 1900년부터 시작되었다. 이곳은 인조 때(1624년) 세운 화산서원華山書院이 있었고, 숙종 때(1700년)에는 전라감사 김시걸이 희현당希賢堂을 세우고 양반 자제들을 가르쳤던 곳이다. 그러나 대원군 때(1869년) 화산서원과 희현당이 폐쇄되면서 양반들의 출입이 뜸해졌고 바로 그 무렵 선교사들이 새로운 문화를 갖고 이곳에 나타났던 것이다. 전주스테이션에는 1901년 해리슨에 의해 첫 주택이 지어진 이래 테이트와 잉골드Mattie B. Ingold, 1902년, 매커첸Luther O. McCutchen, 마로덕, 1905년의 집이 잇달아 건축되었다. 또 남학교(신흥, 1901년)와 여학교(기전, 1902년) 그리고 병원(예수병원, 1902년)이 들어섰다. 신흥학교는 1909년의 양옥 건물에 이어 1928년에는 지상 2층의 본관 건물인 리챠드슨관Richardson Hall을 지었고, 예수병원은 1912년 2층 벽돌 건물(맥코완기념병원)을 완성했다. 14만 여평의 넓은 선교 구내 안에 병원과 학교 시설까지 갖춘 전주스테이션 조성 사업은 대체로 1920년 무렵 완료되었다.

남장로회선교부의 군산 선교는 전주와 비슷한 시기에 이루어졌다. 남장로회 군산스테이션은 1896년 전킨William M. Junkin, 전위렴과 드루Adamer D. Drew, 유대모 그리고 데이비스Linnie F. Davis 선교사에 의해 시작되었다. 당시 군산은 인구 500여 명의 작은 어촌이었다. 그런데 벌써 그 1년 후인 1897년 군산교회의 주일예배 참석자는 40여 명에 달하였다. 금강과 만경강을 오르내리며 진료한 드루의 의료선교 때문이었다. 그 후 1899년 5월 군산의 개항으로 그 일대에 일본인들의 거류지가 형성되면서 선교사들은 기존 시가지에서 동쪽의 구암으로 스테이션을 옮겼다. 그 해 말에는 선교사 불William F. Bull, 부위렴이 가세하였다. 군산스테이션의 활동 결과 전북의 서부와 북부 또 충남 서남부 지역에는 구암교회를 필두로 여러 개의 교회들이 세워졌다. 1903년 현재 군산스테이션 구역 안에는 모두 8개의 교회(구암, 만자산, 남차문, 송지동, 성말, 선돌, 서천, 한산)가 존재하고 있었다.

첫번째. 전주시

✻ 전주 소개

삼한시대 마한 땅이었던 이곳은 삼국시대에 백제의 영역이 되어 완산이라 불렀다. 신라가 삼국을 통일하면서 신문왕 5년(685) 완산주가 되었다가 경덕왕 15년(757)에 지금의 이름인 전주로 바뀌었다. 견훤이 후백제를 세웠을 때에는 그 도읍지가 되기도 했던 전주는 그 뒤 조선 시대에 호남 일대를 다스리는 전라감영의 소재지였다. 조선시대 전주는 한양 다음으로 대접을 받았던 도시였다. 영조 때(1767년) 전주에 큰 불이 나서 천 여 채의 민가가 소실된 적이 있었는데, 당시 전라감사는 사도세자의 처남인 홍낙인이었다. 그는 당시 전주를 복구하면서 이곳을 풍패지향豊沛之鄕이라 하였다. 주지하듯이 '풍패'는 중국 한나라를 세운 유방의 고향으로서 그러니까 홍낙인은 이 곳 출신인 태조 이성계를 한고조 유방에 빗대 전주를 성역화했던 것이다. 그래서 귀빈들이 묵었던 전주 객사는 풍패지관豊沛之館, 남문은 풍남문南門, 서문은 패서문沛西門이라 불렀던 것이다. 패서문은 사라졌지만 서문이란 이름은 전주서문교회를 통해 오늘도 계승되고 있다.

전주에는 전주천을 사이에 두고 기린봉과 마주 보는 산봉우리가 일곱 개 있으니 그것이 곧 전주를 남쪽에서 병풍처럼 두른 완산 칠봉이다. 그리고 완산 칠봉 너머 남쪽에 솟은 산이 높이 794 m인 모악산이다. 이 모악산의 줄기를 이어 받은 다가산은 숲이 우거지고 경치가 좋아 거기에 공원이 만들어져 있다. 전주천은 전주 너른 들판을 지나 고산천과 만나게 되고, 다시 만경강이라는 이름을 얻어 서해로 나아간다.

전주는 전주 이씨의 본관인 만큼 조선 왕조와 관련된 유적이 많이 남아 있다. 즉 전주 이씨의 시조인 이한의 무덤 조경단과 이성계의 4대조인 목조가 살았다는 오목대, 그리고 이성계의 초상화를 모시기 위하여 1410년에 세워진 경기전 등이 있다. 그밖에 중앙동에 있는 풍패지관은 한양에서 내려오는 관리들이 묵었던 객사였다.

✱ 전주 기독교 전래

1892년 11월 내한 이후 1년 이상 한국에서의 적응 훈련과 언어 습득을 마친 남장로회 선교사들은 1894년 2월 자신들의 두 번째 연례회의Annual Meeting of the Mission of Southern Church에서 전주에 스테이션Station: 지역선교거점을 설치하여 테이트Lewis B. Tate를 파송하기로 하는 한편 레이놀즈William D. Reynolds와 신임 선교사 드루A. Damer Drew, 유대모로 하여금 전라도를 순회하도록 결정하였다. 남장로회의 전주스테이션 개설 작업은 동학東學으로 인해 1년 가량 지연되다가 1895년부터 본격화되었다. 그 해 성탄절이 낀 주간에 테이트와 그 여동생 매티Mattie S. Tate, 최마태는 전주로 이사했다. 일요일이면 테이트의 방에는 소년들이, 매티의 방에는 부인들이 몰려들었고, 테이트는 문밖에 서서 그들에게 복음을 전했다. 전주교회(현 전주서문교회)는 테이트에 의해 이렇게 시작되었다. 이어서 1896년 해리슨W.illiam B. Harrison, 하위렴이 부임하였고, 1897년에는 레이놀즈William D. Reynolds, 이눌서가 서울에서 내려왔다.

전주교회 담임목사가 된 레이놀즈는 부임 즉시 유창한 한국어를 구사하며 전주의 장터와 거리에서 전도했다. 물론 주일에는 설교를 담당하였다. 7월 17일에는 레이놀즈의 집례 하에 전주교회의 첫 세례식이 있었다. 이 때 테이트의 사환이었던 김내윤, 함성칠의 부인 임씨, 김창국의 어머니 진주 강씨, 유성안의 부인 김씨(김성희), 김창국 등 5명이 세례를 받았다. 또 8월 1일에는 다시 레이놀즈의 집례로 전주교회의 첫 번째 성찬식이 거행되었다. 9월 5일 주일에는 상당히 많은 사람들이 교회를 찾아왔다. 그래서 예배실을 개수하여 9월 19일부터는 더욱 확장된 공간에서 예배드리게 되었다.

1899년 상반기 선교부는 전주교회에서 사경반Bible Class을 개최하여 교인들에게 깊이 있는 훈련의 기회를 제공했다. 강사로는 레이놀즈와 전킨William M. Junkin, 전위렴이 나섰다. 그들은 성경과 성서신학, 그리스도의 생애, 성서지리 등을 가르쳤다. 사경반은 주일 오후에 나가 5분간 전도하는 시간이 있었고, 마지막 날에는 필답 및 구술고사를 치렀다. 전주교회의 본격적인 성장은 1900년부터 시작되었다. 그 해 봄 레이놀즈는 31명의 세례지원자를 문답하여 그 중 8명에게 세례를 주고,

13명은 학습자로 분류하였다. 나머지는 기독교에 대해 더 많은 관심을 갖도록 독려했다. 1900년 6월 전주교회는 평균 50명이 출석하는, 어느 정도 규모를 갖춘 교회로 변모해 있었다.

✱ 전주 기독교 유적지

전주 예수병원

전북 전주시 완산구 중화산동 1가 149-1

전주스테이션의 모습은 일제시대의 수난기와 해방 후 개발시대를 지나면서 많이 달라졌다. 일제가 신사참배를 강요하자 남장로회 선교사들은 이를 거부하고 1937년 9월 신흥학교와 기전여학교 문을 닫았으며, 1940년 10월에는 예수병원도 문을 닫고 전주를 떠났다. 일제가 병원에까지 '가미다나神柵'의 설치를 강요한데 따른 것이다. 그 후 일제는 다가공원에 있던 전주신사全州神社를 이곳으로 옮겼고, 신흥과 기전의 건물을 징발하여 다른 용도로 사용하였다. 한국전쟁 중에도 건물과 시설이 많이 파괴되었다. 전주스테이션은 1954년이 되어서야 복구될 수 있었다.

그리고 다시 선교사들이 철수하고 난 이후 지금 그 자리에는 5개의 유적 만이 남아 있다. 현재 엠마오사랑병원 건물로 사용 중인 '구 예수병원'은 1912년에 지은 맥코완기념병원이 1935년 화재로 소실되자 그 건물의 보험료를 받아 재건축한 것이다. 1936년 지상 2층의 붉은 벽돌 40병상으로 새롭게 문을 연 '구 예수병원'은 1950년대 몇 차례 증축되었다. 그리고 그 건너편 1949년 지어진 구 예수병원 별관 옆의 산기슭으로 선교사 거주지로는 유일하게 '매튜기념관'이 남아 있다. 이 건물은 예수병원 간호사 매튜Esther B. Matthews, 마애스도가 살던 단층 벽돌집으로 최근 개축되었다. 1915년 한국에 온 독신선교사 매튜는 1923년부터 1930년까지 전주에서 살았다.

'전주 선교사 묘역'은 예수병원(전북 전주시 완산구 서원로 68) 맞은편 예수병원부설 기독의학연구원과 의학박물관(의료선교자료 전시) 건물 뒷산에 위치하고 있다. '구 예수병원'을 내려와 신일아파트를 끼고 왼쪽으로 돌면 '선교사 묘역'이라는 안내판이 있어 쉽게 찾을 수 있다. 지금 이곳에는 모두 17기의 무덤이 안장되어 있다. 먼저 묘역 입구에는 군산에서 옮겨온 선교사들의 묘비 6개가 놓여 있다. 1892년 남장로회 첫 선교사로 내한했던 린니 데이비스Linnie D. Harrison, 후에 해리슨 선교사와 결혼는 전주에서 환자들을 돌보다가 전염되어 1903년 6월 19일 순직하였다. 그 옆의 전킨William M. Junkin, 전위렴 역시 남장로회의 처음 선교사로 내한하여 군산에서 사역하다 건강 악화로 1904년 전주로 임지를 옮겼지만 자신의 몸을 돌보지 않고 지방 순회에 몰두하다가 결국 1908년 1월 운명하였다. 전킨 묘비 앞에 있는 조그만 돌 세 개는 어려서 군산에서 죽은 전킨의 세 아들 시드니Sidney, 프랜시스Francis, 조지George의 묘비석이다. 그 오른쪽의 랭킨 David C. Rankin은 미국 남장로회 선교본부의 협동 총무로 선교 현장을 둘러보기 위해 한국에 왔다가 1902년 12월 28일 평양에서 사망하였다.

다시 그 오른쪽과 아래에는 주로 전주에서 사망한 선교사와 그 자녀들의 무덤이 조성되어 있다. 윗줄 맨 왼쪽은 예수병원을 설립한 매티 잉골드Mattie Ingold

전주 선교사 묘역

Tate의 갓난 딸의 무덤이다. 잉골드는 테이트와 결혼한지 5년 만에 딸을 낳았으나 곧 잃어버리고 말았다. 다시 그 옆은 해방 후 예수병원 원장을 지낸 크레인Paul S. Crane, 구바울의 세 살 난 아들 윌리엄William L. Crane의 것이고, 그 오른쪽에는 이름을 알 수 없는 어린이의 묘가 있다. 그 아래 줄에는 순천과 전주에서 의료선교사로 봉직했던 티몬스Henry L. Timmons, 김로라와 조선예수교서회에서 전문번역가로 활동했던 클라크William M. Clark, 강운림, 그리고 전주 신흥학교 교장과 대전 한남대 학장을 역임한 린튼William A. Linton, 인돈 등 세 선교사 자녀들의 무덤이 나란히 배열되어 있다. 맨 아래줄의 큰 묘비 두 개는 핏츠Laura M. Pitts와 랭킨Nellie B. Rankin의 것이다. 핏츠는 예수병원 간호사로 온 지 6개월 만인 1911년 2월 소천하였고, 1907년 내한한 랭킨은 기전여학교 교장으로 사역하다가 핏츠와 같은 해인 1911년 8월 순직하였다. 당시 두 선교사는 서른두 살 동갑이었다. 그 옆 해진의 무덤을 보고 나오면 묘역 왼쪽에 다시 두 개의 무덤이 있다. 바로 1955년 내한해서 예수병원 부원장으로 사역하다 1967년 운명한 켈러Frank G. Keller와 예수병원 외과 과장이었던 박영훈(1917~1972) 장로의 무덤이다.

전주 신흥고등학교

🚗 전북 전주시 완산구 중화산동 188번지

예수병원 옆의 신흥고등학교에 들어서면 먼저 1927년 건립된 '리차드슨관'의 현관 유적이 눈에 띈다. '리차드슨관'은 원래 신흥학교의 본관으로 사용되다가 1982년 화재로 전소되어 지금 그 건물 일부만 남아 있는 것이다. 또 그 밑에 있는 '希賢堂史蹟碑'(희현당사적비, 1707년)와 '希賢堂重修史蹟碑'(희현당중수사적비, 1748년)는 이곳이 조선시대 희현당 터임을 알려주고 있다. 오랫동안 땅속에 묻혀 있었던 것을 1905년 신흥학교가 들어서면서 발굴, 다시 세웠다고 한다.

그리고 신흥고등학교가 현재 강당으로 사용하고 있는 '스미스기념관'(등록문화재 172호)은 지난 1933년 미국의 리차드슨 부인Mrs. L. Richardson이 자신의 오빠 스미스E. Smith를 위해 기부한 돈으로 지은 벽돌 2층 건물이다.

전주 신흥고등학교 스미스기념관

전주서문교회

 전북 전주시 완산구 다가동 3가 123번지

신흥고등학교에서 내려와 다리 하나를 건너면 바로 우측에 전주서문교회가 보인다. 서문교회가 지금의 위치에 자리하게 된 것은 1905년이었다. 교회가 성장하자 선교사들은 전주 서문밖 대지 780평을 매입한 후 은송리에 있던 테이트 선교사의 사택을 옮겨 예배당으로 사용하였다. 조선 기와 지붕을 올린 붉은 벽돌의 57평 건물이었다. 1911년 증축되었던 이 교회당은 1935년 연건평 230평의 2층 고딕식 예배당을 지을 때 없어졌다. 그리고 그 건물 역시 1983년 지금의 방주형 예배당을 지으면서 사라졌다. 1993년에는 그 옆에 연건평 705평의 지하 1층, 지상 5층의 100주년기념관이 들어섰다.

전북지역　213

전킨 선교사 기념 종각

그런데 100주년기념관 1층 역사자료실에는 전주 서문교회의 다양한 역사 자료들을 만날 수 있다. 즉 이곳에는 서문교회 역대 교역자와 7인의 남장로회 처음 선교사, 서문교회 예배당 변천사, 『방애인소전』, 서문교회의 자랑스런 평신도 이거두리 등을 소개한 사진이 전시되어 있다. 그리고 서문교회는 1908년 제직회록, 1909년 당회록, 1910년 세례문답책과 교적부, 1930년대 예배일지와 여전도회록 등의 자료를 보관하고 있기도 하다.

그리고 서문교회 마당에는 1908년 소천한 전킨 목사 기념종(직경 90 cm)을 달기 위해 만들었던 6.8 m 짜리 한옥 종각이 잘 보존되어 있다. 그 종은 일제 말에 공출되었다고 한다. 그 옆에 있는 4각 화강암의 창립50주년기념비는 1943년 4월 건립된 것으로 그 글씨는 당대 전주 명필 최규상이 썼다고 한다. 교회 정문 앞에는 '전주서문교회창립100주년'을 기념하는 비석이 따로 서있다.

❋ 전주 일반 유적지

전주 한옥마을

🚗 전북 전주시 완산구 전동 83-4

전주 한옥마을은 가장 한국적인 문화를 찾아볼 수 있는 전주의 랜드마크다. 전주 한옥마을은 700여 채의 한옥이 군락을 이루고 있는 전주 풍남동 일대에 자리한 국내 최대 규모의 전통 한옥촌으로, 전국 유일의 도시 한옥군이다. 경기전, 오목대, 향교 등 중요 문화재와 문화시설이 산재한 전주 한옥마을은 전주만의 독특한 문화공간으로 전통문화를 체험하며, 옛 선비들의 멋과 풍류를 느낄 수 있는 곳이다.

풍남동 일원의 도시한옥은 1910년대부터 산업화 사회로의 진행과정에서 발생된 우리나라 주거문화 발달 과정의 중요한 자료이다. 특히 경기전, 향교, 학인당 등 19세기 이전 조선시대의 역사성과 건축양식을 바탕으로 근대 일제에 의한 가옥구조의 변질, 해방 이후 근대 한옥으로서의 변천 등을 엿볼 수 있는 종합적인 한옥주거공간으로 매우 가치가 높다.

한옥마을 주변에 풍남문과 태조 이성계의 어진御眞이 모셔진 경기전, 전주향교 등 조선시대 문화유산이 산재해 있어 우리 전통문화의 숨결을 한껏 만끽할 수 있다. 특히 전주 한옥마을을 투어코스가 마련되어 있어 자세한 설명과 함께 한옥체험을 해볼 수 있는 다채로운 곳이다.

풍남문

 전북 전주시 완산구 전동 83-4

보물 제308호 풍남문豊南門은 원래 전주부성의 4대문 가운데 전주를 상징하는 남문으로 고려 공양왕 원년인 1389년에 전라관찰사 최유경이 전주부성과 함께 창건했다. 건축 양태는 조선후기의 문루 형식으로 비교적 잘 보존되어 있다. 원래 도성이나 읍성, 산성 등은 성문이 있기 마련이고 그 위에 문루를 세우는 것이 중요한 형식이자 관례로 되어 있다. 그러나 조선 영조 43년(1767)에 당시 성내를 휩쓴 정해년 대화재로 불타버려 영조 44년(1768) 전라관찰사 홍낙인이 중건했지만 종전처럼 3층루가 아닌 현 모습으로 수축하여 이때부터 풍남문이라 불렀다.

1905년 조선통감부의 폐성령廢城令에 의해 전주부성 4대문 중 풍남문만 제외한 3대문이 동시에 철거되는 수난을 겪었다. 1978년 문루 보수과정에서 옹성의 기단이 풍남문 홍예문으로부터 12 m 지점에서 발굴됨에 따라 이 기단대로 연장 97.5 m의 여담쌓기와 치석 6,856개로서 옹성 1,933 m²를 축조하여 복원하였다.

문루의 서편에는 종각이 있고 좌편에는 포루가 있었다. 문루는 2층의 팔각지붕인데 정면, 측면이 모두 3칸이고 윗층의 정면은 3칸이나 측면은 1칸이다. 1980년 종각과 포루, 풍남문 바깥쪽 출성인 옹성을 복원하여 현재의 모습을 찾았다. 전주 풍남문은 전주사람들에게는 전주를 대표하는 일종의 상징물이다. 풍남문에는 풍남문이라는 고유의 이름 외에 "명견루"라는 별호가 있다.

전동성당

🚗 전북 전주시 완산구 전동 1가 200-1

전동성당

전주 한옥마을 입구에 위치한 소박하고 아담한 전동성당은 사적 제288호이다. 전동성당은 한국 천주교회 최초의 순교자인 윤지충과 권상연이 1791년 신해박해 때에 처형당한 풍남문이 있던 바로 그 자리에 건립되었다. 1907년부터 1914년에 걸쳐 세워진 전동성당은 처형지인 풍남문 성벽을 헐어 낸 돌로 성당 주춧돌을 세웠다고 한다. 호남 최초의 로마네스크 양식의 서양식 건물로, 순교지를 알리는 머릿돌과 순교자 권상연과 윤지충, 유중철·이순이 동정 부부를 채색화한 스테인드글라스가 눈길을 끈다. 곡선미를 최대로 살린 로마네스크 및 비잔틴 양식의 아름다움과 웅장함이 동양에서 제일가는 성당건물 중의 하나이다.

두번째. 군산

✳ 군산 소개

군산은 전북의 서북단 금강 하류에 위치한 항구도시이다. 군산에 조창이 생긴 연대는 중종 7년(1512)으로 알려져 있다. 원래 전라도 세곡을 용안현 득성창에서 서울의 경창까지 해상으로 수송하다가 중종 7년 군산포로 옮긴 것이다. 그 후 군산창은 옥구, 만경, 함열, 김제, 금구, 전주, 남원 등 부근 7개 고을의 세곡稅穀을 모아 경창으로 보냈기 때문에 칠읍경창七邑京倉이라 했다. 이는 개항 전부터 군산이 배후지의 미곡 집산지로서 국가적 유통의 중심지였음을 보여준다.

뿐만 아니라 개항 이전 군산 부근은 상업지로서 장시가 크게 발달했다. 금강과 금강 지류인 무명천(현 경포천)을 통해 만경, 강경, 서천 방향으로 해상운송이 용이했기 때문에 경포시장과 경장시장이 있었다. 특히 전주가도에 자리 잡은 경장시장(현 군산고등학교 부근 팔마산 자락)이 16세기 무렵 옥구군 경장리(현 경장동)에 개설되어 옥구군은 물론 군산, 서천 방면 이외에도 임디, 전주, 함열, 강경, 한산까지 상거래가 폭넓게 이루어졌다.

군산은 진남포와 목포가 개항된 다음해인 1899년 5월에 마산, 성진과 함께 개항되었다. 군산은 항구로서 내륙으로는 금강의 수로를 이용하여 작은 배로는 약 300리(120km)까지 통할 수 있는 장점이 있었다. 더구나 그 배후에는 전북, 충남에 펼쳐진 최대의 곡창지대가 펼쳐져 있었고, 인근 강경시장은 조선 3대 시장의 하나로 물자 판매액과 출시 상인의 성황을 보인 유명한 시장이었다. 즉 일제는 군산과 강경을 인천–경성, 진남포–평양처럼 밀접한 관계를 맺게 함으로써 미곡의 반출, 수입상품의 유통구조를 구축하려는 의도를 갖고 있었던 것이다.

개항 당시인 1899년 군산은 511명의 조선인이 거주했으며 일본인은 77명(13%)이었다. 그러나 그 후 일본인이 계속 늘어 1905년에는 1,620명(31.4%), 1914년에는 무려 4,742명(47.1%)으로 증가했다. 당시 일본인들은 토지를 직접 매수하거나 구입한 토지를 담보로 더 많은 면적의 트지를 확보했다. 또 미곡상, 고리대, 잡화상으로 군산 상권을 장악했다. 이는 일제강점기 군산이 미곡을 수출하고 또 일본으로부터는 가공품 등을 수입하는 상업도시였음을 나타내는 것이다.

✱ 군산 기독교 전래

1895년 3월 미국 남장로회 한국선교부는 군산에 스테이션을 개설하기로 하고 소속 선교사였던 전킨William A. Junkin, 전위렴과 드루A. Damer Drew, 유대모를 파견하였다. 두 선교사는 당시 1개월 간 군산에 머무르면서 50불로 그들의 집을 매입하고 전도활동을 폈다. 그들이 서울로 돌아갈 때 군산사람 김봉래와 송영도는 절차를 고려하지 않고 세례 줄 것을 요청하기도 했다.

그들이 군산에 다시 온 것은 그 1년 뒤인 1896년 봄이었다. 동학농민봉기로 인해 지체되었던 것이다. 전킨과 드루의 군산 전도는 처음부터 큰 성과가 있었다. 드루 선교사가 그의 집에 진료소를 열자 많은 한국인 환자들이 몰려들었고, 전킨 선교사는 진료를 기다리는 그들에게 복음을 전했다. 그 해 7월 20일에는 김봉래와 송영도가 세례를 받았고, 이듬해 군산교회 신자는 모두 40여 명에 이르렀다. 또 군산 인근에 만자산(대야면 지경리), 남차문(익산 남전리), 송지동(김제 공덕면), 통사동(개정면 통사리) 등 4개의 교회가 새로 생겨났다.

그런데 1899년 5월 군산의 개항으로 일본인들의 거류지가 형성되자 선교사들은 북정구 구릉에 있던 선교 거점을 현재의 구암동(당시 임피 궁말)으로 옮길 것을 결정하였다. 그곳은 기존 시가지에서 동쪽으로 약 3 km 떨어진 해안가 구릉에 위치하고 있었다.

그 후 남장로회 선교사들은 1899년부터 3만평 구암동산 대지 위에 선교 구내를 조성하였다. 일제강점기 군산스테이션 안에는 스테이션 직할 교회였던 구암교회를 중심으로 선교사 불William F. Bull, 부위렴의 집을 비롯하여 모두 6채의 선교사 주택과 안락소학교, 영명학교, 멜볼딘여학교, 예수병원 등이 포진해 있었다.

✱ 군산 기독교 유적지

구암교회

🚗 전북 군산시 구암동 358-6번지

해방 후 귀환한 남장로회 선교사들은 군산스테이션을 복구하려고 시도하였다. 하지만 군산의 선교 구내는 이미 많은 피난민과 무단 침입자들 때문에 아주 곤란한 상황에 직면하게 되었다. 그 때문에 군산 선교사 페이슬리James I. Paisley, 이아곡는 심장마비를 일으켜 1948년 가을 긴급 휴가를 받고 귀국해야만 했다. 결국 선교부는 군산스테이션을 폐쇄하고 선교사들을 철수시켰다. 그 후 이곳의 대부분은 한국전력이 매입하여 사원 아파트 등이 지어졌다. 군산스테이션의 옛 모습을 확인할 수 없는 것이 아쉽다.

또 구암교회 교인들이 뜻을 모아 1916년 새로 지었던 'ㄱ'자형 예배당 역시

군산 구암교회 옛 예배당

지금은 사라졌다. 하지만 그 43년 후에 건축된 석조예배당은 지난 2008년 '군산 3·1운동 기념관'으로 탈바꿈했다. 1919년 3월 5일 벌어진 군산 3·1운동의 발상지인 이곳을 기념하기 위해 군산시가 10억원의 예산을 들여 교회 건물을 기념관으로 꾸민 것이다. 군산의 3·1운동은 당시 구암교회 성도들과 영명학교, 멜볼딘학교 교사와 학생 그리고 예수병원 직원들이 주축이 된 의거였다. 기념관 안에는 기미년 당시 익산에서 만세운동을 주도하다 순국한 영명학교 교사 문용기 열사의 피묻은 의복을 비롯해, 군산만세운동을 이끈 박연세 열사에 대한 일제의 재판기록, 3·1운동 당시 사용된 태극기 목판, 독립군들의 소총과 배지 등 다양한 유물들이 전시되어 있다. 또 그 앞에는 '군산 3·1독립운동사적지' '호남선교100주년기념성역지'라고 새겨진 기념비와 '군산 3·1운동기념비'가 나란히 세워져 있다.

구암교회는 지난 2004년 옛 석조예배당 위쪽에 대지 468평 3층 규모의 '호남선교기념예배당'을 헌당하였다. 교회 건물 양쪽에는 십자가탑과 선교탑을 8층 높이로 세워 웅장함을 더했는데, 그 옆의 작은 동산을 군산구암 3·1동산으로 꾸며 '호남선교100주년기념비'와 '군산 3·1독립운동기념비'를 세워 놓았다. 구암교회는 군산화력발전소가 문을 닫으면서 사원 사택이 폐쇄되었기 때문에, 그 중 일부를 다시 사들여 선교동산으로 꾸밀 예정이라고 한다.

세번째. 익산시

남전교회

전북 익산시 오산면 남전리 618-1번지

익산 남전교회는 1900년 봄 시작되었다. 그보다 먼저 남전리 사람들이 구암교회 혹은 김제 송지동교회를 다니다가 그 해 남전리 이윤국 영수의 집에서 모

익산 순국열사비

이게 되었던 것이다. 그들은 1901년 초가 5칸의 예배당을 마련했고, 1921년에는 'ㄱ'자 예배당을 증축했다. 1920년대 남전교회 교인은 대략 300명으로 추산된다. 또 남전교회는 도남학교(혹은 신성학교)를 운영하여 동네 아이들을 교육시켰다.

3·1운동이 일어나자 전라북도에서는 3월 5일 처음으로 군산 영명학교 학생들과 교인들이 만세를 불렀다. 이날 시위를 주도한 영명학교 교사 박연세가 바로 남전리 출신이었다. 그리고 1919년 4월 4일 익산 솜리장터에서 있었던 만세시위를 주도한 이들은 바로 남전교회 교인들과 도남학교의 학생들이었다. 이날 시위에서 도남학교 교사 문용기 등 4명의 교인이 희생되었다. 문용기 열사의 시신은 오산 상신리 공동묘지에 안장되었다가 1990년 대한민국 건국훈장 애국장이 추서되면서 대전 국립묘지로 이장되었다. 지금 솜리시장 만세시위현장(익산시 주현동 105-9번지)에는 1949년 이리시민들이 세운 '순국열사비'가 서있고, 익산역전에도 이 날의 시위를 기념하는 '3·1운동기념비'가 세워져 있다. 또 1946년 오산면 사람들은 문용기 생가와 가까운 오산면 면사무소 뜰 안에 '순국열사 문용기 박영문 장경춘 충혼비'를 세워 그들을 기렸다.

익산 두동교회

 전북 익산시 성당면 두동리 385-1번지

두동마을 입구에는 1940년 성당면 유지들이 세운 박재신기념비가 있다. 삼천 석지기 부자였던 박재신은 두동교회 설립이야기에 나오는 인물이다. 일제강점기 이곳 성당면은 군산스테이션 소속 선교사 해리슨William B. Harrison, 하위렴의 활동

익산 두동교회 'ㄱ'자 예배당

지역이었다. 두동 마을의 초기 교인들은 인근 부곡교회에 출석하였는데, 바로 박재신의 어머니(황한라)와 아내(한재순), 고모(박씨 부인) 등이었다. 그 중 박씨 부인은 월남 이상재 선생의 막내며느리였다. 처음엔 집안 남자들이 여자들의 교회 출입을 반대했지만 박재신은 아내 한재순이 임신하게 되자 자기집 사랑채를 예배처소로 내놓아 1923년 5월 18일 두동교회가 시작되었다. 또 교회 부설로 배영학교를 설립하기도 하였다. 박재신의 소작인들이 교회에 나오면서 1년 새 교인이 80명으로 증가하였다. 그런데 1929년 박재신의 어린 아들이 목욕물에 데어 죽은데다가 박재신이 그 교회 구연직 전도사와 불화하면서 교회를 떠나고 말았다.

그러자 남은 교인 20여 명이 1929년 채소밭 100여 평에 'ㄱ'자로

'ㄱ'자 예배당 여자석

된 24평 예배당을 건축하게 되는데, 바로 이 건물이 지금까지 남아 있는 것이다. 2002년 전라북도 문화재자료 179호로 지정된 두동교회 구 본당은 전형적인 'ㄱ'자 예배당으로 남자석과 여자석을 분리하여 남녀가 서로 쳐다볼 수 없게끔 설계되었다. 남녀유별의 전통과 서양 종교의 만남이 바로 이러한 형태의 건물을 낳은 것이다. 두동교회는 1960년대까지 이곳에서 예배드리다가, 1964년 다시 새로운 예배당을 지었고, 1991년에는 교육관까지 지었지만 구 예배당을 허물지 않고 보존하였다.

네번째. 김제시

금산교회

전북 김제시 금산면 금산리 290-1번지

금산리는 모악산 국립공원 금산사 입구에 있는 마을이다. 이 마을의 조덕삼은 비단장사로 큰 돈을 벌었던 사람인데, 바로 그 집안의 하인이 뒤에 장로교 총회장을 세 차례 역임한 이자익이었다. 1904년 남장로회 선교사 테이트Lewis B. Tate, 최의덕가 마을을 방문하여 전도하자 조덕삼과 이자익은 나란히 예수를 믿고 1905년 10월 11일 함께 세례를 받았다. 또 그들을 중심으로 금산교회가 설립되었다. 금산교회는 1908년에 'ㄱ'자형 예배당으로 잘 알려진 교회당을 건축하였다. 그리고 1909년 조덕삼의 9살 아래인 하인 이자익이 장로로 장립되었다. 그 후 이자익은 1915년 평양신학교를 졸업하고 금산교회 목사로 부임하여 이곳의 교인들을 지도하였을 뿐 아니라 해방 이후까지 장로교의 유력한 목회자로 활약하였다.

1908년 지은 금산교회의 'ㄱ'자 예배당은 100년이 지났지만 지금도 교육관으로 사용할 만큼 단단하게 남아있다. 27평 규모의 이 예배당은 전형적인 단층

금산교회 'ㄱ'자 예배당

고패집의 한옥 목조 건물로서 역시 두동교회처럼 남자석과 여자석이 분리되어 있다. 천장 남자석의 상량문은 한문으로, 여자석의 상량문은 한글로 써져 있어 이채롭다. 처음에는 초가지붕이었지만, 현재는 시멘트 기와로 올렸다. 전라북도는 지난 1997년 이 건물을 문화재자료 136호로 지정하여 보존하고 있다.

CHAPTER 9

광주·전남 지역

광주광역시 → 목포 → 순천 → 그 외의 전남 기독교 유적지

1. 광주지역

✻ 광주·전남 기독교의 시작

1893년의 장로교선교부연합공의회에서 전라도 선교를 책임지게 된 남장로교 선교부는 어느 정도의 준비 기간을 거쳐 1895년 6월 레이놀즈William D. Reynolds, 아눌서와 유진벨Eugene Bell, 배유지에게 목포스테이션 개설 업무를 맡겼다. 전주와 군산에 이어 이제 전남 선교에 나선 것이다. 그 때 이미 전주에는 테이트 남매Lewis B. Tate & Mattie S. Tate, 군산에는 전킨William Junkin, 전위렴과 드루A. Damer Drew, 유대모가 상주하기로 결정이 난 상태였다. 레이놀즈와 벨은 이듬해인 1896년 2월 목포에 내려와 약 2에이커(2,500평)에 이르는 땅을 매입했다. 그러나 당초 1896년 4월 예정이었던 목포의 자유무역항 개항이 갑자기 연기되었다. 아관파천으로 정국이 불안했기 때문이다.

그래서 한때 전남 선교의 중심지로 나주가 물망에 오른 적도 있었지만 1897년 뒤늦게 목포가 개항되자 남장로교 선교부는 그 해 10월 군산에서 열린 제6차 연례회의에서 전남 목포에 스테이션을 두기로 최종 결정했다. 이 자리에는 선교사들과 아울러 본국 선교본부의 총무 체스터S. H. Chester가 함께 참석하고 있었다. 선교부는 목포 스테이션 개설 작업에 필요한 자금 1,500불을 선교본부에 요청하는 동시에 선교사 벨Eugene Bell을 그 책임자로 단독 지명하였다. 벨은 약 1년간의 준비 작업을 거쳐 1898년 가을 남장로교 한국선교부의 세 번째 지역선교거점인 목포로 이주하였다.

광주·전남 지역

오웬기념각

그 후 선교사들이 잠정적으로 철수하는 1940년까지 목포스테이션은 전남 서부지역의 선교기지로서 복음전파의 핵심적인 역할을 수행하게 된다. 남녀 중등학교(영흥학교와 정명여학교)와 병원(프렌치기념병원) 그리고 스테이션 직할교회(목포양동교회)를 아우르고 있었던 14,000평 규모의 넓은 선교 구내에 상주했던 연인원 400여 명의 선교사들은 이 지역 거의 모든 기독교 현상의 제공자로 있으면서 지역교회의 형성과 발전에 기여하였다. 전형적인 미국 남부 장로교회의 신앙을 소유하고 있었던 소속 선교사들은, 안전한 선교 구내에서 미국식의 일상생활을 영위하는 한편 전도-교육-의료-여성 파트로 각기 역할을 나누어 조직적이고 전방위적인 협동 선교 활동을 펼쳐 나갔다. 또 그 선교사들과 조사助事, helper들의 발걸음은, 내륙은 물론 멀리 남해안 4개 군郡 230개 섬에 걸쳐 있었던 1천 여 개의 마을들에 다다랐다. 설치 이듬해 30여 명에 불과했던 목포스테이션 지경 내의 기독교 인구는 1936년 약 6,400명으로 늘어났을 뿐만 아니라 1개소에 불과했던 예배당은 모두 131개로 증가하였다. 당시 목포스테이션 관할 구역 내의 한국인 안수목사가 모두 4명에 불과했다는 사실을 고려할 때, 총 3,177명에 달했던 세례교인의 상당수는 선교사들이 직접 수세授洗했다고 보아야 할 것이다.

그리고 다시 미국 남장로교 한국선교부는 1904년 봄 열린 연례회의에서 광주에 스테이션을 하나 만들기로 결정하였다. 그리고 이미 목포스테이션 개설 경험을 갖고 있었던 벨에게 그 일을 맡겼다. 벨은 광주가 내려다 보이는 양림동 언덕에 기지를 확보하고 의료선교사 오웬Clement C. Owen, 오기원과 함께 1904년 12월 광주로 이사하였다. 본격적인 선교 구내 조성 사업은 1905년 벨과 오웬의 양옥을 짓는 것으로 시작되어 대개 1914년까지 계속되었다. 그리하여 그곳 10만여 평의 땅 위에는 프레스톤John F. Preston, 변요한, 윌슨Robert M. Wilson, 우일선, 코잇Robert T. Coit, 고라복의 집 등 주택 9채와 병원(광주기독병원), 학교(숭일과 수피아), 성경학원 건물이 들어섰다. 당시 광주스테이션은 지오의 명물이었다. 구경꾼들이 몰려왔고 그들은 모두 탄성을 질렀다. 양림동 언덕에서 발원한 근대화 바람은 이렇게 광주를 강타했다.

전남 동부 지역 기독교의 시작은 남장로교 순천스테이션과 관련되어 있다. 광주스테이션 소속 남장로교 선교사 오웬Clement F. Owen, 오기원의 선교 노력으로 처음 교회가 세워졌던 이곳은 그 후 프레스톤과 코잇의 순회 사역으로 강화되었다. 순천의 가능성에 주목한 남장로교 선교부는 결국 매곡동 언덕을 사들여 스테이션 조성에 나섰다. 이 때 미국 남부의 재력가 조지 왓츠George Watts가 기부한 거액의 헌금이 답지하여, 순천스테이션은 종합적인 계획에 의해 학교와 병원 그리고 선교사 사택을 일괄적으로 지을 수 있었다. 순천스테이션의 통계를 보면 1913년 전남 동부 지역의 기독교인 총수는 1,549명이었는데, 3년 후인 1916년에는 모두 2,507명으로 많이 늘었음을 볼 수 있다.

첫번째. 광주광역시

✻ 광주 소개

백제시대에는 무진주로, 통일신라시대에는 무주로 불렸던 광주가 지금의 이름을 갖게 된 것은 고려 태조 때인 940년부터였다. 그런데 조선시대까지 전남을 대표하는 도시는 광주가 아니라 나주였다. 나주가 수운이 편리하고 그 부근이 곡창 지역이기 때문이었다. 그에 더하여 나주는 고려 태조 왕건의 처향妻鄕이었고, 또 왕건이 나라를 세우는데 큰 도움을 준 지역이기도 했다. 그러나 조선 후기에 이르러서 광주는 나주 못지않은 고을로 이미 성장하고 있었다. 1789년 정조 때의 통계를 보면 광주의 인구는 5,525명으로 나주(5,638명)를 육박하였다. 결국 1896년 전국에 13도제가 실시되면서 나주에 있던 도청이 이곳 광주로 옮겨오게 되었다.

'광주는 무등산 아래에 있고, 무등산은 광주에 있다'고 한다. 높이 1,187 m의 무등산과 그 산줄기는 병풍처럼 광주를 감싸고 있다. 광주의 진산 무등산은 산꼭대기를 이루는 천왕봉, 지왕봉, 인왕봉 아래 세 절경으로 꼽히는 서석대와 입석대, 광석대가 자리하고 있다. 한때 무진악, 무악, 서석산이라고도 불린 무등산의 무등無等은 '높고 낮은 등급이 없다'의 의미 인데, 이는 불교 용어로 석가 모니가 『반야심경』에서 절대평등의 깨달음 '무등등'을 말한 구절에서 유래되었다고 한다.

또 무등산을 중심으로 형성된 사림문화는 호남 정신문화의 기반이 되었다. 조선 건국세력의 역성혁명이나 세조의 왕위 찬탈을 반대하고, 연산군의 학정과 연이은 사화士禍의 와중에서 전라도로 유배 온 절의파 인맥들은 호남의 선비정신의 줄기였다. 또 눌재 박상의 신비복위소愼妃復位疏, 하서 김인후와 고봉 기대승의 사상과 풍류는 호남 사림을 결집시키는 계기가 되었다. 그들은 무등산 자락에 형성된 소쇄원, 식영정, 면앙정, 명옥헌 등의 정자들을 근거지로 주옥같은 시문학과 예술작품들을 남겼다.

광주의 역사는 수많은 저항으로 꾸며져 있다. 무엇보다 지방 관리들의 수탈이 큰 이유였다. 거기에다가 서울과 거리가 멀어 지역민들의 불만이 신속하게 전달되지 않았다. 이른바 소통의 문제였다. 1894년 고부에서 일어난 동학농민봉기의 밀고 밀리는 전투에 가담한 광주 사람은 모두 4,000여 명에 달했다. 1929년의 광주학생운동은 3·1운동 이후에 일어난 가장 큰 민족운동이었는데, 잘 알려져 있듯이 기차통학을 하던 일본 학생이 한국 여학생에게 모욕을 준 것이 빌미가 되어 일어난 이 의거는, 한국 학생들이 일본 학생들과 충돌하면서 시가전의 양상을 띠고 확대되었다. 뿐만 아니라 곧 전국에 번져서 모두 194개 학교 54,000여 명의 학생들이 시위에 참여하게 되었던 것이다. 1980년의 광주항쟁은 한국현대사를 뒤흔들었던 중요한 역사적 사건이었다.

선교사들이 광주에 올 때 광주의 중요한 교통은 영산강의 뱃길이었다. 영산강 상류의 물길은 광주를 통과하고, 서해안과 남해안의 물산은 영산강을 타고 광주로 유입되었다. 영산강은 광주천의 물길이 담양에서 내려온 줄기와 만나서 서쪽으로 내려가다가 다시 나주 금천의 광탄에서 다시 한번 합류한다. 그리고 영산포에서 잠시 큰 강을 이룬 후 남도를 관통하여 서해에 이르는 남도의 젖줄이다. 왕건이 나주를 공략할 때도 영산강 뱃길은 중요한 길잡이의 역할을 했다. 또 서남해안 일대 경상남도와 전라도의 세곡을 모아 개성이나 한양으로 수송하는 기지가 영산강에 있었다. 20세기 초만 해도 양동천까지 화물을 가득 실은 배가 올라 왔고, 일제시대에는 일본 사람들이 목포에서 영산강을 따라 광주로 들어와 지금의 양림동 근처에 터를 잡고 살았다. 영산강 뱃길은 광주 발전의 견인차였다.

✽ 광주 기독교 전래

미국 남장로교 선교사들이 광주에 관심을 갖게 된 때는 대개 1903년 무렵이었다. 당시 목포 인근의 해남과 진도에는 2개의 신앙공동체가 있었던데 반하여 광주지역에는 모두 6곳에 공동체가 있었고 그 교회들은 또 빠르게 성장하고 있었다. 지원근 조사는 바로 선교부가 광주 지역의 교회들을 위하여 파견한 사역자였다. 그는 영광 하나말교회, 나주 바다등교회, 무안 복길교회, 광주 잉계교회와 도둠교회, 장성 배치교회를 돌보았다. 지원근은 도둠에 머물면서 주일에는 잉계교회에 가서 설교했다.

미국 남장로교 한국선교부는 1903년의 연례회의에서 광주스테이션 설치를 처음으로 언급하였다. 그 연례회의를 전후하여 남장로교 선교사들은 목포의 한계와 광주의 가능성에 눈을 뜬 것으로 보인다. 개항장 목포는 비록 선교사들의 안전을 보장해 주기는 했으나 절대 인구가 적은 해안가였고 상주인구 상당수가 일본인이었다. 식수의 부족도 목포의 결함 가운데 하나였다. 대신 내륙 광주는 인구가 많았고 모든 물산이 풍부하였다. 그런데다가 선교의 결과가 좋았다.

그 무렵 광주 지역에서 일어난 박해도 광주스테이션 설치에 영향을 주었다. 즉 그곳의 지방관이 기독교를 반대하면서 심하게 교인들을 박해하고 교인 몇 사람을 체포하는 일이 있었다. 선교사들은 이 사건을 한국인의 교회 밀집 지역과 스테이션이 너무나 멀리 떨어져 있기 때문에 일어났다고 생각했다. 만약 선교사들이 가까이 있었더라면 지방관이 함부로 기독교인들을 박해할 수 없었다는 것이다.

결국 1904년 2월 목포에서 개최되었던 선교사 모임에서 광주스테이션 개설 문제가 집중 논의되었고, 곧 광주에서의 토지 구입과 주택 건설을 위해 목포교회의 김윤수 집사가 광주로 이동하였다. 그 해 10월 프레스톤John F. Preston, 변요한이 광주를 방문한데 이어 12월 중순에는 벨Eugene Bell, 배유지과 오웬Clement C. Owen, 오기원 선교사가 그곳에 머물면서 지역교회들을 방문하였다. 그때쯤 광주의 임시 숙소가 완공되었고, 12월 19일 벨과 오웬 부부는 목포에서 짐을 꾸려 광주로 이사했다.

광주에 도착한 벨과 오웬은 임시 숙소에 이삿짐을 풀고 읍내와 주변 마을에 전도하기 시작했다. 이미 벨은 광주에서 스테이션 개설을 준비하던 1904년 6월부터 12월 사이에 틈틈이 전도한 바 있었다. 광주에 완전히 정착한 이후에도 거의 모든 시간을 전도에 투자하였다. 광주에서의 첫 예배는 1904년 눈 오는 날 성탄절에 벨의 임시 사택에서 진행되었다. 그 집은 10마일 떨어진 산에서 벌채한 목재와 진흙을 이겨 만든 기와와 벽돌을 이용해 건축한 것이다. 벨은 광주 사람들에게 성탄절 예배 사실을 알렸지만 과연 몇 사람이나 올지 알 수 없었다. 그런데 예배 시작 전 하얀 옷을 입은 한국인들이 줄지어 오솔길을 따라서 올라오고 있었다. 벨이 이사하면서 이용한 커다란 상자에 무엇이 들어있는 가를 구경하기 위해 몰려온 사람들이었다. 벨은 무게가 200파운드 나가는 상자 12개를 이용해 이삿짐을 운반했기 때문에 그것은 보는 이들로 하여금 호기심을 자아내기에 충분했다. 여자들과 남자들은 각각 서로 반대칭을 이루는 두 개의 방에 앉았다. 벨은 중앙에 서서 각각 그들을 보며 예배를 인도하였다. 사실 그들은 선교사를 구경하기 위해 왔던 것이다. 이 때 모인 숫자는 모두 40명이었다. 그런데 그 중 세례교인이 3명이었고, 그들은 모두 목포교회에서 세례받았다. 또 그 때 광주 부근에는 모두 8개의 공동체가 있었는데, 총 신자는 300명, 세례교인 28명에 학습교인 79명이었다.

광주교회의 폭발적인 성장은 1905년부터 시작되었다. 당시 예배당으로 사용하고 있던 벨의 임시 사택은 그 해 2월부터 언제나 각 방이 가득 찼고, 방으로 들어오지 못하는 사람들은 마당에서 집회에 참석하는 일이 벌어졌다. 마당의 교인들은 창가에 바싹 다가서서 예배 볼 수밖에 없었.

벨은 1905년 2월과 3월 사이에 광주 인근에 산재한 향촌 마을을 돌면서 183명과 세례문답을 하고 또 그들은 광주의 성경공부반Bible study class에 참석하도록 독려하였다. 4월에는 성경공부반을 개최하였다. 거기에는 약 30명이 참석하였다. 그리고 또다시 6월과 7월 사이에 다시 한 번 시골 마을들을 방문하였다. 이번에는 232명을 문답하였고 70명에게 세례, 70명에게 학습을 주었다. 이때 벨이 순회했던 교회들과 교인수를 보면 하나말Hannamal교회 200명, 영신Youngshin교회 75명, 봉덕Pongcuck교회 35명, 황양Hoangyang교회 40명, 덕산Tucksan교회 30명, 한바틀Hanpattule교회 100명, 장두Changdoo교회 37명, 배치Paichee교회 65명, 택기Taikkie교회 10명, 광주교회 50명 등이었다. 그리고 1905년 11월에 이르면 70명의 세례교인을 더하여 세례교인 총수가 85명으로 증가하였다. 4개의 공동체가 더 생겨났고, 2개의 교회가 예배당을 마련했다. 새로운 공동체들에서는 신약성경 50권과 찬송가 70권을 판매했다. 3개의 공동체는 예배당을 증축하기 위한 준비에 착수했다.

광주 기독교 유적지

오웬기념각과 호남신학대학

오웬기념각: 광주시 남구 양림동 67번지 / **호남신학대학**: 광주시 남구 양림동 108번지

광주스테이션 유적지 답사는 먼저 광주기독간호대학 안에 있는 '오웬기념각'(광주시 유형문화재 26호)을 둘러보는 것으로 시작된다. '오웬기념각'은 광주에서 의료선교활동을 벌이다가 1909년 사망한 오웬 선교사를 기념하기 위하여 그 가족과 친지들이 낸 성금으로 지은 정방형의 르네상스식 2층 건물로 당시에는 숭일학교의 예배당 겸 강당으로 사용되었다. 1914년 건립된 이 기념각의 현판에는 "吳基冕及其祖韋廉之紀念閣"이란 한문 기록과 영문 "In Memory of William L. and Clement C. Owen"이 병기되어 있다. 오웬은 네 살 때 고아가 되어 할아버지 윌리엄에게서 양육되었다. 그래서 그의 삶에 미친 할아버지의 영향은 매우 컸다. 오웬은 미국의 할아버지에게 광주의 학생들을 위해 강당이 필요하다는 점을 편지로 역설했는데 결국 그의 사후 그 바람이 이루어진 것이다. 일제강점기 "광주 신문화의 요람"으로서 다양한 공연 활동이 펼쳐지기도 했던 '오웬기념각'의 설계자는 남장로교의 건축가이면서 장로였던 스윈하트Martin L. Swinehart, 서로득였다. '오웬기념각'을 나와 호남신학대학쪽으로 올라가다 보면 시립사직도서관 입구에 '선교기념비'(1982년 건립)가 눈에 띤다. 1904년 광주에 정착한 벨 선교사가 처음 예배드렸던 사택이 있던 자리라고 한다.

그리고 호남신학대학 구내에는 광주스테이션 유적 중 가장 먼저(1909년) 지어진 것으로 추정되는 '윌슨기념관'(우일선 선교사 사택, 광주시 기념물 15호)이 보존되어 있다. '윌슨기념관'은 의료선교사 윌슨Robert M. Wilson, 우월손이 진료소와 집으로 사용한 지하 1층 지상 2층의 1백여 평 회색 벽돌 건물로 전형적인 미

국 남부식 주택이다. 윌슨은 1908년에 내한해서 1925년까지 광주 제중병원(현 광주 기독병원)에서 활동했다. 벨은 1909년의 선교 보고에서 이미 양림동 언덕에 자신과 오웬Clement C. Owen, 오기원의 주택 외에 윌슨과 프레스톤John F. Preston, 변요한, 코잇Robert T. Coit, 고라복의 사택이 있음을 밝히고 있다.

'남장로교 광주 선교사 묘지'는 현재 호남신학대학 구내 언덕 위에 자리 잡고 있다. 원래 여기에는 12개의 무덤이 있었는데, 순천과 목포스테이션이 정리되면서 그곳에 있던 묘들을 지난 1979년 이곳으로 이장移葬한 결과 그 규모가 크게 늘어났다. 지금은 순천에서 온 10개와 목포에서 옮겨진 4개 등을 합해 모두 26기의 무덤이 이곳 묘역에 위치해 있다.

먼저 원래 있었던 무덤들부터 소개하자면, 폴 크레인Paul S. Crane, 1889~1919의 묘비는 맨 앞 오른쪽에 놓여있다. 폴 크레인은 순천스테이션 소속 선교사였던 존 크레인John C. Crane, 구례인의 동생으로 형보다 2년 늦은 1916년부터 목포를 중심으로 활동하기 시작했다. 그러나 선교 3년 만인 1919년 3월 26일 벨이 몰던 승용차를 타고 서울에서 내려오던 중 수원을 지나 병점의 열차 건널목에서 열차

남장로교 광주 선교사 묘지

와 충돌하는 사고로 목숨을 잃었다. 안타까운 죽음이었다. 그 바로 옆의 오웬(1867~1909)은 벨과 함께 전남 선교를 개척한 인물로 1909년 순천 전도에 나섰다가 폐렴에 걸려 42세의 나이로 순직하였다. 그는 양림동 동산에 묻힌 첫 선교사이다. 오웬 무덤 옆에는 1907년 광주에 와서 수피아여학교 교사로 오랫동안 일했던 엘렌 그래함Ellen I. Graham, 1869~1930, 엄언라이 누워있다. 독신이었던 그녀는 건강이 악화되어 미국으로 돌아갔다가 다시 한국으로 나와 소원대로 광주에 묻힐 수 있었다. 다시 그 옆의 브랜드Louis C. Brand, 1894~1938, 부란도는 1924년 군산을 거쳐 1930년부터 광주제중병원에서 결핵 퇴치 운동을 전개했던 의료선교사로 결국 자신이 결핵에 걸려 소천하였다. 당시 그의 나이 마흔넷이었다.

폴 크레인 바로 뒤에는 벨의 두 번째 부인이었던 마가렛 벨Margaret W. Bell, 1873~1919의 무덤이 자리하고 있다. 그녀 역시 폴 크레인처럼 남편 벨이 모는 차에 동승했다가 사고를 당했다. 마가렛은 남장로교 군산선교사였던 불William F. Bull, 부위렴의 여동생으로 1902년 오빠를 보러 한국에 왔다가 상처한 벨을 만나 1904년 결혼하였다. 벨의 첫 번째 부인 샬롯 벨Charlotte W. Bell은 1901년 목포에서 별세, 양화진에 묻힌 바 있다. 그 후 벨은 군산의 여선교사 다이사트Julia Dysart와 1921년 결혼했지만 4년 후 광주에서 사망, 마가렛의 무덤 곁에 묻혔다. 거듭된 상처와 큰 사고에도 불구하고 선교 현장을 끝까지 지킨 벨의 신앙에 저절로 고개가 숙여진다. 벨의 옆에는 이곳의 유일한 한국인 무덤인 유우선柳佑善, 1956~1983의 묘가 있다. 유우선은 선교사의 추천을 받아 미국에 유학갔다가 하숙집 수영장에서 심장마비로 사망하였다. 다시 그 옆은 닷슨부인Harriet K. Dodson, 1889~1924의 무덤이다. 그녀는 광주제중병원 윌슨 선교사의 처제로 1921년 광주로 와서 선교사 자녀 교육에 힘쓰다가 이듬해 닷슨Samuel K. Dodson, 도대선 선교사와 결혼했다. 하지만 결혼 3년 만인 서른다섯에 사망, 광주에 묻혔다.

묘역 남쪽의 필립 코딩턴Philip T. Codington, 1960~1967 무덤은 1947년 한국에 와 목포, 광주 선교사로 일했던 허버트 코딩턴Herbert A. Codington, 고허번의 다섯째 아들의 것으로 당시 7살이었던 그 애는 광주에서 태어나 1967년 대천해수욕장에서 익사하였다. 당시 대천에는 재한 선교사들을 위해 50여 채의 캐빈으로 이루어진 대규모의 선교사 휴식시설(대천외국인수양관)이 운영되고 있었는데, 허버트는 바로 거기에서 사고를 당한 것이다. 코딩턴 무덤 옆에는 1922년 남편 레비James K. Levie, 여계남와 함께 내한하여 군산, 광주에서 활동하다가 1931년 사망한 레비부인 Jessie S. Levie, 1886~1931의 묘가 있고 바로 그 옆에는 에머슨Amelia J. Emerson, 1860~1927의 무덤이 있다. 에머슨은 일제의 압력에 대항하여 선교부의 재산을 지킨 탈메이지J. V. N. Talmage, 타마자의 장모로, 1910년 외동딸 등 가족과 함께 내한하여 광주스테이션에서 17년간 활동했다. 그녀는 선교사 자녀들을 교육시키는 한편 숭일과 수피아에서는 영어를 가르치다가 1927년 5월 27일 별세하여 이곳에 안장되었다. 다시 그 옆에는 '광주의 전설' 쉐핑Elisabeth J. Shepping, 1880~1934, 서서평이 누워있다. 1912년 내한한 그녀는 서울을 거쳐 광주제중병원 간호사로 오랫동안 사역하다가 1934년 53세를 일기로 소천하였다. 간호협회의 창설자이기도 했던 쉐핑은 많은 고아와 나환자들을 데려다 길렀는데, 양딸이 13명이나 되었다.

다음 목포스테이션에서 옮겨온 무덤으로는 먼저 니스벳부인Anabel L. Nisbet, 1869~1920, 유애나의 것이 있다. 1906년 남편John S. Nisbet, 유서백과 함께 내한한 그녀는 전주를 거쳐 목포 정명여학교 교장으로 8년간(1911~1919) 사역하였다. 1919년 3·1 운동 때 정명의 학생들이 시위를 하기 위해 몰려 나가자 그들을 보호하기 위해 몸으로 막던 교장 니스벳 부인은 그만 밀려 넘어졌고 결국 그것이 원인이 되어 1년 만에 숨을 거두었다. 문필력이 뛰어났던 니스벳 부인은 1892년부터 1919년까지 남장로교의 한국 선교 역사를 정리한 『Day in and Day out in Korea』(호남교회초기역사)를 남겼다. 니스벳 부인 옆에는 니스벳의 두 번째 부인에게서 난 딸Elizabeth D. Nisbet, 1922~1923의 무덤이 있다. 다시 그 옆에는 1923년 목포에 부임하여 선교사 자녀들을 가르치다가 의료선교사 길머William P. Gilmer, 길마와 결혼한 길머부인Kathryn N. Gilmer, 1897~1926의 묘가 있다. 그녀는 길머와 결혼한지 1년만인 1926년 29세의 나이로 세상을 떠났다. 또 그 옆의 채프먼부인Gertrude P. Chapman, 1869~1928은 목포의 간호선교사였던 조카 휴슨Georgiana F. Hewson, 허우선을 방문하러 왔다가 사망하였다.

순천스테이션 구내에 있었던 무덤들로는 우선 1938년 내한한 사우솔Thomas

B. Southall, 서도열의 딸 릴리안Lillian A. Southall, 1938이 잠들어 있다. 그런데 릴리안은 하루 밖에 살지 못했다. 다시 그 옆에는 코잇 형제의 무덤이 있는데, 네 살이었던 형Thomas H. Coit, 1909~1913과 동생Robert C. Coit, 1911~1913은 하루 상관으로 사망하였다. 1907년 내한한 아버지 코잇은 광주를 거쳐 1913년 새로 개설된 순천스테이션으로 임지를 옮기게 되는데, 주택이 마련되지 않은 상태에서 임시 숙소에 머물다가 아이들이 이질에 걸렸던 것이다. 형제 무덤 옆으로는 덤Thelma B. Thum, 1902~1931이 있다. 덤은 1930년 내한 순천 안력산병원 간호사로 근무하다가 1년 만인 1931년 병으로 소천하였다. 같은 줄의 로스부인Cora S. Ross, 1868~1927은 자신의 딸 로저스부인Mary D. Rogers을 만나러 순천에 왔다가 사망한 경우이다. 로저스부인의 남편James M. Rpgers, 노재수은 순천 안력산병원의 의료선교사였다. 두 번째 줄의 무덤 세 개는 사망자의 신원이 알려져 있지 않다. "C. S. R"과 "T. B. T"라고 새겨져 있는 두 개의 무덤은 아마 어려서 사망한 선교사 자녀들의 무덤인 것 같고, 다른 하나는 묘비조차 없다. 셋째 줄의 묘비 두 개는 존 크레인의 자녀들의 것이다. 하나는 1918년 사망한 딸Elizabeth L. Crane, 1917~1918의 묘이고, 다른 하나는 태어난 지 7개월 만에 죽은 아들John Curtice Jr. Crane, 1921의 무덤이다.

광주 수피아여고

광주시 남구 양림동 256번지

호남신학대학에서 내려와 수피아여고에 들어서면 바로 오른쪽 언덕 위에 '커티스 메모리얼 홀' Curtis Memorial Hall(등록문화재 159호)이 보인다. 1925년 소천한 벨 선교사를 기념하여 1926년 건축된 것으로 지하실을 갖춘 단층의 회색 벽돌의 예배당이다. 양철 지붕과 굴뚝, 아치형 창문이 조화를 이루는 이 건물은, 원래 1층 예배실과 지하의 기도실로 꾸며져 있었던 선교사들의 예배 공간으로 지금도 예수피아교회로 사용되고 있다. 선교사 유진 벨은 1896년 내한한 이후 30년 동안 목포와 광주에서 정력적으로 활동했던 전남 선교의 '대부'였다. '커티스 메모리얼 홀'

수피아여고 커티스 메모리얼 홀

에서 내려오면 학교 중앙에 지난 1995년 건립된 '광주3·1만세운동 기념동상'과 최근의 '조아라 기념비'를 볼 수 있다.

'수피아홀'(등록문화재 158호)은 1908년 시작된 수피아여학교가 1911년 지은 지상 2층의 벽돌 본관 건물로, 미국의 스턴스M. L. Stearns 부인이 동생 스피어J. Speer를 위하여 내놓은 기부금으로 지어졌다. 선교사들은 이를 기념하여 '수피아홀'이라 명명하고 학교 이름도 수피아여학교須彼亞女學校라고 불렀다. '수피아홀'은 일제강점기 내내 수피아의 교사로 사용되었는데, 또 이곳은 태평양전쟁 때 일제가 루트Florence E. Root, 유화례와 닷슨M. Dodson, 도마리아 등 여선교사들을 감금시킨 장소이기도 하다. 해방 후에는 전남고등성경학교와 광주기독간호전문학교가 여기에

수피아여고 수피아홀

서 시작되었다. 수피아여고는 최근 개교 100주년을 맞아 '수피아홀'에 100주년 기념관을 꾸며 역사 자료를 전시하고 있다.

또 일제강점기 수피아의 두 번째 교사로 사용된 '윈스보로우홀'(등록문화재 370호)은 전주신흥학교의 '리차드슨관'과 똑같이 스윈하트가 설계한 것으로 화강암 기초석 위에 붉은 벽돌로 미식 쌓기를 한 2층 건물이다. 미국 남장로교회 여신도들이 생일감사헌금을 모아 보내온 돈으로 1927년 지은 이 건물은, 그 모금을 주도했던 윈스보로우W. C. Winsborough의 이름을 건물명으로 했다. '윈스보로우홀'이 건립될 수 있었던 것은 수피아여학교의 '지정학교recognized school'인가 때문이었다. 일제는 1922년 2월, 당시 사립학교들 가운데 총독부에서 요구하는 시설과 재정의 요건을 갖춘 학교만을 5년제의 '고등보통학교Higher Common School'로 지정하여 우대한다는 내용의 '개정조선교육령'을 반포하였다. 이 법령의 근본 취지는 일본의 교육제도를 조선에 적용시킨다는 것이었으나 그 때 5개의 스테이션에 모두 10개의 학교를 경영하고 있던 남장로교선교부는 그 학교들 전부를 한꺼번에 총독부의 표준에 맞출 만큼의 여력이 없었다. 결국 선교부는 1923년 6월 연례회의에서 전주의 신흥학교와 광주의 수피아여학교에 집중하기로 결정하였다. 이것은 다시 1925년 10월의 임시회의에서 재확인되었다. 그 후 선교부는 신흥과 수피아의 지정학교 인가를 위해 재정을 집중 배정하였고, 그 결과물의 하나가 바로 '윈스보로우홀'이었다. 그리고 현재 일반 고시원으로 사용되고 있는 붉은 벽돌의 지상 1층 건물은, 1930년대에 '성경학원'(이일성경학원)의 기숙사로 사용했다고 한다.

광주스테이션 자리에 남아 있는 나머지 유적은 1935년 어간에 세워진 '수피아여고 소강당'이다. 지상 1층의 100평짜리 '수피아여고 소강당'은 원래 체육관으로 사용되던 건물로, 당시 이곳에서 학생들은 농구, 정구, 체조, 핸드볼 등의 체육 활동을 하였다. 이 건물은 '윈스보로우홀'을 건축하고 남은 돈으로 지어졌다..

광주 일반 유적지

전남도청 본관

🚗 광주시 동구 광산동 13번지

등록문화재 제16호로 지정된 전남도청 본관은 1930년에 건립된 건물로 전남지방 한국 근·현대사의 역사의 현장(일제강점기-도청, 80년대-5·18민주항쟁)이며, 지상3층 적벽돌 조적조로 일제강점기에 몇 안 되는 한국인 건축가 김순하에 의해 설계되었다는 점에서 건축적 의미가 있다.

한국의 민주화운동을 상징하는 5·18광주민중항쟁은 군사정권의 폭압과 불의에 항거해 일어선 시민들의 의로운 항쟁이다. 망월동 국립 5·18묘지는 당시 희생자들을 모신 역사의 현장으로 해마다 추모의 발길이 끊이지 않는다. 무고한 시민들이 끌려갔던 상무대는 이제 광주의 내일을 준비하는 신도심인 상무지구가 됐고 그곳에는 5·18정신을 기리는 5·18기념공원과 5·18자유공원이 있다. 또 도심 곳곳에는 항쟁사적지가 있다.

국립 5·18묘지

🚗 광주시 북구 문정동 산34

5·18영령 잠든 신묘역

국립 5·18묘지에는 434명(2005.10월 현재)의 5·18희생자들이 모셔져 있다. 총칼에 대한 두려움을 넘어 최후 항전까지 불사하는 투혼을 보여줬던 그들은 자신과 가족을 지키기 위해 무기를 들었던 우리의 이웃들이다. 분노와 한숨 그리고 애절한 사연이 공존하는 이곳은 5월 정신의 발원지로 해마다 5월이면 유족들의 오열 속에 추모식을 비롯한 다양한 5월 행사가 열리며 자유와 정의를 갈망하는 인권단체들의 방문이 이어져 민주화의 성지로 자리매김하고 있다.

민주열사 묻힌 구묘역

'80년 5·18 광주민중항쟁 당시 산화한 영령들이 17년 동안 묻혀 있던 곳으로 '97년 새 묘역이 완성됨에 따라 이곳에 묻혀 있던 영령들도 치욕의 세월을 뒤로 하고 새 묘역으로 이장되었다. 현재는 고 박종철, 민족시인 고 김남주 시인 등 5·18과 직접적인 관련이 없는 민족과 민주열사 37명과 아직까지 신묘역으로 옮기지 못한 5·18 희생자(2인) 등이 안장되어 있으며 옮긴 이들은 가묘상태로 남아 있다. 광주시는 구묘역을 '80년 당시의 모습을 그대로 간직한 사적지로서의 역할에 보다 충실해지게 하며 그날의 참상을 후세에게 전하는 역사의 장소로 만들려고 계획하고 있다.

5·18 자유공원

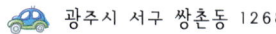 광주시 서구 쌍촌동 1268

5·18광주민중항쟁 구금자들의 처절한 아픔과 한이 서린 곳. '80년 5월 당시 죄없는 시민들을 잡아가 모진 고문을 하고 군사재판을 통해 사형을 선고했던 영창과 법정, 군인막사를 복원해 놓은 이곳은 자유의 소중함을 몸소 깨닫게 하는 역사현장이기도 하다. 상무대 군시설 이전 후 원래의 위치에서 백미터 정도 떨어진 이곳으로 옮겨와 복원했다.

특히 자유공원내 가장 안쪽에는 옛 상무대 영창이 철조망이 둘러쳐진 곳에 자리하고 있다. 많은 시민들이 폭도라는 누명을 쓰고 이곳으로 끌려와 계엄사 합동수사본부의 온갖 고문과 구타에 당하였다. 여섯 개의 방이 부채꼴로 배치되어 있으며 수감자들을 한눈에 감시할 수 있는 감시대가 중앙에 버티고 있다. 한 방에 많게는 150명 씩 총 8백여 명이 수감되어 혹독한 더위와 배고픔을 이겨내야 했던, 죽음과 삶의 경계였다. 군사법정 내무반에 들어서기 전 왼편으로 보이는 건물이 '80년 민주화운동에 참여했던 구속자들이 군사재판을 받았던 곳이며, '80년 그날 수많은 시민들이 부당한 군사재판에 대한 항의표시로 소리 높여 애국가를 불렀던 곳이다. 당시 재판은 법정에 총으로 무장한 헌병을 입장시켜 공포 분위기를 조성한 가운데 비공개로 진행됐으며 군사재판부는 사형, 무기징역 등 실형을 선고했다.

광주학생운동기념탑

🚗 광주시 북구 독립로 237번지 33

광주학생독립운동을 주도했던 옛 광주고보(현, 광주일고) 교정에는 1954년에 세운 높이 약 11 m의 웅장한 광주학생 독립운동기념탑과 기념공원이 조성돼 있다. 또 매년 11월 3일을 학생의 날로 정해 '이름없는 별들'의 숭고한 애국투쟁 정신을 기리고 있다.

2. 전남지역

첫번째. 목포

✱ 목포 기독교 전래

1897년 12월 벨Eugene Bell, 배유지은 목포스테이션의 부지를 매입할 수 있었다. 처음 선교사들은 자신들의 안전과 쾌적한 환경을 위해 한국인들이 밀집해 살고 있는 읍성邑城에서 조금 떨어진 곳의 구릉지를 넓게 확보하고자 했는데, 벨 역시 그런 안목을 지니고 있었다. 물론 이 때 매입한 토지의 양은 그 일부였지만 그 후 벨은 언덕 전체를 매입하게 된다. 선교사들은 처음부터 장차 조성될 대규모의 선교타운을 염두에 두고 몇 차례에 걸쳐 점진적으로 땅을 사들였던 것이다. 최초의 토지매입 계약이 완료된 1898년 봄 벨은 비좁은 초가집에서 한국인들과 지내며 우선 임시주택을 지었다. 벨의 최종 목표는 벽돌을 사용한 서양식 주택을 짓는 것이었다. 하지만 그것은 자재 일부를 서울에서 가져와야 하는 등 시간이 꽤 걸리는 일이었으므로 1년 정도 거주할 한국식 주택을 지어 잠정적으로 사용했던 것이다. 이것은 벨뿐만이 아니라 지방에 내려온 선교사들의 전형적인 단계별 주거 방식이다.

벨은 1898년 12월 새 집으로 이사하였다. 진료소를 겸한 오원Clement C. Owen, 오기원의 사택도 그 집 뒤에 위치해 있었다. 벨의 계획은 목포 양동의 언덕 위 스테이션 구내에 나란히 세 채의 주택을 지으려는 것이었다. 새로운 집을 짓는 사이 벨은 의료선교사의 입국을 고대하고 있었다. 1차적으로는 자신의 가족의 안전을 위해서 의사가 필요했다. 그러나 벨의 머릿속에는 하나의 스테이션에 전도-의료-여성 사역자를 안배하여 효과를 높인다는 협력 선교의 구상이 들어 있었다. 이러한 태도는 몇 년 뒤 벨의 광주스테이션 개설 과정에서도 또다시 반복된다. 광주스테이션의 시작을 몇 달 앞둔 1904년 4월, 그 때는 벨 자신이 직접 미국에 가서 광주 근무 의료선교사를 물색하였던 것이다. 벨은 스테이션 개설의 필요조건을 잘 알고 있었다. 그리고 이 원칙은 다른 선교사들에 의해서도 줄곧 견지되었다.

1898년 11월 의료선교사 오웬이 목포에 도착하였다. 오웬은 1899년 7월 진료소를 열고 환자들을 맞았다. 오웬은 불과 몇 달 만에 400여 명의 환자를 진료하며 스테이션을 일약 도시의 명소로 만들었다. 벨이 바라던 바였다. 1899년 12월 말에는 독신여성 선교사 스트래퍼Fredrica E. Straeffer, 서여사가 합류하여 목포스테이션의 얼개가 얼추 갖추어졌다. 스트래퍼는 여성·어린이 사역을 전담하는 한편 소녀들을 위한 교육을 시작하였다.

벨이 한참 스테이션을 건설하고 있던 1898년 6월 경, 벨의 임시주택에서 주일예배를 본 한국인의 수는 30여 명에 달하였다. 그들은 주로 다른 지역에서 목포로 이사 온 기성 신자들이었다. 당시 목포는 1897년 10월 1일의 개항 이후 새로운 기회를 찾아 사람들이 몰려들고 있었다. 목포에 새로 자리 잡은 '각국공동거류지' 구역의 '일본인 마을'이 도시의 근대화를 추동하자, '목포부 부내면' 구역의 '조선인 마을' 역시 식민지 도시문화의 영향을 받게 된다. 얼마 안가서 목포는 "남선南鮮 굴지屈指의 양항만良港灣"으로서 땅값이 오르고 "다수의 자산가"가 사는 곳이 되었다. 개항 이전의 목포는 대체로 150호 정도의 가구가 목포진木浦鎭의 관할 하에 농업과 어업에 종사하며 살던 그런 곳이었다. 그러나 근대도시 목포의 인구는 1910년 1만 2천여 명을 넘어서 1925년에는 3만 7천여 명에 이르렀다. 목포교회의 기반은 바로 그 도시의 증가하는 인구에 있었다.

오웬의 진료소가 한참 성가를 날리고 있을 무렵 벨도 본격적인 선교 활동에 들어갔다. 우선 신입교인들을 교육하기 시작했다. 그들이 온전한 신앙을 고백할 때까지 별도의 학습반을 드어 평일에 그들을 가르쳤다. 까다로운 문답 시험이 요구되었다. 1900년 8월 목포교회의 첫 세례식은 그 결과였다. 교인들은 주일 오후 두 사람씩 짝을 지어 읍내에 나가 전도했다. 1900년 여름 목포교회의 회중은 75명으로 늘어나 있었다. 전도와 신앙교육에 이어 벨에게 주어진 또 하나의 임무는 지방순회 사역이었다. 벨은 한 때 스테이션이 설치될 뻔했던 나주 외곽의 마을들에서 활동했다. 오웬 역시 진료 외의 시간을 순회사역에 투자하고 있었다. 그 결과 목포 바깥에 모두 8개의 신앙공동체가 생겨났다.

비록 벨 부인의 사망(1901.4.12)과 오웬의 일시 귀국(1902.7~1903.10)으로 레이놀즈William D. Reynolds, 이눌서와 맥커첸Luther O. McCutchen, 마로덕이 잠시 그 공백을 메운 적도 있었지만, 목포스테이션은 그 구성의 핵심 요소라 할 수 있는 안전한 선교 구내의 조성과 기본적인 선교 인력의 충원이 지속되면서 위와 같이 초기 전남 선교의 교두보의 역할을 수행하고 있음을 본다. 1903년 이후에도 스테이션의 성장은 계속되었는데, 선교사가 담임으로 있던 목포교회의 300명 회중은 힘을 모아 벨 부인을 기념하는 '위더스푼기념예배당'을 건립하였고, 소규모의 남·여 학교 과정이 선교사들에 의해 운영되기 시작했다. 또 1903년 11월 목포에 부임한 프레스톤은 벨과 오웬이 광주로 이동하는 스테이션의 전환기에 신임 의료선교사 놀란Joseph W. Nolan 그리고 스트래퍼와 함께 목포 사역을 이어 나갔다. 광주스테이션이 설치되면서 1905년 10월 잠정 폐쇄 되었던 목포스테이션은 프레스톤의 주도로 1907년 10월 다시 그 운영이 재개되었다.

✽ 목포 기독교 유적지

정명여중 구내 목포스테이션 유적지

🚗 전남 목포시 양동 86번지

　1904년 겨울 광주 스테이션이 시작되면서 잠정 폐쇄되었던 목포 스테이션이 1907년 가을 다시 문을 열게 되자 곧 선교사 주택의 건축 필요성이 제기되었다. 선교부는 1908년 6,000불의 예산을 목포에 배정하여 2채의 주택을 짓도록 했다. 그 10여 년 전 벨이 지은 세 채의 벽돌주택만으로는 늘어나는 선교 인력을 수용할 수 없었던 것이다. 그리하여 1909년 단단한 서양식 2층 석조주택 두 동이 목포에 모습을 드러냈다. 이어 1910년에서 1912년까지 모두 3개의 사택이 추가로 건축되었다. 목포남학교 교사校舍 역시 1909년 봄 완공되었다. 하나의 강당과 두 개의 교실을 갖춘 목포남학교는 건축비를 제공한 교회Spartanburg Church, South Carolina의 담임목사 이름을 따서 'John Watkins Academy'로 명명되었다. 그 다음으로 선교부는 1909년에 여학교 건물(105평의 2층 석조)과 병원 신축을 위해 각각 2,600불과 7,000불(병원건물 5,000불, 시설 2,000불)의 예산을 책정하여 건물을 짓도록 했다. 그 후 여학교(맥컬리기념여학교)는 다시 미국의 그레이스 맥컬리Miss Grace McCallie의 지원으로 1922년 최신식의 기숙사와 건물을 신축하였고, 1914년 화재로 전소된 목포병원은 거액의 후원St. Joseph Church, Missouri을 받아 1916년 2층 석조의 '프렌치기념병원'으로 거듭났다.

　그 결과 1924년 현재 목포 스테이션의 1만 4천평 구내에는 5채의 선교사 주택과 남학교, 여학교, 병원, 시약소施藥所, dispensary 그리고 한국인 직원 숙소 등이 세워져 있었다. 그리고 그 자산 가치는 모두 6만불에 달했다. 1940년 남장로교 선교사들이 철수할 무렵 한국에는 모두 8개 지역(5개 스테이션과 서울, 평양, 지리산)에 373개 동의 건물이 선교부 재산으로 등록되어 있었는데, 건물과 토지를 합친 전체 재산의 규모는 100만 달러(320만엔, 현재 가치 3,200억원)를 상회하고 있었다. 북장로회 한국선교부는 그 3배인 300만불의 재산을 보유하고 있었던

정명여중 석조1호 주택(출처: 이덕주, 『예수 사랑을 실천한 목포-순천이야기』)

것으로 파악된다.

  목포 선교와 근대화의 진앙지였던 목포 스테이션의 모습도 이제는 많이 달라졌다. 우선 그 많던 땅이 스테이션 폐쇄 이후 계속 줄어들어 지금은 정명여학교가 갖고 있는 3천여 평과 목포양동교회(기장)가 소유하고 있는 850평이 전부이다. 영흥학교 터는 1980년 상동으로 학교가 이전되면서 고층아파트가 들어섰고, 정명여학교 주변 3천여 평도 지금은 주택가와 상가로 변했다. 길 건너 프렌치병원 건물도 허물어 없어졌다. 현재 양동에서 옛 스테이션의 흔적을 찾아볼 수 있는 곳은 정명여학교와 목포양동교회뿐이다. 다행히 이곳에는 선교사 주택 2채와 교회 건물이 남아 있다.

  학교에 들어서 왼쪽 언덕을 오르면 먼저 보이는 것이 석조 2호 주택이지만 석조 1호 주택부터 소개하고자 한다. 지난 2003년 문화재청에 의해 등록문화재 62호로 지정되어 현재 정명여중의 '100주년기념관'으로 사용되고 있는 건물이 바로 1909년 지어진 목포 스테이션의 석조 1호 주택이다. 한남대 초대 학장을 역임한 남편 린튼William. A. Linton, 인돈의 소천 후 다시 목포로 돌아와 1964년까지 활동한 린튼 부인Charlotte. W. B. Linton, 인사례은 이 집을 가리켜 선교 구내에 지어진 첫 번째 주택이라고 술회하였다. 린튼 부인은 목포 선교를 시작한 벨 선교사의 딸로 1899년 바로 이곳 양동 스테이션 구내에서 태어났으니 목포가 고향인 셈이다. 1960년대에는 린튼 부인 외에 보이어Kenneth E. Boyer, 보계선와 스미스Robert L. Smith, 심득민 선교사 등이 여기서 살았다. 1971년 선교사들이 떠나면서 방치되어 화재를 당하기도 했지만 지난 2001년 보수 공사로 어느 정도 원형을 회복했고, 2010년에는 지붕을 올리는 작업을 하고 있다.

정명여학교 안에는 또 하나의 선교사 주택이 남아 있다. 바로 중학교 도서관 등으로 사용되고 있는 석조 2호 주택이다. 이 건물 역시 1909년 1호 주택과 동시에 세워진 것으로 추정된다. 벨과 프레스톤John F. Preston, 변요한 이후 목포 선교를 이끌었던 해리슨William B. Harrison, 하위렴 그리고 커밍Daniel J. Cumming, 김아각 선교사가 살았다고 전해지는 석조 2층의 이 집은 그 후 양 옆으로 시멘트 건물을 이어 붙여 본래 모습과는 많이 달라졌다. 그런데 이 건물은 목포뿐 만이 아니라 3·1운동과 관련되어 중요한 의미를 지니고 있다. 1983년 이 건물 1층 천장에서 독립운동사와 관련된 귀중한 자료들이 발견되었기 때문이다. 그 자료들은 「2·8독립선언서」 원본과 「3·1독립선언서」 사본, 광주에서 인쇄된 것으로 보이는 「警告我二千萬同胞」라는 격문과 「朝鮮獨立光州新聞」 그리고 만세 시위 도중 널리 불렸던 「독립가」 사본 등 모두 5장으로, 3·1운동 당시 광주의 누군가가 정명여학교와 관련을 맺고 있던 金牧師(커밍 선교사라는 견해가 있음)에게 보낸 것으로 여겨진다. 석조 2호 주택 앞에는 1985년 건립된 '목포독립운동기념비'가 놓여 있다.

목포양동교회

전남 목포시 양동 127번지

정명여학교 정문에서 오른쪽으로 나와 다시 우회전하여 조금 걸으면 석조 건물의 목포양동교회(등록문화재 114호)가 보인다. 1911년 겨울 준공된 목포양동

목포양동교회 석조예배당

교회 예배당은 전형적인 서양식 조적조組積造: 벽돌 등을 쌓아 올려서 벽을 만드는 건축 구조 건물로서 1982년 한차례의 증축 과정을 거쳐 계속 사용 중이다. 예배당 왼쪽 출입구 위에는 "大韓隆熙四年"(대한 융희 4년)이라는 글씨가 태극문양과 함께 선명하게 남아 있다. 그리고 건물 옆에는 '선교107년기념비'와 '순고자 박연세 기념비'가 세워져 있다. 1926년 목포양동교회에 부임한 박연세 목사는 1942년 일본의 황민화정책을 비판하는 설교를 했다가 체포되어 결국 1944년 대구형무소 독방에서 동사凍死하였다. 그의 유해는 지난 1988년 대전 국립묘지에 안장되었다.

두 번째. 순천

✱ 순천 기독교 전래

순천 지역에는 1905년을 전후하여 복음이 전래되었다. 그리하여 여천 장천교회, 벌고 무만동교회, 광양 신황리교회 등이 먼저 세워졌고, 이듬해인 1906년에는 순천읍에서도 교회가 시작되었다. 그 때 순천읍교회(현 순천중앙교회)는 유생들의 교육기관이었던 양사재楊士齋에서 모이다가 다시 1908년부터는 서문밖 한옥 1채를 사서 예배당으로 사용하였다.

그리고 1910년 광주에서 온 김윤수가 선교사들을 대리해 매산등 일대 2,000여 평을 스테이션 부지로 매입하자 순천읍교회는 그 땅 일부 20평에 'T'자형 예배당을 지었다. 바로 지금 순천중앙교회가 서있는 매곡동 144-2번지였다. 그 후 이기풍 목사가 시무할 때인 1923년 대지 800평에 'ㄱ'자형으로 교회당을 개축하였으며, 1935년에는 130평 규모의 단층 예배당이 세워졌다. 이 건물은 1983년까지 오랫동안 사용되었다.

선교 초기 순천은 남장로교 선교사 오웬Clement C. Owen, 오기원의 활동구역이었다. 그 후 그의 사역은 프레스톤John F. Preston, 변요한과 코잇Robert T. Coit, 고라복에게 계승되었다. 오웬을 이어 전남 동남부 지역을 순회한 프레스톤은 순천의 높은 가능성에 주목하고 선교부에 스테이션 설치를 강력하게 요청하였다. 당시 순천 근교에는 벌써 6~7개의 신앙공동체가 활발하게 모임을 갖고 있었다. 결국 남장로교 선교부는 1910년 순천에 새로운 스테이션을 두기로 결정하였다. 남장로교의 다섯 번째 선교 거점이었다. 남장로교 선교사들은 사냥하는 차림으로 순천 일대를 돌며 스테이션이 들어설 땅을 물색했다. 소문이 나면 땅값이 오를 것이기 때문이었다. 선교사들은 맑은 물을 확보할 수 있는 남봉산 자락 매산등 10에이커의 토지를 사들였다. 광주스테이션 개설 경험이 있던 한국인 김윤수가 도움을 주었다.

1911년 안식년으로 귀국한 프레스톤은 순천스테이션 조성 비용을 모금할 목적으로 우선 남장로교의 후원자인 사우스캐롤라니아 그린빌의 직물제조업자 그래함C. E. Graham과 접촉하였다. 그는 전주 신흥학교 校舍 건축을 지원한 바 있었다. 그래함은 다시 프레스톤에게 북캐롤라이나 더램 Durham의 기업가 왓츠George Watts를 소개해 주었다. 그런데 왓츠가 장로로 시무하던 더램제일교회Durham's First Presbyterian Church 담임목사 레이번E. R. Leyburn은 전주 선교사 전킨William M. Junkin, 전위렴의 처남이었다. 왓츠는 순천스테이션에 부임할 선교사 13명에게 매년 13,000불씩 지원하겠다고 약속했다.

순천스테이션은 미국인 실업가 조지 왓츠George Watts가 낸 기부금을 바탕으로 종합적인 계획에 의거해서 1911년부터 1922년까지 조성된 대규모의 선교 타운이었다. 스테이션이 먼저 완벽하게 지어지고 그 다음 선교사들이 입주한 경우는 순천이 처음이었다. 미국에서 보내온 시멘트나 건축자재는 3마일쯤 떨어진 포구에서 하역되었다. 그리고 순천 남봉산 줄기 약 26,000평의 구내에는 선교사 사택, 순천중앙교회, 유치원, 남녀학교(지금의 매산중고교·매산여고), 알렉산더병원, 순천성경학원 등이 순차적으로 들어설 수 있었다.

순천의 첫 선교사들로는 목회사역을 담당했던 프레스톤과 코잇, 남학교의 크레인John C. Crane, 구례인, 여학교의 두피Lavalette Dupuy, 두애란, 의료선교사 티몬스Henry L. Timmons, 김로라와 간호사 그리어Anna L. Greer, 기안나, 여성사역의 비거Meta L. Biggar, 백미다 그리고 주일학교의 프랫Charles H. Pratt, 안채륜 등이었다.

✽ 순천 기독교 유적지

매산중학교와 매산여고

🚗 **매산중학교**: 전남 순천시 매곡동 147-6번지 / **매산여고**: 전남 순천시 매곡동 166-9번지

순천스테이션 자리였던 현재의 순천시 매곡동 매산중학교와 매산여고, 그리고

그 일대에는 모두 7개의 기독교유적이 남아 있다. 전라남도 순천의료원 바로 옆에 있는 순천중앙교회는 순천 기독교 유적지 답사의 출발점이다. 먼저 순천중앙교회 바로 뒤에 있는 건물이 현재 한국선교박물관으로 사용되고 있는 '순천기독진료소'(등록문화재 127호)이다. 원래 이 건물은 왓츠기념성경학원으로 사용하다가 해방 후에는 결핵환자진료소 등이 입주해 있었다. 지금 그 박물관에는 200여 점의 유물이 전시되어 있다. 3층 유물실에는 유진 벨Eugene Bell, 배유지 선교사가 쓰던 테이블 세트 등 20점의 유물이 있고, 2층 전시실에도 다양한 자료가 모두 14개함에 담겨 진열되고 있다. 마당에는 '롯티벨Lottie Bell선교사추모비' 등 여러 개의 기념비가 세워져 있다.

'순천기독진료소'를 보고 다시 조금 올라가면 매산중학교와 매산여고가 보인다. '매산중학교 매산관'은 1911년 개교한 매산학교의 화강암 석조 2층 교사校舍로 1930년 11월 신축되었다. 그리고 매산여고의 지금 '프레스톤선교관'(등록문화재 126호)과 '휴린튼기념관'은 1920년 나란히 지어진 60평 규모 화강암 벽체의 2층 석조 건물로 현재 매산여고의 어학실(교목실, 학생회의실)과 체육실로 사용되고 있다. 매산여고 운동장에 들어서서 먼저 보이는 건물이 바로 '프레스

순천기독진료소

매산중학교 매산관

톤기념관'이고, 그 건너편에 '휴린튼기념관'이 있다. 이 두 곳에는 각각 프레스톤John F. Preston, 변요한과 휴 린튼Hugh M. Linton, 인휴 가족이 살고 있었다. 1903년 내한하여 1940년까지 목포, 광주, 순천에서 활동한 프레스톤은 특히 순천스테이션 건설에 결정적인 공헌을 한 바 있다. 휴 린튼은 한남대학 학장을 지낸 윌리엄 린튼William A. Linton, 인돈의 셋째 아들로 1926년 군산에서 태어났다. 그는 미국에서 대학을 졸업하고 1953년 동생Thomas D. Linton, 인도아과 함께 내한하여 1954년부터 순천 지역의 농촌교회들을 돌보았다. 결핵퇴치운동에 앞장섰던 그는 1984년 4월 10일 애양원에서 순천으로 오다가 교통사고를 당해 순직하였다. 그의 무덤은 지금 순천시 조례동 131번지에 있다.

매산여고를 나와 다시 언덕을 오르면 3개의 유적을 더 만날 수 있다. 순천스테이션 유적 가운데 가장 먼저 지어진 1913년의 '코잇기념관'(전남문화재자료 259호)은 2층의 석조 건물로 매산학교 교장이었던 선교사 코잇Robert T. Coit, 고라복이 생활했던 곳이다. 해방 후에는 미첼H. Petrie Mitchell, 미철, 킨슬러Arthur W. Kinsler, 권오덕 선교사가 살았다고 한다. 1915년 지어진 '순천스테이션외국인학

매산여고 프레스톤 선교관

교'(등록문화재 124호)는 회색 벽돌 단층 건물로 여기에서 선교사 자녀들이 교육받았다. 그 아래로 선교사들이 테니스를 치던 운동장이 공터로 남아 있다. 또 '더램기념관'은 지상 2층의 석조 건물로 원래는 고등성경학교 자리에 있던 것을 해체하여 현재의 위치로 옮긴 것이다. 더램Clarence G. Durham, 노우암 선교사가 조선식 기와를 올려 토착적인 멋이 나는 이 집에서 마지막까지 살았다고 한다.

세번째. 여수

여수 애양원

전남 여수시 율촌면 신풍리 1번지

애양원은 남장로교선교부가 운영했던 나환자의료기관으로 지금도 몇 개의 유적이 남아 있다. 애양원의 역사는 1926년 광주에 있던 나병원(癩病院)이 여수로 이전하면서 시작된다. 그 후 2년 동안 환자들은 모두 41개동의 건물을 지었는데, 현재 남아 있는 '애양원예배당'(등록문화재 32호)과 '애양원역사관'(등록문화재 33호)도 그 시절을 뿌리로 하고 있다. 먼저 '애양원예배당'은 1928

애양원예배당

년 10월 처음 지어진 것으로 짐작된다. 그러나 그 예배당은 1934년의 화재로 전소되었고, 현재의 2층 석조 건물(178평)은 1935년 재건축된 것이다. 물론 그 후에 몇 차례의 증축을 거쳤다. 지상 2층 석조(92평)의 '애양원역사관'은 애양병원 건물로 1928년 처음 건축되었지만, 그 후 몇 차례 증축과 화재 후 중건의 과정이 있었던 것으로 보인다. 그러다가 2000년부터 애양역사박물관으로 활용하고 있다. 그 외에 업무시설인 '토플하우스'(1953년)도 기독교유적으로 꼽힌다.

애양원역사관

애양원교회 뜰옆의 '손양원목사순교기념비'를 보고 언덕을 내려가면 바닷가 오른쪽 양지녘에 3개의 봉분이 나타난다. 바로 손양원 목사 부부와 두 아들 동인, 동신이 나란히 누워 있는 곳이다. 거기서 조금만 더 가면 1994년 3월 문을 연 둥근 형태의 손양원목사순교기념관이 있는데, 주로 손양원 목사의 유물이 보관되어 있다. 잘 알려진 대로 손양원 목사는 애양원교회의 담임목사로 시무 중 1948년 여순사건 때 두 아들을 잃은데 이어 자신도 1950년 9월 순교하였다.

여수 장천교회

여수시 율촌면 조화리 139번지

순천에서 여수로 향하는 길목에 위치한 장천교회는 1905년 10월 조일환의 집에서 시작되었다. 전남 동부지역 기독교의 역사를 대표하는 장천교회는 1912년 여흥학교를 세워 지역 근대교육의 요람으로 만들었다. 이런 연유로 율촌은 여수에서 가장 먼저 개화된 곳으로 이름이 높았다. 처음에는 초가집을 예배당으로 사용하다가 교인이 차츰 늘어나자 1924년 장천교회는 석조 2층 예배당을 신축하

애양원역사관

였다. 그리고 다시 1973년 86평의 석조 예배당을 다시 지었고, 지난 2003년 또다시 그 옆에 현대적인 예배당을 지었다. 그래서 지금 교회 구내에는 이 세 채의 교회당이 나란히 세워져 있다. 한국 근현대 교회 건축 양식의 변모를 한 눈으로 관찰할 수 있는 것이다. 이런 사례는 전국적으로 군위성결교회에서만 발견된다. 1924년의 예배당은 아직도 장천어린이집으로 계속 사용하고 있다.

네번째. 기타

지리산 선교사 유적지

전남 구례군 토지면 구산리 산 106번지

'지리산 선교사 유적지'는 남장로교 선교사들의 여름 휴양시설로 개발되었다. 그들은 1920년부터 별도의 위원회 Summer Resort Committee를 조직하여 전남 구례군 마산면 좌사리 노고단(산 110-2) 일대 약 10만 평을 임대받아 3~40개의 작은 오두막을 지어 사용하였다. 1935년 레이놀즈 William D. Reynolds, 이눌서의 성경 개역 작업도 여기에서 일부 이루어졌다. 해방 이후 귀환한 남장로교 선교사들은 다시 지리산에 휴양시설을 조성하기로 하고 1962년 구례군 토지면 구산리 산 106번지 왕시루봉에 12동의 건물을 지어 이용하였다.

현재 노고단에는 수양관 유적이 반파된 건축 유구상태로 남아 있고, 왕시루봉에는 12채의 건축물과 그 부대 시설이 남아 있다. 왕시루봉 선교사 휴양촌은 노고단의 휴양촌이 파괴되어 더 이상 기능을 할 수 없자 새로운 대안으로 모색된 것이다. 왕시루봉 휴양촌은 해발 1,216 m 왕시루봉의 9부 능선인 1,080 m에서 1,120 m 사이에 남북으로 약 250 m, 동서로 약 80 m의 공간에 독자적인 작은 마을을 이루고 있다. 지금 그곳에는 주택 10동과 마을 입구에 공동시설인 교회당 1동, 창고 1동, 수영장 1개소와 운동시설인 테니스장 등으로 구성되어 있다.

지리산 왕시루봉 선교사 유적지
(샤롯데 벨 린튼 주택)

샤롯데 벨 린튼 주택 내부

대부분 산아래의 구례읍과 인접한 마을이 내려다 보이는 서쪽의 조망권을 확보하고 있는 선교사 주택들은 '하도례Theodore Hard, 미국 정통장로교회 선교사 주택'을 제외하면 산길을 따라 부채꼴의 3열 병렬로 배치되어 있다. '로빈슨Robert K. Robinson, 라빈선 주택'과 '인휴Hugh M. Linton 주택'이 최상단에 위치하고, 중앙에 '샤롯데 벨 린튼 Charlotte B. Linton 주택', '브라운George T. Brown, 부명광 주택', '조요셉Joseph B. Hopper 주택'이 각각 열을 이루고 있다. 맨 아래에 '한성진James Hazeldine, 호주선교사 주택', '모요한John V. Moore 주택', '배도선Peter R. M. Pattisson, 영국 OMF 선교사 주택'이 같은 선상에 자리하고 있다. 그리고 병렬로 배치된 주택들의 한 꼭지점에 홀로 '도성래Stanley C. Topple 주택이 있다. 도성래주택을 제외하고는 길을 사이에 두고 2~3채씩 20~20 m 간격으로 모여 있다. 난방 설비로 온돌이 설치된 하도례 주택은 좀 멀리 떨어져 있고, 역시 온돌의 샤롯데 벨 린튼 주택은 그 뒤에 야외 예배소가 있을 뿐 아니라 전면에 넓은 공간을 갖고 있다. 최근 이 곳 '지리산 선교사 유적지'를 문화재로 지정해야 한다는 논의가 일고 있다.

신안 증도 문준경 전도사 순교지

전남 신안군 증도면 증동리 1304번지

아시아 최초의 슬로시티Slow City로 지정된 증도는 짱둥어가 노니는 갯벌과 최고 품질의 천일염이 생산되는 곳으로 잘 알려져 있다. 문준경 전도사의 유적지를 확인하려면 먼저 증도면사무소 쪽으로 가야 한다. 면사무소 옆에 있는 증동리교회에 문 전도사의 추모비가 있다. 문 전도사는 이 교회 외에 진리교회, 대초리교회 등 10여 개의 교회를 세웠다. 원래 문준경 전도사의 무덤도 이 증동리교회 뒤편 산에 있었다. 하지만 지난 2005년 증동리교회 앞바다 즉 문 전도사의 순교 현장으로 이장했다. 그곳에 가면 깔끔하게 단장된 순교기념비와 묘소를 만날 수 있다.

문준경 전도사는 1891년 2월 전남 신안군 암태면 수곡리에서 태어났다. 17살 때인 1908년 3월 결혼했지만 남편이 제대로 돌보지 않아 20여 년을 생과부로 시부모와 함께 살았다. 그러던 중 목포 북교동성결교회에서 예수를 믿고 경성성서학원에서 공부하면서 1932년부터 이 지역을 순회하며 증동리교회를 중심으로 여러 교회들을 세웠다. 문 전도사는 마을 사람들의 부탁으로 짐꾼노릇, 우체부노릇을 마다하지 않았고, 전도하느라 1년에 아홉 켤레나 고무신을 바꿔 신었다고 한다. 1943년 신사참배 거부로 인해 목포경찰서로 끌려가 고문을 당했지만 문 전도사는 끝까지 신사에 참배하지 않았다. 6·25전쟁 중 섬 전체가 인민군에게 넘어가면서 목포인민위원회에 끌려갔던 문 전도사는 이성봉 목

문준경 전도사 순교기념비

사 등 주변의 만류를 무릅쓰고 증도로 돌아갔다가 결국 총탄에 쓰러지고 말았다. 1950년 10월 5일 새벽 2시 그녀의 나이 만59세였다.

다섯 번째. 영광

6 · 25전쟁기 염산면 기독교인 학살

1950년 6 · 26전쟁 전까지 전남 영광군 염산면에는 두 곳의 교회만 존재하였다. 하나는 1908년 야월리에 설립된 야월교회와 1947년 봉남리 설도에 세워진 염산교회였다. 야월교회는 남장로교 선교사 유진 벨Eugene Bell, 배유지의 방문으로 시작되었다. 염산교회는 야월교회가 설립된 지 거의 40여 년이 지난 후에 세워졌다. 이 교회는 군남면 옥슬리(2004년 염산면으로 편입)교회 교인들이 그 교회를 폐쇄하고 사람들의 왕래가 많았던 염산리로 교회당을 이전하면서 염산교회로 새롭게 출발한 내력을 지니고 있다.

6 · 25전쟁기 염산면에서 일어났던 대량학살은 그 해 9월 유엔군이 인천상륙작전에 성공한 이후 벌어졌다. 염산면 내에서도 야월리와 봉남리의 피해가 상대적으로 컸다. 이 지역에 위치하고 있었던 야월교회와 염산교회 교인들의 피해도 클 수밖에 없었다. 야월교회 교인들은 한사람도 남김없이 65명 전원이 피살당했으며, 염산교회에서는 전체 교인의 3분의 2에 해당되는 77명이 좌익세력들에 의해 학살당했다. 당시 야월교회의 교인들은 대부분 야월리에 거주하는 사람들이었다. 봉남리 설도에 위치해 있던 염산교회 교인들은 대부분 옥슬리 혹은 봉남리에 거주하는 사람들이었다.

당시 피살당했던 야월교회 교인들은 네 집안 사람들 전원이었다. 영수領袖로 있던 김성종 · 조양현 그리고 집사 최판섭 · 김병환 · 정일성 등의 집안 사람들이었다. 김성종의 집안에서는 부인, 아들, 며느리, 손녀 등 모두 33명, 최판섭의 집안에서는 11명, 김병환의 집에서는 7명, 정일성의 집안에서는 13명 등이었다.

염산교회의 77명은 대부분 봉남리 지역민들로 당시 봉남리 학살자 수는 거의 8백여 명에 이른다. 그 때 염산교회는 김방호 목사가 담임하고 있었다. 1950년 3월 10일 염산교회에 부임한 김 목사는 3·1만세운동에 참여했던 민족적인 인물이었다. 김방호 목사는 1950년 7월 23일 주일 낮예배를 본 후 인민군이 교회당을 점령하자 신변의 위험을 느껴 은신해 있다가 10월 26일 끌려가 죽임을 당했다. 야월교회의 교인이던 김성종, 조양현, 최판섭, 최판원, 김두석 등은 염산 설도 앞바다에 수장되었다.

야월교회

🚗 전남 영광군 염산면 541-1번지

야월교회에 들어서면 먼저 순교기념탑과 기념조형물들을 볼 수 있다. 그리고 교회당 옆에는 기독교인순교기념관이 세워져 있다. 기독교인순교기념관은 전국 교회의 헌금과 영광군청의 지원으로 건립되었다. 기념관은 야월교회 순교자뿐 아니라 영광군의 순교자들을 기념하고 있다. 2층으로 된 기념관은 1층에 역사전시실과 기도의 손이 있으며, 2층에는 대예배실과 순교자들의 초상화가 벽 둘레

야월교회

로 배치되어 있다.

염산교회

🚗 전남 영광군 염산면 봉남리 산 191번지

77인순교기념비

마을 입구를 장식한 '순교자의 길' 표지석을 지나 염산교회 예배당 입구에 들어서면 순교자들을 합장한 큰 봉분과 순교기념비 그리고 그들을 추모하는 십자가 돌탑을 볼 수 있다. 예배당 옆에는 순교체험관이 서있다. 염산교회가 설립 70주년을 맞아 개관한 순교체험관은 350평 규모의 2층 건물로 예배실과 함께 순교자체험실과 자료전시실 등을 갖추고 있으며, 건물 1층에는 세 개의 숙소와 식당 등 편의시설이 마련되어 있다. 거기서 조금 떨어진 해안가로 내려가면 6·25전쟁 당시 영광지역에서 순교한 194명(염산교인과 야월교인 포함)을 기리는 '기독교인순교탑'이 나온다. 또 그들의 순교 당시 모습이 조각된 벽화를 볼 수 있다.

CHAPTER 10
제주지역

✱ 제주 소개

　제주도를 언급한 최초의 문헌기록은 중국 진나라 진수(233~297)가 쓴 『삼국지』「위지」에서 찾을 수 있다. 그 책은 제주도 사람들을 '주호州胡'라 지칭하며 그들의 언어와 옷과 생업과 교역관계를 짧게 소개하고 있다. 그리고 고려 때 김부식이 펴낸 『삼국사기』「백제본기」에 다시 제주도가 탐라국으로 기록되어 나타난다. 이것으로 보아 삼국시대 제주도에는 '탐라'라는 고대국가가 존재하고 있었음을 알 수 있다.
　그 탐라가 고려의 한 군현이 된 것은 숙종 때인 1105년 5월이었다. 고려 정부는 이때 탐라라는 국호를 폐지하고 탐라군을 설치한 후 직접 중앙에서 관리를 파견하였다. 그들이 탐라를 다스리면서 그들의 폭정에 항거하는 탐라인들의 민란이 잇달아 일어났다. 또 고려 후기에는 삼별초의 난 이후 고려에 왔던 원나라의 목호牧胡: 제주에서 목마장을 관리했던 몽고인들이 반란을 일으키기도 했다. 원을 멸망시킨 새로운 명나라가 그들에게 마필의 헌상을 요구했기 때문이다.

제주지역

대정교회

 조선시대 제주사람들은 정부의 출륙금지령出陸禁止令으로 큰 타격을 받았다. 1629년부터 1830년까지 무려 200년 동안 제주도민들은 육지로 이주하여 정착할 수 없었다. 육지로의 이주로 인구가 격감하자 섬을 보호하는 차원에서 시행된 것이지만 그로 인해 그들은 외부와 단절된 그립의 삶을 살아야 했다. 출륙금지가 해제된 이후에도 민란과 소요는 끊임없이 계속되었다. 1898년 방성칠의 난과 1901년 신축민요辛丑民擾: 이재수의 난는 그 대표적인 것이다. 신축민요는 천주교도와 도민島民이 무력 충돌한 사건이었다.
 그리고 네덜란드 사람 하멜Hendrick Hamel과 그 일행이 제주도에 표착한 것은 효종 때인 1653년 8월이었다. 하멜 일행은 그 해 1월 10일 무역선 스패로우 호크Sparrow Hawk호를 타고 네덜란드를 떠나 일본 나가사키로 가던 도중 태풍으로 조난되어 제주도에 도착 한 것이다. 8월 21일 하멜 일행은 제주 관아로 압송되어 목사牧使 이원진의 심문을 받았다. 하멜은 저간의 사정을 이야기하고,

자신들을 일본으로 보내줄 것을 간청했다. 정부에서 보낸 문정관과 벨테브레Jan Janse Weltevree, 박연가 도착한 것은 그 해 10월 29일이었다. 벨테브레 역시 1627년 조선에 온 네덜란드 사람이었다. 그 후 그들 36명은 서울로 이송되어 훈련도감 등에 편입되었다. 그 후 하멜 일행 8명은 13년간의 포로생활 끝에 일본으로 가는데 성공했다. 본국으로 돌아간 하멜은 『하멜표류기』를 출간했는데, 거기에는 당시 제주도에 관한 정보가 담겨 있다.

제주 현대사에서 가장 충격적인 일이 제주4·3사건이다. 이것은 경찰·서북청년단의 탄압에 대한 저항과 남한의 단독선거·단독정부 반대를 기치로 1948년 4월 3일 남로당 제주도당 무장대가 무장봉기한 이래 1954년 9월 21일 한라산 금족지역이 전면 개방될 때까지 제주도에서 발생한 무장대와 토벌대간의 무력충돌 그리고 토벌대의 진압과정에서 수많은 주민들이 희생당한 사건이다. 또 제주4·3사건의 희생자 통계는 대략 2만 5천~3만 명으로 잠정 추정하고 있다. 2003년 10월 31일 당시 노무현 대통령은 진상조사위원회의 의견에 따라 남로당 제주도당 무장대와 토벌대의 무력충돌과 진압과정에서 국가권력에 의한 대규모 희생이 이루어졌음을 인정하고 유족과 제주도민에게 공식 사과문을 발표하였다.

제주도를 말할 때 감귤이야기를 빼놓을 수 없다. 감귤은 이미 삼국시대부터 재배되었다. 그리고 「탐라지」「읍지」등에 다양한 감귤 품종이 소개되어 있다. 고구마는 1736년(영조 39) 일본 통신사로 갔던 조엄이 대마도에서 제주도로 보내와 처음으로 제주도에서 시험 재배를 했다고 한다. 제주도의 말은 품종이 우수하여 고려 때부터 조정에 헌상하였으며, 조선시대에는 공마貢馬제도를 만들고 해마다 100마리씩, 조선 후기에는 500마리씩 바치게 하였다.

❋ 제주 기독교 전래

제주 기독교는 1908년 이기풍 목사의 제주 선교로 시작되었다. 1907년 9월 제1회 장로교 노회(독노회)는 평양신학교 졸업생으로 첫 목사 안수를 받은 일곱 사람 가운데 한 사람인 이기풍을 제주도 선교사로 파송하였다. 그의 파송예배는 1908년 1월 평양 장대현교회에서 거행되었다. 그 예배의 설교는 이 목사의 신학교 동기생이자 1907년 평양대부흥운동의 주역이었던 길선주 목사가 했다. 길 목사는 1893년 북장로회의 마펫Samuel A. Moffett, 마포삼열 선교사가 평양에 처음으로 선교하러 갔을 때, 예수를 믿기 전인 이기풍이 마펫의 집에 돌을 던진 일을 떠올리며, 설령 제주도 사람들이 돌을 던진다 하더라도 실망해서는 안 된다고 권면했다.

1908년 1월 17일 평양을 떠난 이기풍 목사는 2월 중순까지 목포에 머물면서 사경회 강사로서 장차 자신을 후원할 남장로회 목포 스테이션 사역을 지원한 후 제주에 도착했다. 그 때는 대개 2월 말이나 3월초쯤이었던 것 같다. 그리고 이기풍 목사는 제주 선교 개시 6개월 만인 1908년 9월 제2회 독노회에 원입인願入人 9명과 주일 출석 20명이라는 선교 결과를 보고할 수 있었다. 이미 그 전에 서울 세브란스병원에 입원했다가 예수를 믿은 김재원과 훗날 제주 출신 1호 목사가 된 금성리교회의 이도종은 이기풍 목사에게 큰 힘이 되었다.

그리하여 제주도에는 1908년 성내교회를 시작으로 그 후 금성리교회(현 금성교회)와 조천리교회(현 조천교회)가 잇달아 설립되었다. 금성리교회는 처음 조봉호의 집에서 모이다가 다시 이덕련의 집을 예배처소로 삼았다. 조천리교회는 천아라의 집을 예배당으로, 성내교회는 일덕리 증인문 안 초가를 매입하여 교회당으로 삼았다. 그리고 1911~1912년 들어서면서 제주 기독교의 성장이 가시적으로 나타나기 시작하였다. 1911년 9월 이기풍 목사는 제5회 독노회에 현재 제주도에는 예배당 세 곳, 기도처 두 곳, 160명의 교인이 있다고 보고하였는데, 이듬해인 1912년에는 다시 교인 400명과 예배당 세 곳, 기도처 다섯 곳이 있다고 노회에 알려왔던 것이다.

　남장로회 선교부 역시 이기풍의 제주 선교를 측면 지원하였다. 남장로회 선교사 프레스톤John F. Preston, 변요한과 벨Eugene Bell, 배유지는 1909년 무렵 2주간 제주도를 방문하여 그를 격려하였다. 또 장로교 노회는 제주의 여성 선교를 위해 이선광 전도사를 파송하여 이기풍 목사와 동역하도록 했다. 이선광 전도사는 1908년 10월 제주도에 와서 5년간 사역하였다.

✽ 제주 기독교 유적지

대정교회

🚗 제주도 남제주군 대정읍 안성리 1639번지

　대정교회는 산방산이 바라보이는 위치에 있다. 그리고 교회 앞뜰에서 1956년 4월 건립된 '목사이도종기념비'와 만나게 된다. 이도종 목사는 1892년 한림읍 금성마을에서 이덕련의 장남으로 태어났다. 이기풍 목사의 전도로 예수를 믿은 이덕련은 아들 이도종을 평양 숭실학교로 보내 공부시켰다. 그 후 이도종은 1926년 평양신학교를 졸업하고 김제읍교회를 거쳐 1930년경 서귀포교회에 부임하였다. 그는 제주 출신의 첫 목회자였다. 해방 후 1947년부터 고산리에 살면서 산북지방의 지역교회들을 맡아 순회 목회하던 이 목사는, 제주4·3사건이 한참 벌어지고 있던 1948년 5월 인성과 화순교회에 심방을 가던 중 대정읍 무릉 2리 인향동 부근에서 무장대에 의해 살해되었다.

목사 이도종 기념비

금성교회

제주도 제주시 애월읍 금성리 436-3번지

　제주도의 첫 교회인 금성교회는 경신학교 출신인 조봉호의 집에서 시작되었다. 그는 1919년 상해임시정부에 군자금을 보낸 혐의로 체포되어 대구형무소에 수감 중 모진 고문의 후유증으로 1920년 순국하였다. 당시 그의 나이 38세였다. 지금 제주 사라봉공원에는 그를 기리는 순국지사조봉호기념비가 세워져 있다. 또 1994년 지어진 금성교회 현 예배당 옆에는 지붕 위에 종탑이 있는 구 예배당이 보존되어 있다. 또 1994년 지어진 금성교회 현 예배당 아래로 조금 내려가면 길 옆에 위치한 구 예배당을 볼 수 있다.

금성교회 구 예배당

강병대교회

강병대교회

 제주도 서귀포시 대정읍 상모리 3846

강병대교회는 6·25전쟁이 일어난 뒤 모슬포에 설치된 육군제1훈련소의 군인교회로 1952년 5월 90평 규모로 그 예배당이 준공되었다. 육군 공병대가 제주도산 현무암으로 지은 강병대교회 건물은 현재 전체의 절반 정도가 그 당시의 모습을 유지하고 있어 등록문화재 제38호로 지정되었다. 예배당 뒤로는 작은 역사전시실이 있어 사진자료들을 전시하고 있다.

이기풍선교기념관

 제주도 서귀포시 조천읍 와흘리 산 14-3번지

이기풍선교기념관은 지난 1998년 이기풍 목사의 제주 선교 업적을 기리기 위하여 건립되었다. 예배동에 있는 사료실에는 이기풍 목사 관련 자료가 전시되어 있다. 또 정원에는 '이기풍목사제주선교백주년기념비'가 세워져 있다.

✻ 제주 일반 유적지

제주4·3평화공원

 제주도 서귀포시 봉개동 산51-3번지

　부지면적 220,394 m²의 제주4·3평화공원은 제주4·3사건 60주년을 맞이하여 이 사건으로 인해 학살당한 민간인과 제주도민의 처절한 삶을 기억하고 추념하며 화해와 상생의 미래를 열어가기 위한 평화·인권 기념공원이다.
　제주4·3사건이란 미군정기에 발생하여 대한민국 정부수립 이후에 이르기까지 7년여에 걸쳐 지속된 한국현대사에서 한국전쟁 다음으로 인명피해가 극심했던 비극적인 사건이었다. 진실을 바탕으로 살아남은 자들의 증언, 유가족의 기록, 4·3과 관련된 역사자료 등과 정부의 진상조사를 바탕으로 이루어져 있으며 과거의 역사를 미래의 후대들에게 전하고자 하는 교육적 전시관이다.
　제주4·3평화공원 조성사업은 제주4·3사건에 대한 공동체적 보상의 하나로 이루어졌다. 1980년대 말 4·3진상규명에 매진하던 민간 사회단체 등은 진상규명과 함께 지속적으로 위령사업을 요구했다. 이런 요구에 부응하여 제주도는 1995년 8월 위령공원 조성계획을 발표했으며 1997년 12월 전 김대중 대통령 후보자는 4·3특별법 제정을 통한 진상규명, 위령사업과 보상을 공약으로 제시한다. 2006년 1월 건축공사를 시작하여 2008년도에 전시물 제작 설치를 끝나 현재 2단계까지 개방하고 있다.
　제1관은 4·3 당시 피신처를 의미하는 역사의 동굴, 제2관 흔들리는 섬, 제주4·3의 前史 부분으로 일제로부터의 해방과 자치 미군정 실시와 뒤이은 3·1발포 사건 등이 전개, 제3관 바람타는 섬, 제4관 불타는 섬, 제5관 흐르는 섬, 제6관 새로운 시작, 1992년 발굴 당시 모습을 재현한 특별관 다랑쉬동굴 등이 전시되어 있다.

제주4·3평화공원

그 외에 야외전시관에는 위령제단과 위패봉안소, 행불인 표석, 상징 조형물, 위령탑과 각명비, 모녀상 등이 있다.

제주 하멜기념비

🚗 제주도 남제주군 안덕면 사계리 산방산 앞

남제주군 안덕면 사계리 산방산 앞 용머리해안에 가면 언덕에 높이 4 m, 너비 6.6 m의 크기로 네덜란드 사람 하멜Hendric Hamel 일행이 우리나라에 표류한 것을 기념해 세운 비(탑)가 있다. 이 탑(비)은 1980년 한국과 네덜란드 양국이 하멜 일행의 표류를 기념하고 양국의 우호증진을 위해 각각 1만 달러씩을 출연하여 난파 상륙지점으로 추정되는 곳에 세운 것이다. 한중일의 중간 해역에 위치해 예로부터 이 지역을 왕래하는 바닷길의 중요한 통로였던 제주도에는 지금까지 표류해온 선박과 사람들이 많았다. 1653년(효종 8) 하멜 일행이 탄 네덜란드 배 '스페로 호크'호가 일본의 나가사키로 가다가 심한 풍랑으로 난파되어 선원 64명 중 28명은 익사하고, 36명이 심한 중상을 입고 사계리 인근 해안에 표도漂倒하였다. 이들은 이후 서울로 압송되어 2년간 억류되었다가 1656년 전라도로 이송된다. 이 사이에 14명이 목숨을 잃고, 1663년 생존자 22명은 순천·남원·여수로 분산 수용되었다. 1666년(현종 7) 9월 4일 탈출에 성공한 하멜 등 8명은 일본을 경유하여 1668년 7월에 네덜란드로 귀국함으로써 13년간의 억류생활이 비로소 끝나게 된다.

고국으로 돌아온 하멜은 이 과정과 조선에서의 생활을 기록한 『하멜표류기』를 저술했고, 이 책이 프랑스·영국·독일 등 많은 나라에서 번역·간행됨으로써 조선이라는 나라가 비로소 유럽에 알려지기 시작했다.

또한 전남 강진군 병영면 성동리 109번지에도 전라병영성 하멜기념관이 세워져 있다. 하멜은 13년간의 유배생활 중 7년간을 강진 병영에서 지냈는데, 강진군은 1998년 하멜의 고향 네덜란드 호르큼 시와 자매결연을 맺고 2009년 12월 3일 하멜기념관을 개관하였다.

집필진	송현강	한남대 겸임교수
	이순자	한국기독교역사연구소 책임연구원
	이진구	서울대 강사

믿음의 흔적을 찾아
한국의 기독교 유적

초판 1쇄 발행 2011년 11월 3일
초판 3쇄 발행 2016년 12월 16일

지 은 이 　한국기독교역사연구소
펴 낸 이 　이덕주
펴 낸 곳 　한국기독교역사연구소

서울 마포구 성산동 226-4 열송재(悅松齋)
www.ikch.org | 전화번호 2226-0850 | 팩스 325-0849

등　　록　　1991년 5월 27일 제313-2011-173호

978-89-85628-71-6　93230　　　　　값 15,000원

* 파본은 구입하신 서점이나 연구소로 연락주시면 교환해 드리겠습니다.